Jackie Collins brings the wild and sexy world of superstardom alive. Her phenomenally successful novels have made her as famous as the movers and shakers, power-brokers and super-stars she writes about with an insider's knowledge. With 200 million copies of her books sold in more than forty countries, Jackie Collins is one of the world's top-selling writers. In a series of sensational bestsellers, she has blown the lid off Hollywood life and loves. 'It's all true,' she says. 'I write about real people in disguise. If anything, my characters are toned down – the real thing is much more bizarre.'

There have been many imitators, but only Jackie Collins can tell you what *really* goes on in the fastest lane of all. From Beverly Hills bedrooms to a raunchy prowl along the streets of Hollywood. From glittering rock parties and concerts to stretch limos and the mansions of the power-brokers – Jackie Collins chronicles the *real* truth.

*By the same author*

The World is Full of Married Men
The Stud
The Bitch
Sinners
The Love Killers
Lovers and Gamblers
Hollywood Wives
Lucky
Hollywood Husbands
Rock Star
Lady Boss
American Star
Hollywood Kids
Vendetta: Lucky's Revenge
Thrill!
L.A. Connections
Dangerous Kiss

# JACKIE COLLINS

# Chances

## &

## The World is full of Divorced Women

PAN BOOKS

*Chances* first published 1981 by Pan Books.
First published in paperback 1982 by Pan Books.
*The World is Full of Divorced Women* first published 1975 by W. H. Allen.
First published in paperback 1984 by Pan Books.

This omnibus first published 2006 by Pan Books
an imprint of Pan Macmillan Ltd
Pan Macmillan, 20 New Wharf Road, London N1 9RR
Basingstoke and Oxford
Associated companies throughout the world
www.panmacmillan.com

ISBN-13: 978-0-330-44665-5
ISBN-10: 0-330-44665-7

1 3 5 7 9 8 6 4 2

A cip catalogue record for this book is available from
the British Library.

Printed and bound in Great Britain by
Mackays of Chatham plc, Chatham, Kent

# Chances

'Once in, there is no out.'

Al Capone

'It's a man's world, and that's the way it's supposed to be.'

Vincent Teresa

'Everybody's got larceny in 'em, only most of 'em don't have the guts to do nothin' about it.'

'Lucky' Luciano

# Book One

# Wednesday, July 13th, 1977, New York

Costa Zennocotti stared at the girl sitting across from him, his ornate carved wood desk separating them. She spoke rapidly, gesticulating wildly, pulling faces to emphasize a point. Christ! He hated himself for having such thoughts, but she was the most sensual woman he had ever laid eyes on . . .

'Costa?' the girl questioned sharply, 'are you *listening* to me?'

'Of course, Lucky,' he replied quickly, embarrassed because she was only a slip of a girl – what was she now – twenty-seven or eight – and yet she was so bright and knowing. She probably *knew* what he was thinking.

Lucky Santangelo. Daughter of his lifelong best friend, Gino.

Bitch. Child. Liberated lady. Temptress. Costa knew her as all of those things.

'So you see,' she fumbled in an oversized Gucci bag and produced a pack of cigarettes, 'no way is it the right time for my father to come back into the country – *no way*. You must stop him.'

He shrugged. Sometimes she could be extremely stupid. How could she expect *anyone* to stop Gino doing exactly what he wanted. As his daughter, she, above all others, should know that. After all, Gino and Lucky, they were two of a kind, they were as alike as two separate people could ever hope to be. Even physically she looked just like her father. The same aggressively sexual face, olive-skinned, with deep set smoldering black eyes, and wide sensual lips. The only difference being the nose. Gino's was masculine and prominent, hers was smaller, more suited to her femininity. They both had jet black curly hair, Lucky wore hers shoulder length in a tangled mass of curls, and Gino, at seventy-plus still had a fine head of hair.

Ruefully Costa reached up and touched his own bald spot –

it was more than a spot – a desert – a barren expanse of scalp that no amount of hair arrangement could conceal. Still . . . he was sixty-eight years old, what else would you expect at that age?

'Are you going to *tell* him?' she demanded. 'Well? Are you?'

Costa thought it best not to mention that at that very moment Gino was in a jet circling the city. Soon he would be landing. Soon he would be back. Lucky would just have to face the fact that her father would be taking over again.

Christ! The shit was going to hit the fan, and he, Costa, was going to be right on target.

Three floors above, Steven Berkely worked industriously away in the quietness of his friend Jerry Meyerson's office. They had a deal going where if Steven wanted total privacy he could use the place after normal working hours. It was great. No phones. No people tracking him down. His own office was always a madhouse – whatever time of the day or night it was. And even in his apartment the phone never stopped.

He stretched, glanced at his watch, and seeing it was nearly nine-thirty, swore softly under his breath. The time just seemed to have slipped by. He thought quickly of Aileen, and wondered if he should call her. He had blown their theater date, but that's what he liked about Aileen – nothing fazed her, she took everything calmly – whether it be a missed theater date or a proposal of marriage. He had proposed three weeks previously, and she had said yes. Steven had not been surprised, there were no surprises in Aileen, but after Zizi, his ex-wife, who needed them?

Steven was thirty-eight years old and he wanted a settled life. Aileen was twenty-three and she would give him one.

Steven Berkely was a highly successful prosecuting attorney. When black first became beautiful he was right in there with a college education, four years of law school, and plenty of enthusiasm. With his knowledge, wit and sharp intelligence, getting where he wanted to go had been comparatively easy. His exceptional good looks had not gone against him either. Over six feet tall, the body of an athlete, very direct green eyes. black curly hair, and skin the color of milk chocolate. He had the disarming quality of not really being aware of just quite how good looking he was. It knocked people off balance. Expecting conceit they found courtesy. Expecting arrogance they found a man concerned with people's thoughts and feelings.

Methodically he sorted through his papers, placing them in tidy sections in his worn leather briefcase. Then he glanced around the office, switched off the desk lamp, and went to the door. He had been working flat out on a special investigation and things were coming to a head. He felt tired, but it was a good tired – born out of hard work – his favorite pastime. It beat sex any day for sheer enjoyment. Not that he didn't enjoy sex, with the right woman it was great, but with Zizi it had been such an obsession. Gimme Gimme Gimme. Foxy little Zizi had wanted it every moment of the day – and the moments he wasn't around . . . Well . . . she had found her own ways of filling time. He should have listened to his mother and never have married her in the first place. But who listened to mothers when your cock was on fire?

With Aileen things were different. She was a nice old-fashioned girl, and his mother approved wholeheartedly. 'Marry her,' she had advised, and that's exactly what he intended to do.

He took one last look around the office and headed for the elevator.

Dario Santangelo bit down hard on his lip to stop himself from crying out. Above him the thin, dark-haired boy pumped solidly away. Pain. Pleasure. Exquisite pain. Almost unbearable pleasure. Not quite . . . Not yet . . . He could silence himself no longer. He screamed, his body shuddering uncontrollably as he climaxed.

The dark boy withdrew his still erect penis at once. Dario rolled over and sighed. The boy stood up and stared down at him.

Dario realized that he didn't even know his name. Another nameless dark-haired youth. So what? He never bothered to see them more than once. Screw it. Screw them. He couldn't help giggling. That was the name of the game, wasn't it?

As he got off the bed and headed for the bathroom the boy stood silently watching him. Let him watch, let him stare, he wasn't having *him* again.

In the bathroom he locked the door and ran warm water into the bidet. He always liked to wash immediately. It was bliss while it was happening, but after . . . Well he liked to forget about it . . . shut it out until the next dark-haired boy appeared on the horizon. He squatted over the bidet and soaped himself, turning the shower attachment onto cold, allowing the icy spray to shrivel up his balls in an invigorating way. It had been so hot all day, so sticky and humid. He hoped the dark-haired boy wouldn't want to stay. Maybe he should give him some money to see him on his way. Twenty dollars usually did the trick.

He put on a terry cloth bathrobe and glanced at himself in the mirror. He was twenty-six, but no one would ever guess. He looked nineteen, nicely slim, tall, with teutonic blue eyes and straight blond hair. He looked exactly like his mother, any relationship to father Gino, and bitch sister, Lucky, was purely non-physical.

He unlocked the bathroom door and walked back into the bedroom. The boy had dressed, slid into his dirty jeans and T-shirt, and stood with his back to the room looking out the window.

Dario went over to the dresser and selected two ten-dollar bills from a small pile of notes. He never kept much money in the apartment – it wouldn't do to tempt his casual pick-ups.

He cleared his throat to let the boy know he was there. *Turn around, take your money, and go* – he silently instructed.

The boy turned around slowly. From the bulge in his jeans it looked like he still had an erection.

Dario held up two ten-dollar bills. 'Car fare,' he said pleasantly.

'Fuck you,' the boy replied unpleasantly, and held up a bunch of keys which he jangled threateningly.

Dario felt a tremor of sudden fear. He hated any kind of trouble or violence. This one was going to be trouble, he had somehow known it all along from the very moment the boy had sidled up to him uninvited in the street. Usually it was Dario who made the first approach, for in spite of his blond hair and blue eyes he didn't look like a fag, he looked exceptionally straight, and he was always careful to wear the butchest of clothes, walk with a purposeful masculine stride. He had always been ultra careful. With a father like his he couldn't afford not to be.

Slowly he backed towards the bedroom door. In his desk lay his insurance, a small snub-nosed .25 caliber pistol. Guaranteed to frighten the shit out of any casual pick-up.

The dark-haired boy laughed. 'Where you goin'?' his voice a peculiar nasal whine.

Dario was nearly at the door.

'Forget the piece,' the boy said. 'I took care of that, an' these here keys, man, these are *your* keys. You get it? *Your* keys.

You know what that means doncha? Means we're shut in this here apartment tighter than President Carter's ass. And I bet he's got a *tight* one – like tight, man.'

Slowly the boy reached into the waistbard of his jeans and produced a lethal looking knife. Ten inches of glinting steel. 'You wanted a screwing fagtime,' he mocked, 'an I'm gonna give you a good one – a real heavy screwin' you ain't gonna forget in a hurry.'

Dario stood perfectly still by the door. His mind was racing. Who was this boy? What did he want from him? What did he have to bribe him with?

And finally – had Lucky sent him? Had the bitch decided to get rid of him once and for all?


For a woman in her early sixties Carrie Berkely looked sensational – four sets of tennis a day kept her body slim and athletic. Her black hair pulled severely back and held with two diamond clips emphasized her facial bone structure. High cheekbones, slanted eyes, heavy lips. Carrie had never been a pretty woman. when young, hers had been a wild erotic look – now with the drawn back hair, understated make-up, and elegant clothes she was a handsome woman. Respectable. Affluent. Controlled. A black lady who had it made all the way to the top in whitey's world.

She was driving a dark green Cadillac Seville. Driving slowly and hugging the side of the street looking for a place. Her lips were set in a thin angry line. And that's exactly how she felt – angry. So many years had passed, and all that time her secret had been safe. And now – an unidentifiable voice on the telephone – and here she was driving through New York streets at night – heading for Harlem, heading for a past she had thought was long behind her.

Blackmail was the name of the game. Pure and simple blackmail.

She pulled up at a stoplight and closed her eyes. Briefly she thought of her son, Steven – so successful, so respected . . . God if he should ever know the truth . . . It did not bear thinking about.

A car blasted her from behind, and she jerked away from the light. She patted her purse lying reassuringly on the seat beside her. It was a nice purse, a Christmas present from Steven. He had impeccable taste. The only slip he had ever made in his entire life was that tramp he had married – Zizi.

And now she was out of his life and would not be coming back. Money . . . what sweet power it held.

Carrie sighed, and slipped her hand inside her purse. The small gun felt cold beneath her palm. More power . . . the glint of metal . . . the ultimate deterrent.

She hoped it was not going to be necessary for her to use it. She knew that it was. And once more she sighed . . .

Gino Santangelo was tired. It had been a long flight, and the final ten minutes were dragging. He had fastened his seat-belt, extinguished his cigar, and now all he wanted was to plant his feet firmly on good old American soil. He had been too long away. Now he was coming home and it was a good feeling.

One of the stewardesses whisked past his seat, smiling brightly, 'Everything OK Mr Santangelo?' she asked. Every ten minutes it had been the same thing – 'Everything all right?' 'Can I get you a drink Mr Santangelo?' 'A pillow?' 'A blanket Mr Santangelo?' 'A magazine?' 'Some food Mr Santangelo?'

The President couldn't have been treated with more consideration.

'I am fine,' Gino said to the girl. She was pretty, but a tramp, he had an eye for such things.

'Oh well . . . ' she giggled, 'soon be there.'

Yes, they would soon be there. New York. His city. His territory. His *home*. Israel had been pleasant. A restful interlude. But he would sooner have spent his seven-year absence in Italy.

He consulted his watch, a jeweled gold creation given to him by a famous blonde movie star ten years earlier. He sighed. Soon he would be home . . . Soon he would have to deal with Lucky and Dario . . . A little fatherly advice was just what those two needed.

'Can I get you anything Mr Santangelo?' Another stewardess bobbed past. He shook his head.

Soon . . . Soon . . .

Lucky left Costa's office and stopped by the ladies room in the corridor. She studied her face in the mirror and was not happy with what she saw. She looked tired and drawn with dark circles under her eyes. What she needed was a vacation and a suntan, but that's not what she would get, not until things were settled.

Carefully she applied more make-up. Blusher, lip gloss, eye shadow. Then she shook her tangled mass of jet curls and placed it with her fingers.

She was wearing jeans tucked into boots, and a pale blue silk shirt with most of the buttons casually undone. Her breasts were clearly visible through the material. She took some gold chains from her shoulder bag and slung them round her neck, then she added two thick gold bangles, and a pair of large hoop earrings.

She was now ready to go out on the town. The last thing she needed was to go home to an empty apartment.

She left the ladies room and buzzed for the elevator impatiently. Her mobile face was creased in a frown. She tapped the heel of her two hundred dollar canvas boots in a nervous rhythm. Costa was getting old. And where the hell did his loyalties lie anyway? Certainly not with her – much as he might pronounce they did. She had been a fool not to see it earlier.

She glanced at her Cartier tank watch. Nine-thirty. Two wasted hours with a senile old man. 'Shit!' The word slipped from between her lips, and she looked around to see if anyone had heard. But of course it was too late for anyone to be there, the huge office building was deserted.

The elevator arrived and she stepped inside. Her mind was racing. If Dear Daddy actually *was* on his way home what would happen? Could she work things out with him . . . ? Would he be prepared to listen to her . . . ? Maybe . . . After all she was a Santangelo wasn't she, and the only one of Gino's two children with any balls. In seven years she had managed to achieve so very much, and it had not been a light task. Costa had been a great help. But would he continue to be on her side with the imminent return of Gino?

Lucky frowned even more deeply. Fuck it. Gino. Her father. The only man alive who had ever told her what to do and got away with it. But she wasn't a little girl any more and Gino was just going to have to realize the fact that he was no longer boss. No sirree. She wasn't about to give it all up. The power – the ultimate aphrodisiac. She was in control. She planned to stay in control. And he was just going to have to accept that fact.

Steven Berkely did not even look up from his newspaper when Lucky got in the elevator. Eye contact was always a mistake, it led to mundane conversations like, 'Isn't it hot today,' or

'Nice weather we're having.' Elevator conversations were a total waste of time. Lucky took no notice of him either. She was thinking of the problems that lay ahead.

Steven continued to read the paper, and Lucky was busy with her own thoughts, when, with a sudden stomach-lifting jolt, the elevator ground to a stop mid-floors, and the lights went out, plunging them both into an inky blackness.

Dario and the bejeaned dark-haired boy moved at the same time. But Dario was quicker – he slid out the bedroom and slammed the door shut in his adversary's face. Fortunately the key was in the lock, and he turned it without hesitation. Now *he* had the boy locked in the bedroom. And the boy had *him* locked in the apartment. Dario cursed his ultra safe security system. He had only ever thought in terms of keeping people out. It had never occurred to him that someone would be able to double lock him into his own apartment. They were both trapped, damn it. And what could he do? Call the police? That would be a laugh, they would have to break the door down to get into his apartment, and then what? The humiliation of having to admit that a crazy transient lay was locked in his bedroom with a knife – and worse – a male lay. They would know he was gay – and oh God – if it got back to his father . . .

No. Dario had no plans to call the police.

Of course Lucky would know exactly what to do in a situation like this. She knew exactly what to do in any situation. But how could he call upon her when she might have planted the boy in the first place? Screw Lucky. Cool. Calm. Assured. More balls than a tennis court. *Screw* Lucky.

A vicious kick against the bedroom door spurred Dario into immediate action. He checked his desk and ascertained with horror that his .25 pistol was indeed missing. So not only did the boy have a knife – he had *his* gun – and it was possible that any second he would shoot the lock off the bedroom door and come walking out.

He felt a shiver of fear run through his body.

It was at that precise moment that all the lights in the apartment went off, and darkness enveloped everything. Dario was trapped, locked into deadly blackness with a maniac stranger.

Carrie Berkely felt sure she was lost. The streets of Harlem – once so familiar – seemed harsh and remote. Locked into the air conditioned comfort of her Cadillac she looked out into streets of despair. Broken hydrants gushed water onto sweaty sidewalks, and lethargic groups of people slouched against walls, or squatted on the steps of broken down houses.

The Cadillac had been a mistake, she should have taken a cab. But everyone knew cabs would no longer venture into the streets of Harlem – especially not in the midst of a heat wave when the natives were hot, angry, and restless.

She spotted a supermarket and drew into the adjoining parking lot. Leàve the car. Walk. After all there were too many people on the street for it not to be safe. And besides which – she still possessed the best insurance of all – a black face. She could ask directions at the check-out counter, it was best to leave the car anyway, although she *had* taken the precaution of obscuring the plates.

She parked the car and walked into the market. Black or not she was getting stared at. Too late she realized she just didn't blend in any more. She looked expensive, smelt expensive. The diamond clips in her hair, the diamond earrings, the diamond solitaire ring she had forgotten to remove.

Two youths fell into step behind her. She quickened her pace.

There was a girl at the check-out busying herself with picking her teeth.

'Can you tell me – ' Carrie began. She never finished her sentence. Before she could the entire place was plunged into darkness.

Air turbulence had never bothered Gino. In fact he rather enjoyed the feel of being buffeted around. If he shut his eyes he could imagine he was on a motor boat in rough seas, or driving a pick-up truck over rocky terrain. He could never understand people who were frightened of flying.

He glanced across the aisle at a thin blonde woman traveling alone. She was desperately clutching a small hip flask, taking long gulps of whatever alcoholic beverage it held.

He smiled comfortingly. 'It's only a summer storm, nothin' to worry about, we'll be landing before you know it.'

The woman lowered her flask. She was middle-aged and well dressed. Probably quite a looker in her time. Gino prided himself on being an expert when it came to women's looks – after all he had had the best, the creme de la creme. Movie stars, show girls, society dames. Yes, he knew a thing or two about women.

'I . . . I can't take all this jogging about,' she confessed, 'I absolutely hate it.'

'Move over here and I'll hold your hand if it'll make you feel any better,' he suggested.

The woman jumped at this chance of reassuring physical contact, and undid her seatbelt. She hesitated for only a moment, a tentative, 'Are you sure?' And without waiting for an answer she was next to him, strapped in, digging long tense fingernails into the palm of his hand.

He didn't mind. Hell – if it made her feel better.

'You must think I'm awfully stupid,' she said, 'but just holding onto someone makes me feel so much more relaxed.'

'Yeh, I know what you mean.' He looked out the window at the sea of lights spread out below. New York City. What a beautiful sight. 'Hey!' he exclaimed suddenly.

'What?' asked the woman tensely.

'Nothin'.' Gino kept his voice nonchalant. He didn't want her any more nervous than she already was. And Christ – would she be nervous if she'd just seen what he had.

New York had vanished before his very eyes. One moment a dazzling fairy city of lights – the next – nothing. A sea of blackness. Jeeze! He had heard of homecomings – but this was ridiculous.

# Gino 1921

Stop it!'

'Why?'

'You *know* why.'

'Tell me again.'

'Gino – *no* – I mean it – *no*.'

'But you like it . . . '

'I don't, I don't. Oh Gino! Ooooh!!'

It was always the same story. *No, Gino. Don't do it, Gino. Don't touch me there, Gino.* And the story always had a happy ending – as soon as he found the magic button they stopped protesting, the legs opened, and they hardly noticed when he removed his finger and replaced it with his fine upstanding Italian prick.

Gino the Ram was his nickname – and it was true that he had screwed more ass than any other boy on his block. Not bad for a fifteen-year-old.

Gino Santangelo. A likable boy. A fast-talking boy now rooming with his twelfth foster family and looking to get out.

He had arrived in New York at the age of three, in 1909. His parents, a young Italian couple, had heard reports of the fortunes to be made in America and decided to try their luck. His mother – Mira, a pretty eighteen-year-old. His father – Paulo, barely twenty – but ready with innocent enthusiasm for all that America had to offer.

Work was hard to find. Mira got a job in a garment factory. Paulo did whatever came his way – which wasn't always legal.

Gino gave no trouble to the various women who looked after him while his parents worked. Every evening at five-thirty his mother would collect him. It was the moment he looked forward to all day.

When he was five years old she failed to arrive. The woman who was caring for him got annoyed when nobody came. 'Where's ya momma? Eh? Eh?' She kept on screaming at him.

As if he would know. He held his tears in check and waited patiently.

At seven o'clock his father turned up. A worried, pinched looking man, his face white and older than his years.

The baby-sitter was enraged by this time. 'You pay extra – you hear me? Five-thirty I want the kids out of here. *No later.*'

There followed a short sharp argument between his father and the woman. Insults were exchanged, then money. Even at five Gino had observed that his father was not one of life's winners.

'Where is momma?' Gino asked.

'I don't know,' Paulo muttered, swinging his son onto his shoulders and hurrying to the one room they called home where he fed him and put him to bed.

The dark was not comforting, Gino wanted his mother desperately, but he knew he must not cry. If he didn't cry she would be back before morning. If he did . . .

Mira never returned. A manager at the factory where she worked disappeared also. An older man with three children – all girls. When Gino was of an age he sought those girls out one by one, and systematically screwed them. It was the only form of justice he could think of – but it was an empty revenge.

After Mira's defection life changed. Gradually Paulo became bitter and violent, and Gino was the butt of his violence. By the age of seven he had been in the hospital five times – but he was a tough little kid who knew his way around. He became adept at hiding from Paulo when it seemed a beating was on the way – and because there was no child to vent his anger on Paulo took to beating his girlfriends – of which there were many. This little practice landed him in prison – and Gino saw the inside of his first foster home. By comparison life with his father had been paradise.

Paulo soon decided that crime paid, and he was an easy recruit for any job going. Jail became his second home, and Gino spent more and more time in foster homes.

When Paulo was not in prison women were his main interest. He called them 'The Bitches.' 'All they want is sex,' he confided to his son, 'an' that's all they're good for.'

Gino – sometimes trapped in the same room, would watch his father go at them like a bull. It disgusted him. At the same time it excited him. When he was eleven he tried it for himself with a raddled old whore who grabbed twenty cents and muttered curses throughout.

Gino – watched by a circle of admiring friends, shrugged as he climbed off. 'It ain't bad,' he admitted, 'beats jerkin' off!'

'Come back again sonny,' the whore cackled. Even at eleven his manhood was a prize.

At fifteen he was street wise. A bright sharp boy who knew how to keep his mouth shut. He was admired and looked up to by the kids on the street. Sought out by the elder boys when they could make good use of him on one of their minor jobs. And idolized by the girls.

Grown-ups were suspicious of him. A fifteen-year-old boy with the bleak hard eyes of a man. Somehow – in spite of his ready smile there was something almost threatening about him.

He was not very tall – five foot six inches, a fact which bothered him, and religiously he worked on his body – running, playing baseball, doing knee bends, push ups, stretch outs.

He had black curly hair – another physical fact he didn't like, so he plastered on the grease to smooth it down.

His complexion was dark and clear and he was not bothered by the unsightly acne which seemed to plague his friends – a definite plus.

He was not good looking in the conventional sense – his

nose too big – his lips too fleshy, but he had a wonderful smile and great teeth.

The combination worked. Gino Santangelo had style.

'Gino – no!'

'Aw c'mon Susie. Let me just put it there, just next to you. I won't put it in – I swear I won't!'

'But Gino . . .'

'There. I told you. Doesn't that feel good?'

'Mmmm . . . I guess . . . But don't move, *promise* you won't move.'

'Course not. I just want to be next to you that's all.' Gently he eased his prick inside her.

'What are you doing?' she squealed.

'Just gettin' comfortable,' he replied, easing his hand down between her legs – feeling for the magic button.

Susie gave a little sigh. He had found it.

'Feel nice?' he inquired solicitously.

'Oh yes, Gino, oh yes.'

All set. No problem. Keeping his fingers on target he started to screw her properly.

She did not object. He knew how to please. He had been taught at the tender age of twelve by his fourth foster mother how to find the magic button. It was a lesson he was forever grateful for. It gave him the edge over the other boys who thought all there was to screwing was a fast shove. Gino knew it was just as important to make the girl like it – want it – even beg for it. He never revealed his secret to his friends who were forever envious of his success rate.

Susie was becoming agitated, wriggling and gasping alarmingly. He increased his stroke.

God but he loved the feel of pussy.

God but he wished he could find a girl who would say no.

'Ooooh Gino!'

He climaxed. Withdrew. Pulled on his pants.

'We shouldn't have done that,' Susie stated gravely. But her cheeks were glowing with pleasure, her small nipples extended and pert.

'Why not? It was good wasn't it?'

She giggled her agreement.

Gino was now dressed and ready to beat a hasty retreat from the disused garage where it was cold and murky. 'Gotta meet the boys,' he excused himself.

'Will I see you soon?'

'Yeh, I'm always around.'

Susie scuttled off in one direction. Gino – hands dug deep into his trouser pockets – strode jauntily the other way.

The boys were waiting for him – a seedy group of misfits hanging around outside a rundown drug store. His best friend was a wiry boy named Catto who worked with his father on the garbage dumps so there was always a vague stink to him. 'Not my fault,' Catto would shrug cheerfully. There was no bath in his house, and to use the public ones on 109th Street usually meant a two-hour wait. Catto's ambition was to find a girl with a bathroom.

Another close friend was Pinky Banana Kassarri, a tall boy given to flashing his large penis which did indeed resemble a pink banana – thus the nickname.

'Get any gash?' asked Pinky.

'Naw – I struck out,' Gino replied with a grin.

'Lying fucker . . . ' mumbled Catto.

They all knew the day that Gino Santangelo failed to score would be an unusual day indeed.

'So what we gonna do tonight?' Gino inquired.

The boys mumbled amongst themselves, coming up with suggestions, then turning to their leader and uttering the usual – 'Whatever ya say.'

'I say we have some fun,' Gino asserted. It was Saturday night, he had just gotten laid, and felt good. It didn't matter that he had no more than ten cents to his name, that his shoes had holes in them, that the foster parents he was living with hated the sight of him. He wanted some fun. He was entitled wasn't he?

They set off downtown like a pack of rats – Gino in the lead. He walked with an exaggerated swagger – bouncing softly on the balls of his feet, rocking and weaving from side to side. There were eight of them hissing and catcalling at passing girls – 'Hey honey – wanna little *my* honey!' 'Wow-Wow-Pretty Baby I could go to *jail* for what *I'm* thinking!'

Gino was the first to spot the car. A long sleek white and brown job parked casually with – he could hardly believe their luck – the keys in! It took only seconds for the boys to some-how jam and squeeze themselves all in, and quick as a flash, Gino – in the driver's seat naturally – shot away from the curb. Since leaving school the previous month he had been working as an auto mechanic – and had picked up a good knowledge of cars. He realized at once that driving came naturally to him – and after an initial clashing of gears they were off and running smoothly all the way to Coney Island.

The boardwalk was deserted, and an icy wind was blasting in from the sea. But it didn't matter. They ran riot along the beach, screaming and laughing – scooping up clumps of sand which they flung at each other.

They were easy pickings for the patrolman who waited patiently by the stolen car, gun in hand.

It was the first time Gino had been in trouble with the police. As the driver of the car, a fact he readily admitted, the brunt of the punishment came down on him. He was given one year at the New York Protectory For Boys – a tough home in the Bronx for orphans and first time offenders.

Gino had never been shut up before. He felt immediately threatened and hemmed in. The brothers in charge of the place were a hard bunch of men. Discipline was the order of the day. And messing with the young boys was sometimes the order of the night. Gino was disgusted. The little kids didn't have a chance.

He was given a job in the tailor shop which he hated. Brother Phillippe ran the shop with a rod of steel, and any boy caught slacking off got a beating with his yard stick. When Gino's turn came Brother Phillippe offered him an alternative. Gino spat in his face. From that day on he never went more than three days without a beating.

When he had been there six months a skinny little orphan not yet thirteen arrived. The boy – named Costa – was easy meat for Brother Phillippe who wasted no time in going after him. The kid objected but it did him no good. The other boys watched blankly as he would frogmarch Costa into the back room and do things to him that caused the small boy to scream out in agony.

Gino, along with the others, did nothing. Six weeks went by. Costa shrunk before their eyes. If thin and undernourished when he came in – he was now a stick. Gino tried to stay out of it. Survival meant keeping to yourself.

The next time Costa was singled out Gino felt himself tense up. The small boy was whimpering and objecting, but Brother Phillippe dragged him by the arm and slammed the door of the back room shut anyway. The pain-wracked cries and screams started almost immediately.

Gino was ready for action. He picked up some scissors lying on a worktop, and followed.

Opening the door he witnessed Costa bent across a table, his trousers and shorts around his ankles. And Brother Phillippe – fly undone – poised for another thrust at the skinny child's ass. The bastard did not even bother to look up so intent was he on his own pleasure. He entered the boy – plunging and tearing at his insides. And Costa screamed in uncontrollable pain.

Gino acted unthinkingly – lunging at Brother Phillippe. The scissors tore through the big man's jacket stabbing him in the arm. 'Get off him y'stinkin' bastard – leave him alone!' he yelled.

Brother Phillippe, taken by surprise, and on the point of coming, tried to shake him off. It was a mistake. Gino's temper was out of control. Suddenly it was his father he was attacking. And in a black haze he blamed his father for everything. His mother walking out. The beatings. The lousy foster homes. The rotten one-room apartments that had been the only homes he had ever known.

As he yelled so the scissors stabbed. And he did not stop until the dirty sonofabitch slumped to the ground. Then the haze lifted and he could see clearly again, and what he saw didn't look too good.

# Carrie 1913–1926

It had been a long hot summer in Philadelphia. Lureen Jones sat on the bed she shared with her six-year-old brother, Leroy, and the tears rolled down her pretty black face. She was thirteen years old and seven and a half months pregnant. No one knew, and there was no one she could turn to. She had no father, no money, and her mother, Ella, a thin wracked woman, sold her body for drugs.

Leroy whined and Lureen lay down on the bed. Sleep did not come easy. Downstairs her mother's 'friends' arrived, and loud music drifted up the stairs. After a while came the noises. Pantings and groanings. Muffled screams and the sound of flesh being hit.

She stuffed cotton wool into her ears and squeezed her eyes tightly shut. It took a long time but at last sleep came.

She was having a nightmare . . . felt like she was suffocating . . . wanted to scream . . . could *hear* herself screaming.

Abruptly she opened her eyes. There *was* screaming. She jumped out of bed and smelled the smoke before she opened the bedroom door and it came piling in.

She began to choke, and forced herself out of the room realizing that the house was on fire. The flames were already licking at the top of the stairs, and the screams coming from below blood-curdling in their intensity.

Funny, but she didn't panic. Tears were streaming down her cheeks but she knew exactly what to do.

She went back in the bedroom, closed the door, opened the window, and yelled at the people milling around outside to catch Leroy. She dragged him from the bed and threw him out of the window.

The flames blew the bedroom door off and were behind her by the time she jumped. She landed with a sharp crack on the sidewalk and lay there in a pool of blood just long enough to mutter to the ambulance man – 'Save my baby . . . Oh God *please* save my baby.'

By the time she reached the hospital she was dead.

The ambulance man reported to a young intern in emergency that she was pregnant, and the intern – fresh and enthusiastic – listened for the baby's heartbeat. It was there – faintly audible. He cornered a doctor who agreed to perform an emergency Caesarean section on the dead girl. Baby Carrie entered the world less than an hour later.

Her chances of survival were slight. She was tiny, hardly able to breathe, and the doctor who delivered her pronounced that she was unlikely to live for more than twenty-four hours.

But Carrie – named by the nurses – was tough. She had survived her mother's fall, cushioned by the water in the amniotic bag that had served as a shock absorber, and she would survive a premature entry into the world.

Week by week she amazed everyone by hanging on. And as the weeks grew into months she gained in strength, and became a normal robust baby. So healthy in fact, that soon it was time for her to leave the loving care of the hospital. There was only one problem – nobody wanted her.

The only relatives she possessed in the world were her grandmother Ella, pulled from the fire in a drunken stupor, and Leroy, her six-year-old uncle.

Ella did not take kindly to the thought of another mouth to feed. In fact she screamed long and loud at the hospital that the baby was nothing to do with *her*. The nurses were shocked that the tiny baby they had nurtured and loved was to be handed over to such a woman. One nurse in particular – a kindly woman called Sonny, with three children of her own – said she would take Carrie.

Ella agreed immediately, so Sonny took the baby home with her, and from that day on brought Carrie up as her own – never bothering to tell her the tragic beginnings of her life.

They were a poor family, but what they lacked in dollars they made up for in love. Carrie soon became one of the family.

The day she was thirteen Ella swooped back into her life, and her young existence was shattered.

Who was this stranger? This withered scarred woman with sunken eyes and falling hair? Things had not gone well for Ella since the fire. Who wanted a whore with a scarred body and disfigured face? She made it for a while, but soon drifted into petty thieving to come up with the money she needed for her drugs. Leroy was her only salvation. He was young and strong, so Ella took him out of school and made him work for her. By the time he was twelve he was the family bread winner. Ella lounged in the one room walk up they rented – stoned and morose – while Leroy worked his ass off. When he reached eighteen he took off fast. Ella was left alone – a weak slothful woman, in poor health, with no money.

It was then she had thought for the first time of her granddaughter – what was the kid's name? Carey – Carrie – yes Carrie. If Leroy could work for her – why couldn't Lureen's kid? After all she was a blood relative wasn't she?

Ella had set about finding her.

They arrived in New York at the end of the summer of 1926, the thirteen-year-old girl and her grandmother. Ella had decided there was more money to be made there, and what the hell, she wanted to be in the big city where it was all happening.

What happened for them was a filthy room, and a job for Carrie scrubbing floors in restaurant kitchens. She looked older than her years, tall, with large breasts, sleek black hair, and limpid eyes.

Ella, now wracked with a bad cough, thought the child had good possibilities – and scrubbing floors wasn't one of them. But she had to wait . . . bide her time. The girl was difficult . . . angry even. You would have thought she would appreciate

the fact that her own grandma had come to find her. But no
. . . it had been a devil of a job getting her away from the
family who had looked after her. Police had been summoned,
but Ella soon established her rights. Carrie *had* to go with her.
Godalmighty she was the girl's *grandma*, her only true blood
relative, and no amount of arguments in the world could
change *that* fact.

'How old are you?' the pudgy chef demanded.

Carrie, on her knees scrubbing the filthy kitchen floor,
glanced up nervously.

'I bet my ass you *ain't* sixteen,' the fat man sneered.

Every day the same conversation – twenty times she had told
him she was sixteen and he never believed her.

'So?' He licked his wormy lips, 'What we gonna do about
it?'

'Huh?' she replied listlessly.

'What we gonna *do*? I mean the manager find out you too
young an' he'll sling your pretty black ass outa here quicker
than a whore suck cock.'

Carrie concentrated on scrubbing the floor. Maybe if she
ignored him he would go away.

'Nigger – I am tawkin' to ya.' He bent down beside her. 'I
don't havta tell no one nothin' – not if you're nice to me I
don't.'

Before she could move, his fat hand was exploring under
her skirt.

She leapt up, knocking the bucket of soapy water over and
screaming – 'Don't you dare touch me!'

He backed off, his pudgy face reddening.

The kitchen manager appeared, a thin miserable man who
hated coloreds anyway. His cold eyes surveyed the mess of
spilled water. 'Clear it up,' he said to Carrie, his eyes staring at
the wall behind her as if she didn't even exist. 'Then get the
hell out of here, and don't come back.'

The fat chef explored the contents of his left ear. 'Silly
girly,' he said, 'I wouldn't have hurt ya.'

Slowly she mopped up the spilled water, not believing what
her life had become. She wanted to cry but had no tears left.
When the woman who called herself her grandma had come
and taken her she had cried enough to last for years. And then
– New York – no more school – and working her hands raw
scrubbing floors. 'You bin' spoiled,' grandma Ella had told

her. 'Well no more my girl. You hear me? Your momma always worked. She cleaned the house an' took care of her brother an' she *loved* every minute of it.'

Carrie *hated* every minute of it. She hated her grandma, and New York, and working. She just wanted to go home to what she considered her real family in Philadelphia.

Now she was fired from her job, and grandma Ella would be steaming, and no more would she be able to hide away the odd cent here and there that she found on the floors she scrubbed. It just wasn't fair.

She left the restaurant after clearing up, and stood on the sidewalk in a daze wondering what to do. Maybe she should look for another job before grandma Ella found out about her getting fired.

Winter was beginning to take root. It was cold, and she had no coat. Shivering, she walked along, passing the five and dime and sniffing hungrily at the smell of sizzling hot dogs. A sniff was all she could afford, besides, they didn't allow negroes to eat in the store.

In New York Carrie had learned about being black. She had heard the word nigger for the first time, and taught herself to shut her ears when she was taunted about her color. In Philadelphia it was the whites who were the outsiders. She had lived in a black neighborhood, gone to a black school. Whites. What made them think they were better anyway?

Men looked at her as she hurried by. Lately men were always looking at her. She kept her sweater pulled firmly around her breasts. She hated the way they jiggled. Mama Sonny had promised her a brassiere, but when she had mentioned it to Ella her grandmother had looked her over with a sharp eye and said, 'Strut your stuff, honey. Show 'em your titties. Give those ofays a hard-on an' you'll *always* have a job.'

It wasn't true was it? If that big fat chef had kept his eyes to himself she would still be working.

She passed by an Italian restaurant that looked warm and inviting. Standing outside she shivered. The wind was biting now, turning her skin to gooseflesh. She clutched at her sweater and wondered what to do. A hobo skirted by her, and the stench of stale liquor reminded her of grandma Ella. Carrie knew she must make a move. If she marched in through the front entrance and asked for work, what was the worst that could happen to her? They couldn't eat her – only insult her. And in New York you soon got used to that.

Gathering her courage she slid inside, suddenly wishing she

hadn't. It seemed like she stood there for hours with every eye upon her, but it was only a matter of seconds before a huge man descended on her. She braced herself, ready to be thrown out.

'Eh!' he asked, 'you wanna table?'

She couldn't believe her ears. A table! Her! A black girl in a white restaurant! Was the man mad?

'I'm looking for work . . . ' she mumbled, 'scrubbing, washing dishes . . . anything – '

'Ah!' he exclaimed, 'you want a job? We go to the kitchen. I don't know we have anything – but we talk about it. You like the hot pasta?'

Carrie had no idea what pasta was, but anything hot sounded good, and anyway she couldn't believe her luck at the man's friendliness. She nodded her head and he put his arm around her and swept her through the restaurant. In the kitchen she met his wife, Luisa, and discovered that his name was Vincento. They fussed around her like it didn't matter *what* color she was.

'She's so young,' Luisa crooned, 'just a baby.'

'I'm sixteen,' Carrie lied, but from the glances they exchanged she knew they didn't believe her. She wanted to be truthful, but grandma Ella had instilled in her a horrible fear. 'You tell anyone your real age,' she threatened, 'an' they'll throw you in a home for bad girls who skip out of school.' It was so unfair. Grandma Ella was the one who had pulled her out of school and ruined her life.

Vincento and Luisa had no job for her in the restaurant, their kitchen was small, and they already had three assistants. But Vincento asked around, and returned with the good news that Mr Bernard Dimes, a regular patron of theirs, needed a cleaner at his house, and if she wanted the job it was hers. If she wanted it indeed!

Vincento took her into the restaurant and introduced her to Mr Dimes, who looked her over with steady brown eyes. 'Can you start on Monday?' he asked.

She nodded, too scared to speak. When she left the restaurant she was in a daze, stunned by her good fortune. What should she tell grandma Ella? The truth? That she would be working in a private house and making more money. Or a lie? That she was still scrubbing kitchen floors.

Much as it went against her nature, a lie seemed more sensible. That way she could save the extra money for herself, and still hand over the same amount.

It worked for a month. Every day Carrie left the rundown room she shared with her grandma, and travelled downtown to Mr Dimes' imposing Park Avenue house. A housekeeper supervised her duties. Carrie only caught sight of Mr Dimes twice, and on both occasions he smiled and inquired after her welfare.

She felt she knew him well. She made his bed every day, changed his silk sheets, scrubbed his bathroom, polished his shoes, did his washing and ironing, and dusted his study, where she sometimes lingered over the silver photo frames filled with celebrities.

Mr Dimes was a theatrical producer. There was no Mrs Dimes, only a series of groomed blonde women who accompanied him on his social rounds. They never stayed over – Carrie was sure of that. She thought he was the most handsome and impressive man she had ever seen. He was thirty-three years old she discovered, and very rich.

One day the housekeeper suggested to Carrie that she might care to live in the Park Avenue house. 'There's a small room in the basement, and it would certainly make it easier for you without all the travellin'.'

Carrie thought it was a wonderful idea. 'I'd love to,' she replied.

'Settled then,' said the housekeeper, 'bring your things and move in on Monday.'

Carrie's mind was racing. She would do it! How could grandma Ella ever find her? She knew nothing of the job, and she would never summon the energy to track her down.

To live in the Park Avenue house would be a dream come true. Her own room! Five dollars a week! In no time at all she would be able to save enough money to get back to Philadelphia and her real family.

It was a Friday, so there was only the weekend to get through. She hurried home, planning her escape. Grandma Ella was waiting for the money Carrie brought home on a Friday night, and grabbing it, she went out.

Carrie settled on her bed. She was too tired to even drag herself down to the corner restaurant and buy a greasy piece of chicken or some grits. Loud jazz music drifted into the room from down the street somewhere. All she wanted to do was squeeze her eyes shut and fall asleep as soon as possible. The sooner she fell asleep the sooner it would be Saturday and then Sunday and then . . .

A hand woke her two hours later. A rough shoving hand that had her by the shoulder.

She came awake slowly, rubbing her eyes, saying – 'What is it grandma? Whatssamatter?'

But it wasn't her grandma. It was a very tall black boy with wide eyes and shaggy hair.

'Who are you?' she shrieked.

'Don' get frightened now,' the boy said with a big grin, 'I'm Leroy. I'm jest lookin' for my mama.'

'How'd you get in?' she started to say. But then she saw that he had kicked his way in. The thin moldy door kept nobody out.

'I guess you all are Lureen's kid. Someone 'tole me mama bin' kind enough to take you in.'

Carrie sat up in bed. She had heard about Leroy. Grandma Ella mentioned him often. 'That mothafuckin' slimey little rat, runnin' out on his own mama. I ever see that little turd agin' I'm gonna crack his head open!'

'She's out. You'd best come back tomorrow.'

Leroy planted himself firmly on the end of her bed. 'Girl! I ain't movin'. I am one tired person. You got any food around here?'

'Nothing.'

'Aw – sheeit. Just like my dear ole mama.' His wild eyes looked over her. 'I suppose she got you haulin' ass for her jest like I did.' His eyes lingered on her breasts, which were not covered much by the thin slip she had on. 'You a pretty little thing. Mama got you sellin' your tail I bet.'

Carrie pulled the cover up around her. 'I work as a maid,' she said primly, wishing he would go away.

'A maid, huh? For some big fat whitey, huh?'

'In a restaurant.'

'A restaurant. Sheeit!' He bit at a hang-nail and studied her through narrowed eyes. 'You wanna sell tail *I'm* the daddy can arrange it for you.'

Suddenly she was very very nervous. It was as if a warning system started going off in her head. Danger. Danger. Danger.

She moved at the same time as he did. But he was bigger and stronger and he had her arms pinned to the bed in no time at all. 'Don't tell *me* ya don' sell ass,' he sneered, and he pinned her wrists with one hand while the other roamed over her body.

'Just you leave me alone,' she gasped.

'Why should I?' he laughed. '*I* ain't buying. *I* get for free. *I* am your uncle – girl.'

With one vicious tear he had the slip ripped off her. She arched her body in a vain attempt to shake him off, but he just slammed her down on the bed, pried her legs apart, and entered her.

The pain was intense. But it wasn't the pain that made her scream. It was the frustration, the fury, the sheer helplessness of what was happening.

'Hey! Hey! Hey!' He was laughing and coming all at the same time, 'you ain't shittin' me – you *was* a virgin. Holy sheeit! You an' me gonna make our *fortune*. We gonna git *rich* from your tight little box. Sheeit!!' Finished, he released her.

She lay perfectly still, too frightened to move or do anything. Between her legs she felt a burning hot stickiness. So this was what it was all about. This was what men wanted. This was sex.

Leroy roamed happily around the room, doing up his trousers and muttering to himself as he checked out their possessions. 'Any money 'round here?' he questioned.

She thought quickly of the few dollars she had managed to save. It was hidden in a rolled up stocking and secreted beneath her mattress. 'No money,' she mumbled, wishing that grandma Ella would come home and discover the unspeakable thing Leroy had done to her.

'Sheeit!' he exclaimed, 'no money, no bootch. Sheeit! Guess there ain't nuthin' to do 'round here 'cept frig a jig.' And then unexpectedly he was on her again, straddling her with his skinny legs, jabbing at her with his thing.

Waves of blackness came over her, she felt herself falling . . . escaping from the pain . . .

'Aw c'mon girl - enjoy it,' she heard him whining, 'ain't no fun for me if you don' enjoy it.'

When she came to she heard voices, words that didn't make any sense. She felt crushed, used, and worst of all totally helpless.

It was grandma Ella talking. Thank God . . . she tried to sit up but all strength seemed to have deserted her.

'You done us all one big favor,' she heard grandma Ella cackle, 'now you've put her tight little fanny in action we can make us some *real* money. Y'know boy, I was gonna wait 'til she was fourteen – but now – well Leroy honey – I guess we done got ourselves the best little hooker in the business!'

# Gino 1921–1923

Brother Phillippe hovered on the danger list for three weeks. Gino didn't know this, he thought he had killed him, and frankly he didn't much care. The scissor incident had made him a hero with his gang.

The newspapers got hold of the story while Gino was in the Bronx County Jail waiting to go before the court. 'JUVENILE SCANDAL' the headlines screamed. 'CHILDREN PROTECT CHILDREN'. All of Brother Phillippe's victims couldn't wait to start talking now that he was safely out of the way.

Costa was pictured in the newspapers – wide-eyed and appealing. His story caught the heart of the nation, and he was promptly adopted by Franklin Zennocotti, a rich lawyer in San Francisco who planned to launch him on a new life as soon as he had given evidence.

Gino was fortunate. Public opinion was on his side. And when it came time for the judge to decide what to do with him, he was given six months probation and released.

He came face to face with Costa outside the courtroom, and the small boy – who had never exchanged two words with him before – clutched him by the hand, and said in a low emotional voice, 'Thank you Gino, thank you for my life. One day I hope I can repay you.'

Gino was embarrassed. He extracted his hand and laughed in a self-conscious way. 'It was nothin' kid, forget it.'

He watched Costa walk away with his new father, and was suddenly jealous. Why wasn't *he* being offered a brand new life? He had been in the newspapers too. How come nobody rushed forward to adopt him?

Oh yeh. He already had a father didn't he. A sonofabitch who was at this very moment in jail.

He glanced at the piece of paper with Paulo's latest address written on it. Although he was in the can, he had married again, and Gino was supposed to go and live with the new wife. A woman he had seen for two minutes in the courtroom. A faded blonde with a pair of big ones.

As soon as he thought of her breasts he got a hard-on. He had been locked up for nine months exactly, and he felt horny as hell. Jerking off had never really appealed to him, especially in a dormitory with ten other guys doing the same thing.

He wanted to get laid. He wanted to get laid immediately. He picked up the cheap suitcase with everything he owned inside, decided to drop it off at his new home, and take off in search of some prime pussy.

As he walked his cock rubbed uncomfortably against his trousers, but he couldn't help grinning. He was out. He was on the street again. It was a marvelous feeling.

The man heaved, grunted, groaned and came. Then he was up and getting dressed, carefully avoiding looking at the woman on the bed.

The woman was named Vera, and she was the blonde with the nice breasts who had married Gino's father.

She closed her legs, pulled her skirt down, and silently watched as the man finished dressing, laid some money on the table, and left.

She was tired. Thank God you didn't need energy to screw Just open your legs and let business commence.

It had been a tough week. Visiting Paulo in Sing Sing. Then dragging down to the courtroom to say that Paulo's kid could come and live with her. Bullshit he could. She had only gone because Paulo had insisted. 'He doesn't havta come and live with us,' Paulo had explained, 'but you gotta say he can so they won't stick him in another home. When he comes round give him twenty dollars and tell him to get lost.'

Vera made a face. Twenty dollars indeed! She would give the kid five.

She got up, picked the money off the table, then listlessly answered a knock on the door.

It was one of her regulars, so there was no need for conversation. She flopped back on the bed, lifted her skirt and opened her legs. As the man unbuttoned his pants she barely concealed a yawn.

Gino bounced jauntily down the street. He was so glad to be out that he didn't even notice the oppressive heat. And it was hot. Way up in the eighties with not a breath of wind. He wondered about his friends – would they still be around? And Susie, and all the other girls who used to put out for him. Which one would get lucky tonight?

He glanced at the piece of paper with the address on once again. Almost there. An open fire hydrant gushed water, and a gang of naked children danced around it. An old man picking his nose sat on the steps of the house which was divided into separate apartments. Number six was on the second floor. He knocked, once, twice. When there was no response he tried the door and it opened.

His new stepmother was screwing on the bed. She didn't seem too put out by the interruption. 'I'm busy now,' she stated flatly.

Gino could see that. He dumped his suitcase inside the door. 'I'll come back later,' he managed. Quickly he shut the door behind him. What the hell was going on?

Then he realized. She was a whore of course. What other kind of woman would marry his father?

He caught the subway to Coney Island. It was crowded and sweaty, the beach even more so. He picked his way among the bodies looking for a familiar face. The old gang had always congregated here when it was too hot to stick around the city. Not finding anyone he knew, he stripped down to his shorts, charged into the sea, and swam out to a wooden raft crowded with bodies. Two sisters looked over and giggled.

'Ya come here often?' he asked. The corny lines always worked well.

Within an hour they were a threesome. Swimming and ducking, racing each other to the shore. It took all his control to stop his hard-on from showing. But he managed. Just.

By the time it started to get dark and the families and screaming kids began to depart, Gino knew he could hold out no longer.

The sisters were making noises about getting home.

'One more swim,' he insisted. 'Race ya to the raft.'

The younger girl demurred, but the elder seemed to think it a good idea. She was about eighteen, with carrot-colored frizzy hair and protruding teeth.

They swam towards the raft, jostling and splashing. Gino let her get in front of him, then just as she was about to haul herself aboard he grabbed her from behind.

She let out a gasp. 'What do you think *you're* doing?'

He knew what he was doing all right. Hands on her breasts, working quickly and efficiently, bringing her swiftly to a point where she wouldn't want him to stop.

He trod water, pumping his legs like pistons, while she hung slackly onto the side of the raft and started to purr a little.

He had her. He moved his body in close and kissed her

salty mouth, never once letting up the action on the breasts.

'We really shouldn't . . . ' she objected weakly, as he started to peel off her bathing suit.

'Oh yes we should.' He dived under the water and maneuvered one of her legs out of the clinging woolen suit.

It was exciting in the water. Anything would be exciting after nine long months.

He pushed his head underwater to kiss her breasts, and spread her legs with his hands, zooming in on the magic button.

'Gino!' she gasped.

He came up for air, wriggled out of his shorts and thrust himself between her legs. The pressure of the water might have made it difficult to enter her, but he was so goddamn hard that *nothing* could stop him.

They clung together, her legs winding round him as they sunk under the sea. He knew he had to come immediately or drown. The choice was his. He chose to come, and they shot to the surface gasping and spluttering for breath.

'You nearly drowned me!' she accused.

'What a way to go!' he laughed.

'I've never done that before,' she complained, struggling awkwardly into her bathing suit.

'Sure you have,' he replied, realizing that in the heat of the moment he had lost his shorts. He dived under the water, but couldn't find them.

Now it was getting cold, and frizzy hair was whining about going back.

'Hey – can't find my shorts,' he said.

Frizzy hair started to giggle.

'We'll swim in 'til I can stand, then you go get me my pants,' he suggested.

'And what am I supposed to tell my sister?'

'Tell her a shark ate 'em. Tell her anything, I don't care.'

They swam back, and when they neared the shore he waited while frizzy hair headed for the beach. He watched her join her sister, throw a towel around herself, and then the two of them ran off without so much as a backward glance. He could hardly believe his eyes. They were leaving him. Bare-assed and freezing. Jee . . . sus!

Quickly he surveyed the beach, took a deep breath, and made a wild sprint for his clothes.

'Who is it?' Vera slurred.

He knocked on the door again, just to be sure. 'It's me, Gino Santangelo. Is it OK to come in now?'

Vera sat up. She had been enjoying a short boozy nap and had forgotten all about Paulo's son. 'Yeah, come in . . . I suppose . . .'

He entered, and they stared at each other.

He saw a tired blonde of around thirty, with streaked make-up and big tits.

She saw a young tough boy with black curly hair, dark olive skin, and deep-set black eyes that were much older than the rest of him. He certainly didn't look like his father.

'You're wet,' she stated flatly.

'Bin swimming.'

'In your clothes?'

'Naw . . . In the nude, but I didn't have a towel.'

They surveyed each other warily.

'You can't stay here,' she said at last. 'We only said you could so's you wouldn't be shut up again.'

'But I thought—'

'I don't care what you thought. This is my place, not your old man's.'

'Yeh,' agreed Gino bitterly, 'and you gotta take care of business.'

'So what?' snapped Vera. 'I make a good livin' at it. I ain't ashamed.'

He reached for his suitcase and turned to go.

'Where'll you sleep?' she asked unexpectedly.

'I don't know,' he mumbled.

'Well . . .' she hesitated, 'I only got one more john tonight. Get outta here while he has his fun, then you can sleep on the couch for tonight. Just tonight mind you.'

Gino nodded. He was wet, tired, and in no mood to wander the streets. Just one night at Vera's was very welcome.

He stayed six months. He got his old job back as an auto mechanic which took care of the days, and at night he hung out with the old gang indulging in a bit of petty crime that did nobody any harm. He also looked after Vera, getting rid of difficult johns, and taking her out on Sundays – the one day she refused to work.

Occasionally she visited Paulo in Sing Sing Prison. Gino accompanied her once.

Paulo greeted him with a sharp, 'You got any booze?'

The first time he had seen his father in a year and that was his opening line. 'No,' he mumbled, nervous in his father's presence, ever mindful of the beatings he had endured at the hands of the thin miserable man in prison uniform.

'Aw c'mon, Pauly,' Vera said, 'y'know we can't bring booze in here. They search us, honest to God – y'know if I could I would.'

'Bitch!' Paulo muttered, and turned his back on both of them.

'He's in a bad mood today,' Vera whispered to Gino, 'take no notice, he'll be better next time you come.'

But he never went back for a second visit. Fuck it. He was too big to get beaten now – if Paulo ever laid another hand on him . . . Yeh . . . One visit to Sing Sing was enough.

Every week he reported to his probation officer who gave him a sharp five-minute talking to. Funny thing, each week there was a letter from California waiting for him. Costa Zennocotti seemed to have decided to give him a blow by blow account of his life. And although he never bothered to answer, the letters kept on coming.

Strange kid . . . Whatever made him think that Gino would be interested in his life. And what a life! School. A nice home. A step-sister who sounded like a real pain. The kid was living in an unreal world.

When his probation time was up he scrawled Costa a semi-literate note giving him a post office box number. If the kid enjoyed writing . . . well who was he to spoil his fun?

The night before Paulo was due to be released he took Vera to a movie. She seemed nervous and edgy, clinging onto his arm as they trudged home through the snow.

'Listen, kid,' she said, 'when Paulo comes home it ain't gonna work out. Know what I mean?'

He nodded.

'We could try . . . ' she continued, 'but hell . . . you know your old man.'

Yes. He knew. Paulo was a mean sonofabitch. He beat up on women. Treated them like dirt. Vera was no angel but Gino liked her, she had been good to him, and they both knew that when Paulo started in on her there was no way he could just stand around and watch.

'I'll move out in the morning,' he said.

'I'll miss you,' Vera replied, tears stinging her watery eyes. She reached out and touched him on the arm. 'If I can ever help y'out . . . '

He nodded. Vera had given him more love and affection than a lifetime of his father.

The next morning he was packed and out before she even woke. He took his one suitcase to work with him, and asked around about finding somewhere to live.

A new mechanic, Zeko, said there was a room going over at his place. Zeko was about nineteen, swarthy faced and greasy looking. Nobody liked him much, but a room was a room, so after work Gino accompanied him to a seedy house on 109th Street.

'Buildin's a shithouse,' Zeko offered, 'no heat, no hot water, no bath, crappers in the hall.'

'So what else is new?'

'I ain't stayin' long,' Zeko continued, 'gotta hot job comin' up gonna take me away from all this.' He winked, 'I'm the wheelman on a big one. I do OK. I'm in. Get it?'

'You ever been inside?' Gino asked.

'Me?' Zeko cackled, 'I'm too smart to get caught.' He wiped his nose on the sleeve of his jacket. 'Listen, we'll dump your case and go and get us a couple of beers and a couple of whores.'

'I gotta date,' Gino replied.

'She have a friend?' Zeko leered.

'Never asked her.'

'So ask.'

'Yeh . . . sure. Maybe next time.'

The room was even worse than he expected. But he took it anyway, he wasn't exactly used to palaces. He didn't have a date, he just had not felt like spending the evening with Zeko. Zeko the Creepo they called him at work.

It took him all of five minutes to settle into his new home. The room consisted of a bed, a worn rug, and a peeling dresser in the corner. That was it. But at least it was his.

Fat Larry's, a drug store over on 110th Street, was the hangout. There Gino met with his friends and generally horsed around.

'What happened with Zeko the Creepo?' Pinky Banana asked as soon as he arrived.

He shrugged, 'I got a room in his place – don't mean we havta become joined at the kneecap.'

'You gonna see your old man?' Catto inquired.

'Naw. I'll give him a few days.'

'Give him a few days and he'll be back inside.' Pinky

Banana laughed at his own humor, letting out a few loud farts for good measure.

'Jeeze!' Gino screwed up his nose, 'ain't it bad enough I got Catto on one side – now you too!'

Pinky Banana guffawed, and eyed a cute little blonde girl busying herself with an ice cream soda. He contemplated a quick flash, but Gino, as if reading his mind, said quickly, 'Not her, I got a hard-on for that one.'

Pinky Banana and Catto rolled eyes at each other. Another conquest for Gino. What *was* his secret?

The girl finished her soda and got up from the high bar stool. She was pretty and knew it. She walked past Gino and his cronies, head held high.

'Girl like you could get into trouble bein' out alone,' Gino sing-songed.

She pretended not to hear.

'Hey,' he said sharply, 'don't ignore me like I'm shit on the street.'

A blush stung the girl's cheeks and she quickened her steps. Pinky Banana laughed.

Gino slapped his hands together. 'I ain't in the mood to go chasing after some stuck-up piece.'

They heard her scream two minutes later. A sharp panic stricken scream from outside in the street.

Gino moved fast, bounding on the balls of his feet, Catto and Pinky Banana beside him.

Zeko the Creepo had little Miss Cuteness pinned up against the wall. She was squeaking like a frightened rabbit while his hands roamed all over her. Her white blouse was ripped down the front revealing her bosom.

'What you doin' Zeko?' Gino asked softly.

'Not your business – punk.' Zeko scowled.

'Yeh? Well I'm makin' it my business.'

Zeko thrust towards the frightened girl. 'I'm not greedy, when I'm through y'can all have a turn.'

'Get away from her – y'slimey creepo.'

'Fuck off Gino.'

They were fighting before anyone knew it. Struggling and rolling on the ground. Kicking and clawing at each other.

Gino was younger and shorter than Zeko, but stronger. He threw a good punch which busted Zeko's lip. Blood came pouring out.

'Y'dirty stinkin' little rat,' Zeko snarled. He reached into his boot and produced a knife.

They were both back on their feet now, warily circling each other. Pinky Banana and Catto had been joined by a neighborhood crowd who screamed for blood. Some were shouting for Gino. Some for Zeko.

Gino didn't hear anything. He had one eye on the knife, and one eye on Zeko's very move.

Zeko lunged suddenly, the knife cutting a vicious slash down the side of Gino's cheek. The blood was more profuse than the pain.

'You cock bastard!' Gino yelled. And the fury came over him. The all-enveloping black fury that he had felt the time he was attacking Brother Phillippe. Zeko wasn't Zeko anymore – he was lousy Paulo.

Suddenly his strength was boundless. He grabbed Zeko's knife arm, and twisted and twisted, not even hearing the sickening crack the arm made, nor Zeko's screams of pain. Pinky Banana and Catto had to drag him off the howling Zeko.

'I think you broke his arm,' Catto announced, not exactly sorry at the thought.

The haze slowly lifted from Gino's eyes. He shook his head, unsure for a moment where he was or what he was doing. He stared down at the whining Zeko. 'Next time it'll be your head,' he warned. He looked around for the little blonde girl who had started all the trouble. She was long gone. Just like a dame.

'We'd better go over to the hospital – get your face fixed up,' Pinky Banana suggested.

Gino touched the dripping blood on his cheek. That's all he needed – a stinking scar. 'Let's go,' he said quickly.

They put ten stitches in his face at the hospital. They asked a lot of questions too, but Gino wasn't saying anything.

Zeko was brought in as they were leaving. The two of them exchanged baleful glares but no words. The law of the streets was keep your mouth shut. Neither of them intended to break it.

Two days later Gino was working in the repair shop, lying under a propped-up Packard, when a stranger visited him. The stranger's shoes came into view first. Two-tone patent. Very racey.

'You Gino Santangelo?' A voice from above the shoes inquired.

'Who's asking?' He slid out from under the car.

'Never mind that. Are you?'

Gino's heart pounded just a little bit faster. Standing above him was Eddie the Beast – right-hand lieutenant of the notorious Salvatore Charlie Lucania.

He gulped, tried to conceal his nervousness, and stood up, wiping his oil-smeared hands on filthy trousers. 'Yeh – I'm Gino Santangelo,' he managed.

Eddie the Beast didn't hesitate. He smashed a punch into Gino's stomach, doubling him in two.

'That's for Zeko,' Eddie said calmly, 'he wanted to send his regards on account of the fact that he's lying in the hospital with a busted arm and cannot convey them personal.'

Gino straightened up, every street instinct telling him not to fight back. So he stood there, stared at Eddie and said, 'That's his bad luck, he asked for it.'

Eddie laughed. 'We heard you was one tough little punk. Looks like the word was right. Come on, Mr Lucania wants to see you.'

Pinky Banana's eyes bugged out of his head.

'I'll be back soon,' Gino told him, keeping his voice light. 'Fix it with the boss, tell him I got sick or somethin'.'

'Maybe ya just might,' Eddie inserted ominously.

Somehow Gino wasn't nervous. He didn't feel that anything bad was going to happen to him. On the contrary, he felt on the verge of some great good fortune.


Charlie Lucania greeted him in the back of a black Cadillac sedan parked nearby. He looked him over carefully, then spoke rapidly. 'Heard lots about you, kid. Some good – some bad.'

Gino remained silent.

'You gotta temper – that's OK. I gotta temper. You just gotta know when to use it. You understand what I'm sayin'?'

He nodded.

'I like t'have good people around me. Bring 'em in young, train 'em, get some loyalty goin'. You understand me?'

Again he nodded.

'How old are you?'

'Seventeen,' he lied. he still had a month to go.

'That's all right. That's good. S'long as you got moxie n' guts.' Lucania leaned forward, 'I picked Zeko to do a job for me. You put him out of action. I'm gonna go easy on you I'm givin' you his job. Next Wednesday night. Eight o'clock. Eddie'll give you the details.'

Lucania leaned back. The conversation was over as far as he was concerned.

Gino cleared his throat. 'Er . . . look . . . I'm glad of the chance . . . but I don't ever want to find myself in the can again.'

Lucania threw him a lazy look. 'You a good driver?'

'The best.'

'So you won't get caught.'

Eddie the Beast opened the car door. 'Come on punk,' he said, grinning. 'Out.'

It was then Gino realized he had no choice.

# Carrie 1926–1927

The man stared at Carrie, and she stared back at him with huge frightened eyes. He was a big negro, well over six feet. But it wasn't his height that frightened her, or his considerable bulk. It was the size of his penis.

She had 'entertained' him twice before, and each time he had nearly ripped her in half. She had complained to Leroy, crying and bleeding on both occasions. He had jeered at her for being a baby. She wasn't a baby. She was a prisoner.

'I don' feel good,' she said to the man, blinking back tears.

'Sure you do, honey,' the man replied, easing off his trousers. 'All the ladies feel good when they see what *I* got in store for 'em.'

Oh sweet Jesus! What had she done to deserve the life she was being forced to live? Since the fateful night when Leroy had raped her she had been kept locked up. Not a moment's daylight or freedom had come her way. Just a perpetual stream of men, and Leroy to collect the money, and grandma Ella to bring her food, sheets and towels when she remembered – which wasn't as often as it should be.

Leroy had rented the room next door, and that's where she had been imprisoned. A human machine, just there to service the men who passed in and out.

At first she had tried to say no. But Leroy had beat her until giving in seemed to be the easy way out.

The man had now removed his trousers and long woolen

underpants, and he stood before her, shirt flapping foolishly down, not covering his large organ.

'You . . . you hurt me with your thing,' she managed, 'isn't there some other way . . . ?'

The man thought for a moment, then a smile spread over his asinine features. 'I could spread it over your little titties then put it in your mouth,' he suggested.

Anything was better than having to take him between her legs. She nodded numbly, and peeled off her slip. She was painfully thin, faded marks of Leroy's beatings remained, and her legs and arms were like sticks. Her large breasts remained, and the man grabbed them roughly, rubbing his penis across them.

She shut her eyes, and wished she could cover her ears, the man's groans were not something she wanted to listen to. She tried to think about the past. The good things that had happened in her life. Mama Sonny. Philadelphia. Her job at Mr Dimes' fine house on Park Avenue.

The man was forcing his thing into her mouth now. It tasted of urine and sweat. She wanted to object, but it was too late, she was unable to speak. He was pushing back and forth, rubbing against her teeth, which longed, spitefully, to bite him.

She had never done this before. Would he push all the way down her throat and choke her?

She gagged, and he withdrew slightly. Then he was clutching onto her breasts as though they were two melons to be squeezed for ripeness, and he was moaning loudly and chanting some sort of prayer.

Then he was climaxing, and great spurts of salty thick liquid were flowing down her throat.

She thought she would be sick. But instead she swallowed, he withdrew, and it was over.

She had prevented him from splitting her in two. That was something wasn't it? She should celebrate really. After all it was her fourteenth birthday.

Grandma Ella died eight months later. Only Leroy didn't bother to tell Carrie for three days. She was virtually starving when he came to see her.

'Get dressed,' he said, shoving a dirty old dress in her direction.

'I need some food,' she pleaded. 'How can you just leave me locked up here with no food. I could die and . . . '

'Shut up – girl,' Leroy said roughly, 'my ma took a trip to heaven and all you can do is whine 'bout yourself.'

Her eyes widened, 'Grandma Ella died?'

'Grandma Ella died!' Leroy mimicked. 'She sure 'nuff did – an' I ain't hangin' round here any longer. I'm a gonna take me a trip out to California.' He rolled his eyes, 'Sunshine an' good times – here comes Le-roy!'

She stared at him. 'You mean I'm free?'

Leroy chuckled. 'Girl – you are my ticket to California. I'm sellin' you.'

Carrie backed away from him. 'You can't do that.'

'Oh no? Jest you watch me, girl. And you'd better behave yourself or I might jest slit your pretty little throat 'afor I go.'

Leroy meant what he said. He dressed her, fed her a greasy plate of fried chicken, and holding her firmly by the arm took her to a nearby house where a big fat woman prodded and poked her as if she were a piece of prime roast beef.

'Lissy, you all will not regret this bargain buy,' Leroy announced. He took hold of Carrie's dress and ripped it from her body. 'See these titties, these legs, that juicy little box.'

Carrie squirmed away from his touch.

'How'll I know she'll behave?' Lissy questioned suspiciously.

'Oh she'll behave,' Leroy said airily, 'she don' know no other job. She loves it. Jest keep her fed an' locked up – you won't have no trouble.'

'I don't know . . .' Lissy was unsure.

' 'Course you do. She's young, you'll make a fortune with her.'

'How much you want?'

'I thought we agreed a hundred dollars. You'll make that back in a matter of weeks – then it's all profit.'

Lissy narrowed business-like eyes. 'Fifty Leroy, that's as high as I'll go.'

'Sheeit!' Leroy was angry. 'You backin' down on me?'

'Take it or leave it.'

'Make it seventy-five.'

'Fifty.'

'Sixty,' he whined.

Lissy relented. 'Fifty-five an' it's a deal.'

They shook hands and money was exchanged. Then Leroy was on his way without so much as a goodbye.

Lissy stared at Carrie. 'You're too skinny,' she stated, 'gotta fatten you up. Come with me. I'll show you your room. An' a good bath wouldn't do you any harm.'

Life at Lissy's establishment was an improvement. Meals were regular. The johns were better, and the room she was kept locked in was luxurious in comparison to what she was used to.

There were other girls there too. At first she wasn't allowed to even see them, but after a couple of months, when she had more than earned back her price, Lissy relented, and gave her a few sweet tastes of freedom.

She would have run. But Leroy was right. She had nowhere to run to. She was a whore now – nothing could change that sad fact. There was no going back to Philadelphia or a job with Mr Dimes. Whoring was her life, and as one of the other girls pointed out, if it was to be her life why didn't *she* make money out of it too?

Shortly after, she approached Lissy. 'I want a share of what I make,' she insisted.

Lissy laughed, 'How come it took you so long to ask?'

By the age of fifteen, Carrie had saved herself a nice little stash of money. With her big breasts, long dark hair, and oriental eyes, she was really something to look at.

Lissy understood when she told her she was moving on. She wasn't happy about it, but there was nothing she could do.

Carrie took herself to see Florence Williams, one of the biggest madams in Harlem. She lived in a beautiful apartment off 141st Street along with three special girls, and after one look at Carrie, Florence was happy to give her a room. The deal was she would get twenty dollars a john, and out of every twenty she would pay Florence five for her rent.

The room she had was a dream. A comfortable bed with a white cover, and matching telephone. In the corner was a china washbasin, and beside it a pile of clean towels – kept that way by a maid who visited the room after every customer.

A maid! Carrie did not enjoy what she was doing, but it was certainly becoming more acceptable.

The other girls at Florence's were friendly. And what's more two of them were white. Carrie was soon to discover that half the customers were white! She was amazed . . . Well she had just never imagined that *white* men would have to pay for it. Seemingly respectable white men who probably had good jobs and wives and all sorts of advantages in life . . .

The other girls laughed when she expressed her surprise.

'Honey, white men a hell of a lot dirtier than some horny

nigger,' Cecilia told her. Cecilia was tall and haughty looking, the last person you would suspect would be selling it. 'Niggers want to give it to you good – show you what a great big wonderful fuck they are. White guys . . . well . . . they like it strange. Tie 'em up and beat 'em up like they're doin' somethin' *real* filtheee. Give me a good old spade any day.'

Cecilia had skin the color of buttermilk, red hair, and long long legs. She spoke in a lazy southern drawl.

The other white girl was all big wide eyes and bounce.

And then there was Billie, a black girl who Carrie suspected was about the same age as herself, although they both claimed to be eighteen.

Carrie thought Billie was real pretty, she liked her a lot. Billie had come down from Baltimore to visit with her mother, and had gotten a job as a maid – hated it – and ended up selling it at Florence Williams' place. 'Beats the hell outta cleaning up after some fat lazy white bitch,' Billie drawled. She had a lovely voice, real nice and smooth, Carrie thought, especially when she would sing along with some of the jazz musicians on the Victrola. 'You oughtta be a singer,' Carrie told her.

'Yeah,' Billie agreed, 'there's a lotta things I oughtta be doin' – and one day I'm a gonna bust right out an' surprise everyone.'

'Sure you will,' Carrie agreed, 'and so will I.' Only she didn't quite know how. Billie had a dream. She had nothing. At least she was safe selling her body. She had no desire to go out in the world again and face people. They would all take one look at her and know immediately what she was.

Sometimes she would wake in the middle of the night and curse grandma Ella and Leroy. Other times she would wake and force herself not to think about them.

The days turned into nights then back to days again, and Carrie really didn't notice the difference. It was as if she was in a permanent daze – even the money she was managing to salt away didn't mean anything to her. Each john blended into the next. Black, white, old, young, it meant nothing to her.

Florence Williams summoned her for a talk. 'You'd better change your outlook little gal. These cats comin' here for a good time. From what I hear you ain't givin' it to them.'

One night, while Carrie serviced a john, there was a big commotion outside her room. Angry raised voices. Billie and a customer. And Florence's calm tone trying to smooth things over.

Carrie found out later that Billie had turned a client down. A real big negro by the name of Big Blue Ranier. A man with connections. He had been with Bub Hewlett – the man who practically ran Harlem.

Florence was furious. 'These guys are in real snug n' tight with the cops,' she fumed. 'You gotta learn who you can say no to and who you can't.'

Billie was unrepentant.

The next morning, as the girls sat around the kitchen eating breakfast, there was a raid. The cops broke in and arrested everyone in the place. They were hauled off to jail in a paddy-wagon.

Within hours Florence Williams and the two white girls were released. Billie and Carrie were not. They were booked, charged with prostitution, and after a horrible night in jail, taken over to the Jefferson Market Court.

When Billie saw who was presiding on the bench she groaned. 'We have had it,' she announced to a by-now petrified Carrie. 'See that old bitch up there. That's Judge Jean Norris – she's meaner than a plateful of turds!'

Billie got off lightly, as far as Carrie could tell. Her mother appeared in court and swore that Billie was eighteen. Then the judge squinted at a piece of paper, said it was a health report and that Billie was sick, and sent her off to a city hospital in Brooklyn.

When Carrie's turn came the judge gave her a real mean stare and asked all sorts of questions which Carrie refused to answer. The only thing she volunteered was the fact that she was eighteen years old.

Finally, exasperated, Judge Norris said, 'If you don't care to answer the court's questions that's up to you young lady. I could be lenient with you, but because of your attitude I don't intend to be. Three months. Welfare Island. Case dismissed.'

Judge Norris was every bit as mean as her reputation.

## Wednesday, July 13th, 1977, New York

'Christ!' Lucky exclaimed. 'What the hell happened?'

Steven, jolted against the side of the pitch black elevator, replied, 'I don't know . . . must be the generator gone out.'

'Who are you?' she demanded, suddenly suspicious. 'If you pulled the switch to try and score you are starting with the *wrong* person – let me tell you *that* up front. I am a black belt karate champion – and if I choose to move on you you'll feel it all the way down to your balls. I'm . . .'

'Excuse me, Miss,' Steven snapped, '*you* are the one standing next to the control panel. Why don't you try pressing the emergency button instead of making speeches?'

'Miz.'

'Oh so sorry, do forgive me. Miz. Do you think you could be kind enough to press the emergency button?'

'I can't see the goddamn button.'

'Don't you have a match or a cigarette lighter?'

'Don't you?'

'I don't smoke.'

'Huh! I should have guessed!' She zipped open her shoulder bag and groped for her Dunhill lighter. 'Shit!' she exclaimed, remembering that she had left her lighter on Costa's desk, 'I don't have it.'

'What?'

'My lighter. Are you *sure* you don't have any matches?'

'Of course I'm sure.'

'*Everyone* carries matches.'

'You don't.'

'True.' She stamped her foot down sharply, 'goddamit I *hate* the dark.'

Steven put his arms out in front of him and edged across the elevator. He touched Lucky and she responded with a swift kick, catching him on the leg.

'Ouch! Why did you do that?'

'I told you, fella. Start anything and you are in big trouble.'

'You really are a nut case,' he complained. 'I am merely trying to find the emergency button.'

'Good for you.' She backed into a corner and squatted down on the floor. 'Hurry up, will you. I hate the dark.'

'You said that once,' he replied coldly. His leg felt like a sledgehammer had hit it. He would probably be sporting a purple bruise any minute. He felt down the panel of buttons, pressing them all for good luck. Nothing happened.

'You find it?' she snapped.

'Doesn't seem to be working.'

'Wonderful! That's why they have emergency buttons so

that when you're in a goddamn emergency nothing FUCK-ING HAPPENS!'

'No need to scream.'

'Don't tell *me* what to do.'

There was silence while they both considered the situation.

Lucky thought – Just my luck. Trapped with some dumb jerk off artist who doesn't even smoke. Uptight schmuck.

Steven thought – What a mouth! She sounds like she's been sharing a room with the New York Yankees!

'So,' said Lucky, forcing her voice to remain calm, 'what are we going to do?'

Good question. What were they going to do? 'Sit tight,' replied Steven.

'Sit tight!' she screamed. 'Are you fucking kidding!'

'Will you stop using that language.'

'Oh sorry,' her voice dripped sarcasm. 'I'll never say kidding again!'

Upstairs in his luxurious office Costa Zennocotti fumbled in a cupboard for some candles. He lit them with Lucky's cigarette lighter lying on his desk. Then he walked over to the window and looked out. The city was spread out before him – lit only by the moon. It was just like the time before in 1965 – only then everyone had said it was a freak cut out, and couldn't possibly happen again. Well it had happened again all right.

He swore softly under his breath as he thought about the forty-eight flights of stairs he would have to climb down. Maybe not. Maybe this time it would be a short blackout.

He sighed and returned to the cupboard where he had gotten the candles. His secretary, a pessimistic girl, kept a special shelf for just such emergencies. Apart from a stock of candles, there was a blanket, a portable battery operated television, and six cans of orange juice. Clever girl. Tomorrow she would get a raise.

Costa took out the television and a can of orange juice. Then he loosened his tie and made himself comfortable on the couch.

The small set sprang into action as soon as he switched it on. 'Charlie's Angels' cavorted across the screen. Costa went to change channels, and as he did so it occurred to him that Lucky might be trapped in the elevator. But no . . . she had left a good ten minutes before the blackout.

He switched to a news channel, and settled back to hear the worst.

'Whatcha doin' out there, asshole?' yelled the dark-haired boy locked in Dario's bedroom. 'Pullin' the fuse on your fuckin' lights ain't gonna help yer. You fuckin' *hear me* asshole?' He kicked the door again and again, and Dario was thankful for the decorator who had insisted he change the flimsy interior doors in the apartment for ones made of good solid oak.

'What's your problem?' he shouted in what he hoped was a firm unafraid voice. 'I thought we had a good time together.'

'You prickass!' the boy screamed. 'You dirty fag!'

Dario was genuinely puzzled. 'If I'm a dirty fag what does that make you?'

'Don't fuck with me brother!' the boy's voice was verging on hysteria, 'I ain't no fag. I like stickin' it to big juicy girls.'

Dario felt more secure now, in spite of the power cut and being locked in his own apartment with this freak. The strong oak door was not going to give out. It was going to hold the maniac until he could call for help.

'Did someone send you?' he asked as coldly as he could manage.

'Aw fuck off,' the boy replied, 'an' turn the fuckin' lights back on – bein' in the dark ain't gonna help ya.'

Dario thought about who he could call for help. The list was limited, he didn't have many friends.

'Turn the lights on, asshole,' screamed the boy, 'or I'll bust right outta here an' smash your fuckin' head in.'

As the lights went out Carrie froze. She did not finish the sentence she was in the middle of. She stood stupidly by the check-out desk in the supermarket in Harlem, her mouth still open.

'What's goin' on round here?' the girl behind the desk shrieked. Her words were almost drowned out by the whoops and hollers of the customers as they realized lights, security, everything was gone.

'Outasite!' shrieked a woman's excited voice, 'let's sure 'nuff help ourselves sisters!'

Before Carrie's eyes grew accustomed to the gloom, the two boys that had been behind her when she entered the supermarket were now on either side of her, hustling and shoving.

'Hey – lady – what's a foxy puff like y'all doin' down this-saway?'

'C'mon. Baby, Baby, Baby . . . You cool baby? You carrin' coffee cream 'tween your long legs baby?'

And as they crooned and hustled and shoved her back and forth they robbed her. Ripping the diamonds from her ears so that the lobes bled. Sliding the diamond ring from her finger. Snatching the diamond clips from her hair. And all the time carrying on a dialogue in husky tones that was almost like the start of a Teddy Pendergrass record.

Carrie was frozen with fear. It brought back every bad memory of her past life. It was all so long ago . . . And yet it could have happened yesterday. 'Leave me alone,' she started to scream, 'leave me alone!'

The boys gave her a final shove, grabbed her purse, and ran.

Gino didn't say a word to the woman sitting beside him, her long fingernails digging into the palm of his hand. He saw every light in New York vanish and he didn't so much as cough.

It came as no surprise to him when the plane, already on a descent pattern, changed course and started to climb.

A buzz of conversation shot through the cabin. Gino was not the only one to have observed the total blackout.

The lady beside him sat upright in her seat. 'What's happening?' she asked. 'Oh my God! Isn't that noise the landing gear coming in again?'

'Don't panic,' he said softly, 'I think there's some kind of problem in New York.'

Her voice rose an octave. 'A problem?' She let go of his hand long enough to swig from her flask. Then she clutched his arm, her face ashen, 'I don't feel well,' she moaned.

'So lay off the booze.'

She shot him a dirty look. Just like a woman, he thought, if there's one thing they hate it's criticism.

'I'm hot,' Lucky complained, 'how long have we been here now?'

Steven peered at his watch, 'About two hours.'

'Two hours! Christ! At this rate we'll be here 'til morning.'

'Probably.'

'Is that all you can say - probably. I mean there must be *some* way out of here.'

'Tell me about it.'

'Shit! You really are a pain in the ass.'

They lapsed into silence.

Lucky could not stand the silence. It was bad enough being stuck in some pitch black box suspended who knew how many levels above ground. But why oh why did it have to be with some idiot?

'What's your name?' she asked.

'Steven Berkely.'

'Mine's Lucky.'

'You could have fooled me.'

'I mean my name is Lucky. L–U–C–K–Y. Get it?'

He wished she would shut up and then maybe he could fall asleep and not wake up until morning and certain rescue.

'Oh God! I can't stand this!' She stood up and hammered with her fists on the side of the elevator. 'Help!' she screamed. 'Help! Hello out there! We're trapped in the elevator! Help!'

'It won't do you any good,' Steven drawled laconically, 'there's no one up here to hear you.'

'How do *you* know?'

'It's late – no one around.'

'Bullshit! How can you possibly make a statement like that. *You're* here aren't you? *I'm* here. The building could be full of people.'

'I don't think so.'

'Oh *you* wouldn't.'

The heat was becoming oppressive. Steven had already taken off his jacket and loosened his tie, but the sweat was pouring off him. He wondered if Aileen was worried. But why should she be worried? They didn't have a date did they?

'Is anyone expecting you?' he asked.

'Huh?'

'Do you have a date tonight? Will anyone be concerned when you don't turn up?'

Now that was a *good* question. Hmmm . . . How to answer . . . No date, just a prowl around a few singles bars. No one to care whether she turned up or not. 'What makes you think I'm not married?'

'You don't sound married.'

'Oh? And what does married sound like?'

'Not like you.'

'Very enigmatic. And you? Are you married?'

'Divorced.'

'Ha! Couldn't cut it, huh?'

He swallowed a rude reply. This woman was getting on his nerves.

'Well?' she taunted.

'I'm going to try and sleep,' he said tightly, 'I suggest you do the same.'

'Sleep! In this sweat box? Are you serious?'

'Yes, I'm serious.'

She decided to turn him on, anything to pass the time, 'I've got a better idea.'

'What?'

'Why don't we fuck?'

Her question hung in the air. He didn't reply.

'Well?' she questioned boldly.

'I thought,' he said slowly, 'when this elevator first stopped, that your main concern in life was keeping me away from you.'

'Sure. I didn't know you then. Now we're old friends.'

'I don't believe you!'

'So believe me. I'm twenty-seven years old, not bad looking, good body. C'mon Steven whoever you are – it'll be *great*. I promise you that.'

'Are you a hooker?'

She began to laugh. 'A hooker! Oh boy!'

'You sure sound like one.'

'Oh I see. Any female who wants to fuck is a hooker. You're one of the old school, huh? A nice old fashioned gent who likes his ladies *real* conventional.'

'I think you need help.'

'Ha! *You're* the one with the hang-ups.' She paused, grinning to herself in the dark. 'So – you don't want to fuck then?'

'No. I certainly don't.'

'Are you gay?'

'No I'm not.'

'Then you're unusual. Most guys offered a free piece would jump at the opportunity.'

'I'm not most guys. Besides, I think you should know that I'm black.'

She laughed derisively, 'What difference does that make?'

'Well lady,' his voice was uptight, 'I wouldn't like you to get one big shock when the lights go up. *Not* that I'm about to oblige you,' he added quickly.

'Did you tell me that you're black hoping it would put me off?' she taunted.

'Nope. I told you because I wanted to get you off my back. Sex with a stranger is not my idea of fun.'

'Shame! You don't know what you're missing.'

'Oh yes I do. And anyway – I don't sleep with white women.'

She snorted. 'God! You're so self-righteous. And why, may I ask, don't you sleep with white women?'

'Because they fall into two categories.'

'And what are they?'

'You really want to know?'

'I wouldn't ask if I didn't.'

'OK. They're either looking for the myth of the giant black penis. Or they are being so damn liberal it's sickening. You know – look at me – I'm sleeping with a black man – aren't I daring.'

Lucky laughed, 'I know the type. But I can assure you *I* don't fall into either of those two categories.'

'I *bet* you don't.'

They were both silent for a few minutes.

Steven wondered why he was revealing so much of himself to her. He was telling her more than enough. He would be sorry when the lights went up and they were both jarred back to reality.

'*I* divide *men* into two categories,' Lucky broke the silence. 'I meet a guy and I know immediately which one he falls into.'

'What categories do you have?'

'The guy I screw right off. And the guy I want to get to know first. The second category are far and few between.'

Steven laughed mirthlessly, 'You sound like you have your problems. You'll be telling me you were badly treated as a child next.'

'My father wasn't exactly the average guy in the street. In fact I had to keep him a big dark secret or I wouldn't have got any action at all.'

'Why? What was he? A policeman?'

'It doesn't matter.' She stood up and stamped her booted foot, 'Shit! When are we going to get out of here?'

'Sit down and keep calm. Getting excited isn't going to help.'

'Listen – I couldn't get *you* excited – so why shouldn't I?'

'Because . . . we've got a long hot night ahead of us. Conserve your energy.'

'You're right,' she slumped back into her corner and unzipped her boots, then she wriggled out of her jeans. 'Whew! That's better!'

'What is?'

'Take your clothes off. I have.'

'We had that conversation . . .'

'Not for sex, stupid. It's just a lot cooler.'

He contemplated her suggestion. But how would it look when they were discovered if he was practically naked?

'I bet I know what you're thinking,' she teased.

'What?'

'You're thinking if I take my clothes off will she attack me? Will she leap on my virgin flesh and . . .'

He couldn't help smiling, 'You *are* mad.'

'Oh sure I am. Bin' mad all my life, it gets me through the day. Take your clothes off – I promise I won't lay a finger on you.'

He wondered what she looked like. He couldn't even make out her shadow the blackness was so dense. He imagined she was blonde, slightly buxom, with protruding teeth and a nice smile.

She wondered what he looked like. Short, studious, probably wore glasses. An Alex Haley, certainly not an O. J. Simpson.

'You didn't think I really meant it when I said let's fuck, did you?' she asked curiously.

He hesitated before replying, he was sure that she *had* meant it. 'Of course not.'

She laughed wickedly, 'Well I did. Nothing like a good fuck to take one's mind off things!'

Costa was dozing on the couch in his office when the phone rang. He groped for the instrument, and sent a table lamp crashing to the floor. Then he remembered that he was still in his office, and he stumbled up, still half asleep, and made his way over to his desk. He lifted the receiver, 'Yes?'

'Costa?'

'Yes. Who is this?'

'It's me, Dario. I thought I'd never find you. I called your club, then your home, then I thought maybe you were still at the office . . . God! Am I glad I reached you.'

Dario. Costa frowned. The only time he ever heard from him was when he needed something.

As if on cue Dario continued, 'Costa. You've got to help me. I'm in trouble. I want somebody . . . got rid of.'

'Don't talk on the phone,' Costa snapped.

'Not iced,' Dario explained, 'just out of my apartment that's all.'

'Will you shut up!' Costa hissed, thinking of how this conversation would sound if there was a tap on his phone. Every week he had his office checked over by an expert . . . but it was not inconceivable.

Dario's voice started to shake, 'Costa. I need help now. There is a maniac in my apartment who is trying to kill me. Right now he is locked in the bedroom but . . . '

'Get out of there immediately,' Costa commanded, 'check into a hotel and contact me tomorrow. I'll see the situation is . . . dealt with.'

'You don't understand,' Dario's voice was rising hysterically, 'I *can't* get out of here. He has my keys. I'm locked in.'

Costa thought quickly, his mind raking for an instant solution. 'The cops . . . ' he began.

'Forget it,' Dario interrupted, 'my father wouldn't like the publicity.'

The picture became clear. One of Dario's pick-ups had turned on him. 'I know someone,' Costa said slowly. 'You just stay put.'

'Oh God!' Dario's voice filled with panic, 'Oh God! I think he's getting . . . out. Costa! You've got to help me – he is . . . he is . . . Oh Christ!'

The line went dead in Costa's hand.

Wide-eyed with fear, blood dripping from her torn earlobes, Carrie backed into a corner as all around her the noise and commotion grew. Her long black hair fell around her face, and the sour taste of bile filled her mouth. *I'm going to throw up. Oh Christ, I'm going to throw up.*

The sound of glass shattering filled her ears, and two excited women ran past her yelling, 'Let's go git us a free Tee Vee.'

She staggered out of the supermarket after them, surrounded by men, women, children, all loaded up with as much food as they could carry. One thought filled her head. Get to the car. Get out of these mean streets.

'Hi there, sister, y'all take these,' a giggling fat woman thrust a packet of paper towels at her, 'I cain't carry 'em, an' I's sure 'nuff ain't leavin' 'em.'

Carrie held the package dumbly. *Where was her car? Where had she left it?* She shook her head. *Goddamn it woman. Pull yourself together. You've got to get out of this place.*

Of course. Her car was in the parking lot. But if she got in her car and left – what then? She had come up to Harlem for a reason. Protecting Steven was more important than getting out of this place.

But then she remembered that her gun was in her purse, and her purse had been grabbed.

She hurried to the parking lot and was just in time to see her car speed past her. Her beautiful dark green Cadillac Seville, all the windows open, the stereo radio blasting out, and her two young assailants sitting comfortably in the front seats. *Of course. The keys to her car had been in her purse.*

She wanted to cry, to scream, anything. Instead she just stood stock still allowing the hate to course through her body. Deciding for sure that whoever had lured her back here was going to die – one way or another.

'Mr Santangelo,' the pretty stewardess bent and whispered in his ear, 'there's been a total power failure in New York and the pilot is taking us to Philadelphia where we can land. I do hope it won't inconvenience you too much . . .'

Before he could reply the captain's voice came booming through the cabin speakers with the same message.

'Can I get you anything Mr Santangelo?' the stewardess asked solicitously.

'No,' he shook his head, 'I'm fine.'

But he wasn't fine. He was pissed off at not being able to set foot in New York. Seven years away and now this.

The woman who had chosen to sit beside him came staggering back from the toilet. 'Philadelphia!' she moaned, 'can you imagine?'

Yeh. He could imagine. Total chaos.

# Gino 1923–1924

The job Gino did for Charlie Lucania was to change his whole life. Wheelman on a bootleg hi-jack – the job was a grudge set up against someone who had double-crossed Lucania. Gino was chosen to replace Zeko because they needed someone clean – if the gang was caught there would be no threads leading back to Lucania.

So Gino found himself out on the road behind the wheel of a brand new Packard which he had picked up at a designated spot. Two free-lance hoods rode with him.

He was nervous as hell, but when the King Of Booze asked you to do something you couldn't exactly turn him down.

Anyway it was his fault that Zeko was out of action – although the creepy little bastard had deserved more than a busted arm.

In a way Gino was flattered to have been picked out. The fact that he had a reputation was a buzz – and he certainly wasn't about to let anyone down. It was a well-known fact that Charlie Lucania was always on the lookout for fresh young talent. 'You build an empire out of loyalty – ' he had been known to say, 'catch 'em young and treat 'em right and they ain't gonna stab you in the balls.'

He drove the Packard well. The job went without a hitch. And the next day Eddie the Beast turned up at the garage and handed him a packet containing fifty crisp one-dollar bills. 'You done good,' Eddie stated, 'we'll be callin' on you again.'

Gino was knocked out. Fifty bucks! For driving a car! Shit – he had never had fifty bucks in his life.

He wanted to celebrate, and what better way than buying himself a new outfit. He had seen a suit he wanted in a tailor's window, black with a white pinstripe – the sharpest goddamn suit he had ever set eyes on. And now he could have it!

He didn't wait until work was finished, he just walked, with Pinky Banana calling after him, 'Hey Gino, what'll I tell the boss?'

'Tell him he can shove his job up his ass,' he replied confidently. After all, hadn't Eddie the Beast said – 'We'll be callin' on you . . . ' Why the hell should he be busting his ass fixing other people's cars for a few lousy bucks a week, when he could pull in fifty crisp new singles for a couple of hours' work?

He bounced off down the street, walking on air. He felt his eyes had been opened. Suddenly he knew what he wanted in life. Money. Plenty. And you didn't get what he had in mind working your balls off nine till five. No sirree. Charlie Lucania had had no golden beginning – but he had grabbed opportunities when they came his way – and look at him now. A big man. A hero. Tough sure, but when you were brought up on the streets tough was the only way to survive.

The tailor took the suit out of his window reluctantly, and then only after Gino had flashed money before his eyes. It was too big, the jacket ludicrously long, and the pants at least three sizes too large. He stared at himself in the tailor's mirror, frustration mounting. 'It don't fit,' he stated blankly.

'I can alter it,' the tailor offered. He had seen the money and wanted it. 'A week. You come back and it'll fit you perfect.'

'Tonight.'

'Impossible.'

Gino narrowed his eyes, 'Tonight,' he said in his toughest voice. 'How much extra?'

A deal was set, proving to Gino that if you had money you could buy anything.

He swaggered off down the street well pleased with himself. He had money to burn and time to spare.

He headed for Fat Larrys, but there wasn't too much action there. Sliding into a booth he ordered himself a double chocolate soda.

He hardly noticed the pretty little blonde at first, but she kept on swaying past his booth, firm breasts jutting purposefully out. Then he remembered. Little Miss Cuteness from the other night. He fingered the ugly black stitches still holding his cheek together. 'Hey you!' he called to her.

She stopped beside his booth, eyes wide and very blue. 'Me?' she questioned innocently.

'Yeh – you.' He pointed to the scar on his cheek, 'See what I got on account of you?'

Her big blue eyes didn't waver. She was uncommonly pretty. He had a sudden hot desire to get his hands on her magic button. 'Aintcha gonna say thank you?'

She tossed blonde curls imperiously, 'Thank you so much for stopping one of your *friends* from attacking me.' She had a breathy soft voice which didn't quite match the sarcasm she was trying to inject into it.

'One of my friends!' He was incredulous. He pointed to his cheek. 'You think I got this from one of my friends?'

'I don't really care where you got it.' She stared at him, 'It looks pretty horrible – that's all *I* can say.'

As she turned to walk away he was on his feet. 'Hey *you*,' he yelled, furious at her sassy attitude, 'don'tcha know who I am?'

She smiled sweetly, 'Some punk, just like your friends.' She walked over to where two girlfriends waited nervously by the door.

'I'm Gino Santangelo,' he shouted, 'G-I-N-O. Remember the name, you'll be hearin' a lot about me.'

'Oh, sure,' she said sarcastically, and the three of them exited.

He shook his head in disbelief. Smart ass broad. And for *that* he had gotten his face ripped up? He should have let Zeko have her – knocked some of the shit out of her.

He wondered what her name was. Where she lived. Who she was. He finished his ice cream soda.

Time enough to find out.

Gino had never visited a whorehouse. Unlike his friends he had never needed to – fresh young pussy was plentiful on the street for him. He had his choice and he took it. He had heard about the girls at Madam Lola's though. Real hot shot whores who charged twelve dollars for opening their legs. Some price. What did they have – fur-lined pussy?

Catto and Pinky Banana usually got it on with a band of hookers who looked like they'd give Dracula a fright. Three bucks for maybe a dose of the clap. That was one trip Gino would never go on. But a real high class whorehouse . . . With tramps who charged twelve bucks . . . Well . . . he figured he should try everything once. Besides which, he had a free afternoon -- and carrying a big bankroll around certainly got you hot.

Madam Lola was a thin high yella woman with flinty blood-shot eyes and a snapdragon mouth. She looked Gino over from head to toe and snapped a sharp – 'Yes?'

He was suddenly aware of his appearance – scuffed work clothes stained with oil and grease and thick dirt under his fingernails. Maybe he should have waited until he picked up his suit. But what the hell . . . He knew enough about whores from Vera . . . If you had the money it didn't matter what you looked like. He reached into his pocket and flashed a few bills.

Madam Lola snatched, but he was not about to get conned. 'How long do I get for twelve bucks?' he demanded.

She laughed. 'How long? Sonny, two minutes is about all *you'll* be able to manage. It's *come* and *out*.' She beckoned him to follow her with long red lacquered nails, leading him through a beaded curtain into a musty room full of velvet couches and small tables piled high with illegal booze. Madam Lola took care of all the right people in all the right places.

The room was disappointingly empty. Gino had imagined a selection of gorgeous girls lying around ready for him to inspect.

'Sit,' Madam Lola said. 'I'll get you a girl.'

'I'd like a drink first.'

'You're too young to drink.'

'I'm too young to fuck but you're letting me. So make it a double scotch.'

She pursed dragonfly lips, 'A tough little guy.'

'The name is Gino Santangelo. Remember it. You're gonna hear a lot about me.'

'Really?' The sarcasm was thick.

'Yeh – really And for twelve bucks I get to choose don't I? Wheel in the girls.'

Humping a whore was different. Gino's choice, a small pretty blonde, was matter-of-fact and businesslike. She led him into a bedroom, stripped off her thin kimono, and lay expectantly on the bed, legs parted. This was a very different situation from doing it in back lots and on rooftops. Gino hesitated, then took off his trousers and shorts and was surprised that he wasn't as hot as he'd thought he was. In fact he was disappointingly limp.

'First time, honey?' the whore questioned sympathetically.

'You kidding?' he replied beligerently.

'No need to be embarrassed.'

*Him* – embarrassed! What a laugh. Gino the Ram. The first time in his life he wasn't able to get it up.

The whore sat up. She had very small breasts – one of them faintly bruised. She reached for his penis.

He backed away. 'No,' he said quickly, 'I wanna do somethin' else.'

'What?' she asked suspiciously.

'I wanna tongue you.'

'Huh?'

'Tongue you – lick you – suck you.'

She looked alarmed. She had been a whore for six whole months and straight fucking was all that had ever been required of her.

'Lie back an' spread your legs,' he said softly.

The small blonde was unsure of herself now. 'It's probably extra,' she whined, 'I'll have to ask Lola.'

'Oh no,' he replied, gaining in confidence every minute, 'cheaper I would think. But I've paid the twelve bucks an' I'm not lookin' for a refund.'

'How old are you anyway?' she muttered, lying back and opening her legs.

He took a deep breath and plunged in, first saying, 'Old enough to take care of you.'

The sensation was strange. He explored her stickiness with his tongue, revelling in the smell and taste of her while she lay very still, her legs rigidly spread.

Instinct took his tongue to the magic spot, and he knew he was on target when she let out a small involuntary groan. He worked his tongue diligently. If he was to learn something new he wanted to be sure he learned it good.

Soon her legs relaxed, and the stickiness turned to a hot smooth wetness, and her groans became louder.

A brisk knock at the door interrupted them. 'Everything all right in there?' Madam Lola's voice sang out.

'Everything's fine,' he replied. 'Just fine.'

The whore was rolling around on the bed now, and Gino returned to his work. He opened her up with his thumbs and she loved that. Then he plunged his tongue deep inside her and felt her spasm.

He was good and hard now. He came up and moved his prick into her.

She was out of control and moaning loudly. Gino joined her in her climax, and they moved across the bed stuck firmly together. They stayed that way for minutes, then gradually the whore realized what had happened, and embarrassed, she extracted herself, and slipped into her kimono not looking at him.

He laughed, pleased with his first effort. 'Good, huh?'

'Where'd you learn that?' she couldn't help asking.

'With you,' he replied, climbing off the bed and getting dressed. 'Now I can go out and try it on the real world.'

The suit fitted excellently, and Gino gave the tailor an extra buck for doing such a fine job.

He admired himself in the mirror. Very sharp indeed. But a black shirt would do nicely. And new shoes would not hurt. He fingered the ugly black stitches cutting a swathe down his cheek, smelt the whore still on his thumbs, and smiled.

'Come back any time,' the tailor said eagerly, 'any time at all.'

'Yeh – I might just do that.' He swaggered somewhat self-consciously out onto the street. He felt like a king. New suit. Madam Lola's. Money still left in his pocket.

As he walked his mind buzzed. He did not want to become like his old man – a fucked-up two-bit gangster whose greatest kick in life was beating up on women. Being locked up was not an experience he wished to repeat. The Protectory had been bad enough – he had no illusions about jail.

But then again who wanted to spend their life lying around

under other people's cars? Getting covered in oil and dirt and grease? Getting paid peanuts?

Not Gino. He wanted money. He wanted all the good things that money could buy. And no way was he going to get what he wanted legitimately.

Paulo was a fool – and fools got caught. Gino had different plans. He was going to be a big man like Charlie Lucania. And the time to start was now.

The job he had done for Lucania had gone like a breeze. All it had taken was a couple of hoods with rods, a driver, and a car. Easy pickings. Fifty bucks for him. Probably twice that amount for the others. So the overall haul must be worth plenty.

He made his way to Fat Larrys, where Pinky Banana and Catto pounced on him.

'Wow-Wowee, where'd ya get it?' Catto sang.

'I want one too,' Pinky Banana rolled his eyes and fingered the material, 'mama, I want one too!'

'No reason why ya shouldn't get one,' Gino said. 'I got an idea . . . All we gotta do is get us a couple rods, steal a motor, an' hey hey – we're in business!'

'Rods.' Catto blinked, 'I don' want any part of that.'

'Not to *use*,' Gino said quickly, 'just to *threaten* with – works like a dream.'

Catto wiped his nose on the side of his sleeve, 'Whacha talkin' 'bout, Gino?'

'Money,' he replied, 'there's plenty about. What the fuck we workin' our asses off for? Whyn't we get out on the street an' take it – just like everyone else?'

It *could* all be worked out of course – if you had enough money. And that was his problem – with the new suit, and the whore, there wasn't that much change left over from the fifty. To get money you needed money. Maybe if he told Vera what he had in mind she would bankroll him . . . He could cut her in on the action . . . Certainly pay her back with a profit.

Later that night he decided to pay her a visit. He had promised he would drop by – let her know how he was getting on. And if he was in luck Paulo would not be around.

Vera was not working. She was also not sober. She lolled on her bed – the only illumination in the room coming from a street light near the window. At Gino's knock she slurred, 'Come in, put your money down, an' get on with it.'

'Hey, it's me,' he said quickly, 'just dropped by to see how you're doin'.'

'Doin' fine,' she mumbled, 'jus' fine.' She paused to reach for a bottle beside the bed, took a swig, then added, 'Who the hell's me?'

'Gino of course!' He reached for the light switch, clicked it on, and wished he hadn't. She was not a pretty sight. Her dirty satin nightdress had been ripped off one shoulder, and exposed her breasts which were covered with livid red cigarette burns. Her face was almost pulped – both eyes swollen and slitted.

She stared at him lethargically, and attempted to smile. Several of her front teeth were missing.

'I look a mess, don't I?' she slurred. And tears welled up in her eyes and slid silently down her bruised cheeks.

He had no need to ask who had done this to her. He only knew that he should get her to a hospital immediately.

He went over to the bed and cradled her body in his arms. She smelt like a brewery, and on top of this there was the pungent odor of sweat and urine.

'Hey,' he said softly, 'I'm gonna leave you for a minute, gonna get an ambulance.'

'Can't do that,' she mumbled, 'gotta stay here, Pauly said I gotta stay here and make money – plenny of money . . . '

Her eyes rolled upwards, then closed. She had passed out.

They asked questions at the hospital, but Gino wasn't giving them any answers. He played dumb. He had made up his mind – this time Paulo wasn't going to get away with it.

When they assured him that Vera was safely in a hospital bed, he left.

He went back to her room and waited, sitting on a chair and staring at the door for three hours.

At four o'clock in the morning Paulo walked in. Gino was on his feet and attacking his father before Paulo knew what had hit him. 'You . . . lousy . . . coward . . . ' he breathed as he kicked and punched. 'Children . . . and women . . . You . . . mean . . . sonofabitch . . . '

It took Paulo a moment or two before he realized what was happening. He had spent a pleasant evening at a local speakeasy nursing a bottle of scotch, and he had come home with every intention of getting laid and then falling into a comfortable sleep. Now he was being attacked, and he had no idea why. The boot was usually on the other foot. *He* did the hitting.

He groaned as a punch landed on the side of his head, and

the full bottle of scotch came rushing out of his mouth along with some of the lasagna he had eaten earlier.

'You stink!' his assailant breathed in disgust, 'ya hear me - you *stink*!'

Paulo thought the voice sounded familiar, but he couldn't quite place it. Then another blow caught him full on the chin and he sunk to the ground.

'Don't you touch her again,' the voice warned, 'next time it won't be so easy for ya.'

Paulo threw up the rest of the lasagna as his attacker left. That Vera bitch. She had a boyfriend. Next time he got his hands on her she'd *really* get it.

Gino ran back to his room and stripped off his ruined suit. He was shaking but elated. It had been some day.

He sat on his bed and thought about it moment by moment. The money. The little blonde. The whore. Vera. Paulo. And his plans to make a bundle.

He stared at the ceiling, hating the cracks, peeling paint and general cheapness of his surroundings. He had never known any better, but he had been to the movies, he had walked along Park and Fifth Avenues and seen the magnificent homes and big cars with chauffeurs. He *knew* there was a better life out there somewhere. And he *knew* the only way to get it was with money.

He went into action the very next day. There were several young street gangs always anxious for new blood. The notorious Minute Men were the strongest - they acquired their name on account of the fact that they always managed to do a smash and grab and be away in less than a minute. Gino considered going with them - but they had a real hot wheelman name of Valachi, and Gino figured it wouldn't work out.

There were Irish gangs, and Jewish gangs, and mixed gangs. Some running minor protection rackets, some into numbers, but most into easy hit-and run thefts.

Gino wanted in with a small outfit that he could take over in time. He vaguely knew a guy called Aldo Dinunzio, who did the occasional job, working with only two other boys. He was smart, kept himself to himself, and the rumor was that he had a cousin in Chicago who was nearly as big as Capone.

Gino approached him and suggested they worked together. Aldo nodded. Gino had a certain reputation in the neighborhood. He was strong, he was tough, and what is more he could really handle a car.

They shook hands in Fat Larrys over a cup of coffee, and Aldo laid out the plans for the next job. A warehouse crammed with furs was just sitting there waiting to be taken. 'We can make ourselves a bundle,' Aldo said, 'but we gotta act fast. A little bird tells me the alarm system is out of action. You, me, two others, and we gotta take care of the night watchman. A five-way split. Could mean plenty.'

'When?' Gino asked.

'Tonight. Are you on?'

'Sure.'

They finalized their arrangements, and Aldo left. Gino was just about to set off for the hospital, when Miss Cuteness and her two girlfriends came in. She ignored him, pert nose in the air. She slid into a booth and buried her face behind a menu.

He went over to the table and stood there. 'Hey,' he said, plucking the menu from her hands, 'what's with you? Don't you have no manners?'

She gazed at him, eyes wide and innocent. 'Have you come to take my order?' she questioned.

'Cindy!' One of her girlfriends stifled a giggle.

'You're so fulla . . . '

'What?' she interrupted him before he could say it.

'Wanna go to a movie one night?' he asked, not quite sure he heard himself correctly, but glad he had asked anyway.

'With *you*?' Her voice said it all.

'Naw – with King Canute.'

'I don't go out with strangers.'

' 'Course ya don't. But I ain't a stranger no more. Like we're old friends now – right?'

'Wrong.'

He grimaced. 'Who needs ya anyway?' He slouched away from the table. Stupid girl. Trying to score points off him. She didn't know what she was missing.

He glanced back in time to catch the three girls convulsed with laughter Kids. Babies. Couldn't be more than fifteen or sixteen. Didn't know from nothin'.

He thought briefly of the whore he had been with the day before and of the things he had done to her. It had been exciting. But it would be more exciting when he didn't pay for it.

Gino celebrated his seventeenth birthday by going on his fifth job with Aldo. Easy money. In just under a month he had managed to stash away fifteen hundred dollars. A fortune! He opened himself a bank account in which he deposited fifty dollars, and the rest he placed in a bank security box. He had plans for the money, and he didn't want to piss it away like he had with the first fifty he made. No more suits or whores. Nothing to make anyone suspicious, especially the neighborhood cops who had taken to stopping by Fat Larrys and checking people out at random. So many gangs, and so many burglaries. The cops were clamping down.

Gino took a daytime job to make himself legitimate. Delivery boy for a pharmacy. Only what he was delivering was a little different from plain aspirin. Narcotics. Twenty-five bucks a delivery. Not bad. Not good. It was a risky job. If he was caught . . .

Every job had its risk factor. Pinky Banana had had a jack collapse on him while he was servicing the underside of a Cadillac. A broken leg, three broken ribs, and lucky to be alive. And for that kind of a risk he didn't even make twenty-five a week.

Gino had visited him in the hospital and talked some sense into him. When he got out no more Mister Straight.

On the personal front nothing much was happening. Miss Cuteness still presented herself at lunchtime in Fat Larrys – but Gino needed none of her insults, so he steered clear. No shortage of girls to take to his room and practice his sexual arts on though. And for Gino it was an art. If the girl wasn't happy, he wasn't happy. Gino the Ram was in full action.

He had not paid Vera another visit. He kept on thinking he would, then he changed his mind and another week went by. He had heard that she'd discharged herself from the hospital. The truth was he was frightened. Shit scared that Paulo would have beaten Vera so badly that he would be forced to do something about it. And he knew that if that happened he might not be able to control himself. The last time he had been prepared, no black rages. But if there was another time . . . If Paulo was sober and fought back . . .

So he stayed away. What he didn't know about he couldn't get upset about.

Costa's letters still arrived regularly from California. And on one occasion a picture was enclosed. Costa, the skinny kid, now a nice-looking youngster pictured with his dog and step-sister. Gino grinned when he saw it. He couldn't help being pleased that things had worked out for the kid. He had escaped into a world as unreal to Gino as taking a walk on the moon.

Two months after his seventeenth birthday Gino was arrested while waiting in a parked Dodge car outside a Bronx warehouse.

Inside the building they arrested Aldo and his two accomplices busy placing bolts of silks and satins onto a trolley ready for loading in the car.

'We were fingered,' Aldo muttered in the patrol car taking them to the police station, 'I just know it. Who'd you tell?'

Gino shook his head angrily, 'What the fuck you mean – who'd *I* tell – no one you dumb asshole. Who'd *you* tell?'

They were booked, and locked in the cells. Gino's stomach churned. He couldn't take being locked up again. And this time it wasn't some boys' home – this time it was the real thing.

# Carrie 1927-1928

Welfare Island. Dirt. Filth. Rats as big as a family cat. Lousy food. An overcrowded ward. And girls alive with all kinds of diseases. Lice. Crabs. Fleas. The Clap. And dikes looking to pounce on anyone who couldn't put up a fight.

Carrie learned the hard way. Two weeks in, and she was jumped by the ward's self-styled boss – a zoftic redhead with squinty mean eyes.

It was nighttime, and Carrie was attempting to sleep on her cramped cot in the overcrowded ward. Suddenly she felt a heavy weight on top of her, and hands on her breasts.

'What the hell . . . ' She struggled awake.

'Shut up and lie still,' Zoftic Redhead warned, 'I'm gonna finger fuck you better than any guy's ever given it to ya.'

'Get off me,' Carrie hissed, her voice hard.

The redhead was surprised. 'Are you kidding? Most gals 'round here would give their left tit for *my* attentions.' She rolled Carrie's nipple between thumb and forefinger, 'Gonna make you a happy little gal.'

Carrie wriggled free and rolled onto the floor where she crouched and glared. 'You leave me alone y'hear. Just leave me alone.'

'Dumb nigger. You sure don't know what's good for you. Never thought the day would come I'd get turned down by a dumb nigger whore.'

'I don't go with women,' Carrie spat. But she didn't add and certainly not big fat ones with greasy skin, bad breath, and a rumored dose.

'There's always a first time,' Zoftic Redhead encouraged. 'You want to know what's good for you then don't turn me down. Understand nigger?'

Carrie shuddered, 'Pick on someone else. I don't want you.' She knew as she said it that it wouldn't be the end of the matter, and sure enough it wasn't. The very next day no one would talk to her. The word had gone out that she had offended the leader, and that was enough for most of the girls. Nobody wanted trouble, so overnight it was as if she ceased to exist. Welfare Island had been bad enough before. But now it was impossible.

At night Carrie lay on her cot, unable to sleep, scared, lonely, and just about ready to give up. She did not see much point to her life. What was she there for? Why had God forgotten her?

Over and over she thought about what her life could have been. And then she thought about what it was, and what *she* was. The redhead was right, a dumb nigger whore, that's all she was.

Soon she started to think about ways she could finish it all, and it provided her with a purpose in life.

One day in the bath-house there was an unusual silence. The other girls were staring at her strangely, and hurrying over their toilet, anxious to get out.

Bad vibrations were strong. But bad vibrations had become such a part of Carrie's whole being that she took no notice. She scrubbed the strong carbolic soap over her body, under her arms, between her legs. To try and stay clean had become an obsession.

'Hello nigger,' Zoftic Redhead appeared, accompanied by four other girls.

They were the first words Carrie had had spoken to her since the incident in the ward six days earlier.

'You know what?' the redhead jeered, as she stepped out of her prison dress, 'I've decided not to hold it against you just 'cos you're dumb.' She took off her brassiere and touched her huge breasts. 'I want you to suck these,' she commanded.

Carrie put down the soap and attempted to edge out of the tiled shower area.

'Not so fast honeypie.' Two of the redhead's friends blocked Carrie, moving in on either side. 'Lie her down,' their leader ordered, 'and get her legs open.'

It was no use struggling. Four of them moved in on her, got her onto the wet tile floor, and held her spreadeagled. The redhead grinned. 'Now dumb nigger, out of the kindness of my heart I am going to teach you a thing or two.'

They kept her there for an hour, spreadeagled and helpless, while they all had fun using her as a receptacle for anything at hand they could shove into her. Zoftic Redhead sat astride her and masturbated as a final act. When they left they were laughing. It had been a good morning's entertainment.

Carrie didn't move. She lay and stared at the dripping shower above her and mumbled about death under her breath. It was enough. Her life was over. She was *ready* for it to be over.

Matron found her two hours later stretched out in the same position, blue with cold, congealing blood decorating her thighs. 'Good God almighty! Who did this to you?'

Carrie did not reply. In fact she did not speak at all for two weeks. She lay listlessly on a cot in the sick ward, and decided it was better than being up and about.

When she was released she went silently back among the other girls. They avoided meeting her eyes, and still they did not speak to her.

She didn't care. She was developing a new quality. Hate. It was a good powerful feeling, and her vibrations silently warned the other girls to keep away.

One day she made a decision. When she got out she was going to look out for herself for a change. She was going to become the toughest, sharpest, meanest, most successful nigger whore in the business.

Winter was cold on the ground when Carrie was finally released. She had been on the island six months, twice the length of her original sentence, but bookkeeping was not one of the high points of life on Welfare Island.

She was eighteen pounds thinner, which meant she was real skinny. Her hair was cropped short on account of the lice, and she shivered in a thin summer dress as the ferry took her across the East River to the docks.

She had exactly ten dollars to her name, but she was hopeful that Florence Williams still had her possessions, including a small box with her six hundred dollars savings in.

A line of pimps waited dockside, ready and anxious to inspect the girls. They looked them over like so much beef, and approached the ones they felt looked promising. It was a situation the authorities were aware of, but no one seemed prepared to do much about it. After all – once a whore, always a whore. Even the police turned a blind eye.

What chance did the girls have? Who was going to turn down a comfortable bed, some new clothes, a hot meal and the opportunity to start making money immediately?

Carrie knew what was going on. A running joke on Welfare Island was which pimp would get lucky. The girls all sent their little messages. 'If Rag Bags is there, y'all give him the clap for me!' or 'Go with the ratty spook with the yellow car and stick *another* knife in him! That mean bastard sure 'nuff deserves it!'

Carrie looked around. She wasn't attracting much attention, she knew she must look a mess. She took a deep breath and stuck out her chest. The result was a swarthy white man who sidled over and muttered, 'Wanna job, darkie?'

She didn't like the darkie. She shook her head.

'Come on,' the man said nastily, 'ain't no one else gonna ask *you*.'

Her eyes narrowed. 'If you saw what I had between my legs you wouldn't talk like that, whitey!' She turned her back on him and saw the pimp she was looking for. He was unmistakable. Tall. Black. Totally bald. White suited. Fur caped. Carrie had heard all about him on the island. His name was Whitejack, and he pimped for Mae Lee, the hottest black madam in Harlem.

Whitejack leaned against the side of a shiney new automobile chewing on a long thin stogie. His attention had not been caught by any of the girls. It was understandable because they were a sorry looking bunch.

Carrie approached him with as much flash as she could muster 'S'cuse me, mister,' she said boldly, 'I'm lookin' for a ride.'

His eyes flicked over her. A lazy head-to-toe inspection. Twice over just in case he missed something the first time.

'You best look elsewhere, honey,' he drawled, totally disinterested

'I just turned sweet sixteen last week,' she spoke quickly,

'sweet, black, hot, an' young, just the way those old ofays like 'em. I worked me a while at Florence Williams, I ain't no amateur.'

'You ain't no hot stuff neither.'

'How about a chance?' she wheedled, drawing her hands down her body. 'Dressed up an' fattened up you got a real winner. How 'bout givin' me a try?'

'Me and Madam Mae are into class, little girl. *Class.* Go shake it elsewhere.'

She glared at him, the wheedling smile leaving her face in a flash. The hate she had learned on the island welled up inside her and she wanted to strike out. But she didn't. She shrugged, turned to go.

He stopped her with a hand on her arm. 'You want a job as a maid?'

She shook his hand off and kept walking. A maid! That was a real laugh. There was no going back for Carrie.

'You!' He was coming after her now.

She stopped, and he moved alongside her. She sensed he was interested at last.

'You really work at Florence Williams place?'

'Check it out. Me, a girl called Billie, two white chicks . . .

'Hmmm . . . ' He blew a thin trickle of smoke in her face. 'You wanna take a chance on Madam Mae likin' you?'

She knew when to be bold. 'You like me, then she's gonna like me. Everyone knows that's the way the story goes.'

He smiled. 'So smart.'

She smiled back, although the smile never reached her eyes, 'And so young.'

'Get in the car.'

'Sure, Whitejack.'

'How'd you know my name?'

'Everyone knows your name out on the island – you sure is some big man.'

His smile broadened. 'Knows how to say the right things.'

'And knows when it's time not to say anything at all.'

He burst out laughing. 'Shee-ii-t, I got me one can talk!'

She laughed with him. 'You sure have!'

They bathed her, fumigated her, de-loused her, fed her, had her examined inside and out by a doctor, dressed her in a pink satin robe, and put her to work immediately.

Madam Mae was as tall as Whitejack, voluptuous, with a

long curling blonde wig that contrasted starkly with her jet black skin. She was a working madam, charging exorbitant prices for her occasional services. She was in her late thirties, and had been an active prostitute since she was twelve years of age.

She hated Carrie on sight, but she knew a good business proposition when she saw one. 'You want to take her on we'll do it,' she told Whitejack. Carrie had not been wrong on *that* score. 'But you stay out of her pants,' Madam Mae warned, 'I don't like sharing what I got with no child.'

Whitejack laughed easily, 'I wasn't thinkin' of it, mama!'

'The hell you weren't!'

'Aw . . . shee-ii-it. You think I mess with that when I got you?'

'I think you mess with anything that breathes I don't watch you real close!'

Carrie was determined to succeed. She wasn't worried about making any deal with the house until she had established herself. A fifty-fifty split suited her fine to start off with. She collected her belongings from Florence Williams, and was surprised but delighted to find her six hundred dollars intact. Florence Williams even asked if she wanted to come back, but Carrie declined the offer. Madam Mae ran a much larger operation altogether, and once she got herself established she wanted to work non-stop. Money was the name of the game. And she was set to make herself a stash.

Madam Mae's clientele was more varied than Florence Williams'. She kept an open house, with ten very hard working girls. Two other blacks, a Puerto Rican, three white-skinned blondes, a fat Mexican girl, a Chinese, and a perfectly formed pretty midget called Lucille.

Carrie had to work hard to stand out. But she had ambition. She wanted to be the best.

From her very first client they started coming back for more. Carrie knew how to make a man feel like a man. They came to her with their limp dicks, their problems, and their stories of woe. She sent them off refreshed, invigorated and properly fucked.

She hated every one of them.

They loved her.

Lucille was the only girl in the house who spoke to her. The others were suspicious, and jealous of hanging onto their regular johns.

'I 'bin here five years,' Lucille confided. 'Whitejack found me workin' in a freak show, he was real kind to me, told me I'd like this better, and honey – he sure was right.'

Carrie had no eyes to start making friends, she just wanted to concentrate on business, but in a way Lucille reminded her of herself. They were both freaks. Both outcasts only good for one thing.

'I'm goin' to get out of here one day,' Carrie confided, 'I'm goin' to be bigger and better than Madam Mae. I'm goin' to have the best place in town.'

'I've heard *that* before,' Lucille giggled.

'Yeah – but I *mean* it,' Carrie replied. And she did. Why else was she subjecting herself to anything that came her way? If she couldn't be the best she may as well be dead.

Her reputation grew. So did her list of regular customers.

'What you got I should know about?' Whitejack asked jokingly one day.

She placed a manufactured smile on her face but her eyes remained cold, 'I told you, didn't I? Sweet, black, hot an' young. You all knows that's what whitey dick likes.'

Whitejack glanced around, they were in the parlor alone together. He reached over and casually placed his hand inside her kimono on her breast. 'You turned out to be a star, girl.'

'Sure. I told you I was good.'

He didn't move his hand. 'I shoulda kept you for myself. Set you up in a room someplace.'

Whitejack was getting hot. Carrie glanced knowingly at his tight white trousers. She could see his prick straining the material. Getting Whitejack hot was some achievement.

She licked her lips. She was looking good and knew it. 'So, why didn't you?'

His hand started to move on her breast, 'Little girls ain't my attraction.'

'I ain't no little girl, Whitejack. I bin around.'

'So you have.' He was moving in on her, pressing his hardness against her thigh.

At that particular moment Madam Mae and two of the girls came walking in the room.

Whitejack backed off double quick, but not before Madam Mae's beady eyes had taken in everything that was going on. She shot him a deadly look. 'We pay for it around here, honey. You all want a little session with the child – you all gonna have to pay.' Her voice dripped sarcasm.

Whitejack recovered his composure. 'Day I pay for it, woman, I am one *dead* man.'

Madam Mae didn't skip a beat, 'You said it, honey,' she murmured sweetly.

The girls laughed, and the doorbell chimed, interrupting any further exchanges.

Three fresh-faced college boys came piling into the parlor. Madam Mae treated them nicely, gave them a drink and put them at their ease. She indicated her girls, 'Take your pick,' she offered, 'anyone you like.'

Carrie smiled prettily at one of them, and took him by the hand to her bedroom.

He was nervous as hell. Sweating, red faced, jumpy.

'What's your name sweet stuff?' she purred.

'Hen . . . ry.' His voice broke on the ry.

'So Hen . . . ry. You and I are going to have us a really beau . . . ti . . . ful time. OK Henry?'

He nodded nervously. He was eighteen years old and this was his first prostitute.

Carrie peeled his clothes off, clucking with admiration at his puny body. When she took off his shorts she couldn't conceal a shudder. Thin and white, like a wriggly white worm.

She sighed, 'Hen . . . ry, you sure are one bee . . . ig bad exciting man! You sure as hell are! You an' me are goin' to have us a time like you only ever dreamed about. Right sweet-stuff? Right?'

# Gino 1924-1926

On July 9th, 1924, Gino Santangelo, after a five-week wait in the Bronx County Jail, was taken to court, pleaded guilty to attempted burglary, and was given an eighteen-month prison sentence. He got off easy. Aldo Dinunzio was sentenced to two years. They were sent to Sing Sing prison together.

Aldo was convinced someone had fingered them and he was hot to get his revenge. 'Who the fuck ya tell?' he asked the two boys who had been on the job with him. 'Who knew about the warehouse?'

They both denied telling anyone. But Aldo kept questioning

and bugging them, and it eventually came to light that one of them had boasted about the job to his sister.

Aldo was satisfied with this information. At last he had someone to blame. 'The bitch!' he mumbled constantly, 'she musta gone to the cops. When I get out of here the bitch won't find her miserable life worth living.'

Gino tried to calm him, but Aldo was having none of it. 'The moment I leave this place. The moment I set foot on the street – the bitch gets it. You wait, you see.'

Gino learned the best way to handle prison life was to keep to himself and stay out of trouble. He shared a small cell with an old man who was in on an intent to kill charge. They ignored each other. It seemed to be the best way to stand being hemmed up together.

The old man would urinate noisily in the bucket provided, and most nights he would sexually relieve himself just when Gino was getting to sleep. It was disgusting, but Gino learned to ignore it. He tried to forget about women and sex and hot warm bodies. He found himself getting a constant hard-on, but refused to jerk off like everyone else. Occasionally he was racked with a wet dream, and he would wake up annoyed and dissatisfied.

He missed sex more than anything. And he daydreamed about the women he would make love to when he got out. The one he thought about most was the little blonde from Fat Larrys. He hadn't even talked to her since she had given him the big brush, but he knew that he would. And once he hit home base on *her* magic button . . . Oh boy . . . Just watch out.

Costa's letters kept on coming, and one day Vera turned up to visit him. She didn't look good. Nothing had been done about the two front teeth Paulo had knocked out, and her skin was lined and swollen from too much booze.

'You little bastard,' she complained, 'short memory, huh? Not a word from you in months. Finally found out where you were, so here I am.'

'Jeeze,' he was embarrassed, his eyes magnetically drawn to the gap in her smile where there should have been teeth, 'it's real nice of you to drag out to see me.'

' 'Course it is. But what's a stepmother for if she can't make one lousy visit. An' I'm tellin' ya now, Gino, I ain't comin' back to this shithole. It was bad enough when I hadda come see Paulo here. You can come see me when ya get out, OK?'

'Where is the old man?'

'The prick took my money and ran. The same day I got out the hospital too.' Ruefully she pointed to her mouth, 'Guess he didn't like the view.'

'I got some dough if you wanna get your teeth fixed,' he said quickly.

She gave a lewd laugh, 'Thanks kid, but I gotta tell you – havin' no front teeth is real good for business. I can do things most guys don't believe!' She leaned close to the wire mesh separating them, 'I'll do it for you when you get out.'

He laughed, 'Come *on*, Vera!'

She giggled, 'Just tryin' to cheer you up. I know all you guys think about here is sex. It must get hard.'

'It sure does!'

'Aw . . . shit! What a joker! Same as ever.' She stood up, 'Gotta go. But Gino . . . thanks . . . You know what I mean. Ain't never had anyone look out for me before – It was a pretty good feelin'.'

'How'd y'know it was me?'

'Are you kidding?'

Doing time in Sing Sing was hard. Gino was assigned to a construction gang – and although the work was back-breaking – the company was interesting. He was making good connections, and learning a lot, mixing with older, experienced men who had been around and knew what it was all about.

The months passed fairly quickly, and with time off for good behaviour, Gino found himself up for parole within a year.

There was a shock in store for him when he came before the parole board. Costa Zennocotti's adopted father had written a letter offering to take him for a vacation. It seemed he had no choice. Straight out of jail and onto a train bound for California without even time to get laid.

He was confused. He hardly knew Costa Zennocotti – only through his letters really. Shit! What kind of suckers wanted to give a vacation to someone like him?

Costa waited impatiently at the railway station in San Francisco with Franklin Zennocotti, his adopted father.

He had grown somewhat, filled out, and although short for his sixteen years, was a nice looking boy.

'I don't know if this is such a good idea . . . ' Franklin said for the twentieth time in weeks.

'Aw. come on, dad,' Costa replied, 'you gave *me* a chance didn't you? And look what happened to me.'

Franklin couldn't help smiling. Costa was right. Look what *had* happened to him. He was the brightest kid around. He got top grades in school, and was a pleasure to have around the house.

Still . . . adopting Costa was one thing . . . Having his *jail-bird* friend to stay was another. But it was only for a month. And Costa had begged, indeed pleaded. 'He saved my life, dad,' he explained simply, 'and if there is something we can do for him . . .'

Costa had never asked for anything before. It would have been difficult turning down his one and only request.

So a vacation for Gino Santangelo it was, and Franklin Zennocotti hoped it wasn't the mistake he felt it might be.

Gino strutted as he left the train. It hid the fact that he was just plain nervous. He fingered the scar on his cheek, and marveled at the bright sunshine.

He took off his lumber jacket and rolled it in a ball under his arm. Then the smell of his own sweat hit him, and he quickly put the jacket back on again.

He spotted Costa immediately, but the little runt didn't seem to notice him. Well of course he had probably changed . . . And then again he did look much older than his years. Everyone thought he was more than nineteen.

He had time to inspect Costa and the man standing with him. They looked so . . . clean. It was the only word that came to mind.

He headed towards them, and finally Costa recognized him. 'Gino!' he exclaimed, and to Gino's embarrassment he ran up and enveloped him in a hug. Shit! Maybe the kid's early experiences had turned him into a fairy.

'It's so good to see you!' Costa said excitedly, 'Come and meet my father.' He dragged him over to Franklin Zennocotti, who gave a tight-assed smile.

Gino knew the expression. It said – I don't like the look of you – why do I even have to talk to you?

'Hey – ' Gino said, extending his hand, 'pleased t'meetcha.'

During the drive from the station he heard about a lot of things that didn't interest him one bit. Swimming galas and tennis clubs and who the fuck knew what else. What really interested him was the diamond-backed brand new Cadillac they were riding in. How he wanted to get behind the wheel of *that*.

The house was straight out of a Hollywood movie. Real big, with pillars and leaded shuttered windows. In the back was a swimming pool. Costa's mother fussed around him, offering him cookies and lemonade and insisting he take his jacket off.

Jeeze! What a set up!

He clung to his jacket, wolfed down a few cookies, and then Costa suggested he show him to his room.

Gino bounced around on the balls of his feet inspecting everything. The view, the bed, the walk-in closet. 'Jeeze!' he kept on exclaiming. 'You really got some set-up here, kid.'

'How did you get that scar on your face?' Costa blurted out, desperate for something to say.

He frowned, and his hand rushed to finger his scar. 'You think it notices a lot?'

'Not really . . . ' Costa kicked vaguely at the carpet. Trust him to mention the wrong thing.

Gino scowled, and moved to inspect himself in the closet mirror. 'Yeh . . . ' he muttered, almost to himself, 'the doctors did a lousy job of sewing it up.'

'I hardly noticed it,' Costa said quickly.

'Bullshit. You fuckin' mentioned it first thing.'

'Shhhh! My mother and father would throw you out if they heard language like that.'

Gino narrowed his eyes. What the hell *had* he let himself in for?

Gino found he had been totally wrong about Costa. The kid was terrific. So goddamn nice it was sickening! And not a fairy, not anything. The kid had never even been kissed, let alone laid. Gino felt it was his duty to do something about *that*. Too much swimming and tennis was not good for anyone. A little fucking would break up the monotony.

'Hey – ' he said to Costa, 'there's gotta be a cathouse around here somewhere.' He had to have a woman, otherwise he was going to bust right open.

'A cathouse?' Costa was blushing before he even got the words out.

'Aw, come on.' Gino encouraged, 'we'll go together. Listen kid – if I don't have a skirt soon I'm a gonna split a gut!'

Costa was excited and horrified. He did know of a whorehouse down near the wharf. Two of his friends had been there and come back with glowing if somewhat impossible reports.

'After dinner tonight we'll say we're goin' to a movie,' Gino decided.

Costa went into a state of unconcealed excitement. His mother regarded him solemnly over dinner. 'You look flushed Costa dear, are you sure you're feeling all right?'

'Fine mother, fine,' Costa replied quickly, glancing anxiously over at Gino.

Franklin caught the look. 'Maybe you should forget about going to the moving picture show and stay home.'

'No, no,' Costa objected, 'there's nothing wrong with me.'

Franklin patted his lips with a napkin, 'Don't be late then. I may have let you off your studies this month, but that doesn't mean I expect you to carouse around every night.'

'Dad, this is only the second time we've been out since Gino's here.'

Franklin regarded his adopted son solemnly. 'Gino did not come to San Francisco to go out,' he said sternly. 'He came here so that we could give him some idea of what life in a proper family home is all about. During his stay I am sure that he has learned a lot.' He fixed Gino with a penetrating stare, 'Isn't that so? Don't you feel that you have learned about respect and caring for other people?'

'Hey,' Gino stated quickly. 'I *always* cared about other people.'

'The people you robbed?' Franklin replied, quick as a flash. He flushed, 'Well . . . they was people I didn't even know . . . the big boys . . . they got things like insurance . . . they expect to get . . . taken . . .'

Franklin glanced quickly at Costa. 'You see, son,' he explained carefully, 'that is an attitude that exists among the more . . . deprived members of society. I was hoping we would be able to help Gino to see things a different way. To understand that no one expects to get . . . taken – as he puts it. And hard working businessmen are no different from anyone else.'

'Bull . . . ' Gino muttered.

'I beg your pardon?' questioned Franklin coldly.

He coughed, 'Somethin' in my throat,' he explained.

Costa pushed his chair from the table and got up. 'We'd better be going,' he said quickly.

The cathouse down by the wharf was a disappointment. Gino felt it was bad news as soon as they arrived.

His worst suspicions were confirmed when he took a look at the woman who opened up the door. She had acned skin, cracked lips, and a bad wig. She winked immediately and hauled them inside. 'Coupla nice randy bucks come for a good time, huh?' She was wearing a faded beaded dress that had seen better days, and her bosom sagged with the weight of a thousand lays. 'It's ten apiece,' she said quickly, 'who's first?'

'Hey – wait a minute,' Gino objected. 'Where's the girls?'

'There was another girl here,' she said, 'couple months ago. But she left to get married. It's just me, tootsie,' she put her hand on his shoulder, 'you first?'

He shook her hand off, 'Naw, not me!'

She turned to Costa, 'Money out, let's see it.'

Costa was anxiously scrabbling in his back pocket for some money.

'Wait a minute,' Gino said, 'I gotta talk to my friend.' He turned his back on the woman and spoke rapidly. 'Let's get the hell out of here. She's a beast. Who the hell wants to stick it into that?'

Costa was glowing with excitement. 'I do,' he said simply.

'Oh Christ!' he couldn't help laughing, 'If you're that anxious . . .'

Costa was already counting out his money. The woman grabbed him by the arm and hauled him off to a side room.

Gino paced around, waiting. They were back within minutes, the woman hitching up her skirt. 'You, now?' she asked, Gino, licking cracked lips.

'Some other time.'

Then they were out of there, on the street, roaring with laughter.

'How could ya? She was a pig.'

Costa was flushed with success, 'It was all right, Gino, honestly it was. I don't think I could have done it with anyone . . . well y'know . . . pretty or young or anything like that. This way was just right. I didn't care what she thought . . . so I just did it.' He giggled, 'I think I liked it!'

Gino slapped him across the shoulders, 'Sure you did, you're my friend ain'tcha?!'

Gino's first Saturday in San Francisco he and Costa went swimming down at the wharf. When they returned a girl was standing in the hall. The most beautiful girl Gino had ever set eyes on. She was of slight build, with white blonde hair, and luminous crystal eyes.

'This is my sister, Leonora,' Costa said casually.

For once in his life Gino forgot about his cock and concentrated on his head. She was so . . . soft. Like no other girl he had ever seen. And his thoughts were like no other thoughts he had ever had.

'So nice to meet you, Gino,' she said, extending a small hand, 'Costa never stops talking about you – it becomes awfully tedious!'

'Yeh.' He could think of nothing else to say, he just gaped at her like some green kid. As far as he was concerned it was the most important moment of his life.

In two weeks he saw her twice. She attended a weekly boarding school for young ladies, and only returned home on weekends. It was hardly a situation that was likely to develop into a romance. And romance was on his mind.

They had never been alone together. Indeed they had never even had a conversation. But still . . . she knew how he felt. He could tell He had caught her watching him across the dining table. Those luminous blue eyes following his every move, the delicate lips quivering, the small hand brushing a wisp of hair from her face.

He didn't lust after her body – the feeling he had for her was completely different. He wanted to look after and protect her. Maybe even marry her.

Jeeze! That thought put a smile on his face. Here he was, nineteen years old, a jailbird with no real prospects. And after paying off the lawyer he had hired to represent him he had exactly two thousand and seventy-five dollars in the world. Hardly a fortune. But not bad. He had ambition too, and whether he made his pile legally or illegally he knew one day he *would* make it . . . And when that day came he wanted Leonora right along there with him.

Finally he got a chance to mention his plans to her. Two more weeks and he would be ass first on the train back to New York. Mrs Zennocotti liked him, but old man Zennocotti was a whole other story. Oh he was polite, even generous. But his eyes showed how he felt about the whole situation. He wanted Gino out of his life as fast as possible. It was written on his face as clear as newsprint.

Leonora Zennocotti was well aware of the way Gino kept on staring at her, and it embarrassed and excited her all at the same time. 'I think he's nice,' she confided to her best friend, Jennifer. 'But he never *says* anything to me. He just sort of gazes across the table. What shall I do?'

Jennifer thought the whole situation highly romantic. 'I wish *I* had someone who sat and stared at *me*,' she lamented, 'Costa doesn't even know I exist.'

'Oh Costa! He's younger than you, how can you like him?'

'Only seven months younger and I *do* like him you *know* I do.'

'Come to stay for the weekend then. It'll be fun.'

Jennifer came home with Leonora, and that very evening, a lot of staring went on across the dinner table.

Mary and Franklin Zennocotti were unaware of the teenage passions zooming around the room. Franklin had a headache, and retired to his room before coffee, and it did not take Mary long to follow him.

For the first time Gino found himself in a room with Leonora without her parents cramping his style. 'How ya doin'?' he mumbled, 'How's school?'

She licked pale lips, 'Fine thank you.' A short silence, then, 'And you? Are you enjoying San Francisco?'

'He's having a wonderful time,' Costa replied.

Leonora pursed her lips. How Costa had changed since Gino's arrival. She liked the fact that he had blossomed forth, but she didn't appreciate his answering his friend's questions for him.

Another silence, then Jennifer broke it. 'Couldn't we all go for a swim? I'm so warm, and it would be such fun.'

'Yeh,' Gino agreed. 'great idea.'

'Poppa would never allow it –' Leonora began.

'Poppa would never know,' Costa interrupted, 'he took his headache pills, and if we are very quiet . . . '

'Why the pool anyway?' Gino asked. 'If we went down to the wharf we wouldn't havta worry 'bout bein' quiet.'

'Oh yes!' Jennifer loved a bit of excitement. 'Please!'

'We can't leave the house . . . ' Leonora declared primly.

'Hey – doncha wanna get t'know me better?' Gino was staring at her again.

She quite literally felt a shock of excitement course through her body, and changed her mind quickly, 'I'll get my bathing suit. Come on Jennifer, I can lend you one of mine. We'll change upstairs and wear our coats over the top.'

'Good girls,' Gino nodded his admiration.

Half an hour later they were swimming in the murky dock-side water. 'This is so exciting!' Jennifer squealed. 'Costa, come on, I'll race you.'

Gino moved closer to Leonora. She had pinned her long

pale hair on top of her head, and they trod water next to a fishing boat. 'I ain't much good with words,' he blurted out quickly, 'but I gotta tell you how I feel.'

Leonora felt her pulse quicken. 'Yes?' she breathed softly.

'Well . . . like . . . y'know . . . Well . . . Jeeze. I don't know what *love* is supposed to be. But Christ! If it's like a cold – I got it – y'know?' He reached for her hand. 'I *really* got it.'

'I know what you mean,' she whispered, 'and I think I've got it too.'

'Hey!' He felt like bursting with happiness. It was a feeling he had never been hit with before.

Together they swam in until they could stand. Then, very gently he took her face in his hands and kissed that mouth. He was careful to avoid body contact, but she was leaning into him, returning his kiss, and he could feel soft breasts, warm thighs, and he *knew* she must be able to feel his hardness that even the cold water was failing to control.

'I love love love you,' he mumbled between kisses, 'love love love you.'

'Me too, Gino, oh – me too.'

His hands automatically went to her breasts, and she didn't push him away. He still hadn't had a woman since leaving jail – but this was Leonora he was with, and he controlled his basic instincts.

'Oh Christ!' he muttered. 'I don't want it to be like this.'

'Why? Let's do what we want to do.' She was kissing him passionately. 'I've *never* felt like this before.'

At that moment Costa and Jennifer came splashing through the water. 'Come on,' Jennifer complained, 'you're no fun. I thought we were going to race.'

Reluctantly Gino let go of Leonora. 'Sure,' he said.

'Yes,' agreed Leonora, her voice still breathy.

'You two race first,' Gino said, 'then we'll follow.'

'We already did,' Jennifer complained. '*Come on.*'

'Maybe we should go,' Costa suggested. He was uneasy about what he sensed was beginning to happen. He had seen Leonora and Gino separate when he and Jennifer had returned. It didn't thrill him. His friend was taking advantage and that wasn't right.

'Yes, let's go,' Jennifer agreed, 'I'm getting cold and this water is ucky.'

They all climbed out. 'We forgot to bring towels,' Leonora groaned.

The girls had only their coats to wrap over their wet suits, and Costa and Gino merely pants and sweaters. The walk back to the house was one long shiver.

Gino put his arm protectively around Leonora and drew her close to him. 'Listen – I know we ain't had much time together – but I know what's right – and we're right – you and I. I knew it first time I set eyes on you.'

'I think I knew it too,' she murmured, 'when I looked at you I felt a closeness that I've never felt with anyone – not even my parents.'

'I'm no angel,' he mumbled, 'done a lotta things I s'pose I shouldn't've done. But I'm no bad person – you know – I never had anyone who cared what I did anyway.'

'I care,' her voice was soft.

He squeezed her shoulder, 'We'll get married,' he said firmly, 'that's for sure.'

Costa glanced round at them and glared. 'Hurry up,' he said brusquely.

'How?' Leonora whispered. 'My father will never allow it and . . .'

'Don't worry. We'll get married. I give you my solemn promise.'

She stopped walking and turned to look at him, 'I wish it were possible. They'll say I'm too young, and you haven't got any money and . . .'

He held her face in his hands. 'Stop it,' his voice was harsh, 'just stop it, OK? We're gonna get married, maybe not right away, but as soon as I can get some money together. We'll wait. It won't be easy, but we'll do it. Right?'

Her beautiful blue eyes were shining, 'Right.'

He bent to kiss her, his mouth hungry.

Costa turned around, saw what they were doing, and ran back to drag them apart. 'Jeeze!' he exclaimed, using one of the words he had picked up from Gino, 'What's going *on* with you two?'

Leonora giggled, 'We're in love, little brother, we're in love!'

'Oh no,' Costa groaned, 'you *can't* be.'

'We are,' she smiled excitedly, 'and we're going to be married!'

'How absolutely marvellous!' chirped Jennifer.

Gino found that he was grinning foolishly, 'I'm gonna be a married man!' he hooted. 'Can you imagine *that*?'

'No I can't,' snapped Costa, 'I don't know what's got into you. I think you've all gone mad.'

'Congratulate us,' Gino insisted, 'I'm your best friend – she's your sister – you should be dancing in the streets!'

'Gino,' Costa's voice was firm, 'think sensibly. What about my father?'

Gino was cocky. 'We won't tell him yet. When I go back to New York I'm gonna make a pile of money and send for Leonora. He won't object when I'm rich.'

Costa shook his head in amazement. He couldn't believe what was happening. And he was frightened, because the only result would be trouble. He was clear headed enough to know that if his father even suspected what was going on it would be Gino on the first train back to New York and out of *all* their lives forever.

Leonora, Gino, and Jennifer were dancing around in the street, giggling, laughing, and dripping wet.

'Let's go home,' Costa said dourly.

'Oh – you're such a grouch!' exclaimed Jennifer, 'don't you like adventures?'

'Only when they have happy endings,' replied Costa grimly, suddenly feeling much older than his sixteen years.

'This'll have a happy ending,' Gino assured him. 'I know it. I'm Gino Santangelo, and when I *know* something you can be sure I'm right.'

Costa nodded, 'I sure hope so,' he said. But in his heart he knew that his friend was wrong.

Gino returned to New York fired with ambition. For the first time in his life he had something – someone to work for. Leonora would wait for him, and their future was in his hands.

The remainder of his visit to San Francisco had flown by – only one more intimate moment alone with her, but they could say more with their eyes than most people could say in a life-time.

Even Costa began to realize how serious they were.

On the night before his departure Gino sneaked into Leonora's bedroom, and they had a long talk, firming up their plans for a future they intended to spend together. They kissed, chastely at first, then it started to become more. 'You can take me if you want,' Leonora had breathed softly. 'I've never . . . you know. But Gino, with you . . . Well I don't want you having to go with . . . other women . . . I know that men have certain needs.'

He forced himself to draw away from her. 'I can wait if you can,' he said simply.

'But we don't have to, Gino.' Her cheeks were flushed, 'we love each other, and if two people are in love then surely nothing can be wrong?'

He looked at her, so soft and lovely and vulnerable. He wanted her so much that he felt his hardness might burst through his trousers there and then. 'It's not wrong, it's just something we should save,' he said.

Whoever thought that Gino the Ram would be coming out with *those* sentiments? Certainly not Gino himself.

In New York the first thing he did was get himself a room. Two blocks away from his previous place and another dump. But he only needed it to sleep in until he got himself in action. Anyway, he had to think seriously about saving every cent and dollar he could – he still had his bank account – which held a big seventy-five bucks – but better than that was his safe deposit box with over two thousand in crisp fresh bills. He reckoned he needed a lot more than that before he could even think of sending for Leonora. He would need a decent place to live, a car, and a lot of money. Franklin Zennocotti would never let his daughter go unless Gino could support her in some style.

His first move was to go straight over to Fat Larrys and check out what was happening. It was early evening and the place was crowded, but no familiar faces, just a lot of green kids sucking on milk shakes.

'Where's the old gang?' he asked.

The counterman looked around furtively. 'Things 'bin changing round here, Gino. Go in the back, knock twice on the door used to lead to the storeroom.'

Gino whistled with surprise. Fat Larrys had become a speakeasy. He made his way through the old storeroom, down a flight of stairs into what used to be the cellar, and there it was – a dimly lit room with round tables, jazz music played by a four-piece band, and leggy waitresses in fluffy little costumes. It must have taken real money to make the transformation.

Sitting at a table was Pinky Banana in a real sharp pin stripe, with a cigar stuck in his fleshy lips, and a glass of hooch which he was feeding to the little blonde sitting on his knee.

And wasn't the blonde Miss Cuteness? Older, because of the lip rouge and permed hair, but with the same arrogant spoilt look about her.

Miss Cuteness. The girl that had occupied his thoughts wholly until Leonora had entered his life. Now she was just another dame. And a cheap looking one at that.

'Hey,' he headed in their direction, 'Pinky?'

'Gino!' Pinky Banana was on his feet at once. 'When they let you out, chump? How was it?'

He made a face. 'What can I tell ya, pal? Only thing I know is I don't recommend it as a vacation spot.'

Pinky Banana laughed and hugged him. 'So I'll buy ya a drink, ya can tell me all about it.'

'Excuse *me*,' Miss Cuteness said sharply, tugging on the sleeve of Pinky Banana's jacket.

'Uh . . . Oh yeh . . . Gino, you remember Cindy, don'tcha?'

'Sure I do,' he grinned at her, 'she was always so friendly how could I ever forget her.'

Cindy glared at him, 'Oh yes,' she said tartly, 'Gino San-tangelo – G-I-N-O – wasn't I supposed to be hearing a lot about you?'

'Y'will, doll, y'will.' He ignored her and turned to Pinky Banana, 'Look at you then! Y'look like you're makin' out pretty good. Last time we was together you was flat on your back in the hospital with a coupla busted gams. What happened?'

Pinky Banana tapped his head, 'I got smart. Remember that talkin' to ya gave me in the hospital? You was right – who the hell busts their ass gettin' covered in other people's shit? I got smart, an' I'm a big man round here now, Gino. You better believe it. A big man.'

They sat down and Pinky Banana snapped his fingers for drinks.

'So, what d'ya do?' Gino questioned.

Pinky Banana lowered his eyes, 'I – uh – take care of things for people. Important people.'

Gino was silent. Didn't want to press any further. Taking care of things could mean anything. Better discuss it another time, not with Cindy breathing down their necks.

'Cindy an' I live together,' Pinky explained, 'got a nice place over on a Hundred and Tenth Street.'

'Say, things really changed around here. You're the last person I'd expect to see gettin' hooked up.'

'And why's that?' Cindy demanded.

She was still as pretty as ever, if a little hard around the edges.

He shrugged, 'I don't know . . . Pinky just never seemed . . .' His words hung there. How could he say that Pinky had never seemed the kind of guy to hook up with one skirt? Pinky, the last of the great flashers. He changed the subject. 'Hey, ain'tcha at school any more?'

She licked heavily rouged lips, 'I hated school, hated home. So I left both of them. I'm seventeen, that's old enough to do what I want. It's *my* life, isn't it?'

Seventeen. Same age as Leonora. But what a difference between the two of them. Cindy – smart – rouged and worldly. Leonora – soft and beautiful – untouched and innocent.

'You seen Catto around?' he asked.

'Catto!' Pinky Banana spat the name out in disgust, 'what a dummy! Still suckin' mommy's milk.'

'Whatcha mean?'

'I mean he's a friggin' pain. Doesn't know what's good for him. *Still* workin' the garbage dumps with his old man. And *that's* what he calls clean money. I don't bother with him any-more.'

'I want to dance,' Cindy demanded.

'In a minute.'

'*Now.*'

Pinky Banana gave an embarrassed grin, 'So, all right. now.'

Gino watched them onto the tiny dance floor. His eyes darted around the room. The place was full. Fat Larry was over in the corner with a man Gino recognized as Eddie the Beast. Several other known hoods were dotted around the place. It shouldn't be too hard to get himself connected.

He sipped at his scotch whiskey and watched Pinky Banana and Cindy. She was putting on some sort of show, wiggling her ass and sticking out her tits. Still a tease. Still pretty. But how-ever pretty it wasn't going to bother *him*. He had Leonora, and she was better than all of them put together.

The next day Gino stopped by to see Catto. He lived in a delapidated tenement building, sharing three rooms with his mother, father, and four younger brothers and sisters. Gino had always been welcomed at their house. 'Mrs Bonnio,' he kissed the careworn woman, 'Is Catto home?'

'Gino! When you get back?'

'Only yesterday. I bin in San Francisco.'

'I thought you bin in jail bad boy!' She gave him an affec-tionate pat, and raised her voice, 'Catto! Catto! Come and see who we got here! You stay for dinner?'

Catto came sloping in, bringing the familiar faint stink of old forgotten garbage with him. 'Gino! You crazy bum!' he embraced his friend, 'we all missed ya.'

Gino returned the embrace. The smell of garbage had never bothered him, he had grown up with it.

Dinner was a family affair, and Gino felt right at home. Later he and Catto took a walk. They talked of old times, then Gino asked, 'What's happening with Pinky? He looks like he's flush. How come he's out makin' it and you're still haulin' shit?'

Catto's face hardened. 'You haven't heard?'

'Heard what?'

'You know what Pinky does to look so flush?'

'If I knew I wouldn't be askin'.' But before Catto replied he suddenly knew, and he was right.

'He kills people,' Catto said blankly, 'for money. They offer him five hundred bucks to do away with you – and you'd better believe it – you're gone.'

Gino was silent. He wasn't shocked. Violence had always been a part of his life. But Pinky Banana . . . A killer? It was hard to believe.

'Shit,' spat Catto, 'I don't see him no more – an' if you're smart you'll do the same.'

Gino was smart all right. But a friend was a friend. And who knew what the future held and when a friend might come in handy?

The old man coughed and spat phlegm into a crumpled handkerchief.

Gino did not look up from his writing. Laboriously he was copying the words he had had the old man write out for him. 'My dearest Leonora, my dearest love . . .'

It was the fourth letter he had written her in so many weeks. Ashamed of his lack of education he had gone to the old man, Mr Pulaski, for help with his spelling and punctuation. Mr Pulaski had the room above Gino, so it was a convenient arrangement. It cost him only a few dollars, and saved him much embarrassment. Plus the fact that the sessions were teaching him plenty.

Leonora had written him two replies. Beautifully scripted letters on pink scented notepaper which he kept on him at all times. Costa had also written him, begging him to heed the talk he had had with Franklin the day he left San Francisco. Gino remembered it well. Franklin had taken him into his study and given him a lecture on what he should do with his life. Crime does not pay . . . etc. etc.

Crime did pay. Gino knew this for a fact. Since returning to New York he had been able to add another two thousand dollars to his safe deposit box. And all he had done was drive the getaway car on a bank job, and been wheelman on a fur loft robbery. Two easy jobs which he had checked out very very carefully, because the last thing he needed in his life was to go back to jail.

His reputation was growing as being one of the smartest and best wheelmen in town. He could handle a car like he could handle a woman – expertly. But his ambition was not to make his fortune behind the wheel of a car. Too dangerous and out in the open. What he really wanted was to get into the boot-legging action where all the *real* money was. Men like Meyer Lansky, Bugsy Siegel, and most of all Lucania were his idols. They had set off with beginnings not much better than his own, and look at them now.

'You have finished?' the old man inquired.

'Yeh.' He sealed the envelope with a flourish, and fished into his back pocket for money.

'Same time next week?'

'Of course.'

'Your young lady, she is a lucky one.'

'You think so?' He was pleased.

'Not many young men write letters like you do . . . '

'Yeh?' he grinned. 'It's simple, pops. I love her.'

The old man clicked his false teeth. 'It is admirable to be in love. My wife and I were married for sixty-two years until she passed away . . . ' his voice quivered, 'she was tired . . . it was for the best . . . I visit her grave every week . . . '

Gino reached into his back pocket and took out an extra two dollars. 'Buy her some flowers from me, pop.'

'Thank you,' the old man was grateful. 'She always liked lilies . . . they were her favorite flowers.'

'Hey, that's good.' He left, bouncing down the street with his customary swagger. Writing to Leonora always gave him an extraordinary high. And besides, the great Lucania had re-quested his presence. It could only mean that things were looking up.

This time the meet was not in the back of a Cadillac, but in Fat Larrys – the front part, where Lucania sat spooning a dish of Italian ice cream, and Eddie the Beast and another couple of hoods kept watchful eyes.

'Sit down, join me,' Lucania was friendly but to the point. He was once again on the lookout for loyal recruits and he wondered if Gino would care to become a part of his organ-ization.

Gino was flattered of course. Although he knew he was only one of many that day who would be offered the chance to pledge alliance to the great Lucania. 'I got my own plans,' he hedged.

Lucania raised an eyebrow, 'It's good to have ambition, just so long as you don't get in anyone's way.'

'Naw,' Gino shook his head, 'my plans are very simple.'

Yes. His plans were simple. He wanted a bootlegging empire all his very own.

And he thought he knew the best way to go about getting it.

Aldo Dinunzio got out of jail fighting mad.

Gino was waiting for him. 'You got connections, I got ideas.'

'Don't talk business, I want to get that bitch that got me locked away.'

'Yeh, of course. But how can you be sure it was her?'

'The fuck I'm sure!' bellowed Aldo. 'You wanna come with me, let's go.'

He accompanied Aldo, hoping to prevent him from doing anything he would regret. Aldo was important to him. He certainly didn't want him getting flung back into jail. Aldo's cousin, Enzio Bonnatti, had become a real big man in Chicago, and this was the connection that Gino figured would work.

Aldo had found out the bitch was called Barbara, and worked in a bank. She lived with her parents and brother in a small neat house in Little Italy, and was engaged to a policeman. 'A fuckin' cop,' Aldo screamed, 'I break his balls too!'

They went to the bank, waited outside at closing time, and one by one Aldo questioned the female employees as they left. 'You Barbara Riccaddi? You? You?'

He had questioned six girls by the time she arrived.

She was tall, with brown hair and freckles. She wore glasses and a longish skirt. She answered Aldo's question with a sharp, 'Yes I am. And I suppose you're Aldo Dinunzio. I've heard what you want to do to me, and let me tell you this . . . '

Aldo was hit with a barrage of abuse the like of which he had never heard before. When she had finished, she stalked off, nose in the air, unfrightened and triumphant.

'Sweet Jesus!' Aldo exclaimed, 'now that's what I call a *real* woman!'

Fortunately, for Gino, Aldo Dinunzio now wanted to make his fortune too.

# Carrie 1928

The problem was keeping Whitejack at a distance.

Only it wasn't really a problem because Carrie found that she had no real strong burning desire to keep him at a distance at all. Why should she? Just because he was marked and stamped 'Personal Property of Madam Mae'. So what? Big deal. The last person that made Carrie shiver and shake in her spike heels was Madam Mae. Big fat old whore. She must be hitting forty any day now – and that was *old*.

Besides, Carrie was getting a little sick and tired of handing half of what she made over to the house. She needed to break away. And to break away properly she needed Whitejack.

Of course he only made moves when Madam Mae was out, or otherwise occupied. 'Where's your balls, big man?' Carrie challenged him one day in the parlor. 'You frightened big momma gonna cut 'em off?'

Whitejack grinned. He had a fine set of teeth, marred only by a solid gold one in the middle, result of an early fight with Madam Mae. They had been together ten years – ever since he had celebrated his twentieth birthday in a whorehouse and been entertained by her. There had been no looking back. Now this hot little Carrie cunt was messing with his mind. She was still skinny as a starved rabbit, but with the greatest pair of jugs this side of Harlem. And what the big F. did all her johns keep running back for? What she have down there trapped between those skinny thighs?

A long hot shaft kept on telling him he just had to find out for himself.

'My balls my business,' he said smoothly, 'an' my oh my – ain't you developed yourself a mouth since you here. Six months ago I remember a scrawny little chick couldn't say boo to nuthin' or no one.'

She stretched, 'A mouth ain't all I developed, big man. I guess I be thinkin' of movin' on soon.'

'You told Madam Mae?'

'No – I ain't told Madam Mae. Why should I? She don't pull *my* strings.'

'She don't pull mine either.' The bitch was getting to him – always making out he was hog tied.

'Ha!' laughed Carrie. 'Big man. Big Mister Whitejack. We all know who runs the show 'round here.'

He glowered, 'Well you all don't know shit.'

'Ha!'

He grabbed her arm, 'Don't you give me none of your lip, you hear me girl?'

'Hey,' she mocked, 'don't tell me I'm gettin' to you – not Mister done it all – Seen it all – *Mister Ice.*'

He was on dangerous territory, but what the hell. Had to silence the bitch. He forced his mouth down on hers. Sucking, drawing at her lips, invading with his tongue.

She responded by clinging to him real tight, bringing her legs up around him so he could feel her body through the flimsy robe she had on.

He was nearly out of control, but his mind was still trying to figure out how he could do the deed without getting caught by Big Mama. She was out – but several of the girls were in, and if any of them wandered into the room . . . sheeit . . . You don't expect secrets to get kept in a whorehouse do you?

'You gonna give it to me, big man?' Carrie was mocking him, 'you *know* you want it. I can *feel* you want to.' Then she was fiddling with the buttons of his trousers. And he was letting her. And he was waiting for the moment she sprang it loose, and then he was going to give it to her like she had never been given it before. He had been actively fucking since he was ten years old – so she was going to get twenty long years of deliciously experienced cock. Lucky girl.

'Oooh baby, baby, baby . . . ' Carrie crooned lovingly, 'you are . . . beau . . . tiful.'

She had shucked her robe off, and her smooth young body was all his. She still clung to him, and somehow, although they were both standing, he was inside her. And it *was* special. Oh *sheeit* was it special!

Nothing mattered. Nothing in the whole goddamn world. Nothing . . . Nothing . . . Nothing . . .

And then he was shooting his load in strong spurts. Coming like he hadn't come for years. Blowing the top of his fuckin' head off.

*Sheeit.* Carrie was right. It was time they *both* said goodbye to Madam Mae.

Carrie dragged on the long thin cigarette – a real heavy drag – causing the smoke to fill her lungs – and her eyelids to droop. Marijuana. Some called it a drug. She called it instant relaxation and peace. A smile wafted across her lips, and she handed the cigarette to Whitejack. He dragged, and handed it on to another friend.

They all lolled on cushions, Carrie, Whitejack, a couple of musicians, and Lucille – the midget hooker – who had insisted on coming with them when they split.

And what a split it had been. Spectacular!

Madam Mae had not taken Whitejack's going lightly.

'You bad assed nigger whore chasing sonofasyphiliticbitch!' she had screamed in a fury, the curls of her platinum blonde wig shaking with anger. 'You walk out on me an' you is *finished* in this town – you hear me – *finished*!'

Whitejack wasn't fond of trouble, why couldn't they just part friends?

'Sheeit, woman . . . ' he had begun.

'Don't you go – *sheeit* woman – to me,' she had yelled, 'with your sweet talkin' whinin' wheedlin' voice. I *knows* you Whitejack. I *knows* you.' Her eyes were wild, 'you leave here today with that dumb child whore – an' don't you *never* set foot in *my* life again. When you get tired of sweet pussy just don't come crawlin' back here for a taste of the real thing. You hear me, nigger?'

'I hear you. The whole block hears you.'

Whitejack had given up trying to be nice. He packed a suit-case of clothes, and ordered Carrie to be ready to leave in ten minutes.

Madam Mae had stood in the hall, wig askew, arms akimbo. 'Fool!' she had spat at Whitejack, as he made several trips down to his car with his many suits stacked neatly over his arm. 'You bald buzzard stupid *fool*! Where'll you be without *me*? You'll come crawlin' back – an' I'll kick you right in your dumb cunt lappin' mouth!'

It was not the exit Carrie had imagined. She had wanted time to make plans. No way had she expected Whitejack to tell Madam Mae about them right off.

But Whitejack had figured she was worth her weight in gold, and why wait? He saw another fine ten years ahead, with Carrie doing all the work. She made him feel like he hadn't felt in years – And if a hooker could make him feel like that . . . Sheeit . . . She must be worth money. Plenty. What a fortune they would make together!

It was quite an achievement getting Whitejack away from Madam Mae. He was the smartest pimp in the business, and that's just what Carrie needed. She was pleased. What a fortune they would make together!

They had set off in Whitejack's sleek white Oldsmobile, with Lucille, the midget, running down the street after them, begging to be taken too. 'Why not?' They had both laughed, high on sudden freedom.

That had been two months previously. And in that two months they had accomplished nothing but fun. A lot of it. Good times, lazy days, and even lazier nights.

Carrie was confused. Whitejack was turning her on to pleasure. And one thing she had never known in her short hard life was pleasure. She had expected to go right to work, but he had different ideas. He rented an apartment for the three of them, then said, 'We are goin' to take us a little vacation, just hang out for a week or two and have us some re-laxation.'

Whitejack's idea of relaxation was a whole new world for Carrie, who had really seen nothing of life but the inside of a whorehouse and Welfare Island. He decided to broaden her horizons.

He liked to dress up real sharp – choosing one of his twenty-three suits, thirty shirts and fifteen pairs of shoes. Before dressing he liked to bathe with drops of ladies perfume in the water. Then he would shave his scalp and oil his bald head with pure olive oil. When he was groomed and ready, he would check out Carrie and Lucille's appearance. He liked them to look outrageous. And that they did, for he had bought them dresses and silk stockings and high heeled shoes in the brightest of colors, and encouraged them both to pile on the make-up. The three of them would then set out on the town in the white Oldsmobile.

133rd Street was Whitejack's hangout. He was known up and down the street in various restaurants, speakeasies and jazz joints. And he made new friends every night, because Whitejack was a generous man, and Whitejack was buying.

Carrie would sit quietly by his side, drinking in all the new sights and sounds. This was a whole other world that she had never even known existed. And when he turned her on to dope it made everything perfect. Because drugs were *the* answer. They dulled reality, and put a sharp diamond spotlight on laughter and good times and having fun.

The three of them went out every night, and came home in the early hours. Sometimes Carrie and Whitejack would make love. It was always hot and exciting, and even began to get to Carrie who had started the whole thing as a business venture.

Suddenly this tall bald man, with the piercing eyes and sweet talkin' voice was *her* man.

Suddenly she forgot about business and revelled in her new life.

Suddenly she was in love.

'Carrie,' Lucille was talking to her through the haze.

'What, honey?' she drawled lazily.

'Whitejack wants us to give these two guys some real hot thrills.'

'Huh?'

Lucille indicated the two musicians lying around on the cushions. 'I think we're back in business.'

Carrie rolled her eyes, '*You* may be honey – but me – I don't think Whitejack would want that. Oh no, that ain't the life for me anymore.'

Lucille shifted uneasily, and keeping her voice low said, 'He *told* me to tell you.'

'Mistake,' she yawned and stretched. 'Must've bin a mistake.' A fine Bessie Smith record was playing on the Victrola, and a nice mellow throb was all around. She had no intention of moving – none whatsoever.

'Here,' one of the musicians was giving her a turn on the weed.

She took the cigarette gratefully, inhaled the strong potion deeply into her lungs, then rolled over to give Whitejack his turn. He was not there.

'You're really somethin' – you know that?' The youngest of the two musicians said, 'I had my eye on you – but I wasn't sure I could get near the honeypot. I thought you was tight with Whitejack – but he told me you an' I can swing any way we want.'

She struggled to sit up. Her head was buzzing. 'Listen,' she slurred, 'you're wrong.'

'Aw come on, I gave that man twenty bucks says I'm right.'

Slowly it was getting through to her that Lucille was correct. They *were* back in business.

But it would have been nice if Whitejack had mentioned it to her himself, and not sneaked away like a thief in the night.

Love. Love was shit. Life was shit.

The musician had his hands on her, peeling down the top of the red silk dress Whitejack had bought her that very week.

'Wow!' he said, 'you got the greatest pair I ever seen in my life!'

She knew that it shouldn't get to her. After all she had long ago lost count of the number of men who had paid for the use of her body. But Whitejack should at least have *asked* her. If they really needed the money she would have understood. He should have let it be *her* decision to go back to work goddamn it!

The musician's tongue was on her nipples, but he never tasted the salt from her tears as she silently began to cry.

It was 2 A.M.

She had been fifteen for exactly two hours.

# Gino 1926–1927

The rise of Gino Santangelo and Aldo Dinunzio in the boot-legging business was solid and steady. They started off small, investing their combined money, and bringing in several truck-loads of high quality whiskey from Canada, taking no risks with strangers, but driving the trucks themselves, only using a few hand picked associates to make sure their assignments did not get hijacked by other mobs.

There was no problem obtaining the supplies, but it was a long and difficult trip getting safely back from the Canadian border to the heart of New York City. The dangers were many; trucks breaking down, police making random stops, and, of course, numerous hijackings.

Gino calculated all the risks, and in spite of the fact that a lot of consignments got lost along the way, his always made it.

Aldo and he worked well together. They trusted each other, and slowly, as they could afford it, they surrounded themselves with a loyal group of henchmen.

A year passed quickly. Gino was now twenty, but he looked and acted much older. His tough swagger gained him respect in the neighborhood. He and Aldo were looked up to and treated royally.

Pinky Banana was the enforcer for the gang. He rode shot-gun on the trips, and blasted the hell out of anyone who tried to stop them. He took a pleasure in his work that was un-natural but useful. He was still with Cindy of the blonde hair and cute ass. Prick tease was a name invented specially for Cindy.

The long hauls up to Canada and back were creating a strain. Tempers were becoming frayed. The Santangelo Gang, as they were known, were beginning to fight amongst themselves. A bad sign. Gino realized the tensions were caused by the trips always full of dangers, so he decided to investigate other possibilities. It was a well known fact that the laws of prohibition had loopholes. One of the biggest was that liquor was allowed to be consumed for medical reasons. If doctors could prescribe it – somebody had to make it. So government licenses were issued to certain companies who could then legitimately manufacture alcohol.

Aldo's cousin, Enzio Bonnatti, had infiltrated several such companies in and around Chicago. And rumor had it that his influence stretched even further than that.

'Why don't we arrange a meet?' Gino suggested to Aldo. He had always wanted to get to know Bonnatti.

Aldo on the other hand, seemed to want to steer clear of him. 'He's a difficult guy . . . ' he hedged.

'Difficult!' Gino scoffed, 'he's your cousin for crissakes. He's as big as fuckin' Capone. *Use* your blood connections . . . '

Reluctantly Aldo agreed, and several phone calls later the two of them set off by train for Chicago.

Sitting on the train was relaxing. Aldo fell asleep, and Gino stared out of the window reviewing his life. It was looking good. He had managed to put by a stash of money. It was almost looking good enough to send for Leonora. He still wrote her regularly every week with the help of Mr Pulaski. Her replies were intermittent, but when they came, so terrific, that he never got angry at her for not writing as often as he wanted.

His letters were full of love and plans.

Her letters were rather childish, dwelling on school and home, rather than their future together.

This was understandable. She did not want to look forward to something that as far as she was concerned could not happen for years. What a great surprise it would be for her when he told her their marriage was only just around the corner.

He found an apartment on which he had paid a healthy deposit. It was small but in a good neighborhood in the Upper Forties just off Park Avenue. Leonora would love it. She could furnish it herself. All he was planning to buy before her arrival was a big comfortable double bed.

He almost groaned aloud at the thought. Bed. Sex. A woman's body.

It had been so very very long. But he had made Leonora a promise, and Gino Santangelo's promise was his bond.

He took Vera to see the apartment and she declared it perfect. 'Gino, your lil' lady gonna love it,' she slurred, 'best goddamn place *I* ever seen.'

Vera was drunk as usual, but it didn't bother him. She was entitled to drink if that's what got her through the day. He had offered her money to move out of her room and into a better place, but she had refused. 'I gotta lot of regular johns – can't leave 'em,' had been her excuse.

Gino knew it'was just an excuse. He had heard that Paulo was back in jail, and for some reason Vera wanted to be where he could find her when he got out.

'I ain't gonna watch out for you if y'take him back,' he warned.

'Sure, honey, I can take care of myself.'

Yeh. Like last time. Gino hoped it would be a long time before Paulo was back on the street again.


It was snowing when they arrived in Chicago. Thick flakes of snow that settled on hair and clothes and then melted into tiny puddles.

'We had to come all this way for weather like this . . . ' Aldo complained. The truth of the matter was that he never liked to be too far away from his stormy relationship with Barbara Riccaddi. Since their first meeting over a year ago he had pursued her relentlessly. At first she had sent him packing with her sharp tongue. But gradually he had melted her down enough for her to break off her engagement to the cop, and spend time on a regular basis with him. She still verbally harassed him at every opportunity, but he seemed to thrive on it. 'First *real* dame I ever came across,' he would say with a faraway smile.

They took a cab straight to the hotel where the meet with Enzio had been arranged. At the reception desk they were told to take the elevator to the fifth floor, where two of Enzio's gang waited to body search them.

Aldo was most insulted, 'He's my fuckin' *cousin*. What kind of sucker ya think I am? Here – ya want my gun – it's yours.' He handed his small .25 caliber pistol over, but they insisted on searching him anyway.

Strapped to the side of his leg – just above the ankle, they found a six-inch hunting knife.

Aldo shrugged, 'Whatcha think? I'm gonna slit my own cousin's throat?'

Enzio walked in then, a powerful figure, soberly dressed in

a dark suit. Aldo had always reminded Gino of a squirrel. Twenty years old, but small and prematurely grey, he had prominent teeth and a passion for eating. Somehow Gino had imagined that Bonnatti would look the same. Wrong. Enzio Bonnatti was a good looking man. Twenty-two years old, tall, with a body in prime physical shape, straight dark hair, heavy set eyes, and a reputation for being tough. When Capone was mentioned, Bonnatti was mentioned. Between them they had a pretty strong hold on Chicago.

He shook hands formally with his cousin and Gino, then nodded to one of his hoods to fix drinks. No requests. Just hefty tumblers of straight scotch.

'So,' he sat down, 'what you two shitheads come sniffin' 'round Chicago for?'

Gino did the talking. Aldo sat silently beside him.

Enzio listened. He really didn't need them. Two small potatoes from New York with no muscle to speak of. What he *did* need was men around him he could trust. The bigger he got the more trouble came his way. A running feud with Capone made his life a misery. He couldn't even take a simple crap without two of his men checking out the crapper first.

Aldo was blood. So he hadn't seen him since he left Chicago to live in New York ten years previously. But he *was* blood. *Had* to be worth something.

And the deal Gino was suggesting wasn't half bad. Could mean big bucks without lifting a finger. A couple of phone calls . . . put out the word to a key connection that it was OK to deal with them.

'Listen – no offense, Gino. I like to talk to Aldo alone.'

'Sure,' Gino stood up. They had been with Enzio two hours. He knew they were in.

Salvatore, one of Enzio's hoods, took Gino to the hotel room booked for them to spend the night. 'Anythin' you want – just buzz the desk,' he remarked amiably. 'A dame – anythin' – no charge.' He also knew which way things were going.

Gino lay on one of the comfortable twin beds, hands behind his head. With Bonnatti behind them they would be into the big time. They would have the clout to be bigger and better. In no time at all they could be up there with Lucania, the Meyer Lansky mob, Siegel, and Costello. There was plenty to go round – it was just a question of breaking balls to get it.

Gino could understand why Lucania was always hunting around looking to recruit new young blood – he *needed* loyalty

– they all needed loyalty. And that's why Bonnatti would help them – Aldo was his cousin – He would be unlikely to stab him in the back . . .

Or at least less likely than a stranger.

When Aldo returned he was jubilant. 'We're in!' he exclaimed, 'you were right, you smart bum! He wants us to have dinner with him tonight – a little celebration. I should've brought Barbara.'

Gino grinned, 'I knew it was all gonna work out – I told you a year ago we should've contacted him.'

'So I like to be sure – this way we don't come crawlin' – we got our own set up an' he likes that.'

Gino clapped his friend on the shoulder, 'We're joinin' the big league, pal.' And as he said it he realized he could safely send for Leonora. Money would be rolling in. Bringing legitimate booze in from Chicago on a regular basis would mean a fuckin' fortune!

The Satin Club, located in the loop district of Chicago, was one of the plushest speakeasies around. The clientele was of the highest quality. Politicians, society folk, high up officials, and of course, beautiful women.

Enzio owned a sizeable piece of the action. He also owned a sizeable piece of Peaches La Moore, the featured entertainer.

Gina and Aldo sat at a table with Enzio, Peaches, and two of her girlfriends. At an adjoining table sat five of his hoods – minus girls.

Enzio figured he had done the two boys a favor. Juicy Chicago pussy. Little did he know about Leonora and Barbara. Neither Gino or Aldo were in the market for Chicago pussy – juicy or otherwise.

'You like the joint, fellas?' Peaches squeaked. She was blonde and stacked, with a voice that could easily curdle cream.

'Yeh – really a swell place,' Gino replied. And he meant it. He had never been in a place like the Satin Club before. The very plushness of it was impressive. And the smell of expensive cigars and perfume got him to thinking that this was the life – and what a kick to bring Leonora here and show her off. She would knock spots off any female in the place. She wasn't all powder and paint. She had true natural beauty.

'I'm gonna sing soon, boys,' Peaches wiggled in her chair, 'you all are in for a treat!'

'Some treat!' joked Enzio.

'Don't be nasty,' she pouted and stood up. 'After all, it was my singin' first got you lookin' in my direction.'

Enzio winked, and leered at her bosom. 'Sure it was honey, sure it was!'

'Come on girls,' Peaches beckoned her two friends, 'it's showtime. We'll see all you big boys later – have a nice cold bottle of champagne waiting. You know how thiiiirsty little Peaches gets!'

Enzio laughed as he watched her undulate her way through the room. 'Dumbhead!' he said affectionately, 'they're all dumbheads. Love 'em and leave 'em – fuck 'em and duck 'em – that's my slogan.'

Gino realized that had once been his slogan too. Before Leonora of course.

A baby grand piano next to the dance floor was drumming out an introduction, and on strolled the MC. He told a few bad jokes, crooned a love song, and introduced the chorus line of girls who high kicked their way across the floor.

'Wow!' muttered Aldo, Barbara suddenly forgotten in the flurry of silver stockinged legs, and seductive feather boas that teasingly nearly covered ten pairs of assorted bouncing bosoms.

Gino found himself developing an embarrassing hard-on. Who wouldn't with the life *he* was leading?

Then Peaches appeared, spectacular in a sequin frock that oozed over her body like a second skin. She stood in the front and squeaked her rendition of 'I Wish I Could Shimmy Like My Sister Kate.'

Gino immediately understood why the voice didn't matter. Every male in the place was mesmerized by the body.

Enzio sucked contentedly on a Havana cigar. 'Somethin', huh?' he sighed proudly.

Aldo kissed the tips of his fingers. 'Cousin, you know how to pick 'em. I think . . .'

He never got to finish his sentence. With no warning all hell was let loose as a group of men carrying machine guns burst into the room. They didn't hesitate, they sprayed the room as if they were watering roses.

There was total confusion – what with the panic, the screaming, the people running this way and that, and the relentless splatter of bullets hitting flesh.

Enzio moved like flash lightning as he hurled the table over and sheltered behind it. Aldo was hit in the arm, but Gino was lucky, natural instinct threw him to the floor the moment the first shot was fired.

'Fuckin' bastards!' Enzio screamed, 'Get the pricks!'

His men were already returning the fire. But two were down and out, and the remaining three were no match for the group with machine guns, who were now backing out of the room, their work well done.

Gino dragged Aldo to a safe spot behind him.

Enzio had his gun out and was shooting round the side of the table, he threw Gino a pistol – 'Give it to the bastards,' he roared.

A woman was wailing louder than anyone, 'My husband! My husband! Oh God – they've shot his face away! Oh my God!'

Gino caught the pistol and aimed at one of the retreating figures. It was the first time he had ever used a gun – but Pinky Banana had given him pointers on what to do.

'You got a hit!' Enzio yelled. 'Fixed the bastard right in the guts!'

The machine gun fire stopped as the group reached the door, and turned and ran for it. They left behind two of their men. The one Gino had shot, and another, wounded in both legs, who was trying to drag himself out.

Enzio didn't hesitate. He raised his gun, fired, and the man, with one final piercing scream, was dead.

'Come on,' Enzio muttered, 'let's get the hell outta here before the cops arrive.'

Gino stood and looked around. The place was a shambles. Broken glass and bodies everywhere.

'You can't do nothin',' Enzio said sharply, as if reading his mind, 'get a hold of Aldo and move it. We'll stick you on a train – you'll get him patched up in New York.'

Gino grabbed Aldo, who although bleeding profusely was well enough to curse his way out of the place while hanging onto his friend.

Enzio led them through the back way into a waiting car. 'Move it,' he yelled at the driver, who obeyed immediately.

'You all right, boss?' the driver asked anxiously.

'No thanks to the mugs out front. How the frig they get past Big Max and Shotty?'

'They jumped 'em – there was a lot of shooting. I just got in the motor and came to the back like you always told me t'do when there's trouble. Right boss?'

'Sure, right.' Enzio's voice was hard. 'Head for the station – I want these two outta here.' He turned to Gino, 'You did all right. I like your style. You're a pretty good shot.'

Gino nodded. He was afraid to speak. He was afraid the trembling in his gut would come puking out with any words he spoke.

They were at the station, and Enzio was almost pushing them out of the car. He wanted them long gone – he had a lot of fish to fry and needed no distractions. 'Take Aldo in the toilet – fix him up. Here – take my jacket.' He removed the jacket of his suit and handed it over. Then he clasped Gino warmly by the hand, 'I'll be in touch – we'll work good together. You proved yourself tonight. I like that – you know when to act and when to stay quiet. I like that a lot.'

Gino managed to nod. He watched the car roar off, leaving himself and Aldo standing outside the railway station – a heavy fall of snow enveloping them.

'I don't feel so good.' Aldo mumbled, 'Why couldn't we go back to our room?'

'Enzio's right, gotta get straight out of town. The less we're known here the better.'

'I should be in a hospital,' Aldo complained.

'Come on,' Gino led him inside the station, 'we'll get you fixed up.'

'What are you – a friggin' doctor all of a sudden?'

'Stop bitchin' – it's a scratch. If you had a bullet in your arm you wouldn't be walkin' around.'

'Holy shit. An expert I'm with.'

Once in the mens room Gino stripped off Aldo's jacket and shirt, and was relieved to find he was right. There was no gaping hole, just a lot of blood from a substantial nick. He tore a towel from the wall and bound it tightly round Aldo's damaged arm. 'That'll hold ya 'til we get back,' he said.

Aldo was ungrateful, 'I should be in a hospital,' he repeated darkly. 'If Barbara was here she'd see I was.'

'Yeh. Barbara would have your scrawny balls for breakfast. Get your shirt back on and let's go find a train.'

Aldo put his bloodstained shirt on, and covered it with Enzio's jacket which was somewhat large on him. He fumbled in the pocket and came up with a bundle. 'Get a load of this!' he exclaimed. It was two thousand dollars in worn hundred dollar bills.

'He must have forgotten to take it out,' Gino said.

'Either that or it's for us.'

'It ain't for us,' Gino replied harshly, 'we'll give it back to him. Put it away.'

But he knew that Enzio had left the money purposely. After

all – two thousand bucks was a fair payment for killing a man wasn't it?

Once safely back in New York, Gino made his plans. Life was short. Just how short he knew only too well. And the newspaper headlines were not slow to remind him.

'FIFTEEN SLAIN. GANG MASSACRE IN CHICAGO SPEAKEASY.'

It could well have been him lying in a Chicago morgue. Unfucked for over a year. A sucker waiting to get married. Waiting . . . it was a dirty word. No more waiting for Gino Santangelo.

He went straight to see Mr Pulaski. The old man was in a bad way. He had been attacked and robbed in the street during Gino's absence. The robbers had taken his gold watch – the only item he possessed of any value – and three measly dollars. In return they had given him two broken ribs, and a kicking that left him black and blue from head to toe.

'Who did it?' Gino demanded, 'you recognize who it was?'

Mr Pulaski grimaced. He was too old and too tired to want to cause any trouble.

Gino was leaning over his bed, a wild look in his eyes. 'Tell me who it was.'

The old man sighed, 'Some people don't know any better . . . boys . . . they don't understand things . . . I would like my watch back . . . '

'Who were they?'

'The Morrisson boy . . . his friend . . . Jacob I think they call him . . . Two others . . . I don't know who they were . . . ' His voice trailed off, and he closed his eyes. He was eighty-three years old and he didn't like the way the world was changing around him. There was no respect anymore . . . Why only the other day a mere slip of a girl had stopped him in the street and invited him to have relations with her. Very young . . . fifteen . . . Maybe only fourteen . . . His eyes fluttered open. 'You want I should write a letter for you?'

Gino was no longer there. Gino was already out on the street, his step purposeful. Little fuckers. He knew who they were. Terry Morrisson and Jacob Cohen. Two neighborhood kids not more than fourteen years of age but always causing trouble.

He would personally beat the shit out of them, teach them a hard lesson about life, get Mr Pulaski's watch back, and *then* go get his letter written.

What a day! Wasn't it enough he had had Barbara Riccaddi screaming at him all morning? Blaming *him* for Aldo's injury. Screaming insults about what a bad influence he was. How if it wasn't for him Aldo would never *dream* of being involved in anything illegal. And all the while, Aldo, behind her back, laughing and making faces. Her whiplash tongue tried but failed to castrate both of them.

He headed for the Cohen household first. A walkup tenement building next door to Catto's family. He hadn't seen his friend in over six months. Catto didn't approve of the way he ran his life and so they had drifted apart. If Catto wanted to waste his life shovelling shit that was his problem. Gino had offered him a chance to come in with him, but the mug had refused. Funny thing was that Catto thought *he*, Gino, was the mug. What a laugh!

A thin harassed woman answered his knock. 'Whatcha want?' her voice was listless.

'Jacob,' he replied.

Her glassy eyes flickered nervously, 'He's at school.'

He pushed past her into the crowded room. 'Like hell he is.'

A baby crawled amongst the mess on the floor. Asleep on a sofa bursting its stuffing was Jacob. Gino woke him with a sharp kick.

'What the . . . ' Jacob sat up and stared.

'I wanna talk to you,' he declared, 'so let's go out the back.'

Jacob glanced quickly at his mother. She averted her eyes. She was no fool. He was just like his old man, a basin full of trouble.

Jacob scowled at Gino, 'What makes ya think I wanna talk to you?'

Gino's hard black eyes narrowed meanly, 'Because I said so punk. Move it!'

An hour later Gino was back at Mr Pulaski's bedside.

'Here, pop,' he handed the old man his gold watch, and saw the veined and liver spotted hands clutch at it tenderly. 'You're a good boy, Gino,' the old man crooned in a weak voice, 'a boy who understands things.'

Yeh. He understood things. Only Jacob Cohen's story had been somewhat different from the old man's. He claimed that old man Pulaski had been flashing it at his twelve-year-old sister for months. 'So she don't mind so much, figures he's a bit cuckoo - but then - the other day - in daylight - I swear to ya it was daylight - he sneaks up behind her in the street and opens up full fire all over her only dress. The old pisser hadda get taught a lesson didn't he?'

Fucking marvelous wasn't it? Gino checked out Jacob's story and it was true. Turned out that he was the only one in the neighborhood didn't know Mr Pulaski was a dirty old man.

In the circumstances beating up on Jacob and his friends didn't seem right. Instead he bawled the shit out of them and recovered the watch.

'Shall I do your letter now?' Mr Pulaski inquired weakly.

'You feel up to it?' he asked anxiously. 'Only it's the big one, pops. I wanna send for her. We're gonna get married. I want this letter to be a real big masterpiece. Think y'can do it, pops?'

'Of course I can, Gino,' Mr Pulaski replied solemnly, 'it will be the most romantic letter that you and I have ever composed together.'

Sure it would. Was there any law that said an old flasher couldn't write one hell of a romantic love letter?

# Carrie 1928

Whitejack was an evasive man. He had a bad habit of not answering questions - instead, saying a plaintive 'Shee . . . ii . . . t,' as though that explained everything.

Carrie could not stay mad at him for long. He was all she had in the world. He was her man, and even though he expected her to go back to work without so much as asking her - well that was just his way.

And nobody could say he wasn't generous. Since leaving Madam Mae's he had paid for everything for all of them - Lucille included - with no complaints.

Now it seemed they needed money, and it was only fair that she and Lucille work for it the only way they knew how. It wasn't like it hadn't been the plan all along.

Whitejack didn't change toward her. He still gave her plenty of lovin' whenever he felt in the mood. But somehow, if the mood took him just when she had finished with a john, she didn't feel like it. In fact it was an effort to moan and groan the way she knew he liked, and to pretend to be having a good time when the truth of the matter was she was tired, her pussy was sore, her back ached, and all she wanted to do was go to sleep.

'Whassamatter with you, woman?' he asked harshly one day, 'you used to be the hottest sweetest piece around. Now all I get is cold ass.'

'I'm just worn out,' she replied, 'I'm turnin' more tricks than when I was at Madam Mae's – and for less money. I thought we were goin' to have a house – do things properly.'

'We need plenty dough 'for we get us a house. Ain't my fault that bitch Mae cleaned out the bank account 'for I could get out my share.'

'I didn't know she did that,' Carrie exclaimed.

Triumphantly Whitejack said, 'You see, woman. I don't bother you with my problems – so why you bother me with yours?' He got up from the bed and stretched, 'Whyn't we take ourselves out on the town?'

She sighed. She would have liked to go out, get away from the small rented apartment, but she had a john coming, and it was important to get regular customers again. 'I can't, but you go.'

'Sure. I'll go. Find us another girl to help you and Lucille out.' He scooped up the twenty dollars that her last john had left on the table. 'How about me gettin' us a big white platinum blonde? How about *that* to go with you and Lucille, huh? The three of you do a show we could *really* be into dough.'

'A show?' Carrie did not know what he was talking about.

'A show – baby – is three chicks suckin' each other off, playin' with each other. Y'know – the kinda stuff you musta done out on the island a thousand times.'

She froze. 'I wouldn't do that.'

There was no animosity in his voice, just a natural friendliness, 'You a whore, woman. You do anything.'

She watched him dress. She watched him go. Then she lay on her stomach and sobbed until there was no tears left.

She didn't hear Lucille come into the room, and was only aware of her presence when she felt a comforting hand massaging her back.

'You think he was Prince Charming honey?' Lucille asked sympathetically. 'He's a pimp, babe, and we are his women. We all got each other – so's no need to fret yourself. You really want to cry, try thinkin' about what it's like bein' me.'

She sat up and stared at Lucille, 'You don't understand,' her voice broke, 'you've *always* been that way. I could've had a good life, but I was forced into being a whore by *my own uncle* – he locked me in a room and sent men in one by one while my grandma sat in the next room collecting the money. I was thirteen years old. There ain't nothin' left for me 'cept this life.'

Lucille blinked, 'I was six when my poppa realized I just weren't gonna get any bigger. So he sold me to the freak show passin' through town – and by the time I was eleven I was servicing every goddamn freak in the show. Whitejack found me when I was sixteen. You could say he saved me. Kidnapped me right out of that hell hole and made me want to live. Madam Mae's was paradise compared to what *I* was used to.'

Carrie listened intently, gradually forgetting about her own troubles.

'These last few months with you an' Whitejack 'bin the very best of my whole life,' Lucille continued, 'you both treat me just like anyone else – not like some freak 'cos I'm a small person. I'd do anything for Whitejack, he's been a good man – An' honey, you should feel the same. He bin good to *both* of us.'

Carrie nodded. He had.

'So what you cryin' 'bout?' Lucille asked, ''cos you're a whore?' She shook her head defiantly, 'So what? I'm a whore – it don't bother me no more. Whitejack's a pimp, it don't bother him none. Come on honey, dry your tears an' let's get back to work.'

Carrie got off the bed and walked to the mirror. She looked awful, her eyes all puffed out, her make-up in streaks down her face. But she felt better. Lucille was right. So what if she sold her body. It was only a job.

'Good gal.' Lucille clucked. 'Start prettying yourself up. We got work to do – an' I just *know* that fella comin' to see you don't want no truck with no midget. See! I can say midget – it don't mean nothin'. You can say whore – same thing.'

She managed a weak smile, 'Thanks,' she said softly.

Lucille shrugged, 'Nothin'.'

Carrie started some repair work on her face. She had left Madam Mae's to get a little more control over her life. What had she really expected? Whitejack to take a job and marry her? What kind of soft thinking was that? Just a couple of months of good lovin', the *first* loving she had ever enjoyed, and she was forgetting her ambitions. Whitejack was right. They needed money to get a house. And if that is what they needed that is what she would get.

Any way Whitejack said. Any way at all.

She couldn't wait to tell him. She knew he was getting fed up with her lately, always complaining and bitching. But now that she had decided to accept the fact that they were back in business things would be different.

She dealt with her john quickly and efficiently – sending him back on the street with a kiss and a promise – 'You all come back now for an even *better* time.'

'Sure will!' he agreed with enthusiasm. And raced home to his wife and three children.

Carrie washed, brushed her hair which was starting to grow back nicely, and took a reefer from the small stash Whitejack kept under the mattress. She lit up and inhaled deeply. It made her feel mellow and relaxed.

She put a Bessie Smith record on the Victrola, and lay back on the bed.

Soon she fell asleep, and she did not realize Whitejack had not come home until she awoke at ten o'clock the next morning.

# Gino 1928

Gino was aware of a great feeling of relief when the letter to Leonora was finally written and mailed. He had waited so long, and now, at last, he was able to put things in motion.

Mr Pulaski had come through with the goods. A letter so romantic and loving that Gino was almost embarrassed to put his signature on it. After all, maybe Leonora would expect him to talk the same way. He didn't want to disappoint her.

He kept on imagining her face when she read the letter. That face . . . so delicate and innocent.

Along with the letter to Leonora had gone the one to her father. The polite formal one requesting her hand in marriage. Everything correct and above board. If all went according to plan, he would soon be on a train to San Francisco and married in a matter of weeks.

Meanwhile there was business to take care of. Bonnatti had not been long in keeping his word, and contact had been made that there was a load of legal alcohol waiting to be picked up from a company outside of Trenton, New Jersey. Bonnatti himself spoke to Gino on the phone. 'You handle this good an' it'll be a regular supply. Take your own truck an' contact the foreman at the plant. He knows the action, an' he's bin taken care of this end. No money changes hands – when you do your deal in town keep my split – I'll be in to pick it up the end of the month.'

'You're very trusting,' Gino joked.

'Sure I am,' Enzio was not amused. 'I figure you're fond of your balls. I also figure you wanna hang onto them.'

Gino laughed, 'When you pick up your dough I got the two thou you left in your jacket pocket. I got your jacket too – had it cleaned an' pressed.'

'The money was a payment.'

'For what?'

'Cut the crap, Gino. You know for what.'

'Hey . . . Enzio. It's not that I don't appreciate it. But I don't want you t'get the wrong idea. I don't wanna work for you – *with* you – yes. But not *for* you. You understand what I mean?'

There was a short silence while the line from Chicago crackled ominously. Then Enzio said, 'What about Aldo? He don't wanna take the money?'

'He can do what the fuck he likes. He brought me to you an' we're partners – but I want to clear our position up – so ya know I ain't some employee. OK?'

Now it was Enzio's turn to laugh, 'I heard tell you was a hot-head. Yeah, yeah. OK. I understand. Give me back the dough if it makes you happy.'

Around the 110th Street neighborhood Gino and Aldo had acquired a lock-up warehouse where they housed cases of liquor awaiting delivery, two trucks, and a beat up old Ford. The trucks were plastered with 'DINUNZIO MOVING AND STORAGE', and once in a while they would be used for such a purpose. But this of course was only a front, and the real purpose of the trucks was to transport booze.

The beat up old Ford, which looked like it would hardly make it from one side of town to the other, had an engine under its hood that would do justice to a new Rolls-Royce. Gino had personally and lovingly fixed it. He was a master mechanic when it came to souping up old cars.

Twenty-one years old, he was doin' pretty good. He had no

complaints. Of course he wasn't in the big time yet. He wasn't no Lucania – but he was on his way – and one thing was sure – no one was going to stop him.

He decided to drive the truck himself on the Trenton job. Hijacking was becoming more and more rife – and to lose this load would mean losing face with Bonnatti – not to mention his balls.

Pinky Banana rode shotgun, and Aldo took the wheel on the Ford. They were all armed and expecting trouble. But none came. It was a perfect run.

Once the goods were unloaded and delivered to grateful customers, Gino, Pinky Banana, and Aldo went to Fat Larrys to celebrate. The place was really becoming fashionable, with society ladies and their escorts bumming their way up from their Park Avenue brownstones.

'The joint is sure jumpin' tonight!' Pinky Banana exclaimed. He bit on a hang nail and with his other hand snapped his fingers for a waitress.

A weary little redhead showed them to a table in the back.

'This ain't no good. Where's Larry?' Pinky Banana questioned in loud aggressive tones, hanging onto the string of her decorative apron so she couldn't retreat.

' 'Scuse me, *sir*,' she snapped, '*Mister* Larry is not here tonight.'

'*Mister Larry!*' mimicked Pinky Banana, 'I knew Mister friggin' Larry when he was just plain friggin' fatso!'

'Sit down, Pinky,' Gino said mildly, 'we'll have a drink and get out of here.'

Pinky Banana's fleshy lips twitched. 'S'OK Gino, don't worry, I'll handle it. *Nobody* gonna shove *me* in the back of this pisshole.'

The waitress was getting frightened now. She was new to the job, and had never set eyes on Pinky Banana before. But she could tell trouble when it was coming her way. 'If you'll let go of me I'll find the manager for you.' Her voice quavered slightly.

'Naw,' Pinky Banana spat beligerently, 'we don't need no manager. You'd better get it straight who I am. I'm *Mister Kassari*, and I'll take that table over there.' He pointed to an empty table center front, right at the edge of the small dance floor. 'Move it, sweetie.' He smacked her sharply on the ass.

She flashed an angry glance at him, then decided her job was more important than an argument with a customer. She led the three of them through the crowded place to the table Pinky Banana had requested. It had a reserved sign on, but let the manager sort *that* one out.

When they were seated, and had ordered drinks, Gino said, 'You're a loud sonofabitch Pinky, y'know that?'

Pinky Banana guffawed, 'Yeah. I know that. So friggin' what?'

Gino shrugged, 'One day it's gonna get you in trouble.'

'So? Ain't no trouble too big for me. I can handle anything.'

'You think so?'

'I know so.'

Gino nodded with no real conviction. He had a bad feeling about Pinky Banana. The power of killing was going to his head.

The waitress returned to the table with their drinks. By her side was Fat Larry. He had changed from the amiable slob who used to run the place when it sold nothing but milk shakes out front. He was still as fat as ever, but his large body was crammed into an uncomfortable formal suit, his hair slicked down with oil, and sweat coursed freely down his cheeks. He threw up his fat arms in mock despair, 'Pinky m'boy. Whatcha tryin' to do to me?'

Pinky Banana sniffed loudly, wiped the back of his hand across his nose, and winked at Gino and Aldo, 'Wait for it, boys, here comes the sob story.'

'I didn't know you was comin' in tonight,' Fat Larry said reproachfully. 'If I'd known of course you would've had this table. But as it is you can see I'm booked out, and this table is promised to a real high class society dame bin comin' here regular for two weeks. This is *her* table.'

'Tough shit,' yawned Pinky Banana.

'Aw come on boys,' Fat Larry wheezed, 'you gotta move.'

Pinky Banana's eyes were suddenly hard and cold, '*Gotta* move, fatso? Did I hear you right?'

Fat Larry visibly blanched. Wasn't it enough he had to pay protection on his place to the mob. Now he had to deal with local hoods too?

Pinky Banana was twitching dangerously.

Gino intervened. He had no desire to get in any kind of brawl. 'This your high society dame?' He indicated a tall woman swathed in fox furs who stood in the doorway survey-ing the room. By her side was a young nervous looking man.

The sweat dripped from Larry's face. 'That's her.'

'So have her and the chump she's with share the table with us. We don't mind do we boys?' He winked at Pinky Banana, 'We could do with a little class education!'

Fat Larry nodded. It was not the ideal solution, but apparently the only one. What was he going to say to Mrs Duke? 'Oh – excuse me Mrs Duke, ma'am, I got three bums refuse to move, so I do hope you don't mind sharing a table with them tonight.' Mrs Duke would *love* that. She had been in every night for two weeks. She was a real lady who always wore beautiful clothes and only drank champagne. Every night she was accompanied by a different young man. Her routine never varied. Arrival ten minutes before the show and departure ten minutes after. Fat Larry failed to see what interest she could possibly have in six high kicking squeaky voiced chorus girls and a bad comedian who told the filthiest jokes this side of the East River. But she seemed to love it. Oh well . . . Bye bye Mrs Duke. Better than a bullet up his ass one dark night. And he wouldn't put that past Pinky Banana if he didn't get his own way.

Fat Larry waddled in her direction.

She raised a quizzical eyebrow, 'Problems tonight, Larry?'

He loved the way her tongue turned over on 'Larry.' Real class. 'Overbooking, Mrs Duke. Stupid waitress is new, didn't realize it was your table.'

'Can't you move them?' Mrs Duke was somewhat amused by Fat Larry's obvious discomfiture.

'Nowhere to move them to, Mrs Duke,' Fat Larry produced a handkerchief from his breast pocket and dabbed at his face. It was true. The place was jammed.

'Are you telling me I can't come in?' Mrs Duke's tone shifted from amused to icy.

'No . . . No . . . ' Fat Larry stammered, 'If you wouldn't mind sharing your table . . . '

'It seems I have no choice.' She swept past Fat Larry in the direction of her table, her escort close on her heels mumbling and nervous, 'Clementine, are you s . . . s . . . sure? Why don't we go somewhere else?'

Gino, Pinky Banana and Aldo watched in amazement as she headed in their direction. They had all expected her to turn down the suggestion.

'You and your big mouth!' groaned Aldo to Gino. 'What we gonna say to her?

'I don't expect she'll be holdin' her breath for conversation with us,' Gino snorted, 'just watch your language.'

'Aw frig!' exclaimed Pinky Banana, 'I ain't watchin' my language for no friggin' taffy nosed skirt.'

'Good evening gentlemen.' She was at the table, cool green eyes looking them over. 'I understand we're sharing this table tonight, perhaps you could move up slightly, and I do believe we'll need another chair.'

The three of them stared at her.

She turned to her escort, 'Frightfully kind of these gentlemen, Henry, don't you think?'

Henry had a bad acne condition around the neck of his shirt which glowed a dull red. 'Yes, Clementine,' he replied stiffly.

Pinky Banana suddenly leapt to his feet and snapped his fingers for the waitress. 'Chair over here!' he yelled. Then he shoved Aldo. 'Move up.'

Aldo stifled a curse. The shove had caught him bang on his bad arm. Sixteen stitches were holding his skin together and he didn't fancy them splitting a bucketful of blood all over the table.

Mrs Clementine Duke smiled at Pinky Banana and extended her hand towards him.

His eyes riveted onto a magnificent diamond ring.

'I'm Clementine Duke,' she said in a crisp New England accent, 'and this is Henry Moufflin Junior.' She shook him firmly by the hand.

'Mr Kassari.' Pinky Banana managed to mumble in return.

'Mr Kassari. A pleasure to meet you.' She extended her hand to Aldo next.

'Aldo Dinunzio,' he muttered.

'Delighted.' Then she was looking straight at Gino, and he was staring straight back at her. Nothing audible was heard but there was a decided click as their eyes met.

'Gino Santangelo,' he said firmly.

'What a nice name.' They held eyes just that split second longer than was necessary.

Mrs Duke broke the stare and turned to Henry. 'Order champagne darling, you're simply going to adore this place – it's so unutterably . . . seedy.'

Gino studied her carefully. He wasn't sure what she had – but she had it all right.

She was an older woman, somewhere in her thirties, but she looked pretty good for her age. Her green eyes were widely spaced and fringed with very long lashes. The slight shadows underneath made the eyes extremely sensual. Her nose was a touch too long, giving her a permanently arrogant look. But it was a perfect nose, and the arrogance only added to the sexuality. Her lips were thin, and her mouth turned down slightly.

She had jet black hair cut dramatically short with straight bangs, and her body, beneath the expensive white satin dress, was thin and muscled. His eyes lingered on her nipples, clearly visible through the satin.

She caught him looking and smiled slightly. She was thinking of the hot excitement she felt. The thrill of being in this dreadful place. The thrill that had been building for two weeks – ever since she had first come to Fat Larrys. She had known that eventually she would find something here – some little morsel that would get her sexual taste buds going again.

Gino Santangelo. What a peculiar name. What a hot looking young man. Bit short, but that never mattered in the bed stakes. She had already checked out his thumbs, and they were long and thick – a sure sign that what he had between his legs would be more than enough. She liked his eyes. Uncompromising eyes. Hard, black, and much older than the rest of him. She liked his hair. Thick and black. Once she got rid of the grease plastering it not too successfully down, it would be an improvement. She liked his face. A strong nose, and thick sensual lips that broke constantly into a wonderful smile. She even liked the scar on his cheek. It gave his face more character.

'Clementine.' Henry Moufflin Jr was busy trying to clink his champagne glass against hers.

She obliged, shifting slightly on her chair. Oh God! She was ready . . . very very ready.

'Fat Larry told us you come here every night,' Pinky Banana said suddenly, having thought a full three minutes about how to open up a conversation with this knockout classy dame.

Clementine nodded, 'Yes.' She didn't like the look of him, too tall and gangly, something dirty about him.

'S'not a bad place,' Pinky continued airily, 'if you can't be bothered goin' downtown. 'Course – we usually do. Jump in the roadster an' pop downtown.'

Aldo choked on his drink. What roadster?

'How about you?' Clementine asked, fixing her eyes on Gino, 'do *you* ever come downtown?'

He shrugged, confused. He didn't want to be thinking about another woman, but this one had given him what seemed like a permanent hard-on. It was her goddamn nipples staring him in the face. One thing was sure – he would never let Leonora wear a dress like that. No siree. Never. 'I get around. New York's my city.'

Her eyes gently teased him, 'I bet it is.'

'My city too,' Pinky Banana joined in quickly, 'the best frig ... er ... the best,' he finished lamely and glared at Aldo who was smothering laughter.

'What business are you in?' Clementine's eyes held Gino's.

'You name it – I do it,' Pinky replied cockily. He did not like the way things were progressing here. 'I ain't never had a job *I* couldn't handle.'

'Really.' Clementine's eyes flickered over him like he was a dog turd in the gutter. 'And you? What do you do?' Her eyes were back on Gino.

He wished she would stop looking at him that way. He knew what she wanted and he wasn't in the market for giving.

He decided to stop her in her tracks. 'I handle shipments,' he said, 's'matter of fact I'll be goin' to San Francisco in a few weeks to handle a shipment for my fiancee's father. I'll be getting married while I'm there.' If that didn't stop her, nothing would.

Pinky Banana frowned, 'What shipment? I didn't—'

Gino kicked him sharply under the table.

'Hmmm ... ' Clementine looked thoughtful, 'my husband is interested in the shipping business ... Perhaps you should meet him.'

Gino didn't believe her line.

Henry Moufflin Jr didn't believe it either. He had invited Clementine Duke out because she was the most desirable tempting woman in the world. He had not expected to end up in some cheap dive with Clementine making eyes at a short, two bit hood. Her behaviour was inexcusable. 'Clementine, dear,' he said quickly, 'why don't we move on from here? I know a most amusing cafe ... '

'Do shut up, Henry.'

His acne glowed.

'Now, let me see,' Clementine was searching her purse for something, 'Ah! Here we are.' She produced a small neatly engraved business card and handed it to Gino. 'This is my card. If you are interested in doing business with my husband do please call on me and we can discuss it. I receive visitors between eleven and twelve most mornings,' she smiled, 'when you return from San Francisco, or even before you go.'

Pinky Banana's mouth hung open. Friggin' bitch. What the

frig was the matter with *him*? Friggin' Gino. Didn't want it, and was getting it thrown right at him. Always had been the one with the dames.

Gino took the card and stuck it in his pocket. Before Leonora this would have been an experience not to be missed. Now . . . what the hell. Some classy broad come slumming, looking to pick herself up something for the night.

She stood up, 'You will call on me won't you?' Her eyes lingered on his. She licked her thin lips and smiled graciously at Pinky and Aldo. 'Thank you so much for allowing us to sit at your table. I *did* enjoy meeting you.'

Henry Moufflin Jr got up abruptly, rocking the table and almost spilling the drinks.

'Careful, college boy,' Pinky Banana muttered darkly.

'S . . . s . . . sorry,' stammered Henry. 'Clementine, I m . . . m . . . ust get the check.'

'Forget it,' Gino said quickly, 'the champagne's on me.'

Mrs Clementine Duke swept off without so much as a thank you.

Gino had not expected one.

At the door Fat Larry blocked her path, 'Mrs Duke. You're leaving before the show. You always stay for the show . . . ' His fat cheeks shook with indignation, 'if those punks bin insultin' you . . . '

'On the contrary, Larry. I had a perfectly delightful time. Your friends were more than charming.'

'They were?' Fat Larry's jaw sagged in surprise.

'They certainly were.'

'Hot shit!' whooped Pinky Banana, standing up and watching Mrs Duke depart, 'that was somethin' – really somethin'. An' hot as a friggin' pistol! Didja get a load of those bedroom eyes?'

'They weren't signalling in *your* direction,' laughed Aldo, 'Gino the Ram makes it again!'

Pinky scowled. He honestly could not understand how any woman could possibly prefer Gino to him. Cindy had assured him time and time again that there was definitely no contest. 'Gino the friggin' Ram!' he spat in disgust, 'he must've forgotten the color of pussy it's bin so long since he's seen any! Some friggin' Ram.'

Now it was Gino's turn to scowl. 'Shut your mouth fuckhead,' he warned.

'Says who?' sneered Pinky Banana.

'Aw come on you two jerks,' Aldo interjected, 'let's cut out the crappin' around and enjoy the show. It ain't every night Barbara lets me off the hook.'

Costa Zennocotti sat in his father's study in San Francisco, gazing out of the window while his adopted father droned on. It was a lecture that would continue for at least another ten minutes and Costa had tuned out. All he heard were the key words. 'Respect' 'Love' 'Ambition' 'Loyalty.' The usual words Franklin liked to jam down his throat.

It didn't bother him. He understood his father, and he knew that every word coming his way was dealt out of a genuine love and concern.

Franklin Zennocotti really had no need to worry about Costa. He did love his adopted parents. He did respect them. He had great ambition, and his loyalty was fierce.

In fact loyalty was the reason he was sitting in his father's study. Loyalty to Gino.

Costa had requested and received permission for a trip to New York. Not an easy goal to accomplish, but he had managed it, and in two hours he would be sitting on a train. He was now getting a final lecture on how to conduct himself in the big city. Not that he would be exactly running wild. It was all arranged that he was to stay two weeks with Franklin's sister and her husband. Then he was to return to San Francisco – attend college – attend law school – and eventually start work as a fully qualified lawyer in his father's firm.

It seemed like his future was very neatly planned. But he didn't mind. It was what *he* wanted as well as what his parents wanted. And he felt that he owed it to them to turn out to be as much of a credit to the family as possible. Especially after what Leonora had done to them. His mother was still reeling from the shock and disgrace of it all.

Leonora. What a devious little miss she had turned out to be. Stringing his friend Gino along. Receiving his letters and giggling over them with her girlfriends. And at the same time going out with any boy that asked her. Sneaking out of the house at night. Playing truant at her ladies college. She was a wild one. For all her innocent looks, big blue eyes, and delicate airs.

Costa had said to her one day, 'Why don't you tell Gino to stop writing you?'

'Why should I?' she had replied.

'Well . . . ' Costa had hesitated, 'I don't think it's fair. After all, he thinks you're his girl.'

She had widened her beautiful eyes, 'Maybe I still am. What do *you* know.'

He knew plenty. He knew she had the reputation in town of being 'easy' and that several boys claimed to have slept with her. He also knew if Gino found this out he would go berserk. He was not proud of himself for having done so, but he had invaded Leonora's room while she was out, and read some of Gino's letters. They left no doubt about his feelings and intentions.

Costa had not known how to handle the situation. He felt it was not his business, but he also felt such a strong sense of loyalty towards Gino, and he did not wish to see him hurt.

Eventually the situation had resolved itself. Sweet innocent Leonora got herself pregnant. Mary and Franklin Zennocotti went into an advanced state of shock when their darling daughter confessed to her condition. When they recovered they insisted a wedding must be arranged as soon as possible. Fortunately the father-to-be was the son of an acceptable San Francisco family. Plans were made immediately, and within two weeks Leonora was walking down the aisle, radiant in white silk.

As she was leaving on her honeymoon she threw Costa a look. 'You'd better tell your friend, Gino, I don't want any more of his mushy letters.'

The day after she left two letters arrived at the house, one addressed to her, the other to Franklin. Costa, recognizing the handwriting, had pocketed them both. When he read them later in the privacy of his room he knew there was only one way to deal with things. He would have to tell Gino personally. An unenviable task, but surely better than a letter. Hence the trip to New York.

Of course he had not told his parents *why* he wanted to go. He suspected that if they had known the sole purpose of his journey they would have said no. So, he talked of museums and parks and art galleries. 'I would just like to get away before college,' he had explained, and miraculously they had agreed. They were good parents.

Franklin was counting out a hundred dollars worth of bills and handing them across the desk to Costa. 'You'll have a good time, son,' he said gruffly. 'My sister and her husband are fine people and will look after you. And be sure to show them plenty of respect.'

'Yes, sir.' The word respect jolted Costa back to reality. 'I certainly will, sir.'

Gino visited Vera once a week at an arranged time. Fed up with interrupting her at work, he told her to keep Wednesday nights free. She did as he told her, looking forward to their evenings together. Usually they went to a movie, and then to a drug-store for a hamburger and milk shake. They made an odd couple. The cheap aging prostitute with the missing front teeth, and the strong looking young man simmering with hidden energy.

'I got enough bucks for y'to give it all up,' he informed her every Wednesday.

'Keep it,' she would reply, 'what would an old hag like me do with free time? 'Sides,' a gummy grin, 'I kinda enjoy my work.'

Gino was not quite sure how Leonora would take to Vera. But he was determined they would meet and hopefully get along. He would explain all about Vera to Leonora, and that should make things right. Leonora was just going to have to accept the fact that there was more to life than a nice family existence in San Francisco.

Every time he thought of her a mounting excitement crept up on him. He was going to be a married man and he couldn't wait!

A married man!

Gino Santangelo.

Leonora Santangelo.

Mr and Mrs Santangelo.

'Whassamatta, Gino?' Vera slurred, 'you're not eatin' your ice-cream.'

'Hey?' he questioned, slapping his palms together. 'Whacha think? Leonora Santangelo. Sound good to ya?'

Vera nodded. 'Sounds wonderful.'

# Carrie 1928

Whitejack stayed away for a week.

First Carrie was worried, then angry.

'That man can look after himself, honey,' Lucille assured her, 'and so can we. He'll be back soon enough.'

'How can you be so sure?' Carrie fretted.

'Oh, honey. I'm sure. No way that Whitejack gonna walk on twenty-three suits!'

And Lucille was right. He breezed in one morning relaxed and full of charm.

'Where you bin?' Carrie screamed.

He held up an authoritative hand, 'Quiet yourself down, woman. I bin gettin' us that big white platinum blonde I told you 'bout.'

'I thought you'd crept on back to Madam Mae . . . '

He laughed, 'Back to that bitch. You kiddin' woman?'

'You could have told me you were gonna be gone . . . I was worried . . . '

He cupped her breast and slid her robe aside fingering the nipple. 'Didn't know I hadda check in.'

'Oh Whitejack!' She felt secure again. She wanted to please him. 'Lucille an' me – we pulled in three hundred bucks this week.' She put her arms around him and pressed close to his body. 'It's all for you, sugar.'

He gave her a gentle shove away. 'Get yourself dressed and packed. Today we move on.'

'What do you mean?'

'I got us a bigger apartment in a better neighborhood.'

Her eyes were wide, 'How'd you do that? I thought we had no money.'

'Leave it to Whitejack. I got us a whole new set up.'


The fat man with the cigar beamed jovially around at his friends. There were about thirty of them all told. An affluent group of middle-aged businessmen, well wined and dined.

The occasion was a stag dinner to celebrate the retirement of one of them. His name was Arthur Stuyvesant, and he was retiring from the investment business.

His fat friend had organized the dinner, and now, cigar aloft, he signalled for the real fun to start. 'Gentlemen,' he announced, hardly able to control the excitement in his voice, 'I have a small surprise for you this evening. Something that I feel is quite unique and will make a memorable ending to a fine dinner.' He nodded at the black man concealed behind a curtain at the end of the conference room, 'Let the entertainment commence.'

Whitejack pinched Carrie on the bottom, 'Move it, woman,' he instructed.

'I don't want to do this . . . ' she began.

He rolled his eyes, 'We bin through all this. *Move it.* You don't like it, we won't do it no more.'

Reluctantly she moved out from behind the curtain.

There was a mutter of approval and some embarrassed laughter from the men. Music started up from a hidden Victrola. Sleazy New Orleans honky tonk. Carrie began to dance. She was wearing a skimpy red dress, rolled silk stockings, high heeled strappy shoes, and ruffled garters. Underneath the dress she wore nothing.

Whitejack watched her undulate between the tables. She wasn't too bad. He slapped the rump of the large white blonde standing beside him, 'Show the little lady how it's really done, Dolly.'

She grinned, horse teeth in a spacious face, 'You betcha, Whitejack.'

She sprung out from behind the curtain, all wobbling breasts and big ass squashed into a tight orange dress.

Whitejack shook his head and smiled. Dolly was a real find. It was she who had explained to him about private shows and the money there was to be made. 'What's a smart jackass like you strugglin' with johns and all that shit for?' she had asked when they first met in one of the jazz joints. 'Give me the right girls an' I can make us *real* big bucks.'

So he had moved in with her for a week to discuss it. She had been delighted when he told her about Carrie and Lucille. 'A spade an' a midget!' she had screamed in ecstasy, 'we will make ourselves one hot fat fortune!'

Whitejack had wasted no time in collecting Carrie and Lucille, his twenty-three suits and assorted possessions, and moving in with Dolly who lived in an apartment big enough for all of them.

Carrie had not been pleased. 'I thought we was settin' up a house,' she had complained.

'Maybe. Maybe not,' he had replied, 'first we'll try it Dolly's way.'

'Are you sharin' that fat bitch's bed?'

' 'Course not.' he had stroked her hair, 'what I wanna do a dumb thing like that for when I got a hot tasty chicken like you?' Whores. Sixteen or sixty. All the fuckin' same.

Whitejack gave Lucille a shove, and she bounced out from behind the curtain to join Carrie and Dolly.

The roomful of men roared their approval. They were loosening up now. Tight assed white mothers. Not a black face among them. Black men knew how to have a good time – they would never need shit like this to give them a kick.

Whitejack watched Dolly. She was a real professional the way she worked the room. She was whipping them up to a frenzy strutting her stuff.

Carrie and Lucille weren't doing so good, but it didn't matter, once they got their clothes off no one would notice their miserable expressions.

Whitejack yawned. He would have to get things sorted out with Dolly. She was not pleased that he had backed off sharing her big comfortable bedroom. 'So why can't you?' she had glowered, 'that little piccaninny got exclusive rights all of a sudden?'

'Only for a day or two, big mama,' he had explained, 'Shee . . . ii . . . t. I be back givin' you what you want 'fore you even know it.'

'You'd better,' she had snorted.

He would just have to wean little Carrie off his red hot cock. That was the trouble really. Once a woman had him she never wanted to let him go.

The girls were starting to take off their clothes. Whitejack yawned again. Fancy paying five hundred dollars to see three sets of tit and ass and some well used pussy.

Shee . . . ii . . . it. There was no accounting for some people's idea of a good time.

# Gino 1928

The Trenton, New Jersey, job having gone without a hitch Bonnatti lost no time in putting more connections Gino and Aldo's way.

'We're gonna havta expand,' Gino told Aldo and Pinky Banana. 'We gotta get more guys in with us.'

Pinky Banana picked his nose. 'I got plenty of guys I can bring in.'

'Shitheads,' Gino snarled, 'their loyalty is up their asses.'

'You don't know that,' Pinky complained.

'*I'll* do some recruitin',' Gino said, 'maybe I can get us a coupla good guys in San Francisco wanna come back East.'

'When the frig you *goin'* to Frisco?' Pinky Banana jeered.

Gino rubbed his scar impatiently. 'Soon,' he answered roughly. Any day he expected a reply from Leonora or her father. He was on tenterhooks waiting.

'You bin sayin' that for weeks.' Pinky Banana sneered. 'Sure you're not gettin' a runaround?'

'Listen fuckhead. Gino Santangelo don't get no runarounds.' He was up and glaring at Pinky Banana.

Aldo's watery eyes darted nervously between them. There was trouble brewing between these two, and any day now it was going to explode.

Pinky Banana extracted his finger from his nose and examined what he had removed. 'So what's the friggin' delay?'

'There's no delay, asshole.'

Pinky Banana gave a maniacal giggle. 'She give ya a runaround, *you're* the asshole.'

Aldo interrupted, 'How long you goin' to be in Frisco, Gino?'

'I don't know. A week or two.'

'What about Enzio? Does he know?'

'Fuck Enzio!' Gino exploded, 'I don't havta report to fuckin' Bonnatti every time I take a piss.'

'You got his share. What happens if he comes inta town while you're away an' wants it?' Aldo asked anxiously.

'So I'll leave it with you.' Gino glared at them both. Couple of deadheads. Aldo, scared shitless of his own cousin. And Pinky Banana – a big dumb ox. 'I gotta go,' he snapped, 'I'll see you tomorrow.' He stamped out of the garage where they had been meeting, and weaved and bobbed his way along the street. Leonora. What the heck *was* takin' her so long to answer his letter? He had expected an instant reply. Fuckin' instant. The delay was killing him.

'Hello, Gino.'

He glanced up, slowed down. 'Hey . . . Cindy.'

She didn't look as chipper as usual. More sullen than saucy. He wanted to keep walking, but she had stopped and laid a hand on his arm. 'How you doin'?' she asked.

He bounced on the balls of his feet, 'I'm doin' good. You?' How come she wasn't razzing him with her usual little sarcasms?

'Not bad. Everything's fine . . . ' And as she said 'fine' two great tears welled up in her eyes and rolled slowly down her rouged cheeks. 'Oh Gino,' she wailed, 'I'm so *unhappeeee.*'

He glanced around the street. People were *lookin'* at them. 'Jeeze, Cindy. Wassamatta with you?'

She was sobbing now. 'It's Pinky,' she gurgled, 'I want to leave him but I can't. I got no money. I can't go home. I hate him and I don't know what to do. *Please* help me, Gino.'

*Please help me Gino.* This from a broad who had handed him nothin' but smart answers and trouble from the moment he had set eyes on her. Little Cindy pricktease, heroine of a thousand jerk offs. He fingered the scar on his cheek and remembered how he got it. Her fault – and she had never given him so much as a thank you. 'Hey,' he said quickly, 'calm down.'

'You don't know,' she muttered darkly, 'just how desperate I am.'

'Aw . . . come on, Cindy.'

She squeezed his arm, 'If you could just give me some money, I could get on a train an' go away somewhere. You see,' she paused dramatically, 'he's told me if I leave him he'll kill me.'

He laughed aloud, 'Crap!'

Her sobs increased, 'I promise you it's true. He's even shown me his gun. He says if *he* can't have me nobody else will.'

Drama on 110th Street at three o'clock in the afternoon. He shrugged. There was nothing *he* could do. Unless of course he gave her the money to get away.

He licked his lips and studied the sobbing girl. She seemed to be on the level. Of course, this could be one of Pinky Banana's stunts, he always *had* been fond of a practical joke, and Cindy Pricktease would be only too delighted to go along with it. 'Er . . . Cindy. Let me think about it.'

Her tears stopped. 'Oh Gino, would you really?'

He nodded.

She sniffed loudly and searched her purse for a handkerchief. 'I know I was a fool for getting involved with him in the first place. But he seemed so nice then . . . And he treated me real good . . . Y'know . . . presents and things. Of course,' she stared boldly at Gino, 'it was always you I really liked.'

He snorted with laughter, 'Come on Cindy. y'don't havta flatter me.'

Her eyes widened, 'But it's true, I swear it is!'

'Sure. Listen, I gotta go.'

She nodded, then pulled him very close. 'I want to show you something,' she whispered.

'What?'

'You'll never believe this,' she continued to whisper, 'I guess I'm scarred for life.' Delicately she held her blouse forward, partially exposing the top of her breasts. Gino peered in. It was certainly some eyeful.

'Do you see the burn?'

'What burn?' He peered more closely, and there, near to her left nipple, was a vicious red mark.

'He did it with a cigarette. I just wanted you to know the kind of things he does.'

Dirty lowdown bastard. Just like lousy Paulo. 'How much ya need?'

'I don't know . . . A few hundred. Would that be enough to get me out to California? I can get a job when I arrive.'

Gino nodded.

'We'll be in Fat Larrys tomorrow night. If you could give it to me then I'd be able to leave the next day.'

'You got it.'

'Promise?'

'I promise.'

She leaned forward and kissed him softly on the cheek. 'Thank you Gino, you're a real friend.'

Costa's train arrived in New York early on a Monday morning. Doctor and Mrs Sydney Lanza were at Grand Central Station to meet him. They eyed him suspiciously at first, exchanging secret glances of surprise that he was so nice looking and polite. After all – the whole family had been in an uproar when Franklin Zennocotti had decided to adopt a boy of such dubious background. But he seemed to be a fine well mannered lad, and they took to him at once.

Their house on Beekman Place was not luxurious, rather more middle-class than the Zennocotti residence. But there were still signs of money around. A table of silver frames, good paintings on the walls, and polished mahogany furniture.

Doctor Lanza conducted his practice in one of the front rooms. An adjoining room did duty as a waiting area.

'The doctor is a very busy man,' Mrs Lanza confided to Costa as she showed him his room. 'He toils hard, and enjoys the good work he does. Healing is God's work you know, and the gracious Almighty chooses his disciples carefully.'

Franklin Zennocotti had forgotten to mention that the Lanzas were devoutly religious people.

Costa nodded, 'I'll try not to get in anyone's way.'

'I'm sure you will observe our rules. Please attend to your own bedmaking each day. And be present at every mealtime punctually. The good doctor abhors lateness.'

'Of course I will,' Costa replied quickly, 'when I'm not out that is. I have plans to explore the city. Visit art galleries and museums . . . that kind of thing.'

Mrs Lanza pursed thin lips, 'I expect you to inform me of your plans the day before. This household cannot be disrupted by your comings and goings.'

'Oh no Mrs Lanza, I'm not going to disrupt anything.'

She crossed her arms firmly across a flat bosom. 'We can *both* be sure of that young man.'

Costa smiled weakly. Fourteen days of Mrs Lanza was not the most pleasing of prospects. 'I thought I might go out this afternoon . . . ' he ventured.

'Not today, Costa, if you don't mind,' she responded crisply, 'meals are already planned, and this household has suffered enough confusion today by your very arrival.'

'Sure Mrs Lanza. I understand.'

But he didn't. And he couldn't wait to get the hell out of the Beekman Place house and find Gino.

Mr Pulaski said, 'No reply yet?'

Gino shook his head.

The old man closed his eyes and pressed his finger to his temples, 'The mails are very slow, very slow indeed. I should not worry.'

'Who said I was worried?' Gino snapped, leaping up from the chair he was sitting on and pacing round the small room. 'I just wonder if my letter got lost or somethin' like that . . . Y'know pops. I was thinkin' . . . Maybe I should just get on a train an' go there.'

The old man opened his eyes and gazed out of the window at the crowded street below. He had been out of bed for two days now and felt frightened of ever leaving his room again. So many people out there . . . waiting to take his money . . . his gold watch . . . Maybe even his life . . .

'Whaddya think, pops?' Gino questioned, standing in front of him, rocking back and forth on his heels, 'Ya think I should do that?'

Mr Pulaski frowned. 'Do what?'

'Go to Frisco,' Gino blurted in an exasperated fashion. The

old guy was gettin' senile. The beating had knocked a lot of the stuffing out of him.

'Perhaps you should wait another week or two,' Mr Pulaski replied, once more catching the thread of the conversation, 'but then again . . . ' He stopped, having suddenly forgotten what he had been about to say.

'Yeh?' Gino asked anxiously, balling up his right fist and punching it impatiently into the palm of his left hand.

'I think . . . ' Mr Pulaski felt a sharp pain and his eyes glazed over. ' . . . think . . . ' The pain was wracking his frail old body. He coughed, and was unaware of the blood that came dribbling unexpectedly out of his mouth and onto his chin. He gazed unseeingly at Gino and thought briefly of his dear departed wife. He began to call her name aloud, but as he did so the pain exploded across his chest and he slumped down in his chair without finishing the word.

Gino watched in horror. 'Mr Pulaski! Pops! Wassamatter?' He grabbed him by the shoulder, 'Wake up old man! Wake up . . . '

He leaned down and peered at Mr Pulaski's face. The eyes were open, as was the mouth. But it was the face of death.

'Oh no!' Gino mumbled, 'Oh Jesus Christ – no.'

He knelt down beside the old man and cradled his head. For the first time in years he was crying. Mr Pulaski. Nice old man. Never did anyone harm. So what if he got a few kicks out of flashing. *So what?*

He wiped his eyes with the back of his hand and stood up. He looked around the old man's room.

Leonora would never meet the composer of the love letters she had received every week for a year. Even more important – Mr Pulaski would never meet Leonora.

'Goddamn it, pops,' Gino muttered aloud, 'couldn't you have waited?'

Breakfast was at seven o'clock in the morning in the Beekman Place household. Hot Scottish oatmeal, thick sweet cocoa, and large chunks of bread.

Costa ate frugally. Mrs Lanza was not impressed. 'A hearty breakfast sets a person on the right road for a healthy day,' she admonished. 'The good doctor always tells his patients that, don't you, dear?'

By 8 a.m. Costa was out of the house. Free at last. He took a big deep breath as he walked along the street. New York smelled different from San Francisco. The air was crisper, more smokey. He knew the city had once been his home, but he had conveniently blanked out all memories of it. As far as he was concerned his life had started the day Franklin Zennocotti had taken him to San Francisco. He refused to think of events before that. He only knew that he *owed* his life to Gino Santangelo. Without him, he would have been finished off at the Protectory.

Protectory. That was a laugh . . .

Gino slept fitfully, huddled beneath the bed covers. He usually slept well, but sometimes he dreamed all night long – and it had been one of those nights.

The knocking on his door took some time to get through to him, and when it did, and he struggled to look at his watch, he wasn't pleased. Eight-thirty in the morning! 'Yeh?' he yelled gruffly.

Costa detected the annoyance in Gino's voice, and wondered if he should come back later. But after all he had come all the way to New York to tell Gino something, and to go away would only be putting off the moment of truth. 'It's me, Costa Zennocotti,' he shouted through the closed door.

'Costa? What the heck you doin' here?'

Gino opened up the door, slapped his friend on the shoulder and dragged him into the small untidy room. 'Hey – ' he exclaimed, 'anyone else I'd've mashed their face wakin' me up at this time of the mornin'. It's good t'see ya. Whyn't y'tell me y'was comin'?'

Costa had thought a hundred times of the best way to tell his friend. Now all his thoughts were jumbled and he knew that the only way to give it to Gino was straight.

'It's about Leonora,' he blurted out quickly, 'I didn't want you to get the news in a letter.'

'What news?' The color drained from Gino's face.

'She got married,' Costa said quietly, 'she married someone else.'

# Wednesday, July 13th, 1977, New York and Philadelphia

'My mouth feels like a couple of bums spent the night there,' groaned Lucky, 'how long have we been here?'

Steven brought his watch up very close to his eyes and squinted at the luminous dial. 'Five hours, ten minutes, and forty-nine seconds.'

'It seems like five months! I've never been so uncomfortable and disoriented in my whole goddamn life!'

'I keep on telling you – just relax. That's all you can do.'

'I seem to remember,' she replied coldly, 'seeing movies where people were trapped in an elevator, and they didn't just sit there doing nothing.'

'Oh,' Steven said, equally coldly, 'and what did they do?'

'Jesus! How should *I* know.'

'Well *you* mentioned it.'

'I mentioned it because I thought that *you* might come up with an answer. I should have known better.'

'*You* saw the movies, not me.'

'Are you always this helpful?'

He was indignant, 'What the hell do you want me to do for crissake?'

'Naughty, naughty! Musn't start using bad language!'

He could easily have strangled her. Put his big strong hands around what he firmly imagined was a chicken neck, and squeezed and squeezed until all the smart ass cracks came vomiting out of her.

'I remember!' she said brightly, 'Hotel. An old movie on TV a few months ago. Rod something or other opened the top of the elevator and climbed up the cable.'

'Forget it,' he growled, 'if you think I'm getting out this elevator forty-something stories up, you've got a good case.'

Her voice was scornful. 'No balls huh?'

'Lady, I don't need 'em. *You've* got enough for both of us!'

Costa slammed the phone down. Dario. Always in trouble. Always.

Such a nice looking boy. Blond and slim and clean cut.

Such a pervert.

If Gino were to ever find out the truth about his only son . . .

Costa swore softly to himself. It took a lot to make him

swear, but you could guarantee on Dario doing it every time.

He thought for a moment, then picked up the phone and dialed quickly. A woman's voice answered. 'Ruth, my dear,' he said smoothly, 'this is Costa Zennocotti. How are you?'

Ruth began a long complaint about the blackout. He interrupted her, 'Is Sal there?'

'Just a minute.'

Sal got on the phone. 'What can I do for you, Mr Zennocotti?'

Costa gave Dario's address. 'Get there pronto,' he urged. 'You'll have to break in – there is a problem with the keys. Remove the obstruction from the premises and deal with the matter as you see fit. Call me tomorrow re payment.' He put the phone down. Dario was lucky, Sal was an expert at dealing with difficult situations. Of course it might already be too late. But would Dario really be missed?

Only by Gino.

Perhaps.

'Mothafucka!' screamed the boy triumphantly as he smashed his way through the bedroom door with a cast iron art deco figure he had found in the bathroom. 'Where are ya motherfucka?' His face twitched as his eyes searched the gloom of the living room looking for Dario. 'Where are ya, cunt?' he screamed, 'hidin' ain't gonna save your faggot ass!'

Dario crouched silently in the kitchen, a carving knife held straight out in front of him.

'Mothafucka!' screamed the boy. 'I'm gonna get ya!'

Carrie walked through the Harlem streets in a daze. It seemed that every resident on every block had come out to see what they could grab. They were smashing shop windows and hauling off anything in sight. Two men staggered past carrying an oak chest between them for all the world like a couple of removal men. A young boy staggered behind with a TV. Transistor radios and tape machines blared out rock music.

Nobody took any notice of her now. She was just another black face, with hair hanging wildly, make-up smudged, blood dripping from her torn ear lobes.

She knew what she must look like, but it didn't matter. Anger was surging through her body now. A hot uncontrollable anger that drove her quickly through the streets searching for the rendezvous.

Life had been so sweet up until two days previously. Then the phone call. The muffled voice saying that if she knew what was good for her she would be outside the meat market on West 125th Street at nine-thirty Wednesday night.

'Who is this?' she had asked, her voice no more than a nervous whisper, because Elliott was in the next room.

'If you don't want your past dragged up, be there.' The muffled voice insisted. Then the line had gone dead. She had been unable to ascertain whether the voice had belonged to a man or a woman.

Wildly she hurried along the street. Somewhere, someone was waiting for her . . . She *had* to find out who it was . . . Had to . . .

The large jet landed smoothly. As soon as it had taxied to a stop, the woman sitting beside Gino changed. She snatched her hand away from his as though he had some disease, and snapped arrogant fingers for the stewardess, 'My mink,' she demanded imperiously.

The girl bobbed her head, 'Coming right away ma'am.' She leaned across, 'Do you have transportation to New York, Mr Santangelo?'

'Nope,' Gino replied, 'I hardly expected to land up in Philly.'

The girl giggled. 'I know. Would you believe it?'

He unfastened his seat belt, 'Can you arrange a car for me?'

'Sure. Although if you're staying in a hotel in New York you might be better off spending the night in Philadelphia – apparently the whole of New York City is without power and they just don't know *how* long it will last.'

He thought for a moment. He had a suite booked at The Pierre, but the stewardess was right, if the city had no electricity it would be foolish to go there. 'Can you recommend a hotel?'

The girl smiled, 'Certainly, Mr Santangelo. I might even stay myself.'

Lucky had fallen into a light sleep. Steven was relieved. Without her constant complaints, being suspended in the black womb the box wasn't that bad. Rather relaxing really. Some people even *paid* for this kind of therapy.

Lucky mumbled something incoherent in her sleep.

He shouldn't really blame her for being rude and dislikable, she was probably frightened.

Ha! He could not imagine a woman with a mouth like hers being frightened of anything.

'Wassamatta?' she gurgled, awakening with a start and rubbing her eyes. 'Jesus H. Christ. We're not still here are we?'

'We sure are.'

'I'm really starting to get pissed off.'

*She* was getting pissed off. In an aggravated voice as though it was *his* fault.

'I gotta pee,' she added sourly, 'like now.'

'I'm sorry,' he replied sarcastically, 'but when they designed this elevator they seemed to have forgotten about supplying toilet facilities.'

'You're such a fucking smart ass.'

He shut up. Let her ramble on to herself. The heat was becoming unbearable. The air conditioning had shut off when the power went – and now – hours later – the elevator was like a furnace. He had stripped down to his shorts, but even so his body was covered with a thick film of sweat as though he had been sitting in a sauna.

He remembered a sauna with Zizi on their honeymoon. Foxy little Zizi. Five foot two inches of dynamic bad woman. His mother had certainly been right about *her*.

'Oooops!' exclaimed Lucky, 'I haven't peed my pants since I was two years old!'

'Christ!'

'Don't get uptight, it'll be your turn next!'

Dario could hear the boy rampaging through the apartment, screaming obscenities and smashing the furniture as he searched.

His heart was beating wildly. *What had he done that was so terrible?* He was gay. So what? It wasn't a crime was it? He had always treated his pick-ups well. Always paid them if they looked like they wanted money.

Jesus! Just because he was Gino fucking Santangelo's son his whole adult life had been one big lie. He shuddered and closed his eyes tight. Any second the boy would find him and then maybe it would be all over.

Carrie could not locate the meat market on West 125th Street. She wandered up and down with the crowd as they surged about on their trip, allowing herself to be pushed and jostled. If only she knew *who* she was looking for.

'It's Christmastime, it's Christmastime!' screeched a scraggy woman as she rushed past.

Carrie stepped into the gutter to avoid two boys intent on wrenching the steel grilles from the front of a jewelry store. Next to them kids smashed the plate glass windows of an appliance store, and people rushed in through the shattered windows scooping up everything in sight. 'Let's *burn* the place down,' shrieked a teenage girl to her boyfriend. The crowd took up the chant. 'Burn! Burn! Burn!'

Carrie hurried on. In fifty years nothing had changed. Harlem was still crawling with rats.

She saw a meat market then. Surely she must have passed it before? The place was jammed with people filling their shopping bags with steaks, chickens, anything they could lay their hands on.

She looked around. There was nobody standing outside waiting for her. Again she thought – *Who am I looking for?*

There was only one way to find out. Wait. And see who turned up.

'How old are you, Jill?' Gino inquired.

'Twenty-two,' the pretty stewardess replied, standing beside the bed minus her clothes.

'Twenty-two, huh?'

'Twenty-two and *vereeee* experienced,' she giggled.

'I bet,' he said. They had been in the hotel bedroom exactly five minutes, and already she was stripped and ready for action as though it was the most natural thing in the world. For her it probably was. But where had all the romance gone?

He was tired, his belly was full, his ulcer was acting up, and he just desired sleep.

The whole thing had been *her* idea. 'I'll come upstairs and check out your room,' she had winked after dinner.

As soon as they entered the suite she had darted into the bedroom and emerged totally naked. Not a bad body. He had seen better, he had seen worse. Slightly too skinny for his tastes. 'Why does a nice young girl like you want to go to bed with an old man like me, huh?' he stalled.

'Mr Santangelo! What a question! Why, you're famous!'

He wondered how insulted she'd be if he told her he didn't want her.

'Now come along,' she said, in her best stewardess' voice, 'let's get your pants off.'

'I'm sixty-nine years old,' he said, hoping to stall her, and also knocking two years off his age because he couldn't willingly admit to being over seventy.

'My favorite number!' she exclaimed, fiddling with his pants, pulling the zipper down and easing them off.

He achieved a half-hearted erection. He hadn't gotten laid in weeks. Somehow, at seventy-one, it didn't seem to matter that much anymore. Not that he couldn't get it up whenever he wanted. It was just that it took someone special to make him really feel like sex nowadays.

'Wow!' she exclaimed, 'you're big!'

He glanced down. Who was she kidding? It wasn't even at half mast.

'Shall I suck you?' she asked matter of factly.

What was he catering to this bimbo for? He pulled his pants back up.

'Why are you doing that?' she asked, alarmed.

'Because I want to.'

'Oh come on. Of course you don't. Just give me five minutes and I'll see you're flying!'

'I have a daughter five years older than you.'

'So what?'

'So I don't want to do it. All right?'

She couldn't quite make up her mind whether to be hurt or angry. Flouncing into the bathroom she emerged in less than a minute fully dressed in her uniform. 'Mr Santangelo,' she informed him coldly, 'you are a cunt tease!' And with that she marched to the door and let herself out.

Gino reached for a cigar. Couldn't win 'em all.

# Gino 1928

Gino took the news of Leonora's marriage badly. He *could not bring himself to believe it. Refused to believe it.* Costa had to repeat the facts over and over until gradually the news began to sink in.

When he realized it was true he went screaming mad. Costa had never seen anything like it before. His friend turned into a wild animal, pacing the room, cursing, pounding the walls with his fists, and finally – sobbing with such a ferocity that Costa felt embarrassed to be witnessing it.

He wondered if he should leave. Gino was quite oblivious to any other presence, but Costa somehow felt it would be best to stay. It was almost as if he'd told him Leonora was dead.

And that was exactly how Gino felt. Leonora had betrayed him – *his* Leonora. It would be better if she had been hit by a trolley car, or drowned or been stricken with some deadly disease. *That* he could have understood. But *this* . . . It was beyond belief.

It took him an hour before he could even begin to pull himself together. Then, gradually, he managed to calm down. He felt empty, used – as if he had received a deadening blow to the stomach.

Costa sat quietly in the corner regarding him solemnly.

Now it was Gino's turn to be embarrassed. 'Hey . . . kid . . . ' he managed, 'you came all this way just to tell me?'

Costa nodded, and produced the two letters he had saved from his pocket. 'I took the liberty of opening these and keeping them. They arrived after she got married. I didn't think – in the circumstances – you would want them delivered. I hope I did the right thing.'

'Oh yeh. You did the right thing.' He stuffed the letters in a drawer, and with his back to Costa mumbled, 'I guess y'must have read them.'

'No.'

He sighed. 'Listen, I don't care. Better *you* should have read them . . . ' His voice became hard. 'Jeeze! I feel so fuckin' dumb!' He rounded on Costa, his deadly black eyes wild again, 'Who the fuck is the guy she married? Some rich prick your father found her?'

'You're right,' Costa lied, 'his family has money, my parents are pleased with the match.'

'And Leonora?'

'She does what she is told to do.'

'What's the bastard's name? I'll have him put away – fuckin' out of the race – you know what I'm saying?'

Costa knew only too well. 'I think she loves him,' he said swiftly.

'Oh.' It was like all the breath had been smashed out of Gino. 'You sure?'

Costa nodded nervously.

'Yeh . . . well . . . I guess if she loves him . . . ' his voice turned harsh again. 'Why didn't she write an' tell me? Why didn't *you*?'

Costa shrugged, 'I had no idea what was going on.'

Glumly Gino thought of the last letter he had received. How long ago had it arrived? Seven, eight weeks – something like that. Her usual letter – nothing personal – But he was used to that, her letters had always been girlish and hollow – yeh hollow. It had never bothered him because he knew only too well that if he hadn't had old Mr Pulaski to write his letters for him, they would have been the same. 'I guess,' he said slowly, 'there is nothin' I can do.'

Costa gestured helplessly, 'I'm sorry . . .'

'She know you was comin' to see me? She send me any message?'

Costa shook his head. No point in passing on the message she *had* sent.

'I just don't know what to do,' Gino's voice was muffled. 'I guess it's gonna take time to sink in. Y'see – I was buildin' my life round Leonora. You gotta understand that everything I bin doin' was for her. *Every dumb fuckin' thing.*'

Costa nodded understandingly.

Gino paced agitatedly round the room. 'I ain't had any kinda life to be proud of . . . But then I didn't exactly get all the breaks to start off with,' he pulled up his shirt and exhibited his chest, criss-crossed with various gouges and scars. 'Each one of those marks got a history. Y'know that?' He pointed out a patch of ridged and discolored skin. 'I was six years old when my old man kicked my ribs in. This scar here was from another beatin' – an' here, an' here. If I hadn't bin a tough little bastard I'd never have made it. My old man got his kicks from beatin' up on me – and when I was too old he started on his women.' He laughed bitterly, 'I had a ringside seat. He fucked 'em – then he beat the shit outta them. I'll tell y'somethin' Costa – that's when I decided my life was gonna be different from his,' he sighed, 'I don't know if y'can understand it – but Leonora was gonna be my life. I knew it the first time I saw her.' He paused, then suddenly became embarrassed. 'Jeeze! How does that grab you for sloppy bullshit? An' what the hell am I tellin' you for anyway?'

Costa reached out and touched him on the arm, 'Because I'm your friend,' he said quietly, 'and it always helps to talk things out of your system.'

'Let's get the hell outta here,' Gino decided, 'I'm gettin' square eyeballs pacin' around this room.'

'Where to?'

'I don't know. Play some pool – catch a movie. Let's just get out.' He pulled on his shirt. 'Gotta funeral this afternoon. Maybe y'can come along.'

'Who died?'

'A friend of mine. An old man who used to do me a lotta favors.

'I'm sorry . . . '

'Yeh. But that's the way it goes ain't it?' He stared blankly for a minute, thinking of Mr Pulaski and Leonora. They were both dead as far as he was concerned. 'One minute you're here – the next you're gone.' He shrugged, 'an' not too many people give a shit. C'mon kid, let's go.'

Gino got through the day. Somehow. He shut Leonora out of his mind and concentrated on other things.

Playing pool was good – total concentration – then winning as usual.

Eating. That wasn't so successful. He tried a doughnut and coffee. But the coffee passed through him like salts, and the doughnut lay like a leaded tire in his stomach.

Conversation. Finding out what Costa had been up to. Pretty boring. The kid seemed to do nothing but study.

Mr Pulaski's funeral. Depressing. Just him, and Costa, and a lousy bunch of flowers he had bought off a street cart.

Finally a movie. *The Thief of Bagdad*. An oldie. He had seen it four times before, but he liked Douglas Fairbanks.

Costa had left halfway through. 'I have to get back, Gino, Mrs Lanza will kill me.'

. So then he was on his own. And he watched the rest of the movie before throwing up the doughnut in the mens room.

Leonora. He was going to have to think about her, there was no avoiding it.

So he did. He walked over to the park, sat in the dusk and gazed off into space. He didn't know how many hours he sat there. *How could she do this to him? How could she make him suffer like this? Didn't she have any feelings?*

Leonora. Pale blonde hair. Soft blue eyes. Full ripe body.

Leonora. Heartless bitch. Unfaithful bitch.

Maybe he cried again, maybe he didn't. He wasn't sure. But he *was* sure that it would be a long time before he ever allowed himself to feel this way again. If ever. Women were not to be trusted. Not even women like Leonora. In the future there would be no promises. No love.

Something prodded him on the leg and a gruff Irish voice said, 'What you doin' here? You'd better move off or I'll arrest you for vagrancy.'

He jumped, and glared at the cop, 'Vagrancy? Are you kiddin'?'

'No, I'm not.' The cop swung his nightstick menacingly.

Gino got up. Fuckin' cops. Crooked bunch of suckers. The Santangelo gang had a regular list of payoffs.

He moved off through the park anyway. Who needed trouble?


Pinky Banana was drunk. He clutched at Cindy on the tiny dance floor and sang out of tune in her ear.

'Pinky!' she complained, trying to shove him away.

'Bitch!' he replied, pulling her even closer and squeezing her ass with his hands.

She squirmed uncomfortably and glanced at the door ever hopeful of spotting Gino.

'Let's go home,' Pinky slurred, 'an' I can do the things you're always beggin' me t'do.'

'I don't beg for nothing,' she retorted sharply.

'Oh no?' he sneered, 'jest clothes an jewels an' furs.'

'Well I ain't got no jewels an' furs yet have I?' she stated shrewishly.

'Play it right, doll, play it right,' he staggered and almost fell.

Cindy snorted in disgust, 'I'm sittin' down.' She pushed her way off the tiny dance floor and returned to the table crowded with Pinky's so-called friends. She hated them all.

Pinky Banana followed her. She hated *him* worst of all. Tears filled her mascaraed eyes. She was caught in a trap of her own making, and the only one who could get her out was Gino Santangelo. And *he* hadn't even bothered to turn up.

Pinky placed a sweaty hand on her knee. She quickly crossed her legs so that the sweaty hand couldn't do any travelling. She knew his charming ways. He would think nothing of sticking his hand up between her legs in full view of his friends. She was property. *His.*

'Look who's here,' Pinky Banana yelled noisily, 'friggin' Gino himself.'

Gino nodded round the table easily. The punks Pinky hung out with were bad news.

'S'what's new?' Pinky burped loudly, 'when's our next trip?'

Gino glared. Pinky's mouth was getting too big for comfort. Cindy shot him a quick grateful look that said a silent thanks for coming.

'I don't know what *your* next trip is Pinky,' he said, 'but keep shootin' your mouth off an' it could be all the way to the can.'

Pinky laughed, and looked around at his cronies, 'My boss y'know. Big man. Lives in a shithole an' likes ta throw his weight around. But he wouldn't know what the frig t'do with a shooter if ya shoved it under his nose.'

Gino smiled thinly. Enough. Pinky Banana was *out*. He stood up.

'Where ya goin'?' sneered Pinky. 'Home t'jack off over a letter?'

Gino's eyes were bleak and hard but his tone was mild. 'You know somethin'? You'll choke on that big mouth of yours one day.'

Cindy's eyes darted between the two of them. She slid out of her chair, 'Just goin' to the little girls room, hon.'

Pinky ignored her as she slipped off. 'Yeah?' he glared.

'Yeh,' replied Gino.

They locked eyes and there was a moment of total hatred between them. Then Pinky laughed uneasily, 'Only kiddin' around, pal.' Something in Gino's eyes always made him back down.

'Sure you are,' smiled Gino.

'Stay. Have a drink,' insisted Pinky.

'Naw. I just come by lookin' for Aldo.'

'Ain't seen him.'

Gino's black eyes flicked around the table. Garbage. And Pinky Banana was one of them. 'S'long,' he said.

'See ya tomorra.' Pinky was now eager to please.

'Yeh,' Gino nodded, 'tomorra.' He made his way out of the room. Cindy was waiting anxiously outside. 'I got your money,' he said.

'I'm so frightened,' she clutched desperately onto his arm.

'Tomorra you'll be able to get on a train an' be outta here.'

'Tomorrow might be too late.' Her voice trembled, 'he threatened to kill me again. He really *means* it.'

'Why'd he wanna *kill* you?'

'Because he thinks I sleep around.'

'Yeh. An' do you?'

'Of course not. Oh, Gino!' She threw her arms around him,

*'Please*, I beg you – get me away now.' Her body, pressed tightly against him, shook with sobs.

He could feel the warmth of her thighs and breasts and his reaction was inevitable. He wanted a woman. He needed a woman. And there was no Leonora to stop him now.

The ache in his groin was almost painful in its intensity.

She felt him grow hard and pressed herself even closer to him. 'Take me home with *you*,' she whispered. 'Look after me and I'll look after you. Tomorrow I can get a train to California. Tonight I need you.'

He made his decision. 'Let's get the hell out of here before he comes lookin' for y'then.'

'You won't be sorry,' she breathed.

She was warm and soft and sugary and sweet. And all the things he had dreamed about.

She was wet, her pussy covered in a fine triangle of blonde hair, and she purred like a kitten.

She had perfect breasts and pointed milky tasting nipples and sharp teeth that teased his cock when he put it in her mouth.

She did not object to anything he wanted to do – and he wanted to do everything.

He had been with many women – but she was the sweetest yet. When he peaked he knew it lasted a good full two minutes – or so it seemed. The come flowed out of him in long satisfying bursts and filled her totally.

She gasped and moaned her pleasure. And when he put his head between her legs and sucked out his own juices she could not keep herself from screaming aloud.

She brought him up and over her so that she could tease his cock with her hot tongue. He squatted above her, pumping in and out of her mouth with his hardness. Then he came a second time, and she accepted and swallowed every drop as if it were some rich precious nectar.

He lay still for awhile and thought about how long it had been, then he took her breasts in his mouth and put his fingers between her legs, while she lay quietly savoring every moment until she started to climax in long quivering spasms.

He wasn't fully satisfied. He needed more. She didn't object. He turned her over and entered her from behind and rode her like they were two dogs in the street. They were both in a frenzy when the third orgasm hit them. It was short, hot, and wild. And only then did Gino feel at peace. He rolled away from her and lay on his back. All the tension seemed to have flowed from his body.

He thought of Leonora with a certain deep sadness, then reached over and touched Cindy's hair. 'You're really somethin',' he said.

She laughed a small wicked laugh, 'I told you, didn't I?'

'Told me what?'

'That you wouldn't be sorry.'

# Carrie 1928

Opium. It beat marijuana any day. It took you higher and higher and then left you to rest on a peaceful cloud way way above everything and everyone.

Carrie had never been happier in her life. Whitejack introduced her to it, as he had introduced her to marijuana. 'Your reward, sweet baby,' he murmured the night they attended a party in the heart of Chinatown.

At first she was frightened. The strange pipe and bowl over fire with several people crouched around it. 'I don't think I want to . . .' she whispered.

'Come on, woman. You had a hard night – this'll help you remember only the good times. Trust me . . .'

So she had trusted him, and drawn on the pipe . . . once . . . twice . . . Everything had become soft and luxurious . . . only good memories and thoughts flowing through her body.

What had happened to her dream of getting control?

Love.

With a pimp.

And what was he to her now? He was still her man wasn't he? He took care of business, and fed her the drugs she was learning to crave. But the craving was beginning to frighten her. Drugs were her love now, and nothing mattered when she was high.

Only some mornings she woke up straight, and thought about suicide as she had thought about it intermittently over the years. Whitejack sensed those mornings, and his answer was to feed her more drugs.

Then it was so easy to forget the bad times and just drift. So many smiling faces . . . So many people who cared for her . . .

And Whitejack of course. Her man. Tall and sharp and powerful. She would do *anything* for that man. And did.

One day Lucille woke her roughly. 'Carrie. You know I love you an' Whitejack. But that man is destroying you, and you'd better get over to the hospital – have yourself cured.'

Carrie was half asleep. 'Cured? What you talkin' about?'

'I'm talkin' about your life.'

Carrie began to giggle, but the giggling soon turned to tears, and Lucille held her close while she sobbed. 'I'm gettin' you out of here,' she decided, 'get dressed quickly – Whitejack an' Dolly still asleep. Believe me hon, you've *got* to get out of here.'

'Yeah?' Whitejack stood in the doorway. 'She ain't goin' anywhere. She walk on me an' I put the cops on her. They send her back to the island I tell them what *I* know.'

'I need somethin',' Carrie wheedled, 'don't feel so good . . '

Whitejack glared at Lucille. 'Get out,' he snarled.

She moved fast, scurrying past him like a disturbed rat.

'Now what's goin' on here?' he asked smoothly, 'somethin' happen to upset my sweet little girl?'

Carrie frowned. Something *had* been going on, she couldn't quite remember what. Hospital . . . Lucille wanted to go to the hospital . . . Yeah . . . Lucille must be sick . . .

'I got somethin' for you,' he was saying soothingly, 'somethin' *real* good. Now you just give me that sweet sweet arm, an' I'm gonna take you all the way to heaven.'

She sighed. Heaven. That sounded good. She extended her arm towards Whitejack. He took it, and wrapped a silk scarf around it tightly, causing the veins to bulge out. From the pocket of his robe he produced a hypodermic syringe. Heroin. No more running down to Chinatown every time she felt the opium kick, or paying out too much money for the rich man's magic white powder – cocaine. Heroin was the perfect drug for her. He could control it, and that way he could continue to control her.

Besides which – he was doing her a favor wasn't he? Transporting her to never never land where *everyone* had a good time.

Carrie smiled at Whitejack and held open her arms. She was nude and normally this might have attracted him. But they had just returned from a party where he had watched her dance, and strip, and make love to Lucille – then a man from the audience – then Dolly – then all four of them in a tangle. If he approached her now and gave her what she called good lovin' she wouldn't know the difference.

Dolly walked into the room and stood surveying the scene. 'You comin' to bed black man?' she demanded.

His eyes flickered between the two of them. No choice really. He liked strong women, and Dolly was certainly the strongest of the two.

Carrie watched them go in a haze. She was tired but she still felt like company. Slowly she got off her bed and wandered over to the window. It was open, so it was no trouble to climb outside onto the iron fire escape. The cold wind caused goose-flesh on her naked body but it didn't bother her. She staggered slightly and almost fell. Giggling aloud, she groped her way carefully down three flights of stairs to the back alley. She stepped on a piece of glass and her bare foot gushed blood. It made her giggle even louder.

A drunk was huddled between two garbage cans clutching onto his precious bottle of bootleg. He watched the naked girl stagger past and decided the booze was finally getting to him.

She emerged from the alley onto the street, and started to do a little dance – a bump and grind routine.

Two boys slouching in a doorway stood to rigid attention. 'Holy crap!' one of them exclaimed. 'Do you see what I see?'

'Sure do.'

They glanced quickly at each other, then checked out the street. It was deserted. 'Looks like it's for free. Let's go get it.'

They emerged from the doorway and moved in on either side of her.

'Hiya fellas!' she giggled.

They pushed her back in the alley and shoved her to the ground, then the elder boy unbuttoned his pants and went to work.

Carrie sighed. 'You're so beaut . . . if . . . ul,' she crooned, 'so beaut . . . if . . . ul.'

The younger boy was frightened. He was used to girls fighting and clawing – *then* saying yes.

The older boy grunted and finished. 'Your turn, Terry.'

'I don't want to, Jake.'

'Aw c'mon. It's free an' she's *hot*.'

Reluctantly Terry undid his pants. He wasn't hard, but he

tried not to let his friend see. He squatted over the girl and pretended to do it.

'Finished?' Jacob asked, after a minute.

'Just a sec,' Terry feigned a groan, and jumped up.

The two boys looked down at Carrie. She smiled in the gloom.

'She's nuts,' said Jacob, 'let's beat it.'

They ran off down the alley, and the old drunk staggered up to see what all the noise was about. He shuffled over to the garbage can she lay next to.

'Hiya,' she mumbled, holding up her arms as if to embrace him. 'Want lil' ole Carrie give ya a real wild time?'

The drunk could not believe his luck. He placed his bottle carefully on the ground and struggled out of his filthy pants.

Carrie welcomed him as he bent over. 'Hya big boy – did I 'member ta tell ya . . . you is beaut . . . if . . . ul.'

The noise hit Carrie first. Early morning noises – children shouting – milk bottles clinking – dogs barking.

Then the discomfort of lying on the ground with her foot throbbing and body shivering.

She opened her eyes and for one long moment thought she must be dreaming. *She was lying in an alley – stark naked – and it was morning.* She sat up in a panic. *Where was Whitejack? Dolly? Lucille? How had she gotten here? What was happening?*

She hunched up, bringing her knees to her chest to cover her nakedness, and shrunk back against the wall. Her head hurt. Her throat was dry. Tears filled her eyes.

*What was she doing here?* She blinked hard to stop the tears. *Think Carrie. Think.*

Vaguely she remembered a party. It was all a blur really. Whitejack gave her a shot of magic and she went on and did her stuff.

Frantically she stood up, pressing her back to the wall. It was then she realized she was in the alley outside her window.

A noise came from nearby. A human sound. It was an old drunk sprawled on his back alongside the neighboring garbage can. He was a pitiful sight. She shuddered.

'Aarrgh . . . ' He turned in his sleep, and the bottle he was clutching slid out of his arms and smashed on the ground.

She jumped. Her foot hurt as soon as it took her weight, but she had her bearings now, and limped quickly over to the fire escape and climbed up it. Fortunately her window was open.

She threw herself into the room, and only then allowed herself to break down in a paroxysm of sobbing. She was truly scared. It was getting so she didn't know herself any more. Drugs were killing her mind. They were killing *her*.

Without bothering to cover herself she stormed into Dolly's room.

'They were asleep – the big blonde – and the tall black man. *Her man*. But he spent every night with Dolly now.

'Wake up, you two!' she screamed. 'You hear me – wake up!'

'Shee . . . it, woman,' Whitejack mumbled, opening his eyes slowly, 'shee . . . it.'

'What in hell's goin' on here,' muttered Dolly, turning in the bed like a beached white whale.

'I was asleep in the street,' shrieked Carrie, 'the goddamn *street*!'

'What you talkin' 'bout, woman,' grumbled Whitejack. 'You taken leave your senses?'

'Get her out of here,' complained Dolly.

Lucille came running into the room. 'What's going on?' she asked.

'Who knows,' he snarled. 'She gone plain mad.'

'I gone plain nothin'!' yelled Carrie. 'You feedin' me drugs day an' night I don't know where I am anymore. *I was out on the street – naked – You hear me? Naked – Naked – Naked.*' Her voice rose until it was one long wailing scream.

Whitejack climbed out of the bed and took her in his arms. He held her tightly. 'You was dreamin',' he said calmly, 'nuthin' wrong with that. Just dreamin', that's all.'

'Was I?' Suddenly she was confused.

'Sure,' he soothed. 'Now you just c'mon along with the man an' I'll fix you up with somethin' take all the bad dreams away.' He led her from the room.

Dolly turned over and went back to sleep.

Lucille shook her head. She had seen bad times come and bad times go and she knew that Carrie was headed for one big bad time.

And there was nothing anyone could do to stop it.

# Gino 1928

Cindy woke first. She propped herself up on one elbow and regarded the sleeping Gino. He lay on his stomach, his face in profile. Asleep he looked quite young. Of course he *was* young – but somehow – when those hard black eyes were in action he didn't *seem* young. Cindy had made up her mind long ago that she was going to share his bed – and hey presto – here she was.

She shivered with excitement. What a lover he had turned out to be. Of course anyone would seem fascinating after Pinky Banana. But her sexual experience was not limited to Pinky – there had been three others – and they were all the same. Gino had a touch she had never known before. He felt her as though he *was* her. He *knew* exactly where to go with his prick or his tongue...

Again she shivered, and thought about waking him up. He looked so peaceful though ... It would be a shame to disturb him.

She had not expected to gain access to his bed so easily. Everyone knew he was planning to get married to some girl in San Francisco. Everyone knew he was religiously faithful. Not so any more...

She stared at his sleeping face and wondered what he was going to do about her when he woke up. Was he going to give her some money and stick her on a train to California? She certainly hoped not. She had no desire to go. But how could she possibly expect him to keep her?

Gently she put her finger to one of her perfect small breasts and played with the nipple until it stiffened and stood out erect. Then she did the same to the other one.

She was hot and wet just thinking about Gino lying beside her. Quietly she leaned over and slid her breasts up and down his bare back. He stirred in his sleep but did not wake.

She continued to rub her breasts against him. He turned over and his penis was standing up and ready even though his eyes were still closed.

She climbed astride him and maneuvered him inside her. Then she rode him hard and fast until her cheeks were glowing red and her breath was no more than short gasps. Then she came in one glorious flash.

He didn't open his eyes, and his erection didn't subside.

She rolled off him and started to 'laugh. 'Gino? You can't possibly have slept through that!'

He lay perfectly still.

She leaned over and sucked him to a monumental orgasm. And only then did he open his eyes, rumple her hair, and say, 'Mornin'.'

'I thought you'd never wake up,' she said brightly.

'I was awake all the time.'

She grinned, 'Well let's say part of you was!'

'Y'like that part?'

'Oh yes!'

He leaped out of bed and headed for the door.

'Where are you going?'

'The crapper – it's down the hall. Don't go away.'

As if she would. She got up from the bed and inspected her face in a cracked mirror on top of the old chest of drawers.

In the can Gino considered the situation. He had to admit he felt good. He had not expected to feel good for weeks, months, years. He was sick to his stomach about Leonora – but no more being the faithful sucker – that kind of action was for the birds.

Starting today he planned to get on with his life. He had plenty of dough stashed away, and a decent apartment. No more saving. For what?

When he got back to the room Cindy was sitting up in bed. 'I'm hungry.' She pouted. 'Got anything a girl can eat?'

Gino dressed on one side of the room, Cindy on the other. Not a word had been spoken about what would happen next.

Cindy bit on her lip nervously. She didn't want to be packed off to California. She wanted to stay. They had made love again. There was no stopping him – he was like a raging Ram. No wonder he had that nickname. But after the lovemaking there was no real talk, just playful banter, until he had glanced at his watch and exclaimed, 'Jeeze! I gotta get outta here.' Then they had both proceeded to dress.

Cindy pulled on silk stockings and secured them with cheap pink garters. She glanced over at Gino. He was pulling on his pants.

He caught her looking and winked. How the heck was she gonna go out in the street dressed like that? She was wriggling into her dress of the previous evening. Pink satin with a low plunge. 'Hey – ' he questioned, 'you gonna travel in that?'

She gestured helplessly, 'I couldn't've taken any of my clothes . . . If Pinky had even suspected I was going . . . ' her voice started to quiver, 'Oh, Gino. WhatamIgonnado?' Her words stuck together in a lump, and they both stopped dressing to consider the problem.

'I thought you wanted t'get on a train. Y'know – get away fast.'

She lowered her eyes, 'That was before last night.'

He hunched his shoulders, 'Yeh?'

'That's right,' she murmured softly. 'Now I don't want to go anywhere. I want to stay here with you.'

'Hey listen . . ' he began.

'No you listen,' she interrupted. 'I know what your deal is – you're gettin' married soon. I'd just like to stay with you for a couple of weeks. Nothing serious. Just fun. Then I'd go – get on the train without a backward glance. What d'y'say, Gino?'

He didn't know what to say. The idea didn't bother him. Two weeks of Cindy and her juicy body was no big hardship. He just wished that she'd never belonged to Pinky Banana . . .

'Jeeze . . . ' He rocked back and forth on the balls of his feet, 'I don't know . . . '

'Your girlfriend would never find out,' she continued quickly, 'we could keep it a big secret. Haven't you got an apartment downtown?'

'How'd y'know about that?'

'Word gets around.'

Yeh. He hadn't exactly kept it quiet.

'If we went there,' Cindy said excitedly, '*nobody* would know about us. It's a whole new neighborhood. Even Pinky wouldn't know.'

She had something there. He nodded. What the hell . . . A couple of weeks . . . What could he lose? 'Tell y'what, kid, you stay here while I go take care of business – when I get back we'll jump a cab over to the apartment an' check it out.'

'Oh, Gino!' she flung her arms around his neck, 'that's wonderful!'

'Hey!' he disengaged her arms, 'like only for a coupla weeks – right?'

She widened her big blue eyes, 'Of course. You'll have me out of there anytime you say.'

'As long as we understand each other.'

'We do, don't we?' She moved close and nibbled on his ear, 'we understand each other pretty good.' Her hand reached for his fly and started unbuttoning.

'Hey!' he slapped her hand away laughingly, 'I got business to attend to.' He looked in the mirror and shook his black curly hair vigorously before plastering a handful of grease on it. Then he was off, with a jaunty, 'See ya kid.'

She ran to the window and watched him walk down the street.

*Gino Santangelo – you weren't that difficult to get. Two weeks. Ha! As long as little Cindy wants to stay you mean.*

Aldo chewed on a piece of garlic, one of his less endearing habits. 'We can't just tell him we want him out,' he insisted, 'you know Pinky – he'll go apeshit.'

Gino sat on the hood of the old Ford. 'Fuck 'im,' he spat. 'I don't care *what* he does.'

Aldo paced the lock up garage, a worried frown creasing his forehead. 'He's bin with us from the beginning—'

'Bullshit. We brought him in to ride shotgun on the trips to Canada. You an' I were together long before that.'

'Yeah, I know, but I guess he kinda figures he's a partner.'

'Jeeze!' Gino snorted with disgust, 'You wanna keep him, is that what you're tryin' ta tell me?'

'Naw . . . I just—'

'You just don't want trouble,' Gino finished the sentence for him.

Aldo shrugged, 'You tell Pinky he's not with us you got trouble.'

'Look – he ain't my partner. He ain't yours. We pay him. We *hire* him. An' now we're gonna fire him. Understand?'

'I guess you're right.'

'You can *bet* I'm right. Pinky's gotten sloppy. He runs with garbage and he's got a big mouth. I don't wanna find myself back in the can 'cos of him.'

Aldo agreed. 'You'll tell him?'

'Goddamn right I will.'

Pinky Banana arrived an hour later. He looked as though he had just fallen out of some whore's bed, and in point of fact he had. He was wearing the same suit he'd had on the night before, and it stunk of cheap perfume. He swaggered into the garage an hour late for the meeting. Without so much as a good morning he growled, 'What's the job? Just give me the time an' place an' let me go home an' get some friggin' sleep. Had some real hot cunt bumpin' me all night – I'm beat.'

Aldo twitched nervously.

Gino was calm. Slowly he said, 'Nothin' personal Pinky, but

we bin' talkin', and it just ain't gonna work out with us anymore.'

Pinky Banana narrowed bloodshot eyes, 'What ain't gonna
work out?'

Gino gestured around the garage, 'The whole set up.'

'What the frig ya talkin' 'bout?'

'I want you out,' Gino said evenly.

Pinky could not believe what he was hearing. 'The fuck ya
do!' he screamed.

'Yeh. The fuck I do.'

Suddenly they were confronting each other. Face to face.
And Gino was poking Pinky in the stomach with his finger and
saying, 'I bin watchin' y'change. I don't wanna have my freedom rest in your loud mouth.'

'Oh, I getcha,' yelled Pinky, slapping Gino's finger away,
'ya gotta cushy set up with Bonnatti an' so ya wanna dump
me.'

Gino's eyes were hard and bleak, 'Whatever you wanna
make of it.'

'Ya soft prick! Ya dump on me an' you'll be so friggin' sorry
ya won't know what's hit ya. The Santangelo gang. What a
friggin' laugh! Without me ya nothin' – they'll be knockin' off
your loads like squeezin' milk from tit.'

Gino turned away, 'Get lost.'

'Don't ya friggin' tell *me* t'get lost.'

Pinky was four inches taller and twenty-five pounds
heavier, but as he swung a punch he got more than he bar-
gained for. Gino was quick on his feet and had turned and
blocked the punch before it was even halfway on its journey.
He countered with a strong right of his own and caught Pinky
square on the nose. There was a squelching sound and a sudden spurt of blood.

Pinky's hands rushed to his face. 'Ya fucker!' he shrieked,
'you've broke my friggin' nose!' Blood seeped between his
fingers and dripped onto the garage floor.

'That's for Cindy,' Gino growled. 'She wanted to send you
her regards.'

Pinky wasn't even listening. He was heading for the door.
'Ya got it comin',' he mumbled, trying to stem the flow of
blood with his handkerchief, 'an' I'm gonna see ya get it.'

'I'm shakin' in my shoes.'

'You'd better mothafucka – you'd better!' screamed Pinky.
And then he was gone.

'Y'see,' Gino announced triumphantly. 'I told you he'd take it OK.'

Aldo was visibly shaken. 'Why'd ya have to hit him?'

Gino stared long and hard. 'You want out?' he questioned.

Aldo shrugged, 'I guess I ain't *that* nervous.' He shuffled his feet uneasily. 'What was the crack 'bout Cindy?'

'She left him, only I don't think he knows it yet.'

'Where's she gone?'

Gino looked blank. 'California I think. Hey – we'd better call Enzio.'

'Yeah,' Aldo agreed, and then added, 'You heard from Leonora yet?'

'Nope.' Gino put his arm around his friend's shoulder, 'Y'know somethin'? the longer she don't reply, the longer I got second thoughts. Marriage . . . shit – I mean I hardly know the girl.'

Aldo stared in amazement. 'I don't believe what I'm hearin'!'

Gino tried to look sheepish, 'Yeh. I know. Strange ain't it? I've bin writin' her over a year, but if I saw her now . . . well . . s'difficult to explain. I got this feelin' I bin buildin' up somethin' too good in my mind. Like I'll get her here an' she'll be just another girl with zits an' the curse an' all that shit.'

'Are you sayin' you're not gettin' married?'

'Naw, I'm not sayin' that. I'm just havin' second thoughts about it all.'

Aldo chewed on his hunk of garlic, 'I know what you mean. Sometimes I think about marryin' Barbara – an' sometimes it scares the crap outta me.'

'Yeh,' agreed Gino, 'that's the feelin'.' He shot Aldo a sideways look. He had planted a seed. It shouldn't be too difficult for it to grow. In a week or two he would say – 'Fuck it – I definitely changed my mind.' And nobody would think twice about it.

Mrs Lanza insisted that she take Costa on a tour of the city.

Fatigue hit her halfway through their trip to the zoo in Central Park. 'Oh my, oh my,' she fluttered, sitting on a bench, 'this really is too much for me, Costa.'

He made the right agreeable noises while she carried on about how she had wanted to show him the city but her heart wasn't strong and she would simply *have* to go home.

He escorted her from the park, hailed her a cab, and thanked his lucky stars he was free at last.

He darted down the subway and made his way over to Gino's place as fast as possible, rushing up the three flights of stairs and hammering on the door.

A small blonde opened up. 'Who are you?' she inquired.

He stared at her. She was uncommonly pretty. 'I'm Costa,' he managed, 'a friend of Gino's. Who are you?'

She licked rouged full lips, 'I'm Cindy, a *very good* friend of Gino's,' she winked cheekily, and her blue eyes – several shades darker than Leonora's – scanned him from head to toe. 'You sure don't look like a friend of Gino's. You're just a kid.'

Costa blushed, 'I am not!'

'Could've fooled me.'

Costa willed the color to leave his face and said sternly, 'Is Gino here? I have come to call on him.'

Cindy broke into peals of laughter, 'Come to call on him! You come to call on girls – stupid – not men!'

He was speechless. His mind was racing. What was she doing in Gino's room anyway? He had witnessed his friend's grief at the news of Leonora's marriage. Had it all been some big act? 'When will Gino be back?' he asked stiffly.

She gave an indifferent shrug, 'I don't know.'

Costa shuffled uncomfortably, 'Can I come in and wait?'

'Oh no,' she said primly, 'I don't even know who you are.'

'I'm Gino's friend, Costa Zennocotti. He was expecting me earlier but I was delayed.'

'You know something,' she winked, 'you talk real nice. Where you from?'

'San Franci . . . ' he began. Then he stopped abruptly as he heard the sound of heavy footsteps mounting the stairs two at a time.

Gino bound into view, looking remarkably cheerful. 'Costa! Where y'bin? Thought you was comin' by at twelve.'

'I was, but I . . . '

'See you met Cindy,' Gino interrupted, then realizing how it must look he added rather lamely, 'She's just a friend I'm helpin' out.'

The three of them crowded into the small room. Costa glanced at the rumpled bed, most of the covers strewn on the floor. Then his glance took in Cindy's dress.

'Listen kid,' Gino said to Cindy, 'I want you to throw my things in a suitcase. I'm just gonna take a walk with Costa – then we'll get outta here.'

She smoothed down her dress, 'Sure, but I gotta get somethin' to wear. I can't walk around in this.'

'Don't worry 'bout it. We'll get you some stuff later.' He put his arm around Costa's shoulder and guided him out of the room.

Once on the street he started to talk. 'I wanna be straight with you, kid. Yeh. I'm screwin' her. But the first time was last night – an' let me tell y'somethin' – that was the first time I bin with a woman since I met Leonora,' he laughed mirthlessly, 'you like it, kid? Gino the Ram bin Gino the sucker. Now I'm gonna make up for lost time 'cos I don't like bein' the sucker.'

'I understand—' Costa began.

'The fuck y'do!' exclaimed Gino, 'I don't even understand myself. What I do know is I want you t'keep your mouth shut. It suits me t'say I'm still engaged.'

'Of course. I won't say anything.'

'You'd better not, kid. Not unless you want your head busted.'

Costa was hurt, 'You can trust me. Surely you know that by now.'

Gino screwed up his eyes, 'Yeh . . . I guess.' Then he jabbed playfully at Costa's stomach, 'C'mon kid, today's movin' day – you're gonna give us a hand.'

The rest of Costa's trip to New York flew by. Every day he spent with Cindy and Gino, helping them to furnish the apartment, going to movies, shopping for clothes on Fifth Avenue, and generally hanging out. Occasionally Gino would vanish back to the old neighborhood for a meeting, but he always returned within hours, and while he was away Cindy would entertain him with her movie star imitations. She did a great Dolores Costello, and a perfect Lillian Gish.

Every night he had to return to the Lanza's residence by 6 p.m. 'It's so goddamn stupid!' Gino exclaimed. 'Tell the old bag you'll be late tonight.' Costa didn't have the courage.

On his last night Gino wouldn't take no for an answer. 'Fuck 'em,' he said, 'what the hell – they can't do nothin'. We're goin' on the town – no argument.'

Costa hadn't argued, and it had been the best time of his whole trip. He had ended up doing the things he had only ever done with the San Francisco whore on the floor of Gino's living room with a girl who had joined them at the speakeasy they went to. God, it was exciting! He staggered back to the Beekman Place house in time for breakfast.

A stoney faced Mrs Lanza greeted him in the hall with his suitcase fully packed. 'Your father will be hearing from me,' she said, handing him his suitcase and slamming the door in his face.

Costa went straight back to Gino's apartment and stayed there until it was time to catch his train. Cindy kissed and hugged him, 'We'll miss ya, kid,' she said, a girlish imitation of Gino.

Once on the train he settled back to savour the trip in his mind. He wasn't concerned with what punishment Franklin would mete out to him. It had all been worth it.

Only one thing worried him. He had not told Gino about Leonora being pregnant. But it wasn't important. When she had the baby he would delay telling his friend about it for a few months. That way he would never know the truth. The last thing Costa ever wanted to do was hurt Gino.

Cindy stretched and giggled, 'Alone at last! What we gonna do without the kid?' She lay back on the large bed and extended her leg through the slit in her champagne satin nightgown.

Gino ran his hand up her leg. 'We'll find somethin' to occupy us.'

Cindy giggled again, and slid down the bed, the satin nightgown riding up around her waist.

His hands travelled up her thighs and pushed their way into her thick triangle of golden pubic hair. She caught her breath and gave a little gasp of excitement as he lowered his head. 'Oh!' she whispered, 'I love it when you do that. I just love it so much!'

'Yeh?' he paused for breath, 'tell me about it, babe.'

She was shivering with bliss. 'I love your tongue, your mouth, your hands. Oohh . . . Gino . . . OOOhhh . . . ' She shuddered, arched her back, and climaxed.

'Talk 'bout the two second wonder!' he complained.

She rolled onto her stomach, 'I can't help it. It's just *soooo* good. Nobody ever did that t'me before.'

'Yeh?' he was pleased.

'Y'know Pinky never licked me there. Pinky said all girls was dirty an' he wasn't puttin' *his* mouth there.'

Gino's hard-on subsided like a deflated soufflé. 'Shit!' he exclaimed sharply.

'Wassamatter?'

He climbed off the bed. 'What the fuck you talkin' 'bout Pinky for?'

'Sorry.'

'I don't wanna know what Pinky did or didn't do.'

'Sorry.'

'Pinky. Jeeze! How y'could ever have shacked up with him in the first place beats me.'

'Sorry.'

'Will y'stop sayin' sorry.'

'Sorry.'

Gino stamped into the bathroom. Fuckin' Pinky Banana. And what was he, Gino Santangelo, doin' with one of his cast offs?

He glared at himself in the ornate wall mirror, filled a tumbler with water, and rinsed out his mouth.

He was busy shaving when Cindy came sliding in. She stood behind him pressing her body close. 'Baby's turn now,' she lisped, reaching for him.

He shook her away, 'Cut it out,' he said sharply, 'I gotta meetin'.'

She retreated, wise enough not to argue.

He finished shaving and walked into the bedroom to dress. He had bought himself a lot of new clothes, and he carefully selected a black suit with a wide white stripe, a dark brown shirt, polka dot tie, and brown patent shoes.

'You look swell, honey,' Cindy breathed. 'Who you meetin'?'

Questions about who he was meeting he didn't need. Maybe it was time to mention her California trip. 'I may not be home 'til late,' he growled, ignoring her question. 'See ya,' and he was gone.

She waited until he was out of earshot, and then she screamed. Bastard! He was ready to dump her. Bastard!

Only little Cindy wasn't ready to be dumped. Little Cindy had to think of a way to make herself indispensable.

That shouldn't be too difficult. Underneath all the strut Gino was an easy touch. Hadn't Pinky always said so?

Gino strode over to Park Avenue, paused there and took the small engraved card from his pocket. *Mrs Clementine Duke. I am comin' to call.*

He noted the address once more. Real hot address in the upper Sixties between Park and Madison. It was a nice day, crisp and sunny, so he decided to walk all the way.

He dug his hands deep into the pockets of his new camel-hair coat, and thought about the preceding weeks. Yeh. They had been OK With Cindy he had made up for lost time sexually – and how! She was a little wildcat, ready to try anything. At first it had been exciting – but she was always there ready to open her legs. An occasional no might have been nice.

Still . . . She would be moving soon. And she had gotten him through the worst time – although she didn't know it.

They had enjoyed themselves fixing up the apartment. It was only a small place – but it was home. Before, it had always been some lousy pisshole with cockroaches roaming the floor, worn furniture, and a bathroom down the hall if you were lucky.

Vera had come to visit a couple of times. Only she and Cindy didn't seem to hit it off too good. It didn't bother him that much because Vera now talked about Paulo as though he was some kind of hero. It pissed him off. 'What you gonna do when he gets out of the can an' beats the shit outta you again?' he had questioned.

'Aw c'mon, Gino, people change,' Vera had whined.

Yeh. And pussy grew on trees.

Business wise, Bonnatti had kept his word and his connections open. The talk was that the trouble he was experiencing in Chicago was encouraging him to forge very strong ties in the East. Aldo and Gino were his key connections. He had already told them that when he came in at the end of the month he had big plans.

Meanwhile Gino kept a tight rein on the liquor runs from New Jersey. He was experiencing trouble – the hijacking situation had never been so bad – but they were lucky. He brought in a new enforcer called Red, who had recently left Detroit and seemed loyal. Not a maniac like Pinky Banana – who was lying low. After all his threats nothing had been heard of him – although Aldo had come face to face with him in Fat Larrys and he had muttered darkly about the revenge that was coming their way. It made Aldo nervous, but Gino just laughed. 'The prick's all mouth,' he said, 'he ain't gonna start somethin' there's no way he can finish.'

'Sure – a mouth with a gun,' Aldo had said miserably, 'and by the way, Fat Larry said that rich dame bin askin' for you – Mrs Duke – she got some business or somethin'. You gonna see her?'

*Yeh. He was gonna see her. Nothing to stop him now.*

He stepped in a pile of dog shit and let out a stream of curses. He stopped to scrape his new patent shoes on the side of the curb.

*Mrs Clementine Duke, I am on my way.*

# Carrie 1928

'We're gonna make a movie,' Whitejack said one day.

'A movie?' Carrie's eyes widened. 'For real?'

'Sure 'nuff,' Whitejack grinned, 'thought I mentioned it before.' Only he hadn't mentioned that it was to be a stag movie. The kind they made in back rooms with a hand-held camera and fiercely hot lights that burned into your flesh. He hadn't mentioned the fact that Carrie was to be the star, and that she was to accommodate four different men during the course of the twenty-minute production.

Not that it mattered. Carrie didn't much care. She was so drugged up by the time Whitejack got her to the sordid little room she would have done anything.

'This girl's a natural!' the director exclaimed joyfully. 'I shoulda gotta dog for her t'work with!'

Whitejack grinned, stood in the background, and then got very pissed off indeed when at the end of the day his director friend – a short white butterball of a man – attempted to shaft him on the payment. 'You cocksucka!' he screamed. 'You pay me the dough you promised or I'll beat your fat white ass to pulp.'

The director paid up. 'Fuck off, nigger,' he sneered, 'an' get your whore outta here.'

Whitejack shoved the man up against a wall and contemplated doing him damage. Then he decided it wasn't worth the trouble, and took Carrie by the arm and hauled her out of the place.

It was the end of her film career.

'She's costin' us too much,' Dolly complained a few days later.

'We're makin' plenty,' Whitejack wheedled.

'Sure we are. But how long you think that gonna last? You *looked* at her lately? Skinny as a rail, eyes like saucers, arms gettin' all marked up. We've got to get rid of her.'

'What you mean – get rid of her?'

'Anyone sees that dumb movie you had her do – it could mean trouble. What is she – sixteen, seventeen? We could be in a real bad position anyone discover we're usin' her like we are. We could go to jail.'

'Who's gonna know? She ain't got no family.' He sipped moodily at his coffee. Dolly was always nagging about Carrie, it got on his nerves. Carrie adored him, and he needed a good solid dose of admiration every day.

'Listen black man,' Dolly got up from the kitchen table, and placed her hands firmly on her solid hips. 'You wanna keep her – go ahead. Only you can say goodbye to *our* deal – I *ain't* prepared to take the risk no longer.'

Whitejack inspected his nails, 'You *threatening* me, woman?'

'No, I ain't threatening – I'm tellin'.' Dolly was not a woman to take any crap. She liked Whitejack and the whole set up, but not enough to risk going to jail over some dumb picaninny. 'I can find us another girl, easy. Got one of twenty, looks fourteen, knocks spots off Carrie. She's blacker than you, an' hotter than shit. You wanna see her?'

He was tempted. 'Who is she?'

Dolly grinned to herself. She knew the way to Whitejack's head was via his cock. For a pimp he sure liked to indulge. 'Just a little find of mine. What d'ya say, black man?'

He took a gulp of his coffee and made up his mind. Dolly was right. Carrie was becoming more dangerous than she was worth. 'What'll we do with her?'

Dolly did not flinch. 'She'll have an accident, somewhere away from here.'

'C'mon,' he objected, 'why can't we just dump her on some hospital doorstep?'

'Real sharp thinking,' scolded Dolly, 'so that when they straighten the teenage junkie whore out she can lead the police straight to us.'

'She wouldn't do that . . .'

'Oh yeah? You wanna place a bet on it?'

He shook his head.

'A nice clean accident,' Dolly continued, 'she could stumble under a trolley car, fall under a subway train, jump off Brooklyn Bridge . . . You can take your choice.'

Whitejack leapt up from the table, '*My choice! I ain't* doin' it woman.'

Dolly's eyes were like two icy marbles. 'Oh you ain't, huh?'

'No, I ain't.'

'So I'll do it then.'

They stared at each other. Whitejack liked strong women but this one beat the band. She was actually ready to kill! He felt a cold tingle all the way down his spine. 'When?' he asked.

Dolly shrugged her ample shoulders, 'How about today?'

'No, not today,' he said hurriedly, 'There's that big party

comin' up this weekend an' I don't want no new girl for that.'

'Next Monday then. We'll start the week off fresh.'

'Yeah, Monday.' He stared at Dolly waiting to see if she flinched.

She didn't. She stared right back at him with icy eyes. 'You want more coffee?' she asked calmly.

His stomach was churning. He kept his voice even. 'Yeah. An' some eggs – sunny side up.'

A flicker of a cold smile crossed her face. She knew he was scared shitless. Cowardly nigger. But she loved him anyway. And the sooner little Carrie was out of her way the better.

# Gino 1928

Quite frankly Gino had never seen a house in New York like it. Well, that was a lie really, because he had – but only in the movies. It was an imposing brownstone residence, set back behind high railings. Its very façade screamed out money.

Gino was impressed. Who the hell was this Mrs Clementine Duke anyway? Some rich broad for sure. What was the scam? Where was the husband?

Tentatively he rang the doorbell, taking a comb from his pocket and attending to his hair in the shiny reflection of the brass door knocker. Wouldn't do to let Mrs Duke catch a glimpse of him unless he looked his very best.

The massive front door was opened by an elderly butler – again Gino was reminded of a Hollywood movie.

'Yes, sir?' questioned the butler disdainfully.

He pulled himself up full height and hit the old guy with a steady glare, 'Hey, Mrs Duke around?'

The butler's mouth twitched. He was used to young men calling, but certainly not of this type. 'Is Mrs Duke expecting you, sir?'

'Yeh, she's expectin' me.' Gino ran his hand through his thick black hair, and was immediately sorry as his hand was now covered by a thin residue of grease. Surreptitiously he wiped it on the side of his trousers.

The butler did not miss a move. His lips wavered on the edge of a supercilious smile. 'Who shall I say is calling, sir?'

'Tell her Gino – Gino Santangelo. S·A·N·T·A·N·G·E·L·O.'

'Very well, sir. Would you wait here please.'

For a moment Gino thought he was going to shut the door in his face. But he didn't.

Whistling, Gino waited until the old boy was out of sight, then he stepped through the front door into the hall. 'Whew! Watta joint!' he muttered. Luxury stared him in the face. Marble floors and staircase, crystal chandeliers, expensive portraits on the walls. And this was only the hall! Jeeze! If you knocked the hall off you could live on the proceeds for years!

Old watery eyes came back then. 'Mrs Duke will see you now, sir. Can I take your coat?'

'Yeh. Why not?' Gino shrugged his way out of the camel hair.

'Follow me please.'

He fell into step behind the butler. They moved through the marble hallway, up the marble stairs, and into a room that resembled a country garden. The butler announced him and discreetly withdrew.

Mrs Duke sat in a high backed white whicker chair, surrounded by palms and ferns. She gave Gino a long icy stare. 'You're late. I said I received visitors between eleven and twelve and it is now,' she paused, and glanced meaningfully at a clock on the mantel, 'exactly twelve forty four.'

'Yeh?' He was not about to be intimidated, 'whacha want me t'do – go or stay?'

'I suppose you had better stay now that you are here.'

'Gee! There's nothin' like gettin' a real hot welcome!'

She smiled, giving a fascinating tilt to her turned down mouth. He swaggered over to a chair and sat down.

'Do sit down, Mr Santangelo,' she murmured.

'You can call me Gino.'

'Thank you so much.'

They regarded each other warily.

She looked older than she had in the dim lights of Fat Larrys, but still a knockout in a short white crossover skirt that revealed long silken legs that he could imagine wrapped around his waist . . . And a soft blouse with those nipples on show – pointing through for all to see.

'Hey,' he said quickly, 'ya wanted t'see me 'bout some business?'

She nodded, wondering who on earth had chosen the preposterous outfit he had on. It didn't hide the fact that she had been right – he *was* an extremely attractive young man. 'Yes Mr Santangelo –'

'Gino,' he interrupted.

'Gino. I did think that perhaps we might be able to do business together.' She crossed her legs.

Gino's eyes followed the movement.

She caught him watching. He didn't look away.

She uncrossed her legs. 'Some tea, Mr San . . . Gino?'

'Yeh.'

She rang a bell on the table beside her chair. It was funny really. Here she was – Clementine Duke – thirty-seven years old – experienced in the ways of the world – rich – a social lioness – married to a billionaire – here she was totally unnerved by some street kid. Good God! He couldn't even be more than nineteen or twenty.

She had thought about him on and off for weeks. Returned to Fat Larrys on countless occasions, and he had never been there, damn it. Until, at last, she had swallowed her pride, and told Fat Larry to have Gino Santangelo call her. 'What business is he in?' She had casually inquired.

'Bootleg,' Fat Larry replied.

Good. They could indeed do business.

'How is your fiancée?' she asked Gino politely.

'She's OK. Why?'

'I just wondered when you would be going to San Francisco.'

He shifted uncomfortably, 'Not for a while . . . Got too many things to take care of here. I . . . uh . . . postponed the wedding.'

Clementine nodded, 'You *are* much too young to get married.'

'Y'think so?'

'Yes. I do. Why you can't be more than—'

'Twenty-two. How old are you?'

'Oh!' Ridiculous! She could feel herself blushing. 'A gentleman never asks a lady's age.'

'Yeh? Well I never said I was no gentleman.'

She struggled to regain her composure, 'Perhaps you should start trying to behave like one.'

'Yeh?' His eyes held hers mockingly. 'Why?'

The butler returned at that moment with a silver tray. He placed it carefully on the table beside Mrs Duke.

'Davies asked me to remind you, madame, that you have a

one-fifteen luncheon appointment,' he murmured respectfully.

'Thank you, Scott.'

The butler retreated once again, and Clementine swivelled in her chair and began to pour the tea. 'I would offer you something stronger,' she said, 'but isn't that *your* line of business?'

'Who told y'that?'

'Oh it's quite all right, I'm not the police or FBI or anything.'

'Funny. I had y'figured for J. Edgar Hoover under the skirt!'

'Hmmm . . . a comedian.'

'I like to make 'em laugh.'

'In that suit you should have no trouble at all.'

He glared at her, 'Wassamatter with this suit?'

She realized she had hurt his feelings and said gently, 'Isn't it a little loud?'

What did she know? Dumb broad. He laughed quickly to show her criticism had no effect on him whatsoever. 'So what if it's loud? I like it that way. Lets people know I'm around.'

'I should think they would know that anyway.' She handed him a cup of tea. 'Now, Gino. Let's get down to business.'

His eyes swept over her, 'That's why I'm here – lady.' Rich bitch. She wasn't going to get the better of *him*.

'My husband and I do a lot of entertaining. Here – ' she gestured vaguely around the room, 'but mostly on our estate in Westchester.'

He nodded. The dame was definitely loaded.

'Obviously our guests like to indulge themselves '

Obviously. He swallowed a coarse laugh.

'Good food, music, dancing,' she paused meaningfully, 'and naturally fine liquor.'

Naturally. What else for Mr and Mrs Duke?

'I don't mind telling you that in the past we have had some . . . unfortunate experiences. Bathtub gin, watered down whiskey, and stuff that I think you would probably call bootleg hooch. God knows how we survived *some* of the . . . poison.'

'But y'did.'

'You can see that.' She stood up and smoothed her skirt down. 'Mr Santangelo. Gino. Would you be interested in supplying us on a permanent basis?'

'Hey—' he began.

'Oh, nothing petty,' she interrupted, 'at least twenty-four cases a month. And naturally if the quality is first class – top prices.' She paced around the room and his eyes followed her legs. 'I know of course that is probably a small order as far as you are concerned, but I would deem it a great favor. And I am sure that if there is anything my husband can do for you in return...'

'What does Mr Duke do?'

'*Senator* Duke, didn't I tell you?'

Gino swallowed hard. Senator Duke. Jesus H. He had fallen right into it. 'Hey,' he said quickly, 'the booze I get is the very best – finest stuff y'can get hold of. It would be er . . . my pleasure . . . to supply you and er . . . the Senator.'

She clapped her hands together, a childlike gesture that was out of character with the rest of her demeanor, 'Oh, good! I *am* pleased.'

He stood up and she walked towards him. With the spikey high heels she was wearing they were about the same height. She stood a few inches away from him. 'I think we can both help each other,' she said quietly, her green eyes boring into him.

'Yeh,' he replied, unsure if she was making a pass or what. He wouldn't have minded a bit. She was one hot classy piece.

She turned away from him abruptly, walked back to her chair and sat down. 'This weekend,' she said, 'we are having a house party. I think we will need two cases of scotch, champagne, gin, brandy—'

'Hang on,' he interrupted, 'write down what y'want, I'll see y'get it.'

'Of course, I'll do that now.' She took a pad and pencil from the table and scribbled out her requirements, then she tore off the piece of paper, got up, walked towards him and handed him the paper. 'This is the address – if you could arrange delivery sometime on Saturday.'

He checked out the paper. 'You ain't settin' me up for a bust?'

She laughed, 'How could you even imagine such a thing!'

'I gotta good imagination. So you better imagine this. Anyone sets Gino Santangelo up gets their neck in a sling. You get my meanin'?'

'Oh yes, I get your meaning.'

He had a strong suspicion she was mocking him again, 'I gotta go,' he said roughly.

She glanced at the clock. 'So do I.'

'Well . . . ' he flexed his arms, 'I guess we're in business.'

'Yes. I guess we are.'

'What about payment?'

She licked her shiny thin lips, 'I thought that you might like to attend our Saturday night party. It should be amusing, I'm sure you'll enjoy it.'

Was she nuts? Asking *him* to her party with her old man a Senator and all.

'Yeh. Sure. I'd like that.'

'The Westchester house. Eight o'clock. And if you don't feel like driving back we have plenty of guest rooms.'

He nodded. Jeeze! He was going to a party with a whole load of big shots. Him. Gino Santangelo.

'By the way,' she continued, 'it's evening dress of course. You do have a tuxedo, don't you?'

He nodded. Have one? He didn't even know what it was.

She smiled, 'See you on Saturday, then,' she wrinkled her patrician nose, 'by the way . . . can you smell . . . something nasty?'

He grinned, 'Yeh. Dog shit. I stepped in it outside the house. Wassamatta? You thought it was me?'

'Of course not.' She looked embarrassed, 'I thought Scott might have been feeding the plants with a new . . . er . . chemical.'

His grin widened, 'Naw. It's dog shit. But y'know what they say,' he winked, 'step in shit an' you'll never be unlucky. I guess it's a good sign for us Mrs D.'

'Call me Clementine.'

'Sure, why not?'

Gino went off to meet with Aldo, a bounce in his step.

'Ya heard about the fire?' Aldo asked.

'Where?'

'Over on Catto's block. His whole family got wiped out.'

He wasn't sure he'd heard right, 'What?'

'Yeah. They was trapped. Only Catto an' his old man's OK, 'cos they was out on the garbage truck early. Terrible ain't it?'

'You seen Catto?'

'Naw.'

'I'm goin' over there.' Gino sloped off down the street thinking of Catto. He hadn't seen him in nearly a year, but what did that matter when something like this happened?

The fire engines were still in the street outside the smoking houses. The sidewalk was awash with water and broken glass. People sat around in doorways, on steps, in their nightclothes.

The women sobbed silently, the men blankly tried to comfort them.

Gino dug his hands deep into the pockets of his camel-hair coat and looked around awkwardly for Catto.

'Mr Santangelo. 'Scuse me, Mr Santangelo.'

Someone was pulling excitedly on his arm. He turned to confront Jacob Cohen — the boy he had seen about Mr Pulaski. 'Yeh? What?' he shook his arm free.

'Ya shoulda seen the flames!' Jacob exclaimed, screwing up his dirt blackened face. 'They was shootin' so high up in the sky I thought the whole city'd burn.'

'How'd *you* get out?'

'I jumped.'

'Your family?'

'All gone.'

The boy didn't seem too wiped out. He scratched his nose. 'I'll be fifteen next week. I don't want 'em sendin' me to no home. I can look after myself.'

Gino sighed. The boy reminded him of himself at that age. Sharp as a rat. 'Whatcha want, Jacob?'

'Fifty bucks. Enough so I can get out of here an' get myself set up in a room. I'll be all right alone. I don't need no one.'

'You'll be looked after in a home. They'll let you out when you're sixteen.'

'Aw c'mon Mr Santangelo. *Y'know* I ain't ready for no boys school. Lend me the money an' I'll pay ya back good. Give me a coupla months — you'll get it back with interest.'

Gino frowned, 'I don't know . . .'

Jacob cocked his head to one side, 'Mr Santangelo. A nice Jewish boy like myself. Would I ever let ya down?'

Gino dug in his pocket, found his bankroll, and peeled off five twenties. 'Here's a hundred. I'll give you six months. Don't forget the interest.'

Jacob could not believe his luck. He grabbed the money and was about to run when Gino stopped him, 'You know the Bonnio family?'

'Sure.'

'You seen Catto?'

'Yeah. His old man hadda heart attack when he heard. They took him over to the hospital. Catto went too.'

Gino flicked another twenty off his bankroll and tucked it into Jacob's belt. 'For you, kid. No interest.'

'Gee, thanks!'

Gino watched him rush off and wondered what would happen to him. But it wasn't *his* problem. He turned on his heel and headed for the hospital.

Cindy was bored. She had cleaned and tidied the small apartment – not too thoroughly – true. But what was she – a maid? Then she had passed the time by trying on an outfit or two, and admiring herself in the mirror.

She had no false modesty. She *was* exceptionally pretty, and men had always gone for her. All she had to do was give them the look. Wide baby blue eyes. Pouty rosebud lips. Stick those bouncing little titties straight out in front – and – voila! She was away and running.

Men were chumps. Girls were smart.

Cindy knew a thing or two about life.

She pirouetted in front of the mirror and decided she should be a movie star. She was certainly as pretty as most of them.

Bored with her image she flopped down on the bed. She wouldn't mind being a spy . . . A glamorous seductive spy hopping from one hot bed to another. Anything that involved screwing really.

She giggled aloud. Oh how she *lovvvved* to make love.

She began to feel sexy – a hot warm feeling that started in her toes and worked its way up to the top of her marcelled head. When she put her hand between her legs the feeling intensified.

She knew what she wanted to do next, and there was no one around to stop her. When she had lived with Pinky, satisfying herself had become a daily event. He had never cared about a woman's feelings. He had just got it out and shoved it in.

Laughter convulsed her body as she quickly took off her clothes. Briefly she wished Gino was home. He *was* the best. He really knew what to do with every bit of his equipment.

Sucker! Where was he when she needed him? This was the first time she had had to resort to her little game since being with him.

Both her hands were between her legs now and she stopped thinking about Pinky and Gino and the whole damn lot of them . . . Who needed men anyway? Who needed the suckers . . .

Gino bumped into Catto leaving the hospital and ran towards

him. He attempted to hug his friend but Catto shrugged him away.

'Well?' he demanded, 'your pop gonna make it?'

Catto's face was impassive. 'He died,' he said vacantly.

'Died?' Gino echoed in disbelief, 'but your old man was strong as an ox.'

Catto started to walk. Gino bobbed along beside him. He didn't know what to say.

They made a strange couple, Catto, tall and thin in his patched levis and shabby jacket. Gino, street sharp in his expensive camel-hair coat.

'Whatcha gonna do?' he asked anxiously.

Catto didn't reply.

'You got money?' Stupid question. How could Catto have any money when he was still working the garbage trucks? Christ! He still stunk too. 'Tell ya what, whyn't ya come back to my place? I gotta nice little apartment over in the Forties.'

Catto shook his head.

'Why not? You ain't got nowhere else t'go.'

'How do you know that?' Catto uttered sharply, 'I ain't seen you in months. How'd you know *anything* about me?'

' 'Cos we're friends . . . ' Gino began.

'Friends, shit! You hang around with Pinky you ain't no friend of mine.'

'I'm through with Pinky, you was right about him.'

'Sure. Now you got other hired killers to work for you.'

Gino laughed, 'Hired killers! You talkin' through your ass.'

'Guy my sister was gonna marry got shot up by a gang bringin' booze inta the city. What difference whether it was your gang or not? You all carry. I don't want any part of you.'

Gino was hurt. 'Hey . . . ' he began.

'You gotta gun on you? You carryin' under that nice smart overcoat?'

'Yeh. I got a piece, but I ain't never used it . . . ' And then he remembered that he had. Chicago. And why the hell was he trying to explain himself to Catto anyway? 'Jeeze!' he exclaimed roughly, 'I came to find you 'cos I heard what happened. I don't need your fuckin' insults. I thought we was friends from way back. I'm sorry I bothered.' He stopped in the street, pulled the collar of his coat up, smoothed down his hair, and turned in the other direction.

'Hey . . . Gino . . . I'm sorry,' Catto came after him. 'I 'preciate your comin' to find me.'

They stood in the street and faced each other.

'Yeh . . . well . . . ' Gino kicked at the pavement, 'what *are* y'gonna do?'

'Get on a train. Get out of here. I'm goin' the first place the train takes me.'

'You need money?'

'Naw.' Catto patted his pocket, 'I got enough.' He had exactly fifteen dollars and twenty-two cents.

'Nothin' I can do then?'

'There is somethin' . . . '

'Name it.'

'If you could arrange for them to be buried properly . . . '

'It's done.'

'Thanks Gino.'

'Aw – forget it.' He shuffled his feet and got a whiff of dog shit. 'Well . . . I'll be seein' you . . . '

'Sure thing.' Catto turned and hurried off down the street.

Gino watched him go, and when his friend was out of sight he made his way over to Fat Larrys, sat in the front, and ordered a dish of double chocolate ice cream with butterscotch sauce.

He felt a shadow loom over him, slowly he glanced up. Pinky Banana stood there, flanked on either side by greasy henchmen.

'How y'doin' Pinky?' he asked easily.

'Like you should friggin' care,' menaced Pinky. 'I hear ya got my cunt shacked up with ya.'

Gino grinned, 'Didn't know y'had one. But if y'say so . . . '

Pinky colored angrily, 'Prick! Ya think y'so goddamn friggin' smart. But y'aint gonna get away with it . . . '

Gino stood up. 'Who's gonna stop me?' he said coldly.

Pinky narrowed his eyes, 'One dark night . . . '

'Yeh. I'm shakin' in my boots.' He pushed his way past Pinky and his henchmen. What the fuck was he doing in the old neighborhood anyway? It stunk.

'Honey?' questioned Cindy, primping at her hair in the mirror.

'Yeh,' replied Gino, struggling with his wing collar and bow tie.

'You know what I'd like?'

'What?' The bow tie fell out of his hands.

'I'd like to learn to drive.'

'This goddamn tie!' he exclaimed. 'It's makin' me nuts!'

She ran to pick it up, then proceeded to knot it on him expertly. 'Can I?'

'Drive? Why?'

'I just do,' she replied earnestly, 'it would be fun, and think how useful it could be. I mean, take tonight. You gotta drive all the way out someplace with Aldo. Two fellas with a trunk load of booze. If the police stop you you've had it. Now if a *girl* was driving...'

She had a point. Only what she didn't know was that the booze had been delivered to Westchester early in the morning. And what she also didn't know was that Aldo was at this very moment hosting a party to celebrate his engagement to Barbara Riccaddi. And the third thing she didn't know was that Gino was driving out to Westchester to attend Mrs Duke's party as an invited guest.

'It's not a bad idea,' he mused, 'I'll give you a few lessons.' He put on his new dinner jacket and admired himself in the mirror. He had bought the suit in a real high class store on Fifth Avenue. It had cost, but it was worth it.

'When?' she demanded.

'Soon,' he replied absently, standing back from the mirror. 'Hey kid, whaddya think? I look OK?'

'Sharp, Gino. Reaaal sharp.'

# The Party 1928

'I need a bang in the arm,' Carrie whined.

'Don't worry, woman,' Whitejack soothed. 'Daddy is fillin' the gun full of beauteeeful H. Soon you will be ridin' a wave.'

She lay impatiently back on her bed. She didn't feel so good. Whitejack was a mean sonofabitch keeping her waiting. If she didn't have to depend on him to get her the stuff she'd scratch the motherfucker's eyes out.

She tossed about on the bed restlessly, the sleeve of her kimono rolled up, her left arm exposed and ready. 'Hurry up,' she snapped impatiently.

He checked out the liquid in the syringe. Little Carrie was a real pinhead. Taken to dope like a dog to a bone. Dolly was right. If they didn't get rid of her soon they would all be in trouble. 'Here we go, woman,' he drawled.

She held out her arm, tightening the belt she had around it so that the veins stood out good and ready. Her arm was already full of puncture marks, but there were still spots left where the needle entered nice and easy.

She groaned aloud as it went in.

'Any minute now you are gonna feel *good* woman, real fine an' good,' he crooned, 'an' you are gonna get that lazy black ass off'n the bed, an start fussin' with your pretty hair, an' pilin' cosmetic shit on your pretty face, an' we are all goin' to some real fine party.' He withdrew the needle.

She rolled around on the bed hugging her knees to her chest. Whitejack stood looking down at her. Gradually she straightened her body out, and stretched luxuriously. A change was coming over her. The tenseness in her face was falling away like a mask, and she was smiling and reaching out languorous arms. 'C'mere honey,' she sighed, 'let's have our own party, just the two of us.'

Wow! She felt so *good*. And Whitejack was such a *wonderful* man.

'Get up,' he said sharply, 'you got half an hour.' He left her room.

She got off the bed and danced around the floor, starting to sing in a shaky little voice, 'You're the cream in my coffee . . . '

Lucille scurried into the room, shutting the door behind her. 'What's the *matter* with you?' she demanded, 'don't you know what they're doing to you?'

'What?' asked Carrie lightly, still dancing.

Lucille glanced nervously at the door, 'You've got to get out of here,' she muttered urgently, 'they're plannin' to . . . get rid of you.'

Carrie pealed with laughter, 'Lucille! Wait 'til I tell Whitejack what you said!'

'Only joking,' Lucille backed off quickly, biting on her bottom lip so hard she drew blood.

'Oh yeah?' teased Carrie, amused by the little woman's obvious consternation.

'Sure,' replied Lucille, forming a grotesque smile. She was frightened. She had no idea what to do. She had overheard Dolly and Whitejack plotting and planning to do away with Carrie. She had stood outside the kitchen door and *heard* them. But what could *she* do? It was information that put her own life in danger.

'We're goin' to a party,' Carrie sang, 'ain't that fun, bun?' She collapsed in giggles.

'Want me to brush your hair?' Lucille asked, tears stinging her eyes.

'Ooh, that would be de-light-ful.'

Lucille picked up a brush and started to attend to her friend's hair.

Gino fairly zipped along in the old souped up Ford. He had been planning to buy himself a new car but had somehow not got around to it. So the old Ford it was. All the way to West-chester. And if Mrs Duke didn't like it – too bad.

He had expected a fancy house, but the mansion that greeted his eyes surpassed even his expectations. Set in sixty acres of lush countryside, it was lit up like a fairy palace.

He drove through wrought iron gates following the sparkling lights that lay ahead. Scattered around the driveway was the most impressive group of automobiles Gino had ever seen. Shiny Rolls-Royces parked next to sleek foreign roadsters. A gleaming bronze Duesenberg with whitewall tires. Pierce Arrows, Cords, and a black and white Mercedes Benz 'SS' that Gino could easily imagine killing for.

Who needed the party? He would be perfectly happy just checking out the cars.

He parked the Ford, got out, and headed for the fun.

Clementine Duke was a wonderful hostess. She knew how to make people relax and feel at ease. She filled her house with flowers, marvelous food, comfortable furniture, and attentive servants.

She also served excellent liquor (contrary to what she had told Gino) imported cigars for the men, and hand made choco-lates and truffles for the ladies.

She mixed her guests – entertaining movie stars, politicians, writers, and jazz musicians. They all mingled freely, and enjoyed it. New romances happened often.

But the main reason why Clementine's parties were so suc-cessful was because nobody was ever quite sure what would happen at them. Nude bathing in the huge marble swimming pool. A charleston dancing competition. A private screening of a new movie. Live jazz bands. Clementine had been the first to feature all these events.

'What *do* you have in store for us tonight, Clemmie darling?' giggled one of her women friends.

'Wait and see, Esther, wait and see,' Clementine uttered mysteriously.

Esther clapped fat beringed hands together, and her large bosoms – clearly visible through a chiffon dress – jiggled in anticipation. 'Something naughty? Oh I do hope so!' She smiled lasciviously, displaying unfortunate buck teeth. 'What time *is* the surprise?'

'Soon enough,' murmured Clementine, and was annoyed to find herself yet again looking around to see if Gino had arrived.

'Don't know why we had t'take a bookin' all the way out in the country,' complained Dolly, 'it ain't like our asses ain't shakin' in the city.' She sat up front in the white Oldsmobile next to Whitejack who was driving.

'Shee . . . i . . . t!' he spat. 'Will you stop moanin', woman? I 'splained to you ten times that this is a special show. Like it's a party fulla 'portant people. We go down big here an' we kin up our price.'

'Yeah. An' what if any those big important people of yours get to takin' an interest in us?'

'What you talkin' woman?' his voice rose, 'I tole ya – tonight we takes it easy. Just the strippin'.'

'Yeah. An' what if they get to wonderin' how old she is?' She jerked a finger at Carrie, sitting quietly in the back with Lucille. 'An' what if they get to wonderin' 'bout the holes in her arms?'

Whitejack pulled the car abruptly off to the side of the road and brought it to a shuddering stop. He crossed his hands over his chest and stared straight ahead. 'I go out my way to please you, woman. You want to bitch my fuckin' head off we just gonna turn this here automobile round an' go right on back to the city.'

Gino paused in the entrance hall and took a quick glance at himself in a magnificent venetian mirror hanging on the wall. Hmmm . . . He didn't look bad at all . . . Certainly not out of place in his wing collar, and expensive tuxedo.

He looked over the setup. A bar occupied one wall of the hall. It was liberally stocked and attended by two barmen in stiff white jackets and striped trousers. Beyond the hall was a large living room with french windows leading out to a tented terrace. All around was the smell of big money. Gino took a deep breath and smiled. He liked the smell a lot.

'I say, aren't you drinking?' A girl had swooped down on him, a large girl with reddish curled hair.

'Ain't got around to it yet.'

She peered at him curiously. 'Delightful champagne. You simply must try some.'

'Yeh.' He edged away. He had no plans to get trapped by just any piece of gash. The talent in the place had to be seen to be believed. Aldo would split a gut if he got a load of the skirt around the joint. And all classy.

He grabbed a glass of champagne from a passing waiter. Leonora would look good here, she'd fit right in.

*Fuck Leonora.*

*He wished he had.*

Mustn't think about her. He had made himself a promise that he wouldn't. Wasted enough of his life being a mug about *her.*

Clementine noticed him the instant he walked out onto the tented terrace. 'Excuse me, Bernard,' she said to the distinguished theatrical impresario, 'but I have to greet a new boy.'

Bernard Dimes nodded agreeably and turned back to his elegant companion.

Clementine walked briskly across the terrace to discourage any of her guests from delaying her. She was right in front of Gino before he even noticed her, so intent was he on drinking in his surroundings.

'Do you like my house?'.she questioned softly.

He jumped, spilling some of the champagne from his glass. Quickly he recovered his swagger. 'Quite a joint.'

'Hardly a joint.'

'Yeh . . . well . . . er . . . it's a joint t'me.' His eyes jumped instinctively to her nipples. Yes. They were still on show. Never let up. He had never seen a woman with permanently erect nipples before.

She took his arm, 'I'm going to introduce you around.'

He felt out of his depth. He didn't want to be dragged through the place like some pet puppy. 'Sure, later.' He dislodged her grip on his arm and took a swig of champagne. He hated the stuff and grimaced.

She noticed and gestured for a waiter. 'Get Mr Santangelo a scotch,' she said, gently removing the champagne glass from his hand. 'I like your tuxedo, Gino,' she murmured, her deep green eyes exploring his.

'Yeh?' He felt like a chump. He had nothing to say to her. He had never in his life made small talk and he wasn't about to start now.

Esther Becker giggled girlishly and poked Senator Oswald Duke playfully in the stomach. 'I understand our surprise tonight is going to be naughty!' she gushed.

Oswald looked at her blankly. He had never really liked Esther Becker. He found her insincere and fatuous.

'I really don't know,' he said stiffly, 'it's Clementine's surprise.'

'Ah yes, you do always allow her to have *her* way don't you?' Esther batted weak blue eyes at him. 'So modern of you, Oswald, but then you do have such a very modern marriage.' She grinned, displaying truly awful teeth. 'I wish Gordon would allow *me* some freedom – just *think* of the things *I* could get up to, maybe even with you Ozzie!' she giggled naughtily.

Oswald had a horrible vision of a naked Esther Becker getting up to things with him. *Her* idea of naughty things. He visibly blanched.

Her grin widened, 'Who does Clemmie have hold of now?'

He followed her gaze across the terrace and observed his wife talking to some young dark-haired chap.

He offered Esther his arm, 'Shall we go and see, my dear?'

Gino had just accepted a hefty glass of scotch from the waiter, when Clementine murmured, 'My husband is coming over. Be nice to him, he can do you a lot of good.'

Gino was more than confused. She was standing next to him sending out silent signals of lust that even a dumb idiot couldn't mistake, and now she was going to introduce him to her husband. What *was* going on?

Before he could give the matter too much thought, the husband was upon them, and an unperturbed Clementine was handing out introductions like she hadn't a care in the world.

He decided that maybe he was reading her signals wrong.

'Delighted to meet you,' Senator Duke said, pumping away with his limp right hand, 'Clementine has spoken of you often.'

Often? Gino snatched his hand away and studied the skirt with the Senator. His eyes were immediately drawn to the floppy breasts encased in chiffon. What was it with these rich numbers? For some reason all of them were out to give a free show.

Clementine gave him a little shove, 'I want you to go with Oswald and get the business matters out of the way, then you can relax and have fun.'

'Quite,' agreed Oswald, 'we'll go to my study.'

Clementine and Esther watched them depart.

'Hmmm . . . ' observed Esther, 'and where did you find *him*.'

Clementine smiled. 'My secret.'

'Shee . . . it!' exclaimed Whitejack. 'Will y'all get a load of this place!'

Dolly was unimpressed by the fairy tale mansion up ahead. She had been to big houses before. She stared stoically to the front and said nothing.

Carrie was singing softly to herself and not taking much notice of anything.

Lucille felt she had better respond, 'Wow!' she enthused. 'It's wonderful!'

' 'Course it is, woman. Din't I tell y'all tonight was gonna be a *special* night?'

'You sure did!' Lucille replied, nudging Carrie. 'Look, hon, isn't it beautiful?'

Carrie glanced vaguely out of the window. Of course it was beautiful, she wouldn't have expected anything else. Everything was beautiful, didn't Lucille *know* that?

Dolly drummed her fingers on the dashboard. 'Where we supposed to go?' she asked impatiently. She just wanted to do the show and get the hell out. These rich parties were the worst – full of drunks and women. Whitejack didn't know from nothing. Dumb black man. He only saw it as a step up in life.

Senator Oswald Duke was a mug. Gino realized that immediately. He wasn't interested in any accounting, he just asked, 'How much do I owe you?' And when Gino told him – sticking an extra two hundred on for good luck – he paid in cash. Gino pocketed the money and felt flush. It was a wonder the rich managed to stay that way if they were all as dumb as the Senator.

'You know, Gino,' the Senator said, 'sometimes I need a small favor.'

'Yeh?'

'A matter that I can't personally be involved in.'

'Like what?'

'Oh,' the Senator waved his hand in the air vaguely, 'different things. Maybe someone owes me money . . . and needs a little persuasion to pay. Or perhaps a former employee threatens to blackmail me over some imagined doing. Trivial matters that affect all men in public office.' He paused, picked up a box of fine cigars from his desk, and offered one to Gino. 'If you were prepared to do the occasional favor for me, I would be more than happy to . . . say . . . advise you on your finances.'

'Huh?'

'I won't beat around the bush. You deal in bootleg liquor. Cash. Right?'

Christ! Maybe the old fart was in with the feds. He said nothing.

The Senator continued, 'Cash is a very valuable commodity – but there is not a lot you can do with it before the tax authorities are banging on your door asking questions.'

Yeh. That was true.

The Senator lit his cigar and stared at Gino meaningfully. 'I can make your money legitimate. Eventually – by doing that – I can make *you* legitimate. Are you interested?'

He nodded. He was interested.

Scott, the butler, materialized at Clementine's side. 'The er . . . entertainers have arrived, madame. I have put them in the blue guest room as you requested.'

Clementine nodded, her green eyes sparkling, 'Take them some refreshments, Scott.'

'Yes, madame.' The old butler bowed slightly, and retreated. He had seen some strange goings on in his time . . . But *this* group . . . He wondered if madame was aware of what a motley assemblage they were. He sighed deeply. She more than likely was. Mrs Duke was a strange one herself.

'Do tell,' Esther Becker insisted, 'Come on, Clemmie, don't be a meanie – tell me what the surprise is.'

Clementine smiled mysteriously, 'I won't reveal what it is. I will only say that it is disgustingly vulgar!'

Esther shivered ecstatically, 'How divine! I adore vulgarity!'

Clementine's eyes swept over Esther's jiggling bosoms, 'Yes dear, I know.'

Carrie dragged deeply on the reefer Whitejack handed her, loving the feel of the rich smoke filling up her lungs. It gave her a tremendous charge.

Dolly peered at herself moodily in the dressing table mirror.

Every platinum blonde curl in place. 'What time we go on?' she asked Whitejack.

He was in seventh heaven. He lay on the large double guest bed in his white suit and white patents and swigged from a full bottle of the finest scotch. 'Who cares woman?'

'I care,' snapped Dolly, 'we got a long drive back. An' you better make sure we get paid *'fore* we go on – not after.'

'You leave the business t'me,' he said, reaching for a smoked salmon canapé.

Business! He didn't know from shit!

The party was a success – as usual. Clementine stood back and watched her guests at play. Dinner was being served now. A succulent buffet table groaning with honey roasted hams, chicken, cold turkey, beef and whole fresh salmons.

She had supervised the dinner herself, making out the menus, ordering the finest cuts of meat, and finally flitting in and out of the kitchen while her two cooks and their assistants, prepared everything. It was indeed satisfying to see the food being devoured with such obvious pleasure. And after the food . . . the entertainment.

She smiled secretly to herself. A big blonde. A young black girl. And a midget! What a perfect combination! As soon as Oswald had returned home from Arthur Stuyvesant's retirement dinner and told her about it, she had known at once that she simply must get them for her next big party. She licked her lips in anticipation.

This would be the most talked about party of the year!

Free from the Senator, Gino wandered out onto the terrace. Before he had time to take a breath the large girl with the reddish curled hair was dogging his footsteps. 'Who *are* you?' she demanded, 'one of Clemmie's gangster friends?'

*One of Clemmie's gangster friends!* 'Hey,' he said, 'wanna fuck?'

She blushed the color of a ripe tomato, 'How *dare* you!'

He was enjoying himself. 'No?'

'I think you are absolutely disgusting!'

He noticed that she made no move to leave his side. 'Wassamatta? Doncha like t'fuck?'

Her eyes widened and her long nose quivered indignantly. But still she made no move. 'You are a sick man,' she said firmly, 'saying revolting things like that to a lady.'

'Didn't realize you was no lady.' He saw Clementine, and instantly became bored with the conversation. 'See ya, kid,' he waved cheerily, and made his way over to Clementine and the group of people she was talking to. Suddenly he realized that one of them was Charlie Lucania. Jeeze! Several flashes darted through his mind at once. Like – what the hell did she need *him* for bootleg if she was friendly with Lucania. Like – wasn't this something – him and Lucania at the same party.

'Ah Gino,' Clementine said, 'I'd like you to meet some friends of mine.'

He noted Lucania's look of surprise, and he drew himself up full height, 'Hey – Charlie,' he said, patting the taller man on the arm as though they were old friends, 'how's it going?'

Scott handed Whitejack the sealed envelope and turned to go.

'Old man!' Whitejack snapped sharply. 'Not s'fast. I gotta count it.'

Scott sniffed disapprovingly. 'I can assure you . . . sir, it is all there.'

Whitejack narrowed his eyes, 'So then y'aint gonna mind if I check it out.'

'Certainly, sir.' He stood stiffly by the door while Whitejack ripped open the envelope and proceeded to count the crisp new hundred dollar bills.

Carrie sidled across to him and started into a glassy eyed bump and grind routine. Lucille went over, took her arm, and drew her away with a soothing, 'Not yet hon.' The big blonde woman sitting by the dressing table snorted in exasperation.

Scott cast his eyes towards the ceiling and made a mental note to tell the housekeeper to have this room fumigated. The smell these four people had managed to conjure up was disgraceful.

Esther Becker attached herself to Bernard Dimes and his woman companion. 'God knows what surprise Clemmie has thought up this time!' she exclaimed, tucking her arm through Bernard's as they made their way into the ballroom at the back of the house. 'She *said* it's something naughty! Can't imagine what, can you?'

Bernard Dimes shook his head and wished that he was at home in bed. He had the beginnings of a cold and he didn't *need* one of Clementine Duke's parties. Not that her parties weren't wonderful affairs. They were. But you had to be fit to attend them, and Bernard Dimes felt dreadful. He was a tall man in his mid-thirties, slightly balding, with thin features, and a pencil moustache. He was a theatrical producer of repute, and Esther Becker and her husband were heavy investors in his shows. Because of this he didn't shake Esther's arm away from his as he wished to. Instead he smiled and nodded and pretended to be having a wonderful time. Bernard Dimes was a rich man, but one lesson he had learned early on in life was that you *never* invested in your own productions.

'I want to talk to you after the entertainment,' Clementine whispered in Gino's ear, 'So don't go away, will you?'

He had no intention of going anywhere.

She squeezed his arm and gazed around with pleasure as the ballroom filled up with her guests. The whole thing was so exciting!

Gino was in a real good mood. Coming face to face with Lucania like that. Equals. And Lucania throwing a cordial greeting his way. Too fuckin' much!

And meeting Lucania's dame. A six foot redheaded showgirl. Wait 'til Aldo got an earful – he'd never believe it!

And the stuff with Senator Duke. Taking their money and investing it. Making it legitimate. Of course it would need checking out. But Gino reckoned he was too sharp to get himself conned. And anyway – the old guy certainly didn't need his money – he was quite obviously rolling.

The scattered tables around the ballroom were filling up. 'Excuse me,' Clementine breathed to Gino, 'I'll be right back.'

Whitejack stood behind the curtain and heard the buzz of excitement coming from the other side. He grinned and pinched Dolly on her fat ass. 'Hear that fuss, mama?'

She smoothed her red satin dress over her ample form. 'I hear it, black man. One number, that's all. Just the strip – nuthin' else. You did tell 'em that, didn't you?'

His eyes flashed wildly, 'Who I have t'tell woman? That cracker?' he indicated Scott who stood a safe distance from them. 'We bin paid. We do what *we* want.'

'Just you remember that.' She pointed at the Victrola set up in the corner. 'One record only.' She spun around to face Carrie and Lucille and was shocked to see Carrie visibly slumping. 'Lookit her,' she hissed, 'she look ready t'go t'sleep!'

'Don't worry, woman. I got me a little blow of coke t'give her just 'fore she go on. She be fine.'

Dolly frowned, then poked Lucille hard in the ribs. 'You

watch her,' she muttered sharply, 'an' remember – one number an *off*.'

'Sure, Dolly,' Lucille replied affably. The big woman frightened her. 'Just follow me when I get on,' she whispered to Carrie. 'Everything'll be fine.'

Carrie nodded blankly, her eyes glazed. She had no idea where she was or even who she was. She felt like she was just about ready to shut her eyes and float off to some place where nobody could ever bother her again.

Clementine peered into the curtained off section of the ballroom and came eyeball to eyeball with Whitejack.

He threw her what he thought was a charming smile.

She was startled. No one had told her about the six foot two inch negro with teeth like slabs of concrete and a totally bald polished head.

She nodded briskly, her eyes skimming quickly over the three females who were quite the oddest trio she had ever seen. 'Whenever you are ready,' she said.

'Ma'am, we is *always* ready,' Whitejack replied, his grin almost splitting his face in two.

She nodded again and retreated. What characters! Even better than she had anticipated.

Whitejack smacked his lips, 'Mama! Mama! Mama! You get a load of the je . . . uuuls on that woman?'

Dolly tossed her curls and ignored his comment, 'Let's get on an' out of here, 'fore you start kissin' the hem of her ass.'

He glared at her, then extracted a small packet of white powder from his pocket and a hundred dollar bill. Deftly he rolled the banknote, poured the white powder into the funnel it made, and beckoned to Carrie. 'C'mon t'daddy little girl, c'mon an' get your nose candy.'

Carrie stared at him blankly. Dolly gave her a shove.

Whitejack held the banknote to her nose and automatically she inhaled, sniffing deeply. 'There you go, girl,' he crooned, 'that happy dust gonna take y'on a real great snow ride.'

He turned to the Victrola and started the loud honky tonk music. Then he pushed Carrie through the curtain.

She staggered slightly in her spike heeled shoes, and just for a moment it looked as if she would fall. But then she recovered her balance, and without even starting to dance she began to remove her dress.

'Shee . . . it!' groaned Whitejack, peering through a chink in the curtain. 'She'll be finished 'fore she's even started.' He grabbed Lucille. 'Get your ass out there an' make her *dance*!'

He almost hurled Lucille through the curtain. She was greeted with shrieks of laughter – mostly female. And she immediately understood what Dolly had been complaining about. A mixed audience was different. The women – secure in their jewels and furs – were hostile, mean and spiteful.

Carrie already had her dress off, and her hands were reaching behind her to undo the lace brassiere when Lucille hissed, 'Dance, please – *for God's sake dance.*'

Carrie got the message, listlessly she began to sway. Lucille moved her tiny body vigorously in time to the raucous honky tonk. They made the oddest couple possible.

The audience laughed in embarrassment and disbelief.

Clementine felt a hot flush sting her cheeks. This wasn't entertainment. This was awful. What was wrong with the black girl? She looked like she might collapse at any moment. And the midget couldn't dance to save her life.

'Really, Clemmie,' whispered Esther, 'what *is* this supposed to be?'

She smiled tightly, 'It gets better.'

'I should hope so! This is pathetic.'

Clementine started to simmer with fury. Five hundred dollars for *this*. She had been conned. Wait until she got hold of Oswald. Was he mad? Telling her what a wonderful entertainment this was.

Then Dolly came on. Big blonde Dolly who knew a thing or two about taking over a room. She saved the situation somewhat with her genuine burlesque routine. At least she could *move*.

'This is disgusting,' Bernard Dimes whispered to his ladyfriend. 'Clementine must have taken leave of her senses. Surely this is only suitable for a drunken stag evening?' He frowned. There was something disturbingly familiar about the pathetic black girl . . . Somehow he felt that he had seen her before . . .

Now all three of them were going into the strip. First the brassiere, then the rolled garters, then the stockings, one at a time, then the panties.

Gino glanced around him. All these rich fancy dudes watching three whores he wouldn't give carfare to. Where the hell had Mrs Duke come up with them?

He stared at naked flesh and felt absolutely nothing except

boredom. Lighting up the cigar the Senator had handed him earlier, he took a sidelong glance at Clementine. She seemed tense.

The black girl was near their table now. She had taken it all off, and her big knockers didn't match the rest of her skinny body. She was taking off her second stocking when she fell. Like a stone she dropped to the ground, legs splayed obscenely open.

'Oh my good God!' Clementine exclaimed.

A ripple of embarrassed laughter rang around the room.

The honky tonk music kept going. The big blonde kept going. The midget was about to stop – but one frosty glance from the blonde made her continue to dance.

Gino leaped up quickly and grabbed the black girl under the arms and dragged her toward the door. Couldn't just leave her lying there. Scott met him at the door, and together they lifted her into the hall. She was out cold.

'Is there a doctor around?' Gino demanded. 'She don't look so good to me.'

'I expect there is a doctor amongst the guests,' Scott said stiffly, trying to avert his eyes from the naked girl lying at his feet.

'Let's get her to a bedroom,' Gino decided, taking off his new dinner jacket and covering her with it.

'I'll have to ask madame . . . ' Scott began.

'I said, let's get her to a bedroom.' His eyes were hard and bleak. They held an expression you didn't argue with.

Simultaneously they lifted the unconscious girl and carried her up the stairs and into the blue guest bedroom where they unloaded her onto the bed. Perspiration beaded Scott's forehead.

'You'd better go find a doctor now,' Gino ordered.

'I'll see what Mrs Duke wishes to do, sir,' Scott replied disdainfully. He was not about to start taking orders from this . . . this . . . person.

'Yeh? Well you'd better fuckin' hurry, 'cos if this girl don't get a doctor soon she is gonna be one dead girl. Tell *that* to Mrs Duke an' see what she says.'

Scott hurried off.

Gino regarded the lifeless girl. He picked up her arm to feel for a pulse, and it was then that he noticed the track marks. Little red puffs of skin with tiny punctures and bruising. Her pulse was disturbingly slow. He held open one of her eyelids and the pupil was wild and dilated. This girl was in bad shape. And she was only a kid – couldn't be more than sixteen or seventeen.

Someone had been feeding her drugs and sending her out to strip for a living. Gino felt the anger begin to burn in his gut. He hated to see a young girl used in this fashion.

Where the fuck was the doctor?

Whitejack groaned when Carrie fell, but he kept the music going and was relieved when someone dragged her out of the way and the act kept right on moving.

A smattering of applause heralded the finale, and a naked Dolly hurled her way behind the curtain and spat, 'You one dumbass nigger. What we gonna do now?'

Whitejack did not take kindly to being called a nigger unless it was a brother or sister did the calling. 'Shut your fat mouth white trash!' he snarled. 'An' get dressed. We'll grab Carrie an' get moving'.'

'Fine with me,' sneered Dolly, pulling her panties on.

'This is Doctor Reynolds,' Clementine said, hurrying into the room with a grey haired man.

Gino stood back from the bed. 'It don't look too good t'me doc.'

'Are you a doctor too?' Doctor Reynolds inquired mildly.

'Only when there ain't anyone else around.'

Clementine put a steady hand on his arm. 'Let's wait outside,' she murmured quietly.

Gino threw the doctor a hard look. 'She's a dope head,' he said roughly, 'take a look at her arm.'

Clementine led him outside. She sighed, 'This has to be the most awful party I've ever given.'

'Aw c'mon. Party's good – you didn't know you was gonna get stuck with them crummy strippers. Whacha think? That they was dancers?'

'I *knew* they were strippers. I *thought* they were good strippers. I was *told* they were an excellent entertainment. I'm just so . . . embarrassed. I'll be a laughing stock.'

'Bullshit.'

Her hand tightened on his arm. 'That's what I like about you. You're so direct and honest.'

Her green eyes were sending out signals again and he wanted to respond. 'Clementine . . . ' he began.

'Where's my baby sister?' a loud voice demanded, and up the stairs and into view came Whitejack, Dolly and Lucille, with Scott trailing behind.

Gino blocked the door to the guest bedroom, 'She your sister?' he asked rudely, checking Whitejack out and knowing him for what he was.

'Sure is,' blustered Whitejack, 'an' I wanna see her.'

'The doctor is with her, Mr . . . ?' Clementine trailed off questioningly.

Whitejack did not bother to supply her with a name. 'She don't need no doctor,' he said brusquely, 'she just gets these faintin' fits now an' then. Nothin' to worry 'bout . . . ' He attempted to pass by Gino.

'Mrs Duke said,' Gino intoned coldly, 'that the doctor is with her. So wait.'

They locked eyes, then Whitejack shrugged. 'Sure, sure. Only it's a waste of everyone's time. We just gotta put her in the car an' take her home to mama an' she'll be as good as new tomorrow.'

'Yeh,' said Gino, 'ready for another trip.'

'Huh?' puffed Whitejack.

Dolly intervened. 'Whyn't I just take a peek at her, get our things, an' we can come back for her tomorrow.'

Gino nodded. The big blonde was smart. She sensed trouble and wanted a fast out.

'You can't leave her *here*!' exclaimed Clementine.

Gino looked at her in surprise. 'Why not?' he asked. 'If the kid's too sick to travel you gonna throw her out on the street?'

'Her brother wants to take her home.'

'Her brother shit.'

Whitejack said menacingly, 'I don't know who you are but if you—'

Dolly interrupted him, grabbing his arm, 'We'll wait in the car. Don't want no fights or nothin'.'

She dragged him down the stairs, Lucille followed, Scott behind her to see them safely on their way.

Clementine was perplexed. 'What *is* going on, Gino?'

'They're leavin'. Fast.'

'Why?'

' 'Cos any minute now your doctor friend is gonna be yellin' all hell 'bout dope and underage an' all kinds a things they could go to jail for.'

'You mean they drugged her?'

'I should think so.'

*'His own sister?'*

'C'mon Clementine, don't be dumb. She's his sister like I'm your brother.'

She was quiet for a minute. 'Oh, I see.'

They waited in silence until the doctor emerged.

'The girl is a drug addict,' he said flatly, 'she's been overdosed. We'll need to get her to a hospital immediately.'

'Oh dear!' exclaimed Clementine. 'Someone fetch Oswald, he'll know what to do.'

'It ain't complicated,' Gino said, 'just call an ambulance.'

'We can't do that! Can you imagine the publicity? Doped girl at Senator's weekend party. It's impossible.'

Gino nodded. She had a point.

'Look here,' Doctor Reynolds said testily, 'the girl is very sick. She must be hospitalized.'

'I'll take her,' Gino decided.

'But if you take her to the hospital won't they think that you had something to do with her condition?' Clementine asked.

'Let me worry about that,' he replied, 'c'mon, let's get her out to my car.'

'Thank you,' Clementine whispered gratefully, 'you have made a decision you will never regret.'

# Wednesday, July 13th, 1977, New York and Philadelphia

'I think I'm hallucinating,' Lucky groaned. 'Either that or I'm going fucking mad! I keep on seeing a big comfortable bed and a cold glass of orange juice.' She moved around on the elevator floor. 'And my ass is killing me! How's yours?'

Steven didn't reply.

'Fine thank you!' Lucky mimicked his voice. 'Of course it is! Your ass is probably made out of rawhide. God forbid *you* should complain about anything.' She waited for him to say something.

He didn't.

'I wonder,' she continued, 'if I could get elevator sores — y'know – like bedsores or something.'

Still the silence.

'Why won't you talk to me you sonofabitch?'

More silence.

'You're an asshole, you know that?' She stood up and stretched. Gotta keep fit. Christ. Is this what they did in solitary confinement in jail? No wonder they had fucking riots.

She touched her toes once, and then sat down again, exhausted. She had discarded all her clothes and bunched them up so that she had something to sit on. Ha! How about the scene in the morning when they were rescued. What an eyeful for the fire department or police or whoever came to get them. 'NUDE WOMAN FOUND IN ELEVATOR WITH BLACK MAN.' Or better still 'LUCKY SANTANGELO, DAUGHTER OF THE NOTORIOUS GINO SANTANGELO – DISCOVERED NAKED WITH BLACK MAN IN ELEVATOR.'

Gino. Fuck it. Why had she thought of him?

*Because he's coming back that's why. And how the hell can I do anything about it trapped in a fucking elevator?*

The screaming boy burst into the kitchen, obscenities still spewing forth from his mouth. 'I'm gonna find ya cocksucka! I'm gonna chop off ya balls an' use 'em for tennis practice!'

Dario held the lethal kitchen knife straight ahead of him in the darkness, and remained crouched in his hiding place.

'C'mon out faggot. I know ya're here, I know it.' A manic laugh. 'I'm gonna slit ya up like a side of beef, an' then I'm gonna roast yer ass an' eat it up!'

Carrie did not draw a second glance standing outside the meat market on 125th Street. She stood there for at least an hour, a bedraggled figure.

Gradually she realized that nobody was going to approach her. She was alone, and was going to stay alone. The power failure must have changed the blackmailer's plans.

Several fires had been started along the street, the fire trucks were already roaring up, sirens screaming. An unruly crowd had gathered, and as the firemen attempted to deal with the flames, they were pelted with bottles and tin cans.

Carrie felt sick to her stomach. She saw a young girl pulled into an alleyway by a group of boys. She saw an elderly man, blood pouring from a cut on his head, stagger by with a heavy stereo set. She saw two men snatch it from him and beat him to the ground.

She ran.

Once rid of the girl, Gino picked up the phone.

'What number are you calling?' the operator inquired.

He began to give Costa's number in New York, then changed his mind. Better not to call. Why alert the feds to where he was? More than likely they were tapping Costa's phone. 'Forget it,' he said to the operator.

He stood up, unzipped his pants and took them down for the second time that night. He couldn't help smiling. Who would have thought that Gino the Ram would be turning down a naked broad? His old nickname. Hadn't been called that for years.

He put on his pajamas, placed his gun under the pillow, and switched on TV.

Johnny Carson.

He settled back to watch.

Johnny Carson.

Now he *really* felt like he was back in America.

'Hey,' mumbled Lucky. 'Whatcha think? You think we could *suffocate* in this sweat box? 'Cos I sure as hell *feel* like I am.'

'There's plenty of air, it's just that it's hot air.'

'Ah ha! You're talking again. Thank Christ for that!'

He sighed and shifted his position on the elevator floor.

*Yes Lucky, my ass is sore and my back is stiff and my legs ache and I want to piss and I'm so thirsty I could kill.*

He said, 'Why do you think that talking's going to help? It's obvious we have nothing in common. I'm uncomfortable enough, I don't need stupid conversation.'

'Thanks a lot! It takes two to argue you know.'

'Which is exactly why I have stayed quiet.'

'Don't you like me?' she demanded.

'Lady, I don't even know you, and I don't think I want to.'

'Why?'

'Here we go again.'

She yawned. 'You *do* know me.'

'What do you mean?'

'I know you.'

'How?'

She smiled in the darkness and affected a black street accent, 'I can smell your balls, man.'

She had succeeded in embarrassing him. There was a frosty silence.

She twitched her nostrils. It was sweaty as hell in the elevator, his *and* hers. In fact it *did* stink. 'I'm sorry,' she said softly, 'I'm going stir crazy. How long has it been now?'

He didn't answer.

Dario held his breath. The boy was near. Within touching distance. His hands, clutching the carving knife, were damp with perspiration.

The boy moved slowly now, sensing he was close to his prey. He had quietened his screaming and sing-songed softly, 'Hey mothafucka . . . cocksucka . . . asskissa . . . '

Dario was ready for him.

Carrie ran right into the arms of a cop who grabbed her roughly, 'Where you runnin' nigger?'

She hadn't been called nigger in more years than she cared to remember. She stared up into his big face, brought her arm back, and whacked him across the cheek as hard as she could.

He was taken by surprise. 'Well I'll be a son-of-a-bitch.'

She wriggled free and ran again. But she was no longer a young girl, and he caught her easily.

'I'm bookin' you, bitch!' he said, fastening cuffs on her. 'Assault of an officer on duty.'

'You don't understand,' she gasped, 'I'm Mrs Elliott Berkely.'

'So what? I'm Dolly Parton – don't mean I shit sugar.'

He pushed her over to a police wagon standing by the curb and bundled her in. It was already full of complaining blacks, and there was no room to sit. She stood shoulder to shoulder, thigh to thigh, with her fellow prisoners.

'Fuggin' disgraaace,' screamed a very tall man. 'All I took was a pair a' sneakers. Some them cats rippin' off sixty dollar patents. Me – all I took was fuggin' sneakers!'

A beautiful young Puerto Rican girl swayed, her eyes closed, 'Por que?' she kept on muttering, 'Por que?'

Carrie felt like asking the same question.

At approximately 2.30 a.m. there was a hammering on the door of Gino's hotel suite in Philadelphia.

He came awake slowly, wondered where the hell he was, groped for his watch, pulled on his silk robe, pocketed his gun, and went to the door. 'Who's there?' he demanded suspiciously, thinking – *What the hell am I doing here? Alone in some lousy hotel in Philadelphia.*

He was back in America now. You don't fuck around on your own in America. Not when you're Gino Santangelo you don't.

# Gino 1934

Clementine Duke was right. Gino never had cause to regret the decision he made that fateful October night in 1928 at Senator and Mrs Duke's party. It was a major turning point in his life.

Now, six years later, as he lay on the bed in the blue guest room, once again in the Westchester mansion, all the memories came flooding back.

He had rushed the little black girl to the hospital, dumped her there, then made a quick getaway before anybody got around to questioning him. What happened to her after that was her problem -- he had enough lame dogs in his life.

Clementine Duke had been truly grateful. She had invited him to her townhouse the following week to discuss the matter. Dinner, she had said. But when he got there dinner was not on her mind.

He would always remember that evening. Just the two of them, no servants around, no Senator. Candles lighting the garden room, and incense burning.

Clementine Duke in a filmy white robe. Those goddamn nipples of hers staring at him. She had held his hand tightly and in a low voice said, 'I suppose you know my husband is a homosexual.'

'A what?'

'A homosexual. A man who does not get excited at the thought of my milky white thighs gripping him round his somewhat portly belly. On the contrary -- he likes men. He likes tight flat bottoms. Preferably young. Preferably negro.'

'You mean he's a fairy?'

'Ah, your street language is so much more descriptive.'

'Jeeze!' Gino whistled through closed teeth, 'You gotta be kiddin'. Fairies don't get married.'

'Oh no? You'd better tell my husband. I think he'd be inclined to argue the point with you.'

'Why are you tellin' me this?'

'Why do you think?' And her green eyes narrowed in a cat like fashion as she took his hand and guided it to her breasts.

He had needed no further invitation. After all – under the rich and classy trappings Clementine Duke was only another broad. He worked her over good. Right there in the candle lit room.

She sighed and moaned and growled his name over and over at her moment of climax. Afterwards she smiled and said, 'I knew you would be wonderful, a little rough, but then you are still so young.'

He was insulted. He had never had any complaints before. 'Hey, whacha mean – rough?'

'I'll show you.' And she had. She had taken him step by step through everything they had done before. Only this time she made him do it all very very slowly, very very softly.

'Instead of sucking my nipples – lick them,' she suggested, 'see how good it is when I do it to you.' She was right. 'When you are inside me, slow down; relax, you're not pumping gas, you're indulging your sensuality.'

'My what?'

'Your lust. Your carnal desires.'

'Hey – talk English.'

She laughed softly. 'It seems to me you've become so intent on pleasing the woman that you've forgotten about your own pleasure.'

'I get pleasure . . . ' he objected.

She shushed him. 'Of course you do. One wild orgasm. I want your climax to last as long as my titillation.'

He pinched her smooth white ass, 'I don't understand a word you're talkin' about.'

'You will, you will.'

And he did Eventually.

Months later, their lovemaking was so good that he could hardly wait for their weekly meetings. He knew what she meant then. He even learned some of the words. Salacious. Hedonistic. Carnal. Their lovemaking encompassed all of those feelings. Good as he had thought he was, he had only been playing before.

Coming face to face with Senator Duke after making love to his wife gave Gino an attack of the guilts.

'Don't be so ridiculous,' Clementine scolded. 'He doesn't care – he has his own interests. Besides, he likes you – thinks you're shrewd. And as long as we are discreet . . . ' To that end she had insisted he keep Cindy as a live-in girlfriend. 'I could never be jealous of her,' she had said dismissively upon meeting the girl, 'keep her around, at least I know you'll get breakfast every morning.'

He got more than breakfast. Cindy had made herself indispensable in his life. She cooked and cleaned, kept his clothes immaculate. Drove him around when he needed her to. And – most important of all – kept a neat handwritten record of his many business transactions. Apart from all of this she was still as pretty as ever.

In the course of six turbulent years Gino Santangelo had risen to the top. With a little help from his friends.

Charlie Lucania – now nicknamed Lucky Luciano on account of a one way ride that he came back from, his surname changed for easier pronunciation.

Enzio Bonnatti, who had fled Chicago and settled in New York right after the notorious Saint Valentines Day massacre on February 14th, 1929. Seven hoods had been lined up in a garage on Chicago's North Clark Street and then machine gunned to death by a rival gang. Some said that Enzio was responsible and had got out before he was hit with retributions – but this was never proved.

Aldo Dinunzio. A hard conscientious worker with just the right amount of larceny in his blood. Married now to Barbara Riccaddi, who nagged the shit out of him. Father of two babies, a third on the way.

And Senator Oswald Duke. The most important friend of all.

Without the Senator who knew what would have happened to Gino Santangelo? Just another hood making his living bringing in bootleg. Small time stuff. Pissing away his profits on suits and cars, parties and women.

Senator Duke made Gino's money legitimate as he had promised. He took a few thousand here – a few thousand there – and invested it in good solid stock.

Gino was uneasy. He liked his money in cash – in a bank box – where he could get his hands on it.

'Trust Oswald,' Clementine had insisted, 'he'll make you rich.'

Gradually, as he watched his money grow in the pages of the Wall Street Journal, he began to believe her. He even argued when, in the spring of 1929, Oswald insisted on selling out and re-investing abroad.

With anger Gino watched his sold out stocks go even higher. 'Shit!' he complained to the Senator. 'Why'd ya havta sell?'

'Wait and you will see,' Oswald replied.

And sure enough, on October 29th, 1929, the stock market crashed, bringing down many men and their fortunes. It also heralded the beginning of the great American depression.

Only Gino wasn't depressed. Gino was in very good shape indeed.

From that day on whatever the Senator advised financially, he did. Ot course there were the favors he was asked to do along the way. Nothing serious. The Senator would place his hand lightly on his arm and say, 'Take care of the matter personally, dear boy. Be sure of that.' So Gino was.

The matters ranged from threatening a young black jazz musician with instant castration if he ever contacted the Senator again, to roughing up some two bit newspaper reporter who was planning an exposé article Oswald did not want published.

The favors were so far and few between that Gino gave them no thought. He didn't mind *what* the old man asked him to do. After all, he was screwing the guy's wife *and* making money. What more could anyone ask?

Enzio Bonnatti had made his move to New York at just the right time. With the collapsing stock market and the ensuing panic and fear, the so-called Roaring Twenties were staggering to an end. Money, once plentiful, was now in short supply. And speakeasies were closing their doors all over town. The result of this was gangland feuds the like of which had never been seen before. There was not enough money to go round, and what there was everyone wanted.

The main war was between two gangsters of the old school – 'Mustache Petes' as they were known. Guiseppe Joe the Boss Masseria, and Salvatore Maranzano.

Lucky Luciano, Enzio Bonnatti, Vito Genovese, and Frank Costello – the young bloods, stood back and watched, ever hopeful that the two men would wipe each other out.

Gino hovered on the periphery. He was Enzio's right arm. Later, his partner.

The Castellammarese War raged for several years, finally culminating with the killing of Masseria in April, 1931, and Maranzano a few months later.

With the old 'Mustache Petes' out of the way Lucky Luciano was ready to take over. And right along with him were his friends and associates.

Luciano wanted to change the face of organized crime and form a nationwide syndicate that could operate together in peace and harmony. He formed a commission of mobsters and appointed himself chairman. But he was at pains to point out that all members would have an equal vote.

Gino, a member of the commission, liked his style. He admired his strength, cunning, and business head. His ethics he didn't give much thought to.

'The man is à killer,' Clementine told Gino one day. 'He *arranged* for that Masseria character to be murdered. He sat and had lunch with him, and then went to the mens room while his hired assassins came in and butchered the man. He should be in jail. I refuse to have him to my parties anymore.'

Gino couldn't help smiling. Clementine's idea of who was in or out depended on whether she invited them to her parties or not. However, he enjoyed his conversations with her. She sure knew a lot for a skirt. You could learn plenty from a woman like Clementine. Even more from her husband.

Oswald informed Gino long before prohibition was officially repealed in December, 1933. By that time he was well into other businesses anyway. Gambling, loansharking, the numbers racket. He refused to touch prostitution and drugs in spite of pressure from Enzio. Because of this conflict they split their interests in January, 1934 and went their separate ways. They parted the best of friends. Aldo elected to stay with Gino who appreciated this mark of loyalty. They worked well together, they always had.

Gino's old enemy, Pinky Banana, had been involved in a bad contract job and had to get out of the city. This relieved Aldo no end, who had always imagined Pinky creeping up to get his revenge one dark night.

Gino's businesses were all profitable in spite of the depression. The numbers racket appealed to everyone from a cab driver to a bank manager. It was a sure fire way of having a thrill. You bet your dime or quarter on a number – and if that number came up you could win two or three hundred dollars. Even more depending on your initial stake.

Gino called it mugs money. And it rolled in.

He had over fifty runners operating in three different neighborhoods collecting bets from customers. They took the money to five central collecting points – usually stores with a special room in the back where the bet was recorded and the cash stored ready for pick-up by Gino's bagman. A lucrative business indeed.

Apart from the money Gino handed over to Senator Duke for investment, he had also accumulated safe deposit boxes crammed full of cash in many of the city's banks.

He realized that he couldn't spend his money without showing a source of income, so early in 1933 he bought himself a night club with money he claimed to have won at the racetrack. By the time prohibition was repealed the place had been renovated, and with a brand new liquor license, Gino was ready to open with a splash. He called the place 'Clemmies' and it was an instant hit.

He had finally persuaded Vera to give up whoring and come to work for him behind the hat check counter. She had agreed – it gave her more of a steady income to save for Paulo's return. He had received a five year sentence for assault with a deadly weapon after only a week out of jail. A week during which he hadn't even bothered to visit her. 'He musta bin busy,' she insisted, now firmly convinced that Paulo was the love of her life instead of a violent petty criminal.

'You're nuts, waitin' for him,' Gino insisted.

'You live your life, I'll live mine,' Vera had replied primly.

Clementine, of course, loved the fact that 'Clemmies' was such a huge success. Her appearances triggered off visits by most of New York's social set, and as owner and front man Gino became a minor celebrity. Women adored him. Clementine was not thrilled by this new development. It was *her* suggestion that he marry Cindy. 'The girl knows everything about you. With federal tax agents sniffing around you simply must protect yourself. Marry the girl – that way she cannot testify against you should they ever get anything on you.'

It *was* a smart idea. 'Yeh,' Gino had said, 'I think I will.'

So here he was, in the blue guest bedroom in the Duke's Westchester mansion, lying on the bed, smoking a cigar, waiting to get married.

Time had not withered cute little Cindy. It had put a sparkle in her eye and jewelry on every available appendage. Diamond Lil had nothing on Cindy. One thing about Gino. He was a generous bastard. And so he should be. How many live-in girlfriends would put up with his two-timing activities? Not many, that was for sure.

OK so she had moved in with him of her own free will. But that didn't mean he had to *lie* to her. Pretend he was engaged, when all the time his San Francisco flower was married to another guy. Cindy had acquired *that* information when the baby was born. *Ten* months after she had moved in with Gino. Costa had telephoned the news. 'Tell Gino, Leonora gave birth to a baby girl.'

She couldn't wait. 'Oh Gino sweetie, your fiancée had herself a baby today. I guess the engagement is off, huh?'

He had turned white, and without a word stalked from the apartment. They never discussed it. But it was obvious he was not about to be a married man.

Cindy continued to make herself a strong part of his life. She knew he was on the way up and she planned to accompany him. Which she had done. And very successfully too.

Now they were to be married. The final step. And she should be happy as a lark. But she wasn't. She was mean and miserable and in the black dumps.

Gino Santangelo was not about to become hers. He belonged lock, stock and cock to that fucking Duke bitch.

Costa Zennocotti knocked tentatively on the door of the blue guest bedroom.

'Yeh. Come in,' Gino yelled.

Balancing a tray that held two glasses, a bottle of white wine, and a dish of crackers, Costa entered.

Gino sat up. 'Hey – what's with the wine crap? I told you to get me a drink.'

'Mrs Duke said you were to have wine.'

'Fuck Mrs Duke.'

Costa put the tray on a table, 'That's what she said, I wasn't about to argue with her.'

Gino laughed. What was it about Clementine that inspired such awe and devotion in young men?

'So pour me a glass,' he said, inspecting his newly manicured nails, 'What you waitin' for?'

Costa obeyed. He had arrived in New York the previous day, flattered and delighted that Gino had elected he should be his best man. They had not seen each other since his trip East in 1928, and although they had corresponded, the change in his friend was quite startling. Costa could not quite place what the difference was – but it was there. Gino had that air of unshakable confidence that comes with age – not the twenty-eight years that he now was – but the confidence a successful man in his forties or fifties possesses. He was no longer the rough street kid. From the top of his head to the tip of his shoes he was groomed.

He had stopped plastering his jet black hair down with

grease. He had cut it short and allowed the natural curl to come through. Also he seemed to have grown taller. Costa didn't know it – but elevator lifts in his hand made shoes helped there.

He wore only the finest clothes. Tailored dark three piece suits, Italian silk imported shirts, fine cashmere sports clothes, Vicuna overcoats. Gone were the pin stripes and flashy colored shirts of earlier days.

Even the jewelry he wore was tasteful. A diamond stick pin in his tie. Solid gold cufflinks to match his expensive Cartier watch. And on his little finger a pinky ring – very simple – just one magnificent diamond solitaire.

Only the scar on his face belied his beginnings, that, and the hard black eyes which still made a flat statement of uncontrolled wildness lurking somewhere within.

Costa consulted his watch. 'Exactly half an hour left,' he said nervously. 'How do you feel?'

'Pretty good, kid.'

'Not nervous?'

'What's to be nervous about? I've been livin' with her six years.'

Costa nodded. Of course he had. Ever since Leonora married someone else . . .

As if reading his thoughts Gino asked casually, 'How's Leonora these days?'

Costa's left eye twitched, 'Just fine.' He didn't want to reveal the truth. That Leonora drank, screwed around, and spent no time at all with her baby daughter.

'And the kid? How old is she now?'

'Nearly six, pretty as a doll.'

A lump formed in Gino's throat, but his voice remained throwaway casual, 'Yeh. I bet. What's she called?'

'Maria.'

He stubbed out his cigar, 'Nice name.' He thought he might knock Cindy up immediately.

'Shouldn't you finish getting dressed?'

Gino stood up. 'You're right.' He squinted at Costa. The kid looked good. Clean cut. A typical Joe College who had completed three years at law school and graduated with honors. Now he was working in his father's office. 'You got a steady girl yet?'

Costa grimaced, 'Don't you read my letters?' he complained.

'Sure do. Wouldn't miss 'em.'

'Then how come you're asking me if I have a steady girl-friend? I wrote you six months ago that I was engaged to Jennifer Brierly.'

'That letter must've gotten lost in the mail. What's she like?'

'Jennifer. You met her. Leonora's friend when you came to stay that time. Remember?'

'Oh yeh . . . sure . . . *veree nice.*' He had totally blanked out on Jennifer whatsit. Couldn't remember her *at all.* 'When you goin' to do the big deed?'

Costa looked serious, 'I don't know. We have to wait until I establish myself. A year, maybe two.'

'Hey,' Gino nudged him slyly. 'You remember that cat house we went to, your first time wasn't it?' He started to laugh. 'I'll never forget the look on your face when you came out. You looked like you just discovered ice cream! I bet you never went back to *her* though.'

Costa grinned, 'I did!'

'Jesus Christ!'

A knock on the door interrupted their reverie. Costa opened up.

Clementine stood in the hallway, chic and elegant in a Chanel suit of pale pink with a black binding. 'May I come in?' she asked sweetly.

Costa jumped, 'Certainly, Mrs Duke.'

'Do call me Clementine,' she swept past him and over to Gino. 'Hello,' she said softly, taking his hand in hers. 'Is the bridegroom nearly ready?'

'For what?'

She licked her thin lips. 'For your wedding of course.'

'How long I got?'

'Twenty-five minutes exactly.'

'Hey, Costa,' Gino said casually. 'Do me a favor an' come back in twenty minutes. I got to have a private word with Clemmie.'

'Anything you say.' Costa threw Clementine an admiring look and exited.

'The kid loves you,' Gino stated mildly.

She walked over to the dressing table and inspected her perfect make-up in the mirror. 'He does?' she murmured dis-interestedly.

'You can bet on it.' He followed her to the dressing table and put his arms around her from behind. 'And so do I – in my way.' Slowly he started to rock back and forth against her body.

'You do?'

He continued to rock.

She felt his erect penis through her clothes, 'Gino!'

He was unbuttoning his trousers, 'I want to fuck you one more time while I'm still a single guy.'

'Don't be so silly! We don't have time. I'm all dressed. Not here anyway. It's impossible.'

'Nothing's impossible,' he said, fiddling with the hook on her skirt. 'You taught me that.'

Clementine realized he was not joking, 'This is ridiculous . . . ' she objected weakly.

'Yeh. Ain't it just?' He had her skirt off, and threw it on the bed. Then he was peeling down her pink lace french panties.

'Be careful of my make-up . . . my hair . . . '

'Bend over the table. I won't disturb a thing.'

She did as she was told, anticipation flooding her whole body. He entered her from behind. Slowly, luxuriously, as though they had all the time in the world.

'Ooooh . . . ' her breath fluttered, 'you certainly learned your lessons well . . . '

'I had a good teacher.'

And as he pumped away he thought about marriage, and Cindy, and having a kid.

And he thought about Leonora for the first time in months.

And when he came it was an explosion that shuddered through him wiping out all memories of the past.

Today was his wedding day. He wanted it to be a new beginning.


# Carrie 1928–1934

It was all a total blank: Doctors, nurses, hospitals. Faces. Voices.

Who cared about any of them? They could all burn in *hell* for all she cared.

'What's your name, dear?'

'Who are you?'

'How old are you?'

'Who did this to you?'

'What's your name?'

'Where do you live?'

'Where is your mother?'

'Who is your father?'

'How old are you?'

Questions. Questions. Questions. Until screaming and screaming finally drove them – the faceless ones – into silence.

The very next day it was the same old story.

And all the time her body aching, and retching, and moaning and stiffening.

Scream. Agonizing cramps. Scream again and again until finally, one day, they wrapped her in something white and stiff and took her away from the hospital.

Another world. A room where nobody cared if she screamed. tore at her hair, scratched at her face.

No questions.

Still the agony, the cramps, the feeling of impending torture.

She lived like an animal, grabbing at the food a uniformed guard brought her, stuffing lumps of bread down her raw throat. Drinking water like a dog, from a bowl fixed to the floor.

For two years she knew no reason. She was out of her head, her mind an absolute blank.

Then one night she awoke at 3 a.m. and it was quite clear to her that her name was Carrie. And why wasn't she at home with her family?

She ran to the barred door and called out for help. But nobody came.

She was confused and frightened. What had happened to her?

In the morning when the guard arrived with her food she hurried to greet him. 'What am I doing here?' she demanded, 'What is this place?'

The guard backed away. These dangerous psychopaths were a pain in the ass. You never knew what they would do next. 'Eat,' he commanded sharply, putting down the bowl.

'I don't want to eat,' she yelled, 'I want to go home.'

A few hours later the doctor came to see her. 'I understand we're talking.'

She widened her eyes, 'Of course I'm talking.'

'Who are you? What is your name?'

'My name is Carrie. I live in Philadelphia with my family. I am thirteen years old.'

'Thirteen?' the doctor's eyebrows shot up.

'Yes, thirteen,' she started to cry, 'and I want to go home. I want mama Sonny . . . I want my mama . . . '

They didn't release Carrie. They kept her. And now that she was no longer like a wild animal they put her to work. She cleaned rooms, scrubbed floors, cooked meals, and crept to her cot bed in a crowded ward at the end of the day where she collapsed, exhausted. And so the years continued to pass.

Once a month she saw the doctor.

'How old are you?'

'Thirteen.'

'Where do you live?'

'With my family in Philadelphia.'

There was no way they could let her out.

Carrie did not understand what was going on. She cried herself to sleep nights. She missed school, her brothers and sisters, her friends. Why were they keeping her in such an awful place?

There were mad people in the place. *Stark raving mad.* Carrie learned to stay away from them.

She was thirteen years old and she had to be careful who she mixed with.

# Gino 1937

'Hey – ' exclaimed Gino, 'you're really somethin' – you know that?'

The redheaded hostess named Bee was not about to fall. 'Mr Santangelo! You say that to *all* the girls!'

He threw up his hands in mock horror, 'Who? Me? You gotta be kiddin'!'

Bee allowed herself a smile, and tossed back her mane of truly wonderful red hair. 'You have a certain . .  reputation.'

'All good I hope.'

'Oh yes.'

'Glad to hear it . . . glad to hear it.' He stood up from behind his massive walnut desk and stretched. He wanted this girl but he wasn't going to jump through hoops. 'How long you been workin' for me Bee?'

She shivered. Was it cold? Or did she have the sudden horrors about getting fired? 'Three months, Mr Santangelo.'

'You like it here?'

'It's a nice club.'

'You had a raise yet?'

'Not yet.' So that was it. A raise or get fired.

'You want me to drive you home tonight and we'll discuss it?'

'Yes.'

He grinned. 'Yes, huh?' His eyes lazily scanned her from head to toe, 'How about yes please.'

'Yes please, Mr Santangelo.'

His grin widened. He was going to enjoy this one. That hair. That white white skin. And great breasts.

'Tell you what, come to my office at twelve o'clock.'

She turned to go.

'Oh, and Bee? Wear your hair up. Pin it on top of your head. Run along now,' he added dismissively, 'I got some calls to make.'

She left and he watched her big ass wriggle out the door. He liked big asses, something to grab hold of. Clementine's was nonexistant, and Cindy's was high and round and small – just like a boy's.

Cindy. Married to the broad for three long years, and not a sign of any kids on the way. It pissed him off. She swore she wasn't doing anything to prevent it, so why wasn't she knocked up?

Aldo padded into the office. Thirty-one years old and getting fat as a pudding.

'When you gonna drop some of that lard?' Gino said roughly.

'I like my food. Terrible thing.'

'You ever get hit by a bullet you'll melt in a pool of fat.'

'Can I help it if my Barbara is a wonderful cook?'

'What's happening?' Gino asked brusquely.

Aldo gave him a rundown.

He yawned. He wasn't cut out to sit behind a desk and scoop in the money. He liked a little action and excitement. The only place he got any action lately was with the broads he screwed. And yet – in a way he was fortunate. With Senator Duke behind him he was protected. He had friends in high places, and he moved easily amongst them. But having important and influential friends did not mean total protection. Lucky Luciano – head of the commission, had been sent to jail the previous year on a trumped up charge of pimping. Trumped up because Luciano had never actually been out on the streets

selling girls' bodies. He had headed a vast crime syndicate –
and one of the businesses involved had been organized prostitution. Anyway – the poor bastard had ended up in jail with
a harsh thirty to fifty year sentence. This had sent a shudder of
fear throughout the mobs. If Lucky Luciano could get sent up,
who next?

Gino liked to think that he couldn't be touched because
since splitting with Bonnatti, most of his dealings were legitimate anyway. He didn't deal in narcotics or prostitution. And
violence was not a part of his operation. A few threats here and
there by his enforcers seemed to keep business flowing
smoothly.

'You all set on the trip?' Aldo inquired.

'All set. Leave tomorrow morning. Cindy's out buying what
she didn't buy yesterday.'

'Broads! They sure can shop.'

'You're telling me.' Cindy cost him a fortune for clothes and
hairdos, jewelry and furs. A cheap wife she was not. But so
what? He could afford it. He was worth well over a million
dollars from his investments alone. Thanks to Senator Duke.
Thanks to Clementine.

He wanted out. Mrs Duke still looked terrific, but he had
just had enough.

She wasn't letting go easy. He made excuses. She gave him
an alternative time. He said he couldn't make it. She said when
could he?

He felt trapped. Here he was, thirty-one years old. He had a
wife. A mistress. A series of casual lays. Yet he was more
trapped than when he was sixteen years old and out on the
street alone.

He wanted something more. He did not know what.

'The trip to 'Frisco'll do you good,' Aldo remarked, easing
himself into a leather chair, 'you work too hard. You can't
even find time to come by the house for dinner. Barbara's
startin' to take it personal.'

'When I get back.'

'I'll hold you to that. Spaghetti and meatballs – my Barbara
makes the best,' he sighed and kissed the tips of his fingers, 'ah
. . . my wife is such a wonderful cook.'

Gino stared pointedly at his friend's gut bulging over the top
of his pants, 'I can see that.'

Aldo laughed self-consciously, 'A contented belly shows a
contented man.'

'Fat. Asshole.'

'Please!'

'Fat!'

A knock on the office door interrupted their joking.

'Yeh?' snapped Gino.

'Me, boss.' The voice was unmistakable. Jacob Cohen. Now known as Jake the Boy. Or mostly just The Boy, although he was now pushing twenty-four. He had received his nickname because of his early start in a life of crime. With Gino's hundred dollar loan to back him at the tender age of fourteen he had gone right to work. Stealing cars. Hit and run robberies. Audacious cons. 'Who did it?' outraged victims would question. 'The Boy,' was always the answer.

Gino had taken him on when he was sixteen. By the time he was twenty he was in charge of collecting for the numbers racket, with several very nice sidelines of his own.

'Come in.' Gino yelled. 'What's with the polite shit?'

Jake burst into the room smiling, 'Don't wanna interrupt you, boss. Understand the new rule is to knock first.'

'What new rule?'

Aldo looked flustered. 'I thought . .   ' he began, 'well it seemed like a good idea . . .'

'What the fuck,' Gino burst out laughing. A week previously Aldo had walked in while he was servicing the cigarette girl over his desk. 'I guess you're right.'

'If Cindy should arrive unexpectedly . . . or Mrs Duke . . . '

'I agree,' said Gino, still smiling. Maybe that's what he wanted – one or the other of them to catch him at it. Then he would be off the hook. Free.

Jake dumped a large bag filled with money on the desk. 'I think Gambino – y'know – the candy store on 115th is stealin'.'

Gino raised his eyebrows, 'You sure?'

Jake scratched his wiry head of hair, 'Sure enough. If it ain't him it's his old lady – she's the only other person gets near the money before it's collected.'

'Give him a warning. Just one.'

'I understand. boss.'

Gino stood up from behind his desk. 'I'm going away tomorrow, Jake. only for a week. Any problems – talk to Aldo.'

Jake glanced over at the fat man and nodded. Why was Gino demeaning him by telling him to talk to the creep. Everyone knew Dinunzio was chicken shit. Frightened of his own shadow. Why Gino kept him on was a mystery. He sat on his fat butt in the office and did fuck all. Oh yeah. He got off his ass to lock the money in the safe the workers brought in. Workers like *him*, Jake, the real guts behind the Santangelo operation.

'Everything else fine?' Gino questioned.

Jake scratched his head again and wondered if he had caught something crawly from his latest girlfriend. 'Everything's stupendous, boss.'

'Good. I'll see y'in a few days.'

Clementine Duke stared coldly at her husband. 'I do not believe what you are telling me.' Her voice was ice. 'How could you possibly be so stupid?'

Oswald gazed unseeingly out of his office window. His voice quavered, 'I've never tried to hide anything from you. You have always known what I was.'

She laughed sharply, 'Not always, Oswald. The way I recall it I waited two years before I found out the truth about you.' She flicked a Camel cigarette from a packet on his desk, lit it and said, 'So – do you have a . . . solution . . . for this . . . problem?'

'Gino Santangelo. He owes me a favor.'

She blew smoke towards the ceiling thoughtfully, 'This would be more than a favor.'

'I know. But he owes me everything he has. He'll do it.'

'You seem so sure . . .'

'He *has* to do it. If he doesn't I can destroy him.'

She licked her lips. In his own way Oswald was probably as ruthless as any street gangster. But then he had power – and enough of that could corrupt anyone. 'When will you ask him?' she breathed.

'The day he returns from San Francisco. The timing will be perfect.'

She nodded wordlessly. Since when did you require perfect timing to ask someone to commit murder?

Bee sat a respectable distance from Gino on the back seat of his black Cadillac sedan. Red drove the car, and Sideways Sam lounged in the front passenger seat.

Gino puffed on a cigar, filling the car with fumes about which no one complained.

Bee, her hair pinned neatly atop her head, felt as nervous as a kitten. She was not an inexperienced girl, indeed she had certainly had her fair share of over-amorous men to deal with. But still . . . Gino Santangelo . . . He was her boss after all . . . And a married man . . . And he was inclined to use women and then discard them with merely a trinket as a remembrance . . .

Bee had no wish to be used and discarded. But how could she make herself different from all the other girls?

'Jeeze!' Gino exclaimed, interrupting her thoughts. 'Whyn't you tell me you lived in a different country?'

'Just another four blocks, that's all.'

'It better be.' He yawned, and wondered if it was going to be worth the trip. Another day. Another broad. They were all the same.

But tomorrow would be different. Tomorrow he was going to San Francisco to be best man at Costa's wedding. Tomorrow he would see Leonora.

The thought ruffled him. How would he feel. How would *she* feel? His initial instinct had been to turn Costa down.

'You can't do that,' Cindy had insisted. 'You promised when he was our best man you would return the honor.'

True. So there was no getting out of it. Besides, it was about time he faced up to Leonora. For insurance he was taking Cindy.

'We're here,' Bee announced.

Red pulled the Cadillac up outside a brownstone apartment house.

'You going in, boss?' Sideways Sam asked.

'Yeh,' Gino replied. What did the idiot think? That he had come all this way just to sit in the car?

Sideways Sam got out and checked up and down the street. Then he opened up the back door of the Cadillac and Bee climbed out, followed by Gino.

She led him up the outside steps, and into an apartment on the first floor. It was plain and simple, but not bad. 'You live here alone?' he asked.

She hesitated for a second, then, 'Yes.'

He roamed around the room. 'Make me a scotch,' he commanded, 'you got ice?'

'Sorry. No scotch either.'

'What have you got?'

'Nothing. I . . don't drink.'

'Don't drink? What d'you do in the club for crissake?'

'The waiters bring me colored water.'

He laughed, 'And the mugs pay for champagne.'

She laughed with him, 'That's right.'

He stretched, 'Jesus! What a life!'

Bee stood watching. 'Shall I . . . take my clothes off?'

He flopped into a chair. 'Is that what you do instead of serving drinks?'

'If you'd like me to.'

The kid was all right. He put his hands behind his head and leaned back in the chair. 'Go ahead.'

Her heart was beating wildly now. She had a plan to make him remember her . . . It would either work or lose her the job at the club. Better than ending up as just another one of the girls.

Slowly she began to disrobe. He never took his black eyes off her.

She removed everything she was wearing except for her high heeled shoes, black silk stockings and red garters.

He stared at her appreciatively. She certainly had a special body. Big and white and smooth. Large pale breasts, topped with generous nipples. Long firm legs. A flat stomach. He liked her style too. Maybe this one would be worth a second visit.

The hardness he felt in his pants was becoming unbearable. He stood up and walked towards her.

She took a deep breath and spoke quickly, 'Mr Santangelo. I think I should tell you. I am recovering from a . . . social disease.'

He stopped dead in his tracks.

'The doctor did say it was all right for me to . . . make love now . . . But I just felt it was only right to tell you.'

'You got the clap,' he said blankly, collapsing back into the chair, 'holy shit! You got the clap an' I nearly screwed you.' He leapt up from the chair as though it suddenly occurred to him he might catch it through the material. 'Whyn't you tell me before?'

'I *am* cured.'

'Jeeze! All the way to the fuckin' village, and you've got a dose!'

'Had,' she corrected.

'Jeeze!' He glared at her. 'Put somethin' on.'

She climbed back into her dress while he edged towards the door.

'I hope I haven't upset you Mr Santangelo.'

'Upset me? No, kid. You only ruined the best hard-on I had all month! See ya.' And he was gone.

She slumped in relief. At least he would remember her now, and hopefully, come back again. She had lied about having a social disease. The only disease she'd had in her life was chicken pox at the age of ten. She couldn't help smiling. The look on his face when she had told him!

Quietly she tiptoed into her bedroom. Her seven-year-old son Marco was asleep in the roomy double bed. She pulled the covers up over him and kissed him lightly on the forehead. If Bee was to get involved with Gino Santangelo it would be properly or not at all. Now she stood out from the crowd.

He wouldn't forget who *she* was in a hurry.

Cindy lay sleeplessly in bed and wondered who her darling husband was bestowing the big favor on tonight. Dear Clementine maybe? After all he was going to be away a whole week and how the heck was the old broad ever going to manage without him?

Or one of the girls in the club perhaps? One of those mindless dumb hostesses who thought that she, Cindy, didn't know what was going on. Gino the Ram. Sure. Everywhere except at home. How did he expect her to get pregnant when he hardly ever went near her?

When 'Clemmies' first opened it had been a project that they were both very much involved in. She had been down there every day with the builders and decorators getting the place ready to open. In the beginning she had hired all the girls for the place. Hostesses. Hat check girls. Cigarette tootsies. No tramps. Pretty girls who were prepared to work hard and earn their money. While she was around Gino never second glanced one of them. After all he had skinny Clementine to keep him busy.

Cindy had steeled herself from the very beginning to accept *that* affair. She was smart enough to know that there was nothing she could do about it. Besides . . . the advantages of being friendly with Senator and Mrs Duke outweighed the disadvantages. She had known that Gino would get fed up eventually. What she had not known was that when he did, he would systematically and thoroughly screw his way through the entire female work force at 'Clemmies'. By the time that happened she was no longer involved with the running of the club. She had given up hiring and firing girls after the first year, and only visited the place when she wanted to be seen. Mrs Gino Santangelo at her usual table. A bunch of saps surrounding her, who although they sniffed around her like dogs sensing a bitch in heat were too scared to do anything about it. Nobody was going to risk anything more than a casual flirt with Mrs Gino Santangelo. Not if they knew what was good for them they weren't.

She tossed restlessly about on the big bed. Mrs Gino Santangelo. Clothes. Jewels. A Park Avenue penthouse. But no one to hold her tight at night. No one to *love* goddamn it. And there was nothing she could do about it. Not if she wanted to stay married to him there wasn't. For Gino gave her only one rule. She was to be faithful or else. That was it.

She reached for a glass of water on the bedside table and thought about the trip. It was something she had looked forward to for weeks. Just the two of them away from New York and the club. Away from it all maybe she could get him to realize that for all his chasing he had something pretty special at home in his own bed.

The front door slammed, and she peeked at the clock. One a.m. Early for Gino. Now he would go to the fridge, fix himself some ice cream, then straight to his study where he usually slept.

Tonight she would not bother him. Sometimes she went to him in a new negligee and tried to rouse his interest. Usually with no result. She lay on her stomach and stuffed her fist in her mouth. Sleep, she commanded, sleep.

When she was just drifting off he came into the bedroom and crawled into bed beside her. His hands started roaming under her nightdress, and she could feel his urgent hardness pressing into the small of her back.

'Gino,' she murmured, sudden joy flooding her body.

Before she had even finished uttering his name he was inside her. Gino. Once the caring considerate lover. Now obviously intent on only his own pleasure.

It was short, sharp, and over quickly without a word exchanged.

Cindy lay in a turmoil of frustration. She bet he never dared to treat his girlfriends like this. And certainly not Mrs Duke.

The bastard! If the way he acted towards her didn't change soon she was going to have to show him a thing or two. Oh yes! She had a plan that would bring Gino fucking selfish Santangelo to his knees!

# Carrie 1937

Early in 1937, Carrie was released from the institution where she had been for nine long years.

She no longer thought of herself as a girl of thirteen. She knew who and what she was. It had all come back to her in sharp fragmented sections. Everything. From mama Sonny to grandma Ella and Leroy all the way to Whitejack.

Her memories tapered off abruptly after a short period with Whitejack. She remembered leaving Madam Mae's with him and Lucille . . . then there was a time of jazz joints and having fun . . . then . . . nothing.

Of course it was the drugs. She knew what she had been. The doctors – especially Doctor Holland who had been looking at her case for the last two years – had told her all about her addiction. It was the biggest battle she would have to face once out of the hospital.

He had argued for a year to have her released. 'The girl is not mad, she's just being kept here as cheap labor.'

Eventually he had forced the institution board to agree with him.

Carrie was now twenty-three years of age. A thin woman with large breasts, dramatically long dark hair, and strangely sad oriental eyes.

On the day she left, she wore a shabby grey coat donated by a charity, along with a brown skirt, and yellow blouse. Her hair was tied firmly back, and her face devoid of any make-up.

She had twenty-five dollars in her purse, and a slip of paper with the name and address of a woman who had a job for her as a housemaid.

Doctor Holland bade her goodbye at the institution gates, 'It won't be easy for you, Carrie, nothing ever is. But I want you to try, and if things get too difficult for you, then please – I am always available to discuss matters with. All right?'

She nodded blankly. The doctor was a nice man who thought he was doing her a favor putting her out in the world again. But hell, all she really wanted to do was curl up in a corner and never have to face anyone or anything again.

She felt strangely empty and inadequate as she left the institution and rode a bus into the center of the city. Everything seemed so different. Maybe she would have been much better off staying where she was. There she had functioned, not thought.

A man on the bus leered at her, and she shrunk into the folds of her coat, and averted her eyes.

Somehow she knew that men were the enemy.

A butler opened the door of the house on Park Avenue.

'I'm Carrie,' she mumbled, shocked because she had just realized that this house was only three doors away from the Dimes residence where she had once worked. 'The new maid,' she explained.

The butler frowned, 'Why didn't you use the back door?'

'I'm sorry . . . I didn't realize . . . '

He tut-tutted and reluctantly ushered her in. 'Follow me.'

She did as she was told, trailing after him as he led her downstairs into a large kitchen where a fat black woman was stirring something over the stove.

'Mrs Smith,' the butler said, 'this is Carrie, the new maid. I'll leave her in your care. I expect that Mrs Becker will want to look her over before she takes up residence.'

'Sure thing, Mr Beal.' She turned to Carrie and drawled, 'You bin in service before, honey?'

Carrie nodded.

'Then you all know it ain't *no* bed o' roses.'

Back in service. The same old routine. Making beds. Dusting. Scrubbing. Cleaning toilets. Scouring baths. Down on hands and knees polishing marble floors. Washing. Ironing.

Carrie started work at 6 a.m. and was sometimes not finished until ten or eleven at night. For this she made less than a hundred dollars a month, and that was considered a top wage for a maid who lived in.

She didn't care about the work too much. It took her mind off other things – kept her good and busy. Once a month she had a day off. She had no idea what to do with her free time, so usually she just stayed in.

She rarely encountered her employers – Mr Becker was very wealthy, so Mrs Smith informed her, and Mrs Becker was always being pictured in the society magazines. 'One day I'll take you in her dressin' room when she's out – she must have more'n thirty pairs of shoes!' Mrs Smith promised.

Whitejack. His name flashed quickly through Carrie's mind. He had possessed just as many shoes.

Whitejack. So tall and sharp and shiny black. So irresistible. She thought of his twenty-three suits, and the way he preened, and his smile.

Whitejack. He had nearly finished her.

She wondered idly where he was now, what he was doing, and if he had a woman.

Whitejack. What would she do if she ever saw him again?

Kill the motherfucker.

# Gino 1937

Gino felt very much out of place at Costa's stag night. He sat at a table and watched the activities through black hooded eyes. Bunch of school kids – crowing and laughing, throwing drinks and bread rolls at each other.

When the usual nude girl popped forth from a giant white cake, Gino thought that thirty-four ex-college boys were going to have thirty-four simultaneous orgasms! Christ! You would think they had never seen a naked woman before.

He had found out early on in the proceedings who Leonora's husband was, and he watched him closely. The love of his life had married a chump. Edward Phillip Grazione. A true asshole who worked in his father's bank, had corn colored hair and pop eyes. A body like a star football player though – which is exactly what he had been at college when he and Leonora had married.

Gino itched to see her again. He almost broke out in a nervous sweat just thinking about it. This infuriated him. He should be long over her by this time.

He was. He just wished that his body would get the message.

'Jennifer – keep still!' Leonora commanded. 'How on earth can I fasten this if you are flying all over the room?'

'Sorry. I'll be good. I promise.' Jennifer Brierly, Costa's fiancée – stood quietly in the center of her bedroom while Leonora fastened her into a waist cinching corset. 'It's so tight!' she complained when the job was done. 'I can hardly breathe!'

'You don't need to breathe,' Leonora replied crisply, 'I think we deserve some champagne, don't you?'

'It's eleven o'clock in the morning.'

'It is also your wedding day. Why don't I run downstairs and grab us a bottle?'

Jennifer nodded. Poor Leonora. She knew her friend drank, but wasn't eleven o'clock pushing it?

'Here!' Leonora returned five minutes later, triumphant. She held a full bottle of champagne and two glasses. 'Voila!' Expertly she opened the bottle without it fizzing over, and filled the glasses. She handed one to Jennifer. 'The toast is marriage,' she said, a bitter twist to her voice, 'may it continue to flourish.'

Jennifer took a sip of the bubbly liquid, then placed her glass on a table.

Leonora held on to hers, taking a few healthy gulps then refilling her glass. 'I hope you realize what you're getting into,' she said, her voice still bitter.

'I'm not getting into anything,' Jennifer replied gently, 'I'm marrying the man I love.'

'Love soon disappears,' Leonora snorted, 'once you become their possession.'

'Costa won't own me, I won't own him. We'll just be together because we both want to.'

'Huh!' Leonora sipped more champagne. 'Let's talk again in two years when romance is out the window. A wife is owned – if she lets herself be.'

'Oh, Leonora, please! I don't want to have this discussion with you right now. I know everything is going badly between you and Edward, but that doesn't mean *every* marriage is destined to be the same as yours.'

'True, true.' Leonora picked up the bottle and filled her glass again. 'I'll see you in a minute.' She walked quickly out of the room, not wanting her friend to see her crying. After all, it was Jennifer's wedding day and she didn't want to spoil it for her.

She had been thinking about Gino Santangelo all day and it was upsetting her. What would he look like now? The same? Broody and dark and dangerously attractive. Or would he, like she, have changed?

She knew she was not the same girl he had fallen in love with. When she looked in her mirror she saw lines and ravages and a mean tilt to her mouth. Why, oh, why, had she not waited for him? Was it his letters, so sickeningly romantic and unlike him? Or was it the fact that there were so many other young men to sample? And once she had sampled one – well, it had seemed only fair to sample all the others.

Then Edward. Then Maria. Then the drink. Then the lovers.

Leonora frowned. Gino Santangelo. A girlhood crush. What was so special about him anyway?

'You sonofabitch!' Gino laughed. 'You're really gonna do it, huh?'

Costa grinned, 'I really am.'

They were in a limousine being driven to the church. 'Be a little hard for me to back out now.' Costa added, 'Besides, Jennifer is a terrific girl.'

'If you're marrying her, kid, then I'm sure she is.'

'She's not staggeringly beautiful or anything,' Costa continued earnestly, 'not like Cindy.'

Gino burst out laughing, 'Cindy! Staggeringly beautiful! Kid – she'd kiss your toes if I told her you'd said that.'

'Jennifer suits me fine,' Costa stated seriously, 'she is the sweetest girl, I don't know why it took me so long to realize it, her being Leonora's best friend and all.'

The name Leonora hung in the air.

Soon they would be arriving at the church.

Soon Gino would be seeing her again.

He swallowed hard and stared out of the window.

Cindy took a cab to the church. She wore a white silk tailored suit that skimmed her body, not missing one of her magnificent curves, over this a white fox stole draped casually. Her blonde hair fell in a sleek fashionable bob, and on top of it she wore a white pillbox hat. Even if she did think so herself – the fact had to be faced – she looked like a movie star. If Clark Gable ever got a look at her he would faint!

The cab driver said, 'You gettin' married or sumpin', sweetheart?'

'I'm a guest,' she replied haughtily, paying him off and entering the church.

Fancy having to take a *cab* to the wedding. The least Gino could have done was arranged a car for her. When she had complained he had merely said, 'I forgot.'

A rather handsome usher looked her over appreciatively. 'Bride or groom?' he inquired.

'Huh?' She blinked the baby blues as wide as possible.

'Bride or groom?' he repeated.

She was stumped.

Another usher stepped forward with a build on him that

would do credit to a Greek God and hair to match the image.
'Are you a relation or friend of the bride or the groom?'

'Why?' Cindy questioned, wondering what this Greek God
looked like without his clothes on.

'Because we have to know who you belong to, so we know
which side of the church to seat you.' He laughed.

'Oh!' she blushed. Nothing like looking dumb. 'Costa's an
old friend.'

The usher smiled and took her arm, 'Lucky Costa!'

Jennifer Brierly walked regally down the aisle, Queen for a
day. She held firmly onto her father's supportive arm.

In front of her walked Leonora, matron of honor, preceded
by the other three bridesmaids, and Maria, Leonora's nine-
year-old daughter.

It was a regal procession, and nobody noticed Leonora's
slight stagger.

Standing in the front pew Costa felt sweat engulf his body. He
wanted to pee. He wanted to smoke. He *needed* a drink.

Gino, by his side, was outwardly calm. It took every ounce
of control he possessed not to turn around and stare down the
aisle. It wasn't the bride he wanted a glimpse of. It was
Leonora who he knew would be right in front of her.

'I don't feel so good,' Costa mumbled under his breath.

'You'll be all right, kid. Just hang on.'

And then Jennifer and her father were coming into view, and
Costa was moving to join her at the front of the aisle with
Gino just a few steps behind. Gino glanced over. His stomach
somersaulted. *Exactly the fuckin' same!* Even in the misty
gloom of the church he could see that.

She stood in profile to him, head slightly tilted, luminous
crystal blue eyes, whispy white blonde hair. She was wearing
some sort of pink frilled dress that gently outlined the curve of
her breasts, the indentation of her waist, and flowed in soft
folds to the floor.

His mouth was dry. He dragged his eyes away and stared
straight ahead. The wedding service was commencing and he
didn't want to miss it.

As far as Gino was concerned the rest of the day passed by in
a blur. There was the wedding lunch and reception. Champagne. Food. Speeches. Toasts.

Franklin Zennocotti giving him the same mistrustful fish eye. Mary Zennocotti warm and motherly.

Cindy flirting around the place looking like an expensive tramp with every young guy in the place hot breathing it after her – *including* Leonora's husband who turned out to be as dumb as he looked.

Costa and Jennifer, lost in each other's eyes. Smiling secret smiles and clutching tightly onto each other's hands.

And then the lady herself.

Leonora.

No longer a girl. A woman of twenty-eight.

Gino – casual. 'How you bin?'

Leonora – even more casual. 'Fine. Yourself?'

Gino: 'Not bad.'

Leonora: 'Good.'

Silence. A very long silence.

Gino – concerned: 'I hear you got a beautiful little girl.'

Leonora – unconcerned: 'Yes. Maria.'

More silence.

Gino: 'I ain't got kids myself.'

Leonora: 'No?'

They stood at the edge of the dance floor while couples whirled past.

Gino: 'I think we gotta dance. Best man an' matron of honor, y'know?'

Leonora: 'Let's get it over with then.'

She was light as a feather in his arms. He held her at a discreet distance and they spun around the floor to the strains of 'Pennies From Heaven.'

He felt elated and sick and foolish and tough. Would she respond if he said anything? Did he honestly want to risk making a fool of himself? He was Gino Santangelo for crissake. He was a big man. He could have any woman he wanted. In New York he was feared and trusted and respected. He counted senators, judges and politicians among his friends. He *screwed* their wives.

'I've had enough,' she said abruptly, 'I want a drink.'

'Sure.'

He spun her off the dance floor. 'Leonora?' he began.

'Yes?' Her luminous crystal eyes were icy, freezing him out. Fuck her. She didn't even have the class to try and explain, apologize, *anything*. 'What do you want to drink? I'll get it for you.'

•

'That's all right,' she removed herself from his grasp, 'My husband will get me a drink.' She walked away without another word.

He felt as though he'd been kicked in the stomach by a horse. What was *with* her? She glared at him like he was *dirt*, like she hated him. What the fuck had *he* ever done except sit around like a faithful sucker?

'Hi.' A little girl stood before him. A small nine-year-old mirror image of her mother.

'Maria?'

'Yes.'

What an exquisite kid. Same eyes. Same hair.

'How did you know my name?' Small head cocked inquisitively to one side.

He smiled, 'Hey, you're famous.'

'I am?'

'You am.'

'Good. 'Cos I wanted you to dance with me next. The best man's supposed to dance with all the bridesmaids,' she grasped his hand shyly, 'my turn now!'

'Little girl. It will be my pleasure.'

Gravely he held out his arms. Very correctly she stepped into them.

Soon they were dancing.

# Carrie 1937

'Mr Bernard Dimes, whose house is just down the street – is havin' a party next Monday. Mrs Becker usually lets us go an' help out in the kitchen. You wanna do it? He pays real good.' Mrs Smith regarded Carrie anxiously, 'What you say? I gotta tell his housekeeper.'

Carrie didn't know what to say. It would be like taking a step back into the past. But still . . . extra money. She saved every dollar she could, although she hadn't quite made up her mind for what purpose. 'I'll do it,' she agreed. At least it would be a change.

She had been working in the Becker household for six months, and the only time she left the house was to go to the market, except for the one occasion she had returned to the institution to see Doctor Holland. He had been pleased with her progress. 'The real test was being back in New York with all the temptations. You seem to have passed with flying colors.'

Had she? Was hiding in her room on her days off passing with flying colors? Or was she merely hiding from temptation?

Perhaps she *should* go out on the street – take in a movie or a show. Walk around and look in the shops.

She would – eventually. When she felt that she was ready.

Mrs Smith and Carrie set off for the Dimes residence at five in the afternoon on Monday. Mrs Smith had dressed for the occasion in her best flowered dress, but Carrie just wore her usual uniform, with her long black hair tied and plaited.

'Ain't you got nothin' else t'put on?' Mrs Smith complained.

'These are my workin' clothes,' Carrie replied dourly.

Mrs Church, housekeeper to Mr Dimes, greeted them at the kitchen door. To Carrie's relief she was not the same woman who had been in residence when she had worked there.

The kitchen had been redecorated and modernized. But all the same Carrie felt a jolt when entering it and looking around. It reminded her of an innocent little girl so very long ago . . .

The kitchen was busy. There was a strapping Swedish girl who wore a waitress ensemble and flopped in a chair awaiting her duties, two barmen, who bustled about organizing ice and wine, and a housemaid who assisted the butler. A special chef in full white regalia was busy producing miniature vol-au-vents.

Carrie quietly attended to the more menial tasks.

At seven the guests started to arrive, and sounds of music and laughter drifted down from upstairs. The barmen and Swedish waitress vanished to take care of their duties, occasionally reappearing with tales of famous faces who were gracing the party. The dirty dishes mounted up as the party progressed. Carrie's hands were red and raw from constant immersion in hot soapy water.

At ten-thirty the butler appeared in the kitchen. He looked around the assorted help, his eyes falling on Carrie. 'Do you know how to fetch coats?'

'What?'

'Oh never mind. You can't possibly be worse than the girl they sent. Come along.'

She dried her hands on a dishtowel and followed the butler up the familiar stairs.

'In there,' he commanded, giving her a little push into a cloakroom filled with fur coats. 'And when I tell you what I want – see if you can find it – and quick.'

It was better than washing up.

Esther and Gordon Becker were among the last guests to leave. 'Wonderful party, Bernard darling,' Esther gushed.

Bernard smiled, 'Thank you. I'm glad you enjoyed it.'

'*I* certainly did, *and* Gordon. Didn't you, darling?'

Gordon snapped back to attention. He had been admiring the black girl who was handing their coats to the butler. Very simple and plain with her long hair braided down her back. Something vaguely familiar about her . . .

'Carrie!' Esther suddenly exclaimed. 'Still here? How on earth will you get through the day tomorrow?'

'Who is she?' Gordon asked.

'Our maid, darling. Esther shrieked with laughter. 'Doesn't even recognize his own servants! Can you believe it Bernard?' Her double chin wobbled along with her mammoth breasts.

'Who recognizes servants?' Gordon joined in with his wife's laughter – determined not to be made a fool of. 'They come and go like rabbits!'

Bernard Dimes' meticulous mind was ticking over. Carrie? The name rang a distant bell. The girl's face was also familiar. Carrie? He hated not being able to remember. 'Do you mind if she stays on a little longer?' he asked Esther.

'Of course not! Only joking! Carrie will be up bright and early whatever time she goes to bed.' She threw her a patronizing smile, 'Won't you, dear?' Then in a loud whispered aside to whoever was listening, 'The girl is a gem! Works like a black!' Giggle Giggle. 'Ooops! Must watch what I say!'

Carrie decided there and then that she was going to look for another job. Mrs Esther Becker could clear up her own mess.

Much later, when the last guest had departed, Bernard Dimes sat alone in his study savoring a glass of his favourite brandy. He rang for his butler. 'Roger, that girl helping you with the coats, if she's still here bring her to see me.'

'Yes, sir. She *was* very helpful,' Roger remarked, 'the kind of maid *we* need.'

Bernard was amused, 'Do you want me to ask Mrs Becker if she'll relinquish her?'

'A good idea, sir.'

Bernard laughed aloud, 'I'm surprised at you, Roger. Stealing staff is hardly your style.'

Roger remained implacable, 'I know, sir. But sometimes it is the only answer.'

Down in the kitchen Mrs Smith swayed drunkenly as she packed a tasty selection of hors d'oeuvres in a paper bag ready to take home. Left over food and drink was one of the perks of the night.

The two barmen were crating empty bottles, and the Swedish waitress had changed into a daring yellow dress and sat reading a movie magazine by the back door. Her husband, the chef, was packing away his equipment.

Carrie stacked clean dishes into a cupboard.

One of the barmen sidled over to her. 'A pretty gal like you wanna have a little fun one night?'

She looked at him blankly.

'Well?' he persisted.

She shook her head.

He was about to pursue the point when the butler appeared. 'Mr Dimes would like to see you, upstairs, Carrie. Right now.'

# Gino 1937

Gino did not enjoy the trip. He did not enjoy the wedding. He hated being closeted in a hotel with Cindy, and after an explosive fight they returned to New York early, hardly on speaking terms.

Cindy was fuming. Gino had confirmed the fact that she was just another possession – like his suits and cars. Oh – naturally he hadn't said it in so many words. But she knew. He had *laughed* at her because in his opinion she had made a fool of herself at the wedding. A fool indeed! What did he know! Every man at the event was probably *still* having wet dreams about her!

'You shouldn't've worn white,' he had stated.

'And why not?'

' 'Cos only the bride's supposed t'wear white.'

'Oh yeah? Who says?'

'I say. It's etiquette or somethin'.'

'Etiquette! Etiquette! I didn't know you knew the word.'

Whack! It was the first time he had ever hit her. She had gone for him like a wild tiger, biting and clawing.

He had fought her off and walked out. Leaving her to brood and sulk in the hotel, while he visited the nearest bar and drunk himself to a standstill. Unlike him. Usually he believed very much in being in control and staying sober. But he was confused. Cindy – showing him up – acting like a little tramp – wiggling her fanny at every guy in sight. And Franklin Zennocotti *still* treating him like some punk kid who didn't know from shit.

And then there was Leonora. He should have been over her years ago – in fact he had thought he was. But there she was – with those eyes, that hair, that body – and it was the same old pain all over again.

And she was so cold and brittle – like *he* had done something terrible to *her* instead of exactly the reverse being true. He just didn't understand it.

He couldn't *wait* to get back to New York.


Aldo chewed on a chunk of garlic and said, 'Thank God you're here.'

Gino paced around the office, anger dogging his every step. 'Jesus Christ! I go away for a few days an' I come back to some fine fucking mess.' His voice rose, 'Can't you handle anything on your own?'

Aldo flushed a dull red. 'The trouble was unexpected, everything's been runnin' so smoothly.'

'Sure. I oil enough palms to make goddamn certain of that,' he slammed his fist sharply down on the desk. 'Where the fuck *is* The Boy?'

'He was hurt bad, Gino. They beat him up real good.'

Gino's eyes glazed to a set hardness, 'The dumb fuck. How come he was travellin' alone anyway?'

'He usually does.'

Yeh. Jacob Cohen. Jake. The Boy. He liked to do things his way. Independent. Sharp as a jagged bottle. Maybe too sharp.

'Repeat the facts,' he snarled.

'But I told you . . . '

'*Repeat.*'

Aldo didn't argue. The anger was flying off Gino in pungent waves. 'He makes the pick ups Saturday. As usual. Is gettin' in his car on 115th Street near the candy store . . . '

'Gambinos?' Gino interrupted.

'That's right. Well . . . just as he's gettin' in the car three guys hit him from behind . . . '

'So he never saw them?'

'No. They got him from behind, beat him good, grabbed his piece, the bag, and ran.'

'Where?'

'Huh?'

'Which direction did they run?'

Aldo shrugged, 'I don't know . . . '

'Sixty grand of my money and *you don't know.*'

'I only know what The Boy told me.'

'He came straight here then?'

'Yes. He was bleedin' – shook up – I had Red drive him home.'

'And tuck him up with a comforter an' a glass of hot milk?'

Aldo looked puzzled, 'The Boy's been with us for seven years. Surely you trust him?'

'I trust I'm gonna take a crap at least once a week – an that's all I trust.'

The realization that Gino might be right crept up on Aldo slowly, then his flush darkened and his voice hardened, 'Why that dirty little kike bastard . . . '

'Hold it,' snapped Gino, 'he don't become a dirty kike just 'cos he's stealin' from us. Like I don't become a dirty wop if I smash your head in with a baseball bat. Come to think of it – that ain't a bad idea – let some air into your brain. I mean Jesus – The Boy is settin' you up. You say this happened yesterday? How much you want to bet he ain't at home waitin' for me to get back to the city.' He paused and glared. 'Nope. My bet is The Boy has gone into hidin' with *my* sixty grand. And *you* asshole – gave him a ride home.'

Aldo said nothing. He just digested the facts.

'I'll check it out myself,' Gino snapped, marching through to the outer offices. 'Sam, Red, let's go. I wanna pay a visit to The Boy, maybe take him a few flowers or somethin'.'

Red and Sam exchanged knowing glances. Jake may have fooled Aldo – but *anyone* could fool him. *They* had known all along it was a set-up. Anyone approaching Jake from a hundred yards with felonious intent would get a bullet up the ass. Jake was the fastest gun on the street. *They* knew that. *Gino* knew that. Wasn't it about time someone wised up Aldo?

Of course, it turned out that Gino was right.

Jacob Cohen's landlady said he had moved out. Suddenly. No forwarding address. 'Nice boy,' she mused, 'quiet, no trouble, always paid his rent on time.'

'And you've no idea where he's gone?' Gino asked.

She shook her head.

'What about girlfriends?'

Pursing her lips, she said, 'My tenants have a right to privacy.'

He slid her a twenty.

'Lots of girlfriends. A different one every week.'

'Anyone special?'

'No. They came and they went,' she sniffed, 'a young buck like that don't want to get tied down.'

Gino nodded. When he found Jacob Cohen he was going to roast his balls over hot charcoal and feed them to the pigeons.

Nobody stole from Gino Santangelo. Nobody.

'Do we have to go?' complained Cindy.

'Yes,' replied Gino shortly. His mood, since getting back from San Francisco, was, to put it mildly, black.

'And I guess that means we have to stay the weekend?' she groaned.

'Yes.' He was as unenthusiastic as she was about Senator and Mrs Duke's upcoming party. But it was their twenty-seventh wedding anniversary, and there was no way he could dodge out of *that*. Clementine herself had insisted, her silky tones mild on the telephone, 'If you don't come, Gino, I am going to start to think you are avoiding me. You missed our last party, and I haven't seen you alone in over three weeks.' A pause. 'I would hate to think that you *are* avoiding me . . . I would hate Oswald to think it . . . '

Was that supposed to be a hidden threat? Gino laughed. No threat. It was his imagination working overtime. If he never wanted to see them again there was nothing they could do about it.

Only Senator Duke knew plenty. About the numbers racket.

About the money skimmed off the top at the club. About the gambling. About the vast sums of cash.

Senator Duke could put him away if he wanted to with one phone call to the Internal Revenue, who were always sniffing around anyway.

But the good Senator would never do that. Because the good Senator had plenty to hide himself. The payoffs he had arranged on Gino's behalf. The stock transactions that weren't always on the up and up. The companies that belonged to Gino, and the fat director's fees the Senator picked up as financial adviser.

Oh yeh. In a way they were partners.

One more party, Gino decided, he owed them that. And at the party he would tell Clementine. It was great fun . . . but it was just one . . . of those things.

Meanwhile he had other matters on his mind. Fucking Jake. Running off with his money. Two days gone by and no sign of him – and for a thousand bucks reward most citizens would turn in their own mother.

He had vanished. No trace. Little prick. But when he surfaced he would get his – in spades.

'What shall I wear to the party?' Cindy asked.

'Whatever you want,' Gino replied disinterestedly.

'Maybe the red silk . . . '

'You look like a tramp in red.'

'Thanks. You sure know how to make a girl feel good.'

'So don't ask me.'

*I won't*, she thought, *I'll wear exactly what I want – even if it's the red silk – even if I do look like a tramp.*

Aloud she said, 'Any word on The Boy yet?' She knew that there wasn't, but she just wanted to watch him burn.

'No,' he replied shortly. 'I'm going to the club.'

'Maybe I'll come, I . . . '

'Not tonight. I have a meeting.'

'Who with?'

He gave her a look.

She shrugged. She knew when to stay quiet. Anyway, her plans were in motion. Soon *she* would be holding the reins.

Clemmies was packed. The place could do no wrong.

Gino stopped to talk to Vera at the hat check counter. She was looking better than she had in a long time. She even appeared to be sober. 'Guess what?' her eyes were sparkling.

'What?'

'He's comin' out.'

'Yeh?' He didn't need to ask who. His stomach turned at the thought.

'S'wonderful news isn't it?'

He nodded blankly. What could he say? That he wished they would keep the slimey sonofabitch locked up forever.

'Gino,' Vera was squeezing his arm, 'I know things ain't never been that great between the two of you ...'

Ha – talk about gross exaggeration.

'But it's important t'me that you get along now. Paulo's changed – bein' locked up all this time is enough t'change anyone.' She paused, took a deep breath, and continued. 'He really admires you. Talks about you a lot. He's *proud* of you, real proud.'

Yeh. Of course he was. Paulo was just about smart enough to realize which side the jam was on.

'I thought,' Vera continued hesitantly, 'that the two of you could get together – talk about things.' Her voice quickened, 'He'll need a job, somethin' straight. Now that Jake's taken off ...'

Gino realized what she was suggesting. 'Forget it,' he said incredulously, 'just forget it.'

'Aw c'mon, don't be like that. He's your *father*. Surely that means somethin' t'you?'

He could honestly say that it didn't. 'When does he get out?' he questioned coldly.

'Coupla weeks.'

'And I suppose you're taking him in?'

'Of course I am ...'

He shook his head, 'You're dumb, Vera, you know that? What's gonna happen? You gonna hold his hand until he beats the crap outta you again?'

'I'm tellin' you, he's a changed man ...'

'We'll see. Just keep him away. I don't want t'see or hear about him.'

She glared. 'You can be a heartless bastard at times. You know that?'

'Sure. How do you think I got where I am today?' He strode off through the club, hard black eyes checking out the action. Nodding briefly at acquaintances and friends. He noticed Bee sitting at a table with another hostess and two men. She caught his eye and looked away.

He flashed onto a memory of her stripped naked and standing before him in her high heeled shoes and stockings. Big white smooth body. You would think she would have told him about the clap *before* she took her clothes off. Nice breasts. Very nice breasts.

He strode by a hostess named America. Raven hair and long legs. He had honored her once. Not a memorable experience but passable. He stopped at her table, leaned over and said, 'I'll drive you home tonight. Meet me in my office at twelve.'

She glowed. *'Yes sir!'* Obviously more memorable for her than him.

Broads. A dime a dozen. All the same whether they wore Givenchy silks or cheap glad rags.

Cindy wore the red silk dress defiantly to the Duke's party. It plunged between her breasts, dipped at the back, and was split up the front. Her blonde hair tumbled around her pretty face in soft curls, held back on one side by a fake red flower.

Gino made no comment on her appearance, but the look he gave her was enough.

She did not care. She tossed her blonde curls, and proceeded to flirt outrageously with every man in sight.

Clementine - chic in basic black - took Gino to one side. 'I think you had better speak to your wife,' she murmured. 'Our little Cindy seems to have found her feet in no uncertain fashion.'

'Yeh?' His eyes were flat as he followed Clementine's gaze and observed his wife in action. 'If she wants to have a good time it don't bother me.'

Clementine swallowed her aggravation, 'You should be bothered. Her behavior reflects on you. She makes *you* look a fool.'

'Oh. If that's the case what do you think *you* make Oswald look like?'

She tried to keep her voice steady, Gino was getting to her - bastard - she who was *always* in control. 'That's different.'

'Why?'

'You *know* why.'

'Sure. *I* know why. But I thought the fact he was a fairy was supposed to be a well kept secret.'

'Don't use that word.'

'You used to like it.'

'Yes, and you used to like spending time with me. What happened, Gino?'

He shrugged, 'I bin away. You know that.'

Yes. She knew that. But she also knew that before he left he was avoiding her. And no man had ever avoided Clementine Duke. Not unless she wanted him to.

She did not wish to pursue the conversation. 'Cigarette,' she demanded coldly.

'Don't have any. I can offer you a cigar.'

She glared at him. Cocky little bastard. If it wasn't for Oswald and her he would still be another ten cent hoodlum working the streets. They had given him everything. Class. Acceptability. Social graces.

She realized with a sharp feeling in her stomach that she loved him. Love was not peaches and cream. Love was jealousy and possession and gut wrenching misery.

*He did not want her anymore.* She knew that to be the truth as sure as Oswald was queer.

'Gino,' she said tightly, 'Oswald has a matter he wishes to discuss with you. Perhaps you would be good enough to meet him in his study at ten in the morning. It is a very . . . private matter. I will take Cindy out shopping with me.'

He looked surprised. What was so private that couldn't be taken care of in town? 'Sure,' he said flatly.

'So . . . I must circulate among my guests . . . I know you will excuse me.'

He watched her walk off. Still a knockout broad.

He watched Cindy in the distance. Prettiest girl at the party.

He wondered why he had absolutely no sexual desire for either of them. Maybe he had started in too early. Too many women and now it was enough already, because even the one night stands were beginning to pall. Once – making love had been like an exciting game. Now – it was boring. Yeh. Boring.

And maybe it was his fault.

He grunted. And thought about Jake. And thought about what he was going to do to him. And smiled. Because The Boy had balls. And he liked that. A good quality.

Yeh. After he had taught The Boy a lesson he would allow him back in the family.

'Why can't we have lunch?' Henry Moufflin Jr demanded for the third time.

Cindy tilted her head to one side and gazed up at him coquettishly. 'I just don't want to see you chewed up and spat out by Gino.'

'How ridiculous!' exclaimed Henry. He was no longer the callow youth who had fawned after Clementine Duke for so many years. He was now thirty-one years old. His acne had cleared up, and he had inherited his late father's very substantial fortune.

'Brave words, Henry,' purred Cindy, enjoying the way his eyes kept on popping down her neckline.

'I mean what I s . . . s . . . ay,' he insisted. His stammer was still in evidence in spite of years of speech therapy. 'I w . . . w . . . ant to take you to lunch. Just lunch. What harm is there in that if I promise to behave myself?'

She thought of the private detective's report she had hidden under the mattress at home. 'Mr Santangelo departed from Clemmies at approximately twelve-ten at night. He was accompanied by two men – one of whom drove a limousine. A young lady also accompanied him. Tall, raven haired. They proceeded to . . .'

'Well?' he persisted.

'Yes,' decided Cindy, surprising herself, 'why not?'

Henry beamed. Why not indeed? He was filled with exhilaration. Gino Santangelo's wife agreeing to lunch with *him.* It would have to be the Plaza of course. Flowers. Champagne. And a suite booked upstairs just in case. Or maybe – even better – a private luncheon *served* in the suite. 'Monday?' he asked anxiously.

'Tuesday,' she replied, wondering what she was letting herself in for, but determined to strike out anyway.

'Superb.'

She giggled, 'I hope so.'

Gino prowled around the Senator's study. He remembered their first meeting in the very same room. He remembered thinking Oswald was a mug and dumb. Yeh. Dumb like a fox.

Restlessly he picked up a silver letter opener and weighed it in the palm of his hand. The Senator entered the room.

'Nice party last night,' Gino remarked cheerily.

Oswald nodded. The heavy bags under his eyes seemed to weigh his whole face down. He was in no mood for polite conversation. 'Gino,' he began, getting right to the point, 'the favors I have asked of you in the past have been small matters easily taken care of.'

Gino placed the silver letter opener carefully back on the desk. He didn't like the way Oswald was rushing his speech, or the way he was talking over his shoulder, refusing to look him in the eye. 'Right,' he agreed cautiously.

'I always mentioned that a time might come when the favor would be . . . big.'

He was immediately alert. 'How big?'

'Very big.'

A silence hung between the two men.

'Keep talkin',' said Gino at last.

The Senator cleared his throat, 'I want a man killed,' he said slowly, 'and I want *you* to take care of it personally.'

# Carrie 1937

Bernard Dimes sat in a padded leather chair in the study that Carrie once used to dust. Her eyes darted quickly round the room – noting few changes. The silver frames were still in position filled with photographs of celebrities. Framed posters still hung on the wall. The large desk was still awash with a clutter of papers that nobody was allowed to touch.

He swivelled to face her when the butler brought her in.

'Shall I stay, sir?' Roger asked discreetly.

'No, no. That's all right. I'll buzz when I need you,' Bernard replied waving him away. 'Sit down, Carrie.' He indicated a chair.

She sat and studied her hands folded neatly on her lap.

'I do know you, don't I?' Bernard inquired gently.

She raised her eyes in surprise. 'Yes.'

'I have a very good memory for faces,' he said. 'Once seen – never forgotten. And if I can't quite place that face it drives me insane! Now, where was it I met you?'

'I b . . . beg your pardon?' she stammered hesitantly.

'Where?'

'Here,' she replied, puzzled.

'Here?'

'Yes, sir. I used to be in service here.'

'You did?' He was surprised, 'When?'

'Oh, quite a few years ago,' she mumbled vaguely, 'I was very young.'

He stared at her, his brow creasing in a perplexed frown. 'No . . . not here . . . Somewhere else.'

'I did work here.'

He was unconvinced.

'Mr Dimes. I worked for you in this house – oh – way back in 1926. I had to leave suddenly because of a . . . family reason.'

His frown deepened.

'Yes,' she continued excitedly, 'don't you remember? I met you in an Italian restaurant. The owner brought me over and you gave me a job. You *must* remember?'

He remembered a skinny little girl – certainly not this woman sitting before him. Oh – her hair was braided, her clothes unflattering, and her face bereft of make-up – but Bernard Dimes had not been a producer for twenty-three years without being able to recognize a beautiful woman when he saw one. 'So,' he questioned, 'after all those years are you still satisfied to be just a maid?'

She studied the pattern on the carpet, 'I guess so.'

'What's the matter with you, Carrie? No ambition?'

She looked up at him in surprise. He was talking to her like a person. 'Yes, I have ambition,' she said, startling herself, 'but it's not easy getting any other kind of a job.'

He stared at her. And then he said, 'I guess that's true. But you are a very attractive girl, you should be doing more with your life.'

She shrugged, 'I know . . . '

He looked at her thoughtfully, then on impulse, got up from his chair, walked over and handed her a card. 'Be at the Shubert Theater. Ten o'clock tomorrow morning. There may be something in the chorus.' He stared at her gravely, 'You don't want to remain a maid all of your life, do you?'

She shook her head.

'I'll clear it with the Beckers. Don't worry.' He rang a bell and the butler appeared instantly. 'Roger, take Carrie downstairs.'

She left the room in a state of shock.

Bernard watched her go. He was as surprised at the turn of events as she was. He had asked to see the girl because of a nagging sensation of not being able to place her. And then . . . sitting in his study looking at her, the strangest feeling had come over him. She radiated a hidden sexuality that enthralled him. *Why not give her a chance in life?*

He lit a cigarette and blew smoke rings towards the ceiling. Something was still bothering him . . . He *had* seen her somewhere before, but it was not when she had worked for him.

He racked his brains but it would not come. Eventually he

would remember . . . If he thought about things long enough they always fell into position.

The director picked his teeth with the edge of some book matches. 'Where'd you find her?' he asked.

'She works for a friend of mine,' Bernard replied vaguely.

'She sure looks good.'

They both regarded Carrie from their anonymous seats in the stalls. She stood on the stage, blinded by the lights, nervous and perspiring, clad in a borrowed leotard.

'What you want me to play, sweetie?' the young pianist asked.

'I don't know,' she mumbled.

'You gonna sing or dance first?'

'Er . . . dance I guess.'

'How about "Pennies From Heaven"?'

'How about some honky tonk?'

'Hey – now you're talkin' my language!' He started to play enthusiastically – a real New Orleans rendition of 'Hard Hearted Hannah.' Carrie began to dance.

'Good God!' exclaimed the director 'She moves like a stripper!'

Bernard sat bolt upright in his seat.

Indeed she did.

Clementine Duke's party.

Westchester, 1928.

He knew he would remember – eventually.

# Gino 1937

Gino drove the black Cadillac sedan erratically.

Cindy tucked her legs under her on the front seat and said, 'Say – are you drunk or somethin'?'

'What kind of a crack is that?'

'You're drivin' like you are.'

'Fuckin' Senator. Thinks he can call the shots. *I* don't dance on *anyone's* string.'

'Who said you did?'

He glanced quickly at his wife and wondered if he should

tell her. No. Why let her in on his humiliation at Senator Duke talking to him like some two bit hoodlum. Expecting him to say – yeh – I'll kill for you – just tell me where and when. Cocksucker. And he had thought they were friends. What a laugh!

'Nothin',' he muttered.

'Sure, nothing. That's why we raced out of the place like a couple of fugitives. Your girlfriend wasn't pleased.'

'She's not my girlfriend. I've told you that a hundred times.'

'Sure,' Cindy yawned, 'and Jean Harlow don't bleach her hair!'

They drove the rest of the way in silence. Gino was as mad at himself as with anybody else. *He hadn't actually said no.* He had listened and said, 'I can arrange to have it done for you.'

And the Senator had replied – '*You* must do it, Gino, nobody else can know.'

Fuck. He had sat there and *allowed* himself to be taken for a cheap killer. He was a businessman – not a criminal who lived by the gun. But he had sat there while Oswald had unfolded the details. Blackmail, of course. Sexual, of course. A long story.

Senator Duke hadn't actually said – 'If you don't take care of this matter personally I will destroy you.' But the words hung in the room.

And could Gino take care of it? Probably. He had the power.

Of course – thinking it over – he had been unwise to allow Senator Duke so much knowledge of his activities. But how could he help it? The Senator was a director of most of the companies he owned, and his lawyer handled all legal documents. His broker took care of Gino's investments. The only thing the Senator didn't know about was the safe deposit boxes all over town.

So – what to do? Murder some faggot blackmailing creep? And by doing that Oswald Duke would have even *more* on him.

Or – forget the whole thing and take his chances?

Gino was stumped.

It had not been a good week.

It got worse.

The very next day three of his collectors got hit on the street. Two beaten, one shot. Another fifteen grand down the drain. Jake the Boy was in business.

Gino didn't think twice about it. He put out a contract on The Boy. Having balls was one thing. Making Gino Santangelo look like a fool was another.

Senator Oswald telephoned at midday, 'Have you made a decision?' he whispered.

'Yeh.' Gino replied, 'Don't worry, it'll be taken care of.' He would take care of the matter in *his* way.

Later he dismissed Red and Sideways Sam for the night, took the old Ford from the basement garage of the club, and drove to the address Oswald had given him. The car ran like a dream. It should, he still worked on it lovingly once a month.

The address was down in the village. A dump. He parked the car a block away and walked to the building. He checked the names scribbled under buzzers and found Kincaid Z. Second floor.

The time was 2 a.m. But the building rocked with the noise of a jazz band in session.

He knocked on Kincaid Z's door, and a black boy opened up immediately as though he was expecting someone.

Gino jammed the door with his foot and slid inside.

The boy backed nervously into a corner without saying a word. He had wild frizzy hair and the eyes of an addict. He was wearing bright red lipstick, and a flowered housecoat.

'You Zefra Kincaid?'

'Who's asking?' the boy replied in a strange falsetto voice.

'Are you?' Gino's hard black eyes bore into him.

'Yes,' the boy whispered.

'I want the letters. '

'What letters?'

With one swift step Gino was on him. The palm of his hand under the boy's chin forcing his head back. His knee jammed deeply into his stomach.

'I . . . want . . . the . . . Senator's . . . letters . . . now.'

'Yes,' the boy's eyes were frozen with terror and pain. 'I'll get them.'

Gino let him go and sighed. His instincts were always right. No need to kill this petrified little freak. Just put the fear of God in him with a few well intended threats, then dump him on a train out of town.

The boy was shaking as he went towards a cupboard in the corner. Idly Gino wondered where Oswald had found him. Where would their paths ever cross, the Senator and the teen-aged fairy junkie?

The boy opened the cupboard, and with a wild scream an

apparition leaped out. A six foot bewigged maniac wielding a butcher's knife and heading in Gino's direction.

For one moment he was paralyzed with horror. And in that moment the maniac struck – the knife embedding itself deeply in Gino's shoulder.

# Thursday, July 14th, 1977, New York and Philadelphia

Lucky drifted in and out of sleep. She was no longer aggressive toward Steven – she just wanted out. They had been trapped in the elevator for nine long hours, and all the fight had gone out of her. She felt filthy dirty. Her lips, mouth and throat were parched dry. Her head ached. Her stomach cramped. She wanted to throw up, yet at the same time was starving hungry.

'You awake?' she murmured.

'Can't sleep,' Steven replied.

'Neither can I.'

He felt sorry for her and sorry for himself. And very pissed off that in New York in 1977 you could get trapped in an elevator for hours on end without anyone doing a thing about it.

'What are you going to do when you get out?' Lucky asked.

He couldn't help smiling in the dark. She sounded like a forlorn little kid looking forward to getting released from jail.

'Take a bath.'

She laughed softly, 'So am I – a long hot bath, and a glass of cold white wine to drink in it. And music playing – some Donna Summer or Stevie Wonder.'

'How about Millie Jackson or Isaac Hayes?'

'You like that kind of music?'

'Sure do.'

'Really?'

'You sound surprised.'

'I didn't have you figured for the kind of guy likes soul.'

'What did you have me figured for?'

'Oh I don't know. Middle of the road. Herb Alpert, Barry Manilow.'

'Thanks a lot!'

'Wouldn't it be great if we had music here?'

'Marvin Gaye.'

'Al Green.'

'Willie Hutch.'

'Otis Redding.'

They began to laugh. 'Hey – ' she exclaimed, 'we've got something in common.'

'You ever listen to old music? Billie Holiday. Nina Simone?'

'Sure. Love it.'

'You do?' Suddenly they were discussing music, carrying on like old friends. So intent that they almost missed the voice yelling down the elevator shaft – 'Anyone in there?'

'Hey!' Lucky leapt to her feet. 'I think we've been found.'

Steven jumped up too. 'We're in here!' he shouted. 'Two of us. *Can you get us out?*'

Dario tensed his whole body as he crouched on the kitchen floor of his apartment. All he could hear was the boy's chant of obscenity as he got nearer and nearer . . . Closer to the knife that protruded from Dario's sweating hands . . .

'Asskissa . . . cocksucka . . . monthafucka . . . ' The voice was almost upon him. 'Asskissa·. . . cocksucka . . . Aargh . . . '

The boy walked into the knife. Dario had not moved. *The boy had just walked right on into it.*

Silence.

Dario's hands slipped noiselessly from the handle. He felt sick. Had he killed him?

Carrie's indignity was complete. Hauled down to the police station in a filthy wagon with a seething furious mass of humanity. 'The dregs of society,' Elliott would say. And what would he say when he found *her* among them?

She closed her eyes and tried not to think about it.

She could picture the scene. His patrician features creased in amazement, 'But what on earth were you doing in Harlem, Carrie? I don't understand.'

She had told him she was dropping by to see Steven. 'I won't be long,' she had said. Steven lived three blocks away. Elliott, who had been watching a movie on television, waved vaguely.

How long *had* she been? Hours. Elliott would be frantic. He would have phoned Steven, found out she never arrived there . . . They would *both* be frantic.

Desperately she wracked her brains for a cover story. And when it came it was perfect. Everyone would believe her.

'I said, who is there?' Gino repeated gruffly.

'Mr Santangelo . . . It's me, Jill. I thought you might have changed your mind.'

Christ! Broads! Two thirty in the morning and she was back knocking on his door. 'Forget it,' he growled.

'Just open the door a minute,' she wheedled, 'I have to ask you something. *Please.*'

Always a sucker when they asked nicely. He slipped his gun in the pocket of his robe and turned the lock on the door. Maybe he *was* feeling a touch horny. Why not do her the big favour?

Opening up the door he began to say, 'Hey – now listen kid – what . . .'

His words turned to a strangled curse as a camera flash exploded in his face.


Laboriously a top panel was removed from the elevator, and a man in overalls stuck a torch through, pinpointing it on Lucky's face.

'For crissakes,' she snapped, bringing a hand up to cover her eyes.

The torch swivelled around and hit Steven who was busy putting his clothes back on. 'Turn that thing off,' he commanded, 'we've been in pitch dark for nine hours and I'm not about to have a torch in my eyes.'

The man in overalls laughed crudely and switched the torch off. 'You two sure look a mess. Just took ten people outta an elevator in the Sherman Building. Goddarn – they was joined at the hip!' He cackled some more, 'sweating like a regular herd a' cattle . . . an' the stink! I . . .'

'Can you get us out of here?' demanded Steven shortly.

The man cracked his knuckles, 'That's why I'm here.'

'Let's quit the talking and do it,' Steven said sharply. 'Are you from the fire department?'

'Naw,' the man sniffed, 'fire department's all backed up. The whole city's a mess. I'm from elevator maintenance.'

'Don't tell me there's a city power blackout?'

'You got it.'

Lucky was struggling into her clothes. 'Let's just get *out* of here,' she hissed.

'Right,' Steven replied, then to the man on top of the elevator, 'What are you going to do – force the doors?'

'Can't do that. You're between floors. Everyone who ever gets stuck is always between floors.'

'So how . . .?'

'Put a rope around you. Pull you out.'

'Oh God!' exclaimed Lucky, 'I don't like the sound of that.'

'Let me get this straight,' said Steven, 'you tie a rope around us and pull us up through the top of the elevator. Is that it?'

'Sure is. Safe as pullin' a tooth.'

'What's so safe about pulling a tooth?' Lucky demanded, the thought of rescue reviving her somewhat.

'You don't *have* to be taken out, ma'am. You can stay here 'til they turn the power on if you want – it don't bother me none.'

'Let's do it,' Steven decided, 'if he says it's safe – then it's safe.'

'Oh – if *he* says,' Lucky spat disdainfully, 'who the hell is *he*?'

'Look,' said Steven patiently, '*I'm* going. You want to stay that's up to you.'

'Wonderful. Really wonderful. You mean you would just leave me here, all alone?'

' 'Scuse me folks,' the maintenance man said, from his position on top of the elevator. 'Why don't I just come back? I got six more elevators to check out in this building – maybe I can find me some folks *want* to get out.'

'We're leaving,' said Steven grimly, 'throw down the ropes.'

Before Dario could stand, the boy crumpled and fell on top of him. He shrieked with horror, pushing and shoving until he was able to roll the boy off. He was shaking, his whole body one quivering mess.

He staggered up and ran from the kitchen. *He had killed someone. Get to a phone. Get hold of Costa immediately.*

The apartment was dimly lit by the moon. It enabled him to see his way to the telephone. Frantically he picked up the instrument and started to punch out the numbers.

It was then that he heard the noise. A picking scraping noise outside his front door.

*Someone was trying to get into his apartment.*

It wasn't easy getting attention in the crowded police precinct. After all – she was just another black face jammed in a pen with a whole bunch of them. But Carrie was in control of herself again, and quickly, lucidly, she spun her web of lies in a firm voice. 'Please phone my husband,' she begged at the end of her tale, 'and let him come and get me.' The cop she had been talking to nodded. It was a plausible story, and easily checked. Fortunately for Carrie, he made the phone call, and within an hour Elliott Berkely arrived at the precinct with his lawyer. He looked frantic, just as Carrie had expected. Within fifteen minutes she was released, apologized to, and out in the car with Elliott.

'Christ almighty! This city!' he exploded. 'Now they arrest the victims while the criminals roam the streets.' He started the car, and patted his wife comfortingly on the knee. 'What you must have gone through. Are you sure you're all right?'

'It's just my ears ...'

'Don't worry, we'll go straight to Doctor Mitchell's house. He'll take care of you. My God, I was so worried, I ...'

She tuned out as he carried on, and wondered what the blackmailer's next move would be. Elliott had bought her story, after all it was partly true. Her car *had* been stolen. She *had* been assaulted and robbed. The only make-believe was that two youths had climbed into her car on Sixty-Fourth Street while she waited at a stoplight. *They* had forced her at gunpoint to drive to Harlem, where they had thrown her out of the car. She had been caught up in a rioting mob, and arrested. Perfectly believable.

Elliott drove his Lincoln Continental slowly through the unlit streets where looters were still on the rampage and intermittent fires burned. 'What a hell hole!' he muttered, 'look at them – they're like animals. Thank God you were arrested – it was probably safer than being out on these streets. Vermin!' he spat emphatically. 'They deserve everything they get.'

Elliott had never been a liberal.

A cold shiver ran through Carrie's body when she considered the consequences of his ever finding out about her past.

'What the fuck ...' exploded Gino, attempting to close the door.

'An interview, Mr Santangelo,' insisted a hoarse male voice, his foot blocking the door. 'Please. Just a few questions.'

Gino could make out the stewardess, Jill, and next to her some creep with a camera strung around his neck. They were both drunk, any idiot could see that.

'You'd better both fuck on out of here,' Gino bellowed, 'and get your fucking foot out of my door before I blow it off.'

The jerk with the camera backed off, 'I thought you said he'd cooperate,' he hissed angrily at Jill.'

She shrugged drunkenly. 'I told you I'd bring you to him – didn't say he'd give you a kiss an' a cuddle.'

The photographer tried once more. 'Mr Santangelo – talk to me now and you won't have to talk to dozens of us tomorrow.'

Gino slammed the door of his room. He was too old for this shit.

# Gino 1937

Initial thought. Kill.

Blackness sweeping over him in uncontrollable waves.

Pain of course. But pain could be ignored.

Slam bewigged maniac in balls with knee.

Watch in slow motion as wig falls off and giant crumples.

Respite temporary.

Flowered housecoat leaping on his back.

Black rage.

Can feel blood oozing from wound.

Sound comes from throat. Animal sound.

Smash flowered housecoat against wall. Wild snarling teeth beneath lipstick.

Kick.

Smash.

Both of them now.

Reach for gun.

Crushed beneath two of them.

Pull trigger. Once. Twice.

Dead weight slumped across him.

Someone tearing at his face.

Slashes down his cheeks. Nails gouging for his eyes.

Pull trigger again.

Just once.

Bee slept soundly on one side of the large comfortable bed, her seven-year-old son, Marco, on the other.

The knocking on her front door became part of her dream. She was in a boat. the sun was shining, then the shark – swimming right up towards the boat and knocking . . . knocking . . . knocking . . .

She sat up in bed with a start. The knocking was for real.

Quickly she glanced at her alarm clock. It was 2.30 a.m. She looked over at Marco. He slept peacefully, thumb firmly in his mouth. Hurriedly she climbed out of bed, put on her housecoat, and padded barefoot to the door. 'Who's there?' she demanded, in a furious whisper.

'Let me in,' came the reply.

A man's voice which she almost recognized, but not quite. 'Who is this?' she insisted.

'Gino Santangelo.'

Her stomach flipped. Hadn't she scared him off the first time?

'Open up this fucking door,' he growled urgently.

She was in two minds about what to do. Let him in and fight him off? Or – not let him in and lose her job?

She needed the job. Reluctantly she slipped the catch, but before she could pull the door open he fell into the apartment.

'Oh my *God*!' she stifled a scream. 'What *happened* to you?'

He was a mess of blood. It was everywhere. His face was a red mask. His jacket soaked through.

For a moment she nearly panicked. But then good sense took over, and she half dragged him inside so that she could close the door properly.

'Get me a drink,' he groaned.

'I . . . I don't have anything . . .' she stammered.

'Oh yeh . . . I remember now . . .' he laughed feebly, 'you're . . . the . . . one with no booze . . .'

'You need a doctor,' she said firmly, 'who shall I call?'

He groaned. 'Don't . . . need . . . no . . . doctors . . You . . . can . . . take . . . care . . . of . . . me . . .'

'I can't.'

'Yes y'can. It . . . ain't . . . as . . . bad . . . as . . . it . . . looks.'

She pulled her housecoat tightly around her. What if he died? Here on her floor? 'Have you been shot?' she asked timorously.

'Stabbed,' he managed. 'No big deal. Help me get my clothes off.'

She thought about Marco asleep in the bedroom. 'Mr Santangelo,' she begged, 'let me call someone. Mr Dinunzio or your wife. They'll know what to do, I . . .'

'No phone calls,' he interrupted, 'five thousand bucks says you'll take care of me *an*' keep your mouth shut.'

Five thousand dollars! She was already spending it! Marco's education. New clothes for both of them. A small car. A vacation.

'What do you want me to do?' she asked quickly.

Cindy woke early, and was annoyed to see that Gino hadn't even bothered to come home. 'So what?' she muttered darkly to herself. It pleased her to know that regularly, every Friday, she would be getting a written report of her husband's activities. When and *if* she decided to divorce him she would be holding all the cards in the pack. Every little tramp he had ever shacked up with would be accounted for. She couldn't help giggling aloud. Gino thought he was so smart. But she was smarter! It was a fact!

She dressed carefully, curious about her lunch with Henry Moufflin Jr. Up until now she had faithfully adhered to Gino's rule. *No fuckin around while you're married to me.*

Some rule. He did nothing but.

Well, she had had enough. She had taken steps to protect herself and was all set to have herself one heck of a good time.

If Gino didn't like it – too bad.

He came awake slowly, only two aware of the throbbing pain in his shoulder. His face felt like sandpaper as he reached up to touch it with his left hand. The fuckers had split open his old scar. The sheet around his shoulder was soaked in blood. In the clear light of day he realized that he was going to have to see a doctor and get himself stitched up.

Wearily he tried to sit up, but black waves of pain hit him, and he lay back down. It was a miracle really that he had ever gotten out of Zefra Kincaid's seedy little room alive. He had killed to do so. They would have killed him if he hadn't.

Goddamn it. Oswald Duke's grisly task had been done. There was even an extra body thrown in for good luck.

And the letters had been there. A bundle of ten or twelve crammed behind a pillow. Senator Duke's distinctive handwriting on each and every one. Gino had stuffed them in his pocket and staggered from the apartment. A jazz session was still blasting forth from behind closed doors. Nobody had heard a thing. He had made it to his car, then, slumped behind the wheel, he had realized that driving all the way back uptown was impossible. Fortunately he remembered the hostess with the clap . . . Bee . . . She lived nearby. Only a couple of streets away. He had managed to drive there.

'Good morning,' Bee said gravely, entering the bedroom and hovering beside the bed. 'How do you feel?'

He remembered her kindness. Kindness that came with the promise of five thousand bucks. 'Like I got ran over by a train.'

'Hmmm . . . ' she regarded him solemnly. If he could see himself he would realize just how true that statement was. Both his eyes were blackened and swollen. His face was gouged with scratches, the old scar split obscenely open, a lump of congealed blood holding it together. His lips were thick and puffy.

She didn't want to think about his shoulder wound. When she had cut off his jacket and shirt the previous night, blood had come pumping out in torrents, causing her to scream aloud in shock.

Marco had run into the room. 'Mommy! Mommy! Wassamatta? Who is this man?'

Gino had looked at the boy, then back at her. He hadn't said a word.

'Just a friend of mommy's darling,' she soothed, 'go back to sleep.'

The small boy had retreated uneasily. Later she had carried him to the couch, and helped Gino into the bed. She had slept fitfully on a chair.

In the morning she had hurried Marco off to school before he could ask any more questions. By the time he returned home in the afternoon she hoped that Gino would be gone.

'I want you t'make a coupla calls for me,' he mumbled.

'Yes, of course.'

'Don't say nuthin' on the phone.'

'I understand.'

'Call Aldo. Tell him I need t'see him urgent – then give him your address.'

'Right.'

'Tell him to bring Doc Harrison.'

She produced a slip of paper and wrote down the number he gave her. 'You can depend on me.'

And so he did. For the next ten days he depended on her entirely. She bathed him, fed him, waited on him day and night, and watched him recover.

He had the strength of a horse. In ten days he was ready to go home. The doctor said it would have taken any other man weeks to get on his feet again. 'You lost a massive amount of blood, quite frankly you were lucky to survive.'

Yeh. He was lucky all right. Nobody knew the story of what had really happened that night. Not even Aldo. 'I was visiting Bee,' Gino had told him, 'an' a coupla punks jumped me in the street. Didn't even know who I was. Took my money an' ran.'

To Bee he gave no explanation at all and she did not ask any questions. He liked that. They became friends in the ten days he was there. She was a great cook, and played a mean game of cards. The kid was all right too. A tough little boy who entertained him with schoolboy jokes.

'Where's his old man?' Gino questioned one day.

She blushed, 'There never was one.'

'Aw c'mon. So you weren't married. So what? There hadda have been a guy.'

'Yes. There was a guy. He was fifty-two, I was fifteen. Same old story. He raped me. He was a friend of my father so nobody believed me. I was thrown out of the house, so I came to New York, and I've been here ever since.'

'And y'made out OK.'

'I made out, let's put it that way. And I kept my son. Corny isn't it?'

'Sure. Truth always is.'

He never touched her sexually, although when his strength came roaring back he was tempted.

'You really had a dose?' he asked her one day.

She smiled, 'Nope. But I wanted to keep you off.'

'Oh yeh? Why?'

'Because who needs to be another one of the girls?'

He thought about grabbing her and tumbling her into bed with him. Then he thought again. They were friends, why spoil everything?

The day after he left he sent her over an envelope. It contained fifteen thousand dollars and a scrawled note. The note said, 'You'll make some poor sap one hell of a nurse! The five as promised – the ten to bank for Marco.'

She was overwhelmed. Gino Santangelo could do no wrong in her book. And she put to the back of her mind the double killing in her neighborhood that had taken place the very same morning that he had come staggering to her apartment covered in blood.

First lunch with Henry Moufflin Jr. Fun.

Second. Exciting.

Third. Devastating.

Fourth. A sexual coupling of intense proportions.

Wow! Ecstacy! Henry Moufflin Jr was in love and Cindy was enjoying every minute of it.

He was a rich society puppet who jumped whichever way she pulled the strings.

He wanted to shower her with jewels and furs and gifts.

He wanted to drown her with champagne and smother her with caviar.

He wanted her to divorce Gino and marry him.

She weighed up the pros and cons.

Gino ignored her.

Henry adored her.

Gino screwed around.

Henry would be forever faithful.

Gino talked down to her.

Henry put her on a pedestal.

Gino had no class.

Henry was loaded with it.

Of course –

Gino was rough and tough and good looking.

Henry was a bit of a wimp.

Gino was powerful *and* had money.

Henry just had the money.

Gino – when he wanted to be – was a magnificent lover.

Henry had a lot to learn.

She could teach him. Why not? What fun to teach him what to do with his fingers and tongue and somewhat shakey erection.

She made a decision – very much influenced by the fact that according to Aldo, Gino had had to leave unexpectedly on a secret trip. And yet according to her detective's report Gino was holed up in some whore's apartment down in the Village.

She scanned the report one more time. It stated that Gino had visited two whores in the Village that night. One apparently was not enough for him any more. He had staggered out of the first building, drunk, and then gone onto another apartment where he had liked the taste of pussy so much he had gone to ground. Bastard.

Well, he wasn't making a fool of *her* any more. She would divorce him and marry Henry.

And the sooner the better.


There were countless messages to contact Senator Duke waiting for Gino when he got home.

Aldo drove him. It was five o'clock in the afternoon but the maid was the only person waiting in the apartment.

'Where's Cindy?'

Aldo shrugged, and averted his eyes. *He* wasn't going to be the one to tell Gino that his wife was running all over town with another guy, he would find out soon enough.

'Hey – ' Gino said to the maid, 'where's Mrs Santangelo?'

She jumped nervously. The sight of her master's face was making her sick to her stomach. 'I . . . I . . . don't know, sir. She left no message.'

He scowled, 'You tell her I was comin' back today?' he asked Aldo.

'Yes. I told her. Perhaps if you had telephoned yourself . . . She wasn't too happy about you just takin off . . . '

'The hell with what she wasn't too happy about. She's my wife for crissakes, she should be here.' ·

Aldo shuffled his feet uneasily. Maybe he had better warn Gino about what was going on. 'Listen,' he began.

'I don't feel so hot,' Gino interrupted, 'I guess I'll go to bed. You got all the figures for me?'

Aldo nodded, dug into his inside pocket, and handed over a sheaf of papers.

'Any news on The Boy?'

'Nothing. He's gone to the mattress. He'll have to surface eventually. Don't worry, we'll get him.'

'Who's fucking worried?'

Luncheon was delicious. Room service provided cold lobster, chilled champagne, and strawberries with cream.

Henry Moufflin Jr provided a suite full of red roses, some romantic music on the gramophone, and a small exciting black velvet box, which he would not let Cindy open until after lunch.

'Oh Henry!' she squealed. 'You're so *mean* to me!'

He chortled happily, 'And you are s . . . s . . . so very good to me, my darling.'

She wolfed down the lobster, gulped the champagne, stuffed the strawberries one by one into her pert open mouth. 'Now, honeybunch?' she asked excitedly. 'Can cutsie pie open it now?'

'Y . . . y . . . yes. Now.'

Her big blue eyes sparkled as she grabbed for the small box like a hungry puppy getting hold of its first bone. She had plenty of jewelry. But a girl could never have enough.

She opened up the box and gasped. The sumptuous ring that rested proudly on a bed of black velvet knocked her eyes out. It was a huge ruby in an antique setting of diamonds and emeralds. Incredibly beautiful and lavish, it surpassed anything she owned.

'Oh my God, Henry!' she breathed softly, *'Oh my God!'*

'Do y . . . y . . . you like it?' he asked anxiously.

'Like it? *Like it?* I'm *nuts* about it!' She leaped up and threw her arms around him, kissing him generously.

He blushed with pleasure. It had not been easy extracting a family heirloom from the grasp of his patrician mother.

Cindy slipped the ring on her finger, and waved her hand in the air admiring it.

This action so excited Henry that he began to drag the clothes off his hairless body at full speed. Soon he stood before Cindy, naked, with a limp hard-on.

She was still admiring the ring. Her mind doing quick mathematical calculations trying to figure out how much it was worth.

'Cindy,' Henry begged plaintively.

She had forgotten he was even there. 'Ooops!' she exclaimed, 'is my baby Henry all ready for a little fun and games?'

'Yes,' he said eagerly.

'Well my ickle bickle Henry is going to have to sit back an' enjoy the show.' She pushed him down into a chair. Adjusted the record until it was at the start, and to the strains of 'I've Got My Love To Keep Me Warm' began to provocatively remove her clothes.

Henry sighed ecstatically.


Alone in his luxurious apartment Gino read through Senator Duke's letter again. The man might be a financial genius, but he was also a prize fool.

Twelve letters, written over a period of twelve weeks.

Twelve damning, compromising letters written to Zefra Kincaid while Senator Oswald languished in southern France for an extended vacation after breaking his leg on a yacht outing.

From the letters Gino was able to piece together the whole story. Zefra Kincaid. A young boy the Senator had found in his nighttime travels through the dark world of the homosexual community. The boy – very young. The Senator – very rich.

A weekly relationship had developed. A meeting in an indifferent hotel on the West side where no questions were asked. A relationship that continued for three long years. The boy being fifteen years of age when it started.

The Senator had quite obviously kept the boy. But when

Zefra began to grow from boy to man, the Senator had tired of him.

Gino could imagine the rest. Blackmail. And the Senator had called upon Gino to do him a favor. And he had done just that.

The double killing had not received much press. After all, the victims were black, certainly not headline material. 'NAR-COTICS DOUBLE MURDER' had been the heading to the short story. Gino sighed. No great loss to the community.

He glanced at his watch and started a slow burn. It was nine o'clock and still no Cindy. He had phoned Clemmies but she wasn't there. Vera had gotten on the phone and started to harangue him about giving Paulo a job when he got out of jail. 'He'll need support,' she had wailed.

Yeh. He'd give him support all right. The same sort of support *he* had received as a kid.

He got out of bed and went to the bathroom to study his face. Not a pretty sight. Doc Harrison had opened up the old scar and then stitched it neatly back together again. When the black thread came out it wouldn't look too bad. Fade back to normal in no time the Doc had said.

The scratches all over his face were fading too, although they still made a vicious pattern. He ran his hand through his black curly hair and narrowed his eyes. Christ! Stick him in a gangster movie now and he'd sure look the part. Move over, Cagney . . .

He laughed aloud. He had no regrets. He was a born survivor.

The Senator's letters were in a neat pile on the bed. He picked them up and locked them in the safe. No way was good old Oswald getting them back. No way. They were his insurance policy against any more favors.

Clementine smiled at the Beckers, waved to Bernard Dimes, and urgently whispered to Oswald for the tenth time that day, *'Why* do you think he's avoiding us?'

Oswald motioned to a waiter for a refill of his brandy, 'I don't know,' he hissed back.

They were attending the opening night of Rodgers and Hart 'Babes In Arms', a new musical comedy, and they were socializing in the bar during intermission.

It had not been an easy ten days. Gino had done the favor, but had failed to contact them.

'He had to take an unexpected trip,' Aldo informed the Senator.

'Mr Santangelo is away,' the maid at his apartment said.

'How should I know where he is. *I'm* only his wife,' Cindy had sniffed.

'He'll have to come back eventually,' Clementine mused.

'Of course he will,' Oswald had agreed.

'How could he put us through this?'

'I don't know m'dear. It's shocking.'

'It certainly is.'

Clementine thought about the loss of his body. His strong hands. His bleak eyes. The way he had of bringing her to a climax so exquisite, so . . .

'Hiya!' Cindy stood before them, a vision in pink crepe de chine and dyed pink fox. Cindy wearing and flashing the famous Moufflin ruby.

'G . . . G . . . Good evening Clementine, Senator,' stammered Henry, cheeks glowing above a tight wing collar.

Clementine looked from one to the other. Was the girl mad? Surely Gino would never let her get away with making a public fool of him?

'Cindy,' she nodded coldly, 'Henry.'

'Wonderful show, ain't it?' enthused Cindy, putting her hand to her face to make sure her ring was on show.

'Wonderful,' replied Clementine dryly, 'do you have any news about Gino's return?'

Cindy grinned. Stuck up Mrs Duke having to ask *her*. She shrugged casually, 'You know Gino. He comes an' he goes as he pleases. He's probably shacked up with one of his broads!' How she enjoyed watching the grand old lady squirm.

Clementine was furious. Little tramp. How would Cindy feel if she knew that the only reason Gino had married her in the first place was because she, Clementine, had insisted. Deliberately she turned her back.

Cindy giggled, and stage whispered to Henry, 'The old bag is jealous 'cos *I've* got you, toots.'

Henry was immensely flattered, 'Do you really th . . . th . . . think so?' he stammered.

'Sure do!'

Midnight came and went. No Cindy.

Gino prowled around the apartment cursing. One a.m. Two a.m. Three a.m. No Cindy.

He fell asleep at last, his imagination running riot at the things he would do to her. No wife of his was going to get away with whoring around. He tossed and he turned, and woke occasionally to check the time. He dreamed about Leonora and Bee and Jake the Boy and Zefra Kincaid, and he awoke at seven o'clock with an ache in his gut, a pain in his shoulder, the stitches in his cheek pulling.

The maid brought him black coffee, fresh orange juice, and the morning papers. He was lying in the lap of luxury, but he thought longingly of Bee's shabby warm apartment where breakfast was hot freshly baked rolls and milky tea. And reading matter was F. Scott Fitzgerald. Yeh. He had done a first at Bee's. Read a book. 'The Great Gatsby' from cover to cover. And then again. Reading wasn't half bad. He wondered why he'd never tried it before. He could identify with a guy like Gatsby, a loner, a figure of mystery.

The telephone rang. Clementine's voice, tight and worried, 'Thank God you're back.'

Cindy and Henry argued.

'But I w . . . w . . . want to come w . . . w . . . with you,' he insisted.

'Nope.' She was very firm.

'Your h . . . husband doesn't frighten me.'

'Glad to hear it. But I can promise you he frightens a lot of people. He's mean and rough and plays dirty.'

'But C . . . C . . . Cindy . . . ?'

She leaped out of bed and stretched athletically. '*I* can handle him honeybunch. *I* can play *just* as dirty as *he* can.' Naked, she danced around the hotel bedroom admiring her ring.

Henry sat up in bed. 'My mother can't wait to meet you. I thought perhaps next weekend would be suitable.'

She high kicked, giving him a full view of hidden glories. 'Very suitable. This morning I tell Gino. This afternoon I move out. And a quick divorce will follow. I promise.'

'G . . . G . . . Good,' he stammered, 'come back to b . . . bed my darling. Just one more time before you g . . . go.'

She giggled. Anyone would think a girl hadn't dipped her head to him before. She jumped on the bed, pulled back the covers, and his shakey erection awaited her. A most peculiar organ actually. Very long and thin with no substance, no real hardness. Certainly not *her* fault. Lovingly she took him in her mouth.

He groaned. 'Oh C . . . C . . . Cindy . . . Oh . . .'

Thoughtfully Gino hung up the telephone. His black eyes

burned as he picked up the newspaper and turned to the Walter Winchell gossip column.

The item was there, just as Clementine had said it would be. In clear print. For all to see. And read. And snigger.

*'Cindy Santangelo, wife of notorious club owner Gino the Ram Santangelo, was out on the town last night seeing the sights and opening night of 'Babes In Arms' with Henry Moufflin Jr.'*

That's all it said.

That was enough.

He threw the newspaper to the floor in a fury.

At twelve noon Cindy arrived home. She swept into the apartment tottering slightly on heels that were just that much too big for her. She was swathed in pale pink fox from head to toe.

The maid greeted her with a nervous bob. 'Mr Santangelo is home, ma'am. He's in the bedroom.'

'Thank you,' Cindy said regally. 'Take the rest of the day off.' She swayed into the bedroom, ready for the battle she was sure lay ahead. The sight of Gino brought her up short. 'What in hell happened to you?'

'I had a car accident.'

'Bull!' She walked closer to the bed and peered at him, 'You look *horrible.*'

'You don't look so hot yourself. Where have *you* been?'

She shrugged off her fox coat. 'Ha! *He* vanishes for ten days and where have *I* been. You've got some nerve.' She flounced over to the dressing table, sat down and carefully removed her fox hat.

'Cindy,' he called, very softly, almost a whisper, 'you read your daily papers?' He threw her the paper, which landed by her feet. It was folded and opened at Winchell's column.

She screwed up her face for a moment, and thought about not picking the paper up. But curiosity got the better of her, and she plucked it from the floor.

She read slowly, laboriously. Reading had never been one of her strong points. When she saw her name mentioned in Winchell's column a little smile flitted across her face. *She was famous.* Oh boy oh boy!

She finished reading and placed the newspaper carefully on her dressing table. Maybe she should start a scrapbook.

Gino was infuriated by her attitude. 'Well?' he demanded,

'how you gonna explain that? And how you gonna explain where you were all night?'

'With Henry,' she replied calmly. 'And I'm gonna be with him again tonight.'

He could hardly believe what he was hearing. 'The fuck you are!'

'The fuck I am! And *you* ain't gonna stop me.'

'Oh no?' He began to climb out of bed.

'Oh no.' She stood and faced him brazenly, hands on hips, a sneer on her lips. 'Not if you know what's good for you.'

'Huh?' He started to laugh. This broad was nuts. Who did she think she was playing with for crissakes? *Smart ass Cindy. Don't fuck around with the big boys.*

'I've got plenty on you, Gino Santangelo,' she said, 'P-L-E-N-T-Y.'

'What the fuck you talkin' about?'

A triumphant shadow flickered across her face. '*I* have had you followed by a private detective. *I* know everything. Ha! A ten day trip all the way to the Village and some dumb cunt. *I have it all in writing.* When we get our divorce you'd better be nice to me or I'll take everything. You hear me?'

His voice was deathly ice, 'You . . . had . . . me . . . followed?'

'I sure did,' she said jauntily, 'an' I guess that puts me in the drivin' seat.' She paused for breath, then continued, 'And another thing. Those federal tax agents bin sniffin' around while you was gone. You don't cooperate with me, honey, an' I'm gonna lead 'em to every bank in town an' show 'em your safe deposit boxes. *And* the copies of the books I got.' She fluffed out her platinum blonde hair, 'I want a divorce Gino. I got the goods on you so I don't expect you to give me *no* trouble.'

# Carrie 1938

Carrie could hardly believe her luck. She had got a job in the chorus of Bernard Dimes's new musical. It was the second time in her life he had been there just when she needed him.

He told the Beckers she would be leaving, and personally drove her to a small apartment in the Village that he had arranged for her to share with another girl.

'Why are you doing all this for me?' she asked.

'Because everybody deserves a break – and I have a feeling not too many have come your way.'

She wanted to hug him. Instead she said, 'I'll do my best not to let you down.'

That had been in December. It was now August, the show was a success, and Carrie was happy. She was working hard at a job she liked, and Goldie, the girl she shared the apartment with, was nice. The only subject they ever argued about was boyfriends. Goldie had plenty. Carrie wanted none.

'You're abnormal,' Goldie would joke, 'how come you never thought of being a nun?'

'I had a boyfriend once,' Carrie lied, 'but he died.'

Goldie was immediately sympathetic and left her alone for a while. But only for a while. It seemed that most of her dates had a friend who wanted fixing up, and Goldie was always trying to get her to come along. She always said no. Nightclubbing, jazz joints, and parties were events she steered well clear of. She was sure she could resist temptation . . . but being sure wasn't enough . . .

Every Saturday night Bernard Dimes turned up backstage for a short visit. He usually had an elegant woman on his arm, but that didn't stop most of the girls in the show being absolutely mad about him.

Goldie adored him. 'He's the most attractive man I've ever seen!' she sighed. 'So worldly. I wish he'd ask *me* out.'

Carrie considered Goldie's usual boyfriends. Brawny muscular types all in their twenties. 'He doesn't seem your type,' she ventured.

'That's it,' Goldie enthused. 'He's different. Why I bet the way he makes love is even different!'

On his weekly visits to the theatres he always had a kindly word for Carrie. How was she getting along? Was everything all right? He seemed to take an interest in every member of the company – that's how he had known that Goldie was looking for a roommate.

He frightened Carrie in a way. He had so much authority. He was always the master of every situation. Mr Bernard Dimes appeared to be in total control of his life.

In her own mind she knew that she was thinking about him far too much. Was she – like all the other girls in the show – falling a little bit in love with him?

Bernard Dimes – with his money and his style and his tall beautiful women. He would never desire *her* in a million years.

Bernard Dimes was forty-five-years-old, unmarried, extremely successful, and a very lonely man indeed. Oh he had many acquaintances, but few people he could term as real friends. He enjoyed the occasional sexual liaison – but his standards were exceptionally high, and few women could maintain his interest.

Beautiful women *were* important to him. If they were witty and intelligent that was an extra plus, because Bernard had found that having an elegant companion was a definite asset when raising money for a new production. He had a stable of females he could call upon for various events. Each one of them adored him. And marriage was on their minds. Bernard had never even considered the possibility. After all – what conceivable advantages could marriage bring him? He had the best of their services as it was.

Then Carrie came into his life. A black waif with a face of such exotic unusualness, deep expressive eyes and jet black silken hair that a man could imagine sweeping over his chest . . .

At first he had wondered where he had seen her before. Just a casual interest. Then on talking to her, the strangest sensation. He wanted to help her . . .

And then the rush of remembrance. She was the girl from Clementine Duke's party. The pathetic drugged creature who had collapsed in the middle of her degrading dance.

He had not mentioned his memory of that occasion for fear of embarrassing her. But when he checked with Esther Becker's housekeeper about where they had found her he learned that she had been in an institution for quite a few years.

Desperately he wanted to ask her about her life. She had such sadness in her beautiful eyes. Almost a hopelessness. He wanted to *know* her.

Every Saturday, when he visited the theatre, he thought – yes – tonight I will ask her out. He never did. He smiled politely, inquired after her welfare, and wondered hopelessly what a woman like that would be like in bed.

For the first time in his life, Bernard Dimes was in love.

And for the first time in his life a situation had arisen that he did not know how to handle.

One Saturday it was Goldie's twenty-first birthday. She had a date with her favorite boyfriend – Mel. And he was bringing along a friend – Freddy Lester. It was after show time, and the girl who had agreed to be Freddy's date had turned her ankle and was hobbling around in agony.

Goldie looked beseechingly at Carrie, 'Please!' she begged.

Carrie did not see how she could reasonably say no. After all, it *was* Goldie's birthday. And anyway – she had to learn to trust herself sometime – she couldn't be a recluse for the rest of her life. 'OK,' she agreed reluctantly.

'We'll have a *wonderful* time!' Goldie enthused, 'Mel is *the* most fun guy I've ever been out with, and if *he* says Freddy is a hunk then you can betcha skirt he *is*!'

Carrie nodded. A hunk. Goldie's favorite description of any halfway decent looking male. A hunk. All the same in the dark.

'I'd better lend you something to wear,' Goldie carried on excitedly. She turned to inspect the supply of clothes that littered the dressing room they shared with four other girls. 'Susie, can Carrie borrow your skirt? Oh and Mabel, your strappy shoes – the ones with the three inch heels. *Pleeease!*'

Goldie could be very persuasive. Carrie ended up in Susie's tight black slit skirt, Mabel's stiletto heels, and an off the shoulder white blouse of Goldie's.

'Hmmm . . . ' Goldie stepped back to survey her, 'very nice. Sexy, with just a touch of class. Do you *have* to wear your hair all knotted back? Can't you let it down?'

Carrie obliged. Why not? She was actually getting quite excited at the thought of an evening out. She brushed her waist length black hair, and secured one side off her face with a white flower.

'You look terrific!' exclaimed Goldie. 'Just keep your hands off Mel!'

A discreet tap on the dressing room door heralded Bernard Dimes' Saturday night arrival. He smiled, and nodded round the small cramped room. Then he handed Goldie an extravagantly wrapped gift.

She opened it with a lot of ooohing and aaahing, although she knew it would be chocolates. He never forgot a birthday, and it was always chocolates. 'Umm,' she purred, 'how delicious. *Tank you*.' She batted her spikey eyelashes at him. 'They'll put pounds in *all* the wrong places.'

He glanced over at Carrie. She looked different. Then he realized that she was obviously dressed to go out. He was disappointed, having earlier decided that tonight he *would* invite her to dinner. Oh well . . . He had waited months as it was. Another week or so wasn't going to make any difference.

Outside the stage door entrance of the theatre Mel waited anxiously.

His friend, Freddy, who was quite good looking and knew

it, said, 'I hope she's six feet tall. I've always had a yen for tall girls.'

'What do you care, as long as she puts out?' Mel replied dismissively. 'If she's anything like Goldie, it's two drinks and she's all yours.'

'Can't wait! I haven't been laid in two days!'

Goldie and Carrie emerged from the theatre. 'Be sure to order champagne,' Goldie whispered, 'it makes them realize you're something special.'

Mel and Freddy stepped sharply forward.

'Hiya fellas,' greeted Goldie, in her best Mae West voice.

'Happy birthday gorgeous,' said Mel, grabbing her in a bear hug, and kissing her full on the mouth.

Carrie and Freddy stared warily at each other.

'Whoops a daisy!' exclaimed Goldie, pushing Mel away, 'you're spoiling my lipstick you big oaf.' She grinned at Freddy, 'Hello, I'm Goldie as if you didn't know. And this is Carrie – your dream date for the night. Aren't *you* the lucky one!'

Freddy's expression did not indicate that he was the lucky one at all. He nodded quite curtly at Carrie, and the four of them set off down the alley to Mel's car.

Once there Mel opened up the doors. Goldie climbed into the front, and Carrie got into the back. Mel and Freddy stood outside.

'What's the matter with you?' Carrie heard Mel ask his friend.

'Je . . . sus!' Freddy replied, in what was supposed to be a whisper. 'She's a fucking dinge!'

'So?' replied Mel, matter of factly. 'Haven't you ever heard of black pudding?'

'Sure,' replied Freddy, 'but I've never taken it out in public.'

'Aw, c'mon.' laughed Mel. 'Let's get this show on the road.' They climbed into the car.

In the back, Carrie sat gazing miserably out of the window. Their hateful words hung in her ears – *Fucking dinge. Black pudding.*

Her eyes filled with salty tears that slid silently down her cheeks. She kept her head determinedly turned towards the window so that no one would observe her misery.

Goldie and Mel chatted merrily away in the front seat. Freddy sat rather stiffly in the back. He cleared his throat a couple of times and finally said, 'So you and Goldie share an apartment then?'

'Yes,' Carrie replied, willing her voice to sound steady and normal. No way could she let him see that she was upset. If he realized that she had heard it would only make things worse. She decided to let him off the hook. 'You know I have an awful headache,' she announced. 'Maybe I should just go on home.'

Goldie replied immediately, 'Definitely *not*! It's taken me six months to get you out and you're staying. That's that! Right, Mel?'

An enthusiastic, 'Right.'

Carrie sank miserably back into the seat. There was no getting out of it.

They started off in a small jazz joint on Fifty-Second Street. Neat little combo playing, champagne flowing.

Goldie was in high spirits, rarin' to go. And when Carrie stated she wanted to stick to fruit juice, she let her have it full blast. 'Hey listen chickie. It's my *birthday* an' I plan to have *fun*. If you're gonna moon around with a long face it's goin' to spoil *everything*. Now have some champagne for God's sake, an' put a smile on your face!'

Carrie obliged. She had forgotten the potent taste of champagne, although when Whitejack was flush he had bought it by the bucket. She figured one glass wasn't going to send her on the road to ruin. And she had to get through the evening somehow.

One glass turned into two, then three, then on to another club, and frothy white daquaris that were so delicious she had at least four. After all they were such little drinks, what harm could they do?

By the time the four of them piled into Clemmies they were feeling no pain. Carrie and Freddy were the best of friends, giggling, laughing, dancing. And when his hands accidentally on purpose kept brushing against her breasts she didn't mind one little bit. She felt so free. So alive. It was the first time in years she could honestly say she was living.

'You are simmly great, y'know that?' Freddy slurred.

She responded by locking her hands around his neck and gazing into his eyes. *Fucking dinge* no longer reverberated through her mind. 'Thank you,' she murmured sincerely. It had been a long time since anyone had told her that.

'No, I mean it,' Freddy insisted, as if he was expecting her to argue, 'I really mean it.'

'Hey,' said Goldie nudging Carrie, 'you see that guy over

there. That's *the* Gino Santangelo. He owns the joint. I met him once, he's a *real* bad boy.'

Her eyes swivelled to check him out. 'I've taken on a lota bad boys in my time,' she boasted.

'Carrie!' exclaimed Goldie, giggling, 'I've never seen you like this!'

'Yeah. You don't know nothin'!'

Goldie nudged Mel, 'She's really bombed.'

Mel grinned, 'How'd you like to make yourself fifty bucks, Carrie?'

'What didja have in mind big boy?'

'I betcha fifty bucks y'can't make it with the great Mr Santangelo.'

'Yeah?' Her eyes gleamed. 'You lost yourself a bet.'

Before any of them could stop her she was on her feet and sashaying across the crowded club.

Goldie clapped her hand to her mouth in amazement. 'Oh my God, Mel! What have you done? This isn't like her at all.'

He laughed in a nasty fashion, 'C'mon doll, she isn't gonna do anything she hasn't done a hundred times before.'

'No, no,' Goldie attempted to argue through an alcoholic haze, 'she's not that kind of girl . . . '

Mel silenced her with a great big wet kiss, then began to whisper promises of what he was going to do to her later.

Goldie forgot about Carrie and concentrated on herself.

Freddie grimaced drunkenly. 'Thanks a lot old buddy,' he complained. But already his eye had been taken by a tall brunette sitting by herself two tables away.

As Carrie proceeded across the room she was on her own.

# Gino 1938

Gino sat at his usual table. Cock of the hoop. A constant stream of customers trailed over to pay homage.

He wore his customary three piece dark suit, white silk shirt, tasteful tie. His black hair was slicked down. The huge diamond ring on his pinky caught the light occasionally and gleamed expensively. Only the scar on his face gave him a slightly sinister look. That, and his hard black eyes which one woman had recently compared to Rudolph Valentino's. He had liked that compliment. Rudolph Valentino. Yeh.

He had been wearing black for nearly a year now. Well it was only right wasn't it? A mark of respect for his dear departed wife, Cindy. She had slipped and fallen from the twenty-fifth floor window of their penthouse apartment. A terrible tragic accident. And Gino not even in the city at the time. He had been in Westchester, staying with his good friends Senator and Mrs Duke.

Yes. A dreadful disaster. A crushing blow for him to be left a widower at only thirty-two.

He had arranged a magnificent funeral with an impressive turnout.

Cindy would have been honored.

Unfortunately Henry Moufflin Jr had been unable to attend. He had been involved in a rather bad car crash, and was in Europe recuperating. The rumor was that he loved Europe so much that he might never return to the States.

That very same week there had been a fire in the offices of Sam Lawson – a private investigator. He had been burned to death along with all his files. Coincidentally Sam Lawson had been the private detective that Cindy had been using. Gino felt it only right to send a wreath as a mark of respect. Cindy would have appreciated a gesture like that.

He sipped his scotch on the rocks and inspected the female heading his way. Black. Exotic. And breasts that would stop traffic.

She reached his table, stopped and smiled. 'Mr Santangelo?'

'Yes.'

'I hear you own this place. I just thought I'd stop by and tell you what a classy spot I think it is.'

He smiled. He liked bold women. Sometimes. 'Sit down, have a drink.'

Carrie sat. She felt marvellous. Just drunk enough to feel she could own the world if she wanted to.

'Champagne?' he questioned.

'Naturally.'

He clicked his fingers and a waiter was instantly by his side.

'A bottle of the best champagne.'

'Yes, immediately, Mr Santangelo.'

Gino studied her. A rare unusual beauty. One glass and he would take her home.

One more glass and she would go.

'Do that again,' Carrie moaned, 'uum . . . please.'

He was licking her. Patiently darting his tongue in and out with skilled expertise. It had been a long time since he had tongued a woman. But this one was so creamy and eager . . . It was almost like she hadn't had a man in years. And he liked that. It got his sexual juices and desires going full force.

Not that he wasn't well occupied sexually. There was Bee – always available – warm and solid. There was a girl singer in the club – very sexy but he suspected that she didn't bathe as often as she should. And of course there were the various one night adventures with everyone from Copacabana showgirls to rich society dames.

She moaned again, this time more loudly.

He stopped with his tongue and rolled on top of her. She gripped him with her smooth brown legs and urged him on.

For one fast moment he almost got carried away. But not quite. His mind was always a spectator. Sharp and wary. Observing the action like a particularly alert bystander. Even in orgasm.

The girl was reaching a climax. A prolonged session of concentrated energy as she came. He could feel her throbbing around him, and as if on cue he willed himself to climax too.

Now it was over, and he wanted her to go home.

He got up from the bed. 'Hey – hey – hey,' he said, 'betcha didn't learn to do *that* in school.'

The champagne was still coloring Carrie's mind. She felt powerful and in control and *oh so good*. Gino Santangelo had not used her. She had not used him. It had been a mutually enjoyable experience.

Lazily she stretched. Her body felt reborn – like someone had come along and hammered out all the tenseness.

'My car's downstairs, the driver'll take you home whenever you're ready,' Gino said easily. 'Oh – and here's a little present for you. Buy yourself something pretty.'

He handed her a hundred dollars. He always gave the women he took to bed money for a gift. It was an idiosyncrasy of his, and no one ever objected. Even the society girls tucked it into their purses and sauntered into Tiffanys or Cartiers the next day to pick up a little something to remind them of Gino Santangelo.

'You sonofabitch!' she screamed, leaping up from the bed, '*You think I'm a whore?*'

'Hey . . . Of course not . . .'

'How dare you! How *dare* you!'

This one was obviously nuts, struggling into her clothes like a wildcat, glaring at him and screaming.

'Hey listen – if I thought you was a whore I'd have given you the going rate. This money's a present.'

'Fuck you!' she screamed. 'If I was a whore it would have cost you a hell of a lot more,' and throwing the money in his face she stormed out of his apartment.

He shook his head in amazement.

Women.

He'd never understand 'em.

# Carrie 1938

Carrie ignored Gino's car and driver waiting downstairs, and began to walk along Park Avenue. She was sobering up in a hurry. *Fucking dinge* was coming back to haunt her. And a red hot fury was building inside her.

What had she been thinking of approaching Gino Santangelo like that? Who else but a whore would go over to a man's table, sit down, and half an hour later be sharing his bed?

*Fucking dinge. Whore.* The words flew through her head. She had tried so hard to be decent. And now – after one night – she was back where she had started. Why hadn't Goldie stopped her? Why had she gone out with her and her lousy friends in the first place?

She walked seven blocks before she got a cab, and then the driver gave her a dubious look and said, 'I ain't goin' to Harlem, honey.'

She gave him a cold stare in return, 'Nor am I – *honey*.'

He didn't like that. He maintained a frosty silence all the way back to the Village.

She paid him off and climbed the three flights of stairs to the roomy loft. Once inside she was dismayed to find Freddy in bed. *Her bed*. She could not believe her eyes.

Angrily she shook him awake, 'Get out of here,' she insisted in a furious whisper.

'Aw c'mon, toots,' he mumbled, bleary eyed and still drunk. He had no intention of getting up and going home.

'Will you get out of my bed?' she hissed.

'Whyn't you come in an' join me? I've bin waitin' all night,' he slurred.

'Whyn't you drop dead?'

He gripped her wrist, 'C'mon sweetie pie, be a sport.'

'Leave *go* of me.'

He was surprisingly strong. He was able to pull her onto the bed with ease.

'I'll scream if you don't stop,' she raged.

'Don't you do that, sweetie.' And he placed the heavy palm of his hand over her mouth, stopping her from screaming, and holding her down all at the same time. With his other hand he pulled up her skirt and ripped off her panties.

She went numb. The strength just drained right out of her.

He took this as a sign of acquiescence, and somehow he got out his penis and began jamming it into her.

She made little choking noises in her throat. His hand preventing her sobs of anguish from emerging.

'You're wetter than a bathful of oil!' he crowed, 'I betcha lovin' every minute of it. Huh, honeypuss? Huh?'

She willed her mind to go blank. And when he took his hand away she did not scream. She waited until he finished, and then said quite calmly, 'That'll be thirty bucks, mister. Thirty big ones.'

'What?' he mumbled.

'You screw a whore, you pay,' she said in a cold unruffled manner. 'Especially when you screw a fucking dinge.'

'But . . .'

'Pay or I holler rape.'

He paid.

Carrie could not wait to get away from Goldie. She moved out the very next day, after phoning the theatre and telling the stage manager she wouldn't be coming back.

With her one suitcase she tramped around trying to find a single room for rent. No luck. Eventually she got the message when enough doors were slammed in her face. She took a bus and went back to the streets she knew.

Harlem looked grimier than ever, but it was where she belonged. She found herself a room and hibernated. She had just enough money to sit out a couple of months before making any decisions about what to do next.

Six weeks later she realized with a dull shock that she was pregnant. It was a bombshell, because she had always thought she was unable to conceive. 'You just ain't fertile,' Whitejack had assured her on many occasions.

Now she was pregnant and she had no idea who the father was, Gino Santangelo. Freddy Lester. It could be either,

She didn't know what to do or where to turn,

# Gino 1939

Bee mumbled in her sleep and rolled towards Gino. She was bare assed – he liked his women bare assed in bed.

She still resided in her Greenwich Village apartment, but there had been changes made. For one thing, Gino had bought the building. He had arranged for her apartment to be enlarged, so that there was a separate bedroom for Marco and a great big kitchen where she could prepare his favorite meals. The decor was more or less the same though, Gino liked it that way – nice and homey. And since he had never had what he considered a proper home . . .

He still kept a permanent residence of his own. A penthouse, practically identical to the one he had shared with Cindy. It was designer decorated and extremely plush. He spent very little time there.

He had bought himself a building just off Wall Street in partnership with Oswald Duke. He was getting into legitimate business in a big way, while also keeping a firm hand on his not so legitimate ventures.

He owned a liquor company. Two laundry firms. A trucking business, and a string of automobile showrooms. All going concerns. Not bad for a boy who started off with only a kick up the ass for company.

Every day he attended his office, struggled through the Wall Street Journal, dictated a few letters, and fled on over to his small office at Clemmies where he felt more comfortable.

For pleasure he owned three cars. Sixty suits. And a library of books which he was slowly ploughing through. Gatsby remained his favorite.

In his safe Oswald Duke's indiscreet letters were a constant reminder that he was vulnerable, and should never do anyone a favor again.

Oswald had been suitably grateful. Clementine was a different story altogether. She simply refused to accept the fact that their affair was over. She lost her cool, elegant demeanor, pestered him constantly. The tables had certainly turned. When he had first met Clementine she had been at her peak and he had been a green kid desperate for anything she had to offer. Now *he* was at his peak, and surely ten years of sexual service was enough repayment? Why didn't she just bow out gracefully and become his friend?

He placed his hands firmly on Bee's big white ass and squeezed. 'Wakey, wakey.' She rolled over to face him, large nippled breasts giving him ideas. 'Go put your hair up,' he demanded.

Obediently she climbed from the bed. He liked the fact that she never gave him any arguments.

Naked, she walked towards the dressing table, sat, and began to pin her luxurious red tresses atop her head.

He lay back and watched her, throwing the covers off himself and watching his erection grow at the same time.

By the time she was ready – he was ready.

She stood, locked the bedroom door, and walked sensuously back towards the bed. Then she knelt on the floor and from this position took him in her mouth, sucking methodically while he sat silently on the side of the bed, his hard black eyes open and staring.

After fifteen minutes of this action he was ready, and as he peaked, his fingers scrabbled desperately through her hair, finding the pins and pulling them out, so that at the exact moment of orgasm her thick red hair tumbled and fell around his throbbing hardness.

He had the timing off pat.

'Vera called,' said Aldo.

'Vera?' Gino questioned. 'When did she get back?'

Aldo shrugged, 'I don't know, she didn't say. Just wants you to call her.'

Gino swore softly under his breath. Two years of silence meant all had gone well. He had packed Vera off to Arizona with twenty thousand bucks in her pocket and Paulo by her side.

'I don't want to see him,' he had told her flatly. 'The money's so's I don't *ever* have to see him again. Get it?'

'Yes, Gino.'

'Now you take him out to Arizona and make a new start. Buy a little shop or somethin'. Settle down.'

'Yes, Gino.'

'If y'feel like writin' I wouldn't mind hearin' from you. But if I don't hear, I'll know everything's OK.'

She had taken the money and run. Not a word. Not even a postcard. Now she was back. And what the hell did *that* mean?

'The final payment from The Boy came in. Plus all the interest. It was delivered this morning,' Aldo announced.

Gino smiled, 'It did?' When he had put out a hit on The Boy he had received a phone call. Jake had been seen in a restaurant on La Cienega Boulevard in Los Angeles. Seen. Followed. Shot at. Escaped. The Boy had phoned Gino. 'Trust me,' he had pleaded, 'I know what I did wasn't smart. Just trust me an' call off the contract – I'll see you get back every dollar. With interest.'

Balls. Gino had always admired them. He had given The Boy a shot.

'You're mad!' Aldo said at the time.

'We'll see,' Gino had replied.

Now he smiled. All the money repaid. And The Boy forever in his debt. He liked that. He liked it a lot.

'Where's Vera staying?' he asked.

Aldo gave him the number of the seedy hotel over on the lower East side.

He propped the phone under his chin and dialed.

She had lied to him on the phone. She was lying to him now. He had an instinct for such things. 'Vera,' he said softly, 'do you really expect me to believe that the whole twenty grand went down the drain in a dry cleanin' business?'

They were lunching in the Waldorf Astoria grill room. Vera, a nervous wreck in a cheap blue costume, her hair limp and straggly, her face bloated and puffed.

'Honest, Gino,' her eyes studied the tablecloth, 'we had a run of real bad luck. Kept pumpin' money into the business, and things just kept goin' wrong.'

'What things?'

'Oh, new fangled machines an' things,' she said vaguely, her eyes stuck firmly on the cloth.

He sighed. Why question the poor bitch? He would bet money there never was any dry cleaning business. Paulo had never worked an honest day in his life.

'Your dad really tried,' she added lamely, raising her eyes at last, and looking pleadingly at him. 'You see, just a bit more dough would've kept us afloat.'

'Is that why you came back? For more money?'

She jumped guiltily in her chair, 'Well I knew that if I explained it to you . . . '

'Where is Paulo?'

'Er . . . ' her bloodshot eyes darted frantically this way and that. 'He er . . . thought it best . . . I mean *I* thought it best . . . knowin' the way you feel an' all . . . '

'Is he in town?'

She picked up the napkin from the table and screwed it into a ball. 'He's a changed man, honest. I wouldn't lie to you. And you gotta remember. *He's your father.*'

Why the hell did he have to remember that for crissake? 'He's here isn't he?' he asked blankly.

'Yeah,' said Vera, grabbing her scotch from the waiter and gulping it down quickly. 'He'd like to see you. You're his only child Gino . . . '

Sure. And what if he wasn't a very rich and powerful only child? Would the sonofabitch still want to see him then?

Like hell he would.

'I told you,' he said wearily, 'the twenty grand was for keepin' him out of my way.'

It was almost as if she didn't hear him. 'He ain't bin in jail for two years. He's behaved himself. He treats me real good.'

Yeh. With twenty grand to play with why shouldn't he? 'What is it you want from me, Vera?'

'Just t'give your daddy a chance.'

'Don't use that word,' he said angrily.

'What word?'

'My daddy an' all that crap. Just cut it out.'

'You can't escape the fact that that's what he is to you. Your daddy.' She stared very hard at him, her eyes tearing. '*I* gave him another chance. Why can't you?'

He picked up his drink, tossed it down.

She sensed a moment of weakness. 'I ain't never asked you anythin' in my life,' she wheedled. 'Give the man a shot. Just for me at least *see* him.'

He nodded. He didn't know why. 'OK. I'll see him.'

Her bloated face lit up. 'I knew y'wouldn't let me down.'

'I said I'll see him. That's all. Doesn't mean I'm gonna give him a hug an' a kiss an' forget old times.'

She stood up. 'I'll get him,' she said.

'You'll what?'

'He's in the lobby. I knew y'wouldn't disappoint me.'

She was off before he could stop her. He cursed silently, fingered the scar on his cheek, and began to sweat.

He signalled the waiter for another drink, and flashed onto his last memory of Paulo. How many years ago? Sixteen, seventeen? A long time ago. Not long enough. He had been a boy. But even then more of a man than his father. With satisfaction he remembered the beating he had given him.

His eyes fixed onto the entrance to the grill room. And Vera came in. Only she wasn't with Paulo. She was with a skinny old man who walked with a limp and had greasy grey hair plastered across his scalp. And as they grew closer, Gino realized that – yes – it was Paulo after all. And was this what age did to a man? For he always remembered his father as being thin and wiry with thick brown hair and regular features. The man approaching had the face of a punch drunk fighter. He was bearing down on Gino, a smile splitting his boozy face, and then he was clapping him on the shoulder and saying, 'Hello, son. Long time no see.'

*Hello son.* Gino did not believe his ears. *Hello son.* What did the creep think this was? Some lousy tear jerking movie?

'Paulo,' he said shortly, shrugging his shoulders to remove the creep's hand. 'Take a seat.'

Paulo sat. Vera sat.

'Well son . . . ' Paulo began.

'Cut out the son shit,' he said coldly.

The smile wavered, but managed to remain on Paulo's face.

'Gino,' Vera whined, 'take it easy, huh? We ain't got no fights goin' any more.'

'It's all right, I understand,' Paulo said magnanimously.

Gino fixed him with his hard black eyes. 'What is it you want from me? More money to piss away?'

'We lost that money legit,' Paulo blustered.

'Yeh?' Gino sighed wearily. 'You want a job, I'll give you one. But y'ain't gettin' any more lumps of dough outta me. I'll find somethin' for you t'do, but one wrong move an' that's it. You understand me?'

Paulo threw him a surly glare.

'He's a changed man,' Vera interjected quickly, 'you'll see for yourself, Gino. Y'won't be sorry if y'give him a job.' She nudged Paulo hard, 'That right sweetie?'

The boozy smile was back on his face. 'S'right.'

Gino stood. 'That's settled then. Have him at Clemmies tomorrow night at six o'clock.' He clicked his fingers authoritatively for a waiter. 'Serve them lunch,' he said brusquely, 'and send the check to me.'

'Certainly Mr Santangelo, sir.'

Gino left the restaurant without another word.

He stopped outside and spat in the gutter.

Paulo always had that effect on him.

# Carrie 1939

Abortion. Expensive and dangerous and was that what she really wanted? Yes.

A dirty apartment. All of her savings. An old black crone with a pair of rusty scissors.

Searing pain and humiliation.

Bad hooch poured down her throat to keep her quiet.

Back in her room. Huddled. Alone. One day of bleeding and then nothing except despair. She was still pregnant.

Random thoughts. Contact Gino Santangelo. Freddy Lester. Never.

Kill herself? Maybe. She toyed with the thought. Suicide was comforting. Always there if you needed it.

She had twenty three dollars left in the world, and another human being growing inside of her. She couldn't just lie in the room she was renting and wait. There were no Prince Charmings in her life who were going to come charging up to Harlem on a white horse ready to rescue her. She had conquered drugs and survived. Was she going to crumble now?

She was only in her twenties.

She decided to continue living.

The months went by slowly. Jobs were not easy to get. She had a variety. First a singer in some seedy dive. Then a waitress. Then a hostess in a cheap club. She left them all because eventually each boss at each place decided sex with him should be part of her duties.

Money was tight, and her belly was swelling. Strangely enough, as the baby grew inside her, it gave her hope for the future. *Their future.* Two of them. She was quite ridiculously excited at the thought.

She managed to get a steady job as a cashier in a restaurant, and it was a job that lasted because now she was very pregnant, and called herself Mrs Brown to discourage advances.

On the night of May 17, 1939, Carrie was admitted to All Saints Hospital, New York. And at 3 a.m. on May 18, she gave birth to an eight pound baby boy. The birth nearly killed her.

She named the baby Steven.

# Gino 1939

Rumblings of a war in Europe were shaking America. Hitler, the German dictator, had invaded Poland, and Britain and France were at war with Germany. President Roosevelt had declared America neutral, but who knew what the future held?

Senator Oswald Duke and Gino Santangelo sat down one day and worked out ways to make money from the situation.

Oswald suggested the purchase of several appliance factories that in a time of crisis could be converted into making machinery and ammunition. Gino agreed. Oswald also suggested that they buy an industrial rubber plant, a chain of gas stations, and stockpiled in warehouses across the country, coffee, sugar, and canned goods. 'You never know,' Oswald decided sagely, 'these are the products that everyone will be screaming for if the war in Europe spreads.'

Gino went along with everything the old man suggested, he had never been wrong yet, and it was always a good idea to keep an eye on the future.

On New Years Eve, 1939, Gino closed down Clemmies for the night, and threw a lavish private party. Everyone attended. It was the best party of the year.

As far as he was concerned it was the worst.

Two things happened that he didn't like.

First, Clementine Duke got drunk, threw a drink in his face, and sneered, 'Murderer!' for everyone to hear.

He wanted to slap her fine porcelain skin, and kick in her skinny ass. Instead he wiped the booze off his face, grinned to show it didn't matter, and said, 'Mrs Duke is drunk again folks, let's get on with the party.'

His guests surged around him, shutting out Clementine's white and furious face. Oswald gripped her by the arm and took her home.

The second upsetting incident concerned Paulo. Gino had given him a job as gofer – go for this, that – and so far it had worked out. But now, as Gino took a quiet walk around backstage, he came across Paulo, trousers round his ankles, screwing a petrified young dancer from the chorus line of Clemmies.

'What in hell's goin' on here?' he asked in a soft menacing tone, trying not to look at his father's sagging ass.

The girl squealed loudly. 'Oh Mr Santangelo. I'm sorry. He said I had to do it because of well . . . because of who he was' . . . He said if I didn't I would lose my job . . . '

Paulo pulled his pants up and hurriedly slouched off.

Gino stared at the girl. She was only a youngster, one of the older ones would never have fallen for such a line.

'Never do anything you don't want to do,' he said very slowly. 'Never. You understand me?'

He went looking for Paulo, but could not find him, so he was left with a gut full of anger, and nobody to take it out on. Bee got the brunt. 'That motherfuckin' sonofabitch!' he raved.

When the party was over, and they went to her apartment, she pinned her lovely red hair atop her head and did the one thing she knew pleasured him the most.

For once it did not soothe him.

He could not sleep. He lay beside Bee's warm body and listened to her deep contented breathing. It was her goddamn deep contented breathing that was keeping him awake. Who the hell could be expected to sleep with that racket going on?

He got out of bed, went into the kitchen, opened the refrigerator, and filled a plate with ice cream.

He thought of Clementine. The tight lines on her face, the bitterness around her mouth as she had drunkenly screamed 'Murderer!' at him.

Bitch. What made her think she could get away with behavior like that? He would have to talk to Oswald about her.

Murderer. Nobody could prove a thing. The newspapers had speculated about Cindy's untimely death. He had hit them with a slew of lawyer's letters. After all he was a bereaved widower for crissakes. And what is more, he had an alibi tighter than an ant's ass.

Scavengers. They were always tracking him for this or that. It wasn't bad enough that he had the tax authorities continually breathing down his neck, he had reporters coming out his ears. They loved to create newsprint characters, and he was a natural. There would probably be a report of the entire party in one of the New York rags tomorrow. 'GINO THE RAM SANTANGELO AND THE SENATOR'S WIFE.'

The ice cream failed to satisfy him, just as Bee had failed to satisfy him earlier. He went back to the fridge, and piled his plate high with more. As he spooned it into his mouth he reflected on Paulo. Why he had ever allowed Vera to talk him into giving the prick a job was a mystery. Six weeks later and he was using the 'I am Gino Santangelo's father' line to screw the help. Great. Terrific.

And where was Vera anyway? *She* had been the one he had invited to the party.

Where *was* Vera? The thought began to bother him. He hadn't seen her in weeks.

'Hi.' Nine-year-old Marco stumbled into the kitchen, hardly able to keep his sleepy eyes open. 'Can I have ice cream too?'

'Go back to bed, kid. Your mom'll bat your ass.'

'Aw please,' Marco wheedled, 'Mom promised to get me some paper hats an' balloons. Did she?'

He ruffled the boy's hair, 'Yeh. She got them.'

'Where? Can I have them?'

'No you can't,' Gino replied firmly, 'and keep your voice down or you'll wake your mother.'

'Aw ... please ...'

'No. Sit down, have some ice cream and shut up.'

The boy grinned and sat at the kitchen table.

Gino went to the refrigerator and fixed yet another dish of ice cream which he placed in front of Marco. Bee would be furious, she said he spoiled the kid. But who wouldn't? Marco was one of the main reasons he hung out at her place so much anyway.

'Hey – ' Gino said suddenly, 'how about you an' me takin' in a movie tomorrow? I heard a lot about 'Stagecoach'. Douglas Fairbanks. Cowboys an' Indians. Whatcha think?'

'Really?'

'Sure, really. We'll see it together, just the two of us.'

Marco beamed and stuffed his mouth.

'Listen – ' Gino said, 'I'm gonna get dressed an' get outta here. Tell your ma I'm gonna get some work done while there's no one around to bother me. An' I'll pick *you* up at noon. Now you finish up in here an' get your ass back to bed. It's four o'clock in the mornin'.'

He went into the dressing room and dressed hurriedly. It may be four o'clock in the morning but he was going to pay a little visit to Vera and check out her health. Christ! He should have done it before.

He was also going to tell her the truth about Paulo and the girl – and if that didn't open her eyes . . .

Nothing would give him greater pleasure than watching Vera tell Paulo to take a hike. And if she did, he would set her up in any little business she wanted. Vera – on her own – could soft touch him as much as she wanted.

He pulled on casual clothes, and whistling tunelessly left the Greenwich Village apartment. He had a gut ache, usually a warning signal of trouble, but he ignored it. After all – who wouldn't have a belly ache after two big dishes of ice cream!

The hotel they were shacked up in was a dump. A real flea bag on the East side with a broken neon sign that flashed an occasional 'Rooms Available'. As if the clients who frequented such a rat trap would even know what available meant.

New Year's Eve revellers were still wandering the streets. Blousy women blowing paper horns and wiggling their fat asses. Ageing drunken men in shiny suits with bloodshot eyes and false teeth.

Gino pulled the old Ford up outside. A prostitute lounged carelessly against the wall outside the hotel. 'Wanna have a wunnerful time big boy?'

He ignored her, and strode into what passed for the lobby. Behind the desk a sharp nosed man argued with a drunken couple. 'Ten bucks or y'can scram.'

'Aw c'mon,' the woman whined, 'make it five, Pete, we're only gonna *be* an hour most.'

The sharp nosed man was adamant, 'It's New Year's Eve. Charges are double. You don't like it, then piss off.'

The woman's date fished in his pocket and slammed two grimy five dollar bills on the counter. The sharp nosed man scooped up the money with one hand and reached behind him for a key with the other. Not a word was spoken. The couple took the key and headed for the uncarpeted stairs.

'Yeah?' snapped sharp nose, peering at Gino.

'You got a Mr and Mrs Paulo Santangelo here?'

'Who's askin'?'

Gino did not bother to answer. He reached for his wallet and extracted a twenty which he slid across the desk. 'I'd like the key.'

Sharp nose didn't hesitate. He had an amazing sleight of hand when it came to money. He stroked up the twenty and handed Gino a key all in one movement. 'Second floor,' he muttered, 'take the stairs, the elevator's broke. You never got no key from me.'

Gino nodded. The dump was worse inside than out. He walked up the stairs. The smell of the place was enough to make anyone sick. He didn't bother to knock on the door, just fitted the key and walked right in.

He was not prepared for the scene which greeted his eyes.

Vera was hunched on the bed, nude. The harsh ceiling light showed up every purple bruise on her well used body. Across her arms and breasts were fresh red weals. Blood flowed from her crushed nose. In her hands she clutched a .38 gun which was pointing at Paulo. She was breathing in great hysterical gulps and in frenzied tones was screaming, 'I'm . . . going . . . to . . . kill . . . you . . . This time . . . I'm . . . going . . . to . . . kill . . . you . . .'

Paulo stood blankly at the foot of the bed clad in shorts and a filthy undershirt. From his right hand dangled a heavy leather belt complete with lethal looking buckle. His greasy grey hair was mussed and untidy. In his bloodshot eyes was an expression of true terror mixed with total disbelief.

Neither of them noticed Gino at the door.

'Bastard!' Vera screamed, and squeezed the trigger.

The bullet hit Paulo squarely between the eyes. He staggered back, the expression of disbelief fixed in his eyes forever.

'Bastard!' Vera screamed again, but before she could fire a second time Gino jumped her and desperately struggled for possession of the gun. 'Vera! Vera! What are y'doing?' he yelled, pinning her on the bed and wrestling the gun from her tightly clenched fists.

'Oh Gino!' she began to sob. 'Oh God . . . Oh God . . .'

He felt he was in the middle of some terrible nightmare from which he would shortly awaken. And Bee would be by his side with her big warm breasts and comforting thighs.

So why didn't it happen? Why was he still in this sleazy room with a naked hysterical Vera lying beneath him? And his father now slumped on the floor, blood pumping from a broken mess which had once been his face.

If only he had gotten to the room a minute earlier . . .

If only he had been in time to stop her . . .

Why? Paulo was dead. Wasn't that what he had wanted all along?

He got off the bed still holding the gun. Vera was rolling back and forth now, racked with sobs.

Soberly Gino stared at the heap that had once been his father. He tried to remember a good time. But he could not remember one. He bent to the pathetic body, listened for a heartbeat, heard none. He had not expected to.

'Why did you do it?' Vera screamed, suddenly sitting up. 'Why did you do it Gino?'

'Calm down,' he said softly, his mind running over the possibilities of how to get her out of this mess, 'I didn't do nuthin'.'

'Yes,' she whispered, 'you did it. You took away his balls. This is all *your* fault.' She started to scream again, 'You did it, Gino! You did it!'

She collapsed back into wild sobs.

Gino gazed at the ceiling and wondered what move to make next.


Margaret O'Shaunessy and Michael Flannery got engaged on New Year's Eve. He presented her with a cheap imitation emerald ring and a hotel room key.

'I got us a room, just like I said I would,' he crowed excitedly. Flushed with celebratory beer they raced to the hotel.

Margaret was not impressed with her surroundings, but when Michael started to lovingly remove her clothes she began to relax. 'We got the whole night together,' he informed her. 'You don't like it the first time we can do it again and again and again.'

She did like it the first time. But they did it again and again and again anyway. Until at last they lay exhausted and just talked, going over their plans for the future.

Around three-thirty in the morning they fell asleep.

At about three forty-five a lot of noise started coming from the room next door. Margaret woke immediately. She could hear angry voices – male and female. She could not make out exactly what they were saying, but an occasional word came across clearly. 'Bitch . . . dirty slut . . . can't stand you . . . ' Then a short silence.

Margaret hoped that the couple next door would be quiet now. But this was not to be. The man yelled loudly, 'I'll beat the shit out of you – cunt.' And this declaration was followed by a terrible series of lashing sounds.

Margaret sat bolt upright in bed. Michael snored peacefully on. She wondered whether to wake him. The noises coming from next door were truly horrible. She could hear the woman crying and groaning as she was hit.

Tentatively she poked Michael in the ribs. He did not move. He was some heavy sleeper. She snuggled back under the covers, holding the pillow around her ears to try and cut off the sounds.

It was no good. The woman's cries were getting louder. The noise certainly more violent.

Determinedly Margaret set about waking her fiancé up. By the time she got any sense out of him at all she was really angry. 'I could have been raped and murdered in this room Michael Flannery, and *you* would have slept through the whole thing,' she admonished.

He grinned sheepishly, 'What's the matter my little beauty?'

'Shhh . . . and listen.'

Michael sat up, 'Listen to what?'

The noise had stopped.

'Oh Michael, the people next door were fighting and screaming. You've never heard such a carry on. I think someone was getting beaten. I think –'

'I'm . . . going . . . to . . . kill . . . you . . . '

The wildly screamed words hurtled through the thin walls.

Michael jumped off the bed.

'Bastard!' the same hysterical woman's voice yelled, then a shot. Then another, 'Bastard!'

Michael Flannery struggled into his trousers. 'You stay here Margaret, I'm going to call the police.'

'Michael! You can't leave me!'

But, shirt flapping, he was already out of the door.

'Oh dear father, help me, please!' Margaret uttered, running for her clothes and hurriedly putting them on her shaking body. She had never been as frightened as this in her whole life. It was a punishment, of course. A chastisement for having sex before marriage.

'Why did you do it?' the woman next door wailed. *'Why did you do it, Gino?'*

Margaret O'Shaunessy was to repeat those words more times than she would care to remember in the following months. They were the only words she clearly remembered.

# Carrie 1941

'What's yer name, girly?' The fat man in the mustard suit scratched his balls and regarded her through screwed up eyes.

'Carrie,' she replied, trying to sound pleasant, but inside she was seething. Girly indeed. She was twenty-eight-years-old and a mother – yet she still got called 'Girly'.

He continued to scratch his balls furiously as though she weren't even in the room. 'Yer got yerself a job,' he decided. 'Money ain't much – but a girl looks like you won't have any trouble pickin' up tips.' He winked, 'An' more. Depending.'

She had a strong desire to say, 'Fuck you fatty – you can shove your lousy job.' But instead she said – real polite, 'Thank you Mr Wardle. Shall I start tonight?'

He left his balls alone for a moment and patted her warmly on the shoulder, 'Yeah, sweetie. Tonight'll be fine. Wear somethin' shows off them pretty titties.'

She left the dingy office. Walked through the even more dingy dance hall, and took a bus home.

Home.

One room for baby Steven and her in a run down tenement building in the midst of Harlem.

Home.

No bathroom. Rats at night. Walls that perspired in the summer and leaked in the winter.

Yet it *was* a home for her and Steven. And for two years she had been able to pull in just enough money to keep them both.

It had not been easy. After the difficult birth she had been exhausted. But the hospital had allowed her no long leisurely rest. After two weeks it was out on the street with only the welfare money in her pocket and a baby in her arms. She had found a woman to care for Steven during the day, and had gone back to her old job as cashier in the restaurant. The job did not last long. Now that her belly was no longer swollen, the boss began to get ideas. He was old with thin yellow hands, which made her shudder, and a wife who watched him like a hawk. He pounced one afternoon in a store room in back, his yellow hands pawing every inch of her. She left that very same day.

Two years of the same kind of job. And always a boss, always the same story. What was it about her that caused men to want her so much? Did they think that being black meant being easy?

She could not figure it out. She always wore her hair back, no make-up, and plain clothes. It did not put them off.

As she moved from job to job, struggling to make ends meet, it occurred to her that she was a fool. If men wanted her so much why not make them pay for it? One night of whoring would net her more money than a week's work.

But could she sell her body again? That feeling of being no more a person, just a thing, a piece of meat . .

Of course drugs could get her through it . . .

She closed her mind to *that* thought. She had baby Steven to consider, and she wanted more for him than a mother who was a junkie whore.

The new job at the Fun Palace Dime a Dance near Times Square was another direction. Firstly Carrie wanted a nighttime job so that she could spend the days with Steven. Secondly the only daytime jobs on offer were for scrubbing or being some lazy white woman's maid.

She knew that she was laying herself open for advances, but so what? She had to fight men off anyway – on a crowded dance floor it should be easy.

A bouncy Mexican girl named Suzita taught her how to do it. 'Zay get too close – knee 'em in zee groin. One, two, like *so*. Zay back off dead quick!'

Carrie found she was right. A quick knee was far more effective than a hundred no's.

Suzita did a little business on the side. Any customer she liked she provided 'extra' services for. 'Zees is good,' she told Carrie. 'Zees way I get to pick and chooze. Why you not do it too? You need extra money. It eazzy money. Only take guys you like.'

Carrie shook her head.

Suzita laughed. 'You change your mind. I know.'

Three weeks after that conversation, Steven was taken ill with an unidentified virus infection. Almost overnight he turned from a strong healthy two-year-old into a very sickly child indeed. Carrie took him to doctors and specialists, but none of them could seem to find out what was wrong with him.

After several weeks it was suggested that he was put into hospital under observation. By this time Carrie was frantic. Before she had managed to scrape by. Now it was suddenly bills bills bills. And working as a dime a dance girl wasn't going to pay them.

Suzita was helpful and sympathetic. She took Carrie around to the hotel she used, introduced her to the desk clerk, and said in her quaint accent, 'You like eet Carrie. Izz not bad work. Plenny dough.'

Carrie nodded blankly.

That evening she dressed with care. Even Mr Wardle was impressed. 'I wouldn't mind spendin' a dime on yer myself, girly,' he said as he wobbled past.

She shuddered. She may be going back to work, but it was on *her* terms. She was going to be like Suzita and pick and choose.

That night there wasn't much to pick and choose from. She finally settled on a nondescript little man with ridiculous small glasses balanced on the end of his nose. 'How about you an' me goin' round the corner to a hotel I know?' she questioned, as they lurched around the dance floor to the strains of a tired tango.

He pretended not to hear her, but a nervous tic indicated that he had. Two dances later he summoned up the courage to ask a barely audible. 'How much?'

Carrie willed herself to think of all the mounting doctors bills. 'Twenty-five,' she said.

'Yes,' he gulped.

He was waiting when she left the dance hall. She wanted to run away and leave him standing there in his stupid little glasses. She thought longingly of having something to dull her mind. Silently they walked to the hotel.

The desk clerk winked and requested ten dollars. The man paid up without an argument. The desk clerk handed the key to Carrie and winked again. She had to remember to slip him a five when she left.

In the room a neon sign flashed on and off outside the window. The blanket on the narrow bed was grey. The carpet had a hole in it.

They stood inside the room, embarrassment heavy in the air. She pulled herself together and requested the money.

He handed her fifteen dollars.

'Twenty-five,' she said quickly.

'But the room was ten,' he objected weakly.

'Twenty-five or no . . . ' her words trailed off.

He produced a further ten dollars. She pulled her dress over her head, unfastened her brassiere, removed her panties.

He turned his back and took off his trousers.

She lay down on the bed. Just like old times.

He mounted her carefully. His penis was so small she couldn't even feel him inside her. In five minutes it was over, and he dressed and scurried off like a frightened rabbit.

Carrie lay on the bed and gazed at the ceiling. She was back in business. It was a day to remember. December 7th, the same day the Japanese bombed Pearl Harbor. The next day America declared war on Japan.

America declared war. And she was a whore again.

Whoring was a business she knew inside out. And much as she hated it, she performed as a professional. Soon, any johns she got were coming back for more.

Suzita was impressed, 'You is one quick operator. I like zees.'

Mr Wardle – owner of the Fun Palace – did not. He called her into his cramped office one night and said, 'You're using my place to pull tricks. You wanna do that – fine. I want a cut.'

'Take your job and shove it,' she replied.

'You're fired girly.'

'You can't fire a person who just quit.'

Baby Steven was beginning to recover. Home was no longer good enough for him. He needed a dry clean place with a small terrace where he could get some fresh air. She suggested to Suzita that they find an apartment together and operate a small house. Suzita agreed. Within weeks Carrie found them a roomy apartment in the mid Thirties. The place was big enough for Steven to have his own private section, and she hired a sixteen-year-old black girl to care for him.

The city was alive with soldiers, sailors, and marines, all looking for a good time. Most of them were going to Europe and wanted a last fling. War was good for business, and soon the money was rolling in. A tall redhead named Silver joined them.

It wasn't long before they found themselves with one of the most popular whorehouses in town.

# Gino 1947

'You got everything, Santangelo?' the prison guard asked.

Yeh. He had everything.

'I guess it's goodbye then.'

Yeh. It was goodbye. Seven years was enough time for anyone to spend in jail for a crime he didn't commit. Seven long years of boredom and monotony and bad food and no women and sadistic guards and prison riots and *no fucking freedom to do anything*.

Gino fingered his scar and walked to the prison gates.

The warden was a mean son-of-a-bitch. He had known the press would be scamming around the prison like locusts at a feast, but he had refused permission for Gino to be released secretly in the dead of night. Bastard.

But Gino was strong. He could handle it. Prison had not broken him. The fittest survived, and he was the top of the whole fucking heap.

His step was full of bounce as he headed for the gate. But his gut ached, and what he really wanted to do was smash a few heads. That Irish cunt, for one. Margaret O'Shaunessy with her dumb pop eyes and soft childish voice. Star witness for the prosecution at the famous Santangelo murder trial. 'SON MURDERS FATHER' the headlines had screamed. Tried and found guilty by the press before Paulo's body was even cold. And Margaret O'Shaunessy's damaging little voice, 'I heard a woman screaming "Why did you do it Gino".'

And poor dim witted Vera. By the time the cops finished with her she was actually convinced that he, Gino, *had* pulled the trigger. Unbelievable!

It was true that thanks to Michael Flannery the cops *had* broken in and found him standing over the body with the murder weapon in his hand. And also true that he had not at first given a truthful account of what had taken place. For some stupid reason he was thinking of protecting Vera. But eventually he *had* told the truth. And nobody had fucking believed him! Nobody! He was branded a murderer – a killer – long before the trial. What kind of man executed his own father?

His lawyers were a bunch of highly paid fuckheads. They were prepared to defend him at an exorbitant price, but they were not prepared to believe him. Somehow, being believed, was the most important issue of all.

Friends immediately dropped by the wayside. The Dukes

vanished off to South America, leaving instructions with their legal representatives to terminate all partnerships with Gino Santangelo. This suited him fine. He, in turn, instructed his lawyers to buy Oswald Duke out. It took all of his available cash flow, plus a considerable selling of assets, but he did it.

Judges, politicians, society folk, they all vanished out of his life while he chain smoked in jail and waited for his trial.

His connected friends stayed true. Sending in messages, arranging whatever comforts they could. Aldo . . . Enzio Bonnatti . . . They were loyal friends.

And Bee. Visiting him weekly in spite of being hounded by the press.

Costa Zennocotti had turned out to be the truest friend of all. He had given up a thriving legal practice in San Francisco and flown to New York with his wife, Jennifer. 'I'm taking over your case,' he told Gino tersely.

'Hey – listen . . . ' Gino began to object. He appreciated the gesture, but what did Costa know about defense on a murder trial?

'I'm good,' Costa said, 'and what's more I believe you.'

The magic words.

And without Costa fighting for him so eloquently in the courtroom who knew what might have happened? As it was the murder charge was reduced to manslaughter, and he received a ten year jail sentence.

Before Vera's eventual death from alcoholic poisoning Costa managed to extract a written and witnessed confession from her. It was seven-years too late. Gino got a pardon, and a paltry offer of compensation. What amount of money could possibly compensate for seven years of a man's life?

As he emerged from jail on a spring morning in 1947, he was a bitter man. He had missed a war, he had missed the death of Franklin D. Roosevelt. He had missed new songs and plays and fashions. He had missed flowers and grass and just walking down Fifth Avenue.

He had missed seven years of life.

'What the hell you wearin'?' Gino asked.

Bee smiled. 'It's the latest fashion,' she replied, 'the New Look. Don't you like it?'

'What was wrong with the old look?'

She shrugged, 'You don't want me to appear old-fashioned, do you?'

He had been back in his apartment for fifteen minutes and

felt totally disoriented. Costa had been at the jail gates with two bodyguards to push their way through the hordes of photographers and reporters. Gino had not said a word. He had ignored the flash bulbs and microphones shoved under his chin, and let Costa do the talking. 'He has no comment boys, no comment. Come on – give the man a break.'

Outside the Park Avenue penthouse more reporters waited. The same story. He had nothing to say to the fuckers, let them print what they wanted – they did anyway.

Costa had escorted him upstairs, and Bee had run to greet him.

'I'll leave you two alone,' Costa had said, 'and Gino, can we meet early tomorrow? That's if you're up to it of course.'

'Yeh, yeh. Early tomorrow suits me fine.' If he was up to it indeed. What did they think he was? A fucking invalid for crissakes? He was a forty-one-year-old man.

'Shall I fix you a drink?' Bee inquired solicitously.

'Scotch. Plenty of ice. And make sure it's in one of those crystal glasses.' The New Look. He could hardly even see her legs. Some look.

She fetched him the drink and stroked his cheek. The gesture almost drove him crazy. 'Get out of those goddamn clothes,' he ordered. 'I want you in nothing but stockings, garter belt, and high heels.'

She laughed softly, 'I thought you'd never ask.'

He closed his eyes, and just the thought of her nakedness gave him a powerful erection. Seven years of not having a woman. Some of the guys didn't even bother to wait. Some of them picked on the weaklings as soon as they got in, and jammed it up their ass before they even got their toothbrush out.

Being Gino Santangelo meant getting immediate respect. Often he wondered if he could have taken it if he wasn't who he was.

Bee walked back into the room. She had followed his instructions to the letter. She had even pinned her luxurious red hair up.

'Hey – ' he said softly, 'just walk around the place. I wanna watch you.'

She had magnificent skin. Smooth and white. And her large orange tipped breasts showed no sign of sag.

The black garter belt cut tightly across her waist, and then the little bits and pieces came down her voluptuous thighs and held in place black silk stockings. On her feet were delightfully high heeled strappy sandals. He loved the way the garter belt emphasized her pubic area. The soft white belly, the maze of reddish hair. 'Turn around,' he instructed, his voice thick with desire.

She did as she was told, and he admired her large white ass. He did not want to rush anything. He had waited too long to throw a five minute fuck into her.

'Hey,' he said, 'remember the first time you stripped off for me?'

She turned around and smiled, 'How could I ever forget it? You were so angry!'

He laughed, 'What did you expect? Tellin' me you had the clap. Very funny I don't think.'

She held her arms above her head and stretched. He watched her breasts pull up, and knew he wasn't going to be able to control himself much longer.

'Why don't I undress you?' she suggested, as if reading his thoughts.

'Sure.'

She walked towards him, 'Stand up.'

He stood. She was taller than he was in the outlandish heels. Close up he noticed little lines around her eyes which hadn't been there before. Seven years can't have been easy for her either. Materially he had looked after her, but what about the lonely nights?

As she peeled his clothes off, he asked, 'You have any other guys while I was away?'

'Gino,' she replied very softly, 'there *are* no other guys. Only you.'

It wasn't an answer to his question, but it satisfied him.

She removed his shoes and socks, and then she was kissing his toes, sending little shock waves through his whole system.

'Where'd you learn this?' he asked.

'You're full of questions today.'

He reached for her breasts, and rolled her nipples between his fingers until they became hard. Then he pushed them together and tongued them until she started to whimper. 'Gino . . . ' she murmured, 'I don't think I can wait anymore. Let's . . . go . . . in the bedroom.'

He was inclined to agree with her. His cock was on fire, but still his head insisted that he wait. Keeping his hands on her breasts he began to kiss her on the mouth. She had a wonderful mouth, wide and sensual, with breath that tasted ever so faintly of peppermint. Her tongue darted out to meet his.

With his hands cupping her big breasts and his tongue in her mouth he felt he was in heaven. The texture of her nipples was like rough silk. He had forgotten the feel of woman, and he had no plans to stop until he was as familiar as he'd ever been.

Suddenly her whole body stiffened, and little cries of ecstacy escaped from her mouth. She was climaxing, and he hadn't even gone for the magic button yet.

'Hey – ' he asked softly, 'what's your hurry? We got the next twenty-four hours.'

'Well?' questioned Jennifer Zennocotti. 'Did everything go all right?' Ten years of marriage had changed her from a freckly faced girl into an attractive mature woman. She was, at thirty-nine, a few months older than her husband, but her whole demeanor was that of an even older person. She radiated warmth and kindliness.

Costa had never regretted marrying her, even though the marriage had produced no children, a fact which greatly saddened them both. 'We got him home. The reporters were everywhere but they didn't upset him.'

Costa loved working. Since arriving in New York to defend Gino, he had taken exactly one week off, to fly to San Francisco and tell his father that he would be staying in the East and starting his own practice. Franklin Zennocotti had been furious.

'You belong here,' he stormed, 'eventually you will take over my entire law firm. What more do you want?'

Costa did not like to seem ungrateful, but what he did want was his own identity. And besides that, he felt it his duty to continue to defend Gino. The way the newspapers had represented the case was a disgrace. Gino the Ram Santangelo. Mobster. Criminal. Even when Vera confessed, the newspapers had hinted that she was paid to do so. Costa had never paid her one red cent. But he *had* kept after her over the years begging her to tell the truth.

He had also accepted Power of Attorney to deal with Gino's many business affairs. And in his capable hands the legitimate businesses had flourished. He refused to touch the more shady side of things, leaving Clemmies, the numbers racket, and the gambling to Aldo. When Aldo was drafted into the army and sent overseas, with Gino's permission, Enzio Bonnatti took things over.

'That's fine with me,' Gino said from his jail cell. 'At least I know things'll get taken care of an' when I get out I can take over again.'

Clemmies was closed down a year later by the narcotics

squad. Bonnatti sent his apologies through the prison grapevine. Gino was pissed off – but he was hardly in a position to do anything about it.

About that time Aldo came limping back from the war in Europe. He had shot himself in the leg to avoid any more active duty. 'An y'know somethin'?' he said to Gino, on a visit. 'It was worth it! Now I'm a friggin' hero!'

Costa was never drafted because of a severe asthma condition. Enzio avoided the problem by passing large amounts of money in all the right places. 'I got flat feet,' was his only comment if anyone ever asked him. And not many dared.

'Was Bee there to greet him?' Jennifer asked.

'All dressed up and happy as a lark.'

'I should think so. That woman is a saint! To wait for a man all that time, when he's not even her husband.'

Costa couldn't help laughing, 'I'd hardly call Bee a saint.'

'Your ass has gotten bigger.'

'Don't say that!'

'Bigger and better.'

'You're only saying that because you've been deprived.'

'Yeh. That's what you think!'

He grabbed her by the cheeks of her ass as they lolled in bed. 'Gino! Not again!'

He grunted and eased himself in from behind.

She raised her big white bottom and he pumped easily in and out. It was the third time, but the pleasure was still as sharp.

They had stayed in bed all afternoon in the silent apartment, only the constant ringing of the phone disturbing them. Eventually he had taken it off the hook.

'You know what?' he said, when they were finished. 'Maybe we should think about getting married.'

Bee was silent.

'Hey – ' he said, 'where's the gasps of amazement and the "oh Gino it's what I always wanted"?'

She spoke very slowly. 'It *is* what I've always wanted. You know that.'

'So – what's the problem?'

'Love.'

'Love!'

'Yes. I love you. *I* say it. You never have.'

'Aw, c'mon, kid. I just fucked you three times. If that isn't love what is?'

She sighed. 'You don't understand. Fucking isn't loving.'

'Listen. We bin together quite a few years. I give you everything you want – right?'

'Yes. Of course you do, but . . .'

'I paid for Marco to go to a swell school. He must be some
kid now. What he needs is a brother or sister. You get my drift?'

'You want us to get married and have children?'

He jumped out of bed and paced the room excitedly, 'You
got it! Why not! We're neither of us gettin' any younger. I
thought about it a lot in the can. I want kids, Bee, an' we'll
make great kids together.'

She propped herself up on her elbow and began to smile,
'Yes . . .'

'Of course yes! I can see 'em now. Cute little fuckers with
red hair and fat asses!'

She began to laugh.

'You *can* have more kids can't you? It hasn't been too long?'

'I'm thirty-two-years-old. Once I stop taking precautions I
think they'll pop out like rabbits!'

Now they were both laughing.

'We'll do it properly,' he said, 'tomorrow I'll take you to
Tiffanys and buy you the biggest flashiest diamond ring you
ever seen. We'll get engaged. You like it? Then – when I get
you knocked up we'll get the license an' do it.'

'You mean I've got to get pregnant first?' she complained.

'Yeh. But I promise you one thing – we'll have a lot of fun
makin' sure that you do!'

Gino bounded into his office the next morning full of energy.
He was in such a good mood that he even had a smile and a
wave for the press boys gathered outside his apartment and
office building.

Costa had reached him very late the previous evening to
tell him of a phone call from San Francisco. 'Franklin had a
heart attack – I'm flying to the coast.'

'Don't worry – I'll find my own way around,' Gino assured
him.

Miss Marchmont, Costa's extremely efficient personal secretary, was on hand to greet him and show him any papers or
books he might wish to look at. He skimmed through a few
things. Buying out Oswald Duke had been the best move he had
ever made – all the ventures they had been involved in together
were going great.

It made him restless, sitting in an office with seventeen
secretaries trying to catch a glimpse of him. Costa had a good

system going. All the various businesses had their own key personnel, he just kept an overall eye on things.

Seven years in jail, Gino thought, and now I am richer than ever. It certainly beat working.

Miss Marchmont made him uneasy. She had an expression on her face that indicated a bad smell under her nose.

'Uh – I've seen all I want,' he said after a couple of hours, 'you need me I'll be at Riccaddis restaurant.'

He fled. He didn't enjoy sitting around in offices. Besides, he couldn't wait to get together with Aldo.

His old chauffeur and bodyguard, Red, drove him to the restaurant. Red had been working for Enzio Bonnatti, but as soon as he had heard of Gino's release he asked for his old job back. He was a fine driver. Within six blocks he had shaken the following reporters.

'You done good!' laughed Gino.

'Can't stand those fleabags,' muttered Red, 'writin' lies an' persecutin' honest men.'

'Yeh,' agreed Gino. He made a mental note to check out how much he was paying Red and give him a bonus.

Riccaddis was a small unassuming Italian restaurant tucked between a dry cleaning business and an undertakers. Aldo had purchased the place for Barbara in 1945. It was the perfect front for him to carry on his business activities. Barbara did the cooking and baking, and her brother tended bar and managed the restaurant. This was Gino's first visit.

Aldo came to the door to greet him. It was an emotional reunion, the two men embraced. Then Barbara came running forward, her strong face creased with tears. 'Gino! So good to have you back, so very very good.'

They led him inside the restaurant and all around were friends and acquaintances standing back and smiling. Enzio Bonnatti was there, Jennifer . . . Bee . . . And Marco, a good looking seventeen-year-old.

'Jesus! What's going on?'

'Nothing, nothing,' Barbara insisted.

A banner on the wall proclaimed, 'WELCOME BACK GINO.'

He felt delighted, foolish, embarrassed. He walked around shaking hands, kissing cheeks, and drinking wine, while Italian opera issued forth from the juke box. He cornered Bee, 'Why didn't you warn me?'

She smiled and squeezed his hand.

Aldo and Barbara's four children ran about singing and

waiting table. Aldo had scored with a matched set, two girls and two boys. They were all Gino's godchildren, nice kids, kept in line by a very strict Barbara. They served their mother's home made lasagna, then hot rich spaghetti with meatballs – Gino's favorite, followed by delicious creamy zablagione.

Gino sat at a table with Enzio, Aldo, and other male friends. He smacked his lips and said, 'Barbara, you're the best cook in the world!' Everyone agreed.

Later in the afternoon, when cigars were lit, and small potent glasses of Sambuca tossed down, the men discussed business. Matters that concerned them all. Of course Gino knew what had been going on in his absence, the prison grapevine gave out more information than the New York Sunday Times. But all the same it was good to be back in a position of power where his opinion was sought out and respected.

Enzio and Aldo had attended a recent meeting in Havana where Lucky Luciano, now released from jail, presided over a gathering of major underworld chiefs from all across the States. The talk had been of cooperation with each other – an end to rivalries, feuds, and gangland killings which generated so much bad publicity.

'You shoulda seen Pinky Banana,' Aldo recalled, 'wearin' more diamonds than a jewelry shop!'

Pinky Banana was now a powerful force in Philadelphia, an overlord of narcotics, prostitution and murder for hire.

'Yeh?' Gino's interest in Pinky was minimal.

The talk drifted onto other matters, and it was well into the evening when they parted company.

Gino finally left Riccaddis at nine. He was stuffed with pasta and relaxed. The talk had been stimulating, and Aldo and Enzio had certainly done a fine job of looking after his interests while he was away. He took with him several satchels jammed full of cash – over three hundred thousand dollars – and there was a lot more to come.

Bee clung onto his arm lovingly, 'It's so good to have you home, Gino,' she said warmly.

Yeh. He was kind of enjoying it too.

## Thursday, July 14th, 1977 New York and Philadelphia

Steven tied the ropes under Lucky's arms, and held his hands as a step for her to climb onto to reach the opening in the top of the elevator.

She complained all the way. 'Jesus! Help! I'm not a fucking acrobat you know.'

As soon as the maintenance man had hold of the top half of her, Steven put both hands firmly on her ass and shoved.

'Watch it!' she shrieked. Crouching gingerly on the roof of the elevator she muttered in an uptight voice, 'I am . . . one very . . . frightened person.'

'Nuttin' to worry about,' the maintenance man said, checking that the ropes were secure under her arms. He raised his voice and yelled – 'Haul her up, George.'

George, somewhere out of sight, obliged. And dangling like a puppet on a string she was pulled to safety and the forty-seventh floor. George and the two other men assisting him peered at her curiously.

'Whew!' she sighed. 'Do me a favor and get these ropes off me.'

Silently they obeyed.

'Anyone got a drink?' she demanded.

One of the men indicated a nearby drinking fountain. Quickly she went over and drank three paper cups full of luke warm water, then she looked around the candle lit hallway, 'No lights yet, huh?'

The men were busy throwing down the ropes for Steven. Lucky took a candle and made her way to the ladies room. She stuck the candle on a washbasin and peered at herself in the mirror.

'Christ!' she exclaimed. 'Watta hag!' She ran some water in the basin and rinsed her face. It felt wonderful.

All she wanted to do now was get home, have a bath, and sleep for a week.

Dario froze. Someone *was* trying to get into his apartment. He stopped punching out numbers on the phone and looked around for a weapon. He picked up a solid bronze statue and stood by the front door. 'Who's there?' he questioned in the toughest voice he could manage.

The picking scraping noise did not stop.

Dario raised the statue ready to strike.

The door clicked open suddenly, but as his arm travelled down with the heavy bronze, something happened. He was grabbed, tripped up, and imprisoned on the floor. The statue crashed uselessly to the ground. A few swift moves had rendered him helpless.

'What's going on . . . ' he started to say, but the feel of cold steel between his eyes shut him up in a hurry.

Someone had a gun on him.

Once more he was a prisoner in his own home.

Doctor Mitchell attended to Carrie's ears, dosed her up with sedatives, and Elliott drove her home.

They climbed the stairway to their seventeenth floor luxury apartment escorted by a boy with a flashlight who was assisting people upstairs at a dollar a throw. 'Free enterprise!' joked Elliott, giving the boy a five for his trouble.

The sedatives were beginning to take effect. Carrie felt drowsy . . . very drowsy . . . 'I must phone Steven,' she mumbled.

'Forget about Steven for once,' Elliott replied crisply, 'you're going to bed and that's that.'

She didn't argue.

Gino could not get back to sleep easily. He was restless after the incident with the photographer and that dumb stewardess. Coming to his door and trying to take pictures in the middle of the night. What had happened to privacy? A person's rights?

He attempted to get back to sleep, but his mind was racing with thoughts of Lucky and Dario and his old friend Costa. He ached to see them all again. Especially Lucky. His beautiful wild daughter. Especially Lucky . . . Seven years was a long time . . . Maybe too long . . .

Eventually he fell asleep.

Lucky emerged from the ladies room as Steven was hoisted onto the forty-seventh floor.

He patted his rescuers gratefully on the back and thanked them profusely as they undid the ropes around his body.

Lucky stared at him. He was definitely in the O. J. Simpson league – even in the flickering candlelight she could see *that*. 'Hello,' she said, 'nice to *see* you.'

He looked at her, and he too was surprised. Where was the buck toothed buxom blonde he had imagined? This slim young woman with the wild black curls and direct eyes was a very foxy lady indeed.

He grinned, 'I told you we'd make it.'

She grinned back, 'All in one piece too.'

'You don't look like I imag . . . '

'Nor do you,' she interrupted. 'Hey – how do we get out of the building?'

'I guess we walk down the emergency fire stairs.'

Steven turned to George, who was now hauling the maintenance man back onto firm ground. 'Walking's the only way to get out of here, right?'

' 'Less'n you wanna fly out the window.'

'Thanks guys. I really appreciate all you've done.'

George chewed on his lower lip, 'How much you appreciate it, fella?'

'Very much indeed.'

'Lay a little cash on him,' Lucky hissed, 'and let's go.'

'Oh!' Steven fumbled in his back pocket and produced a ten dollar bill. 'Here – have a drink on me.'

George took the bill, and stared at it, then he handed it disgustedly to the maintenance man and said sarcastically, 'Ten bucks for our trouble. I reckon we 'kin get a coupla beers to split between the *four* of us.'

Lucky opened up her purse and fished out two fifties. 'Here you go, boys.' Then she grabbed Steven by the arm and said, 'For crissake let's *move*.'

He went with her as far as the emergency door, and when it clanged shut behind them he stopped and said furiously, 'You just embarrassed me.'

'Huh?'

'Giving them all that money. They get *paid* for doing a job – they didn't even deserve the ten.'

'What's all this deserve shit. They just *saved* us – pulled us out of the fucking black hole of Calcutta for crissakes. They *deserve* anything I care to give them.'

'Ten was enough,' he said stubbornly.

'Ten was an insult,' she replied.

He glared at her. Foxy lady or not she was still one big pain.

'Well?' she demanded. 'Are we going to walk down the stairs or are we going to stay here and fight?'

'You can do what you like. We're not joined at the hip.'

She glared at him. One of the best looking men she had ever seen but still an uptight schmuck. 'Fine. I'll say goodbye then.' She slung her purse over her shoulder and began the long descent.

He stood on the concrete landing, the early morning light filtering through the slatted windows.

'Oh, by the way,' Lucky yelled up the stairs, 'your fly's undone.'

He looked. It was.

Smart ass woman.

Dario hardly dared to move, the gun was grinding into his forehead and he thought he might puke.

'Who are you?' a voice growled.

Who was *he*? What was happening here? 'Dario Santangelo . . .' he managed.

'You'd better be able to prove that,' the voice said, releasing him. As he stood up a bright flashlight was beamed onto him. 'So prove it,' the voice demanded.

Prove it, prove it. How was he expected to do that?

'I . . . I live here,' he stammered. Then it occurred to him that perhaps this was a contract hit, and once he identified himself . . .

He snapped. It was all too much. If he was going to get killed then let it be. He sprang forward with an anguished roar.

Carrie fell into a sedated sleep. She dreamed wild nightmares and woke bathed in sweat in the early morning.

Elliott slept in his own bedroom across the hall.

She tried the light beside her bed. only to discover that the electricity was still out. Her ear lobes were throbbing and her body felt stiff.

She pulled on a robe and padded down the hall to the kitchen. The small battery alarm clock she kept beside the stove told her it was six-forty-five. She opened up the fridge and poured herself a warm glass of grapefruit juice. Modern living. She couldn't even fix a piece of toast.

Was it too early to call Steven? Usually she called him every morning at eight-thirty, but wasn't today an exception?

What was she going to say to him? Tell him about her wonderful adventure the previous evening? Steven would have a fit. In his own way he was even more conservative than Elliott.

A twinge of pain in her left hand disturbed her. Arthritis,

Doctor Mitchell had told her when she first complained months ago – 'After all Mrs Berkley – you're no longer a spring chicken.'

*Thank you Doctor Mitchell.* She was sixty-four-years-old, looked forty-eight, and certainly never felt old.

Arthritis! Is that how one ended up – a crippled old woman – bones and joints stiff and tired.

Vogue magazine certainly did not see her as an old woman. Vogue magazine had recently featured a full page picture of her with a caption that read 'SIXTY PLUS . . . AND STILL GOING STRONG'. The article had started off by saying – '*Mrs Elliott Berkley – one of the great exotic beauties and hostesses of our time . . .*'

She noticed that her hand was shaking as she sipped the grapefruit juice. She put the glass down and wandered through her tastefully decorated wholly original ten room apartment. '*Tastefully decorated . . . wholly original*' – quotes from the Vogue article.

She rubbed her eyes and thought about going back to bed, but she knew that she wouldn't be able to sleep.

When would the blackmailer strike again? She would live in fear until she knew.

By nine o'clock in the morning Gino was showered, dressed and ready to get the hell out of Philadelphia. He placed a tense call to Costa, telling him to meet him at the Pierre, then he went downstairs where an apologetic hotel manager waited.

'Mr Santangelo. I'm so sorry about last night. The car you ordered is ready. If there is anything I can do for you . . . ' He walked beside Gino to the revolving doors. Outside waited a group of reporters and photographers.

'Shit!' Gino snapped. 'What *is* this?'

'You're news, Mr Santangelo,' stated the hotel manager apologetically as he escorted his notorious guest out to the waiting limosine.

Gino covered his face as best he could. 'The blackout is news. Jackie Onassis is news. I'm just a tired old man who wants to live out the rest of his life in his own country – quietly – undisturbed.'

His words hung in the air. They were untrue. And everyone knew it.

# Carrie 1943

It was Carrie's birthday. She was thirty-years-old.

Suzita, Silver, and the other two girls now resident in the apartment, baked her a large chocolate cake with thirty blazing candles on top of it. She wanted to cry. It was the first birthday cake she had ever had.

Little Steven danced around excitedly in a white silk suit, while the girls fussed and petted him, exclaiming – 'Ain't he the cutest little fella in the world!' He *was* cute, with his milk chocolate skin, black curly hair, snub nose and huge green eyes. Carrie gazed at him lovingly. Having Steven made it all worthwhile and she was determined to give him the best of everything.

They were a protected house now. A large chunk of the week's taking had to be paid to a collector. 'We don' fight zee mob,' Suzita had insisted, when a polite young man had come calling two years back with a proposition.

Carrie had agreed, although her natural instinct had been to tell him to get lost.

'Say!' Suzita trilled, lifting Steven onto the table next to the cake. 'Sing for mommy Happy Birthday like zee good boy.'

One of the girls took a picture. Steven grinned, revealing missing baby teeth, and began to lisp the song.

Carrie's eyes filled with tears. She was glad that she didn't know who his father was – somehow it made him all the more hers.

Bernard Dimes sat in the dimly lit theatre and watched his actors and actresses going through their paces. The rehearsals for his new show were progressing smoothly.

The director called a ten minute break, and walked over to where Bernard was sitting. Amiably they discussed things. Costumes. An actor's temperament. Accommodation in Philadelphia and other cities they would shortly visit. 'I had a funny experience the other night,' the director said, almost as an afterthought.

'What was that?' Bernard asked politely.

'Hell! I don't even know if I should tell you.'

Bernard sipped his coffee from the thin paper cup.

'But I guess I will – 'cos you know *anyway* that I have my kinks.'

Bernard smiled. The entire company knew about the director's kinks.

'I went over to this brothel on Thirty-Sixth Street. Someone told me about this wild Mexican whore who specializes in what I like. And guess who is running the place?'

'Who?'

'That black kid we had in the chorus a few years back. The one that ran out on us . . . Used to share with Goldie. Remember?'

'Carrie,' stated Bernard, his stomach lurching.

'That's it! Carrie! I said to her — what's a nice girl like you doin' in a place like this. You know what? She pretended not to know me. How d'you like *that*?'

'How was the Mexican?' Bernard asked, trying to keep his tone non-committal.

'Wild! Why? That's not your scene is it?'

'I have an investor who might be persuaded to part with a touch more cash should I be able to recommend such a service.'

'Really? Who?'

'Leave the finances to me. Just write down the address in case I have to pass it on.'

The director shot him a quizzical look, but he scribbled on the card Bernard handed him anyway.

Bernard tucked it into his pocket, and did not remove it until he arrived home that evening. Then he took it out and studied it, memorizing the address and thinking that of course he would never go there. He thought of Carrie as he had thought about her over the years since she had vanished.

Goldie had been no help at all in his search for her. '*I* don't know why she ran off. She had a wonderful evening out with me and my boyfriend and a very *nice friend* of his. She *was* rather a *strange* girl.'

Yes. She was. Different. Unusual.

Bernard made a decision. He got in his car and drove to the apartment house on Thirty-Sixth Street, parked outside and stared at the building. The minutes ticked by, then the hours. He watched the different people going in and out of the entrance. Mostly men. A constant stream of them.

He watched until dawn, and his neck was stiff and his body aching. Then he drove slowly home.

Early lessons she had learned from Florence Williams and Madam Mae stayed with her. The madame of a house should be warm, friendly, and a touch stern. She should treat the men like guests at a fun party. Learn their favorite brand of cigarette or cigar. Their favorite drink. Their favorite sexual game. She should suggest which girl they might like to try. And greet them like a long lost friend at every visit. A madam *never* offered her own sexual services. She only obliged very special clients. Screwing the madam was like getting the best table in a restaurant.

Suzita did not object at all to Carrie taking charge. 'Suits me,' she had said, shrugging shapely shoulders, 'you do all zee work. I have all zee fun!'

Carrie tried to keep a very professional house. Her girls were spotlessly clean, never under sixteen, and dedicated to their job. One of the reasons the place developed a good reputation.

After an initial brush with the police, she learned to pay off and was not bothered again. What with the protection *and* the police sometimes it seemed that life was one big pay off. But there was plenty of money coming in. She rented another small apartment in the building and moved Steven and the girl who looked after him there. The further he was away from her activities the better.

Every day at twelve noon she took him for a walk. He sat in his stroller, bright as a button, and they would wander over to Fifth Avenue and window shop, Steven loved his walks with her, and she never let him down. After all, Steven was her only reason for living.


Bernard Dimes began to spend a great deal of time sitting in his car outside the building on Thirty-Sixth Street. He did not know why he was doing it, something just seemed to compel him.

He took to driving past at every opportunity. In the mornings before going to rehearsal, at lunch time, in the evenings on his way home, and then finally, after dinner, he would park outside and just sit there.

What was the matter with him? Was he going mad? He was in his fifties and yet he felt fifteen. Too nervous to go in and see her. Not strong enough to stay away.

'Bernard, dear, you're awfully jumpy lately,' one of his polished blondes complained, 'something troubling you?'

Yes. Something was troubling him. He was in love with a person he hardly knew. He was in love with sad exotic eyes and a graceful black body. *He was obsessed.*

Carrie smiled at Enzio Bonnatti. It was his second visit. She had obviously pleased him the first time. She handed him his scotch, fixed exactly the way he liked it, two ice cubes and a splash of water.

He lay on the bed in her room and talked about his wife – Francesca. He obviously thought a lot of her. According to him she was young, beautiful, sympathetic and intelligent.

If she was all of those things how come he wasn't home with her?

Carrie had learned not to ask questions. Just to nod and mumble an encouraging 'I understand'.

Enzio was fully dressed, but as he began to describe in every intimate detail his wife's lovemaking techniques, his erection grew.

Francesca was the perfect wife. The perfect mother. She had a perfect body. A perfect cunt. Only Francesca refused to go down on him.

Carrie knew exactly when to unzip his pants and take him in her mouth. That was all Bonnatti required of her. Nothing more. Nothing less. He did not pay. He did not need to. Enzio Bonnatti controlled every whore house in the area.

'You're a smart girl,' he said to her conversationally, when she returned from the washbasin in the corner of the room, 'but a good whore would swallow it.'

'Next time,' she said quickly.

'What makes you think there'll be a next time?'

'I . . . I hope so.'

He laughed, 'I want you to start pushing a little dope for me, nothing heavy. The niggers'll go for it, an' those dumb college kids.'

She felt dismay flood her face. 'Er . . . Mr Bonnatti . . . I don't think so . . . '

'You don't?' he studied her intently. 'I do.' The way he said 'I do' was deceptively mild.

'I'd . . . sooner not,' she stammered, losing control.

'And I'd sooner you did. I'll send one of the boys round with some stuff. Just watch who you offer it to. And stash it away somewhere safe.'

She was upset, 'If the place was raided I could go to jail for having drugs on the premises.'

Enzio stood up. 'An' I thought you was smart. *If* you have a raid you'll know about it before. Plenty of time to dump the goods.'

She nodded blankly. The time had come to get out of the business.

'Nice kid you got,' Enzio remarked, as if reading her thoughts. 'I got boys myself. You wanna take good care of him – the city can be a tough place.'

When had he ever seen Steven? She was filled with a hopeless fury.

Enzio was at the bedroom door now. 'Don't think of skipping on me, chickie. I like the way you run things. Keep up the good work an' the kid'll stay healthy, an' so will you.'

Bastard! Bastard! She was caught in another trap.

'I wouldn't think of it Mr Bonnatti,' she said dully.

'Of course you wouldn't. Didn't I say right off you was smart?'

It was her. No mistaking the purposeful walk and the long jet hair. She was pushing a stroller, and Bernard nearly careened into the back of another car with excitement.

He maneuvered his car into a parking space and proceeded to follow her on foot.

She walked briskly, pausing occasionally to gaze in a shop window. He shortened the gap between them until he was almost upon her. *Talk to her* – a voice screamed in his head – *say something – anything.* He tapped her on the shoulder and she spun around like a nervous colt. 'Carrie!' he exclaimed, 'I *thought* it was you.'

Her smile was sickly, 'Mr Dimes . . .'

'Fancy bumping into you just like that!' He wondered if he was overdoing it.

Her eyes flickered this way and that as if looking for an escape route.

'How are you? And who is this little fellow?' He was bending over the stroller.

She was stunned. Bernard Dimes. After all this time. 'My son,' she said quickly, 'er . . . that's why I took off like I did. I got married.'

He looked quickly at her wedding finger. It was bare. 'Congratulations.'

'Thank you.'

An awkward silence enveloped them. How could he say, 'I want to be with you.' She was looking at him as though he was the last person in the world she wanted to see. 'Perhaps we could have dinner one night,' he said at last, in a strained voice. 'I'd like that very much.'

She shook her head, 'I told you. I'm married. But thank you all the same.'

'Then perhaps you and your husband would care to see a preview of my new show  We're out of town for the next six weeks, but after that there will be a week of previews and . . .'

She was hardly listening to him. She was so ashamed and embarrassed. Oh God! If he ever found out what she was . . .

'I must go,' she said, interrupting him.

'Of course.' He held her eyes with a very intent look. 'If you should ever need me . . . I'm still in the same house.'

'Goodbye.' She rushed off down the street pushing the stroller at a furious pace.

'Mommy! Mommy! Mommy! Too fast!' Steven chanted.

She slowed down and thought about the encounter. Bernard Dimes wanted her. There was no mistaking the look in his eyes. Bernard Dimes like all the others. But different. He was a very rich man.

'Candy!' demanded Steven, 'Peas mommy. *Peeeas*.'

She stopped at a candy store and purchased some chocolate. 'Bad for your teeth,' she grumbled, handing it to her son.

'Bad! Bad! Bad!' Steven chanted.

She sighed. Bernard Dimes wanted her body, that was all. He couldn't be of any help to her. Bonnatti had sent a delivery of narcotics to be sold and *that's* what she had to worry about. Now not only a whore and madam, but a pusher too.

She looked at Steven dribbling chocolate down his chin and felt a cold tightness around her heart. She *had* to do something. But what?

# Gino 1948–1949

Gino kept his promise. He bought Bee the biggest diamond enagement ring he could find, and then he sat back and waited for her to get pregnant. And waited . . . and waited . . . and waited . . .

'The doctor said it could take a few months,' she explained, 'it doesn't always happen just like that. We have to do it at certain times, keep trying.'

Making love at arranged times did not thrill Gino one little bit. In fact the more Bee marched cheerily into bed saying,

'Now's the right time,' the less he wanted to perform. 'I'm not a fuckin' monkey!' he snorted, 'I can only do it when I want to.'

She sulked, 'The doctor says . . .'

He wanted to kill the fucking doctor.

Bee was in the kitchen one morning fixing breakfast. She didn't look too good in the mornings with her shiny face and mussed hair.

Marco sat at the table reading a well thumbed copy of Mickey Spillane's 'I, The Jury'.

Gino knocked it out of his hand, 'I ain't spendin' a fortune on your education for you to sit around readin' crap like that.'

Marco flushed. 'It's real good stuff Gino.'

'Read Fitzgerald, Hemingway, somethin' decent.'

'How many eggs?' Bee asked matter of factly, just like a wife.

He gazed around the large comfortable kitchen and decided he hated the Village apartment. It was a dump. What was he doing here anyway?

Bee turned to ask him how many eggs again and the sun coming through the window hit her across the face. She looked old and tired. Christ! If she looked like this now

'No eggs. Nothin'. I gotta lot of work to do.'

He walked out of the apartment and out of her life just like that. He never saw her again, although he continued to pay all her bills, and allowed her to keep the diamond ring. He heard, a couple of years later, that she had married an accountant and gone to live in New Mexico. Marco kept in touch.

Out of jail over a year. Out of his relationship with Bee. All business interests booming, and hot pussy whichever way he turned.

Gino concentrated on having a good time.

The situation in Las Vegas was appealing to him. Las Vegas – once a barren desert pisshole – discovered by Bugsy Siegel who opened up the infamous Flamingo Hotel in December 1946 and got assassinated for his trouble in June 1947. He had been caught 'skimming' the mob's money, and there was only one punishment for that.

A year after Siegel's demise, Meyer Lansky financed the building of another luxury hotel and casino, the Thunderbird. Soon, several more big hotels were planned.

Gino liked the idea of getting in on the ground floor. And he had a syndicate of investors anxious to get involved. He had a feeling that Las Vegas was going to get hotter and hotter. Where else could you get sun, sand, and legal gambling? And only a few hours drive from Los Angeles too.

Jake the Boy was quite a force out on the coast. He had taken over where Bugsy Siegel left off. He was good looking, a swaggerer, and friend of the stars.

Hollywood. A glamorous name to most people. Home for The Boy. A Beverly Hills mansion with palm trees in the garden, and a movie starlet named Pippa Sanchez in his bed.

Gino arrived on a balmy morning.

The Boy met him in a white Lagonda drophead coupé and drove him straight to his house. He had a special guest wing for Gino to stay in. Very Hollywood. Marble floors. White furnishings. Gold taps in the bathroom.

Gino had arrived to discuss his syndicate financing the hotel Jake wanted to build in Vegas. Jake was flush. But not flush enough to finance the building of a multi-million dollar hotel by himself. He needed Gino – he needed him badly. 'It'll be the biggest an' the best!' Jake enthused, 'I want to call it the Mirage. Every star in Hollywood'll come to the opening. It'll be the best hotel in the whole friggin' world!'

Gino liked the sound of it. He liked The Boy's enthusiasm and style. Over the years they had become friends. The Boy had even visited him a few times in jail on lightning trips East. 'I owe everything I got to you Gino,' Jake was fond of saying, 'you gave me my first hundred bucks.'

Pippa Sanchez had arranged a group of girlfriends around the pool for his arrival.

'Y'can take your pick,' Jake said airily, 'blonde, brunette. redhead, I didn't know which you'd prefer.'

Gino eyed the selection of nubile flesh lounging in varied swimsuited poses, their young bodies carefully oiled. 'It all looks good to me,' he said.

Jake laughed and smacked his lips, 'Take my advice, try a California blonde, they're like no other broad. When they come I swear it's suntan oil oozes out!'

'It's a long way from the mean streets, huh?'

'It sure is!' Jake agreed.

Gino felt himself begining to sweat in his heavy three piece suit. 'I want to shower and rest up.'

Jake remembered his manners, 'Sure, sure I'll send one of the girls in with drinks. And then maybe we can sit around the pool. You want to get a tan while you're here don't you?'

'I want to get our business done,' Gino replied shortly. 'What have you arranged about Vegas? I'd like to see the place as soon as possible.'

'It's all arranged. Tiny Martino is lendin' me his private plane. We fly up in the mornin'. Spend the night at the Flamingo, fly back the next morning.'

'Tiny Martino huh?' Gino was impressed. He had watched Tiny Martino dozens of times on the screen. Bee always said he was funnier than Chaplin. 'He coming with us?'

'Maybe, maybe. He's a good friend. In fact, he's made me a promise to open the season for us at the Mirage.'

The way Jake spoke, the hotel was already built and finished. Gino hadn't even seen the plans yet.

Pippa Sanchez swayed across the terrace towards them. She was short, with a dynamic body and a sweep of dark curls. She wore a white swimsuit and white high heeled sandals, her body was naturally tanned. In her native Mexico she was a star. In Hollywood she was just another contract starlet. Jake the Boy was mad about her.

'So,' she said dramatically, extending her hand, 'you are *the* Gino Santangelo I've heard so much about.'

He took her outstretched hand and squeezed, 'That's me.'

She studied him through thickly lashed dark eyes, 'Nice to meet you at last,' she husked.

'Likewise.' He wondered if the choice of flesh included this one. If it did he wanted her.

Jake must have read his thoughts, quickly he said, 'Pippa's my girl. We bin together – how long honey?'

'A year or two,' she replied casually.

'One of these days we'll make it legal!' he laughed.

'Sure. And one of these days pigs will play leapfrog on your ass!' Pippa responded.

'Actresses!' Jake exclaimed. 'Stay away from 'em Gino.'

'Yes,' agreed Pippa, in her low down throaty voice, 'stay away from them. We *bite* you know!'

Gino smiled. He liked a broad who could join two words together.

It was Costa's sixth trip home since the funeral. After Franklin's death he had found himself in a quandary. What to do? Stay in New York and look after Gino's interests? Or return to San Francisco and take care of his mother, Leonora and the family law firm?

Jennifer was no help when it came to making a decision. 'You must do what you feel,' she insisted. 'If you go back to

'Frisco you'll always be Franklin Zennocotti's little boy. And if we live with your mother she'll become too dependent on you. And Leonora is certainly not going to stand any interference in *her* life. She's thirty-eight-years-old. If she wants to drink . . . and . . . er . . . have . . . men . . . How can *you* stop her? Especially if her own husband can't.'

Costa had to admit that Jennifer was probably right, but it didn't make him feel any the less guilty when he made his monthly visit home. That was one of the reasons he approved of Gino's getting involved in Las Vegas. With business on the coast he could spend extra time there.

Jennifer had not accompanied him on his latest trip. This suited him fine, because after two days he planned to travel on to Los Angeles and meet up with Gino. He thought about all this while driving his mother to a family dinner.

Leonora and her husband Edward lived in a sprawling ranch type house. A black uniformed maid opened up the door and led them into an oak panelled living-room. Leonora lounged on a bar stool. She had added quite a lot of weight to her once svelte body. She wore slacks and a blouse, and held a martini glass which Costa noticed never left her hand.

Edward stood behind the bar, moodily cracking ice. He too had put on a lot of weight, and his handsome face was florid and puffed.

One could see that they had once been a magnificent looking couple – but only just.

'Ah, the visiting New Yorker,' Leonora remarked sharply, 'I don't know how you manage to drag yourself away from your criminal friend so often. Does he allow it?'

Costa ignored her. She did nothing but make cracks about Gino, it seemed to give her some kind of perverse pleasure.

Edward came out from behind the bar and they shook hands.

'How's business?' Costa asked.

'Banking is a constant source of boredom. I'd like to give it up and spend all of my days on the golf course.'

'Oh,' remarked Leonora sarcastically, 'I thought that's what you *did* do.'

Maria came into the room at that point. A delicate looking girl of twenty. She reminded Costa of Leonora at the same age. Only Maria's temperament was entirely different from her mother's. She was shy and withdrawn, almost old fashioned in a nice way.

'Good evening, uncle, grandma.' She kissed them both warmly on the cheek.

'Oh, God!' exclaimed Leonora. '*You're* not home for dinner again are you? Don't you *ever* go out on dates? When *I* was your age I had them lining up at the door.'

'When you were her age you were married,' Costa pointed out quietly.

'Didn't stop me!' Leonora waggled a finger at her daughter. 'It's not natural never going out. What's the *matter* with you?'

Maria's face flushed, 'There's nothing the matter with *me* mother.'

'Don't you start with me young lady,' Leonora screamed, 'did you hear her, Eddie? *Did you hear her?*'

'Oh, shut up,' Edward snapped.

Leonora mimicked his voice, 'Oh shut up! She could sit in her room for the rest of her life just coming out to insult me for all *you* care.'

'Leonora . . . please . . .'

Maria glanced quickly at Costa and her grandmother. She was painfully embarrassed by her parents' behavior and it showed.

He took a deep breath and interrupted the bickering couple. 'Jennifer has a great suggestion,' he said, 'how about – for Maria's twenty-first birthday present if she comes to spend a month with us in New York?'

Maria's face lit up.

'New York,' snorted Leonora, 'mixing with all your gangster friends. I should think not.'

'Oh mother!' pleaded Maria. 'Please!'

'She won't be mixing with any gangsters,' Costa explained patiently, 'Jennifer has a lot of delightful friends. Plenty of respectable families with nice eligible sons.'

Leonora pursed her lips, 'I've never even been to New York myself.'

'You've never wanted to,' Edward snapped.

'Perhaps if *we* went too . . .'

'I can't take a month off My father would have a stroke.'

'We'll have to see . . .' Leonora decided reluctantly.

Costa winked at Maria and mouthed – 'It'll be OK.'

She smiled at him gratefully.

'When the hell's dinner,' snarled Leonora. 'I swear I'm going to have to get rid of that dumb girl who crawls around this house pretending to be a maid.'

Costa sighed. Another wonderful evening at Leonora's house.

*

The desert sun was boiling hot as they walked around and inspected the site Jake had picked out for the Mirage.

'Once the money is in we can start to build. I got an option on the land. Architects plans. Builder's standin' by. All I need is the word from you. It's a can't miss operation. It'll be like erecting a bank!' Jake enthused.

Gino had already made up his mind. He was in. But let The Boy sweat a little. 'You got the plans here?'

'Sure, sure.' Jake snapped his fingers at a hovering minion, 'Get me my case outta the car.'

He took Gino by the arm, and they strolled across the dusty barren stretch of land. 'Over here an olympic size pool – maybe a couple of 'em so's the kiddies can come too. Mom and the kids can play in the sun, while the old man loses the family fortune.'

'I like it.'

Jake's man came running up with his case. The Boy took it, snapped it open, and produced the plans. He bent down on the ground and started to open them up.

'Forget it,' Gino said, 'I'll look at them later.'

Jake, on his knees, began to say, 'I thought you wanted to see . . . ' then he changed his mind and stood up, leaving his bodyguard to fold the plans and put them back in his case.

Gino had strolled off. Jake ran anxiously after him. 'Over here a whole lot of tennis courts.'

'Tennis courts? I don't think that's a good idea.'

'Why not?'

'Give 'em too much to do an' they'll never get to the tables. Gamble and sunbathe – nothin' else.'

'You're right. Nothin' else.'

'Except the supper show. A star name. It'll lure 'em here in the first place.'

'And beautiful girls.'

'Whores?'

'Naw. Waitresses to serve 'em drinks while they're losin' it. Showgirls. A few whores, but high class ones that the bell captain'll have on tap.'

'Right. Hand picked.

'I'll pick 'em myself!'

'Jeeze! It's hot.'

'You want to go back to the car?'

'Why not? I've seen all I need to.'

Jake was sweating, not so much from the heat but from

Gino's nonchalance. When they were firmly ensconced in the back of the car he blurted, 'Well? We got a deal?'

Gino smiled. 'That blonde wasn't bad last night. But I've had better.'

'I'll get you somethin' better tonight. Pippa's got friends you haven't even seen yet.'

'Pippa.'

'Huh?'

'Your exclusive property?'

Jake's smile faltered, 'Kinda. We bin together a while . . . ' He trailed off, and the sweat stood out in pearl like beads on his forehead. 'Of course – if you want her, feel free.'

Gino grinned, 'We could call it a loan for the night. Right?'

Jake smiled in a sickly fashion, 'Right.'

'After all, when you ran off with my sixty grand it was only a loan wasn't it?'

Jake nodded gloomily. Pippa Sanchez was the only broad he'd ever felt anything for in his life. The rest were tramps.

'So I'll borrow Pippa. For a night. It makes things fair – don't you think? Sort of evens up the score.'

'Sure Gino,' Jake's voice was strained, the bastard had him by the balls *and* they both knew it, 'She's all yours.'


# Carrie 1943

She paced around her bedroom, a craving within her that she thought had gone forever. In the closet, hidden in the back, were the drugs. The very thought of them caused a shiver to run through her whole body.

She wondered if Bonnatti knew of her previous addiction. If he *was* aware of it why would he send round a supply of dope for her to sell? Could he be *that* cruel? Or stupid?

Of *course* he could not know. Her past was her own secret. Or was it'

It was early evening, and only a smattering of clients had arrived. The sound of Frank Sinatra drifted through the apartment. Ever since the girls had gone en masse to watch the skinny Sinatra perform at the Paramount Theater they had all been mad about him – and his records were a constant background to the comings and goings of clients.

Carrie preferred something a little more bluesy herself. Bessie Smith or Billie Holiday. She had often wondered if it was the same Billie Holiday she had been at Florence Williams with. And upon seeing a picture of her one day in a magazine she had realized with a thrill that it was indeed the very same girl. She hugged the secret to her. Who would believe it if she went around boasting 'I knew Billie Holiday – we used to work in a whore house together.'

Suzita knocked on her door, 'There eez some strange cat askin' for you, I didn't let him in. He say he good friend of yours. He look like peemp to me.'

'I'll get rid of him,' she replied, smoothing down her tight yellow dress, and walking out of the room.

Through the peephole in the front door she inspected Suzita's 'peemp'. He was a tall skinny black in an absurd pinstripe suit and a big hat. They didn't get a lot of blacks. The ones they did get were usually musicians. Negroes were not encouraged, the white johns didn't like it.

She opened up the door a few inches, keeping the sturdy security chain firmly in place. 'Can I help you, honey?' she drawled. Charm usually got rid of them quicker than a whole lot of screaming. If this black cat wanted action she would send him over to Madam Zoe's on 94th Street, where they would welcome him with open legs.

'I wanna see Carrie,' he demanded in a whiney voice.

'I'm Carrie, honey, an' I'm all booked up for weeks an' months. But I know a place where you'll get the sweetest piece of ass this . . .'

He was peering at her through the dimly lit crack in the door. 'Hot jumpin' shitass craps! *You* is Carrie?' His voice was filled with surprise.

'Sure am. Now listen fella . . .'

'*I* is Leroy,' he crowed, '*You* remember *me* girl? *I is your uncle!*'

She thought she would faint. Just drop to the floor there and then. *Leroy.* It couldn't be. *Leroy.* It was impossible. *Leroy.* Surely the bastard was dead by now.

His very name stirred memories she never wanted to dredge up. *Leroy.* Son-of-a-bitch. Prick.

'I don't know what you're talkin' about,' she said calmly, her heart beating so fast that she thought he must be able to hear it.

'Le-roy!' he yelled excitedly. 'Your *uncle* girl!'

'You got things wrong mister. You'd better get away from here before I call a cop.'

'I ain't goin' nowhere. Call all the cops you want. *I* is staying.'

She thought quickly. Could this really be him? And if it was, how could he possibly know it was her? It had been at least sixteen or seventeen years since he had seen her. She had been a child then – no more than a baby. 'Mister, you get your ass out of here.'

'Why?' he snapped, 'I want a girl. I got money. I kin pay.'

'I can tell you a place t'go where you'll be welcomed. All my girls is busy . . .'

'I'll wait.'

'You can't do that.'

'I'll wait.'

Stubborn mean bastard. It was Leroy all right. She would never forget the selfish whine in his voice.

Suzita joined her at the door. 'Shall I call our protection?' she whispered.

'Yes.' What could he say that would do her harm? She slammed the front door in his face and went with Suzita to call someone from the Bonnatti mob.

'He theenk he know you?' Suzita asked curiously.

'I guess so.'

'You ever seen heem before?'

She shrugged nonchalantly. 'Never seen him in my life.'

Suzita giggled, 'He look like real mean peemp.'

'Yes,' agreed Carrie. That's probably what he still was. A mean pimp. Her uncle. Her only living relative. What a laugh! She walked into the living-room and fixed herself a drink.

Suzita rushed back to the front door, and remained there, eye glued to the spy hole, until two of Bonnatti's hoods came and forcibly removed Leroy. 'He won't be back,' she giggled, 'they beat zee sheeet outta heem.'

As the weeks drifted by Carrie managed to forget about Leroy. She was too busy to brood about the fact that he was out there somewhere. A beating would have frightened him off anyway He was always a yellow sonofabitch She wished the two Bonnatti heavies had sliced his skinny black body up and thrown him in the East River. Any man who made a thirteen-year-old girl take to whoring for him did not deserve to live. If he came back she would kill him herself.

The thought excited her. She bought a small gun from one of her johns and kept it close to her at all times. It gave her a feeling of power. Whenever a man used her body now it was *she* who had the upper hand. Some white dude lying on top of her pumping away – he could be the most important guy in America – but when he was screwing her he was inches away from death. She kept the small gun under her bed, fully loaded. Nobody knew it was there except her. Nobody. And even when she entertained Bonnatti – one of the most powerful criminals in New York – her gun was close at hand.

Oh, if he only knew! Enzio Bonnatti who travelled with three bodyguards at all times. Enzio Bonnatti who had people taste his *food* before he ate. Enzio Bonnatti. Pig. They were all pigs. All the same. They couldn't wait to act out their little perversions.

The men were the whores. At least the woman had a reason for doing it.

Black Bitch! It was her all right with her sassy walk and big tits. She may not be a kid any more, but he could recognize her – he wasn't some dumb asshole.

At first he hadn't been sure. Wasn't able to get a real good look at her through the crack in the door. Bitch! Wouldn't even open up the door and let him into her whore house. *What's the matter, Carrie? Black dick not good enough for you any more?* He could remember the time when black dick was *all* she'd get, and plenty of it.

Well known fact – black dick was bigger than white dick. Smelt better and lasted longer.

Leroy cackled as he ducked and weaved down the street behind Carrie, keeping his distance, mustn't let her spot him. She had certainly turned into a looker, legs like pistons and hair down to her ass. Shit!! Finding her was the best luck he'd had all year!

He extracted a wad of chewing gum from his mouth, and replaced it with a fresh piece. Fortunate that he'd gone into that jazz joint a few weeks back, and got to sittin' around and blowin' a little weed with some of the musicians. Fortunate because the talk had turned to chicks an' things – and while he'd been trying to sell them a taste of his live-in piece – sixteen-years-old, Swedish, and some fast worker – the talk had got around to Carrie's place – a cathouse on Thirty-Sixth Street that had girls a man would cry for. Girls that did anything – for a price – and were the best looking bunch of slits in the city.

The name stayed with him. Carrie. It couldn't be . . . could it? The name wasn't that usual . . . and he found out the chick running the place was black. Carrie . . . what hot luck if it was.

Now he had checked her out . . . It was. Sizzlin' crap! He was onto a good thing.

He whistled as he bopped along the street, chewing on his gum. Things had not been going his way of late. Ten good sunshine years in California sellin' pussy had been followed by six bad ones in San Quentin gettin' dicked by the residents. On his release he had skipped out of the state before he got drafted, run on back to good old New York City, and spent his time boppin' around the bars and dives. Miss Sweden he had discovered serving chicken a la king in a cheap restaurant off Times Square. Now he had her sellin' ass – enough to just about support both of them in a dingy Harlem walk up. Not the life style Leroy had imagined for himself. In California he had been drivin' a Cadillac for crissake. And he had been runnin' ten girls. He was thirty-six-years-old. Time to start lookin' out for his future. As far as he could see little niece Carrie *was* his future. After all – he had taught her everything she knew. Didn't that mean she owed him? In his book it did.

He stopped behind a big fat woman while Carrie lingered in front of a store window. Bitch! She had got him beaten up good. She would pay for *that*. He didn't like mean white dudes messin' with his features. A man could get hurt that way.

Next time he approached her things would be different. Next time she would crawl to him, kiss his feet, even suck his balls if he wanted her to.

He had a plan.

It would work.

She moved away from the shop window, pushing the cute little kid in the blue stroller.

Leroy bopped right along behind them, whistling softly to himself.

# Gino 1949

After the blue skies of sunny Los Angeles, New York City in July was hot, muggy and depressing. For the first time in his life Gino thought about buying a house. A nice spread out of the city with grounds and a pool. Somewhere to spend his weekends. Long Island maybe.

He could understand why The Boy liked Los Angeles. He lived like a king there, surrounded by beautiful broads and all the trappings of success. Like Bugsy Siegel before him he was treated with a mixture of respect and fear. His unsavory reputation created an aura of glamor around him. In Hollywood, if you were glamorous, you were in.

Pippa Sanchez had confided to Gino that The Boy liked to kick his women around. She had shrugged nonchalantly when he asked her if she minded, 'Why should I mind? Being with Jake gets my name in all the columns. It's better than dating some stupid actor. Besides . . . he doesn't mean to do it . . . it just makes him feel . . . strong.'

'Strong huh?' He decided that The Boy needed a watchful eye kept on him at all times. After all he was going to be sinking a lot of dough into the Mirage, and he wanted to know where every dime went. Pippa seemed the ideal person to tell him.

He propositioned her. In exchange for certain monetary rewards would she be prepared to split her loyalties?

Yes she would. She would continue to live with Jake and she would report to Gino, by telephone, once a week.

She did not come cheap.

He had never imagined that she would.

They spent one long languid night together. But her smoldering sensuality did not turn him on as much as he had thought it would. She was back in The Boy's bed the following night, and Gino tried a few more Hollywood blondes before flying back to New York with Costa.

He had made up his mind. No more long affairs. There wasn't one woman he would even consider spending a week with . . . let alone a month or two.

The thought of buying a house appealed to him. A Gatsby style mansion where he could entertain. He missed having Clemmies and playing at being a host. He enjoyed important people drinking his booze and eating his food. Yeh. He could throw great parties just like Clementine Duke used to. Now that he was out of jail and back in action and loaded, big shot friends were no problem. They had all come flocking back, and more besides. Sometimes he wondered if there was one true friend among them. He knew that there wasn't. Money bought you a lot of things – but real friendships were not for sale. The secret was – never trust anybody. That way you could never get hurt.

Gino found it the only way to operate.

*

Jennifer and Costa Zennocotti had rented a house in Montauk for the summer. Nothing fancy, just a comfortable roomy place near the beach, with a swing in the scented garden, and two resident dogs. Jennifer loved it. She took off her New York clothes and lived in a summery cotton shift and bare feet.

Costa spent the weekends there. He found it so relaxing. The moment he drove up on a Friday night he felt every bit of tension leave his body. And working with Gino meant a tension filled life. The man was a dynamo, with a mind as sharp as a knife. Take the Las Vegas deal for instance. Gino needed no papers – the deal was in his head. Of course there *were* papers. Legal documents signed by Gino and The Boy. The venture was going to cost plenty. But if indications of the action at the Flamingo and Thunderbird were anything to go by, opening the Mirage was going to be like opening a bank.

The third week in August, Maria came to stay. She was bubbling with excitement, full of questions, and obviously delighted to be away from home.

'How is Leonora?' Jennifer asked. 'It's been such a time since I've seen her.'

'Mothers fine,' Maria replied and thought of the screaming argument she had overheard between her parents on the eve of her departure.

'I'm going to have a big party for your birthday,' Jennifer decided, 'It'll be such fun. There are a lot of young people I want you to meet.'

Maria nodded brightly, and wished that she could forget all about her birthday. She did not want to be reminded of the fact that she was going to be twenty-one-years-old. At twenty-one you had to make decisions about life, and Maria had no idea what she wanted to do.

All through July and August, Gino viewed houses on the weekends. Big ones, small ones, island retreats, country cottages, mansions. He found nothing that satisfied him from the green pastures of Connecticut to the wilder shores of Long Island.

He was getting fed up with looking. And the real estate brokers were getting fed up with him.

The last Sunday in August he took off on his own, dispensing with driver and bodyguard. He viewed a large property in East Hampton. The woman realtor showed him around proudly, 'I think you will find, Mr Santangelo, that this is just the house you have been looking for.'

He checked the place out carefully. She could be right. It

was an old house in a state of disrepair. But the potential was staring him in the face, *and* he had the money to spend.

The main structure was Victorian, white paint flaking off pillars and balconies covered with intricate trellis work. The rooms were large and many, with big bay windows, and an outdoor veranda that ran around the entire upper floor.

'I like it,' he said.

'It *is* quite unique,' the realtor replied, 'only on the market because the old lady who lived in it all her life died, and the family wish to sell.'

'Kinda rundown.'

'Ah yes. But the price does take that into account. And fixed up it will be magnificent.'

He could not make up his mind. He had looked at so many places he was getting confused. Moodily he kicked at some rubble lying on the floor of the glass conservatory that stretched across the rear of the house. 'I'd havta spend a bundle on it.'

'Oh, I'm sure it would be well worth it.' The woman glanced at her watch. She had another appointment for which she was already ten minutes late. 'Well, Mr Santangelo. What do you think?'

'I don't know yet. If I decide yes I'll give you an offer on Monday.'

'Other clients *have* seen it.'

'Monday.'

'Of course.' She looked at her watch pointedly again, 'I do have to be on my way, Mr Santangelo. Have you seen enough?'

'Sure. You can go. I'll just take a walk around the garden.'

As the sound of her car faded into the distance he realized how peaceful it was. Just the birds chirping, no other sound at all. What did he need all this peace for? Maybe the place was *too* quiet.

He wandered around the gardens, noting the overgrown grass and the roses growing wild everywhere. He tried to imagine how it would look when it was all fixed up. Maybe a big marble terrace leading off the conservatory, tennis courts, and a large blue Hollywood style swimming pool. Yeh. The place could look sensational. Still, he couldn't make up his mind, and it occurred to him that he needed somebody else's opinion. Costa's or Jennifer's. She had good taste, she could tell at a glance what the place would turn out like. And he wasn't that far from Montauk, he could just drive on over to their rented house and fetch them.

•

Maria dived into the swimming pool, swam vigorously for ten lengths, climbed out and collapsed onto a lounger. She felt marvelous, six days with Jennifer and Costa was a revelation. No fights. No long drinking bouts. Just peace and harmony and two people who obviously cared for each other very *very* much.

She shook her long white blonde hair out and closed her eyes, offering her face and body to the sun. Costa and Jennifer had gone out for the day to visit friends. They had wanted her to go with them, but she had declined the invitation, pleading a headache. She had no headache. She had just felt like spending a day alone. One of the dogs began to bark. She reached out her hand and called softly, 'Here boy, here.'

The dog ran to her quickly, wagging its tail.


Gino pulled his Mercedes convertible up in front of the Montauk house. He could hear a dog barking, but there were no other cars in the drive.

He got out of his car and rang the doorbell, hitting the button sharply several times. When there was no reply he roamed around the small house, impatiently shading his eyes and peering through windows. Then he made his way around the back, where a shaggy spaniel loped over to greet him.

And then he saw her, lying by the swimming pool. Leonora. *His* Leonora. And his heart began to beat double time, and sweat broke out all over his body, and his throat went quite dry.

He stood rooted to the spot, and stared. Like a kid. Like the village idiot. And a sharp pain twisted in his gut as he said, very very quietly, 'Leonora.'

'Huh?' She moved her arm from across her eyes and sat up.

It was not Leonora. It was a girl who looked exactly like her. And then he realized that this must be her daughter, Maria. Costa had mentioned something about the girl coming to stay.

He felt like a fool. How could he have possibly thought . . .

'You're Gino Santangelo, aren't you?' she said, getting up and hurriedly covering her bathing suit with a terry cloth jacket.

He took a deep breath. 'Yeh. How'd you know that?'

'Oh. I've seen your picture in the newspaper, and well . . . I met you once before at Costa and Jennifer's wedding,' she laughed self-consciously, 'I was only a child – I guess you wouldn't remember me. I'm Maria, Leonora's daughter.'

'Yeh. Well you sure grew some didn't you?' He was as uncomfortable as hell, and didn't know why.

She wrapped her jacket tight around her and said, 'They're out.'

'Who?' he asked foolishly.

'Jennifer and Costa.'

'Oh. Yeh.' He stared at her intently. The resemblance to Leonora when he had first met her was uncanny. And yet . . . Something was different. Something made this kid more than just a mirror image of her mother.

As if reading his thoughts, she said, 'You thought I was mommy didn't you?'

'Hell, no.' *Hell, yes.*

She smiled sweetly, and brushed a lock of damp hair from her forehead. 'It's all right. I'm quite used to it. Lots of people are amazed by the resemblance. People who knew mommy a while ago that is . . . She looks . . . different now.'

He fingered the scar on his cheek. 'How'd you like to come with me to look at a house?'

'What house?'

'A place I might buy.' He had not the faintest idea why he had asked her. 'Go get dressed, I need another opinion.'

'Is it far?'

'What difference does that make? You're lyin' here doin' nothing.'

She nodded, feeling strangely excited.

'Hurry up.'

'Yes.'

She rushed into the house, flew upstairs to her bedroom, and quickly slipped into a cotton dress. Then she brushed her wet hair and wondered with a shiver of excitement why she was going.

The big bad Gino Santangelo. Murderer. Gangster. Hoodlum. She had developed a crush on him when he had twirled her around the dance floor at the tender age of nine, and ever since, over the years, she had read about him in the newspapers. He had a fearsome reputation. Her mother called him 'scum' and forever berated Costa for being his lawyer.

'You comin'?' he yelled up the stairs.

'Yes, yes.' She rushed from her bedroom and clattered down the stairs in clumsy sandals.

'I raided the kitchen,' he announced, 'Jen won't mind.'

He had taken bottles of Coca Cola, a loaf of French bread, and a packet of ham. 'We'll have lunch there.'

'I'd better leave them a note,' Maria decided, 'just in case they get back early.'

'Good idea.'

He watched her as she scribbled out a message, her long hair falling over her exquisitely beautiful face. She was so clean and innocent and lovely. Just like Leonora had been all those years ago ... Just like Leonora ...

# Carrie 1943

The scraggy teenager with saucer eyes, a sulky mouth, and dirty flaxen hair cut in a series of spikey ends, stared at Leroy in horror. 'I can't look after some kid, man. You crazy or somethin'?'

Leroy stood over her, legs planted firmly apart, and brought his hand down hard smacking her across the face with a resounding wallop. '*You* will do what'n *I* want. You hear me, girl?'

She made a face at him, and tried not to cry. 'Bully,' she muttered.

'What you say?'

'I said sure Leroy. If that's what you want. But how'm I gonna work if we got a kid here?'

He scratched his stomach. 'You stooge. We only gotta *keep* the kid a day or two. Then the bitch pays up to get him back, an' we hightail ourselves off'n somewhere nice.'

'Florida?' her bovine face lit up, 'I always wanted to go there.'

'Sure 'nuff.' Florida like a rat's ass. No way would he head anywhere that pointed south. But it didn't matter what the Swedish tramp wanted. When he had the money he would dump her – fast. She was useless. Enjoyed her job too much. Kept johns lingering on her bed for hours at a time. Not like Carrie. She had them in and out in five minutes. *And* they left with a smile on their faces. He should never have sold her, he'd be ass deep in luxury by this time. But sold her he had, and the bitch owed him, and he planned to get what was rightly his. Money. Plenty of it.

'I'll be back in a coupla hours,' he said, 'have everythin' ready so's you don't have to leave here for a week at least.'

'I thought y'said two days.'

Leroy sighed. 'If'n things don't go as we planned it *might* be a day or so longer. We gotta be prepared. Now move your ass.'

'I don't . . .'

He didn't wait to hear what she had to say, he slapped her again and repeated, 'Move your lazy ass.'

She obeyed.

Leroy grinned. He sure knew the best way to keep 'em in line.


Young Steven's nursemaid was a gawky black girl, too large in every department. Her hair was unruly frizz, braces decorated her teeth, and glasses perched on her nose. Her appearance was one of the main reasons Carrie had hired her. She wanted Steven to have as stable an upbringing as possible, and by engaging a plain looking nursemaid she was insuring that the girl wouldn't go running off to get married.

Leroy had moved in on the girl weeks before when she went to the market for the groceries. Leroy had charm he had never even used, and it all came pouring out to bewitch Steven's nursemaid.

She was flattered beyond belief, simpered, smiled, went on a diet, bought new clothes.

On her Sunday nights off Leroy took her dancing or to the movies. And he found out everything about Carrie and Steven that he wanted to know.

Snatching Steven was going to be one big piece of chocolate cake.


Carrie stirred in her sleep and woke up with a start. She reached for the bedside clock and was surprised to see that it was only ten o'clock in the morning. Usually she slept until at least eleven-thirty, giving her just enough time to shower, dress, and be ready for her walk with Steven at noon.

She lay back in bed and stretched her arms, arching her whole body. Another day. Another grind.

There was plenty to do. Enzio Bonnatti sent his collector round every Monday to fetch the money and replenish the drug supply. Then there was a police detective who had a regular three o'clock Monday appointment. Monday was also laundry day, and pay off day for the cop on the beat.

She rolled over in bed and tried to get back to sleep. It was impossible. She just felt . . . strange. Couldn't put her finger on it.

She thought, as she did every morning, about the drugs in the cupboard. How easy it would be to start the day off lost in the hazy smoke of a reefer. Then, in the evening, a few blows of cocaine to get her through the long working night.

How easy . . . And how wrong . . . She knew what it would lead to.

Leroy goosed the girl from behind, causing an alarmed but happy squeak to emerge from her lips.

'Bright 'n early doll, jest like I said.'

She gazed at him through the thick lenses of her glasses and jiggled the blue stroller where Steven sat contentedly sucking his fingers.

They stood in the middle of the street and chatted idly. Then, quite naturally, Leroy took over pushing the stroller. 'I got a beeg surprise for you,' he said.

'What?'

'Don't know if'n I kin trust you.'

'What? What?' Her glasses jumped onto the end of her nose and she pushed them back up.

'OK,' he laughed, 'this is what I want you to do . . . '

Carrie dressed slowly. The uneasy feeling had not left her. She tried to shake it off but it would not go.

She played a favorite Bessie Smith record while drinking her morning coffee, and as usual considered all avenues of escape. All avenues needed money. She was saving, but it would take time.

Suzita came into the kitchen and flopped down into a chair, 'Honey! I eezz tireder than a beetch on heat!'

Carrie didn't feel like conversation. She felt like seeing Steven. Holding his baby warmth up against her body and absorbing all his goodness and innocence. Soon he would be five years old.

How was she ever going to get out of the life she led without him discovering what she did for a living?

Steven's nursemaid did not disappoint Leroy. She left him with the child as though she had known him for years, and waddled off to the jewelry store where he had told her a 'surprise' would be waiting for her if she just gave the man behind the counter her name.

She'd get a surprise all right. A big surprise when she came truckin' on back and found him and Steven gone.

He cackled aloud, and began to push the stroller at a very fast pace indeed.

'Toofast . . . toofast!' Steven chirped.

'Shut up, kid,' Leroy muttered, '*I* is in charge of you now. An' *I* say shut your goddamn mouth 'fore I slap it shut.'

# Gino 1949

Jennifer opened up the front door and the dogs came bounding through the house to greet her. She sat on the floor petting them and realized with a feeling of regret that soon it would be time to leave the Montauk house and head back to the city.

'Costa, can we get a dog?' she pleaded.

He considered the question. 'If you want one I don't see why not.'

'I think maybe a French poodle, or perhaps one of those funny little sausage dogs.'

'Good idea,' he stroked the back of her neck, 'How about some iced coffee and chocolate cake?'

'You can't possibly be hungry. It's only five o'clock and you ate an enormous lunch,' she exclaimed.

'I'm hungry.'

Laughing together, they walked into the kitchen, the dogs trailing behind.

'Where's Maria?' Costa asked, and then he saw the note. He picked it up, read it, and frowned. Silently he handed it to Jennifer.

She scanned it quickly and said, 'Oh dear!' Leonora had given them one strict rule concerning Maria's trip East. Under no circumstances was she to be allowed to meet Gino Santangelo. 'What are we going to do?' she wailed.

Costa shrugged, 'I don't know.' He read the note again. Maria's neat handwriting. '*Have gone to see a house with Mr Santangelo. Back later. Love and kisses, hope you had a nice day. M.*' He laid the note carefully on the table, smoothing it out with his fingers. 'I just don't know.'

Jennifer made an angry noise, 'Honestly! What do you think happened? Do you think he just turned up here?'

'Yes. Knowing Gino.'

'But we invited him all summer long and he never came.'

'I know.'

They stared at each other.

'Shit!' exclaimed Jennifer.

Costa burst out laughing. 'Shit! *You* said shit! I've never heard you swear the whole time we've been married!'

'Well, you've heard me now. How could he *do* this? Leonora will be *furious*.'

'Listen,' Costa said quickly, 'she doesn't have to find out. We'll tell Maria the situation . . . she'll understand . . . she knows what her mother's like.'

Jennifer nodded. 'You tell her.'

'Sure. No problem.'

Jennifer smiled. 'No problem.'

'Say shit again. I like to hear you talk dirty.'

'Costa!'


Gino broke through a side door to gain access to the house. 'You can't do that,' Maria admonished.

'I just did it,' he laughed.

'Hmmm . . . so you did,' she couldn't help laughing with him. 'May I look around?'

'Sure. Be my guest.'

Maria fell in love with the old house. She ran around exclaiming about this and that, her cheeks flushed, her eyes shining. 'You *have to* buy it,' she insisted, 'it is absolutely the best house ever!'

'You think so?'

'I know so!'

He began to see the old house through her enthusiastic eyes. When he told her about his plans for a big marble terrace and luxurious Hollywood swimming pool she threw up her hands in horror. 'No! You'll ruin it. If you have to build a pool make it a simple one. You *can't* destroy any of the natural beauty. You mustn't change a thing – just a coat of white paint and a few repairs.' Suddenly she realized that maybe she was being rude, foisting her ideas on him as if her opinion was of importance. 'I'm sorry, Mr Santangelo,' she said, stopping her whirlwind rush about the place, 'I get carried away . . . take no notice of me.'

He could hardly believe she was twenty, she seemed more like a sixteen-year-old – so fresh and unspoiled. 'Hey – ' he exclaimed, unable to keep his eyes off her, you can call me Gino.'

He felt like Clementine Duke speaking to *him* the first time he had visited her house. Christ! He was getting old. Forty-three years to be exact. And yet he still felt the same deep inside. As far as he was concerned he would always be twenty.

'OK . . . Gino,' she said hesitantly.

'That's better.' He was pleased.

Their eyes met in the still of the hot balmy afternoon, and Maria could have sworn that her legs turned to jelly. She felt distinctly faint. Spontaneously her hand reached out and lightly touched the scar on his face. 'Where did you get it?' she asked softly.

Nobody had dared to ask him that question in years – and yet it didn't bother him. 'A fight,' he said vaguely, 'long time ago.' And he thought about Cindy. Bright blonde tarnished Cindy. And for a moment he was sorry it had ended the way it had. 'Why d'you wanna know?'

She took her hand away quickly, 'I was just curious.'

'Curiosity killed the cat . . . '

'And satisfaction brought it back . . . ' She laughed softly like a child. But she wasn't a child, she was a woman and he knew instinctively that she *could* satisfy him, and he wanted her like he hadn't wanted a woman in a long time.

She gazed at him expectantly, almost as if she was waiting for him to make a move.

He took her hand and led her out to the garden. 'Let's eat,' he said, 'you sit here while I get the food from the car.'

Obediently she sat down on the grass, her long tanned legs tucked neatly under her.

He fetched the loaf of French bread, the slices of ham, the warm Coca Cola, and they sat in the garden picking at the food ravenously.

'How long you bin with Costa and Jen?' he asked, striving for light conversation.

'Six days exactly. It's been lovely.'

'Yeh. They're a real swell couple.'

'Oh yes. They're wonderful.'

He studied her face, the soft skin lightly kissed by the sun, the huge blue crystal eyes fringed with long lashes, the warm generous mouth. None of it touched with make-up. 'And so you're movin' back to New York with them next week?'

'Yes. Jennifer is busy planning my birthday party.'

'Birthday party?' he was surprised. 'How long you stayin'?'

'Just until the end of September.'

Gino swigged from the coke bottle, 'Kinda an early party. Your birthday's not 'til December is it?'

'I'll be twenty-one on September the fifteenth.'

'December.'

'No, September.'

He was silent as he digested this information. If Maria had been born in September that meant that when Leonora got married she was already pregnant. His virgin girl friend was goddamn *pregnant!* While he was pouring out his heart and soul in love letters and being faithful – *she* was out screwing around. Wonderful. Terrific. Shit. No wonder Costa hadn't wanted to tell him.

But it was all so long go . . . who cared anyway . . .

'Why did you think that my birthday was in December?' she asked curiously.

He shrugged, 'My mistake.'

She picked at the grass with her fingers, 'Did you and my mother . . . um . . . was she ever . . . your girlfriend?' Her heart was beating wildly, and she knew she should never have asked such a personal question, but she simply *had* to know.

'Where'd you get that idea?' He questioned in a guarded fashion.

'Oh I don't know . . . Mommy never said anything . . . but I just picked up on things here and there.'

'Well you picked up on the wrong things. I knew your mother. I went to stay with Costa – we were friends, that's all.'

'You aren't friends anymore. She doesn't approve of you at all. In fact, I'm not supposed to know this, but one of the provisions of my trip was that I wasn't allowed to meet you.'

'Is that so?'

She nodded, looked straight at him, raised her hand boldly to his scar and said, 'But I'm glad I did.'

It seemed only natural that he should take her hand from his cheek and press it to his lips. 'You're beautiful,' he muttered. It wasn't an empty compliment. He meant it.

'Thank you.' Her voice was no more than a whisper.

Silence enveloped them. He kept a hold of her hand. Her big blue eyes were fixed upon him expectantly.

Very slowly he reached over and began to undo the buttons on her thin cotton dress. She said nothing. Briefly he remembered the first time he kissed Leonora. Swimming in San Francisco Bay, the cold oily water and her shivering young body pressed against him.

This was not Leonora.

This was Maria.

He undid the buttons down to her waist, and reached his hand inside the flimsy material. Her breasts were warmly damp, she wore no brassière, which excited him.

'Aren't you going to kiss me first?' she asked in a tiny voice.

He withdrew his hand from her dress and held her face with both hands. Then he began to kiss her very slowly. He pushed his tongue into her mouth, and tentatively she responded, copying everything he did. When he probed she returned the pressure. When he paused she did so too.

Her mouth and lips were so sweet – like succulent fruit.

'I want to kiss your scar,' she murmured hardly realizing what she was saying. And then she was tracing the outline of it with her fingers, and following this up with her soft entrancing lips.

The sun, burning down on them, was very hot indeed.

Gino struggled to remove his clothes, taking everything off except his shorts. He was glad that he had stayed in such good physical shape. Not an ounce of fat on his entire body.

Carefully he peeled her dress from her shoulders, exposing perfect breasts. He bent to kiss them.

She was very quiet, not saying a word but allowing him to do what he wanted.

He began to unbutton the lower half of her dress. Then he peeled down her panties and buried his head in the blonde fluffy triangle. She reared away. 'No, no, please don't do that.'

He stroked her carefully, and laid her down on the grass.

She looked like Leonora. But she was Maria. He had no trouble realizing that.

'You're very beautiful,' he muttered. As he spoke he divested himself of his shorts and started to roll on top of her, '. . . beautiful . . .'

Her long legs were open, and he was as rigid as he'd ever been, but he was having difficulty entering her. 'Jesus Christ!' he exclaimed suddenly, rolling off. 'You've never done this before, have you?'

'It doesn't matter,' she whispered. 'I want to do it.'

'Oh, Christ!' He lay on his back and stared up at the cloudless sky. The fact that she was a virgin had brought him down to earth with a bang. *She was Leonora's kid for crissakes. What the fuck did he think he was doing. Getting his own back perhaps?*

He reached for his shorts and pulled them on.

'What's the matter?' She sat up, instinctively covering her breasts.

The gesture was sweet, reminding him of the fact that she was a decent innocent girl and what the hell was *he* doing with her? 'I made a mistake,' he muttered, 'I'm sorry. Get dressed, kid.'

Two bright spots of color stung her cheeks, 'I'm not a kid. I'm a woman. And what we were doing here today is perfectly all right with me.'

'Yeh? Well it's not all right with me, so be a good girl and put on your clothes and I'll drive you back.'

Her eyes filled with angry tears, 'You are insulting – Mr Santangelo.'

'Hey – what are you talkin' about?'

'If you knew anything at all about women you would know that you can't treat me like this.'

'Like what?'

'Like calling me *kid* and *good girl*. I *know* what I am doing, and I *want* to do it,' she reached out her arms to him and very softly murmured, 'please.'

'Look ki . . . er . . . Maria. This is somethin' that shouldn't be happenin'.'

Her eyes were huge. 'Why?'

'Because I'm much older than you.' He felt ridiculous in just his shorts. He wanted to get dressed and be on his way. All of a sudden he wanted Maria out of his life.

'Are you asking me to believe that you have never made love with a younger woman?' she demanded incredulously.

'I'm not sayin' that.'

'Well . . . what?' She stared at him, genuinely puzzled.

He stared back. She was the most beautiful creature he had ever seen.

She sensed the hunger in his eyes and lay back on the grass. 'I don't know what love is,' she said softly, 'but I do know that I want you to be the first man in my life. I want that very very much.'

He remembered San Francisco. He remembered Leonora saying . . . 'We don't have to wait, Gino . . . ' But he had insisted hadn't he? He had mumbled some garbage about how they should save making love until they were married . . . He had played schmuck all down the line. And now he was about to do it again . . .

'Maria,' he said roughly, 'if it's what you really want . . . '

She reached out for him, 'Oh, yes, Gino . . . oh, yes . . . '

Jennifer and Costa both heard the car roar up in front of the house at the same time.

Jennifer's mouth was set in a thin angry line. She glanced at her watch just to make sure that it really was twelve o'clock at night.

'Now stay calm,' Costa urged, 'she's back now, and it won't happen again. I'll talk to Gino, don't worry.'

'How can I stay calm?' Jennifer snapped. 'I'm furious. Not even a phone call to tell us she'd be out half the night.'

Costa put a finger to his lips, 'Sssh.'

They heard the front door slam, and then in walked Maria and Gino. All of Costa's worst fears were confirmed. The two of them were glowing like Christmas trees. A stupid grin split Gino's face in two, and Maria was flushed and bright eyed.

'Hey-hey-hey!' Gino exclaimed. 'And how's my favorite old married couple?' Jennifer turned a frosty cheek as he bent to kiss her.

Costa said coldly, 'Why didn't you phone? We were worried.'

Maria looked guilty, 'I left a note, uncle.'

'Yes,' agreed Costa, 'a note that indicated you would be gone an hour or two. Do you realize what the time is?'

'I took her to a sea food restaurant,' Gino said breezily, 'best lobster I ever tasted.'

'Oh yes!' agreed Maria. 'It was wonderful!' She looked at him and smiled.

He smiled back and winked.

Costa sighed. 'Why don't you run along to bed, Maria. Mr Santangelo and I have some business to discuss.'

'It's all right,' she said cheekily, 'I'm allowed to call him Gino.'

Jennifer stood up, 'Come along dear, say goodnight, I want to talk to you.'

Maria smiled very softly at Gino. 'Goodnight. And . . . thank you.'

He grinned, 'We had a good day, huh?'

She glowed, 'A *very* good day.'

Costa waited until the women left the room, and then he asked sharply, 'Drink?'

Gino settled himself into a comfortable chair, 'Yeh. A brandy would be OK.'

Costa went to the bar and silently poured the amber liquid

into a balloon glass. Then he handed it to Gino and said, 'What's the game, my friend?'

'Huh?' Gino looked vague.

Costa was very angry. 'Don't shadow box with me. I know you too long and too well. What the fuck are you playing at?' It took a lot to make Costa swear. When he was angry his face broke out in red blotches and his eyes narrowed until they were merely slits.

'I took the kid out to see a house I'm thinkin' of buyin'. Then I took her to dinner. What's the big deal?' Gino said unconcernedly.

'Why Maria?' Costa snapped.

'Why Maria what?'

'Why are you picking on her?'

Gino swirled the cognac around in his glass, 'Aw c'mon, I don't know what you're talkin' about . . . '

'I'm talking about what my eyes see. She's my niece, Leonora's daughter for God's sake.'

'Yeh?' Gino was beginning to get aggravated, 'The one she had in September or December?'

Costa had the good grace to look embarrassed, 'It wouldn't have done any good telling you then.'

'Very true.' Gino yawned, and changed the subject, 'You got a spare bed here? I don't feel like drivin' back to the city.'

'I'd appreciate it if you did.'

Costa was taking the shine off his day, 'Why?'

'Because I have very specific instructions from Leonora that Maria is not to meet you on this trip. We can't help today, but . . . '

'Fuck Leonora,' Gino blazed.

'Look. Be reasonable.' Costa paced around the room, wondering how he had ever got himself in this position. 'What difference does it make in your life if you never see the girl again?'

Gino tipped his brandy glass, draining the last drops of the rich liquid. He shrugged, 'You're right. What difference?'

Costa looked immensely relieved.

Gino placed the glass firmly on the table and gave Costa a long hard look. 'I'll be seein' you, pal.'

'Tomorrow. You'll be in the office, won't you?'

'I may take a trip to the coast, check out how The Boy's doin'.'

Costa tapped his fingers on the table nervously. He had made his point, now he wanted them to part friends. 'Unexpected isn't it?'

'Yeh. But I figure maybe I should get outta the way. What with the big party Jen's planning, it's better I ain't around . . .'

'I'm sorry, it's just that Leonora feels . . .'

'What *does* the bitch feel?' Gino raised his voice. 'That her precious daughter will get corrupted in my company? That I'm a bad boy? Well you can tell her from me that I think she stinks – y'get it? Stinks.'

Costa nodded silently.

Gino slammed his way out of the house.

This time he didn't stay at The Boy's house in Los Angeles. He rented a place of his own – a huge mansion in Bel Air that had once belonged to a silent movie star.

He moved in with bodyguards and entertained a procession of prime female flesh. They were beautiful all right, but they were boring. Each and every leggy one of them wanted to get into movies. While waiting for the big break they got into bed with anyone they thought could help them.

He visited Vegas and checked out the construction of the Mirage. Progress was fast – it was looking good.

Pippa Sanchez came to his house in Bel Air and prowled around like a particularly lethal cat. She had kept her word and told him tales of Jake's doings – it all seemed very on the up and up. The Boy wasn't stealing – yet.

She stripped off her white dress in Gino's bedroom, and went through the acrobatic motions of making love.

He wondered if The Boy knew what she was up to. He hoped that he did.

'You should finance a movie,' Pippa remarked casually, 'you can afford it. Why don't you?'

It wasn't a bad idea. 'Find me a script. If I like it, I'll do it.'

It was the first time he had ever seen her smile. *Why* was she smiling? He hadn't offered her a part.

On September 15th he phoned one of his secretaries in New York, dispatched her to Tiffany's, and told her to buy the biggest and best aquamarine set in diamonds she could find. He dictated a note to go with it, and had it sent to Maria. The note said, *'Happy Birthday, this'll never outshine your eyes.'*

When Maria opened it and read the note she cried. It was nothing new, she had been crying on and off since Gino's departure.

He sat by his pool in Bel Air and thought about the girl who would be twenty-one that day. He thought about her face and her skin and her eyes and her body and her smell.

At six o'clock in the evening he got a plane back to New York.

He did not care what was right or wrong. He did not care if Leonora had hysterics, or Costa never spoke to him again.

He knew what he wanted, and he was going to get it.

# Carrie 1943

For days Carrie had been crying until there were no tears left. Then a hot burning fury swept over her, and she stormed into the restaurant where she knew Enzio Bonnatti lunched every day. She swept over to his table, ignoring his bodyguards who leaped to their feet, and began to harangue him. 'I want my baby. You hear me? I want my baby! You told me when he was taken you would get him back. Well WHERE IS HE? I *told* you who took him. Your boys talked to the girl that looked after him. So where is he? Why haven't I got him back? It's six days! I pay you protection . . . I WANT ACTION!'

The bodyguards had a hold of her now, vice like grips on each side. 'Move it, nigger,' one of them snarled.

'Where's my little boy?' she screamed at Enzio, who studiously broke bread and attempted to ignore her. 'I WANT MY BABY! AND IF YOU CAN'T GET HIM BACK I'M GOING TO THE COPS. YOU HEAR ME – THE COPS. I'LL TELL THEM EVERYTHING . . .'

She was frogmarched from the restaurant.

Enzio glanced at his luncheon companion, a rather statuesque showgirl. He shrugged, 'Never saw the girl before in my life. I get that all the time.'

Outside the restaurant Carrie was dumped unceremoniously into the back of Enzio's car, while one of his bodyguards went back inside to find out what should be done with her.

'Take her to her place, lock her in a room, I'll be by after lunch,' Enzio muttered from the corner of his mouth. There was nothing worse than a hysterical whore. Maybe it was time to ship her out of the city down to one of his South American connections. He had other things on his mind – he didn't need aggravation about her stupid kid.

Leroy sat on the floor and tossed peanuts into his mouth. Like miniature bullets he fired them off – one by one – and his aim was great – they all landed right on the center of his large pink tongue.

Four-year-old Steven watched fascinated. Sixteen-year-old Lil squatted on the bed painting her toenails. A fly buzzed around the musty little room, and settled on a chunk of ham left uncovered on a shelf.

'Today's the day,' announced Leroy, suddenly leaping up, 'I guess'n the bitch will give me anythin' I want now. She must be sweatin' shit!'

'We gonna get rid of the kid today?' Lil asked excitedly.

'Maybe . . . maybe not . . ' he replied, giving nothing away as usual.

'It's bin nearly a week,' she sulked.

'Tough shit,' he snapped.

'I wanna get back to work,' she whined, 'we need the dough.'

'We'll have dough comin' out our assholes!' smirked Leroy.

Steven looked from one to the other of them with serious green eyes. He didn't understand why he was with these funny people, but he had learned that it was best to keep quiet. They hit him when he didn't.

Leroy danced around the room getting himself dressed. 'Today's the day,' he sang.

Lil concentrated on her toenails.

Steven remained in the corner quietly watching them.

Enzio's slap stung the side of Carrie's face. 'No whore talks to me like that. Who do you think you are, *puttana*?'

She was defeated, her hands picked at the material of her dress, 'I'm sorry Mr Bonnatti.'

'Sorry!' He laughed mirthlessly, 'I've had people killed for less than you did today.'

She was silent.

'I don't like being threatened. I don't like no talk of telling the cops. Not that you *could*. You know nothin'.'

Her voice was a whisper, 'I'm sorry . . .'

'Sure you are. You've had time to think things over.'

'I want my son back, Mr Bonnatti, you promised . . .'

'I promised nothin'. I said I'd have a couple of the boys look into it.'

'If you could . . .'

He was impatient, 'I will, I will. But in the meantime maybe you should take a little rest . . .'

'No!' She was startled.

'What d'y'mean – no?'

'I'm not going anywhere without Steven.'

He sighed, 'You run a good house, I ain't shittin' when I say y'could be worth a lot to me. I don't wanna havta throw you out on the street, but if you cause me trouble – believe it – I will.'

She was desperate. 'Mr Bonnatti. Please. I just want my son back. I'll do anything you ask. Work for nothing . . . anything . . .'

'I'll get the kid back – but no more scenes – y'get it?'

She grabbed his hand and kissed it, 'Thank you, Mr Bonnatti. I know you can find him . . . You'll do it . . .'

He unzipped his pants, 'Give me a blow job while I'm here,' he requested casually.

She didn't understand for a moment, and then, when the realization set in, she knelt unhappily to her task.

Enzio Bonnatti was a pig.

But he was the pig who would find her baby.

Leroy bopped happily down the street. He checked out his reflection in a shop window and liked what he saw. He would like it a whole lot better when Carrie came up with plenty of dough. And she would. He had no doubt about *that*.

He went into a diner and ordered a cup of coffee, then he went in back to a pay phone and dialled the private number of her whorehouse.

A chick answered with a real heavy accent. 'Get me Carrie,' he demanded.

'She ees busy right now mister.'

'I'm callin' 'bout Stevie baby. Unbusy her.'

The chick snapped to attention. 'Steven? Her Steven?'

'Put her on this phone, bitch, 'fore I hang up.'

He hummed a tune and read the graffiti on the wall while he waited. 'MARLENE FUCKS. WHO DOESN'T?' He wondered who Marlene was. Probably wrote it on the wall herself.

Carrie got on the line real frantic sounding, just like he had expected. 'You got my baby?' she cried frenziedly, 'Is he all right? You haven't hurt him? Where is he?'

Leroy spoke slowly, 'How much y'gonna pay to get him back?'

'Who is this? Is this Leroy?'

'Well, what d'y'know. Thought you di'n't know who I *was*. Thought you *had* no Uncle Leroy.'

'I'll pay everything I got. Only I want him back today.'

'Hot steamin' crap! How yore memory come rushin' *back*, girl.'

'I'll meet you. Where? When?'

Things were moving faster than he had anticipated. He thought quickly. 'One o'clock tomorrow afternoon. Top of the Empire State building.'

'Tomorrow?' her voice shook. 'Why not today?'

'One o'clock. Bring five thousand bucks if'n y'ever wanna see the kid alive again. An' don't you tell nuthin' to no one.'

As he hung up he could hear her sobbing. Shit man. She deserved a little misery in her life treating him the way she had.

He returned to the counter, took a gulp of his coffee, and sauntered out of the place without paying. Nobody stopped him. It was a good sign.

'Leroy,' he muttered to himself, 'soon you is gonna be one rich mutha!'

Enzio Bonnatti said, 'He just made it easy for us.'

Carrie nodded limply. She didn't know whether to be glad or sorry that he had heard the entire conversation.

'What shall I do?' she whispered.

He frowned, 'Keep the date. Leave the rest to me.'

'You will get Steven back?'

'Tomorrow you'll have your kid back, then perhaps we can get on with running a business here. I'm sending up more dope – shift it faster – encourage the suckers to use it.'

'Yes Mr Bonnatti.'

'Good girl.'

Her eyes were dull, 'Thank you Mr Bonnatti.'

One o'clock, and Manhattan was teaming with people on their lunch breaks.

Leroy cursed as he entered the towering Empire State building and took a series of elevators to the 102nd floor. He was sweating profusely when he reached the observatory. Moronic dumb ass meeting place. He wiped the perspiration off his upper lip and put on a pair of very dark sunglasses.

It seemed the world and its wife had decided to make the trip. The place was jammed. He looked around for Carrie. Couldn't see her, and wondered if she would recognize him today. He remembered her as a skinny black chick with slanty eyes and big tits. She hadn't changed. Just got better looking.

He couldn't see any black faces at all. If she didn't turn up he would skin her whiney little kid alive. Steven. What kind of name was that for a nigger anyway?

Carrie walked to Thirty-Fourth Street and Fifth Avenue. She arrived half an hour early and huddled miserably in a coffee shop watching the minutes tick by on a wall clock.

Enzio Bonnatti had not confided what was going to happen, he had just assured her that she would have Steven back that very same day – 'Unless he's dead,' he had added chillingly. *Unless he's dead.* The casually spoken words tormented her all night, and were still tormenting her. If Leroy had harmed Steven in any way at all she would personally kill the scumbag. Shoot him with her gun which rested reassuringly in her purse.

The clock was five minutes off one o'clock when she paid for her coffee and left.

Big Victor and Split watched her go.

'Some ass,' Big Victor leered.

'If you like darkies,' Split commented.

They looked exactly what they were, a couple of hoods. Big Victor was a heavy man with hangdog eyes and a sloppy mouth. Split was younger, thinner, with unruly greased hair and a prominent nose.

'I never paid for it,' Big Victor remarked causally, picking at his teeth with a finger. 'Can't understand mugs that do.'

Split nodded his agreement, and they set off after Carrie.

Leroy saw her coming, and hot shit she was something!

He forgot himself for a moment and stared. Sharp as a Dizzy Gillespie solo! *Something!* He wondered if a little bit of lovin' might be part of the deal.

She hadn't seen him, she was looking around kind of panicky.

He was glad he had worn his favorite suit. Brown with a wide white stripe. And he adjusted his white knit tie, which went nicely with his tropical shirt. When she saw him, with his wide brimmed hat and his dark glasses she would probably think he was a movie star or something!

He bopped towards her, catching her from behind with a, 'You musta bin a beau . . . tiful baby – 'cos momma – lookit y'now!'

She almost jumped in the air with shock, and then she turned around and glared at him. 'Leroy?'

He preened. 'The very man himself!'

Hate filled her eyes. She wanted to pull out her gun and shoot him there and then, but Enzio's instructions were to identify him – talk a couple of minutes – and walk away when his men took over. She hadn't *seen* any of his men. 'Is Steven all right?' she asked quickly.

'Sure 'nuff havin' the time o' his life.'

Her voice was flat, 'What do you want?'

He laughed. 'Some greetin'. You look hot – talk cold. Whyn't you warm up some an' we kin discuss things, huh?'

Her eyes darted around the crowded observatory. 'Yes.'

He thought she was objecting to the crowds, 'We'll get outta here. We'll go someplace else.'

'Where?'

He took her arm in a proprietory way, 'That's for me t'know an' you to worry about.' He began to walk her towards one of the elevators.

She glanced around desperately, and saw them. They had to be Enzio's. They looked the part. She almost sighed aloud with relief.

A line of people waited to board the down elevator. 'We shoulda hadda look over the city while we was up here.' Leroy remarked, 'I bet it's some view.' He pinched her arm when she failed to answer. 'We'll do it again, huh?'

She nodded, dizzy with fear. The two men were behind them in the line, so close that she could smell the garlic on their breath.

An elevator arrived, spilling out a new batch of sightseers. A couple of sailors grinned at her and made appreciative noises. This seemed to please Leroy who held her arm even tighter. How was she ever going to get away?

They got into the elevator, the two men close behind.

She thought about Steven and once again wanted to get out her gun and put a bullet through Leroy's oafish stupid grinning mouth.

One day she would. Yes. One day she would.

Big Victor said, 'We'll take him on the sidewalk.'

Split agreed.

'I'm gonna enjoy this job,' Big Victor remarked, 'smart ass nigger pimp's gonna get everything he should.'

Split ran a hand through his greasy hair. 'You think the boss is screwin' dark meat?'

Big Victor spat contemptuously, 'Naw.'

'So why we doin' this?'

'Beats me. I don't ask questions. Maybe he's got a soft spot
for kids.'

'Yeah – but a darkie kid?'

They both shook their heads in puzzlement.

Out on the sidewalk Leroy adjusted his dark glasses and tipped
his hat at a more rakish angle. He was enjoying himself. Having
a *good* time. Passing guys were checking Carrie out like she was
ripe fruit on a market shelf. 'You done pretty goddamn good
for yourself, chicken,' he remarked happily, 'I guess I done
you one *beeeg* favor when I set you on the road.'

She stared at him, hate and disbelief mixed on her face.
Before she could say anything Big Victor and Split were
moving in. Crowding Leroy, one on each side of him. 'Look
out man – watch it . . . ' he began to say, then realization he was
being taken and an outraged splutter of curses.

'Just take it easy,' Big Victor said in a low cold voice, 'an'
walk along with us, otherwise my gun's gonna spew your black
guts all over the sidewalk.'

Carrie turned to walk away, but not before Leroy held her
with his shifty eyes and spat – 'Bitch! The kid'll get it for this.'

Split jammed something into the side of him and he let out a
low moan of pain and stopped talking.

Carrie hurried away, frightened to look back, frightened to
do anything.

She wanted Steven back. And until she had him safely in
her arms again she couldn't even think straight.

Swedish Lil was getting bored. She looked at the stupid kid, and
the stupid kid gazed back at her with his big serious eyes.
'Whatcha starin' at?' she snapped angrily.

Steven did not reply. He was confused. He wanted his
mommy and his toys. He didn't like it where he was. Tears
brimmed over and fell down his cheeks, 'I want my mommy,'
he cried.

'Shut up!'

'I want my mommy.'

'I said *shut up* brat.' She threw a shoe at him. It missed, but
it shut him up. She yawned, said, 'Shit!' jumped off the bed and
did a few leg bends.

Life with Leroy was turning into one big bore.

It took longer than they anticipated. About five minutes longer. Pimps were all the same – black, white or orange. They could dish it out, but they sure as hell couldn't take it.

Leroy was no different. The first spill of blood on his sharp brown suit and he was spitting teeth and blubbering like a baby.

The rest was easy. The drive to Harlem. The hot smelly little room. And the hot smelly little broad who Big Victor whacked on the ass and said, 'What's a white chick like you doin' hangin' out with a bad ass nigger? Get yourself packed an' out of here. I'll be comin' back to check.'

Lil glared at him, then at Leroy – a snivelling whining wreck in the corner. 'Shove it!' she said rudely, 'both of you. I'm *gettin'* out – you can bet on *that.*'

The kid was all right. Filthy, stinking, a few bruises, but all right. Split slung him over his shoulder and carried him out to the car where he dumped him on the back seat. Steven was rigid with apprehension.

'A nice clean job,' Big Victor remarked.

'Yeah,' agreed Split, 'y'get a load of the floosie? Couldn't've bin more than fifteen.'

'A dirty chick.'

'Yeah. Real low down dirty.'

'Just the way you like 'em, huh?'

Both men laughed.


Carrie got her baby back, but he wouldn't talk, wouldn't say a word. Just stared at her with big accusing eyes as if everything that had happened to him was *her* fault.

She hugged him, bathed him, put liniment on his bruises, fed him.

He gazed at her and said nothing.

She cursed Leroy silently and hoped that Enzio's hoods had killed the son-of-a-bitch.

Suzita was taking care of things upstairs while Carrie nursed her son in the small apartment that was their private sanctuary. The fat stupid nursemaid was long gone. It was just the two of them alone together.

At around 11 p.m. Suzita phoned down, 'Mr Bonnatti just arrived,' she whispered, 'he's askin' for you. I told eem you was just downstairs for zee minute only.'

'Oh, God!' raged Carrie, 'I can't come up. Not tonight. I can't leave Steven.'

'He look plenty mad.'

Carrie drummed her fingers impatiently on the receiver. Did Enzio Bonnatti think he owned her now? Was she supposed to jump as soon as he called?

The answer was yes, and she knew it. 'I'll be up,' she said, 'in a minute.'

She went into the bedroom and studied Steven who slept restlessly. If he woke she should be by his side. Goddamn Bonnatti. Goddamn all men.

She slipped out of her robe and into a dress, then she pressed a kiss onto Steven's forehead and crooned, 'I'll figure something out for us, sweetheart. I'll get us out of here. I promise.'

Enzio Bonnatti was lying on top of her bed fully dressed and smoking a cigar. 'I get your kid back – you take off. What is this? A rest home?'

'I have to find a new nurse for him,' she muttered resentfully.

His eyes hardened, 'So find one. You're supposed to be runnin' a business here.'

'Yes, Mr Bonnatti. Just give me time.'

'You'll be gettin' a delivery tomorrow of some very fine white stuff. Six thousand dollars worth. I want the cash in my pocket like in a week. Get it?'

'Yes.'

'Yes, yes. What's the matter with you? You're sullen as an old pole cat. Don't I get a little appreciation around here?'

What did he want with her? Why didn't he leave her alone? He was Enzio Bonnatti. He could have any woman he wanted. Why her?

'What do you want me to do?' she asked flatly.

'Such enthusiasm!' he mocked.

She tried to push a smile onto her face, but it didn't quite work.

He drew on his cigar and regarded her as though she was a small bug whose only function in life was to entertain him. 'Get your clothes off – I wanna see y'naked.' He gestured with his cigar to a chair. 'Sit astride it.'

She did as he requested, and all the time she was thinking of Steven and hoping that he wouldn't wake and wondering how the two of them could escape from this whole degrading scene.

Enzio began to talk about his wife. The things he said about her were disgusting, but it excited him immediately. The more he talked of his wife the more aroused he became.

She tried to look interested, but it was difficult sitting naked in a chair like an object. She wanted to scream, get up and run. Enzio Bonnatti never thought of her as a person with feelings. She was just another whore, and he had stables of them all over the city.

Much later, she lay in the gloom of the small downstairs apartment, Steven tossing and turning beside her. Was this the freedom she had worked so hard to get for them? Running whenever Bonnatti called. Pushing his drugs.

And would Leroy be back? Sniffing around and making her live in fear? Forcing her to watch Steven every second of the day and night? She could see no escape. And yet . . . Bernard Dimes. Could *he* help her? A stray thought, but the way he had looked at her that day in the street . . . If she went to him . . . told him the truth . . . It was worth a shot. Anything was worth a shot.

She fell asleep at last, and like her son she slept restlessly.

Big Victor and Split delivered the small bags of white powder called cocaine. They breezed in like long lost friends, winked and joked with Carrie, and demanded a free fuck on the spot.

She put Big Victor with Silver, the other hood with Suzita, and fumed in the kitchen while the delivery boys had their fun.

Steven sat at the kitchen table, still silent, a plate of scrambled eggs in front of him. Once this had been his favorite meal, now he didn't want to eat it. He pushed the food discontentedly away.

'Aw, come on, sweetheart, be a good boy for momma,' she pleaded.

He regarded her with big solemn four year old eyes, pushing the plate until it crashed to the floor and broke into pieces.

'Goddamn it . . . ' she began angrily, raising her arm as if to strike him.

He didn't flinch.

*What was she thinking of? Was she going mad?*

She ran to him and hugged him tightly. 'I'm sorry honeybunch. Momma's sorry.'

He was unmoved in her arms. A small stubborn package of flesh.

One of the girls strolled into the kitchen, wearing nothing but a yawn and a loose negligee. 'Hiya Stevie, baby. Coochi coochi cool!'

Carrie snatched him up, 'Tell Suzita I'm going out,' she snapped.

'Sure.'

She hurried to her room. The bags of cocaine were on the middle of her bed waiting to be put away. *Goddamn it! She wasn't going to be Enzio Bonnatti's pusher any longer.*

She sat Steven on a chair and stuffed some clothes in a shopping bag. Then, from a drawer, she took a stack of twenty dollar bills neatly joined with a rubber band. Pay off money. Briefly she felt sorry for Suzita who would be left to explain . . . but what could she do?

She scooped Steven under one arm, the shopping bag under the other, and quietly left the apartment.

Downstairs she collected his stroller, and within five minutes she was out on the street and walking fast.

Carrie was on her way to a new life, and no one was going to stop her.

# Gino 1950

Maria smiled. She had the greatest smile in the world, *and* the biggest belly. She sat in the garden of their house in East Hampton and said, very quietly, 'Gino. I think that you had better take me to the hospital.'

He went into a panic. 'Jeeze! Who shall I call? What shall I do?'

'Phone the hospital, tell them we are on the way. Stay calm.'

'I *am* calm! Jeeze! How do you know it's time?'

She smiled serenely, 'It's time.'

'Holy shit! You stay right there.' He raced into the house to summon help.

Mrs Camden, the nanny they had hired, was knitting, drinking tea and listening to the radio.

'Move it!' Gino screamed. 'She's ready!'

Nanny Camden did not move as fast as he would have liked. She placed her knitting on a table, patted her neat white bun to make sure every hair was in place, and then – very slowly – got up.

Gino was almost jumping up and down with frustration. He

alerted his chauffeur and bodyguard, then dashed upstairs to get Maria's suitcase. She had been packed and ready for weeks.

He could hardly believe that the moment had finally come. Forty-four-years-old and he was going to be a father! He had almost given up on the idea.

'Hey – baby – how do you feel? You OK? Can you walk?'

'Of course,' Maria laughed, as she made her way slowly towards the car, Nanny Camden on one side, Gino on the other. 'You did alert the hospital didn't you?'

He slapped his forehead, 'Shit! I forgot. Don't go away.' He rushed back into the house, his heart banging at an alarming pace. Quickly he called the hospital, 'Mrs Santangelo's comin' in now, have everything ready!'

The nurse on the other end of the line was cool as ice on tit. Gino could have strangled her. What was the matter with everyone – didn't they have any sense of occasion?

He raced out to the car. Maria was settled comfortably in the back, Nanny Camden beside her. He squashed in beside them and held onto his wife's hand.

'Wouldn't you be more comfortable in the front, Mr Santangelo?' the nanny asked pointedly.

'No, no, don't you worry about me.'

Maria gave a little grimace and clutched her stomach.

'Jesus! What's the matter?' Gino yelled, 'Red – will you move this fuckin' car!'

Nanny Camden pursed disapproving lips.

The large green Cadillac reached the hospital in record time. Maria was immediately whisked inside and Gino suddenly found himself redundant.

'Just take it easy, sir,' a young nurse told him, 'if you want to go out for coffee . . . '

Out for coffee! Was the girl mad! He did the traditional thing and paced the long hospital corridor.

Maria. His wife.

It had not been easy for either of them. So much opposition . . . so much screaming and yelling . . . And Maria whisked back to San Francisco like *she* was a criminal.

'I want to marry her,' he told Costa.

'Are you crazy? You don't want *her*, you just think you do because she looks like Leonora.'

'That's bullshit. I love her.'

'Come on, Gino. Be reasonable. You're not being fair to anyone – least of all her. She doesn't understand what all this is about. She's just got a schoolgirl crush on you.'

'Maria is no schoolgirl, Costa. She's twenty-one-years-old and I'm going to marry her.'

'Forget it. Leonora will *never* let that happen.'

But it turned out that Leonora had no choice. Maria was pregnant and thrilled about it. She managed to telephone him and tell him the news. He made immediate arrangements for her escape. They met in the state of Maryland a week later and were married the same day.

Leonora swore that she would never talk to her daughter again. Edward reluctantly went along with her decision.

Neither Maria or Gino much cared. They were ecstatically happy. He bought the East Hampton house where they had fallen in love, painted it white, put in a simple natural swimming pool, and kept the gardens unbridled and wild.

For the first time in his life he knew a state of bliss that he had only ever dreamed of.

Maria was perfect. He idolized her. And he never once thought about her resemblance to her mother.

'You have a beautiful baby girl. Seven pounds five ounces. She's gorgeous.'

'Jesus H. Christ!! Jesus!!'

'Mr Santangelo. Please!'

He picked up the nurse and danced her along the corridor. *'Mr Santangelo! Put me down!'*

He dumped her unceremoniously onto her feet, 'My wife? How is my wife?'

'She's fine. The doctor is just sewing her up and . . .'

'What d'y'mean – sewing her up?'

'Perfectly normal procedure. A few stitches . . . the doctor will explain everything to you.'

'Goddamn it! I'm a father!' He whacked the nurse on the behind, 'Hey – you want a cigar?'

The baby was the most exquisite creature – next to Maria – he had ever set eyes on. Small, dark, crunched up, hairy. Exquisite!

Day after day he sat in the hospital just staring, hardly able to believe that this beautiful little creation was his.

'You like her, don't you?' Maria inquired with a smile.

'You said it!' He grinned at his young wife who sat up in bed like a flaxen doll, her face shining with happiness, long fair hair braided.

'So,' said Maria softly, 'it *is* about time we gave her a name. She's six days old and I'm fed up with calling her baby.'

'I've bin giving it a lot of thought.'

'Good.'

'How about Lucky?'

'Lucky what?'

'Lucky Santangelo of course! You like it?'

'If you do.'

He bent and kissed his wife, 'I like it.'

'Then Lucky she is.'

'And will be.'

One thing they never discussed. His business life. She questioned him once and he shushed her with a finger on her lips, 'Don't ever ask. I'll do what *I* think is best for us.' He didn't need another Cindy who knew where every body was buried. Not that Maria in a million years could ever be like Cindy. She brought so much warmth into his life, just looking at her made him feel good. She had so many great qualities. The baby was just the icing on the cake.

It hurt him, for her sake, that her family had rejected her. She never mentioned it or complained. But when the baby was born and Jennifer was visiting he heard Maria ask, very softly, 'Did you tell my mother?' And Jennifer had sighed, 'Yes, of course. But you know, dear, Leonora will never forgive you . . .'

He wasn't supposed to have heard. But he had. And the disappointment on his beautiful wife's face was enough to spur him into action.

He had to make a trip to the coast to check out the Mirage. The hotel was built, a million dollars over budget, and was now in the final decorating stages. He wanted to see for himself where all the money had gone, and while he was in California he would drop in and see his mother-in-law. What a quirk of fate *that* was.

Maria did not want to go with him. It was too soon after the baby's birth, and, as she said, he would only be away a few days. Jennifer was moving into the house while he was away. The nanny, a housekeeper, and two bodyguards would also be there. As Gino's power increased, so did the number of his enemies. It was a fact of life he had learned to live with. Bonnatti had survived two assassination attempts in the last year. Unruly young mobsters climbing the hills of greed had no respect for elder statesmen. Gino remembered wryly how he used to feel about the Mustache Petes – the old fashioned dons who used to control the rackets in the early twenties. He had regarded them as a joke with their funny looks and courtly manners. In his time he too had had no respect.

He kissed his wife and baby goodbye and set off for the coast reluctantly.

The Boy looked even more affluent than usual. Maybe it was the sleek suntan . . . Maybe the ready smile . . . In spite of Pippa Sanchez's reassuring phone calls Gino immediately sensed The Boy was stealing.

'Congratulations! Such wonderful news!' Jake's greeting couldn't be warmer 'I have a little gift for the baby – it's nothin' – really.'

Gino opened up the expensively gift wrapped package. It contained a solid gold brush and comb set with *Lucky Santangelo* inscribed on it. 'Thanks, Jake,' he said.

'I told you – it's nothin'.'

They met for dinner at the Beverly Hills Hotel, and Pippa Sanchez was by The Boy's side.

'I've sent you fifteen scripts,' she husked, 'don't you like *any* of them?'

'Not enough to put my money into,' he replied.

Pippa scowled.

Jake gave her a hard nudge under the table, 'It's all she thinks about – her career,' he joked, 'I told her – it's a full time career just lookin' after me!'

'I can believe it,' Gino said unblinkingly.

Pippa slid off to the ladies room, throwing them both disdainful looks.

'Broads!' exclaimed Jake. 'By the way, you want one tonight? I got a real hot little number. She's so hot that . . .'

'No,' Gino interrupted sharply, 'I'm a married man now.'

'Oh yeah. So you are. But still . . .'

'My investors are not too happy about the sudden rise of costs. In fact, they are pretty goddamn pissed off.' Gino's hard black eyes bore into Jake's.

The Boy was undisturbed. 'Hey! Come on! We've built a hotel to be proud of. Wait'll you see it. It's got everything.'

'For the money it's cost it should have.'

'I don't wanna boast,' Jake said, 'but just wait until y'see it. Your really gonna flip.' He paused to wave at a movie star passing their table, 'Janet, baby, y'look terrific. How's Tony? We'll get together soon.'

Gino threw the dice. 'There's a rumor come to my ear that not every dollar has ended up in the hotel. There's a rumor that quite a few have ended up in your pocket.'

Jake flushed angrily, 'Who said that? Who the fuck said it?'

Gino shrugged, impressed with The Boy's performance, 'Just a rumor . . . Nothin' to get excited about . . . if it ain't true you got no worries . . .'

This time Tiny Martino flew up with them. He was a red headed bear of a man who had dominated film comedy for twenty-five years. He was a star in every sense of the word, but he treated Gino like visiting royalty.

'I never played a room in my life,' he said, 'but for The Boy here, and you, Gino, I'll open up the Mirage, and what is more I'll do a two week stint twice a year.'

When Gino heard the salary they were paying for the privilege he nearly had a seizure.

'He's worth every dime,' Jake insisted.

'The dime's don't bother me. It's the dollars that hurt. We could get two Sinatras for that kind of money.'

'Two Sinatras wouldn't bring 'em in like Tiny.'

Yeh. Maybe The Boy was right.

Gino had to admit that the Mirage did look magnificent. Jake had done the job he had set out to do and more besides. The other hotels on the Strip paled beside the Mirage, with its marble floors, crystal chandeliers, and silk draperies. Workmen were still swarming around the place putting the finishing touches. 'Well?' Jake questioned proudly, 'What'd'ya think?'

'I think you've built a fuckin' palace,' Gino said slowly, 'maybe too much of a palace.'

'Huh?' The Boy's eyes were bright and watchful, 'What's that supposed t'mean?'

'I mean we're supposed to be caterin' to people – just ordinary people. What's with all the luxury an' stuff?'

'You'll see,' Jake replied sagely, 'it'll pay itself off. When the peasants come to Vegas – they'll come here.'

'They'd better.'

'They will.'

There was plenty of time to find out if The Boy had been stealing. Gino instructed Costa to send in the best accountants to check out the books. He wanted every brick and stone accounted for. In the meantime he could afford to sit back and

wait. If the Mirage took off like Jake assured him it would –
then what was a few hundred thousand dollars between friends?
Jake was a smart son-of-a-bitch. Gino hoped he was smart
enough not to try and take from him twice.

San Francisco was hot, but there was a nice breeze blowing in
from the ocean. Gino checked into the Fairmount Hotel and
called Leonora.

A maid answered the phone, and requested his name.

'I'd like to speak to Mrs Grazione,' he said, 'Tell her it's a very
good friend from New York.'

'Yes, sir.'

There was a long silence. He drummed his nails impatiently
on the table. Leonora. He could think her name, say it aloud,
and it meant nothing – a total blank. Maria's mother. That's
all she was to him now.

'Hello. Who is this?' Her voice. Unmistakable.

'Hey – Leonora. This is Gino.' He could feel the frosty
silent hate coming at him through the phone. One good thing,
she didn't hang up. 'I'm only in San Francisco for a day,' he
added quickly, 'and I think it's important that we meet.'

Pure ice, 'Why?'

'Because . . . er . . . well I think it's only fair to all concerned.
Don't you?'

'Not particularly.'

'I'd appreciate it.'

'Would you?'

'Very much.'

A long stoney silence. He waited.

Finally she said, 'You have your goddamn nerve, you really
do. I never thought . . .'

He cut her off mid-sentence. 'Whatever you have to say I'd
sooner you said it to my face. I can come to your house or meet
you. Which will it be?'

Perhaps it was the command in his voice but unexpectedly
she said, 'I'll meet you. Where are you staying?'

'The Fairmount. Will you . . .'

This time she cut him off. 'The bar. Six o'clock.' And the
phone was slammed down.

He sat in the bar drinking Jack Daniels and idly keeping track
of the time. It was six-twenty-three precisely.

She walked in at six-twenty-four wearing a long mink coat

and dark glasses. Her white blonde hair was scraped back into an elegant chignon. She approached him without hesitation, slid onto the next bar stool, clicked her fingers at the barman and ordered, 'A double martini. Very dry. No olives.' Then she turned, lifted the dark glasses and stared at him, 'You bastard,' she drawled coldly, 'how I hate you.'

She reminded him of a seasoned call girl – a grotesque caricature of her former self. Gone was the simplicity and soft- ness – it had been replaced with eyes like blue chips and a tight mean mouth. He estimated that she must be almost forty. She looked every minute of it.

'Nice greeting,' he said.

She threw her mink coat off her shoulders and flicked a cigarette into her mouth. Then she leaned forward for him to light it. He could see right down the cleavage of her olive green dress, and he could smell Chanel No. 5 and other womanly odors. She made him uneasy.

He lit her cigarette. She drew on it deeply, blew smoke in his face and said, 'Well? What do you want?'

*This* was the woman he had been in love with half his life? *This* was the woman he had wanted to marry? Jesus! What an escape!

'Congratulations,' he said slowly, 'you're a grandma.'

She laughed aloud. 'Is *that* what you wanted to tell me?'

'I figured someone should. Seeing as Maria hasn't heard one word from you I thought perhaps you didn't know.'

She laughed again. A high pitched sound that caused people to turn and look at her. '*Who* is Maria?' she inquired mockingly.

He was deadly angry. 'Your daughter, your little girl. And you have another little girl in your life. A granddaughter named Lucky. She was born three weeks ago.'

Leonora narrowed her eyes, 'I don't have a daughter. I don't have a granddaughter. Do you understand, Gino? They don't exist.'

He kept his voice low, 'You goddamn bitch.'

'Oh dear. Have I upset you? The great Gino Santangelo. I *am* sorry.'

Now he knew why she had come. To gain a little satisfaction, to play her little game. 'Maria would like to hear from you,' he said flatly, 'I don't care what you want. Name it – you got it. Just get in touch with your daughter. Let her know that she matters to you.'

'Oh, I see. Whatever I want I can have. Is that it?'

'That's it.'

'How very generous.' She finished her drink with one gulp and pushed the empty glass in front of him. 'I'll have another drink for a start.'

He signalled the barman.

'Hmmm . . . ' She looked thoughtful, 'how far are you prepared to go with this . . . offer?'

'Whatever you want,' he said heavily. How he hated this woman.

'Let me see . . . ' she mused, 'a new mink . . . a foreign sports car . . . or . . . how about an apartment in New York? What do you think, Gino? Would that be asking too much?'

He had known that everyone had their price. 'So. An apartment in New York then?' he asked tightly.

'Yes.' She hesitated. 'No. Oh goodness, it's such a *difficult* decision.' She stubbed out her cigarette and immediately produced another one. She followed the same charade for him to light it, leaning forward exhibiting even more of her breasts.

He wanted to get out of the place and breathe some clean fresh air. He was getting smothered with her perfume, cigarette smoke, and human greed.

'I've decided,' she announced brightly.

'What?'

'Just one simple fuck.'

He stared at her, his black eyes hardening.

She smiled. 'Just one, Gino. The one you've owed me all these years.'

He honestly could not believe what he was hearing. 'You drunken bitch. Do you know what you're sayin'?'

'You honestly believe that your money can buy anything and anyone don't you?' She slid off the bar stool and shrugged on her mink coat. 'I wouldn't fuck you if you were the last man on earth.' Her eyes gleamed dangerously. 'When you married my daughter she ceased to exist – and that's the way it is. So get that into your moronic head.'

He stood up. 'You know what I'd like to do to you.'

Her voice was loud now, a triumphant screech, 'Why don't you threaten me, Gino? Why don't you set one of your *mobsters* on me. You're just a common little criminal, and you can't buy me. Get it? *You can't buy me.*'

He breathed deeply and concentrated on Maria. *Think of Maria!* a voice screamed in his head. If he didn't he knew he would smash Leonora to pieces.

She hurled a few more insults and left. People were staring at him. He signed the check and stalked out. Maria could have anything she wanted, but she couldn't have her mother, and he would *never* come begging again. Never.

# Carrie 1943–1944

As she hurried along the street pushing the stroller with Steven in, Carrie experienced many different emotions. One minute she was elated that she had had the courage to make a bolt for freedom. Then she felt fear that maybe Bonnatti would come looking for her. *Never again would she sell her body. Never again would she subject herself to the perversions and humiliations of transient men. It was over.* Whether Bernard Dimes helped them or not.

She hummed softly to herself, stopping to buy Steven a shiney black stick of licorice.

He accepted it quietly, huge green eyes staring as though she was the enemy. She heaped silent curses on Leroy. Hoped the loathsome scarecrow pig had got everything he deserved.

Occasionally she glanced nervously behind her, just in case she was being followed. She spotted no one, but to make extra sure she darted in and out of Macys, then crossed the street to Gimbels, where she rushed up and down the aisles like a whirl-wind. Satisfied, she took a cab and had the driver stop a block from Bernard Dimes' Park Avenue residence. Her step slowed, her courage faded. *What was she going to say to him?*

She halted half a block from the house and considered other possibilities. They were limited. If she went to a hotel or tried to leave town Bonnatti might find her. No. What she needed was the protection of a respectable member of the community. If there was only herself to consider she would take her chances. But there was Steven to think of . . .

She started to walk again, her step firm. And soon she was ringing the doorbell of the Park Avenue house, and there was the familiar face of Roger, the butler, staring, half recognizing her but not quite sure.

She was cool, poised. 'Is Mr Dimes at home?'

'Who shall I say is calling?'

'Carrie.'

'Carrie?' His eyebrows shot up. 'Is he expecting you?'

'Yes.'

Roger ushered her and Steven into the hall. She took a deep breath and wondered again what she was going to say.

'One moment, please,' intoned Roger politely.

The moment stretched like a lifetime. Maybe Bernard Dimes would refuse to see her and solve the problem of what she should say altogether.

Roger returned. 'This way, please.'

She followed him into the study, pushing Steven in front of her.

Bernard Dimes got up from behind his desk. The sleeves of his silk shirt were rolled up, and his desk was piled high with papers. Steel rimmed glasses decorated his aquiline nose, and his grey hair was somewhat mussed. She had never seen him like this before. 'Carrie!' he exclaimed warmly.

'Mr Dimes,' she glanced uneasily at Roger.

'Will you be requiring anything, sir?' Roger asked.

Bernard glanced at his watch, 'Is tea ready?'

'Right away, sir.' Roger withdrew from the room as Bernard emerged from behind his desk. 'This is a very pleasant surprise,' he said.

'I hope so.' She gazed around the panelled study, unable to meet his eyes.

'I hope so too.' There was a long awkward silence. He noticed that she looked tired and drawn and seemed somewhat jumpy. He approached her and took her by the arm, 'Are you all right?' he asked concernedly.

She shrugged, ready to say – yes – of course I am – when suddenly the cool and the poise and the control all went flying away. She stood before him, her face crumpled, and the tears came.

'What is it Carrie – ' he began.

Roger came into the room holding a silver tray of tea. Bernard pushed the stroller in the butler's direction and said – 'Take the child downstairs.' Then he led Carrie to a chair and made her sit down. 'Why don't you tell me all about it,' he said gravely. 'Talking always helps, you know.'

As soon as Roger left she was sobbing out the whole story – no holds barred. And it *did* help. It was like a heavy burden being lifted from her shoulders. Bernard listened intently, fed her hot sweet tea, snapped at anyone who phoned, wiped her tears away with a soft linen handkerchief, and seemed truly concerned.

The light outside the study window faded, and dusk arrived. She was at the end now, telling about Leroy and Steven and Enzio Bonnatti. 'I came to you,' she said simply, 'because I know you're a good man . . . and there *is* no one else . . . But I understand if you can't help us . . . ' She felt so very tired as her words trailed off into nothingness, 'really I do . . . I understand . . . '

He said in a low firm voice, 'I *can* help you, Carrie. I *want* to help you.'

'Thank you,' she grasped him by the hand, 'thank you . . . so much . . . I just felt sure you would . . . I just felt so sure . . . '

One year later to the day they were married. It was a simple ceremony at City Hall. Five year old Steven jumped around excitedly.

Bernard invented a new background for Carrie. It amused him. According to *his* story she was an African Princess whom he had met on safari in Kenya. It was amazing how many people believed this to be true.

The world of the theater was shocked. Bernard Dimes getting married! Marrying a negress! And the rumors about her past . . . Scandalous! But they couldn't possibly be true . . . could they? Bernard certainly wasn't saying.

Several tall elegant blondes swept around New York in a fury. They had all tried so hard for so long to land him. What did a *black* girl have that they didn't?

So the two sets of stories about her circulated, and Bernard loved every minute of his friends' and acquaintances' confusion.

'I'm frightened,' Carrie said.

'Of what? The past? It's behind you now. You have me to take care of you.'

She listened to her husband. He was a wise man, and she could not believe how fortunate she was to have found him. He had taken her and Steven in a year previously without any fuss. Sent her to his beach house on Fire Island, where she had learned to enjoy solitude for the first time in her life. Every weekend he had arrived from the city with gifts for her and Steven, until gradually the child emerged from the shell he had retreated into, and once more became a normal talkative little boy.

Sometimes she worried about Bonnatti. 'Your connections

with those people are *over*. They can't touch you. They can't hurt you. You've got to understand that,' Bernard assured her.

Slowly she began to believe him.

Bernard's house was situated on Ocean Beach which had a cosmopolitan community. The pace of life was right for her, and Steven adored it. He especially enjoyed Bernard's weekly visit, and so did she. She found herself waiting breathlessly for the ferry to arrive late on a Friday afternoon. She longed to see the tall distinguished man who treated her like a human being and showed her every kindness. He never approached her sexually. He slept in the guest bedroom and insisted that she and Steven share the main one. This delighted her at first, but eventually began to bother her. Had she been wrong? Didn't he want her? Was it because of her past?

After six months she could bear it no longer. She went to him one night in a long filmy nightgown, her jet hair loose and flowing. He was asleep, snoring lightly.

She sat on the side of his bed and gently touched his face.

'What is it?' he asked, struggling to become fully awake.

It was ridiculous, but she was suddenly shy. 'Don't you want me, Bernard?' she whispered.

He sat up in bed and took her face in his hands, 'Yes, I want you. I want to marry you.'

She was surprised and thrilled. And yet somehow she had known he would ask her. She felt that she wanted to give him the most pleasurable night of his life.

He was a restrained lover. Gentle, undemanding, fast.

It didn't matter one little bit. She lay in his arms and shivered with ecstacy. As far as she was concerned it was the most wonderful night of her life.

Now she was Mrs Bernard Dimes. And at thirty-one years of age she could finally start her life.

# Gino 1951

The Mirage opening was an extravagant affair. True to his word The Boy produced a planeload of stars – and the stars produced extensive press coverage of the event. Exactly what The Boy had predicted.

The natural follow up to this was excellent business, with people all over America clamoring for reservations.

Jake sat back and smiled, 'I told y' I was buildin' a gold mine!' he boasted on the phone to Gino a few months after the opening. 'The joint is burstin' at the seams! We're the only hotel doin' capacity. What d'y'think of *that*?'

'I think that's very good news,' Gino replied evenly. He had placed his men in key positions on the staff, and reports filtering back to New York were that the golden pot could be even fuller. Jake was definitely taking. What a *dumb* fuck he was.

'Whyn't y'show a little enthusiasm,' Jake urged, 'Jesus! I've worked my balls off on this goddamn hotel, an' we're all makin' a friggin' fortune. The syndicate should be proud of me.'

'Oh, they're proud of you all right. I'm sure they're gettin' ready to show their appreciation in a very special way.'

Jake was pleased, 'Yeah?'

'Yeh.' He hung up the phone and wondered at The Boy's stupidity. So smart in some ways, and yet so dense in others. Unfortunately he would have to be made an example of. You didn't steal from your own. Not if you wanted to live you didn't.

A knock on the door interrupted his thoughts. It was Nanny Camden with Lucky. 'She's just going for her nap Mr Santangelo,' Nanny said.

He looked at his little baby and grinned. Only a few months old but the kid had style. 'Hey, she looks better every day. Probably gonna be a movie star!'

'Yes, Mr Santangelo,' Nanny said dryly. Every father she had ever worked for thought his daughter possessed special possibilities.

'Have a good nap sweetheart,' he crooned. Nanny took the child from the room.

A few minutes later Maria came rushing into the living-room of their New York house – a little gift he had bought her because he didn't care to winter in East Hampton although she would have happily lived there all year round.

'Gino!' she exclaimed, looking like a blonde fairy tale princess in her high fur boots and fitted cloth coat trimmed with astrakhan. 'I have *wonderful* news!'

Whenever she walked into a room he smiled. 'What is it, sweetheart?' he inquired lazily.

Her cheeks were glowing from the crisp January day, and her beautiful blue eyes sparkled, 'I'm pregnant again!' she announced triumphantly. 'And *this* time I'll have a boy! I promise!'

He was overwhelmed by the news. 'You're kidding!' He leapt up, kissed and hugged her. Her nose was cold, and she snuggled up against him like a puppy finding warmth and refuge.

'Isn't it marvelous?' she sighed, 'I'm so happy!'

He undid the buttons of her coat, slid his arms around her slender waist and squeezed. 'What's all this about havin' a boy? I don't care *what* it is – boy – girl – twins.'

'You *want* a boy,' she teased. 'All men want boys.'

He squeezed her harder. 'Bullshit!'

'Not so tight, you're hurting me.'

'I am?' He took his arms from around her waist and began to massage her breasts. 'That better?'

'Gino! Not now.'

'Why not?'

'Because . . . Anyone could walk in.'

She had a strong streak of prudery in her which he loved. 'It's our house,' he pointed out.

'I know,' she tried to squirm away from him, 'but it's daylight . . . and . . . everyone's around.'

He tried not to laugh, 'So I'll lock the door.'

She looked at him shyly. 'All right.'

He was surprised by her sudden acquiescence. They had been married exactly one year, two months, and she still excited the hell out of him. She had a natural enthusiasm for sex but a certain reluctance to let herself go. It was the most stimulating combination.

She refused outright to have anything at all to do with oral sex – but he was bringing her around. He knew that when he got her to a certain point she would become totally and absolutely his. Slowly he started to undress her.

'Lock the door,' she whispered.

He did so quickly. Meanwhile she closed the heavy damask drapes, and went to lie on the soft flowered couch.

He approached her gently, stroking her thighs, removing her clothes, making her gasp little notes of pleasure.

She tried to take off her boots but he stopped her, 'Keep 'em on, they look sexy.'

'Gino!'

Carefully he moved his hands over her flat supple stomach, marveling at the fact that another child was growing inside her. *His child.* He bent to kiss her belly, and gradually he moved down until he reached the silky golden bush. For a moment he thought she was going to let him progress further, but she reared away and pulled him up to kiss her on the mouth.

'Why not?' he mumbled. 'It's supposed t'be a celebration.'

'Not now,' she whispered, 'not here.'

'Why not?'

'Oh Gino! *I* don't know.'

'You'd love it.'

'One day.'

'When?'

'Soon, I promise. Just give me time . . .'

'Sure.' He ripped off his clothes. 'We got the rest of our lives, huh sweetheart?' Then he was riding her beautiful body smoothly, bringing her to an orgasm that left her weak and exhausted.

'I love you,' she murmured.

'Yeh. An' I love you too – you an' Lucky an' whatever you got wrigglin' around inside you.' He held her for a while until the telephone interrupted their reverie. 'Yeh?' he growled.

'Gino. This is Enzio. I want a meet.'

'Important?'

'Very.'

'Riccaddis.'

'Six o'clock?'

'Y'got it.'

Enzio Bonnatti had his problems. Dealing in narcotics and prostitution among other things put him in a far more dangerous position than Gino. He had to struggle to keep his hold at the top, but keep it he did, eliminating enemies like so many flies on a hamburger. He favored violence as an answer to any problem. Gino disagreed with him about that. 'There's two ways to power,' he would say, 'blood and murder – which only brings more killings. Or you can use your brains an' make big dough – like me – that's the guy whose gonna stick around forever.'

Enzio would laugh, 'Easy, my friend, if nobody gets in your way. But the fuckers always do.'

Enzio was right. They always did.

He sat at a table in Riccaddis, a strong looking man, with a napkin tucked into his shirt collar, and a full plate of Barbara's delicious spaghetti bolognaise before him.

Gino slid into a chair on the other side of the table.

'Ciao Enzio.'

'Greetings, my friend.'

'Is Francesca well?'

'She is. And Maria?'

'Perfect. Got a belly full again.'

'Congratulations. We toast the unborn one.' He signalled for an extra glass which he filled with rich red wine.

The two men clinked glasses solemnly, 'Salute,' Enzio said, and added, 'May you be blessed with a boy.'

Gino laughed, 'What's all this boy shit. I don't care *what* it is!'

'I have two sons to take over when *I* go,' Enzio pointed out gravely, 'you havta think of such things.'

'Well I ain't goin' anywhere for a long long time. Y'can lay odds on *that*.'

'Good. Then I suggest you take care of your friend in Vegas without waiting too much longer.'

'Yeh. I know. I know. Only I wanna be sure I have the right guy ready to step in an' replace him. Runnin' that whole Vegas set up ain't as easy as it looks. There's a lot of temptation, an' I don't want us to have t'go through the same exercise twice.'

Enzio twirled long strands of spaghetti around his fork and stuffed his mouth full. Dribbles of sauce landed on the napkin. 'There is a rumor, came to me today, that The Boy has sold his piece of the operation to Pinky Kassari in Philadelphia.'

Gino was incredulous, 'Pinky Banana? I don't believe it!'

'You better believe it. My source is very reliable.'

'Aw come *on* Enzio, I just spoke to Jake . . . He would've said somethin' . . . '

'He's screwin' around – an' I don't like it. I don't like it one little bit,' Enzio twirled another forkful of spaghetti and crammed it into his mouth. 'You want to deal with it or shall I?'

Gino was glowering. His mind was racing. The Boy had turned out to be nothing but a cheap two bit hustler. And what about all the dough he, Gino, had put in Pippa Sanchez's direction? Not so much as a word from her that The Boy even *knew* Pinky Banana, let alone that he was selling out his piece of the action to him. 'I'll get on a plane tonight,' he said tightly, 'it's my responsibility – I got the syndicate together. Don't worry about a thing.'

'I ain't worried, Gino. Like you – I'm just pissed off that this yiddish dogshit should think he can get away with it.'

'Yeh. But he *ain't* gettin' away with it.'

Enzio mopped his dish clean with a piece of sour dough bread. 'That's what I hoped you'd say.'

Plenty of time to think on the plane.

Plenty of time to work out the perfect plan of action.

Red, and a new recruit known as Little Willie sat across the aisle playing a mean game of gin rummy and downing straight bourbon.

The Boy presented no problem really, although Gino felt a certain regret that he would have to be got rid of. A shame. But it was the jerk's own fault.

Pinky Banana *might* present a problem. It depended on the deal he had going with The Boy.

Pinky Banana. A slob with a gun. That's how Gino remembered him. It was difficult to imagine him now being referred to as Mr Kassari, and running a mob. But he had made his mark in Philadelphia, and was looked on as one of the top boys there. Boy. He must be forty-four now – they were the same age. Gino had only one thing to say to him – *Take your money back Pinky, get the fuck out of our operation.*

He checked into the Beverly Wilshire Hotel, Red and Little Willie in adjoining rooms. He still kept the rented house in Bel Air but he had no desire to advertise his presence in Los Angeles. Better he should take The Boy by surprise.

While Red arranged for a private plane to fly them to Vegas, Gino phoned New York and spoke to Maria for well over half an hour. Her voice on the phone was soothing, for he was more than a little disturbed about what had to be arranged. 'I'll be back in a few days,' he assured her, 'get plenty of rest, drink lots of milk, and take those vitamin pills the doc recommended when you was pregnant with Lucky.'

She laughed softly on the other end of the line. 'Gino! You sound like someone's mother!'

He was not amused. 'I give y' good advice, y' sneer. What kind of a patient are you, anyway?'

'I'm not a patient,' she chided gently, 'I'm a perfectly healthy expectant woman.'

'I love y' when you're all blown out an' fat.'

'Gino! Goodbye.'

He got horny just talking to her. He took a cold shower, dressed carefully and checked with Red on the arrangements.

'All set, boss,' Red informed him, 'I got a plane booked for six o'clock.'

Pippa Sanchez was not in Vegas with The Boy. She had a small part on a Clark Gable movie coming up, and was spending the week in Hollywood getting into shape. That's what she had told Jake. In point of fact she was servicing an elderly casting director who put the occasional interesting cameo role her way and in return expected energetic appreciation. If The Boy ever found her screwing anyone else he would kill her. Or so he had told her on many occasions.

Pippa was a girl used to her freedom. When Jake had instructed her to sleep with Gino Santangelo she had been surprised – yet secretly pleased. Variety was the spice of life as far as she was concerned, although that didn't mean that she wasn't very fond of Jake. He was good for her image. And in the long run image was more important than anything. She was ever hopeful of persuading Gino or Jake to finance a movie. For over a year she had been working on Gino, sending him scripts, telling him of the fortunes to be made out of a successful production. No results as yet.

She was thinking about this as she parked her pink Thunderbird in the driveway of the house she shared with The Boy. Thinking, and biting her lower lip, and wondering if the screen writer she had secretly hired was any further along with the script she had commissioned. Not being able to interest Gino in a story was one thing. Having one specially written about him was another. Of course it would have a wonderful woman's role for which she would be perfect.

Inside the house it was quiet, except for the whir of the huge refrigerator in the kitchen. How Jake hated that refrigerator. 'Throw it out!' he was always screaming, 'I can't stand the fucking noise.'

The refrigerator stayed. It was the only one she could find big enough to cater for all The Boy's needs. He had this fear that Tiny Martino, Errol Flynn, or some other big film star would drop by and request something to eat that he might not have. As far as Jake was concerned that would show him up as just an East coast bum with no idea how to run a proper home. It didn't matter whether Jake was in town or not, his large noisy refrigerator was always kept full.

Pippa slipped off her dress. Underneath she wore a small shiny black bikini imported from Europe. It suited her voluptuous form admirably.

She padded through the white living-room and out to the inviting swimming pool. For a moment she poised on the side, sucking in her breath, and then she dived, sleekly, smoothly, cutting through the bland chlorinated water like a scythe. Pippa was an excellent swimmer.

Gino watched her. He sat on the window seat of the pool house silently observing. He had arrived at the house fifteen minutes before, given Jake's manservant a hundred bucks to make himself scarce, and settled down to wait. The wait had not been as long as he had expected.

She swam the length of the pool twenty times and then stepped out.

He emerged from the pool house. His clothes were incongruous for the hot Californian sun. A dark suit, vest, blue shirt, narrow conservative tie. He made a sinister figure in the afternoon sun.

She gasped in surprise, 'Gino! My God! Where did *you* come from. You frightened me.'

Slowly he said, 'I'm disappointed in you, Pippa.'

She grabbed a short terry cloth beach wrap and threw it across her shoulders. Her mind was racing. What was he doing here? Did The Boy know?

'Disappointed?' She attempted a laugh, 'I don't understand . . . ' He wasn't sweating. He should be, dressed like he was in the boiling sun. 'Aren't you hot?' she asked, toying with a gold crucifix that hung between her breasts.

'I want you to get packed,' he said, 'you have exactly one hour.'

She was sweating now, the tiny beads of perspiration mixing with the water from the pool still on her body. But Pippa was not a nervous type. She had led too hard a life to be intimidated easily. 'Something wrong, Gino?' she inquired, pulling herself together.

'Very,' he replied coldly.

She pulled the terry cloth wrap around her, and tied the belt tightly. 'Why don't we go inside, have a drink, and you can tell me all about it.'

'You don't have time,' he said evenly, 'you're wasting minutes. You have under an hour now.'

'What's going on?' she snapped, dark eyes flashing dangerously. She was over the fear of him sneaking up on her and ready for battle. He might tell The Boy what to do, but he certainly wasn't about to take over *her* life.

'You stole from me,' he said without a flicker of emotion,

'you took my money and reported to me each week about Jake and told me nothing. *Nothing.*'

'There was nothing to tell . . . ' she shrugged, 'nothing . . . honestly . . .'

And as she said it she was lying, and what was worse he *knew* she was lying. Why had she ever confided in The Boy? Told him about the money Gino Santangelo was paying her to report on him? Fool! But she hadn't thought so at the time . . . Not when Jake bought her a diamond necklace and showered her with other gifts and gave her five thousand dollars worth of chips to play with at the Mirage tables. *Any time she wanted, Any time at all.*

She had known he was stealing all along, but so what? She and The Boy had spent many an evening in bed giggling over the fact that Gino Santangelo would *never* be able to prove how much was being siphoned into The Boy's pocket. *Never.*

'I don't want to hear your stupid excuses,' Gino said harshly, 'if you were a man, we wouldn't even be discussing this. You would be lying at the bottom of that pool or your face would be through the windshield of a car. You understand what I'm saying?'

She understood, and the fear and the sweat came rushing back. 'I'm sorry,' she gasped, 'I'm really sorry . . .'

'Sure you are,' he said amiably, 'an' *that's* why I'm letting you off so easy. Let's go. I'll watch you pack.'

'Where am I going?' she whispered.

'Spain.'

'Spain?' She was horrified, 'I can't go abroad, I have a movie to do in a week. I . . .'

He cut her off. 'Spain. And you'll stay there for at least two years. If you come back before that . . .'

He didn't need to say any more.

The Boy loved Vegas and Vegas loved him. They were compatible – The Boy and the garish tinsel city in the middle of the desert.

The Mirage was everything he had expected and more. He strutted around the place, and in his mind he began to plan something even bigger and better. What a coup! Hotel after hotel, and each one even more magnificent than the last.

When Pinky Banana Kassari had approached him about selling out his piece he was ready. He asked a ridiculous price and to his surprise Pinky agreed immediately. He knew he should consult Gino, get his permission — but what if he said no? In the end he decided to make the deal and tell Gino when it was too late to stop it.

It was too late to stop now, and Jake and Pinky celebrated with a magnum of champagne, a tableful of stars, and three showgirls who could balance ten cent pieces on their nipples. All the same Jake wished that Pippa was with him to share the evening. She drove him mad with her goddamned career. He was going to have to do something about *that*. Maybe invest some of his new found fortune in a movie vehicle for her. Christ knows she had been carrying on about it for long enough.

'What's the little redhead's special trick?' Pinky leered.

'You wanna take her upstairs an' find out?' Jake leered back, secretly hating the prick but grateful to have the first half of his payment in cash safely installed in his bedroom safe.

'Maybe I'll take all three,' guffawed Pinky.

'Be my guest.'

'I plan to,' Pinky wiped saliva from the side of his mouth. He had not improved with age. His eyes seemed smaller and meaner, his lips more fleshy, and his greasy hair had receded, making his face seem bigger and even more oafish.

He dressed in flashy bad taste, and had gone through three wives. He was currently on his fourth, a brassy blonde former stripper who waited in Philadelphia with three Pekinese dogs whom she refused to leave for short trips. The only children he had produced were fat boy twins from his first marriage — who held the promise of turning out exactly like their father.

Pinky was vicious, powerful, greedy and corrupt. And for twenty-two years he had harbored a grudge against Gino Santangelo. Buying out The Boy at any price was a good way to finally get close enough to do something about it.

Gino slid into Las Vegas as unobtrusively as he had hit Los Angeles. Surprise was an element he enjoyed, and he wanted to see the surprise on The Boy's face when he joined him at the celebration dinner he was having with Pinky Banana.

Yeh. He knew what was going on. Now.

Once Pippa started to talk, she talked. And others. Anxious to save their necks because they knew that the shit was about to hit the fan — and they wanted to be well away from the splatters.

A dark limousine met his plane on the runway, and whisked him straight to the hotel. He strode through the lobby, Red and Little Willie in close attendance. Eyes followed him, voices whispered. He was a recognizable face.

The casino manager rushed over to greet him, but Gino was not about to be delayed. 'Later, later,' he muttered brusquely.

'Cunt is a commodity,' Pinky said expansively, 'merchandise. Only good for a few months on the shelf, then you gotta get in new stocks.'

Jake stifled a yawn. Who needed this asshole's thoughts on the matter? On *any* matter?

'I gotta string of whorehouses in Philly with the hottest freshest cunt in town,' Pinky continued, warming to his subject, 'y'see, I *know* how to run the business. Bring 'em in – work 'em out – an' ship 'em off to one of my connections in South America. It's the only way.'

'Sure,' agreed Jake, giving a wink and a nudge to one of the showgirls, indicating that she should go to work on Pinky.

She wrinkled her nose, but Jake was the boss. 'Mr Kassari,' she cooed, 'I've been admiring your suit. Such *fine* material.'

He was pleased, 'Ya think so, doll? Well I've been admiring your tits. How does *that* grab ya?'

However it grabbed her she never got to say, for at that exact moment Gino Santangelo entered the private dining-room and panic hit the table. The Boy went white, visibly paling beneath his suntan. Pinky Banana's jaw fell slackly open.

'Hiya fellas,' Gino said easily, 'this a private party or can anyone join in?'

The celebrities down the other end of the table were unaware of any happening. They continued to drink and laugh and joke.

The three showgirls figured *something* was amiss because of Jake's very apparent nervousness. 'Gino!' he exclaimed. 'What y'doin' here?'

'What kind of a welcome is that?' Gino said, pulling up a chair and sitting down.

'B . . . but we just spoke on the phone . . . ' Jake stuttered, 'you was in New York.'

'So now I'm here,' he smiled, 'an' so is my old friend Pinky Banana I see. How y' doin' pal? Long time, huh?'

Pinky threw a poisonous look at Jake, then attempted a smile in Gino's direction. 'I dropped the Banana a long time ago.'

'Yeh. Where'd you drop it?'

Pinky glowered.

The Boy knew he was in trouble. He began to wriggle. 'Hey, I'm glad you're here. A lot's bin goin' on an' I wanted to talk to you,' his words were tumbling out fast now, 'I'll take y'into my office an' lay it all out for you. What y'think? Shall we go now?'

Gino fixed him with deadly black eyes, 'You dumb fuck,' he hissed, 'it's too late for any explaining, too goddamn late.'

Three months later, early in the morning, Gino was paying his customary visit to Lucky in her playroom. She was ten months old, a gorgeous baby with black gypsy eyes and a shock of dark hair. 'Who's daddy's girl?' he crooned, lifting her from her crib. 'Who's daddy's little princess?'

Lucky gurgled happily. He was holding her close to him, enjoying the warm baby smells, when Maria came hurrying into the room. She looked upset. 'Gino,' she said, thrusting a newspaper at him, 'didn't this man used to work for you?'

He took the paper, scanned the headline.

### 'JAKE COHEN DISCOVERED IN DESERT GRAVE'

*Jake 'The Boy' Cohen's decomposed body was discovered today in a gruesome desert grave ten miles outside of Las Vegas. Two hitchhikers made the grisly discovery at 10 a.m. after a fierce sandstorm had uncovered the make-shift grave.*

The story continued. Gino's eyes flicked quickly across the newsprint. Poor old Jake. He had it coming and he got it.

'Well?'

With a start Gino realized that Maria was standing watching him. 'Yeh,' he said casually, 'same guy.'

She waited for him to say more, but he didn't. He turned back to Lucky and began playing with her again.

Maria did not question further. She touched his cheek softly, 'Breakfast? How about something special today?'

He laughed and grabbed her ass, 'I got somethin' special,' he joked.

'Gino!'

She was always shockable. He loved it.

Riccaddis at lunch time was packed. Barbara and her children zoomed around the place balancing dishes of pizza, and carafes of wine.

Gino ordered lasagne in spite of the fact that he had put on a few pounds. Enzio never tried anything except the spaghetti bolognaise, and Aldo stuck to plain veal.

'I lose plenty of weight on this,' Aldo said, wolfing the veal down in three great mouthfuls and signalling one of his children to bring over more.

'Yeh,' said Gino laconically, watching his friend go to town on the second piece, 'plenty.'

Enzio ate his spaghetti slowly, stoically, his bib tucked carefully in place.

The three men sat at a corner table in the back of the restaurant. By the door two tables were occupied by their various bodyguards. Taking chances was a thing of the past.

'We got a war,' Enzio said at last, 'and I for one want to put an end to it.'

Gino nodded his agreement. 'We take out Pinky – no more war.'

'It has to be done,' Enzio said, 'no son-of-a-bitch is going to screw around with *me*. I don't care *who* he is.'

Gino nodded, 'Right.' Pinky Banana had given them nothing but trouble over the Las Vegas deal. Gino had tried to handle it fairly. He had even offered Pinky his money back – and when he refused made sure it was delivered via messenger. The messenger had turned up two days later in the Mirage parking lot with a bullet in his head and the money on his person. 'You ain't cuttin' my balls off *this* time. Y'got rid of me once, an' it ain't happenin' again. I got a piece of the Mirage an' I aim to keep it,' Pinky had told Gino on the phone. The struggle was on.

Gino's people were firmly installed in the Mirage – but Pinky was determined to take over – by force if need be. Three murders took place. The casino manager, a cocktail waitress, and a croupier. Murder was bad for business. Takings at the Mirage began to slump as the publicity began to grow.

'I'll arrange a contract,' Gino said, 'there's a head hunter in Buffalo who'll take him out.'

Enzio agreed. 'The sooner the better.'

On April 1st, 1951 Pinky Banana woke late. His current wife – whom he had lovingly nicknamed Piranha – was asleep beside him. She snored, a fact which drove him crazy.

The bedroom smelled of dog shit. Pinky kicked his wife awake. 'Your fucking dogs!' he screamed, 'they've done it again!'

Piranha rubbed her eyes which were heavily caked with yesterday's mascara. 'What?'

He was enraged, 'Your fucking dogs have shit all over the fucking carpet!'

Piranha sat up in bed. She was naked and sported the most pneumatic breasts in the whole of Philadelphia. Sometimes Pinky thought he hadn't married a woman, he had married a pair of tits.

'So what?' she whined. 'A stink never hurt no one.'

'You should know,' sneered Pinky, 'when was the last time *you* took a bath?'

Piranha sprang into action, 'Don't you call *me* dirty y' filthy slob.' She went to whack him across the face, but he caught her by the arm and held her off. 'Let me go!' she yelled, 'leave go of me!'

Her three Pekinese dogs reacted to the sound of their mistress' voice, and roused themselves from their slumberous positions around the room. Two of them leaped on the bed, while the third stood on its hind legs against the side and barked excitedly.

'Shut those fucking animals up!' Pinky screamed.

Piranha encouraged them, 'Come on sweeties, come to help poor mommy.'

All three dogs began to bark, and the two on the bed leaped on Pinky. He threw them off with a roar, letting go of Piranha, who took the opportunity to claw at his face with her lethal long red fingernails.

'Cunt!' Pinky screamed.

'Prick!' she screamed back.

The dogs joined in. Pinky took one of them by the scruff of the neck and hurled it across the room. It landed in the corner with a broken whimper.

Piranha stopped her attack and rushed to the dog. 'You bastard,' she shrilled, 'you've hurt Puff Puff!'

'Fuck Puff Puff!'

'Fuck *you*!'

Pinky jumped off the bed into a mound of dog shit. 'Je . . . sus Chrieeest!' he yelled, hobbling into the bathroom.

Piranha was busy flinging a coat over her nakedness. Then she picked up the whimpering dog, took the keys of Pinky's Cadillac from his bedside table, and ran out of the house. 'Don't worry, pet,' she whispered to the little dog, 'moma's gonna get you to the vet real quick.'

Pinky was busy washing his feet when he heard the explosion. At first he thought it was an attack of some sort and threw himself to the floor double quick. Then, when he realized it wasn't, he got up, cautiously left the bathroom, and saw the smoking wreck of his Cadillac burning outside the bedroom window. 'Holy shit,' he muttered reverently, 'that coulda bin me!'

Gino's son was born on September 1, 1951.

*His son!*

The most joyful moment of his life.

They named the boy Dario.

Gino celebrated for a week.

Maria smiled and said, 'I told you I'd give you a son didn't I?'

He smothered her with kisses – his beautiful child woman wife, and counted his blessings for finding a woman like her.

Dario was a small baby, only five pounds ten ounces, and quite unlike Lucky in looks. Bald, skinny with matchstick legs and arms, pale skin and blue eyes.

Lucky, now a sturdy one year and three months, was the image of her father. She had the same dark olive skin, the same black eyes, and the same curly jet hair. He loved her very much, but the birth of a son was something else.

Maria spoke to him firmly before she left the hospital. 'We must be very careful,' she insisted, 'I don't want Lucky to be jealous of the new baby.'

'Jealous!' Gino exclaimed. 'Are you kidding? I love 'em both.'

'Be sure that you love them both the same then,' Maria warned.

'Of course, of course,' he lied. He couldn't help it. A son was a direct extension of himself. A daughter could never be that.

'That fuck is like a cat with nine lives,' Enzio exploded. 'I've never known anything like it.'

'We've achieved our purpose,' Gino said calmly, 'no more trouble in Vegas. Business is booming. Pinky won't try to muscle in again.'

'If you think that, you're wrong,' Enzio said sharply.

'If I'm wrong, we'll get rid of him once and for all.'

'Shit!' Enzio snapped, 'I say we should keep a hit out on him.'

Gino sighed, 'You've killed his wife. He's been warned. He'll stay away.'

'For now perhaps.'

Gino laughed confidently, 'I *know* what Pinky's like – don't forget we started out on the streets together – he's always had a yellow streak an' he ain't gonna start anythin' else. You can bet on it.'

'I ain't a betting man.'

'So don't bet. I'm tellin' you, Enzio. Just take my word. He'll stay in Philadelphia an' never come sniffin' around us again.'

'I sure as hell hope you're right.'

'Oh, I'm right. I *know* I'm right.' Gino lit up a long thin Monte Cristo cigar and grinned, 'You wanna see the baby? Come – I'll show you. Dario Santangelo. The best goddamn baby in the whole goddamn world!'

## *Thursday, July 14th, 1977, New York*

Steven stared after Lucky's retreating figure, waited until she was out of sight, and set off down the concrete fire stairs behind her. He was tired, dirty, and angry at having been trapped in an elevator for a whole night. Especially for being trapped with a girl like Lucky. Rude, arrogant and language like a truck driver. Some looker, though. Even after a night in the elevator she still shone.

He stopped himself from thinking about her. What was he doing? He hadn't thought about another female since he had made up his mind that Aileen was the one for him.

Dario regained consciousness slowly. He didn't know where he was for a moment, then he remembered and sat up frantically, a leaden feeling in the pit of his stomach.

He realized with a dull shock that he was on his own bed. His head ached. His stomach ached. His balls ached.

'How are you feeling?' someone asked.

He blinked. A candle was lighting the room. A figure was sitting in a chair by the door. Dario struggled to get off the bed, but as soon as his feet hit the floor nausea and blackness overcame him.

'It's all right,' the figure by the door said, 'I'm Sal. Costa Zennocotti sent me to help you out. I'm sorry I laid one on you – but I had to be sure of who you were.'

Dario held his head and groaned, 'Thanks a lot,' he muttered bitterly.

'No hard feelings.' The figure got out of the chair and walked towards him, and with a shock Dario realized that Sal was a woman.

By the time Elliott Berkely awoke, Carrie was dressed and nervously pacing around the apartment.

'I thought you would want to stay in bed today,' he said disapprovingly, 'after all you did have a nasty shock yesterday.'

'I feel fine,' she managed to sound quite bright. The last thing she needed was to spend a day in bed.

'Damn!' exclaimed Elliott, trying the switch in the bathroom, '*Still* no electricity? What's *happening* to this city?'

She shrugged. What was happening to her life, never mind about the city.

The driver made good time into New York. Twelve-thirty and they were speeding through the crowded Manhattan streets, edging carefully through non-functioning traffic signals, roughly riding the pot-holed roads.

'You'd think they'd get the city streets fixed,' the driver complained, 'all the money the government pisses away . . . ' It was the first words he had spoken during the entire journey.

Silence suited Gino. Who needed conversation?

Twenty seven flights down, and her legs were aching, her feet hot and cramped in the high fashionable canvas boots. Screw fashion. She wished she had on sneakers, shorts, and a T-shirt. She couldn't help smiling as she imagined Costa's face if she had turned up for their meeting in such an outfit. Why not? Why the hell not? She was a big girl wasn't she? She could do anything she liked couldn't she? Anything. No more was Big Daddy in control. Calling the shots. Telling her what to do. Frightening the shit out of her.

Gino Santangelo. Big man. Father. Daddy.

Gino Santangelo. Tyrant.

Christ! He would be back in the country any day now. *Any day*.

She paused for breath, sat on the concrete steps and let out a long sigh. A confrontation with her father was an awesome prospect. Awesome but challenging.

She bit on her thumb and closed her eyes for a minute. All she wanted to do was sleep. Somewhere in the distance she could hear the clatter of someone else descending the fire stairs. Steven whoever he was. Uptight schmuck.

Wearily she pulled herself up and set off again. Only another twenty flights to go.

'Wait a minute,' Dario managed, 'you're a woman . . . '

'Well, what d'y'know!' replied Sal mockingly, 'I knew there was somethin' wrong when I got out the shower this mornin'!'

Dario lay back on the bed and groaned, 'You sure don't hit like a woman.'

Sal grinned. She was thirty-four years old. 165 lbs, and strong as an ox. She had close cut curly hair and a Shirley MacLaine face. She was a freelance enforcer renowned for her skill in getting any job done quietly and fast. She came expensive, but earned every last cent. Dressed in a black track suit, with her husky voice, it was understandable that Dario had not realized straight off.

'Listen,' she said, 'your "problem" in the kitchen has got a bread knife stickin' straight out of his guts. Who is he?'

Dario groaned again. 'I don't know . . . He tried to kill me so I . . . ' his voice trailed off helplessly.

Sal shrugged, 'No sweat. I guess y'want the body out of here. It'll cost of course . . . '

'It doesn't matter how much, Costa'll take care of it.'

'Good. So get some sleep. Stay in here for a couple of hours. By that time we'll both be out of your life. Right?'

Dumbly he nodded. Soon I'll wake up, he thought, and none of this will have happened.

'Here, take a couple of these, they'll help you relax.' He accepted the turquoise capsules gratefully. Within minutes he was in a deep sleep.

Sal regarded him thoughtfully. Dario Santangelo huh? Son of Gino. Maybe now was her time to take a shot at a fortune.

Costa slumbered the night away in his office. The couch was comfortable. Why, at his age, even contemplate the long climb downstairs? After arranging for Sal to take care of Dario's problem he had called the airport and found out that Gino's flight had been re-routed to Philadelphia. He knew that Gino wouldn't be pleased. All the years of delicate negotiation to get him back into the country . . . But still . . . A night in Philadelphia wasn't the end of the world – and Gino would be foolish if he attempted to get into the city tonight. The Mayor had declared a state of emergency and it looked like the blackout was not a short inconvenience.

So Costa had loosened his tie, taken off his jacket, and slept fitfully.

Gino's nine a.m. phone call awakened him.

'I'm on my way in,' Gino said shortly. 'Meet me at the Pierre around midday.'

Costa did not think twice about huffing his way down fifty-one flights of hard concrete stairs. Gino wanted to meet. Even after all these years when Gino wanted Costa jumped.

'I suppose we'd better cancel the dinner party tomorrow night,' Elliott said reluctantly. He hated anything to interfere with his meticulously planned life.

'I'm sure the power failure won't last as long as that,' Carrie replied soothingly.

'Hmmm . . . ' he frowned, 'You know what I feel like doing?'

'What?' she questioned, hoping that it was getting out of the apartment and spending the day at his office.

'I feel like going somewhere. The Bahamas, Hawaii, maybe the Virgin Islands. What do you think?'

What did she think? She thought it was a terrible idea. To go away and know that someone somewhere in New York was waiting to expose her. Impossible.

She forced a laugh, 'Don't be silly, we can't go away now.'

'Why not?'

'Because we just can't. We have a full social calendar right through until September. Dinners we've promised to attend, openings, parties . . . ' she was talking too fast and she knew it.

Elliott interrupted her. 'Nothing that can't be cancelled.'

'You know you hate letting people down.'

'A few weeks away. You need it my dear.'

'I'm quite happy to stay in the city,' she replied quickly.

'I don't understand you – ' he began, 'after what happened yesterday . . . ' The telephone interrupted. He picked up the receiver. 'Hello? . . . Hello?'

'Who was it?' She asked tremulously as he replaced the receiver.

'A wrong number. Even the telephone system is failing. This city is falling to pieces . . . '

Carrie shivered. It had been her blackmailer on the phone. She knew it. She was sure.

Gino strode through the lobby of the Pierre to the reception desk. His walk was slower, his step more tempered. But he still generated a certain raw energy.

'Mr Santangelo, we've been expecting you, sir,' the desk clerk said, handing him the key to his suite.

A woman standing by the desk turned to stare at the sound of his name. When her husband joined her, she nudged him, whispered something, and they both stared.

'Mr Zennocotti is already upstairs, sir,' the desk clerk continued, 'I have it on good authority that power will be restored soon. If you require anything at all, please don't hesitate to call.'

Gino nodded, looked around, and took a deep breath.

New York. It had a certain smell. Like no other city.

He was home.

He finally felt it.

And what a feeling it was!

# Book Two

# Lucky 1955

Memories up until the age of five were fragmented happy blurs. Warmth. Security. And beautiful gentle mommy with the soft pale hair and velvet skin. Beautiful mommy who always smelled good, laughed a lot, and wore pretty dresses with cuddly furs.

Daddy. Bigger. Rougher. The bearer of gifts. Dolls and teddy bears. And hugs so tight that sometimes Lucky thought her breath had been squeezed right out of her body.

Baby Dario, smaller, delicate. Lucky learned early to look after him.

He cried a lot. She was a happy baby. He was difficult to feed. She grabbed at anything that came her way. He was a slow walker. She was toddling around at fourteen months. At four he barely spoke. At five she garbled on about everything and everyone.

On her fifth birthday her parents threw a big party. Fifty children. Clowns. Donkey rides in the garden. A huge chocolate cake shaped like her favorite dolls house.

She was so excited she could hardly breathe. She wore a frilled pink dress, ribbons in her curly black hair, and short socks with white patent leather shoes.

Gino swept her up in his arms and called her his little Italian Princess over and over. Then he gave her his present, a fine gold chain with a tiny diamond and ruby studded locket. Inside the locket was a picture of the two of them together.

'Daddy!' she squealed, smothering him with kisses.

'You spoil her,' Maria smiled indulgently.

'Some kids are made to be spoiled.' And he threw Lucky into the air.

She screamed with excited terror, but he caught her and hugged her to him. She breathed deeply the smells she liked best. Daddy smells. Snuggling close to him she said, 'Good boy, daddy, good, good boy.'

He put her down and winked at Maria. 'This kid's the greatest, takes after her old man.'

Maria smiled sweetly, '*Looks* like her old man – has all *my* best qualities.'

Lucky clung to his leg, begging to be picked up again, but she had lost his attention, he was grinning at his wife, 'Oh yeh?'

Maria was grinning back, 'Oh yeh,' she mimicked.

'Oh *yeh*,' Gino roared happily, shaking Lucky from his leg and throwing his arms around his wife, 'says who?'

Lucky jammed her thumb into her mouth and watched her parents silently. Silly grown ups. When they got in this mood they *never* took any notice of her, and it was *her* birthday.

Removing her thumb from her mouth she lisped, 'Gotta tummy pain.'

Maria pushed Gino away and bent to her daughter. 'Oh no! Not today. Where does it hurt, darling?'

'All over.'

Maria gave Gino an accusing look, 'You shouldn't have thrown her about, you're too rough with her.'

'Yeh?' Once more he swept his daughter up into his arms, 'You got a pain, kid? You got a pain?' He began to tickle her. She screamed with laughter. 'Where's the pain? Huh? Huh?'

'Stop it, Gino,' admonished Maria.

'Aw c'mon. She loves it.'

And Lucky did love it. She laughed so hard that tears formed in her eyes and slid joyfully down her cheeks. 'Pain all gone, daddy, all gone,' she yelled happily.

He continued to tickle her.

'Stop it! Stop it!' she cried.

'Yeh? You want daddy t'stop?' he joked. 'Well I ain't goin' to. How does *that* grab you?'

'Gino, she's getting too excited,' Maria said mildly, 'she won't enjoy her party.'

He stopped the tickling, squeezed her tightly, and whispered, 'Daddy loves y' kid.' Then he put her down.

At that point Nanny Camden appeared with Dario. She held the blond toddler's hand firmly. Dario had a habit of wandering off and getting lost.

'Hey – ' Gino exclaimed, 'I know it ain't your birthday but I got somethin' for you too.'

Dario did not let go of Nanny Camden as Gino handed over a large gift wrapped package.

Lucky jumped for joy – she was not a jealous child, and the thought of her baby brother getting a present too only served to delight her. 'Open it, silly,' she instructed him, and when he made no attempt to grab at the parcel she opened it for him, pulling and ripping at the colorful paper with much enthusiasm. Inside was a large model car – shiny red with whirling black wheels. Lucky seemed more fascinated with it than Dario – he gave it a cursory touch, then swapped nanny's hand for his mother's warm grasp.

'Hey – hey – hey!' Gino exclaimed, 'y'like it?' And now he swooped on Dario, picking him up and throwing him in the air just like he had done with Lucky.

The child burst into tears, bawling at the top of his lungs. Then he was sick.

Gino handed him back to nanny and wished that the kid would toughen up – be more like his sister.

'He's only just finished his lunch,' Maria reproached. 'What do you expect when you throw him around like that?'

Gino shrugged and returned his attentions to his daughter. Together they zoomed the shiny red car around on the floor. Maria got out her camera and photographed them. 'Smile,' she instructed, and two identical grins beamed up at her.

A week later Gino set off on a trip.

Lucky didn't mind him going away too much because he always brought back wonderful presents. She did miss him though. Sometimes mommy let her talk to him on the telephone. That was a big treat.

When daddy was away the house filled up with people, and mommy didn't like that. Lucky knew, because she had heard them fighting about it. This time there were no other people in the house. When she asked why, mommy said it was because daddy was only going to be gone one night. Lucky wondered if this meant no presents.

In a small house in the garden lived Red and another man. Lucky liked them. They gave her piggy back rides and threw her in the swimming pool. Nanny Camden didn't like them. She called them 'uncouth louts.' Lucky didn't know what 'uncouth louts' meant. Dario cried when they tried to play with him. He cried a lot. Lucky was the only one who could get him to laugh.

Daddy gave her a big kiss when he left and an even bigger one to mommy, who later took her into the big bedroom and let her try on her clothes and shoes and jewelry. Lucky had great fun playing dress up. It was one of her favorite games and only allowed as a special treat.

She hoped that she might get two special treats and be allowed to sleep in the big bedroom. But it was not to be. Nanny Camden bustled her off for a bath at six o'clock, and at seven o'clock mommy came into her bedroom to kiss her goodnight.

She reached up and held a strand of her mother's silky pale hair. 'Why haven't *I* got yellow hair?' she inquired.

'Because you've got lovely black hair, just like daddy,' Maria said softly, 'that makes you lucky twice. Once for your name, and once for your nice curly hair.'

Lucky giggled. Sometimes mommy made good jokes. 'Dario's got yellow hair.'

'So he has. Now go to sleep.'

'Will daddy come home tomorrow?'

'Yes he will.'

'Can we all swim together?'

'If he's home early enough.'

'Good.' She popped her thumb in her mouth. Within minutes she was fast asleep.

Lucky was an early riser, jumping out of bed anywhere between 6 and 7 a.m. Dario and Nanny Camden never got up before 8.30, but she didn't mind. She had learned to fix her own breakfast and enjoyed running about by herself. Of course she wasn't allowed out of the house until the grown ups were around because of the bells that would go off if she opened any doors or windows. She had tried it once and daddy had gone mad! Yelling and shouting and running around with a *gun* in his hand. Just like television. It had made her giggle a lot, but Dario had cried.

When daddy was home he got up early too. Sometimes.

Lucky knew how to ping the switch to make the kettle boil. She knew how to make daddy's coffee – just the way he liked it. When she made it for him she got extra kisses.

Mommy usually got up late. Nine o'clock. Or half past. Daddy smacked her bottom and called her lazy. When they kissed it made Lucky shy.

The birds were talking to each other, chattering away, Lucky could hear them outside her window. She jumped out of bed and ran to watch them. And what a surprise! Mommy was up and in the swimming pool. Resting on the striped raft that floated lazily in the middle of the pool.

Excitedly Lucky wriggled into her yellow bathing suit. Daddy said she had a fat tummy. Gutso, he called her. It made her giggle.

She ran downstairs and was delighted to find the glass doors open.

'Mommy!' she called happily as she raced outside. 'Mommy mommy mommy – me swim too. Pleeeease!' She ran towards the pool giggling and laughing and happy as could be.

As she neared the pool she realized that her mother was asleep. The most beautiful mother in the world – that's what daddy called her, and Lucky agreed – was lying motionless, her long white blonde hair fanning out in the water, her arms and legs trailing limply from the sides of the raft.

Two things struck Lucky at once. Mommy was a naughty girl. She was in the nudie rudie.

And the water in the pool was a different color. It was pink.

She stood at the side and said, 'Mommy.' Then louder, 'MOMMY MOMMY MOMMY!'

She knew that something was wrong but she didn't know what. Where was daddy? He would know.

Silly daddy. He'd gone away.

She sat down, her short little legs dangling near the water. She would wait until mommy woke up. That's what she would do. She would just wait.

# Steven 1955–1964

When Steven was sixteen years of age he was summoned home from the private school he attended, and Carrie told him, red eyed and heartbroken, that Bernard Dimes had passed away in his sleep. He had suffered a fatal heart attack.

Steven was stunned by the news. While he knew that Bernard was not his natural father, he loved him just as much as if he was. After all, Bernard was the only father he had ever known. They had spent many good times together – in New York and at their summer house on Fire Island.

Steven stood loyally by his mother at the funeral, a tall good looking boy. And after that, at the Park Avenue house he held her trembling hand while a stream of Bernard's friends and acquaintances stopped by to pay their respects.

Carrie was very brave. She held her head high, and hid her tears with a long black veil.

A week later Steven was back in school.

'I can manage,' Carrie had insisted, 'your studies are more important than being with me.'

She *always* put his studies first. *Always.* It was a drag, but he had learned not to fight with her. His mother had a temper that could scorch ice. She expected top grades in everything. Early on he had learned to get them. If he didn't . . .

At thirteen he had goofed off, spent the term boxing and getting involved in the whole sports scene. It was great, but his school marks were really down. Carrie had blown a fuse. Wacked him, and burned his ass so bad he hadn't been able to sit down for a week! It had taught him a lesson.

'When you are black you have to try harder,' she snapped coldly, 'just you remember that.'

Steven couldn't figure *that* one out. He had never come across racial prejudice. He lived in a beautiful house with loving parents. The fact that one was white and one black had never bothered him. They had plenty of friends who didn't seem to care either. All types of people came to their house – famous stars of the theater, foreign producers, musicians, actresses from the films, opera singers.

In school he and a boy called Zoona Mgumba were the only black students. But they were just a part of the melting pot in the very expensive private school. The others were all sons of diplomats, financiers, or traveling dignitaries. Carrie had picked out such a school for Steven because she wanted him to worry about his grades, not about the color of his skin.

Bernard had argued that it would be protecting the boy from the real world. But Carrie had insisted.

Zoona Mgumba's father was something very important at the United Nations, Steven never quite figured out what. Zoona's main activity in life was jacking off – weapon in hand – he was always 'beating his meat' as Jerry Meyerson, Steven's best friend, called it.

Jerry was all right. Tall and gangly with a shock of red hair. Like Steven he was very into work, and being close friends they helped each other enormously.

Unlike the other boys, work came first, discussions on sex a

poor second. Who had time to discuss the merits of *this* pair
of stapled tits against *that* pair? Some of the boys spent hours
drooling over dirty magazines – especially Zoona – who was
eventually thrown out of school for whacking off in full sight
of three mothers during parents day.

By graduation Steven's sexual experiences were sadly
limited. Like Jerry he thought about girls, but who ever got to
meet any?

'We'll kill 'em in college,' Jerry boasted, 'the campus will be
teeming with girls, and you and I together – what a combination!'

Steven and Jerry were planning to study law – and they had
managed to swing it so that they both got to go to the same
college just outside Boston.

Jerry was right. Girls *were* everywhere. Short, fat, thin, tall.
Big breasts, little breasts, long legs, rounded asses. It was like
being on a diet all of your life, and then suddenly you were let
loose in a candy store.

Jerry went mad. Getting into a girl's pants became numero
uno on his list of things to do. After six months of trying, his
success rate was nil. His studies were pretty bad too.

Steven helped him all he could. He was enjoying himself
enormously at college. He liked the work – found it a challenge – and he had become an enthusiastic member of the
basketball team. It took his mind off girls and sex – he could
see the trouble Jerry was having, and he didn't need those
kinds of problems in *his* life. He had problems – but they were
with his mother. Since Bernard's death Carrie had all but
become a recluse. She sat in Bernard's study in the Park
Avenue house for hours on end. Just sat there. Staring. Day
after day.

Home on vacation Steven tried to jolt her out of her apathy.
He suggested they go to the Fire Island house for a break.
'I'm selling it, Steven,' she said sadly, 'too many memories.'

He asked about their financial situation. Were they all
right? Should he quit college and get a job?

She assured him that Bernard had left them well provided
for. And icily she added that if he ever quit college she'd kill
him.

He could not get through to her at all, and it worried him.
His mother was a very attractive woman in her early forties.
She should be out enjoying herself, not locked away in a dead
man's study surrounded by memories.

One day he had a great idea. 'Hey – mom,' he said brightly, 'whyn't we take a trip to Kenya? You must have a whole slew of relatives there and we could go see some of them.'

Her reaction was not what he had expected. She didn't say – 'I'll think about it,' or even 'maybe.' She just said, very coldly, 'Never go back in life Steven. Remember that.' End of discussion.

He knew what everyone else knew about her, the things he had read in magazines and articles. But sometimes – in the middle of the night – he woke in a cold sweat and thought – *Who am I? Who is my real father?*

The only information he could ever get out of Carrie was – 'He was a good man – a doctor – He died when you were one.'

He tried not to let her silence on the past bother him. She had her reasons. If she didn't care to tell him who his natural father was that was just something he would have to accept. So he did.

1957 was an event filled year for Steven. He turned eighteen, was called nigger for the first time in his life, got laid, and learned how to defend himself.

Being black was not the same as being white. Carrie had told him enough times, but he had never really listened. Now he knew. For a fact. And he started to become concerned about civil rights and the way things could be changed. Martin Luther King interested him, and the campaign for desegregation he was running down in the South.

He began to be very aware of his blackness, and now he understood what Carrie meant when she had said things like, 'When you are black you have to try harder.'

He was an excellent student as it was, but suddenly he did start to try harder, and excellence turned to brilliance.

His first sexual experience that went all the way was with a very pretty black girl called Shirley Sullivan. Classic college sex in the back of a friend's car with Shirley's skirt around her waist, her panties around her ankles, her sweater pushed up under her chin, and one tit pushed painfully out of a bra cup.

Steven was fully dressed, penis at attention rigidly sticking out of his trousers. It was messy and undignified. It was also the best thing he had ever done in his whole goddamn life!

He went with Shirley for seven wonderful months, asked her

to marry him, and was heartbroken when she jilted him for a pre-med student from another college.

He learned a lesson. Girls said one thing. Meant another. And were not to be trusted.

After Shirley he spread out. It wasn't difficult. He was now over six feet tall and incredibly good looking. Girls fell at his feet. Even white girls. He tried a few. They were no different. Pussy was pussy whatever color it was wrapped in.

Steven entered law school when he was twenty. That same year, Carrie married again. She surprised everyone by marrying Elliott Berkely, a snobbish, twice divorced, theater owner. A man who stunk of old money and old ideas although he was only forty-five years old.

To Carrie, Elliott was no Bernard Dimes. He was not a man she could ever dream of being truthful with. But contrary to what she had assured Steven, money was becoming a problem, and to see him safely through college and law school and keep up their lifestyle, an answer had to be found. Elliott Berkely was that answer. He had been pursuing her for years – and although she didn't love him. one morning she woke up and thought, 'Why not?'

When they married she already had a signed document guaranteeing Steven's education for as long as it would take. She also persuaded her son to change his name to Berkely.

Security was the name of the game. Security for Steven.

Zizi blew into his life like a blisteringly hot wind on a freezing day. He was twenty-five years old, a graduate of law school with a Bachelor of Arts and Law degree. He had passed his bar exam and was working as an Assistant Public Defender to gain courtroom experience.

Zizi was a dancer of sorts. She appeared as a witness on an assault case, and Steven took one look and got a hard-on there and then. He didn't know why. It was just one of those things. She grabbed the instant attention of his cock, and there was no escape.

Zizi. Five foot two of dynamic tits, snakey legs, flashing eyes, purring voice. Hot lover.

Zizi.

Carrie hated her on sight.

# Lucky 1965

Lucky Santangelo stood at the front door of the Bel Air house, watching the chauffeur load her suitcases into the trunk of a long black limousine. She was almost fifteen. A tall coltish girl with a jumble of jet curls and huge widely spaced black gypsy eyes. She was thin and rangy, her figure as yet undeveloped, deeply suntanned, and no make-up decorated her strong good looks.

Dario Santangelo sat disconsolately on the hood of the limo, much to the chauffeur's annoyance. He had picked up a handful of pebbles from the driveway, and now threw them moodily at an outdoor light. They pinged infuriatingly.

As dark as Lucky was, that's how blond Dario was. Thirteen and a half, with perfect features, longish white blond hair, and startlingly blue eyes.

He stared at his sister, then made a face at the chauffeur who was too busy with the suitcases to even notice.

Lucky giggled, winked at him, and silently mouthed, 'Jerko!' It was their favorite word, the word they used to describe most people they knew.

A woman emerged from the house. Tall, bossy, she issued a few instructions to the chauffeur, glanced at her watch and said, 'Come along, Lucky, get in the car, we don't want to miss our plane now, do we?'

Lucky shrugged, 'I wouldn't mind . . . ' she began.

'Now, now, miss,' snapped the woman, 'none of that.'

Behind her back Dario mouthed, 'Jerko! Jerko! Jerko!' making ears of his hands and waggling them insolently.

Lucky stifled a laugh, although she really didn't feel like laughing, she felt like crying.

Marco appeared. He was assigned to accompany her whenever she left the Bel Air house. She liked Marco. He was *soooo* good looking. Unfortunately he treated her like a kid. Had never even given her so much as a sideways glance of interest. Today he wore a light jacket, sports shirt, and tight jeans. He must be at least thirty, but he was lean and muscular, not fat at all like some older men she had seen.

For the thousandth time she wondered about his private life. Did he have a girlfriend? What did he like to do when he wasn't on bodyguard duty?

'Get off that car right now,' snapped Miss Bossy at Dario, 'and say goodbye to your sister.'

Dario threw the remainder of his pebbles in one triumphant lunge at the light. The glass shattered.

'Dario!' screamed Miss Bossy. 'Wait until I tell your father what you just did.'

She would have a long wait, Lucky mused. Gino's visits to the Bel Air house were getting further and further apart.

Dario slouched in her direction, trying to look cool, trying to look like he didn't mind the fact that she was being sent away to boarding school. 'S'long, sis,' he mumbled, 'if you feel like writing I don't mind.'

She took a step forward and hugged her brother. Normally he would have shoved her away, but today he let her hold him and she whispered very very softly, 'Don't let 'em get you down, I'll be back before you know it.'

He gave her a damp embarrassed kiss and fled inside the house before anyone could notice his tears.

Lucky climbed into the car. She was frightened and apprehensive, but in a way she was relieved. At last she was going out into the world. Ten years of nannies and private tutors were coming to an end. Ten years of privacy, and loneliness, and hardly being able to do anything. She was sorry about leaving Dario, but still . . . She needed companionship . . . Girls of her own age . . . And soon Dario would go off to school too.

It was Aunt Jennifer who had insisted that she be sent away to school. 'You can't keep the children locked up and protected forever, Gino,' Lucky had overheard on one of her father's rare visits. 'I've heard of a very good girls boarding school in Switzerland. It will do Lucky a world of good . . .'

She dozed on the plane, reluctantly, because she really didn't want to miss anything at all. Miss Bossy sat rigidly beside her keeping a sharp eagle eye on things.

Lucky thought it ridiculous that she needed a traveling companion at her age, but Gino had insisted. 'You go, she goes. When she delivers you safely to the school she leaves. That's it. No discussion.'

Gino. Her father. King of the no discussion.

She loved him so much it hurt. Yet sometimes she wondered just how much he really cared about her and Dario. He spent so little time with them . . . They lived in Bel Air . . . He lived wherever it suited him at the time. New York, Las Vegas, he had apartments all over. She knew the phone numbers but had never seen the homes. Sometimes, lying in bed late at night, she could remember a far off time when she was very little . . . He had always been around then. Hugs. Kisses. Attention. Real love and caring. She could remember her mother too. A beautiful pale angel with a sweet soft voice and skin like velvet . . .

Abruptly her memories would stop. Too painful to continue. Something would flash across her memory – a lightning vision. Pool. Raft. Body. Naked. Blood.

She must have said something in her sleep, Miss Bossy snapped crisply, 'Yes, dear, what is it?'

'Nothing.' She jogged herself awake, 'Can I get a Coca Cola?'

The air in Switzerland was so clear that Lucky felt she wanted to take large gulps of it to free her lungs of the Los Angeles smog.

A car met them at the airport, transporting them on an hour and a half's drive into lush green countryside. L'Evier, the school she was to attend, nestled at the foot of rolling hills and dense woods. It was very picturesque and totally unlike the manicured greenery of Bel Air and Beverly Hills.

Miss Bossy had the car wait while she took Lucky inside, deposited her with the principal, and left with a brisk efficient, 'Goodbye dear, see that you behave yourself.'

Miss Bossy had been in charge of Dario and Lucky for three years. She had given them about as much love and affection as a plank of wood. Lucky was not sorry to see her go.

'Miss Saint,' the principal said, 'welcome to L'Evier. I am sure, like all my girls, you will enjoy it here. I demand respect and obedience. Remember those two words, honor them, and your time at L'Evier will be happy and fruitful.'

Miss Saint. What a name to get stuck with. Lucky Saint. God! For years she had known what her father did. The bodyguards, the alarm bells, the bars on the downstairs windows, the dogs. It all spelled out the fact that he was a man who had to be careful. But fancy having to change her name just to go to a stupid school. What did it matter whether she was Santangelo or Saint? Who could possibly care?

In his penthouse suite at the Mirage Hotel in Las Vegas Gino got the call to tell him that Lucky had arrived safely. He lit up a long thin Havana cigar and sighed.

The last ten years had been difficult. But he had protected

his children, kept them safe, hadn't seen them as much as he would have liked to. It was better that way ... safer ...

After Maria's murder ... So many killings ... Personally he had taken care of Pinky Banana ... Personally ... He could still hear his screams of pain ... his anguished squawks for mercy. What mercy had the animal shown Maria?

Abruptly he stood up. Walked to the window and stared out. The Strip was crowded with hotels now – neon signs shooting up into the desert blackness lighting up the night. The Boy had been right about Vegas.

A discreet knock on the door. Red ushered in a man who wished a favor. The man was florid faced and nervous. He was part owner of a rival hotel, an important man to some. In Gino's presence he was servile, fawning. He requested his favor in hushed conspiratorial tones. Gino said he would see that the matter was attended to.

The man backed from the living room wringing his hands with thanks.

Gino knew that the favor would be repaid tenfold. He enjoyed storing favors. It gave him a sense of tremendous power. Not that he needed to sense it. He had it. Plenty of it. Enough to keep politicians and judges and policemen right in his back pocket. Clowns on a string ready to dance for him whenever he needed them. Whenever and wherever.

He ground out the expensive cigar after only three puffs. Cigars were like women. Expendable. No matter how much they cost there were always plenty more.

No more like Maria though. No more like his dear departed wife ... his love ... his life ...

'Lucky Saint,' the blonde girl said incredulously, 'What the hell kind of name is *that*?'

Lucky's first encounter with Olympia Stanislopoulos, a short frothy girl with piggy eyes set in a round face, cascades of the most glorious golden hair, breathtaking whiter than white skin, and rounded adult breasts that wobbled through a grubby tennis shirt.

Lucky glared defiantly, 'I don't see anyone criticizing Ringo Starr or Rip Torn or Rock Hudson,' she spat.

'Oh!' jeered Olympia, 'I didn't realize I was sharing a room with a budding movie star. Soooo sorry!'

Off to a bad start, a week later they were the best of friends. Olympia was sixteen and a half, rebellious daughter of a

Greek shipowner and his American society wife. Her parents
were divorced and she was shuttled back and forth between
the two, each one seeing who could spoil her more. She had
been thrown out of two American boarding schools, and in
despair her mother had enrolled her at L'Evier. 'Daddy doesn't
give a shit about my education,' Olympia giggled, 'he figures
I'll marry some rich cat he picks out for me in the old home-
land. Mommy thinks I should have a career. They're both
wrong. *I'm* going to have a good time, that's what. Boys and
booze and grass and fun! Wanna join me on my quest for the
good life?'

It sounded like a marvelous idea. 'Sure,' said Lucky, her
sense of adventure surfacing for the first time, 'but how are we
going to have a good time when we're locked up here?'

Olympia winked, 'There are ways,' she murmured mysteriously, 'Just watch and learn!'

It was easy. Lights out at 9.30 p.m. Lucky and Olympia out
at 9.35 p.m.

Their bedroom window was conveniently situated next to a
handy tree, and it was no trouble at all to shin right down and
out onto the damp grass. Then a race across the grounds to the
bicycle shed, borrow two bikes, and a ten minute ride to the
nearest village.

The first night they did it, the two of them sat in an outdoor
cafe and drank steaming hot coffee laced with slugs of Tia
Maria.

Olympia was soon busy eyeing a group of teenage boys sitting nearby. The boys eyed her back. Soon they all joined up.

Olympia held court grandly, throwing back her golden mane
of hair, and sticking out sensual rounded breasts.

The boys grouped admiringly about her. 'I simply *must*
learn the language,' Olympia sighed, 'it's soooo boring not
being able to understand what they're talking about.'

Lucky understood. She spoke fluent German, Italian and
French – private tutors were good for *some* things. She
wondered if she should tell Olympia that in quick asides to
each other the boys were saying – 'Fantastic titties!' 'I sure
hope she screws!' 'Or sucks!' 'Or both!'

Drunk as she was Lucky knew that they should be getting on
their bicycles and getting the hell out. Boys only ever wanted
one thing. Nanny after nanny had taught her *that* much. And
now it seemed they were right. 'Let's go,' she suggested.

'Why?' pouted Olympia, 'I'm having fun. Aren't you?'

It would have been perfectly obvious to anyone not as self absorbed as Olympia, that no, she was not having fun. She was sitting at the end of the table, ignored, while the boys all buzzed around Olympia and her magic tits.

'I want to go,' Lucky hissed, 'and I think you should too.'

'So go,' Olympia said airily, 'nobody's stopping you.'

And nobody was.

She got up, collected her bicycle, and cycled off. Half way back to school she stopped and was sick by the side of the road. Had it been fair of her to leave her friend?

Quite fair, she decided. Olympia was obviously no slouch when it came to looking after herself.

Climbing back through the window she fell onto her bed fully dressed and was asleep within five minutes.

She never heard Olympia return three hours later, she was too busy dreaming of Marco.

'Hi,' said Marabelle Blue in a soft breathy voice, 'I've been dying to meet you, Tiny often talks about you.'

Marabelle Blue. Latest contender for the famous Monroe throne.

Gino stared. Only for a moment. She *was* something.

Tiny Martino laughed, 'I've been wanting to get you two together for some time, but Marabelle never stops working. She goes from movie to movie – she's hot on the trail of non-stop stardom,' he laughed some more, 'and what a crock of shit *that* is – *I* can tell you.'

Marabelle gave a low throaty chuckle. She was wearing a grey chiffon dress with specks of diamante, it clung tighter than foil, barely covering her large tempting breasts.

Gino felt a stirring in a place where he didn't often feel a stirring any more. Since Maria . . . nobody permanent . . . no woman who held his interest past a week or two . . . no woman he wanted to wake up with . . . Ten years of being alone was a long time.

'Do you ever go to the movies Mr Santangelo?' husked Marabelle. She was exuding a strong perfume. Heady . . . exotic . . . A very womanly smell.

Gino shrugged, 'Not much, but I will. Tell me the name of your last film?'

'*Bad Girl*,' she purred.

Her eyes were blue. He had always had a weakness for blue eyes. '*Bad Girl*, huh?'

'Yes.' She lowered her eyes in a surprisingly demure way, 'Silly title, don't you think?' She raised her eyes to look straight at him. A strangely disconcerting move.

Here was a broad with everything on show, sex oozing out of every pore, and yet she had a vulnerable little girl quality. He cleared his throat. 'Yeh. I guess so.'

He wondered how he looked to her. He was fifty-nine years old, but he didn't look it. He was fit and tanned. He had all his hair and teeth. Worked out religiously. He could pass for forty- forty-two. Not that he wanted to. Growing older was all right. But still . . . Who wanted to look old?

'My next movie is called *Womanly Wiles*, even sillier, don't you think?' She giggled, and brought her hand up to cover her mouth.

He noticed her hands were workworn with nails bitten down to the quick. They didn't match the rest of her. The lush body, the sexual face, the fall of platinum blonde hair loosely waved.

'Where you shooting it?' he asked casually.

'L.A,' she replied, licking her full glossed lips with a snaky pink tongue, 'Why don't you come and visit on the set one day?'

Lucky dragged herself awake the next morning, shoved Olympia, and silently and hurriedly they dressed, making it to assembly with only seconds to spare.

It was the lunch break before they got a chance to speak, then they collected plates of salad, and flopped out on the grass.

'Why did you run off?' Olympia inquired languidly. 'You missed all the fun.'

'What fun?'

'*Fun*, kid, *fun*. You know – groping and petting and getting felt up. Ummm . . . ' Olympia closed her eyes and smiled, 'It was delicious!'

Lucky couldn't help it, but she was shocked. 'With *all* of them?' she gasped.

Olympia laughed. 'Of course not, dumbo. I picked out the one I liked best.' She looked concerned, 'Didn't you like *any* of them?'

Lucky bit on her lower lip. Actually she *had* quite liked the look of one of them, but he hadn't even glanced in her direction, all eyes had been firmly focused on Olympia.

Anyway, what did she, Lucky, know about boys and sex and

all that stuff? Exactly nothing. Oh, she knew the technical details – what went where and all that jazz. But as far as experience was concerned, one big zero. She had never even been kissed.

'Well?' demanded Olympia.

'Oh!' Lucky jumped, 'er . . . I don't know . . .'

'Have you ever done it?' Olympia asked suddenly.

'I've been around,' Lucky replied coolly.

'Have you ever screwed a boy?' Olympia asked matter-of-factly.

Lucky threw it right back at her. 'Have you?'

'Almost,' replied Olympia mysteriously. 'Almost is much more fun.' She stuffed some potato salad in her mouth. 'If you like, I'll teach *you* how to do Almost.'

Lucky nodded quickly. She didn't know what Almost was, but it sounded interesting.

Instruction from Olympia was a hit or miss affair. Ideas and thoughts came to her at the most inopportune times, and when they came she insisted on passing them on there and then. In the middle of a cookery class she might whisper, 'Always start off with kissing. Make it last, that way you can get to enjoy it. If boys had *their* way they'd stick it in, whip it out, and that would be that!'

During science: 'If he goes for your tits let him – it's the *most* fun. By the way, where *are* your tits?'

A day of thought, and then, 'The best way to develop tits is to get a boy to work on 'em. How do you think I got mine?'

As the weeks passed by, instruction hotted up. 'If a boy says he just wants to lie next to you and he won't do anything – forget it! He's lying.'

'If he wants to kiss you down there – let him.'

And finally – the piece de resistance – 'Sucking a boy can be fun. Only don't let him come in your mouth – it's worse than onions – you'll taste it for days!'

Fully instructed on sex, Olympia decided the next thing Lucky had to get together was her look.

'You know, you're really quite a knock out,' Olympia exclaimed one day, after she had made Lucky up and back combed her hair.

Looking in the mirror, Lucky felt a tingle of excitement. She *did* look terrific, at least eighteen or nineteen. What would Marco say if he saw her now?

'I think it's time we sashayed our fine young asses down to the village again,' Olympia said with a wicked grin. 'Let's see if everything I've taught you works!'

It wasn't long before Gino Santangelo was a regular visitor on the set of Marabelle Blue's new film. He would be driven onto the lot in his sleek black Cadillac – rumor had it that the entire car was reinforced with an inner steel lining and that the dark tinted windows were bullet proof – and would emerge from the car, flanked by two bodyguards, to sit stiffly in a special chair on the set watching Miss Blue at work.

She was quite a sight. She fluffed take after take, but when she got it right she was magic.

Marabelle Blue. Christened Mary Belmont. Came to Hollywood at sixteen having won a talent contest. Starved for a year. Got wise and used her God given talents to survive. Met and married a veteran Hollywood stunt man who guided and helped her, saved her from becoming just another hooker working the casting couches.

Then the sudden bright meteoric rise to fame. Husband pushed into the background. Bad for her image. Marabelle understood. She had been around. She was just twenty years old.

Gino took her to bed on their second date. She was every bit as good as he had known she would be.

He felt fine. Here he was fucking a broad that half the males in the world would give their left ball for. Maybe even the right one too.

Marabelle Blue.

He didn't love her, but she was permanent.

Lucky felt strange wearing Olympia's clothes. The skirt was too short, the white boots tight, the sweater clinging.

The two girls cycled into the village having used their usual escape route. And this time Lucky was getting attention too. Oh, the power of clothes and make-up!

Ursi was the name of the boy she liked. He was eighteen and spoke some English. After a decent interval of coffee and small talk he invited her, very politely, to go for a walk.

Olympia gave her a wink and a nod. This was the big time! Let's see if she could do Almost too!

Ursi walked her as far as the woods, then he took off his jacket, laid it on the ground, and without a word they sat down. Immediately he pounced, groping hands everywhere.

She nearly panicked, but then she remembered Olympia's words of advice. She pushed him away and said calmly, 'What's the hurry? Take it easy.'

The promise in the words soothed him, and he began to kiss her on the mouth, wet sucking kisses which she couldn't help finding a bit disgusting. She squeezed her eyes shut and hoped that things would improve. They did. When his hands strayed to her budding breasts things got better immediately. It was true what Olympia had said – this *was* fun.

Ursi had her sweater pushed up, but he was obviously disappointed with her lack of curves, because after a few minutes his hands were already fiddling with the catch on her skirt.

'No!' She stopped him sharply, '*I* want to see *you.*'

Happily he fiddled with his trousers and extracted his erection.

Lucky held it carefully. He was a well developed boy. 'Oh my!' she said in awe, 'Wow!'

Her words excited Ursi into a frenzy of passion, and before she knew what was happening he was thrusting himself back and forth against her hand and coming in a series of triumphant spurts.

She leaped away from him. 'Hey – ' she complained, 'watch out for my skirt.'

'Oh honey,' he sighed in his careful English, 'you is nice nice girl!'

Lucky grinned. She felt the power. She wanted more.

# Steven 1965

'The trouble with you, Steven, my dear, is that you have no real sense of what it means to be black. You have no black consciousness.' So spoke Dina Mgumba, fiercely radical wife of Zoona Mgumba. Yes, Zoona had settled down. After years of jacking off in every possible direction he had met Dina at a civil rights demonstration, fallen in love, and become a changed man overnight.

Lounging on the couch, Zizi gave a loud obvious yawn.

Dina shot a steely look in her direction. 'What's the matter dear?' she inquired coldly. 'Are we boring you?'

'*You* are boring me Dina *dear*,' Zizi replied, equally coldly. There was no love lost between the two of them.

'I think it's time to go home,' Jerry Meyerson said, raising his lanky frame from an easy chair. 'Come along, pet.'

Pet was the name he gave to all his girlfriends, which was good, because only a computer would have been able to remember their names. Jerry's girls changed weekly, sometimes daily. And they all looked the same. Pretty, mousey, little blondes who Jerry claimed were – 'Dynamite in the old sackerooney.'

Half-heartedly Steven said, 'No. Stay. Have another drink.'

Jerry laughed ruefully. 'Wouldn't I just love to. But I've got a real hot whiplash case first thing in the morning and I'm going for big damages.'

Zizi yawned again, and rolled off the couch. 'Goodnight Jerry, everyone.' She walked towards the bedroom in the small apartment, and paused by the door, 'Hurry up,' she directed the words at Steven, 'I feel *reaaal* horny tonight. Don't keep me waiting lover.' She slammed the bedroom door behind her.

Dina pursed her lips disapprovingly. She didn't say anything, but her expression said it all.

Steven knew the expression. His mother gave it to him constantly. 'How about dinner next week?' he asked, falsely enthusiastic, because he knew that however hard he tried Zizi and Dina would never get along. 'We could take in a movie first – I'd like to see the new Polanski film "Cul-de-Sac".'

'That's what you're in, man,' muttered Dina.

Zoona gave her a look. Dina was not a girl to be silenced with a look. 'We can't make it anyway,' she said, 'We'll be goin' down to Alabama for the march. I imagine you *won't* be joining us?'

Steven shook his head. He had worked hard in the civil rights movement. In 1963 it had taken up most of his time. He had been in Birmingham when the riots and beatings culminating in the arrest of Martin Luther King took place. He had marched with 200,000 freedom marchers on Washington. He had felt the need to be involved, but not perhaps as deeply as a black man who had lived the deprivations and humiliations of being born and living out his life in the South.

Carrie had finally convinced him that he could do more good for the black race by becoming a successful and respected lawyer. When he had met Zizi that clinched it. No more travelling around the country on marches and demonstrations and sit ins.

Dina had taken it as a personal affront. She and Zoona and Steven had been a team, working together, sweating, crying, *forcing* change. Now they were merely friends who saw each other for dinner and what Dina called 'Dumb ass conversation',

'Nope,' said Steven, 'I won't be coming on the march.'

Dina's lip curled, but she said nothing.

Goodbyes were exchanged, everyone left, and Steven surveyed the wreck of empty glasses and overflowing ash trays. Zizi wouldn't clear it up, even though she shared the apartment with him, she never lifted a finger.

He wondered what he saw in her.

And a powerful hard-on told him what.

He forgot about clearing up and went in the bedroom.

Zizi lay nonchalantly on the bed reading a movie magazine. She was naked, apart from a gold ankle bracelet and six gold bangles on each wrist. She had a spectacular dancer's body. Although only five foot two inches tall, she was perfectly proportioned. Half black, half Puerto Rican, her skin glowed with a sepia tint. She had dyed her naturally dark hair blonde, and the contrast of the light hair and her fiery amber eyes was lethal. At twenty-nine she was three years older than Steven.

'Why are you so rude to Dina?' he asked patiently.

She spread her legs sensuously, 'Why don't you cut out the talk and show me what the black movement is *really* all about.'

'I want to get married, mom,' Steven said, feeling like a nervous teenager.

Carrie, busily arranging flowers in a vase, didn't even turn around.

'Did you hear what I said?' he mumbled, swatting at a bee that buzzed around the flower and plant-filled room of his mother's luxurious apartment.

'You know,' Carrie said slowly, still attending to the flowers, 'for a smart boy you sure can behave like a fool.'

He was on his feet. His mother was so unfair. She hardly even *knew* Zizi. 'Why don't you want me to get married?' he demanded.

Carrie turned and faced him. 'You're twenty-six years old, Steven. I can't stop you. If she's the kind of girl you want to spend the rest of your life with . . . '

'What do you mean – "kind of girl". *What* kind of girl?'

'Do I have to spell something out that I'm sure you already know?'

'Shit!' he exploded. 'You're so old fashioned and prudish.'

Her eyes sparkled dangerously, 'Watch your mouth. I'm your mother you know.'

'Too fucking right!'

She smacked him with all her might across the face. 'Is that what she's taught you? To lose respect for me? To use gutter language like some pimp from the ghetto?'

He backed towards the door. 'What do you know about ghettos and pimps? You live in a dream world where everyone's the good guy. I love Zizi, and I'm going to marry her whether *you* like it or not!'

# Lucky 1965

Dario Santangelo patiently awaited his sister's return home for the summer vacation. He had so many things he wanted to tell her. Miss Bossy had left, and been replaced with an older woman who was more of a general housekeeper. It was a relief. No one to watch and spy on him. He couldn't wait to get away to school after the summer vacation finished. After all, he was nearly fourteen, and like Lucky he was starved for outside companionship.

Moodily he picked at a pimple on his chin. Lucky was his *best* friend. It had been *awful* without her.

Lucky glanced around the arrival lounge, saw Marco waiting, and thought – *Oh my God! What'll he think of the new me!*

She had departed L.A. three months earlier a fourteen year old kid. She was returning, a fifteen year old sophisticated young woman.

Marco looked right through her. *He didn't even recognize her!* She tapped him on the arm and brightly said, 'Remember me?'

He was startled. 'Lucky?'

'You got it in one!'

'Jesus!' It slipped out before he could help himself. Gino would have a fit when he got a load of his sweet little girl. She had cut off her wild abundance of jet curls, and now her hair was short – very short – and clung to her scalp like a weird hat. Her make-up was not to be believed. White, stark, clownlike, with spikey false lashes top *and* bottom, purple eyeshadow, and a chalky lipstick. Her outfit defied description. A geometric pattern black and white mini dress that barely skimmed her ass, worn with white shiny boots.

'Well?' Lucky questioned, putting her hands on her hips and surveying him boldly. 'How do you like the new me?'

'Uh . . . it's certainly different.'

'*I'm* certainly different.'

'Oh?'

'You can betcha! You could call me a woman of experience,' she winked, 'know what I mean?'

Holy shit! Gino would crap himself.

He signalled for a baggage porter. 'I'll take you out to the car.'

Marco had been in Gino Santangelo's employ for six and a half years, and he liked the work. Before that he had been a cab driver, a lifeguard, a lumberjack in Canada – you name it, Marco had tried it. His restlessness had begun after a traumatic six months in the army in Korea. When your two best buddies get shot down beside you, nothing seems the same any more. 'Go to Gino,' his mother, Bee, had finally said. 'He's always had a soft spot for you. He'll give you a job.'

Her words were true. Gino welcomed him warmly 'You'll be with me,' he had said, 'you'll watch and learn. I need loyalty – people around me I can depend on one hundred percent.'

Six and a half years had flown by. In that time he hadn't been bored once, and he had learned plenty.

'You look gruesome!' exclaimed Dario.

'Thank's a lot,' replied Lucky, killing him with a withering stare, 'that's a fine welcome home.'

Dario belched loudly, 'Want to hear my new Beatles album?' he asked eagerly.

'No I don't.' She stalked grandly into the house.

Dario trailed after her. She *did* look horrible. And she seemed so sort of . . . different. He decided to tell her his news immediately, put her in a good mood.

He followed her upstairs. 'You didn't write,' he accused.

She yawned, and sat down on her bed, 'Didn't have time.'

He shut the bedroom door. 'I know something you won't believe.'

'What?' Her tone was disinterested. She was wondering why Marco hadn't declared his instant and undying love for her.

'It's about dad.'

'Yes?' She was interested. In three months all she had had from Gino was a phone call on her birthday, and an expensive stereo set delivered to the school and promptly confiscated.

'He's got a new girlfriend.'

'Who?'

'A movie star.'

'Who – you little rat?'

'Don't call me names.'

'WHO?'

'Marabelle Blue.'

'You're kidding?'

'It's the truth.'

'Holy shit!' She extracted a cigarette from her purse and lit up.

Dario was impressed, 'When did you start to smoke?'

She inhaled, showing off, and allowing the smoke to trickle slowly from her nostriles. 'I've always smoked.'

'Liar!'

'Tell me more about daddy and her. How do you know?'

'Everyone knows.'

'*I* don't.'

'It's in the papers.'

'When?'

'All the time.'

'That doesn't prove anything.'

'He brings her here.' Dario paused, savoring his moment of triumph. 'I've seen them screwing!'

Lucky leapt off the bed, excitement outdoing her new sophisticated reserve. 'You haven't?'

'Oh yes I have.'

For the next hour they talked about nothing else. How Dario, heading for the kitchen and a glass of water in the middle of the night, had heard noises coming from Gino's bedroom. How he had bent down and reviewed the proceedings through the keyhole and seen *everything*!

Lucky wanted details. And then she wanted them repeated once, twice, and a third time. Dario was quite hoarse by the time she was satisfied. 'OK,' she said finally, 'I'm going to take a shower now, we'll get together later.'

Reluctantly he left her alone, first imparting the news that

Gino would be having dinner with them that evening. 'He's in Las Vegas, but he said he'll be back.'

She stripped off her clothes and stood under the shower keeping the water good and cold. Her newly developed breasts reacted nicely, the nipples hardening and sticking out. How right Olympia had been, a little boy massage did wonders for the tits.

'I don't get along with kids,' Marabelle quivered, her lower lip trembling.

Gino stretched his arms in front of him, cracking the joints in his knuckles. 'They're not kids, they're teenagers.'

'Same thing.'

'Different thing.'

Nervously Marabelle peered at her face in the mirror. They were in her dressing room at the studio, Gino having come directly there from the airport. 'What shall I wear?' she quavered.

'Nothing special. They're only kids.'

The dinner table was silent. Gino sat at one end, broodingly angry. He sent his daughter to a very exclusive expensive private school, and she came back looking like a circus freak.

Lucky sat on his left hand side, sulking. Her father hadn't seen her in three months, and instead of saying how much she had grown up, he just went off on a whole nagging jag about how awful he thought she looked.

Dario sat opposite Lucky, staring at Marabelle Blue, his eyes fixed firmly on her breasts.

Marabelle herself faced Gino. Her lower lip trembled. She didn't attempt conversation. She had *known* his kids would hate her.

After dinner they all got up and went their separate ways.

Dario tried to tag along with Lucky, but she wasn't having it. She went to her room, locked the door and sobbed for an hour. When she recovered she picked up the phone and placed a person-to-person call to Olympia in Greece. 'Help!' she begged. 'Can you invite me to come stay with you for the summer?'

'Sure,' replied Olympia. 'Why not? We can have a ball – you and I – an absolute ball!'

They did. Right from day one.

Dimitri Stanislopoulos, Olympia's father, lived in great style on a marvelous sun kissed Greek island. In residence were many house guests who flitted back and forth between his sumptuous villa and private yacht. They were only too happy to welcome a pretty young girl, even if she was Olympia's friend and therefore out of bounds to their straying hands.

'The trouble with daddy's friends is they're all so old!' Olympia giggled, 'but amazingly rich. What are *your* father's friends like?'

For a moment Lucky was tempted to tell the truth. Daddy's friends. Some of the most notorious and infamous gangsters in the United States. But she remembered her promise. She was *never* to reveal her true name. *Never.* She shrugged, 'Old I guess. Boring.'

Olympia nodded knowingly.

For two weeks they lay in the sun, water skied, and scuba dived. 'I'm so healthy I could faint!' Olympia complained. 'Let's take the Riva to the mainland tonight and get us some *action*!'

Lucky agreed. It seemed so long since they had done Almost. *Everything But* was their motto. 'Two little virgins are we,' Olympia would giggle, after a particularly randy necking session, 'and we aim to stay that way!'

They found a couple of local fishermen on the mainland, and after a suitable amount of time drinking and chatting they retired to a nearby beach.

Lucky lay back on the sand, reveling in the feel of the boy's lips on hers. His large hands were rough on her breasts. He didn't speak much English, but they understood each other perfectly.

After a time, when his hands ripped at her shorts, she made him stop. Then, before he knew what was happening, she had maneuvered his hardness out of his trousers and was going down on him in a fast businesslike fashion.

Only after he was satisfied did she allow him to remove her shorts and pants. Then she lay back with her legs open while his fingers brought her to a shuddering climax.

It was the perfect way to make love. No risk. No hassle.

Lucky grinned as she pulled on her clothes . . 'Two little virgins are we . . . '

Slowly Gino realized Marabelle was cheating on him. He was outraged. Discreet inquiries revealed that the other man in her life was a very important Senator based in Washington. A well known, happily married politician. And what is more, Miss Blue was under constant surveillance by the F.B.I.

Gino found out all this information bit by bit, and it shook him. But Marabelle was special. He wasn't ready to dump her.

One clear September morning he took a plane to Washington, phoned the Senator, and arranged a very private very discreet meeting.

Senator Peter Richmond was, at forty-five, boyishly handsome. He lived his life to the full. He had an attractive wife, four healthy clean cut children, and he screwed anything that winked in his direction. Marabelle Blue had done more than wink. She had appeared at a Washington fund raising benefit, settled her baby blue eyes on him, and had him there and then in her dressing room. Since that first magical fuck they had been meeting two or three times a month across America.

Marabelle liked screwing a famous politician.

Peter liked screwing a famous screen goddess.

Gino didn't like any of it.

He spoke to Peter Richmond softly, mildly, as though they were the best of friends. By the time the meeting finished they were.

Senator Richmond was shocked when he learned of Marabelle's affair with Gino Santangelo. He couldn't thank Gino enough for warning him. The repercussions if it ever came out! Marabelle Blue sharing her favors between a politician and a hood! What an escape!

Of course he did not voice his thoughts. He nodded and listened and thanked Gino, who pledged his full support should Peter ever see fit to run as a presidential candidate.

Gino flew back to Los Angeles a happy man, content and smiling. He could be useful to Peter Richmond. Peter Richmond could be useful to him. Everything settled, and he hadn't even had to show him the pictures or play him the tapes. Gino patted the manila envelope in his pocket. It would go into his safe along with the yellowing faded bunch of Senator Duke's letters.

He had never had to use those . . . And for seven years now Senator Duke had been dead. But Gino still kept the letters. A souvenir of times past.

Back in school Lucky read of Marabelle Blue's suicide attempt in the newspapers. Gino phoned to tell her of their engagement, which took place six weeks later. He was too late, she had already seen it on the television news.

How could he? She cried long into the night. Olympia came to her bed, climbed in, and cuddled her. 'What is it, baby?' she crooned. 'What's the matter?'

Lucky wouldn't tell her. She just clung to her friend, until mutually they began to caress each other.

Soft breasts, hard nipples, warm thighs, milky wetness.

They brought each other to a climax, and slept in each others arms.

Early in the morning Olympia slipped from her bed. By some reciprocal unspoken word they never mentioned the incident. It had happened. It had been good. It was not something either of them wanted or needed again.


# Steven 1966

Steven and Zizi got married on a freezing cold February morning. Zizi wore black thigh length boots, a bright red miniskirt, and a furry black jacket.

Jerry Meyerson acted as best man. Zoona and Dina were witnesses. Zizi had invited no one. She claimed she had no family, and friends were not an important part of her life.

The wedding ceremony at City Hall was short and impersonal. Afterwards, they all went to a bar where Jerry bought champagne, and Zizi did an impromptu dance which embarrassed Steven. They had their first fight forty-five minutes after the wedding ceremony. Nobody was surprised. Steven and Zizi – who had been living together for nearly a year – fought constantly. The only surprise was that they had finally married. Talk about attraction of opposites.

Jerry had spent weeks trying to talk his friend out of it. 'What have you got to gain?' he questioned. 'You've got all the advantages now – why tie yourself up?'

Steven shrugged. 'I don't know Jerry . . . She wants it.'

'Sure *she* wants it. They *all* want it. Why give in?'

'Listen, I kind of like the idea myself . . .'

'Crap.'

'No, really . . .'

'Crap.'

Steven didn't want to tell Jerry the real reason he was getting married. The real reason was that Zizi had threatened to leave if they didn't. 'You want me – you marry me,' she told him, "cos honey – *you* don't – there's plenty others will.'

He believed her. Men were always looking her up and down in the street, following her with their eyes, undressing her mentally. She didn't seem to mind. In fact she loved it. If they were married, Steven reasoned, she would have to stop all the flirting and settle down. Maybe have a baby. If Zizi was pregnant other men would *have* to stop giving her the eye.

The thought of her with another man created a jealous fury in Steven that frightened him. He knew that she could inflame passions and angers in him that were potentially dangerous. Theirs was a volatile relationship, he thought that marriage would make it stable and calm.

He was wrong. He found that out on their honeymoon. Zizi, in a string bikini that left nothing to the imagination, flaunted her body beside the pool at the resort hotel they had chosen to go to in Puerto Rico. She was on home ground, and loving every minute.

Steven could only watch in helpless fury as she undulated her way around flirting with everyone from the lifeguard to a leering group of American tourists whose fat wives were not pleased.

It was the first time they had been on a vacation together, and back in their room he complained. 'You're showing too much, when you stepped out of the pool I could see everything – nipples and pubic hair – everything.'

'Oh mah gawd!' she drawled in an exaggeratedly shocked voice, 'not nipples *and* pubic hair!'

'Don't joke about it.'

She unhooked the top of her bikini and let it fall to the floor. 'Sorry honey, you're right.' She turned to face him, provocatively moving so that her breasts swung in a tantalizingly sexy fashion.

In spite of his anger he was hard immediately. She had that effect on him.

Slowly she brought a finger to her lips and licked it, then she drew the finger down to one of her extended nipples and circled it slowly.

He watched as the nipple grew even bigger, and he grew even harder. He had made love to her hundreds of times but the thrill, the expectation, was always as hot as the first time.

How could he possibly stay mad at her? She might flirt around, but when you got right down to it she was his – only his – and that's what really mattered.

Carrie had a full report on the wedding from Jerry Meyerson. He was a nice boy. She had liked him from the moment Steven had first brought him home when they were both sixteen. Over the years she had watched him grow from a gawky teenager into a successful young lawyer. He called her Carrie, never failed to drop by at least once a week, and harbored a secret crush on her which they were both aware of but meticulously never mentioned.

Carrie was flattered. She was fifty-three years old, and the admiration of a man young enough to be her son was always acceptable.

Of course she did look marvelous. She was a face in New York society. Other women envied her. She was treated with respect, her opinions on everything from make-up to home decoration quoted constantly.

Often she wondered what would happen if they all knew the truth about her. Would her opinions and ideas be courted then? Would charities beg her to be their patron? Clothes designers fight for her to wear their clothes?

No way.

How strange life was. Who would have thought she would have ever made it to where she was today? And Steven. How proud she was of him. He was a fine lawyer – even if he did insist on working as a public defender. He made a living, but it was nothing to the money he could be making if he would only go into private practice. She was prepared to finance him – but when she suggested this to him, he had turned her down flat. 'I *want* to help people who really need my help – not some fat cat with dollar bills sticking out his ears. The people I help have to make do with what they can get. If they get me – and I can do something for them, it makes me feel good.'

She didn't argue. She knew that when he got older and wiser he would change his mind.

Then Zizi had come into his life and ruined everything. From the moment Carrie first set eyes on her she had known she would.

'It won't last,' Jerry assured her. 'They were even fighting after the wedding.'

Carrie nodded. She knew it wouldn't last. She just wondered how long it would take.

She had not seen Steven since he had told her of his marriage plans. Much as it hurt her she had frozen him out of her life in the hope that it might make him see sense. 'Where have they gone?' she asked.

'San Juan, where else would she drag him?' Jerry replied.

She stood, indicating their meeting was over, 'You will keep in touch, won't you? I'm here if Steven needs me, but until he gets rid of that person I don't think I want to see him. Perhaps it will help him to make a decision if I'm not around.'

'You could be right.' He kissed her chastely on the cheek and wondered why *his* mother looked like an Elizabeth Arden face mask while Carrie resembled Lena Horne.

'I'll see you in a week,' he said.

'Thank you, Jerry.'

# Lucky and Gino 1966

'You have brought disgrace upon this entire establishment,' said the school principal with a censorious glare, 'L'Evier has *never* known behavior like this before. *Never!*' She removed her pebble like spectacles, and for one wild moment Lucky thought that the austere English woman was going to burst into tears. But she didn't. She merely squinted, curled her thin lips disparagingly, and continued with her diatribe. 'To bring boys into the school is bad enough. But to *smuggle* them into your *room*, and to be found . . . in *bed* with them . . . '

Olympia stifled a giggle.

The principal caught her eye and said ominously, 'You may well laugh, young lady. I do hope that your laughter continues when your father arrives to remove you from this school that you have besmirched with your . . . *disgusting* behavior. You are *both* expelled. I have managed to contact your father too, Lucky. He will be here in the morning, and so will Mr Stanislopoulos.' She replaced her spectacles firmly on her long thin nose, 'In the meantime,' she continued, looking with distaste at the two girls, 'you are to go to your room and *stay* in your room until you are fetched tomorrow. Is that quite clear?'

'Shit!' exclaimed Olympia, flopping down on her bed. 'Daddy's going to be really pissed off. He *hates* it when I'm thrown out, and he has to come and get me and make small talk and apologize for his *naughty* little girlikins. He made me *swear* I wouldn't get myself thrown out of this one. Shit!'

'My father won't come,' Lucky said dourly, 'he'll send someone.

'Why won't he come?' Olympia questioned curiously.

Lucky shrugged, 'He's a busy man.'

'They're *all* busy men.'

'My old man's busier than most.'

'What *does* he do?'

Lucky shrugged again, then said carefully, vaguely, 'He has a million interests. Hotels . . . factories . . . publishing . . . You name it, he has a piece of it.' She opened her closet and inspected her clothes.

'Does he have a piece of Marabelle Blue?' Olympia asked casually.

Lucky spun around and faced her friend. 'How long have you known?' she snapped, two bright spots of red lighting up her cheeks.

Olympia yawned and stretched, 'A while. I was waiting for *you* to tell me. Jesus! I wish *my* father was a notorious criminal instead of a boring old millionaire.'

'I'm not allowed to tell anyone.'

Olympia snorted, 'Since when did that stop *you?* Not allowed indeed! Ha!'

Lucky couldn't help feeling relieved that at last someone knew who she was. She had always *wanted* to confide in Olympia, but Gino had forced her to make such a solemn promise . . .

'I'd *love* to meet him, I've only ever glimpsed pictures of him in newspapers and things but he looks marvelously rough and kind of sinister.'

'Sinister?' Lucky laughed – what a strange description for the man she could remember hugging and holding, smelling and kissing. They might have drawn apart over the years, but she would hardly call her father sinister.

'Tell me?' questioned Olympia excitedly. 'Has he really *killed* people?'

'I don't know,' replied Lucky shortly, 'everything that's written about him is exaggerated. He told me that himself. I think he's just got a reputation because of . . . ' her words trailed

off. Because of what? How the hell would *she* know? Gino
was her father. She loved him. Or hated him. Depending. The
man she read about – Gino the Ram Santangelo. Who *was* he?
*She* certainly didn't know. And she certainly didn't want to
find out.

Or did she? Maybe. Maybe not. Maybe one day. Only
maybe...

Getting engaged to Marabelle Blue had been an ace mistake
on Gino's part. The woman was a suicidal slut who craved
constant attention. He couldn't understand why he had done it.
Had he been sorry for her or what? Six months of living
together and he *still* couldn't figure it out. All he knew was he
wanted her to go. She talked marriage day and night and it was
getting difficult to stall.

When he had removed Peter Richmond from her life, he had
removed her security blanket. She needed a Peter Richmond
around. She *needed* to know that she was beautiful and desirable, and that a man would allow his future to hang in balance
while he fucked her. Gino wanted her. But Gino wasn't risking
anything by going with her. Peter Richmond's sudden defection
was a blow indeed. Marabelle couldn't handle it. The most
desirable movie star in the world took to her bed and sobbed
like a small punished child.

Gino kept in touch, talking to her maid on the phone every
day, hearing first that Miss Blue had a bad cold, then a headache, then a toothache.

The studio was not amused. She was in the middle of shooting a movie, and her sudden sickness was costing them thousands of dollars a day. After four days they sent their lawyers
and doctors to her house. The next morning she reported for
work, pale and drawn. She had a fight with the director and
walked off the set early in the afternoon. By six o'clock in the
evening she had overdosed on a variety of pills and was rushed
to the hospital where her stomach was pumped out just in time.

Gino was in Las Vegas when he heard. He flew back to Los
Angeles immediately, and went straight to the hospital.

Marabelle was like a child lying in bed. She looked about
twelve with stringy yellow hair, pale blue eyes and blotched
skin.

'What are you? Some kind of a nut?' he asked affectionately.

'I'm sorry,' she sobbed, 'I always screw things up . . .
always...'

'Hey – you wanna get engaged, kid?' It was out before he knew it. Then it didn't seem like such a bad idea. Gino Santangelo. Marabelle Blue. Every guy in America would eat his fucking heart out!

Marabelle liked the idea a lot. There was only one small problem, she already had a husband. The veteran stuntman she had married in her early Hollywood days.

'We can fix you a quickie Tijuana divorce, no big deal,' Gino had said. 'In the meantime you can move in.'

A few weeks after she took up residence in the Bel Air house, he realized he had made a big mistake. Her movie had finished shooting and she had a long break before the next one. She spent her time lying in bed, watching television, devouring movie magazines, and eating. Marabelle Blue – fantasy sex symbol – couldn't even be bothered to comb her hair.

Gino could not believe what was happening. 'You going to get up today?' he would ask.

She would smile contentedly, 'Maybe.' But more often than not she wouldn't. She would lie in bed like a sloth, and by the evening the room would smell of oranges, pickled onions, and Marabelle herself – she *never* bathed.

Gino was soon disgusted. But how to get rid of her? She wasn't just an ordinary woman, she was a movie star with accountants and agents and managers and producers and directors and hangers-on and fans.

There were times when she was forced to get up, apply a two hour make-up, mask her platinum blonde hair with a scarf because the black roots were an inch long, and bathe, because how could she go to costume fittings stinking like a pig?

What the fuck had he got himself into? He sent for Costa, 'Get her out of my house,' he told him tersely, 'I don't care what it costs. I'm going to New York, and I want *you* to tell her it's over.'

He knew he should tell her himself, but Christ! It was like dealing with a retarded child. He had tried to have a conversation with her a few nights before. Her lower lip had trembled, her eyes brimmed with tears, 'Aren't you happy, baby? Don't I make you happy?' And before he could stop her she had slid out of bed, thrown off her nightgown, held open her arms and lisped in her best Marabelle Blue movie star voice, 'Come on and fuck me, baby, that'll make you happy.'

He would sooner have thrown a fuck into a rancid cat. Fuck her? Wasn't smelling her enough?

Costa went to the house while Gino was away and told her that she must go. She took the news calmly enough, her eyes barely leaving the flickering television set.

That very same evening she slit her wrists with a razor, and barely made it through the night. The maid discovered her naked and bleeding on the bathroom floor, and immediately contacted Costa, who was able to arrange a cover up that prevented it hitting the papers.

Gino flew back to Los Angeles, furious and trapped.

Marabelle was childlike and contrite. 'I'm sorry,' she sobbed, 'I'll try harder, really I will. When we're married it'll all be great.'

'I must be gettin' old to have even thought about marryin' her,' Gino confided to Costa.

'You? Old? *Never*, my friend.'

'I'm nearly sixty,' he said ruefully, 'that ain't springtime.'

Costa slapped him on the shoulder, 'We're both getting on. The difference is I'm younger than you and yet I look years older!'

'You lead a clean life, that's what does it. I bet you've never even *looked* at another woman. You and Jen are *still* a couple of kids together.' His eyes hooded over, and Costa knew, without his saying anything, that he was thinking of Maria and how things could have been. 'How's Lucky?' he asked quickly. 'Does she write often?'

'Nope. She's a funny kid. Didn't even stay over Christmas — came home for two days, then was off to stay with that friend of hers again.'

'I guess with Marabelle in the house...'

'Christ! When I get rid of her I'm really gonna spend some time with the kids – get to know 'em. They come back from school with their loud music and funny clothes and honest to God, Costa, I feel I've got a couple of strangers in the house. I've been so busy anyway... Next summer I'll take 'em away somewhere.'

A week later he struck on the ideal way to get rid of Marabelle. 'Call up the schmuck she's married to,' he instructed Costa, 'let's see how much it'll cost.'

Dario Santangelo was five feet eleven inches tall. Straight, slim, and clear skinned. With his white blond hair, fine features, light suntan and natural clothes sense, he looked older than his years. Most boys in his grade at school were short, pimply monsters, always fighting, jerking off, discussing girls or cars or the most effective ways of farting in class.

Dario was immediately regarded as somebody different – an outsider. He didn't fit in. He was clever. The teachers liked him. The boys hated him.

His dreams of having a wonderful time at school were soon shattered. To gain favor he confessed his real identity. He was Dario Santangelo. His father was the infamous Gino. The result of his confession was that the boys hated him even more and went out of their way to make his life as miserable as possible.

He stopped trying to be liked and retreated into a shell where their sarcastic barbs and insults could not penetrate. Regularly he wrote to his sister, telling her how great school was, how terrific the other boys were.

Lucky never replied. It was as though she had forgotten all about him. For so many years it had been just the two of them – and then she had gone away to that school in Switzerland – met some stupid girl with a dumb name – and withdrawn from his life. Just like that. At Christmas she had hardly spoken to him at all.

He decided to stop writing to her. Pay her back. *He* would ignore *her.*


Lucky couldn't sleep. It was nightmare time. Flashes. A blue swimming pool. A sunny day. A raft in the pink water . . .

She sat up in bed sweating. She wished she was Olympia with a real mother and father. What difference if they were divorced? At least they were both around.

She kicked the covers off the bed and wondered who Gino would send to bring her back. She hoped it would be Marco. She wanted him to hear all about her escapade. Let him hear the gory details of her and the boy she had smuggled into the school. Let him hear about the two of them naked under the sheets, and Olympia, across the room, naked with *her* boyfriend for the night. Hah! He wouldn't think she was such a kid *then.* She was fifteen. Old enough. Experienced. Very.

Many's the night she had escaped from the confines of L'Evier and practiced the fine arts of Almost. Even naked, in bed with a boy, you could get away with Almost.

With Marco she would like to go All The Way. Yes. Olympia said she would only consider going All The Way with Marlon Brando. Lucky decided to settle for Marco.

Gino boarded a plane in New York, sat back, and lit up a fine
Monte Cristo. At first he had considered sending someone to
fetch Lucky home. Marco, Red, or even Costa. But Jennifer
had convinced him he should go himself. 'It's your duty as a
father, Gino,' she explained, 'it shows that you are genuinely
concerned.'

'I *am* genuinely concerned for crissake. When I get hold of
her I'll beat the livin' shit outta her.'

'No,' Jennifer said softly, 'you'll do no such thing. You'll
talk to her and find out why.'

'She's fifteen, Jen,' he exploded, 'what's a kid of fifteen doin'
fuckin' around?'

'What were *you* doing at fifteen?' Jennifer inquired quietly.

Gino frowned. Poor old Jen was getting past it. Only a fool
would make a remark like that. He was a man – at fifteen
he could do what the hell he liked. It was different for
girls.

Now he was on a plane and he still wasn't sure why. Whatever had to be said could be said anywhere. New York. Los
Angeles. Vegas. Anywhere.

So why was he going? Just because Jen *said* he should?

'Can I get you anything, sir?' inquired a stewardess.

He ordered a double scotch, sat back and thought about
Marabelle. At last she was gone. What a brilliant stroke coming
up with her husband. Who better to take her off his hands?

The old stunt man had come to see him. A weather beaten
face clad in cowboy clothes that had seen better days. 'How's
Mary?' he asked anxiously.

'Mary?'

'Marabelle,' Costa interjected quickly.

'Oh yeh.' Gino shook his head sadly, 'she's one sick kid –
her own worst enemy.'

The old man nodded, 'Mary has . . . problems.'

'Problems. Shit! More than problems.'

'Are you going to marry her?'

'Tell you what – I'm goin' to give her back to you with a
nice little present. I got you both a house on the top of
Mulholland Drive. It's yours – just get her out of my life by
six o'clock this evening.'

It was done. Bye bye Marabelle Blue. And good riddance. It
cost a hundred thousand but it was worth every cent.

They faced each other across the principal's office. The daughter on one side of the room, darkly defiant. The father on the other, darkly furious.

The principal was speaking, her clear concise English accent cutting across the vibrations. ' . . . So you see Mr Saint, it is not for us at L'Evier to punish such behavior. It is up to you as a parent to guide your daughter along the acceptable path of life. I do think . . .'

He tuned out and studied Lucky – seeing her properly for the first time in years.

She was tall, like her brother – *When had she grown?*

She was slim, long legged, and had the figure of a young woman. Her looks were striking. The deep olive skin, jet hair, huge broody eyes.

*She was him.* Christ! There had always been a resemblance . . . Maria had called them the terrible twins . . . But now . . . It was more than a resemblance. She *was* him. A female him.

She was also a stranger. A young woman he didn't know at all. *And it was his fault.* He had been so concerned with keeping Dario and her protected and away from him. He loved them both so much . . . And yet he was frightened of the fact that this was so. He had purposefully withdrawn. Taken his love and run. Because he knew he could not handle a repeat of what had happened . . . He was strong but not that strong.

Maria . . . Maria . . . Maria . . . Jesus! How long did it take for the pain to leave? The gut wracking ache that greeted him every morning on waking. The nightmares. The futile hope that somehow someday she would come back. He had cast a bitter bloodbath of revenge. But revenge meant nothing really.

Across the room, Lucky studied her father equally intently. Why had he come? Why hadn't he sent one of his lackeys? Quite frankly, she was amazed.

Olympia and she had observed his arrival from their window.

'Shit!' Olympia exclaimed. 'It *is* your old man. I thought you said he wouldn't come.'

'I d . . . didn't think he would,' Lucky stammered, completely thrown.

'Well, he did . . . and hmmm . . he's *veree* attractive isn't he?'

Looking at her father across the room Lucky tried to decide whether he was attractive or not. He didn't look his age – that was for sure. He dressed impeccably. The three piece dark suit, gleaming white shirt, silk tie. His black hair was thick and fashionably long around the collar of his shirt – the grey flecks suited him.

As she stared she remembered the way he smelled. *Daddy-smells*. Oh, God! Why wasn't she five again? Why couldn't she throw herself into his arms and allow him to hug and squeeze her until she screamed for mercy?

Her eyes filled with tears. Furiously she willed them to go away. How *weak* to cry. Who cared about getting slung out of school? *She* certainly didn't.

They were out of the school, sitting side by side in the back of a chauffeured limousine, and not a word had been exchanged. As the car sped towards the airport Lucky wished that Gino would say *something*. Was he very mad? She cleared her throat, thought she might say something herself, then changed her mind.

The silence persisted all the way to the airport, all the way to the plane, all the way to New York.

Once in New York they got off the plane, cleared customs, and walked out to the usual black limousine. She was surprised. She had expected to be loaded onto another plane and shipped straight off to Los Angeles and the privacy of Bel Air. Instead it was obvious she was to stay in New York – at least over-night – and that was exciting.

The limousine took them to an exclusive apartment house on Fifth Avenue overlooking Central Park. Gino strode into the lobby, and she followed. Into the elevator, up twenty-six floors. Then they entered a duplex apartment that looked like something out of a Frank Sinatra movie. All chrome furniture, fur rugs, and mirrors. So this is where Gino lived in New York. Quite a place.

'Hello, dear.'

Someone was speaking to her at last! Aunt Jennifer, looking plump and motherly in a pink two piece suit, with pearls at her ears, round her neck, and on her wrists.

Lucky felt her eyes filling with tears again – Shit! What kind of a stupid little cry baby was she turning into?

Aunt Jennifer held out her arms and she ran right into them. She was immediately enveloped in a cloud of perfume and comforting warmth.

'Come on, dear. Let's go in the bedroom and talk,' Aunt Jennifer said in a kindly tone, 'there's nothing better than a good talk about things to clear the air.'

Covertly Gino watched Jennifer take Lucky off, and heaved a sigh of relief. Women. He had been dealing with them all his life. But Lucky wasn't a woman. She was his daughter, for crissake. And by God if they had known who she truly was at that rat assed fancy school he would have had to have found the horny little foreign creep who had forced his way into her room and strung him up by his dirty foreign balls.

Lucky was a very striking girl – a fact he had only just realized. He had still thought of her as a kid, but no. She was of an age where horny little creeps – foreign or otherwise – would be after her body. She was fifteen – only a few months off sixteen. And who did she have to counsel and advise her? Certainly not him. Jennifer was the logical person to talk to her – and explain that if he, Gino, *ever* heard of a boy trying to take advantage of her again he would break his fucking head in – *and* hers.

She was Gino Santangelo's daughter, and by God she'd better learn what that meant.

How easy it was to fool the grown-ups. Aunt Jennifer was a dear sweet woman, but she also had one foot in the stone age! Her dialogue was unbelievable. Words like modesty and self-respect and honor came pouring out of her gentle unrouged mouth like so much garbage. It soon became clear to Lucky what she wished to hear. What Big Daddy wished to hear. Yes – the boy had forced his way into her bed. But she had fought him off, protected her honor, and prayed for help, which had come in the shape of the gym teacher, who had burst in and saved her ... from a fate worse than death ... Was she going too far? Aunt Jennifer didn't seem to think so.

Conveniently, the fact that she had been naked never came up. Nor the fact that Olympia had also had a boy in *her* bed.

Whitewash was easy. Aunt Jennifer's concerned and worried frown vanished in no time. 'Your father will be so relieved ... ' she murmured, 'not that he ever doubted your ... virginity.'

*Virginity! Aunt Jennifer! Really!*

'Where's Marco?' Lucky inquired artlessly.

'Marco?' Aunt Jennifer looked vague.

'Daddy's Marco,' Lucky replied impatiently, '*you* know.'

'No, I don't,' Jennifer blinked very quickly several times, 'Marco ... Marco ... Ah yes ... Bee's son.'

Bee's son. Who in hell was Bee? Lucky remained casual, 'Yeh. Where is he?'

'I don't know, dear. In Los Angeles I expect.' Funny how the girl sounded just like Gino on occasion – as well as looking exactly like him.

End of conversation. Aunt Jennifer was ready to report to Big Daddy.

'Hey – ' Lucky asked anxiously, 'am I going to be staying here?'

Jennifer looked surprised, 'Hasn't your father told you? You've been enrolled in a private boarding school in Connecticut, you'll be going there tomorrow.'

'Oh!' she was deflated. No. Gino hadn't told her. But that was just like her father wasn't it. Making *his* plans. Doing what *he* wanted. And forget about what *she* might want.

A private boarding school in Connecticut. Shit! Double shit! Treble shit! The *last* thing she needed in her life was more school.

'You'll like it there, kid. They got swimmin' an' ridin' – y'like horses don't you?' Gino felt more easy in his daughter's company now that Jen had assured him she was still his little girl.

'Horses!' Lucky made a face, 'I *hate* horses!'

'Hey,' he picked up an embroidered linen table napkin and dabbed at his mouth. Goddamn asparagus. How many times had he told his fucking dumb cook he *did* not want asparagus served at his table? 'Hate is kinda a strong way t'feel about horses. Y'know, man's best friend an' all that crap.'

'Dog is man's best friend, father,' she said, putting on her grandest tone to try and make him feel small.

'Money is man's best friend, kid,' he corrected, having the last word as usual. 'An' don't you forget it.'

How she hated him. He was short, brash, badly spoken, coarse.

How she loved him. He was handsome, macho, beautifully dressed, sexy.

She picked disconsolantly at an asparagus tip, licking the dripping butter with her tongue. 'I was thinking,' she began tentatively.

'Yeh?' He had half an eye on the television set which he insisted was kept on at all times. A hangover from Marabelle Blue perhaps?

'Well . . . I mean . . . In a couple of months I'll be sixteen. Why do I have to go back to school at all?'

'Education can teach y' a lot.' A horse racing result on the news grabbed his full attention.

'Obviously,' she muttered.

'Huh?'

'I'd sooner *not* go back to school,' she said stubbornly.

'Yeh?' he smiled lazily, 'an' what would you do all day?'

'I could do all sorts of things.'

'Like what?'

'Like be with you, come around with you, learn about all your businesses – things like that.'

That jolted him. His eyes swivelled right off the television set full power onto her. *A fifteen year old child. A girl. Was she kidding?*

'I'm not joking,' she said sharply, 'isn't that what kids are supposed to do? Take an interest in the family business?'

She had to be putting him on, making some sort of obscure teenage joke. He wished Jen and Costa had been able to stay for dinner, it would have made things much easier. 'Listen, you'll finish school, go on to college, meet some guy an' get married. Sounds good to me.'

She narrowed her deadly black Santangelo eyes and spat boldly, 'Sounds lousy to me.'

He fixed her with a killer. 'Don't develop a smart mouth, kid, you'll do as *I* say, an' one of these days you'll thank me.'

She glared at him.

'*I* never had no fancy education,' he lectured, 'foreign school an' the whole bit. *I* was out bustin' my ass to earn a buck long before I was your age – so just you remember how fortunate you are.' As he said the words he remembered Maria lying in the hospital after their daughter's birth. So pale and soft and beautiful.

He remembered the day they had named the child . . . Lucky . . . Christ! If only he could bring Maria back . . . If only . . .

'New girl . . . New girl . . . New girl.' The words were hissed wherever she went. A fine private boarding school in Connecticut – more like a fine private jail – with uniforms and guards masquerading under the title of teachers – and uptight snotty schoolgirls who Lucky hated on sight.

After two days she knew she had to get out.

After a week she knew it was a necessity.

She had a list of telephone numbers for Olympia, and on the pretext of phoning Gino she cut math and tracked her friend down.

Olympia was in Paris, staying at her father's house on the

Avenue Foch taking a Russian language course. 'I'm so bored!' she screamed down the phone. 'Can you imagine the kind of people studying Russian? Yuck!'

'I would say it's certainly better than being stuck in *this* dump,' Lucky groaned, 'I've *got to* get out. Any ideas?'

'Yes,' Olympia replied crisply, 'hop a plane and come join me. We'll pinch one of daddy's cars and zip on down to the south of France. It'll be ab . . . so . . . lutely marvie! Are you game?'

'Oh sure. And just suppose I *could* get out of here, *what* would I use for money? I have exactly twenty-three dollars and fifteen cents.'

'No problem,' said Olympia gaily; 'this place is crawling with telex machines. All I have to do is put an order through for a ticket to be left for you at Kennedy. We'll use *my* name. *You* get out of there, *I'll* do the rest. You got your passport?'

'Sure.'

They talked for a few more minutes, making plans, and by the time Lucky replaced the receiver she was as convinced as Olympia that it would be easy. And it was.

She slipped out of the school at dawn the next day, hitched a series of rides to the airport, picked up a ticket at the Pan American desk for Miss Olympia Stanislopoulos, and by noon she was on her way.

Upon arrival at Orly airport she telephoned Olympia as agreed, who squealed with delight and told her to just hang on until she was able to get there.

Three hours later they were on their way to the Cote d'Azur, Olympia driving a snappy white Mercedes convertible.

'Jes . . . sus!' she exclaimed happily, 'this is the most fun I've had all year! One thing about you Santangelo – chicken shit you ain't!'

Lucky grinned, 'It was easy!'

'Told you it would be,' Olympia swerved to avoid a scraggly cat as the powerful car zoomed through the outskirts of Paris. 'Did you leave the notes I mentioned?'

'One to Gino, one to the school. Very sincere garbage all about how I needed time to think things out, not to worry, and that I was on my way to L.A.'

'Beautiful! By the time they figure things out we'll be long gone and having a wonderful time.' She reached into her purse and popped a strong Gitane cigarette into her mouth. 'I told the housekeeper here that I had to go see my mother. The old crow hardly speaks a word of English — besides which she can't stand the sight of me and was de-light-ed to observe my departure. We're on our own babe! *Let's have incredible fun!'*

# Gino 1966

Power. It was important. Very. When you had it, it was never enough. There was always something missing. Another pinnacle to climb . . . The perfect deal . . .

Often Gino wondered why he worked so hard. Running here there and everywhere . . . Putting people in his pocket . . storing favors . . .

'You got legitimate power and clout,' his dear friend Costa had told him on countless occasions, 'why not stay on the legit end of things?' Costa held the license for the Mirage, which was making a bundle. But he was a lawyer, with a lawyer's mind. He always wanted to take the easy way. Pay the fifty dollar fine and keep your hands clean. Poor old Costa. Always fighting. Always warning. But happy enough to become a millionaire many times over.

The casino/hotel in the Bahamas — opened two years previously and called the Princess Saint, was doing pretty good too. Then there were the gambling interests in Europe. And the rest.

Yes. Business was booming. Bank accounts all over the world. Money sent out of the country, laundered, sent back clean. Invested. Put into trust funds. New businesses.

Gino enjoyed his life. It was a good life. A little aggravation here and there. Nothing he couldn't handle.

He had ridden through the bad times virtually unscathed. First the Dewey Commission in the thirties. Then the Kefauver Committee set up to investigate organized crime in 1950. More recently Bobby Kennedy in the early sixties as Attorney General determined to investigate every aspect of criminal activities — and then Valachi — a small time hood, singing his guts out about who did what to whom — with times and places and dates.

Gino honored the silence of being connected and never

opened his mouth. The authorities were unable to ever pin anything on him. He walked free. He had the luck – as Aldo put it. Aldo, not in good health now, virtually retired, helping his wife at Riccaddis.

Gino had an idea. A plan. A dream really.

He wanted to build the biggest, most luxurious, most beautiful hotel that Las Vegas had ever seen.

Since the birth of The Boy's dream child, the Mirage, Las Vegas had grown beyond recognition. Compared to some of the newer establishments such as Caesar's Palace, the Mirage was a toilet. Oh a fancy toilet – with its own faithful following – but still a toilet. Gino wanted bigger and better. He wanted to put up a hotel that would leave *his* mark on the city. Something special that would get talked about worldwide.

He had found a site and was now in the process of discussing ideas with various architects. 'It'll cost *a* fortune,' Costa had groaned, when Gino first mentioned it, 'and the headaches! My God! Building costs are going up every day and we'll have to put a syndicate together, and who's going to want to put in money and wait years to get anything back? And the tax people are breathing down your neck as it is.'

Sometimes Costa was an old woman. Gino would build the finest hotel in the world. It would be called the Magiriano. A combination of Maria and Gino. A fitting tribute to their love.

With Lucky packed off to school once more Gino did not linger in New York.

Connecticut. Good choice. Lucky would soon settle down. Recommended by Peter Richmond's wife, Betty. A horsey woman with an abundance of good breeding and charm. 'We sent Loretta there before college, she praised it to the skies,' Betty assured him, talking of her eldest daughter.

Idly Gino wondered what it would be like to sleep with a woman like Betty Richmond. He couldn't imagine it. Naked she must be bonier than a leg of lamb. He could understand why Peter Richmond had enjoyed the soft womanly curves of Marabelle Blue.

The two men had become friends of sorts. A discreet friendship of course. Nothing public. But there were so many favors Gino was able to put the Senator's way. Little favors. Big favors. Always discreet favors.

Gino enjoyed doing them. It always pleased him to cultivate friends from a different social level. Besides which, he knew quite certainly that one day Senator Peter Richmond was going to be a very important man indeed.

From New York he flew directly to Washington. He was a weekend house guest on the Richmond's Georgetown estate, the first time he had been accorded that privilege. Of course he knew why they had asked him. Betty Richmond was planning a gala evening for one of her many charities, and she wanted him to offer her the use of the Mirage for the night.

He knew, but he wasn't letting on. If Betty Richmond wanted she was going to have to ask. 'Yes,' he would say, 'Of course my dear, of course. How could I ever turn you down?'

It was all a game. But there were rules to follow. One day she would find that out.

The ping of balls hitting tennis rackets. The sharp call of the score. Gino strolled to the side of the court and watched.

Betty Richmond was playing her son, Craven, and the way Gino saw it, beating the shit out of the poor kid. It wasn't bad enough they had hung a name like Craven on him, they also had to trounce him at every sport going.

Betty waved, hardly interrupting her strong forward swing. Craven leaped to hit the shot, missed, and sprawled miserably on the ground.

'Game!' Betty sang, then, ignoring her son's fall, she skipped brightly over to greet Gino. Kiss, kiss. One sharp peck on each cheek.

She was a handsome woman. Tall and strong with piercing brown eyes and hair like muddy cotton candy. She wore tennis whites, springy gym shoes, and her hair was caught in two girlish bunches. At forty-one she just about got away with it.

'And how are we today?' she inquired. 'Ready for a game?'

Gino laughed, 'Ready for a drink.'

Betty frowned, 'Exercise, everybody needs it.'

'I know. You tell me every time I see you.'

'And every time you promise me you're going to take something up.'

'I will, I will.'

She took his arm and squeezed.

He winced. The broad didn't know her own strength.

'One quiet game,' she wheedled.

'No way. Your idea of a quiet game an' mine are two different things.'

Craven loped over then. He was twenty-one, six feet four

inches tall, and skinny as a board. Not unpleasant looking, he would certainly never win any prizes as the world's most dynamic man. 'Hi, Gino,' he said.

'Hello, kid. How's it going?'

'Rather good, actually. I've been offered this job. Nothing very special, but . . . '

'Later, Cray,' snapped Betty. 'Put the balls away before the dogs get them.'

'Yes, mother.'

Betty linked her arm through Gino's, 'I'm *so* glad you could come,' she said, walking him towards the house, 'there's something I've been meaning to ask you for simply ages . . . '

Not a woman to waste time, Mrs Richmond. She would make a wonderful First Lady. Active. Sportive. Direct. What more could America want?

Later that night Gino lay in the guest room staring unseeingly at the ceiling. His newly acquired ulcer was giving him trouble . . . Rich food . . . shouldn't touch it . . . But who could resist fresh oysters with a squeeze of lemon, succulent roast beef and newly picked raspberries steeped in a Grand Marnier sauce?

Betty Richmond gave great table. The dinner party had been nice. Just twelve people. The Richmonds, their son Craven, three couples, and two spare women for Gino to look over. What made the Richmonds think he was in the market? He, who could have his pick of Hollywood starlets, New York models, Las Vegas showgirls?

He was fifty-nine years old. Maria would have been thirty-seven. He celebrated her birthday every year with a solitary dinner at the pool of the East Hampton house. Yes. He had kept the house. Surrounded it with an electrified fence and allowed the garden to grow back to its former wilderness.

Maria was buried in the garden underneath the tree where they had first made love. The inside of the house was left exactly as it had been on the day of her death. Nobody was allowed to go there except himself. He went on her birthday. Every year. He looked forward to it. What other woman could possibly live up to Maria and her memory?

A knock on the door surprised him. He glanced at his watch. Two-thirty in the morning. 'Who is it?' he called out.

The door slid open. Betty Richmond stood in the doorway. She wore a peach satin robe tightly wrapped, her cotton candy hair was loose and frizzy around her shoulders. 'Come to tuck you in,' she said firmly. So firmly that he almost missed the slight slurring of her words.

He relaxed the grip on his gun prudently placed beneath the pillow, 'I'm very comfortable, thank you Betty,' he said slowly.

'Sure you are,' she drawled, shutting the door behind her and approaching the bed. 'But I'm not.'

Before he had time to consider what to do, she had shucked the peach robe from her broad shoulders, and stood naked in front of him. 'I would like you – *Mr* Santangelo – friend of the family – friend of the whole goddamn world. I would like you to fuck me.'

He was momentarily shocked. The woman was a whore.

He kept his voice very low, 'Put on your robe. Go back to Peter.'

'Why? Don't you want me?'

Tread carefully . . . A woman scorned . . . 'I didn't say that. But the situation . . . '

'The situation is that Peter has gone to visit a girlfriend, and is probably jamming his inadequate cock into her dumb mouth this very minute. I don't intend to sit here and wait.'

'And *I* don't intend to find myself in the middle.'

She shrugged. Muscles everywhere you looked. Small sharp breasts, wide hips, strong thighs . . .

'I thought you found me attractive . . . ' she began.

'I do,' he interrupted quickly.

She climbed into the bed without an invitation. 'I won't tell Peter,' she husked, 'I promise.'

There followed the most athletic fucking he had ever known. She squeezed his cock in and out like an elongated tennis ball. In. Out. Round. About. Up. Down. Off Center. On center. Game!

A second round. The same exquisite workout. Then she left, and he slept. And in the morning he thought maybe it had all been some wild dream.

# Lucky 1966

Olympia drove as if she was the only person on the road. Fast and furious and everyone had better get out of her way or else. The journey to the south of France took twenty-two hours, with five stops for gas, countless sandwiches and numerous cans of coke.

'You got a driver's license?' Lucky asked after one gruelling four hour session on winding country roads at breakneck speed.

'Driver's license? What's that?' Olympia replied cheerfully.

Lucky didn't question further. She sat back, closed her eyes, and hoped for the best.

Between them they had a princely ninety-four dollars, and that was being rapidly depleted every time they stopped. Tempting little pensions and hotels had to be ignored.

'When we get to Cannes we'll go to my aunt's villa,' Olympia decided, 'she *never* goes there – well only for a week in September. It's a great place – probably all locked up, but I know a way in. I used to spend the summers there with my nanny when the parents didn't have time for me.' She laughed ruefully, 'Not that anything's changed much – but it ain't easy to bundle me off now that I can talk!'

Lucky knew the feeling. Dining with Gino in his New York apartment she had had the distinct impression that he would have been a lot happier elsewhere. She made him uncomfortable, she sensed it. And he rendered her speechless – a shadow of her normal self. Why, she hadn't even had the nerve to ask him where Marco was.

She wondered what Big Daddy would do when he learned of her defection. He'd be steamed, but so what? There was nothing he could do about it except send her to another school. And she would just keep on skipping out until he got the message.

What was so wrong anyway about wanting to learn about his business? She had no intention of following the route *he* had planned for her. School. College. Marriage. No way. She wanted to be like him. Rich. Powerful. Respected. She wanted people to jump when she gave the orders – just the way they always had for him.

'We're in good shape,' sang Olympia, belting full speed down a narrow freeway hewn out of rock. 'We just passed the Saint Trop turn off – another hour and we're there.'

Lucky wiped the sweat from her brow with the back of her hand. It was only May, but the noon sun was exceptionally hot, and they were exceptionally exposed in the small open car. 'I bet we stink!' she laughed. 'Two little stinking virgins!'

Olympia said, 'Correct that statement.'

'Huh?'

'I was going to tell you when we arrived. Y'know, like lying by the pool sipping dry white wine. All that bit.'

'You mean you . . . did it?'

A smile hovered on Olympia's luscious lips. 'Yup.'

Lucky sat eagerly forward, 'When? Who? How was it?'

Olympia swerved to avoid a boulder that had rolled down onto the highway. 'Horrible!' she said, wrinkling her nose. 'Stick to Almost. It's much more fun!'

Just as Olympia had expected, her aunt's villa was shuttered and closed to all intruders. Set high in the hills above Cannes the house rested in magnificent gardens of mimosa and jasmine.

Olympia jumped from the car, opened up the huge wrought iron gates, then drove through the grounds to the door of the pale pink villa. 'Nice, ain't it?' she stated.

'Fabulous,' sighed Lucky, 'are you sure she's not going to mind us breaking in and taking over?'

'She's not going to know, is she?' replied Olympia wisely, 'and anyway – the only thing she'd mind is if Balenciaga or Balmain went out of business. She's a clothes zombie.'

They parked the car and Olympia demonstrated her own special way of gaining entry. She shinned up a peach tree, flicked the still broken catch on an upstairs shutter, forced the window, and climbed in.

Lucky waited patiently by the front door. Within minutes Olympia was using the spare set of keys inside and opening up. 'Welcome to Casa Good Times!' she giggled.

The house was decorated with a sense of French good taste and Greek money. Most of the furniture was covered with dust sheets, but some of these had slipped, leaving a glimpse of a chintz couch here, a polished leather table there. Cobwebs abounded.

'I told you she only uses the place for one week a year,' Olympia explained, 'the work force arrives a few days before she does and clears up. Do you realize we could probably stay for months? And nobody would think of looking for us here.'

Lucky hadn't exactly thought in terms of being on the missing list for months. Weeks maybe . . . But months? Gino would worry, not to mention Aunt Jennifer and Uncle Costa, and of course Dario. She *must* write to him . . . She had been meaning to but something always got in the way. 'Who did you go All The Way with?' she asked eagerly.

'A positively foul little French commie bastard. Kept on telling me my father should be shot and that I didn't know anything about life. I smuggled him into the house one night and he pinched a silver ashtray and refused to settle for Almost. It was too awful. I bled all over the leather couch in daddy's study. I can't bear to think about it. Thank God you called the next day. I certainly couldn't have gone back to that awful Russian course and faced him.'

By nightfall they had the villa as they wanted it. 'We'll just use one room,' Olympia decided, 'that way it will be easy to clear up when we leave.'

Lucky thought a large room on the ground floor next to the kitchen would be best. It had two convertible couches, a green baize card table, and three big comfortable chairs.

'Maid's quarters,' Olympia announced disparagingly.

'It'll do,' insisted Lucky.

They had two small bags between them containing make-up, and a few light clothes. It took them no time at all to unpack.

In the kitchen they found the refrigerator stacked with wine, beer, and Seven-Up. And a cupboard contained caterers boxes of potato chips, tins of nuts, and twenty-four cans of tuna fish. 'We can have a feast!' Lucky exclaimed.

'Oh, no,' said Olympia, 'not tonight. Tonight we tootle on down to town and get us a *real* meal. I fancy a great big bowl of bouillabaisse or maybe some fresh lobster with mayonnaise . . . um . . . Delicious, huh?'

'But we've got no money.'

Olympia grinned, 'Lucky, for a smart girl you can sometimes be *soooo* dumb. Who needs money when we've got our fine young bodies?'

The famous Cannes Film Festival was coming to an end, only the stragglers were left. Unlucky hustlers still trying desperately to lock up a deal. Unlucky producers with nothing on their current agenda to shoot. Unlucky would-be actresses with big tits and false smiles.

Warris Charters was in the unlucky producers category. He

had come to Cannes with what he thought were two hot properties. He had been wrong on both counts.

Hot Property number one. Pippa Sanchez. A foxy Mexican actress who had starred in a couple of very successful Spanish productions way back in the fifties. She was forty if she was a day – although she insisted she was only thirty-five – and indeed she only looked thirty-five. But Warris knew. He had done his homework on Miss Sanchez when she had first approached him in Madrid, a month earlier.

She had come after him at a party. 'Mr Charters, I saw *Kiss and Kill* – loved it. And I have a script I just know you will adore.'

*Kiss and Kill*. His one claim to fame. Made in Paris in 1959 for seven hundred thousand dollars, it had so far grossed sixteen million. A fluke. Everything else he touched turned to pure unadulterated shit.

Hot property number two. Pippa Sanchez's script. A fast paced violent period piece called *Kill Shot*. The story of a gangster in the '20s and '30s. A killer with a heart of gold.

Warris thought it was wonderful stuff. Pure hokum. But after twenty-three years in the business he felt that he knew a winner when it came his way.

'Whose script is it?' he asked her.

'Mine,' she said fiercely, '*I* commissioned it. *I* own it. I have a contract with the writer gives me everything.'

'So what do you want to do, sell it?' Warris asked carefully, frightened to show too much enthusiasm.

'No,' said Pippa firmly, 'I want to star in it. The woman's part was written for me.'

Sure. Twenty years ago, Warris thought cynically. But still . . . If she was prepared to let him go with the script for nothing . . . If he could get a deal together . . . *That* was the time to tell her that no way was she right for the part.

So they went to Cannes, Warris Charters and his two hot properties . . . And the only interest they had raised was the night they fought publicly on the Hotel Carlton Terrace.

Warris clutched a Pernod and Malvern water as he sat in the Blue Bar restaurant on the Croisette in Cannes, and thought about his bad luck. He was thirty-two years old, a former child movie star who had fled from Hollywood at the age of thirteen when his voice broke. At twenty-five he had produced *Kiss and Kill* and gone back to Hollywood as a boy wonder. Two flops later, he was wandering Europe, cruising the film capitals trying to get something together. In desperation, flat broke and on drugs, he had married a rich seventy-two-year-old Spanish widow. When she died a year after the marriage her family had thrown him out of the house without so much as a bar of soap. So much for marrying money.

Warris whistled softly between his fine white teeth. He did not believe the sight he was seeing. Two chickies, delicious little morsels of jail bait, were alighting from a sleek white Mercedes. The blonde took his eye immediately. Tits that came at you like machine guns. Golden hair literally falling down her back. And hot pants so short that chunks of delectable ass were exposed for all to see. Her companion – at first glance – was not such a looker. Tight faded jeans and a T-shirt on a tall rangy body. A jumble of jet black hair obscured her face.

Yes. It was definitely the blonde for Warris. He deserved a treat.

He watched the girls leave their car and stroll casually towards the restaurant. Instinct told him they were looking to get picked up.

As they approached his table he quickly stood and inquired in schoolboy French if they would care to join him.

The dark one replied in fluent French. Something about they were meeting someone but maybe while they were waiting . . .

Then the blonde said something in English, and Warris exclaimed, 'American? So am I.'

He ordered Pernod all round, and wondered if they had any money. He was down to his last fifty bucks, but he did have some very good grass burning a hole in his pocket. Maybe he could tempt them to buy . . .

Hmmm . . . Lucky thought. Not bad. Not good. Not my type. Which was fortunate, because he was obviously turned on by Olympia. Weren't they all? Maybe it was true about gentlemen preferring blondes. Who wanted a gentleman anyway?

She studied Warris Charters through slitted eyes as he did his number on Olympia. Slim, slight, very good looking if you liked men with corn colored hair, mean green eyes, and pale eyelashes. Frankly she didn't. She liked them dark . . . very dark . . . the darker the better. Like Marco. Gorgeous sinister Marco with the brooding dark looks and macho style.

She sipped her Pernod, decided it tasted like some sort of vile medicine, and wondered when food was going to get mentioned. Olympia seemed to have forgotten all about dishes of bouillabaisse and fresh lobster mayonnaise.

'Hey,' she said, 'I'm starved. Can we eat?'

'Yes,' agreed Olympia, 'I must say I'm a tiny bit hungry myself. What's good here, Warris?'

He glared at Lucky. Why did she have to open up her mouth about food? Who needed it? Who could afford it?

He leaned confidentially close to Olympia. 'I got something a lot better than food in my pocket,' he whispered.

Her small eyes lit up, 'You have?'

'Grade A stuff. Now why don't you and I . . .'

'And Lucky.'

'Oh, sure, and Lucky. Why don't we find us a nice quiet spot and have us a little fun?'

Olympia nearly clapped her hands with delight. Here was a man after her own heart. 'Where?'

Warris thought quickly. His small room in a back street pension was hardly suitable, he had moved from the Hotel Martinez two days earlier to save money. And the beach wasn't the greatest idea in the world. 'Where are you staying?'

Olympia hesitated for only a moment. Lucky could hardly believe it when she said, 'We have a villa in the hills. If you like we could go there.'

What happened to secrecy? 'We won't tell anyone where we're living,' Olympia had said on the drive down to town. Now, half an hour later, she was inviting Warris Charters back. Too much.

'Great!' he enthused, calling for the check. 'Let's go.'


Pippa Sanchez studied herself critically in the full length mirror. She turned this way and that until she was perfectly satisfied with what she saw. What she saw was the mirror image of what she had been seeing all her life. Perfection. Dark skin. Raven hair. A taut sexy figure. She might be forty-two years old but she was still perfection. Not a line, or a sag, or *any* tell tale sign of creeping age. So why the hell wasn't she a great big movie star?

Why? Because the schmucks that ran the movie industry had never cast her in the right parts that's why. She was always the 'other woman' the 'sexy whore' the 'vivacious dancer.' Morons! What did they know with their foot long cigars and silicone blondes?

She had stayed away from Hollywood on purpose. First,

when she had read of Jake the Boy's grisly death, she had been too frightened to return. Second, Spain was good for her. She never stopped working, she had appeared in dozens of movies, two of them very big successes. And she had married a Spanish movie star, divorced him after five turbulent years, and for the last seven been alone. By choice of course. Men ran after her like dogs in heat. She had affairs – picking and choosing. But her career came before anything else. She didn't want to end up as just a Spanish film star. So what? Who cared? She wanted *international* fame – *Hollywood* fame.

Throughout the years she had nursed her script, *Kill Shot*. As far as she was concerned it was a marvelous property, with all the makings of a big hit. Love. Humor. Pathos. Violence.

It *should* be good. It was based on Gino Santangelo's life.

The trouble was he never got to read the property. She was run out of town before it was ever completed.

Diligently she had kept up a correspondence with the writer, and in 1955, when Gino Santangelo's wife was murdered in an East Hampton swimming pool, she had ordered the ending changed to accommodate the event. What it did to the script was dynamite. Pippa was so excited that after a prudent amount of time she sent a copy to Gino with a letter reminding him about his desire to invest in the movie industry. A secretary's terse note returned the manuscript six months later, '*Mr Santangelo does not have time to read film scripts . . .*'

Over the years a lot of people had not had the time to read it. Then enter Warris Charters, and Pippa had known – just known – that he was her man.

Now Cannes. And nothing. No deal. No production. Nothing.

To say Pippa was disappointed would be putting it mildly.

She checked out her reflection once more before setting off to meet Warris. It was time the bastard returned her script. He was just another two bit hustler and she wanted him out of her life. Who needed Warris Charters to shop her precious manuscript around? *She* certainly didn't. She would raise the money herself – somehow – somewhere.

Smoking grass was nothing new to Lucky. She liked to think of herself as very experienced. In point of fact she had indulged exactly twice before. The first time with Olympia on her father's island lying out in the hot sun. Wonderful! She had fallen asleep and woken up in time to devour four portions of chocolate mousse at dinner.

The second time was with a couple of Swedish hippies bumming their way around Europe. She and Olympia had come across them on the mainland and spent one long giggly day together.

Warris Charters produced very strong, very good Acapulco Gold. He had two joints already rolled, and he shared them with the two girls generously.

The three of them lay on sunbeds out by the darkened swimming pool. Olympia lit candles and opened up some wine. 'I wish we had some music,' she complained.

Warris wasn't complaining about anything. He was thinking to himself that he had fallen into some cushy set up. The villa. The car. These two little chickies obviously had bread. He deserved a vacation. A rest before getting back to the grind of keeping body and soul together.

Olympia dragged deeply on the thin cigarette and let out a contented sigh of enjoyment before passing it on to Lucky.

Food was still on Lucky's mind, but she entered into the spirit of the occasion, taking the cigarette, inhaling the magic weed, languorously allowing the effect to take over her body.

Ten minutes of silence while they indulged, passing the two joints back and forth, Lucky giggling as the sound of the chirping crickets reached a crescendo. 'Wow . . . very noisy little animals . . . ' she slurred, 'veree noisy indeed!'

Her comment induced hysterical laughter from Olympia and Warris. She smiled, feeling like the world's greatest wit.

'Let's swim,' suggested Olympia, standing up and stripping off her clothes. She turned to Warris allowing him to inspect her ripe and luscious curves. He was literally ripping off his trousers, then his shorts. Naked, his erection stood out like an eight inch flagpole.

'Ummmm . . . ' murmured Olympia, and as he went to grab her she jumped into the pool.

By the time Lucky was undressed both Olympia and Warris were cavorting under water. Suddenly Lucky didn't feel like swimming any more. The hell with swimming. She was hungry.

Nude, she wandered into the house, found a can and opened it. Hungrily she devoured the oily chunks of tuna. It was delicious.

She felt very tired then. A hollow weariness born from nights of no sleep at all.

Outside Olympia and Warris were still at play, she could hear their screams and shouts. They wouldn't miss her if she just crawled ever so quietly into bed . . . ever so quietly . . .

Warris was not to be found in any of his usual hangouts. Pippa visited the Blue Bar, the Carlton Terrace, and the Martinez Bar, more than once. Finally, when it was late enough, she gave up, allowing a chirpy English dress manufacturer to have the pleasure of buying her a bottle of champagne. The best of course. Pippa was only interested in the best.

Later she allowed the man to make love to her. He wasn't bad, full of enthusiasm. But he wasn't Jake the Boy. Nobody was The Boy . . .

The insistent dive bombing of a mosquito forced Lucky to open one eye. It took moments before she acclimatized herself to her surroundings. Then she remembered.

She sat up quickly and checked out the other bed in the room. No Olympia. No Warris.

She crawled out of bed, put on a bikini and an old shirt, and found Olympia in the master bedroom, blondely nude, sprawled and wanton. Warris slept beside her on his stomach, giving Lucky ample opportunity to study his small firmly muscled ass. He did have a nice ass.

For the next three days Warris was a fixture. Olympia was in love and had no intention of letting him go.

Watching them together Lucky was jealous, but there was nothing she could do, so she just lay by the pool concentrating on her suntan and wondering if Gino was looking for her yet.

There was a tiny village near the house, and there they were able to buy hot rolls of French bread, freshly sliced ham and cheese, and an abundance of fruit.

'I could live here forever!' Olympia sighed dreamily.

'Well, *I'm* getting bored.'

'So take the car and go have fun.'

'You know I can't drive,' Lucky said testily.

'Teach her to drive, honeybuns,' Olympia requested of her lover.

Warris jumped to attention. After three days in her company he had learned she was one very rich little girl indeed. She was a Stanislopoulos, and that name was as good as Onassis. She was also one very hot little girl indeed. And after he had conquered her initial revulsion about fucking, she took to bouncing about on the bed like an Indian takes to curry. He was teaching her everything he knew, and she was lapping it up in every way. Of course having the friend around was a drag. He didn't like her and she didn't like him. Teaching her to drive would be a perfect way to get rid of her.

Lucky mastered the mechanics of driving a car within the first half hour, then, full of confidence, she dropped Warris back at the villa and set off on her own for the day. She decided she *loved* driving. The feel of all that power under the accelerator was a turn on. She took off in the direction of Italy, went as far as San Remo, parked the car and wandered around for a few hours, then drove back to the villa along the curving coastal route. Exhilarated, she arrived home at midnight.

Olympia and Warris were dancing a rhumba to music from the radio. Olympia wore her bikini bottom and very high heels. Warris was in slacks and a shirt. They danced very seriously together, Olympia's large bosoms doing a special jiggle all their own. They were both stoned as usual, Warris having rolled the last of his Acupulco Gold into one final joint.

'You're back,' Olympia giggled. 'We thought we'd doll ourselves up and trip on down to the casino. Do you want to come?'

'You bet,' Lucky said quickly.

'So let's get changed. I'm sure auntie has *something* in her closet that will do.'

Pippa Sanchez was in a boiling fury. For Warris Charters to run out on her was one thing. But for him to run out with six xerox copies of her beloved script! Forget it! This was the kind of behavior men got their balls sliced off for!

Pippa refused to leave Cannes until she found him. The sneak was hiding out, probably waiting for her to go so that he would have her precious property all to himself. Once a bum always a bum. She should have known. She should have *smelled* him. The Boy had taught her that – 'Always sniff out trouble when it's comin' at ya . . . that way your nose'll always look after ya.' So how come his nose hadn't looked after him?

Goddamn it. Pippa put on her tightest sexiest red dress and ventured out on the town with a Bolivian jeweler she had met. If he was as rich as he *seemed* to be maybe he would be interested in making an investment in her movie.

Dressed up to the nines in Olympia's aunt's clothes, they

roared into Cannes, Warris at the wheel of the white Mercedes.

'I've got to change,' he said, 'I'll drop you two at the Blue Bar and be back in ten minutes.'

'Why can't we come with you?' Olympia pouted.

'Because . . . it's better this way.' He had no intention of letting them see the dump he was staying in. Besides, what he wanted to do was check out, and load his two Gucci suitcases into the back of the car. Might as well take advantage of the situation he had found himself in.

'OK,' Olympia sulked, 'but if I meet a better looking dude don't expect me to hang around.'

'Ten minutes. Watch her, Lucky.'

She smiled thinly. Watch her indeed! She'd personally grab the first half-decent looking guy that came along and force Olympia's tongue down his throat. Anything to get rid of this jerk, who she hated more and more each day.

He settled them at a table, ordered drinks and took off.

'Hey – ' said Lucky, 'you noticed that guy over there. He hasn't taken his eyes off you.'

Olympia preened, 'Where?' she asked quickly, sticking her chest out.

# Gino 1966

Gino lay on the king sized bed in the bedroom of his suite at the Mirage and watched the girl dress. She was very thin. Long legs, bony shoulders, a minuscule waist. He couldn't understand why he had picked her. Not his normal type at all.

She turned to face him as she pulled her halter topped dress over her small breasts. 'That was wonderful,' she breathed, 'Will I see you again?'

He remembered why he had picked her. A certain something in the blue eyes . . . wistful . . . innocent . . . Not so innocent when he got her into bed. She had crawled all over him like a plague of ants, her hot tongue licking everything in sight.

Women. They had changed. He was no prude but their

sexual habits were becoming ridiculous! A demanding woman was guaranteed to kill even the most vibrant of hard-ons.

'Here,' he said, handing her an envelope from his bedside drawer, 'this is for you. Buy yourself a little something.'

'Oh!' she took the envelope, weighed it delicately from hand to hand. 'You don't have to.'

I know I don't have to, he thought. I want to – gets you out of my hair – no complications. 'Take it – enjoy,' he said.

Now she was dressed and standing at the edge of the bed expectantly. He wanted her out. 'So . . . ' he began, 'the night is young an' you're a very pretty girl. I'll call the maitre de and have him hold you a table for Tiny Martino's late show, compliments of the house. You'll love it. Take a friend.'

Once she was out he got up, did a few push ups, took a shower, and dressed carefully. Then he buzzed for Marco on his personal intercom system.

Marco appeared within three minutes flat. One of his best qualities was always being around when you needed him. That and loyalty that you couldn't buy. Marco was family. It meant a lot to Gino. Recently he had promoted him to manager of the Mirage. He wanted him to be the best. When the time came he wanted Marco to run the Magiriano.

'What's happenin'?' Gino asked.

Marco shrugged. 'Everything. Tiny Martino lost his salary on the roulette wheel. That Jap businessman is into us for seventy-three thou. I sent four hookers up to the judge's suite just like you requested. A normal night.'

Gino chuckled. Out of his varied business interests the Mirage was his favorite. He was at his happiest in the air conditioned comfort of Las Vegas.

'Has Senator Richmond's wife checked in yet?'

'Not yet. The suite's all ready. Four dozen yellow roses. The best tennis pro is keeping himself available all day tomorrow.'

'Good, good.' Gino wanted to make certain Betty Richmond was well looked after. He had been entertained royally at her Georgetown estate, and he wanted to be sure to repay the compliment. Whether he wanted to sleep with her or not was another matter. Physically she did not turn him on. But in bed, with those strong thighs wrapped around him, that pulsating cunt . . . Jeeze! He was getting an erection just thinking about her! And so soon after little Miss what-was-her-name. Not bad at all for a man who would be sixty in two weeks' time.

Betty Richmond was afforded the royal treatment upon her arrival. Her son, Craven, hovered around superfluously.

They entered their suite preceded by fifteen pieces of luggage.

'Hmmm . . . ' she snorted, striding around throwing open windows, 'this is the most tasteless decor I've ever seen.'

'Yes, mother,' agreed Craven, 'tasteless.'

'Vulgar.'

'Absolutely.'

'Gold taps indeed!'

'Awful!'

'Well . . . what can you expect?'

'She's here,' announced Marco.

Gino nodded. A day late but as long as she'd arrived. 'What's she doing?'

'Playing tennis. Killing the pro.'

'You're kidding!'

'She has a stroke like Little Mo!'

Gino laughed, 'Send her a message. Tell her I'd like to dine with her. She can be here at six-thirty.'

Later Marco returned to say that Mrs Richmond thanked him for his kind invitation, but she already had a dinner engagement, and could she meet with him later – say ten o'clock.

Gino was furious. *She* was coming to ask *him* a favor and he was getting the run around. Unbelievable!

'Tell Mrs Richmond ten o'clock is not convenient,' he said tightly, 'eleven o'clock if she wants to make it.'

Marco carried the message, returned with the news that Mrs Richmond said eleven o'clock would be just perfect – *her* suite.

'Fine,' snapped Gino. '*My* suite.'

Betty Richmond turned up at five past twelve looking athletic and suntanned in a blue dress, her cotton candy hair pulled back and tied with blue ribbon. 'I'm so sorry,' she gushed, 'but this is such a fascinating place – you just don't know *who* you're going to bump into.'

'Yeh,' he glanced pointedly at his watch.

'I do hope I haven't kept you up,' she said anxiously. 'Is it too late to discuss the gala evening? Would you rather meet at breakfast?'

'Now's fine,' he snapped. 'I spoke to Tiny Martino – and he says that maybe – just maybe mind you – he'll do it.'

'Oh he will,' she said airily.

'I said he *might*.'

'No, no. It's all right. He definitely will. I met him tonight – charming man – he gave me a very firm yes.'

Gino frowned. Jesus! What did she need him for? She could organize the whole thing herself. He wished that he had never promised her a goddamn gala evening for her goddamn charity in the first place.

At seven o'clock the next morning Gino was awakened by his telephone. The personal line, the one that was only used by a few close associates in an emergency. It was Costa calling from New York. 'Gino. I have bad news.'

'What?'

'It's Lucky. She's run away from school.'

'Oh *Christ*!'

'She left a couple of notes.'

'Saying?'

'Something about working things out, not to worry, she's heading for L.A.'

'Jesus Christ!'

'I've told the school to keep it quiet. They're cooperating.'

'That's something.'

'What do you want me to do?'

'I don't know . . . Jesus! That *stupid* girl.' He thought for a moment. 'Look – don't do anything. Just hang on – I'll get a flight in this morning – we'll talk about it when I get there.'

'I think that would be best.'

'See you later.' He hung up the phone and sighed. Lucky. Dumb kid. She needed her ass paddled, and he was going to have to do it. When he found her, that is.

# Lucky 1966

Two extremely polite Frenchmen dressed impeccably in dinner jackets and dark trousers argued quietly and firmly with a harassed Warris Charters.

'But I'm telling you – they're *both* over twenty-one,' he insisted.

'I'm sure they are, sir,' agreed one of the men pleasantly, 'but we have our rules, and unless the ladies can produce their passports . . . ' he gave a gallic shrug.

Lucky wanted to giggle. The whole scene was so ludicrous really. She and Olympia all dolled up, an angry red faced Warris, several amused onlookers.

'Oh God!' Olympia said loudly. 'This is ridiculous. Let's go.'

'No,' said Warris stubbornly, 'rules are made to be broken.'

'Not in *this* casino, sir,' said one of the men implacably.

'Fucking frogs!' screamed Warris suddenly. 'What the fuck do you know about *anything*?'

Even as he lost control one of the men was gesturing for a doorman or two to remove the obstruction. They moved in on him, a firm hand under each elbow. This really infuriated him, and he began to scream insults even louder.

'Wonderful!' sighed Lucky, rolling her eyes at Olympia. 'Who's your friend?'

Olympia tossed her long blonde curls imperiously.

At this point a fiery dark haired woman in the tightest most revealing dress Lucky had ever seen, alighted from a white Rolls Royce accompanied by a tall grey haired man. 'Warris!' she yelled wildly. 'You sneaky crapshooter! Where have you been?'

Warris stopped struggling and screaming. He shook himself free and adjusted his clothing. 'Pippa ː ː ː ³ he mumbled sheepishly, 'I was going to call you.'

'Sure,' she replied sarcastically, 'and the President took a shit in Washington Square!'

Olympia stepped into the fray. She wound herself around a somewhat shaken Warris and said in a proprietary fashion, 'Who is this woman, darling?'

Pippa squashed her with a look, 'I didn't know juvenile pussy was your bag,' she said derisively to Warris, 'wassamatter – all the big girls found out you're a crap artist?'

'Pippa, I'd like you to meet Olympia Stanislopoulos,' he said stiffly, 'of *the* Stanislopoulos family.'

'Oh!'

'And Olympia sweets, I'd like *you* to meet Pippa Sanchez – a business associate of mine.'

What am *I* – chopped liver? thought Lucky. But she couldn't help enjoying the scene, it was certainly a kick to see Warris firmly entrenched in the shit.

'So,' boomed the grey haired man, speaking for the first time, 'these are friends of yours, Pippa, dear. Why don't we all go and have a drink?'

The Vieux Colombier was a large cavern like place situated along the coast at Juan Les Pins with live jazz groups and a spacious dance floor. Lucky loved it immediately, it was about time *she* had some fun, and judging from the guys around the place tonight was her night. While Olympia and Warris had been fucking their brains out, she hadn't even indulged in Almost. The time had come to even up the score.

Pippa and Warris were engaged in earnest conversation. Olympia was batting her eyelashes at Pippa's Bolivian friend. So Lucky sauntered through the dimly lit club to the ladies room, and got herself accosted by a nice looking boy in tight jeans.

'You American?' he asked, grinning.

She grinned back and nodded.

'Dance?' he gestured towards the dance floor filled with wildly gyrating couples,

'*Love* to,'

Something was bothering Pippa. As she spoke earnestly to Warris about her precious script *something* was nagging in her head.

' . . . If I can just get to her old man,' he was saying, 'do you *realize* how much money the Stanislopoulos family has?'

'Who is the other girl?' Pippa asked. 'The dark one, Olympia's friend.'

'Oh, don't take any notice of her, she's a pain,'

'Who is she?'

'Some kid , , , They were at school together or something. Why?'

Pippa shook her head, 'I don't know, she looks familiar . , , '

'Sure – like a million other beatniks.'

Pippa nodded. 'When do you think you will meet Olympia's father?' she asked.

'Soon. I have to play it carefully, can't push anything.'

Pippa watched the dark haired girl jive past on the dance floor. What *was* it about her . . ,

'Are you screwing this Olympia?' she asked. Her attachment to Warris had always been strictly business except for one drunken night the second evening of the festival when they had both thought they had a deal going. The fucking had been good, the deal had fallen through. Neither of them had felt inclined to try again.

'No, no,' Warris replied sarcastically, 'I'm just up at the villa taking care of the house plants. *Of course* I'm fucking her.'

'She's very young. What makes you think her father is going to like the idea?'

'By the time I meet daddy he'll have no choice. Maybe I'll marry her. How does *that* hit you?'

Pippa smiled and murmured, 'Shh . . .'

Olympia was returning to the table with the Bolivian jeweler who had taken her on a tour of the place. 'Where's Lucky?' she sighed, fanning herself with the back of her hand.

'Who?' questioned Pippa sharply.

'Lucky. My friend.'

Of course! It had to be! It was! She had *known* the face was familiar. Gino's face. Gino Santangelo! And the girl must be his daughter – *had* to be. How many girls called Lucky were there in the world? Pippa could remember quite clearly taking the solid gold brush and comb set The Boy had bought for Gino's baby, and having it inscribed '*Lucky Santangelo*'. Fifteen years ago, Jesus God! Warris thought *he* was falling into something with the Stanislopoulos girl. Little did he know . . .

Pippa beamed, 'Warris,' she said brightly, 'let's celebrate. Order champagne. I think tonight is going to turn out to be a very important night for *all* of us.'

# Gino 1966

His daughter had been missing four days and Gino was burning up with fury. He had visited the school she had absconded from, read her notes, threatened the headmistress, returned to New York, and waited for news.

In the house in Bel Air, his people waited for Lucky to turn up. When it became obvious that she wasn't going to, Gino started his own detective work. He went back to the school with Costa, and questioned the girls in her class, finding out nothing. The headmistress was furious, she told him quite frostily that she thought they should call in the police. It took Costa two hours to convince her this wouldn't help matters, plus a healthy donation towards the school's new building fund.

Gino then tracked down the mother of Lucky's best friend, Olympia, who assured him that her daughter was studiously studying Russian in Paris, and knew nothing about Lucky's disappearance.

Next he called up Dario at his school in the hope that his son might know something, but he drew another blank.

Dario replaced the receiver after his father's call and decided that it was incredibly exciting news. Why hadn't he thought about running away? He *hated* school, it just got worse every day. If only he knew where Lucky had run to he could join her. But no . . . he didn't have any idea where she'd gone. Sulkily he returned to class.

His art teacher, Eric, said, 'Everything all right Dario?'

'Yes, sir.'

'You sure?'

'Yes, sir.'

One of the boys sitting behind him mimicked 'Yes, sir,' and snickered.

Dario ignored him. He had developed a healthy disregard for anything the other boys did. He found that a cold un-emotional attitude towards everything gave him a very slight edge. It was better than reacting and getting into fights all the time.

The art teacher approached his desk and surveyed his charcoal sketch of a swimmer. 'Hmmm . . . ' he murmured, 'not bad, Dario, not bad at all. Stay behind after class I want to talk to you.'

'Yes, sir.'

Gino imagined all sorts of things. He imagined Lucky hitching her way to California in her tight faded jeans and clinging T-shirt. He imagined some clown of a truck driver giving her a lift. He imagined the struggle, the rape, his daughter's lifeless body being thrown from the truck into a ditch.

She was only fifteen-years-old. A baby. If any bastard had so much as *touched* her . . .

Jennifer and Costa stayed with him constantly. Jennifer fussing around, making sure that he ate, reassuring him of Lucky's safety. 'She's like you, Gino, dear. She can look after herself.'

'She's a *child*, Jen.'

'Oh no. She's all grown up. I can *feel* that she's all right. I *know* it.'

Gino frowned, and decided that he should speak to Olympia Stanislopoulos himself, make sure that she hadn't heard from Lucky.

Olympia's mother had departed on a cruise, but a secretary was able to give him the girl's number in Paris. He tried it for a day, getting no reply. Finally he tracked her father down in Athens. He was not pleased about being interrupted in the middle of a meeting. 'Olympia is most definitely in Paris taking a language course,' he said shortly, 'I'll contact her and have her phone you.'

'Thank you,' Gino said, equally brusque, 'the sooner the better.'

Eric, the art teacher, said, 'I've noticed that you don't seem to fit in here. You're very . . . different.'

'Yes I am,' Dario replied defiantly, 'I'm not like those other little creeps.'

'I know. I can see that. You're more . . . sensitive . . . intelligent.'

Dario had never thought of himself as either sensitive *or* intelligent. 'Yes,' he agreed quickly, 'I guess I am.'

'I knew that,' Eric said quietly, 'I sensed it the first time I saw you.'

Suddenly he felt uncomfortable. Eric was staring at him in a very strange way.

'You're like me,' Eric continued, 'I was . . . different at school. The boys hated me because I liked art . . . good books . . . the finer things in life . . .'

'Really?' he tried to look interested, but he was beginning to get bored with Eric and the story of his life.

'Perhaps you'd like to spend a weekend at my place,' Eric said casually, 'I've noticed you never go home on weekends. We could have a good time, you'd enjoy yourself.'

Dario considered the possibility of enjoying himself with Eric. The man was twenty-four if he was a day. He had sandy colored hair, a stocky build and watery grey eyes. 'What'd we do?' he asked carefully.

'Whatever you'd like to do. Go to the movies, bowling, swimming, eat plenty of good food. What do you say?'

'Yeah,' he said slowly, 'why not?'

Eric smiled, 'Why not indeed? Only it must be our secret. We mustn't tell a soul. School rules and all that . . .'

Dario grinned. Suddenly he felt important and liked. It wasn't every boy in the class Eric was inviting for the weekend.

It took Dimitri Stanislopoulos exactly twenty-four hours to call Gino back. 'We have a problem,' he said tightly. Suddenly it was we:

'Yes?'

'Olympia has left Paris, taken one of my cars and gone.'

'Ahhh . . . ' Gino sighed, feeling immediately better. At least he knew Lucky was with a friend.

'She's a very strong minded girl,' Dimitri said wearily, 'uncontrollable I suppose you could say. Also easily influenced. I expect together with your daughter Lucky . . .'

'Have you any idea where they could be?'

'No idea at all. But I have put an immediate report out on the car . . . It shouldn't take long to find them.'

'I hope not. If your wife hadn't been so insistent about Olympia being in Paris . . .'

'My wife believes what she's told. I wish that you had contacted me sooner.'

'Yeh. So do I.'

They finished the conversation, agreeing to meet in Paris the following day.

'You'd better come with me, Jen,' Gino pleaded, 'I can't handle her alone.'

'You *must*,' Jennifer replied, 'she's your daughter. You *have to* develop a closeness before it's too late. *Now's* the time. Talk to her, get to know her, find out *why* she did it.'

He would try. After he had beaten the living shit out of her, he would try.

# Lucky 1966

How had Pippa Sanchez become a part of their lives? The previous evening she had dumped the Bolivian jeweler, collected a small bag from her hotel, and squeezed in the Mercedes all the way to the villa. 'You don't mind?' she had said sweetly to Olympia. 'Just until we finish our business.'

'Sure,' Olympia agreed.

Now it was morning and Lucky stood in the kitchen glaring at her friend. 'Whyn't we take off?' she demanded, 'this whole scene is becoming boring. I thought we were going to have fun.'

'I *am* having fun,' Olympia insisted, 'Warris is a terrific guy.'

'Yeh. So how about the Mexican firecracker? How come *she's* moved in?'

'Only for a couple of nights. They have business together.'

'Well *I* don't like her. She keeps on giving me the creepy fish eye.'

'Maybe she wants you!' Olympia giggled.

'Maybe you can shove this whole gig up your ass!' Lucky stormed, '*I'm* taking off.'

'With what? You've got no car, no bread, no nothin'!'

'That's right, remind me.'

'Aw, c'mon – what *you* need is a fella. Tonight we'll find you one.'

'I found one last night but what happened? No room in the car to bring him here – according to darling Warris.'

'Tonight'll be different,' Olympia assured, 'find one you like and *I promise* we'll get him here – somehow.'

Lucky was placated, 'OK.'

The two girls walked out into the sunlight. Warris was sprawled beside the pool, next to him Pippa displayed her beautifully oiled body on a sunbed. 'Very nice house,' she purred, 'how long have you girls lived here?'

'A while.' Lucky replied cagily.

'No school?' Pippa inquired.

'We're finished with school,' Olympia said, plumping herself down on Warris' stomach.

'You're heavy!' he objected.

'You didn't say that last night,' she giggled.

'Things were harder then!'

Lucky dived into the pool, a fast racing dive which took her three quarters of the way through the water. A lizard scurried up the side of the pool, its scaly body glinting in the hot sun.

'Ooch!' Olympia squealed, 'I *hate* creepy crawlies!'

'They can't hurt you,' Pippa explained.

'No, only frighten the shit out of you,' Warris laughed.

'*I* know,' Pippa said, 'how about having a party here tonight?'

'A party?' Olympia asked, 'but we don't know anybody.'

'I do,' Pippa husked, '*I* know everyone. All the fun people.'

Olympia's eyes lit up, 'Do you?'

'Of course,' I even know a group of musicians who'll play for nothing – just drink and food and a good time.'

'Sounds great, but where do we get the drink and food? I'm a bit pushed for cash at the moment . . . waiting for my allowance to come through . . .'

Pippa leapt up, 'Don't worry about a thing. Leave everything to me. Can I take the car?'

'Certainly. But . . .'

Pippa grinned, 'I'll arrange the party. You lie in the sun.' She slipped an orange beach dress over her bikini, 'See you later.'

'Wow,' Olympia giggled, 'she sure is one terrific lady.'

Warris pulled at the top of her bikini and sprung a breast free, 'So are you my sweet, so are you.'

Olympia's eyes skimmed appreciatively over his brief white bikini pants, 'Show me what you got for a little girl.'

He stood up and took her by the hand, 'I'll do better than that, I'll show you what I got for a big girl. Come inside with me.'

Lucky was oblivious to everything. She was swimming lengths, churning up and down the pool like an automaton.

Pippa drove the white Mercedes down the winding narrow road fast. She hummed softly to herself. Life was good. It had not taken her long to get her beady eyes on things. The girls were runaways. Any idiot could tell that. No money. No plans. A house that obviously wasn't theirs half covered in dust sheets. Yes. They were runaways all right. From school . . . from home . . . *Someone* must be missing them.

Gino Santangelo. The very thought of his name brought a shiver to her spine. Was he looking for his daughter? It was a probability. And if he was . . . Who better than Pippa Sanchez to tell him where he could find her?

He would be grateful. Perhaps grateful enough to finance her movie . . .

She smiled, felt briefly sorry for Warris, then decided that not confiding in him was the only way. After all, he was more interested in catching the Stanislopoulos girl, and who could blame him?

Pippa's smile broadened. How easy it was. *I'll arrange a party, can I take your car?* Now they were all trapped up at the villa with no means of escape. And instead of arranging a party she was going to arrange for Gino Santangelo to fly in from wherever he was and she was going to lead him – personally – to Lucky. It couldn't be more perfect!

She turned the volume up on the car radio and put her foot down hard on the accelerator.

Now what actor would be right for the Gino Santangelo role? Marlon Brando? Tony Curtis? Paul Newman? How great to have power over casting. Yes. Marlon would be perfect, just the right blend of sexiness and toughness. Just the right . . .

The corner took her by surprise, it was a hairpin bend and she was driving much too fast. The English tourists in a lumbering hired Citroën were too far in the middle of the road anyway.

The Mercedes and the Citroën met head on. The thundering crash could be heard for miles.

Pippa Sanchez died instantly. Her dreams intact.


# Gino 1966


Gino flew into Paris alone. Reports from Vegas were that Mrs Peter Richmond was making unprecedented demands. She had departed Las Vegas the day after Gino, leaving her son Craven there to implement her instructions about the forthcoming gala evening. Her phone calls from Washington were hourly.

'It's crazy,' Marco told him on the telephone, 'she wants half the guests to have comp suites for the night. She wants special food, flower arrangements like you wouldn't believe! The evening will cost us a fuckin' fortune!'

There was nothing Gino could do, he had agreed to give her the evening, he couldn't back down on his word. She had taken him for a fool though, one fuck of that bony body was supposed to be payment enough. One fuck, as though she was measuring how much the evening was worth.

'Do whatever she wants,' he said, 'I'll get back as soon as I can.'

Mrs Richmond would learn the hard way. Gino Santangelo was nobody's fool. She would have her gala charity evening, just the way she wanted it. One day she would pay. When *he* was ready for her to do so.

'Any news about Lucky?' Marco asked.

'I just got here. I'll let you know.'

'Cigarette, Dario?' inquired Eric.

'Thanks.' He took the cigarette, lit up, and lay back on the sunbed that took up most of Eric's cramped terrace.

The small apartment was a few miles from the school in San Diego. Dario had arrived on Saturday morning by bus. Eric had met him at the bus station. They had spent a pleasant enough day driving around the town, shopping, browsing the book stores and a few art galleries. Now that they were back in the apartment Eric hovered like an attentive blowfly.

Dario had to admit that he was enjoying all the attention. At school, any attention that came his way was hostile. At home, if Lucky was around, *she* took center stage.

'There's a rumor at school that your father is Gino Santangelo,' Eric said, clearing his throat nervously. 'Is that true?'

He nodded.

'I don't think . . . well I mean I shouldn't think that you even *would* . . . but . . . I . . . er . . .'

He grinned. He felt a lot older than his age. He felt knowledgeable and worldly, 'It's OK Eric. I'm not going to tell him that I'm here.'

Eric breathed an audible sigh of relief, 'It's just that . . . '

'You don't have to explain.'

Eric clutched his hand, their first physical contact. Dario allowed his hand to be held. His heart was beating fast. He *knew* what Eric wanted. He wasn't *that* naïve. Whether he was going to let him do anything was another matter.

'You're such a beautiful boy,' Eric gasped, his voice throbbing with emotion. 'I noticed you the first day you came to my class. I saw you and I thought – that boy is different – that boy has known much pain and sadness. Was I right?'

Their hands were hot and sticky together, yet Dario had no desire to pull his away. He felt a sexual stirring – the same kind of stirring he had felt when seeing Marabelle Blue in bed with his father – sneakily watching Lucky undress – viewing the other boys in the shower. 'Yes,' he said, enjoying a romantic vision of himself as someone who had experienced great pain and sadness. Well it was true wasn't it? His life *had* been very lonely . . .

Eric's mouth was descending upon his. He felt no revulsion, only a strange blank curiosity.

'I think I could love a boy like you . . .' Eric was saying, his words muffled and blurred.

Dario surrendered himself to the kiss. Surrendered himself to what followed . . .

For the first time in his life he felt loved, wanted and totally secure.

Dimitri Stanislopoulos was a large beak nosed man with a mass of thick white hair, wild roaming eyes, and an annoying habit of prefacing each sentence with a terse – '*I* think . . . '

After fifteen minutes in his company Gino was thoroughly fed up with what *he* thought.

Together they visited the housekeeper at Dimitri's Paris residence. The elderly woman was surly and unintelligible, her slight mastery of the English language deserting her totally when faced with the two men.

Dimitri spoke to her in rapid French, his arms flailing around like windmills.

She replied in a gruff resentful mumble.

'Stupid cow!' Dimitri complained. 'She's nervous I'm going to blame her – boot her out.'

'What did she say?' Gino asked impatiently.

'Nothing we didn't already know. Olympia took the car last Monday – said she was going to visit her mother.'

'That's five days ago. They could be anywhere by now.'

'I think you will find the firm of detectives I have employed will trace the car today. They are the finest. And let us face it – two pretty young girls in an expensive automobile should not be hard to trace.'

At three o'clock in the afternoon Dimitri Stanislopoulos' firm of investigators had news of the car. It was a wreck, a write off. It had been involved in a serious accident on a narrow road above Cannes. In the car was the body of an unidentified female.

Gino and Dimitri were on a plane to the South of France within the hour.

# Lucky 1966

Clouds were spreading a pattern in the sky, and the sun was eclipsed. A biting wind began to blow.

'Mistral,' Warris said crossly, 'goddamn it! It'll ruin the party.'

'Why?' pouted Olympia.

'Because my sweet, a great big storm is going to blow up, and who is going to want to come riding up into the hills?'

'Oh, what a shame! I was looking forward to a *fantastic* party, weren't you, Lucky? *Lucky?*'

'What?' she jumped. She had been thinking of Bel Air. The huge cool house with the immaculate gardens. Her room. Big and white with a television, her collection of records, books, and all her old toys. 'I think I might go home,' she said casually.

'Whaaat?' Olympia's eyes widened.

'Yeh, really.'

'*Come on.* Why?'

She shrugged vaguely, 'I don't know . . . I just kind of feel like it.'

Olympia's piggy eyes narrowed, 'But you can't do that.'

'Why not?'

'Because you can't, that's why. We started off this adventure together and that's the way we have to finish it – together.'

Lucky scowled, 'Not necessarily.'

'But this morning you promised me you'd stay.'

'I didn't promise. I *want* to go.'

'You're so selfish,' Olympia pouted.

Ha! *She* was selfish. Ha! All morning Olympia had been closeted in the bedroom with Warris. It was two in the afternoon, and they had only just emerged. She was fed up with feeling like the odd one out. 'Listen,' she said, 'I'm going, there's nothing you can do about it.'

Warris watched the two girls, and as he watched he realized for the first time how very striking Lucky was. He had never really looked at her before, but beneath the tumble of jet hair and deep olive skin was true wild gypsy beauty. To think he had been living in the house with her all this time and never really *seen* her. She was far more attractive than Olympia, who was really quite ordinary if you took away the tits and the long blonde hair. There was nothing ordinary about Lucky.

'You're giving me a headache, I'm going to take a nap,'

Olympia snapped at last. 'Talk some sense into her, Warris, explain that if she goes back she'll just get shoved into another dumb school. *Tell her!*' She flounced off to the main bedroom and slammed the door.

Warris and Lucky sat in the storm darkened living-room silently staring at each other.

'Why'd you want to go?' he asked at last.

'I don't have a reason,' she replied tardily, 'and *she's* not keeping me here.'

Warris stood up and stretched, 'When Pippa gets back I'll drive you to the airport if you want. How are you going to pay for your ticket?'

'I'll figure that out when I get there,' she paused and eyed him suspiciously, 'will you really take me?'

He moved slowly towards her, 'Sure. Why not.'

She was sprawled on the floor, her long tan legs stretched out in front of her. She had on shorts and a knotted denim skirt.

He stood over her and held out his hands, 'Get up, we'll figure out a way to pay for your ticket.'

She took his hands and he pulled her to her feet. 'How?'

'I don't know, I'll have to think about it.'

He did not leave go of her hands, he moved very close and before she had a chance to stop him he was kissing her.

'Hey,' she objected, shoving him away, 'will you cut that *out.*'

'Why?' suddenly his hands were everywhere, 'I've noticed the way you've been watching me and Olympia together. Don't you think I know that you're hot for me too?'

'You're full of shit!'

'Say that when I've got you pinned down, when I've got my cock inside you, when I . . .'

She kneed him as hard as she could. He was momentarily stunned, bent double with pain, holding onto his balls as though his life depended on keeping them intact. 'You bitch!'

She watched him warily. She wanted to laugh, he looked so funny. Then again she knew that would only infuriate him more and who knew what the creep would do then?

He fell onto the couch, still bent double. 'Why don't you fuck on off to the airport?' he mumbled. 'Because *I'm* not taking you – no fucking way. And the sooner you go the better it'll be for everyone.'

'What am I supposed to do – walk?'

'Who gives a shit *what* you do.'

Inexplicably her eyes filled with tears. How had she got into this mess? Trapped in a villa in France with Olympia and this horrible man? If it wasn't for him they would be having a marvellous time. He had spoiled everything. She stared out of the french windows and thought about what she could do. The rain had started, a deluge of water falling heavily from the black clouds. How she wished she was a little girl again with someone to take care of her and tell her what to do.

'Don't worry,' she muttered, 'I'm going. As soon as the rain stops, I'll be out of here.'

She left him lying on the couch and went to pack the few clothes she had brought with her.

Screw him. Screw her good friend, Olympia. She was going and *nobody* could stop her.

The thoughts that went through Gino's head on the flight down to the South of France were not pleasant ones. What if the body in the car was Lucky? What if it was his little girl?

He tried to remember their last meeting. The New York apartment. A stilted dinner. He had one eye on the television while she mumbled something about not wanting to go back to school. He hadn't listened. He wished that he had. The next morning she had been whisked off in the usual black limousine – he hadn't even gone with her. Well, shit – he was still angry about Switzerland. What was he supposed to do? Give her a kiss and a hug and ignore the fact that she had been caught naked with a boy in bed? Fifteen-years-old. Fifteen for crissakes.

Dimitri Stanislopoulos maintained a healthy silence too, deep in thought wondering why God had seen fit to bestow a daughter on him who was more trouble than all his ex-wives put together.

At last the private plane landed at Nice airport. A car had been sent out onto the tarmac to meet them. It was raining hard, black storm clouds whirling around in a strong wind. Gino consulted his watch. It was seven o'clock at night. His stomach growled – reminding him that he hadn't eaten all day, but who could eat at a time like this?

He climbed in the car, his heart heavy, dreading the drive that would take them straight to the morgue.

Lucky debated with herself about what to do. She had packed her few things, then sat and waited all afternoon for either

Pippa to get back or the rain to stop. It was now seven o'clock. The rain was as heavy as ever, and there was no sign of Pippa.

Olympia had emerged at four o'clock and busied herself with removing dust sheets and putting out glasses in preparation for the party. She and Lucky studiously avoided talking.

Warris slept on the couch, his snoring aggravating both girls.

At six Olympia lit the house with candles, woke Warris and said, 'Where the bloody hell is your girlfriend?'

He was sulky and bad tempered, his balls still aching from Lucky's well placed knee. 'She'll be here,' he mumbled.

'She's certainly taking her time.'

'She'll *be* here I said.' He got off the couch, and the two of them went back in the bedroom slamming the door behind them.

Lucky sat staring out the french window, watching the sudden flashes of lightning, and the relentless rain sweeping down and flooding the garden. She was depressed. It was bad enough being cooped up, but now she felt really trapped.

It was with relief she finally saw the lights of a car approaching. If Pippa refused to drive her she would just take the Mercedes and go. It was as simple as that.

She picked up her small bag, flung open the french doors, and hurried outside.

The rain enveloped her, turning her into a drowned rat as she ran towards the car.

Too late she realized that it was not Pippa, it was not the Mercedes. Holy shit! It was Gino. It was her father!

# Steven 1967

Zizi loved to go out dancing. Steven preferred to stay at home listening to music – he liked jazz, a little rock – but his particular passion was soul. He could sit for hours with the stereo full blast drowning in the sounds of Isaac Hayes, Marvin Gaye, Aretha Franklin.

Zizi preferred strident disco music and Latin American sounds. They fought constantly about what record should be on the turntable. 'I hate the shit you listen to,' she would complain.

'Where's the beat? The fire? Let's go out and dance it up.'

Her favorite place was in Spanish Harlem. Small, crowded, noisy. She was always the center of attention. Steven would watch her undulating around the tiny dance floor with one of a dozen different partners, and he would do a slow burn. They had been married a year and the jealousy he felt wasn't getting any better.

Zizi loved it. She taunted him, enjoyed watching him lose his cool, was thrilled if he punched a guy out.

'You have a very destructive relationship,' Jerry told him one lunchtime, 'what kind of a lawyer goes around starting fights? You're going to end up in one of your own courts. How do you think *that'll* grab the judge?'

'You're right. But what can I do? She's in my blood, Jerry. I love her.'

'Love! Who are you kidding? She's got you by the rocks and she's squeezing.'

Steven picked absently at his salad, 'You've been talking to Carrie.'

'Of course I have. How do you think *she* feels?'

'The trouble with my mother is she's too straight laced. If she had *her* way I'd have married a twenty-year-old black virgin with a college degree, a diploma in domestic arts, and a good family.'

'Are there any twenty-year-old virgins with college degrees?'

Steven sliced at his steak, 'I wish you'd talk to her, maybe arrange a meeting between us.'

'I'll try.' Jerry knew it was impossible, knew that as each week passed Carrie became more and more determined to have nothing to do with her son until he got rid of 'that garbage' as she referred to Zizi.

'I'd appreciate it,' Steven said, 'you know sometimes I feel like I've got no friends anymore.'

'What am I – a chicken sandwich?'

Steven laughed, 'You're a good friend. The only one I got.' As he said it he realized it was true. He had his work. He had Zizi. That was it.

'You given any thought to my offer?' Jerry asked casually over coffee.

'I've given it a lot of thought, and don't think that I'm not flattered – but private practice just isn't my bag.'

'Don't knock it if you haven't tried it.'

'I'm not. All I'm saying is that it's not for me.'

'Maybe you'll change your mind,' Jerry gestured for the check.

'It's my lunch today.'

'Forget it,' Jerry said, reaching for a credit card, 'it's all deductible.'

'I may only be working for the city,' Steven said tightly, 'but I can still pay for lunch.'

'You like?' questioned Zizi, standing, legs splayed, in front of Steven's work desk in their small apartment.

He was absorbed in some papers, his mind clicking this way and that, preparing for the following day's case. Abstractedly he glanced up.

She was in a gold lurex dress split to the crotch. 'Nice, huh?' she crowed.

It was the worst dress he had ever seen. Flashy. Hookerish. Cheap. 'I hate it,' he said.

A dull flush suffused her face. 'It cost you one hundred and twenty bucks,' she spat, 'so you'd better like it.'

His mind was still on the case he was preparing, absent-mindedly he said, 'Take it back, they'll refund your money.'

He was totally unprepared for her fury. She sprang, upsetting all his papers, scratching his face with long fingernails 'You hate everything I do!' she screamed, 'You criticize me all the time, you prick! What makes you think you're so hot?'

He restrained her, clamping her arms to the side of her body. 'What's the matter with you – ' he began. And then it was upon him, as it had always been upon him every time he came in contact with her. The world's greatest hard-on. At least it felt like that.

He was pushing at gold lurex, screwing it up around her waist, not caring if it was spoiled. And she was encouraging him, hot throaty little moans and sighs. Jerry was right, she had him by the rocks *and* she knew it.

'This way Mrs Berkely. Beautiful darling! Beautiful! Show me those teeth – just a grimace – not too much. Perfect!'

The photographer clicked happily away while Carrie went through her repertory of expressions and poses. It was second nature. She had done it so many times before.

It was funny wasn't it? You could become a celebrity – a name – without doing anything at all. Talent was not needed. Only money, style, and the right husband.

She had married two 'right husbands' – only Bernard had been a warm and giving human being – while Elliott was a humorless snob. It often amazed her that he had ever married her. She was black – he loathed blacks. To him they were inferior people. He never saw the color of *her* skin, only her style and panache. She was his own genuine African Princess. God! If Elliott ever knew the truth about her background he would probably kill himself – *and* her.

She did not love Elliott but she certainly enjoyed the life-style.

'Last roll,' said the photographer gaily, 'perhaps you can change into the Yves Saint Laurent. Would you mind awfully?'

No, she wouldn't mind awfully. She retired to the dressing-room in the photographic studio accompanied by two dressers, a hairdresser and a make-up artist. They fussed around her and helped her put on the dress.

She watched her reflection in the mirror and marvelled at what she saw. When had she changed from a nothing black whore into the elegant stylish creature she saw before her?

With Bernard of course. He had created her.

'You look divine, darling,' cooed the hairdresser.

She had to admit that she did. But it hadn't been easy getting there.

# Lucky 1966

Four weeks had passed. The South of France was a distant memory. The Bel Air house reality. The Bel Air prison, more like. Since returning, Lucky's freedom had been limited. A housekeeper called Miss Drew appeared on the scene. She never let Lucky out of her sight.

The rain soaked night in France lingered in Lucky's memory. The shock of Gino arriving, his face as angry as the thunder clouds. He had held her by the shoulders, his nails digging into her flesh, and without saying one word he had shaken her so hard that her teeth had actually rattled.

It was all a nightmare. Olympia's father emerging from the car and saying, 'I knew it! I knew they would be here!' And the three of them standing in the rain, soaked to the skin, and

Lucky wondering desperately how she could warn Olympia who was probably in bed with Warris because that's where they spent most of their time.

Then into the house they had all marched, Gino gripping her by the arm as if frightened she would run off, and Dimitri, exclaiming in shocked tones, 'My God! They've wrecked my sister's home!'

It was at this point that the storm had really erupted. Vivid streaks of lightning, great roars of thunder. And while Gino screamed at her, 'How was Pippa Sanchez involved with you?' Dimitri flung open the double doors of the main bedroom, and there was Olympia exposed for all to see, naked, her rounded ass up in the air as she diligently bent down between Warris' spread legs and gave him one of the best blow jobs he had ever experienced.

There was a nasty silence, broken only by the slurping sounds Olympia made with her mouth.

Dimitri did not hesitate, he moved forward and whacked her ass with all his might. It was unfortunate that Warris had just begun to come, for as Olympia leapt up yelling, 'What's going on?' Warris shot his sperm in a perfect arc all over Dimitri's arm.

'Christ!' screamed Dimitri.

'Christ!' screamed Warris.

The news of Pippa's death brought a temporary lull to the proceedings. Warris had crumpled into a chair, his head in his hands, 'Holy Jesus! I don't believe it.'

'What was she doing here anyway?' Gino demanded.

'She wasn't here,' Warris mumbled, 'she was just a friend of mine, she borrowed the car, that's all.'

The towering fury of the two men knew no bounds.

'You get the hell out of this house,' roared Dimitri.

'Fast,' added Gino, 'while you're still in one piece.'

The rest was a blur of raised voices, Olympia hysterical, accusations all round, Warris being made to pack and leave, staggering out into the storm ridden night clutching his two Gucci bags. And then another silent plane ride with her father, his face like granite. A plane ride that took them all the way to Los Angeles and the Bel Air house. No conversation. *Why didn't he talk to her? Why couldn't they communicate?*

She wasn't even punished. But it was punishment enough to be left alone, for the very next day Gino was gone, and she was left with Miss Drew, athletic thirtyish Miss Drew who never moved from her side.

She wondered what punishment Olympia had received – probably just another school in another city. One day they would run out of cities for Olympia. When she tried to call her at one of her various homes she found that all the numbers had been changed. 'Your father does not wish you to communicate with Miss Stanislopoulos,' said Miss Drew primly. Obviously.

She awoke on the day of her sixteenth birthday to find that Gino was back. Just like that, a smile on his face, a cup of coffee in his hand, he was sitting on the patio overlooking the swimming pool when she came down for breakfast.

There was so much she wanted to ask him. How had he found her in France? What did he think? Was he glad to have her back?

'Hi, daddy,' she said tentatively.

He threw her a great big smile, 'I solved our problem, sweetheart.'

Our problem? What was *our* problem? Another school? If it was she would just take off again.

'You got a pretty dress?' he inquired.

Showed how well he knew her. She hated dresses, never wore them. 'Why?' she queried suspiciously.

' 'Cos I'm takin' you on a little trip, want you to meet some friends of mine.'

'Where?'

'Vegas. For the big charity evenin' I'm giving Mrs Peter Richmond at my hotel.'

'Vegas?' Lucky glowed. Las Vegas was somewhere she had always wanted to visit. 'Really?'

'Sure. We'll hop a plane 'bout one o'clock, go pack a bag.'

She couldn't believe her luck, 'Honestly?'

He laughed. 'Yeh, honestly. And pack somethin' decent – I don't want to see you in those crummy jeans and that old work shirt you live in.'

'Sure thing.' She raced up to her room and inspected the contents of her closet. Marco was in Vegas. Had to find something sensational to wear.

Miss Drew came to the door and peered in smiling thinly, 'I understand you'll be off for a few days.'

A few days! Wow! It was getting better and better. 'Yeh,' she said, 'Gino . . . er . . . daddy's taking me to Las Vegas with him.'

'How nice.'
'You bet!'

'Happy birthday, kid.' Gino clinked champagne glasses with her and handed her a small package.

Suddenly it was like everything in her life was going right. She was sixteen – she was sitting in the Mirage Hotel in Las Vegas next to her father – and he was paying attention to her. Marco sat across from them. Dark broody Marco, even better looking than she remembered him. The only drag was the way she looked . . . But if it made Gino happy . . .

Upon her arrival in Las Vegas he had insisted that she visit the hotel beauty parlor to get her hair fixed. The woman in the salon had rigid instructions from her father on how she should look. Neat groomed curls. Horrible! Gino said she looked lovely.

He had personally picked out a dress for her. Pink. Frilled at the neck and the hem. *The* most revolting dress she had ever seen. Ugh! Gino said she looked lovely.

Feverishly she tore at the small package, and then gasped when she opened the velvet lined box. Diamond ear studs! Impulsively she threw her arms around her father and hugged him tight.

Laughingly he pushed her away.

It was like all her dreams were coming true at once. She was so happy she could burst.

Marco said, 'Those are some earrings.'

Proudly she held them up to her ears.

'Go put them on an' take a look, the ladies room is in back,' Gino said, smiling.

She rushed off.

'You told her yet?' Marco asked, watching her departing figure.

'Not yet. I'll get around to it.'

'How do you think she'll take it?'

Gino leaned back in his chair, his black eyes suddenly bleak, 'I don't particularly care. It's for her own good. One day she'll thank me.'

Marco nodded unsurely, 'I guess.'

Gino's voice was hard, '*I know.*'

Betty Richmond was dressed and ready. Her husband, Peter, was still fiddling around at the mirror.

'Do hurry,' she scolded, 'you know how I hate to be late. Especially for *my* evening.'

'Gino Santangelo's evening you mean.'

'*My* evening.'

Peter fixed his tie and grimaced, 'You know how the old saying goes – lie down with dirt and you get up covered in it. That, my sweetheart, is what is going to happen to us.'

'You should know, Peter, *you've* been lying down with dirt all your life,' Betty replied acidly. 'If you hadn't we wouldn't be in this position.'

'Oh for Christ's sake . . . ?'

'*Come on.* I refuse to be late.'


In the ladies room Lucky studied her diamond earrings. They were stunning. She picked up a brush and attacked her hair managing to make it a little less neat, but there was nothing much she could do about her dress – more's the pity. She made a face at her reflection, then grinned impudently and stuck out her tongue. So what? Surely Marco had the sense to see beneath some cruddy dress?

She hurried back to the table which had filled up somewhat. Marco appeared to have vanished. Squeezing into her place next to Gino, she recognized a few famous faces. There were also several other couples, elderly and affluent – diamonds and jewels dripping off the women – cigars sticking from the men's mouths. Across the room she thought she recognized Elvis Presley and Tom Jones and Tina Turner and Raquel Welch. Too much! 'This is incredible!' she whispered to Gino.

'Good,' he replied easily, 'I'm glad you're enjoying it.'

Senator Richmond and his wife were making an entrance. Lucky had seen their pictures in the popular magazines on many occasions. The Senator was always doing something active – playing polo, canoeing, power boat racing. He was suntanned and healthy looking. So was his wife.

Gino stood as they approached and introduced her. 'This is my daughter, Lucky,' he said proudly. The Senator gave her a firm handshake, while Mrs Richmond inspected her from head to toe. Then some tall freak stepped into the picture, 'And this is Craven Richmond,' Gino added. 'He'll look after you tonight.'

Before she had time to figure out what was happening, Gino moved out from the table and Craven Richmond slid into his place.

'Aren't you going to sit here, daddy?' she managed, sounding like a fool.

'I'll see you later, kid, have a good time.'

She should have known it was all too good to be true.

The evening turned out to be a drag. Sitting through a whole bevy of elderly talent – one eye on Gino who sat at the center table with all the really important people – and one eye on the lookout for Marco, who never reappeared. And who could blame him? The show was the pits. No rock stars, no decent music, just a series of old superstars who Lucky couldn't care less about – but who sent the audience into a paroxysm of applause.

And Craven Richmond by her side. Attentive, polite, BOR . . . ING!! He was the kind of guy she and Olympia had lots of names for – Jerk – Creep – Square.

After the show there was a private party hosted by Gino. She couldn't shake Craven, she couldn't get near Gino, and when she saw Marco he was deep in conversation with a girl she could easily kill. All she wanted was to get out of there.

'I'm tired,' she told Craven.

'So am I,' he agreed.

'I think I'll go to bed then.'

'Let me walk you to the elevator.'

*Let me walk you to the elevator!* She wanted to scream!

He escorted her to the elevator, 'How about a game of tennis in the morning?' he asked politely.

'I don't know what time I'll be getting up . . . '

'I'll call you at ten, we can arrange a time then.'

'Gee . . . I . . . er . . . ' She couldn't come up with an excuse.

Craven bent down and kissed her chastely on the cheek.

He was tall. A real freak. 'Tomorrow,' he said, 'don't worry, everything will be just fine.'

She stepped in the elevator and quickly pressed the close button. What a jerk! And what did he mean – don't worry, everything will be fine? Idiot. She hoped she would never have to spend another evening with *him* again.

Up in her room in Gino's private suite she couldn't wait to wriggle out of the horrible pink dress. She kicked it in a corner of the bathroom and strode around in just bikini pants. She never bothered with a bra – she didn't have enough up top, and she hated the confining feel of it. She stared at herself in the mirrored bar and practiced a little walk around like the showgirls she had watched earlier. It amused her and she started to giggle. Fancy strutting your stuff for a living. What happened when your stuff started to go off?

She rummaged in her bag and came up with a pair of dirty white jeans and a T-shirt which she quickly put on. It was only twelve-thirty, this was her first night in Las Vegas, *and* her birthday. She had no intention of going to bed – not yet anyway.

She took a twenty dollar bill from the dresser in Gino's room, shoved a couple of pillows under the covers on her bed to make it look like she was sleeping there, pocketed the key to the suite, and set off.

At 2.15 a.m. Gino kissed Betty Richmond on both cheeks, shook Peter Richmond by the hand and said, 'I'm for bed.'

'It was a wonderful wonderful evening,' Betty said, glowing with energy.

'It certainly was,' agreed Peter, clapping Gino on the shoulder, 'surpassed everyone's expectations.'

'Yeh,' agreed Gino modestly, 'I guess everyone had a good time.'

Up in his suite he took off his jacket, loosened his tie, poured himself a brandy and sat for a while on his terrace staring out at the twinkling neon lit strip. It *had* been a successful evening. Everything had gone according to plan.

He was disappointed that Lucky had left early without so much as a goodnight. Funny kid. Probably tired out with all the excitement. He had watched her exit with Craven, approached the boy when he returned five minutes later. 'Lucky all right?'

'Oh, yes, sir, she was just tired.'

'Don't call me sir, makes me feel a hundred.'

'Sorry sir . . . er . . . Mr Santangelo.'

'Gino.'

'Yes *sir.*'

Quietly Gino went to her room, peered round the door. She was asleep. A good place to be. He went to his own room, stripped off his clothes, and fell onto the bed. Within minutes he too was asleep.

'You little cocktease!' The man's voice was filled with fury. 'Now you're gonna put out or I'm gonna make you. Get it – cunt?'

The man had her pinned against the brick wall of the parking lot at the Mirage. Her own fault. She had met him at some seedy joint, and they had spent a couple of hours together playing the slots and cruising the string of cheap bars and gambling halls in the downtown area where she had won herself two hundred dollars. By the time he offered to drive her to her hotel they were old friends. He had parked in back and they had begun to neck. She didn't object to that. He looked like Marco. He was fun to be with. And she hadn't indulged in Almost for simply ages.

When things got too hot and heavy in the car she jumped out. He followed, pinning her again the wall.

His fly was already undone and he was pressing his distended penis against her leg. One of his hands roamed roughly under her T-shirt, the other ripped at the fastening on her jeans.

'Will you stop it?' she muttered through gritted teeth. She wasn't frightened, just mad as hell.

'Listen cunt – no way are you gettin' *me* all hot an' bothered an' leavin' me with a stiff prick. *No fuckin' way.*'

His hand ripped at her jeans tearing them down. And then his fingers were diving between her legs, pushing and probing.

Her timing was off – too much cheap wine – she should have moved earlier. Summoning all of her strength she gave him the famous Santangelo knee, smashing into his balls as hard as she could.

He let out a strangled cry of pain and let go of her.

She ran, almost tripping, hauling up her jeans, dodging swiftly in and out of parked cars. Stupid jerk. If he had been nice about things she would have bent her head to him, allowed him to do the same to her.

It was four o'clock in the morning, but as she rounded the corner to the front of the hotel she could see it was still all happening. Cars arriving, others leaving, drunken revellers spilling out counting their winnings or bemoaning their losses.

She fastened her jeans properly, the zipper worked but the top button was gone. Quickly she pulled her T-shirt down to cover the damage, slid through the entrance, skirting the casino section of the lobby, hugging the walls and heading purposefully for the elevators in back.

'Lucky?'

She kept moving.

'Lucky.' The voice, closer now, was accompanied by a hand on her shoulder.

She turned, wide eyed and innocent. It was Marco. The *real* Marco – not some carbon copy bum. 'Oh!' she gave a sigh of relief. 'It's you!'

He was looking at her strangely, 'What are you doing?'

'I . . . couldn't sleep . . . took a walk.'

'Where did you take a walk?' The smell of stale wine was coming off her in waves.

She shrugged vaguely, 'Just around.'

'Does Gino know you're out?'

'He's asleep,' she said, taking a chance that he was, 'I didn't want to disturb him.'

'Baby – if he knew you were out you'd disturb him all right.'

The way he said 'baby' made her shiver. 'I'm hungry,' she said impulsively, 'is there anywhere I can get a sandwich?'

'I'll have one sent up to you.'

She gave him a bold look, 'I don't feel like going up yet.'

He scratched his chin and thought about what to do. If Gino woke up and found her gone he would hit the ceiling. Where had she been anyway? She looked like she'd been in a dog fight. 'OK we'll get you a sandwich. Come along.' He took her to the coffee shop, settled her in a booth, summoned the waitress, and told her he'd be right back.

Then he did the right thing. He phoned Gino and told him.

Gino said, 'Sonofabitch. Where the fuck has she been?'

Marco said, 'I don't know. I'll try and find out, then I'll bring her up.'

Lucky sat happily in the booth munching on a Sinatra Special sandwich and swigging a coke. Marco slid in beside her.

'This is terrific!' she said, full of enthusiasm. 'You and I should do this more often.'


Gino pulled on a bathrobe, went to her bedroom, found the pillows plumped up under the covers, swore softly to himself. His daughter was a wild one. Had to be protected from herself. He had made the right decision. Now he was sure of it.


Marco escorted her to the door of the suite.

'Shhh . . . ' she whispered, giggling, taking out the key and waving it around, 'mustn't wake Big Daddy.'

He felt a twinge of guilt – squealing on the kid wasn't nice – but it *was* for her own good.

'I'd ask you in,' she giggled, opening up the door, 'but *he* wouldn't like it. Of course you *could* ask me back to your room . . . '

She had been making plenty of cracks like that, coming on

to him strong. Gino would have a fit if he knew. 'Goodnight, Lucky,' he said quickly, giving her a little shove in the small of her back.

'Hey – don't I get a kiss?' She grabbed him before he could back off, arms around his neck, open mouth on his.

He pushed her away fast, and headed for the elevator.

Behind him he heard Gino say, his voice hard, 'Come on in Lucky, you and I are gonna have a little talk.'

They faced each other, father and daughter. It was just the two of them. Alone.

Gino's eyes raked her up and down missing nothing. The dirty torn jeans, the rumpled T-shirt, the unruly hair.

'Where you bin kid? Out gettin' laid?'

She flushed, 'What?'

'You think I was born yesterday, kid? You think just 'cos I ain't as young as I was I don't know what goes on?'

'I'm sorry . . . ' she began.

'Don't give me that sorry shit,' he rasped, 'I've had that sorry shit comin' out my ass. Who the fuck do you think you're foolin' with?'

She was startled by his language, by the way he was using it towards her. 'I just went for a walk,' she said lamely.

'A walk, huh? Is that how your clothes got in such a mess? Is that why your arms are all covered in bruises? Your jeans hanging down? A walk, huh?'

'A man attacked me,' she admitted sulkily, 'I was wandering around the parking lot and he jumped me.'

'Oh, yeh? Like the boy in Switzerland, huh? He just happened to get in your room, take *his* clothes off, take *your* clothes off, and climb into bed with you. While across the room your girlfriend was doin' the same thing. How come neither of you screamed for help, huh? Answer me that, huh?'

She stared moodily at the floor.

'And France,' Gino continued, 'shacked up in that villa with your whore friend. How many guys did you have there? How many, kid? Or did you and your friend settle for sharing that pimp who was living there with you?'

'No!' she objected sharply. 'It wasn't like that.'

'Don't give me any more crap, your hear me?' He was very very angry, his eyes a deadly black, his hands shaking with emotion. 'I figured out what I'm gonna do with you – figured it out good – an' you should get down on your knees and thank me.'

'What?' she whispered fearfully. Whatever it was she would escape.

'You got hot pants – you wanna fuck around . . .'

She flinched.

'Well, you're my daughter – *Gino Santangelo's daughter – I will not have it.*'

'I don't . . . fuck around . . .' She could hardly say the word in front of him, 'I don't – honestly . . . daddy.'

He ignored her. 'You're gettin' married, kid. I found you a husband an' you're gettin' married. And any screwin' around you do will be in your marriage bed and nowhere else.' Suddenly he was screaming, 'You understand me, kid? You understand me?'

'But I don't want to get married . . .'

He hit her then. The first and only time. Across the face. Hard.

She spun across the room such was his strength.

He went after her, picked her up, cradled her in his arms, began to talk fast, 'I'm sorry, kid, I'm sorry. Trust me. I know what's best – you gotta do what I say – you gotta learn to listen to me.'

Deep in the warmth of his arms she started to cry. He smelled good, so very very good. Daddy smells. Security. Love. Why wasn't she five again? Why wasn't her mother alive? 'OK daddy, OK I'll listen to you, I'll do it. I love you. I love you so much, I'll do *anything* to make it right with us.' She never wanted to leave the strength and warmth of his arms again. Never. Ever.

'Good kid,' he said softly, 'it'll be for the best, you'll see.'

'Who?' she whispered, knowing in her heart it would be Marco.

'Craven Richmond,' Gino said proudly. 'It's all arranged.'


# Steven 1970

After five years of a marriage that got progressively worse Steven was forced to admit that his mother had been right all along. Zizi *was* a cheap little tramp. A hotshot hustler who would not understand love and decency if it was given to her during the kiss of life. It took him a while to find out, but when he did, he found out good. Coming home early one day he had discovered the security chain in place. Knowing she was inside he rang the bell continuously until a dishevelled Zizi had appeared with a young guy hovering beside her. Before Steven could say anything the boy slid past and vanished nervously down the stairs.

'He was just delivering the groceries,' she objected when he accused her, 'I *always* put the chain on. Habit.'

He wanted to believe her – so he did. Although he knew she was screwing around.

Soon after, he was having a drink with Jerry, discussing this and that, when Jerry blurted out – 'I went to bed with your wife.'

'Huh?' He thought Jerry was joking around as was his way.

'It wasn't my fault!' Jerry said desperately. 'It happened a week ago. You remember – when I dropped those papers by your apartment and you were out. She was all over me, damnit. I didn't have a chance.'

Steven looked at his friend in total disbelief. 'Why are you telling me this?'

'Look – I'm not proud of what I did – but hell . . . I don't want to walk around with it on my conscience. You're my friend. I *had* to tell you.'

Steven had stormed from the bar and headed home.

In the apartment Zizi was practicing for a dance exhibition with two of her Puerto Rican friends. Angrily he threw them out. A ferocious fight had ensued. She couldn't wait to tell him everything. Yes, she had screwed Jerry Meyerson. And many others too. She was bored, fed up, screaming to do something interesting with her life like go to Hollywood and become a famous dancer in the movies. 'I'm prettier than Rita Moreno,' she screamed, 'I have more talent, I'm *wasted* married to you!'

'So why don't we get a divorce?' he questioned coldly, staring at her and realizing for the first time in five years that his cock was no longer on fire. Why hadn't he realized before that she dressed like a hooker? Talked like a hooker? Even acted like a hooker?

'Suits me *fine* Mister,' she flashed, 'you are one tight-assed *boring* man. With *boring* friends and a *boring* job.'

Why hadn't she told him that *before* she screwed half of New York?

He wanted her out of his life as fast as possible. No fuss, no bother. So he bought her a plane ticket to Hollywood, gave her a thousand dollars, agreed to pay her maintenance, and started divorce proceedings.

It was two months after her departure before he got up enough courage to call Carrie. Ridiculous really. Thirty-one years old and he was in a sweat about confronting his mother. He had been more hurt than he cared to admit by her total rejection of him. Now he knew she had been right, and while he didn't condone her unforgiving attitude. he could certainly understand it.

Jerry had kept him in touch with what was going on. Carrie was well, working hard at her favorite charities, keeping up her reputation as one of the great New York hostesses. 'You know your mother is amazing,' Jerry said, 'she has the energy of a woman half her age.'

Jerry and he had remained friends in spite of what had taken place. Steven wasn't happy about what had happened . . . But it certainly wasn't worth blowing a fourteen year friendship over.

With Zizi gone he suddenly found that his life took on a new texture. He was working extremely hard as usual. But the bonus was not having Zizi at home nagging, sulking, generally distracting. Now he could visit his friends when he wanted, go to movies *he* wanted to see, play the soul music *he* loved without having to listen to a stream of complaints. Christ! He hadn't realized it before but she had cut off his balls while they were married. He determined that it would *never* happen to him again. *No* woman would get into his blood like foxy little Zizi had.

Looking back on their relationship he found it hard to figure out. What *had* she had that was so special? Jerry and he went out one night, really laid one on in a bar, and discussed it.

'It was her pussy. You could smell her a mile off,' Jerry said wisely. 'She was a bitch in heat and all us cats got the scent.'

'Thanks,' Steven said bitterly, 'that's my wife you're talking about.'

'Ex-wife. And you learned what *not* to look for in a woman. Must be worth something.'

'Yeah. I guess you're right.'

Jerry slapped him on the back, 'Course I'm right. Now *have I got a girl for you* . . .'

'Thanks but I'm taking a break.'

'Hey . . . nobody takes a break from pussy . . . '

'You're looking at just the guy.'

'Shit!'

'Don't worry about it, I know I can count on you to do enough screwing for both of us.'

Jerry laughed, 'Right on, buddy boy – right on!'

Carrie paced around her luxurious apartment. She was expecting Steven any minute. It was foolish – but she was nervous. Nervous of seeing her own son!

It had certainly taken him long enough to contact her. She knew to the exact moment Zizi had left town. She *should* know, the girl had called her the week before. 'Hey – Mrs Berkely – this is the *other* Mrs Berkely. Y'know – the one you love to hate. I have a little proposition for you.'

'Yes?' Carrie had said coldly.

'You remember our conversation just before your baby boy an' I got married?'

'Yes.' She remembered offering the tramp five thousand dollars to get out of Steven's life – permanently. Zizi had laughed in her face.

'Well . . . baby boy an' I are talkin' divorce.'

Carrie's heart had soared joyfully. She said nothing.

'So . . . ' continued Zizi, 'as I know you are an interested party I figured I should let you in on it. You see, our discussions could go either way . . . All I would have to do to keep things together is sweet talk a little . . . y'know the sort of stuff I mean . . . '

'How much?'

'Ten thousand. Cash,' purred Zizi, 'and I want it in two days.'

'If we . . . make a deal . . . can I take it that Steven will never see you again?'

'I'll be in L.A. within a week.'

'You'll sign a paper?'

'For ten thou I'll stand on my head in Times Square!'

Yes, thought Carrie, I bet you would.

'Well?' snapped Zizi.

'I'll phone you back within the hour,' she replied, 'I have to make certain . . . arrangements.'

'I don't want a double cross, no runnin' to baby boy tellin' him I'm hittin' on you for bread. You do that, honey, and the mistake is yours. I can sweet talk that cat any time I want to – you'd better believe it.'

'I believe it all right.'

Carrie had replaced the receiver thoughtfully. She hoped

that Steven was over the tramp at last, but she couldn't be sure. Best to pay the money and get the girl off *both* their backs. Fortunately she would not have to go to Elliott for money, she still had fifteen thousand dollars left over from Bernard's estate.

She paid the money. Had a document drawn up for Zizi to sign. And waited for Steven to call.

He finally had.

The doorbell rang. She jumped, and tried to compose herself by sitting down and picking up a magazine.

The maid opened up the front door, and moments later Steven walked into the room. Tall and handsome. Well dressed and classy. She had made sure he had every advantage in life. Advantages that had never come her way. He could go anywhere . . . do anything . . . And now that Zizi was gone . . .

He swooped down on her and said one word, 'Mama!'

She rose to hug him.

'I love you – stubborn woman!' he said. 'How come it took me so long to find out you are always right?'

# Lucky 1970

'Can I get you anything, Mrs Richmond?'

*Yes please, a divorce.* 'What?' Lucky shaded her eyes and stared at the good looking pool boy. Lazily her dark eyes inspected every inch of him. He was stocky, with firm thighs, a bulging crotch, and a chest heavily matted with blond hairs. 'How about a Pina Colada?' she drawled.

'Yes ma'am.' He trotted off.

She raised herself from the sunbed she was lying on, and surveyed the scene around the pool at the Princess Saint Hotel in the Bahamas. Things had not changed in the four years she and Craven had been going there. The action never varied. Scads of tourists frying their asses off. Fat black Bahama Momas waddling around holding trays aloft. A surly steel band playing their renditions of old Beatles hits.

Walking towards her she saw Craven. Her husband. Four years of marriage and still she couldn't stand the sight of him. It wasn't that she hated him, she couldn't say that. He was just a constant aggravation. A dull person with no conversation, no personality, and no drive.

Craven Richmond. Her husband. What a joke! On his skinny body he wore an Aloha print shirt, white bermuda shorts, tennis shoes with short orange socks. Liberally spread across his nose and around his mouth was a thick coating of white zinc ointment.

She lay down quickly and closed her eyes. She didn't have the energy to indulge in the usual conversation.

With her eyes closed, and the hot sun beating down on her body she thought about the first time they had come to the Bahamas. Their honeymoon. Another joke. Big Daddy had thought he was marrying off some hot panted little raver. Marry her off. Protect the great Santangelo name. Little did he know she was a virgin. Had never done the dirty deed. Oh sure – had done everything else – but when it came down to actually screwing . . .

Craven had never done the dirty deed either. Twenty-one years old when they married, he was more of a virgin than she was!

After a sick making wedding in Vegas, they had found themselves on a plane to the Bahamas. Two strangers. She had only been sixteen for one week. And what a week! When Gino said he had it all arranged, he *meant* it. It seemed everyone knew about it but her. Craven was delighted at the prospect. Betty Richmond coolly affectionate. Peter Richmond tolerant.

Planefuls of Richmond family flew in for the wedding, which was flashy, distasteful, and fully covered by the press. In one fell swoop she went from little Lucky Saint who nobody knew – to Lucky Santangelo – Gino's beautiful daughter – marrying Craven Richmond of *the* Richmond family. Even Dario was allowed out of school for the event. She hardly recognized him – he had changed from a little boy to a young man. Long blond hair and sly blue eyes.

'I bet you're a killer with the girls!' she joked.

'What girls?' he asked blankly. 'It's a boys school.'

'Wait until college. You'll slay 'em.'

The communication they had once shared seemed to have gone.

Marco was at the wedding – damn him. The Betrayer, she called him in her mind, and carefully went out of her way to ignore him.

Upon arrival in Nassau, a steel band met them at the airport, and a convertible Cadillac whisked them across to Paradise Island, where the manager of the Princess Saint waited to greet them. A Marco clone. Dark, broody, dangerous looking. Lucky gave him a cool greeting. Craven was more effusive.

She had to admit she was impressed with Paradise Island, it certainly was the right name for the stretch of coast land which housed several beautiful luxury hotels. From the windows of their beachfront villa they were confronted with uninterrupted stretches of white sand, clear turquoise water, and exotic palms and ferns. She couldn't wait to slip into her bikini and lie out on the beach. Craven rushed to join her in checked bermudas. She was horrified by the sight of his skinny white body exposed at last. Incongruously his legs and arms were deeply tanned. It only made everything else seem whiter.

Why had she gone through with it? To make Gino happy? Or because there was no choice? Sixteen and married to a man she didn't even know – let alone love.

It was a windy day, but Lucky was immune to getting burnt because of her natural dark skin and her deep seated South of France tan. Several times she warned Craven, whose face and body were turning a particularly bright pink. 'I'm all right,' he insisted, 'never had sunburn in my life.'

There was always a first time. That night Craven lay in screaming agony while she plied him with unguents. 'We got a real lethal sun here, ma'am,' the black guy in the hotel drug store told her with a wide smile, 'once burnt nevah forgotten!' Very true. Craven was unable to leave the room for five days. Unable to do anything else either.

Lucky waited patiently. She was married. She wanted to screw. If she closed her eyes tightly maybe she could imagine Craven was Marco. There had to be *some* compensation to being married.

On the sixth day of their honeymoon it became quite obvious that unless she made the first move no moves were going to be made. Craven's sunburn was much improved. He had peeled – twice – and was now ready to approach the sun again – carefully.

Instead of putting on the pajama top she usually wore to bed she stripped off in the bathroom. She wasn't embarrassed to enter the bedroom naked and stroll provocatively towards a startled Craven, whose dick shot up like a soldier at attention through his pajama trousers.

'Hiya, honey,' she drawled, doing her best Mae West imitation, 'wanna get a taste of somma my honey!'

His erection deflated. It took her an hour and a half to persuade it to reappear. By that time they were both too tired to do anything about it.

Another three days went by before the marriage was consumated. Then Lucky sobbed herself to sleep. It was the most disappointing event she had ever experienced. Was that it? A few jerky bumps, a roll over, and straight to sleep?

Apparently Craven thought it was. He seemed quite inordinately pleased with himself. He developed a knowing leer which drove her mad, and a desire to fuck once a night – before cleaning his teeth – for a duration of exactly three minutes each time. She could not interest him in Almost. He didn't want to know about Almost. Sucking tits, caressing pussy, putting his cock in her mouth, and tongueing her, were all no-no's. Craven knew what a man did and he had no intention of indulging in 'perversions' as he called them. He didn't even care if she came or not – and who the hell *could* come with a stop watch and a limp hard-on for company?

Four years. What a waste.

'One Pina Colada, ma'am.'

Lucky opened her eyes and sat up.

Craven said, 'Mornin'. How are you today?'

She took the drink from the pool boy, had another quick glance at his bulging crotch, smiled, and signed the check with a flourish.

Then she turned and looked at her husband. She was no longer sweet sixteen, she was twenty, and divorce was on her mind *all the time*.

'Ah, the zinc kid,' she drawled. Craven *knew* that covering his face in zinc ointment drove her crazy!

'I didn't sleep well,' he whined, 'there was a mosquito in the room all night. Didn't you hear it?'

Craven always had a complaint about *something*. He was like an old man. 'Nope. Did you get a little prick?' she inquired innocently.

He stared at her oddly, 'A sting, Lucky, a sting.'

'Oh, yes. A sting.' A little prick was what she got. Occasionally. If she was fortunate. Or unfortunate. Depending which way one looked at it.

Two months after the honeymoon, Craven had cut down his lovemaking routine to once a week, then once a month, then to whenever the feeling took him – which wasn't often. She had reconciled herself to the fact that he didn't like sex much.

Gino had forced her to marry because he thought she was some kind of budding nymphomaniac. It didn't take her long before she decided to prove him right.

She took her first lover before the honeymoon was over. The Marco clone who managed the hotel. Her father's employee. Perfect. *She* seduced him, went to his penthouse suite on the pretext she had a message from Gino, and once there took off her clothes and challenged him with her eyes to say no. He was scared to turn her down. Scared to do it. Either way he was a loser. She was Gino Santangelo's daughter. It made things mighty difficult.

Power she decided, sure was a wonderful feeling! And being fucked properly was even better.

She had not looked back. If she saw a man she desired, she had him – if he was havable – most of them were. Of course she was discreet. It would never do for word to get back to Big Daddy that marriage – instead of stopping her from screwing around – had actually forced her into it.

'How long have you been out here?' Craven asked.

'An hour. Why?'

'I just wondered.' Fussily he arranged his things on the sun-bed next to her.

As soon as he was settled, Lucky got up and dived gracefully into the olympic size pool. She was well aware that nearly every male in the place second glanced her. At sixteen she had been a wild daisy – at twenty she was a wild rose. Dark skin, black eyes. Still lean and slender, but her breasts had filled out, giving her body a sudden voluptuous look. She had let her hair grow very long, and it tangled and curled its way below her waist.

She wore very little make-up, it wasn't needed. Just black kohl around her eyes, a deep red lipstick, and touches of gold glitter here and there.

Vigorously she swam the length of the pool, ducking her head beneath the cool water, surfacing for breath only occasionally.

Again she thought about her life.

Mr and Mrs Craven Richmond lived in a very nice apartment in Washington. She drove a red Ferrari. Wedding present from Big Daddy. Craven had a cream Lincoln Continental. He also had two hundred thousand dollars plus four years interest in a Swiss bank account. Gino had *paid* Craven to marry her. Blackmailed Betty and Peter Richmond to allow it. Betty had told her – without revealing the facts – spitefully, bitchily, during the course of a family argument. One day Lucky determined to find out what the blackmail was.

The fact that Gino had *paid* someone to marry her was devastating. So awful that at first she refused to believe it. But one day she had flown to New York and confronted her father.

'So what?' he had questioned. 'You're married into one of the best families in the whole friggin' fifty states. Big deal so I gave him some money to get started.'

Get started doing what? Craven had no job. He hung around his father, played tennis with his mother, and Lucky was expected to tag along to all of the Richmond happenings. Golf. Horseback riding. Table tennis tournaments. All faithfully chronicled by the popular press. She soon learned that Peter Richmond wouldn't lift a finger unless there was a photographer around, and then it was all stops out.

This was not the life she had imagined for herself. She was frustrated in every way. 'I want to get a job,' she told Craven. 'I can't just hang out like you do, my brain is turning into a tennis ball.'

'It's not a good idea,' said Craven.

'It's not a good idea,' said Betty.

'It's not a good idea,' said Peter.

One thing about the Richmonds – they stuck together.

'Have you thought about getting pregnant, dear?' Betty asked one day.

Had she thought about it? The very idea gave her nightmares.

'I speak four languages – I have an extremely active mind – I don't want kids yet, Betty – I *must* get a job or I'll go crazy!'

Reluctantly they let her work part time in Peter's office. After a week she gave it up. Working for Peter alongside his backslappers was worse than doing nothing.

She filled her days with shopping, reading, lunches with girlfriends who were not really friends – more acquaintances. She drove her Ferrari for hours up and down the freeway just for something to do. Fast – the stereo tape blazing good black soul. She indulged in many short sharp affairs – but none of them lasted more than a few days – her choice. Very occasionally she saw her father. He flew into Washington or she and Craven flew into New York. Always for an event. A dinner. A presentation. They were always surrounded by people. Dario turned up a couple of times. The brother she had once been so close to was now a secretive stranger, and they had nothing to say to each other any more.

She felt trapped in a life she didn't want. A life that Gino had forced upon her.

So why did she stay? She *still* hadn't figured out why. She hated her father with a passion. Yet at the same time she desperately wanted to please him.

Staying married pleased him.

Fucking around pleased her.

She hauled herself out of the pool only to find Craven waving frantically. She took her time strolling casually back to their sunbeds, 'What's the matter?' she asked, shaking out her wet hair so that droplets of water went all over him.

'It's your father,' he said irritably, 'they're paging you. He's on the phone.'

'Yes?' Her heart soared a little. She hadn't seen or heard from Gino in months. Was he suddenly missing her?

Without bothering to wrap a towel around her she hurried over to one of the glass covered phone booths. 'Yes?' she kept her voice deliberately casual.

'Lucky? Hi kid, how you doin'?'

'Just great. And you?'

'I got problems – nothin' that can't be worked out.'

*He* was telling *her* about *his* problems. This was a first.

There was an awkward silence, then he said, 'Listen, kid – I want you to fly into New York.'

A million questions came into her head, 'When?' she asked quickly.

'Today, tomorrow – you don't havta break a neck but it has to be soon.'

'I'm in the middle of my vacation,' she explained calmly.

'Your whole life's a friggin' vacation!' he exploded.

'What's it all about anyway?' she asked impatiently, ignoring his outburst.

'I don't want to discuss it on the phone,' he said tightly, 'just get your ass into New York. It's important or I wouldn't ask you.'

'We'll get a plane tonight,' she decided.

'No – don't bring Craven. Come alone. This is private family business.'

The thought of flying to New York without Craven delighted her. 'OK,' she said slowly, still wondering what it was all about, 'I guess I'll see you later.'

'Get an early plane – we can have dinner together. Dario's coming in from the coast.'

Now she was really confused. Dario. Her. Gino. The whole Santangelo family. Was Gino sick? Did he have some dreaded disease and five minutes to live?

'Are you . . . all right?' she asked softly.

'Sure. Couldn't be better. I'll see you later, kid. Call Costa when you got your flight number and there'll be someone to meet you at the airport.'

A low buzz told her he had hung up.

Earlier that day Dario had received the same call, and was just as surprised as his sister.

On the whole his father left him alone. 'Get yourself a good education and you got the world by the balls – ' Gino was fond of saying. Dario took his advice. He stayed at school until he graduated at seventeen, then he persuaded Gino to let him study art at the San Francisco Art Institute.

At first his father was skeptical, 'Art? What kinda education is that?' But at the same time he was proud that his son obviously had artistic talents. He confided in Costa – 'I'll let the kid have fun – do what he wants to do. He can screw around in art school – fuck all the girls he wants, and then when he's twenty-one I'll teach him everything I know – *that'll* complete his education good. One of these days he'll take over the Santangelo empire – I don't want to push him into it before he's ready.' So Dario was given his freedom.

With unlimited funds generously supplied by Gino, he rented an apartment in San Francisco and settled down with Eric, who gave up his job and moved from San Diego to be with his protégé.

Dario was quite happy with the relationship. Eric catered to him in every way, and it was good to just sit back and be adored. He didn't feel abnormal or bad about the way it was – the only guilt he ever felt was when he considered the possibility of his father ever finding out. Unthinkable.

He and Eric kept very much to themselves. They didn't join the thriving hippie community, or attend the gay clubs, or get involved with any other people at all. This suited Eric fine. He didn't want anyone else getting their hands on Dario.

At the Art Institute the girls pursued him relentlessly. He simply wasn't interested. Eric was fulfilling all his needs.

Time passed quickly. Dario had seen his father only occasionally. One Christmas, then some weeks in the summer when he made a dutiful visit to Las Vegas. A few New York trips. And that was it.

In Vegas, Gino threw the odd girl in his son's direction. 'This is Jenny, she's new in town.' 'I want you to take out Crissy – she just broke up with her boyfriend.'

Dutifully Dario took them out – even kissed them goodnight in case they were reporting back to his father. Eric would kill him if he ever knew!

Kissing girls was no big deal. In fact it did not turn him on one bit. He hated the gooey feel of their lipstick, and the cloying smell of powder and paint. The thought of a naked woman was disgusting to him now. All that soft flesh. Huge bosoms. Hidden places. He remembered a naked Marabelle Blue and he shuddered.

'Why do you have to go to New York?' Eric questioned.

He combed his hair carefully and wondered if he should get it cut before facing his father. 'I just do. Family meeting, whatever that means.'

'What *does* it mean?' Eric asked peevishly.

Dario shrugged, 'Who knows? I'll just have to find out.'

# Gino 1970

Impatiently Gino waited for his children to arrive. Lucky would be first – she was only a two hour flight away. Then Dario – he was due in at Kennedy around seven-fifteen. What a shame, Gino reflected, that the boy wasn't the older of the two. Somehow it was more fitting for the male child to be the eldest. And also – why weren't their looks reversed? Why couldn't Lucky be the image of Maria? And Dario, dark and masculine? Not that Dario wasn't masculine. Gino had seen his son in action, chasing the girls in Vegas, and obviously having one hell of a time at that Art Institute he attended in Frisco. To think – a son of his at an Art Institute! He grinned, and wished – as he wished every day of his life, that Maria had lived to see her children grow. What would *she* have done with Lucky?

He felt he had made a wise choice marrying her off. Even at such a young age. She had every advantage being with the

Richmonds. One day Peter Richmond would run for President . . .

It had all been so easy. People were suckers to manipulate. To convince the Richmonds to accept Lucky as a daughter-in-law had taken only mild persuasion, money, and the mention of the rather torrid photographs and tapes of Peter with Marabelle Blue that Gino had locked away in his safe.

Betty Richmond had been furious. She had even presented herself at his door with the hope that one more fuck of that boney body would persuade him to forget the whole idea.

He had dismissed her as she had dismissed him. Score – even.

A week later Lucky and Craven were married. Only time would tell if he'd done the right thing. He hadn't seen that much of her, but when he did she seemed fine. A little tense perhaps. Why didn't she have a baby? Then he would *know* he had done the right thing. He resolved to talk to her, tell her he would like to be a grandpop. After all . . . time was passing . . . He wasn't getting any younger.

Costa entered the room. He had aged considerably since the death of his beloved Jennifer the previous year. Cancer had taken her mercifully quickly.

Gino felt so sorry for his friend. No children. No family. Only Leonora still alive, a hopeless alcoholic by all accounts. He didn't even want to think her name. To remember her filled him with disgust. The way she had treated Maria – her only child. The bitch had not even bothered to come to the funeral – and over all the years she had never once attempted to see Lucky or Dario. Not that he would have allowed it. Never.

'Red's gone to the airport,' Costa said, 'he'll have time to bring Lucky here – then go back for Dario.'

'Good,' Gino replied, running a hand through his unruly mop of hair. Sixty-four. His hair was as thick as ever. His cock could get hard whenever he wanted. Only his stomach let him down. Goddamn ulcers. Drove him mad. Sometimes the pain was so bad he rolled on the floor in agony.

'Something smells good,' Costa said, sniffing eagerly.

'You should get yourself a cook, fatten up – there's nothin' worse than a scrawny old man.'

'How about a scrawny old woman?'

Gino laughed, 'You're right! I take out nothin' over twenty-nine. Their conversation stinks but their necks look nice!'

He wished he could get Costa to start going out. When a man lets the hard-on out of his life something happens. It was happening to Costa. A grey stooped look. Jennifer was a year buried. It was time.

They made light conversation. Gino at the head of the table, Costa facing him, Lucky to his left, Dario to his right.

He was certainly proud of his children. They were both very good looking in highly individual ways. Of course Dario's hair was much too long – but wasn't that the way of young boys today – the fashion? He couldn't help saying, 'You should get your hair cut, Dario, you look like one of those hippies or somethin' out of a rock group.'

'I like it,' Lucky said quickly, rushing to her brother's defense as she had always done when they were children.

'*You* would,' Gino chided, 'I don't like somethin' – you love it – it's always bin that way.'

'Has it?' She was genuinely surprised.

'Sure. Ain't that right, Costa?'

Costa nodded.

Lucky laughed. 'I can't help it if we always have different opinions.'

She felt good sitting at the table with Gino and Dario. It was nice being with her family – she couldn't remember the last time they had all sat down together for a meal. At least her father looked well – so it wasn't his health that had brought them together.

She thought about Craven's face when she had told him she was going to New York and that he couldn't go with her.

'Why not?' he had whined, the zinc ointment making him look even more ridiculous than usual.

'Family business,' she had replied airily, 'you know how important families are.' A nice zinger right between the balls. *His* family ruled their life. Bossy Betty and Randy Peter as she had nicknamed them. If only Peter Richmond would run for President – get it over with. He had no chance as far as she was concerned – he was no Kennedy. Besides – he had *her* as a daughter-in-law, and that had to be a major strike against him.

The roast lamb was delicious. It was followed by the traditional dishes of Cassata that Gino liked so much. He ate quickly, spooning the dessert into his mouth in big chunks. It wasn't as good as the old days – nostalgically he remembered the Cassata Fat Larry used to serve – rich, creamy with real bits of fruit – but it wasn't bad.

When dessert was finished and coffee served, he left the

dining table, opening up the door to make sure no one was lurking outside, closed it again, and returned to the head of the table. 'I guess you're wondering why I wanted you both to come,' he said.

Lucky glanced quickly at Dario. Wondering! She was shitting bricks!

'I gotta take a little vacation,' he continued, 'somewhere out of the country.'

What was so earth shattering about that? Lucky reached for a cigarette.

'Maybe I'll be gone a few weeks – maybe a few months. It's difficult to say right now.'

'How come?' Lucky asked, suddenly very alert.

Gino shrugged eloquently. 'How come? That's a good question.' He fingered the faded scar on his cheek, barely visible now. 'Hey Costa – you wanna tell the kids what this is all about.'

Costa nodded and formally cleared his throat. 'Your father has to leave America for a while,' he said dourly, 'a short while – we hope – it all depends on . . . certain circumstances.'

'Yeh, yeh, we're getting the picture,' Lucky said impatiently, 'he has to go – but why?'

Gino frowned in her direction. 'Just shut up and listen.'

Costa cleared his throat again. Lucky noticed that his hands were shaking and she felt sorry for him. He certainly looked twenty years older since Aunt Jen had gone.

'You see, it's like this,' he said, 'for some years now the Internal Revenue Service has been after Gino for what they describe as tax avoidance on what they see as concealed assets. This all goes back some time, but as I am sure you both know the IRS never lets up.'

'Dirty sonsofbitches!' Gino interrupted bitterly, 'I've paid enough goddamn taxes to run the White House for twenty years!'

'Things have come to a head,' Costa continued, 'I won't bother you with the details – but we have it on excellent authority that a grand jury is being set up specially to investigate his tax affairs and that they're going to subpoena him and it'll mean a jail sentence for sure.'

'But if you've paid your taxes . . . ' Lucky said in a puzzled voice, 'I don't understand . . .'

'Don't be so dumb!' Gino snapped, 'I thought you were a smart girl. *Sure* I've paid taxes – more than enough. But there's plenty I haven't paid on – plenty.'

'So if you pay it now . . .'

Both men laughed.

'It's not as simple as that, Lucky,' Costa said gently. 'It's far too complicated for you to even begin to understand I'm just telling you the bare facts . . . if I started to go into it properly it would take me a solid week.'

'Yeh,' agreed Gino, 'but it ain't nothin' that can't get worked out. And *I* don't plan to sit in some crummy jail while it's fixed. That's why I'm leavin'.'

'Where will you go?' she asked anxiously.

'Maybe London – we got a piece of the casino action there. Maybe France. I don't know yet.'

Her eyes sparkled, suddenly she saw an escape route. 'Can I go with you, daddy?' She hadn't called him daddy in years.

'What are you talkin' about? Go with me? What a suggestion! You got your life here, and a pretty good one at that.'

'Who says?' she muttered darkly.

Ignoring her, Gino turned towards Dario, who was toying with a spoon. 'Hey – you're very quiet, kid, don't you have no questions?'

Dario jumped. He hadn't been concentrating. It didn't bother *him* if Gino had to leave the country. He never saw him anyway. 'No questions,' he said quickly, 'I understand.'

'Good.' Gino rose from the table and walked to the window. 'As a precaution I'm signing over a lot of things to you two. Nothin' to bother yourselves with – you'll just have to put your signature on some papers occasionally. Costa will have my power of attorney, he'll be takin' care of everything. Dario,' he stared at his son, 'I want you to move to New York. There's a lot of things I want you to know about – Costa'll start teachin' you.'

At last Dario showed some emotion, 'Move to New York!' he cried. 'Why?'

'I just told you why,' Gino said patiently, 'you're my son, that's why. You're a Santangelo that's why. And you've been pissin' around at that dumb art school for long enough. It's time you came into the business.'

'But I don't want to live in New York,' Dario objected, 'I hate New York.'

Gino's eyes were bleak and cold, 'Ain't askin' you kid, I'm telling you. Get it?'

Nervously Dario nodded.

'What about me?' Lucky demanded.

'What about you?'

'Well if Dario's going to learn the business *I* want to as well.'

'Don't be a silly girl,' Gino said mildly.

She felt four years of frustrated rage boiling up inside her. Her black eyes were as bleak and as cold as her father's. 'Why not?' she demanded. *'Why not?'*

'Because you're a woman,' Gino replied calmly, 'a married woman who will stay by her husband's side and behave like a proper wife.' He paused, then added, *'And* it's about time you had a baby. What are you waiting for anyway?'

'What am I waiting for!' she exploded, 'I'm waiting to have a life first – that's what I'm waiting for.'

Gino looked to Costa and threw up his hands in mock despair. 'A life. She wants a life. It isn't enough that she's had the best that money can buy . . . '

'Including a husband,' Lucky yelled angrily, 'you bought me a husband with your lousy money. You—'

'That's enough.'

'It's *not* enough. I want more,' she screamed, 'why should Dario get a chance and not me?'

'Cut it out, Lucky,' his voice was like ice.

'Why should I? Why the *fuck* should I?'

His black eyes were as deadly as hers. 'Because *I'm* tellin' you – that's why. And watch your language – ladies don't talk like you.'

She put her hands on her hips and arrogantly faced him, 'I ain't no lady,' she mocked, 'I'm a Santangelo. I'm just like you – and *you* ain't no gentleman.'

He stared at his wild black eyed daughter and he thought – Christ! What have I raised here? I've given her everything money can buy. *What more does she want?*

'Why don't you just shut up and sit down?' he said wearily.

This made her even angrier, 'Oh sure! Shut her up – she's only a woman – what does she matter? Shut her up and marry her off and who cares whether she's happy or not?' She took a deep breath and hissed, 'You're a fucking male chauvinist who thinks women are only good for screwing and cooking. Keep 'em in the kitchen or the bedroom where they belong. Is that what you did with mommy before she was murdered? Did you lock her –'

He cut her words off abruptly by hitting her across the face with all his strength.

Costa jumped up from the table. 'Gino!'

Dario watched uneasily, but did not move.

Lucky was desperately trying to control the burning tears which threatened to slide down her face. 'I hate you,' she hissed, 'I really hate you. And I never want to see you again.'

'Lucky . . .' Gino began.

She stormed from the room. Behind her she heard him say – 'Kids! What can you do? You try your best . . . A woman in business . . . you gotta be nuts . . . Emotional . . . Jeeze . . . they're all so goddamn emotional . . .'

She wasn't emotional. She was full of a hard cold anger.

Why had she run? Why hadn't she stayed to state her case? Why hadn't she convinced him to give her a chance?

*I don't want to be married, daddy. I don't want to stay by Craven Richmond's side and behave like a proper wife. He can't fuck properly. He can't do anything properly.*

*You made me marry him. I did it to please you and because I was too young to realize that your word wasn't law. Now I want out. I want to be like you.*

*And I will.*

*Oh yes I will.*

*Nobody's going to stop me. I promise you that.*

*And haven't you always said that a Santangelo's word is their bond?*

*Yes. I'm your daughter.*

*You'll see.*

*Everyone will see.*

# Steven 1971

Since reconciling with his mother, Steven had been busier than ever. It was difficult to resist her wish that he go into private practice. He *did* owe her – especially after the Zizi business. So, to please Carrie, he joined Jerry's law firm as a partner. He stuck it out six months and then – splitting amicably with Jerry, returned to public service.

'I *know* what you want for me,' he told his disappointed mother, 'and believe me – *I* want it too. But I have to feel that I'm doing something worthwhile – and representing rich ladies suing even richer corporations is *not* my idea of worthwhile.'

Carrie tried to understand. It wasn't easy when she saw Jerry getting richer and more important, while Steven slogged away at what he considered worthwhile.

Recently he had started dating again. 'Your pecker'll fall off if you don't give it some use!' Jerry had complained. Good friend Jerry who had fucked his wife. Best to forget about *that*.

Tentatively he re-entered the sexual rat race. He proceeded slowly, carefully. The first girl he took to bed was a law student with a magnificent afro. The first girl since Zizi. He had been celibate for a year – not such a big deal. It was like sticking your toe into luke warm bath water after months without a wash. He enjoyed it. He could also live without it.

After Afro, girls crept back into his life on a purely disposable basis. Never again would a woman lead him around by his cock. Never.

He worked hard, dated when it suited him, and saw a lot of Carrie to make up for lost time. As glamorous and assured as she appeared, Steven did not really feel that she was happy. He tried to talk to her, but she put up barriers when it came to talking about *her* life.

Then the Bert Sugar case occurred. And the course of Steven's career was radically changed.

Bert Sugar was a no account petty criminal. Arrested for the brutal rape of a fifteen-year-old girl, he was locked up and the arresting officer told him – 'You're going to whack off for the rest of your life, you bastard. 'Cos when they finish splittin' open your dirty ass in the pen you can *bet* you won't *ever* wanna do anything else.'

'I'm innocent, Mr Berkely,' Bert Sugar told Steven tearfully at their first meeting. 'It's a frame.'

Looking at the miserable pathetic man, Steven was prepared to believe him. He didn't look like he had enough strength to take a piss, let alone commit rape.

So Steven defended him – brilliantly. *And* got him off, in spite of the fact that the prosecution thought they had enough evidence to lock Bert up and throw away the key forever.

Steven was convinced that Bert Sugar *was* innocent. He discredited witnesses, spoke movingly of the pitifully deprived life Bert had led, and persuaded the jury to give the man a chance.

Bert Sugar walked out of court a free man.

The victim's mother, a black woman, accosted Steven outside the courtroom. Her eyes were full of fire as she gripped Steven by the arm and wailed, 'Brothah! May God forgive you for what you gone done today.'

He tried to pull his arm free, but she had a grip of steel.

'You is wrong,' she continued to wail, 'you let the white devil go free. You will pay. We *all* will pay.'

He had extracted his arm from her grasp finally and walked away. Of course she didn't want to admit that Bert Sugar was not the man that had attacked her daughter – she wanted a fall guy – Bert was perfect. He lived near them, he had no job therefore was home all day, he had been seen near their apartment within minutes of the crime. All circumstantial evidence. The girl couldn't even identify her attacker – he had gained entry to the apartment through a window, sneaked up on her while she was asleep in bed, blindfolded her, tied her up, beaten and raped her repeatedly.

Steven was glad he had defended Bert Sugar. With anyone else the pitiful little man wouldn't have stood a chance.

Within twenty-four hours Steven's sense of triumph turned to sick horror.

Bert Sugar, upon his release, had gone straight to a neighborhood bar. There he had sat downing bottles of Budweiser and boasting about the 'little black cooze he had fucked good' and 'the dumb nigger lawyer who had got him out of jail'.

Drunk, Bert had reeled from the bar at eleven o'clock. He had returned to his victim's apartment, knocked the mother unconscious with a length of piping he had picked up in the basement, entered the place and proceeded to attack the petrified girl, ripping her nightdress viciously off and trying for another rape. Only this time Bert Sugar couldn't get it up. Bert Sugar had had far too much to drink.

The police arrived in time to pull him off of the hysterical girl. They did not arrive in time to save her mother. She died from head injuries on the way to the hospital.

Steven was destroyed. It was *his* fault – his misjudgement. Because of *him* a woman was dead. *He was an accessory to her murder.*

Nobody could calm him down. Eventually Carrie persuaded him to take a vacation. A friend of Elliott's had a cottage in Montauk and it was arranged that Steven could stay there as long as he wanted. Carrie said she would go with him.

He insisted that she didn't, 'Please, ma, I just want to be alone, think things out.'

He liked the solitude. The wind, the rain, the long walks on the deserted wintry beach.

He thought long and hard about his life, what he had achieved, what he *hoped* to achieve.

He thought about his relationships with people. Carrie – who was she really? He loved her but he didn't really *know* her. Somewhere in the back of his mind he could remember things long ago. Women . . . lots of them . . . singing Happy Birthday. Where *was* that? He had asked Carrie – she had shrugged. The same when he asked about a skinny man called Leroy. He remembered being with someone called Leroy. The name stuck. Carrie said she had never heard the name in her life.

Zizi. One long bad dream. He was over her with a vengeance.

When he returned from Montauk he had made a big decision.

'I'm changing sides,' he told Jerry. 'no more defense – in future I'm going to be a prosecutor. I think I can do more good . . . so many things in this town need cleaning up, and if I can do my bit to help . . .'

Jerry noticed the glint of a zealot in Steven's eyes. 'Private or public?' he asked, as if he didn't already know the answer to *that* question.

'Public, of course,' replied Steven frowning.

'Of course,' Jerry laughed, 'so what else is new?'

# Lucky 1970–1974

When Gino left town in 1970, it was not a quiet exit. Headlines screamed gleefully about getting rid of one of America's most powerful criminals. Photographers jostled and fought at the airport to get the best shots of him.

He wore his customary dark suit, a fedora hat pulled low over his forehead, and oblique dark glasses. He did not smile, or turn, or react in any way at all to the hordes of photographers. It pissed him off that they knew about his departure.

Once aboard the airplane he was furious to discover that some of his travelling companions were press. He should have realized then and there that something was up.

The flight to Rome was uneventful. What happened after they landed was not. It was the beginning of a nightmare that Gino would never forget.

He was refused admittance into Italy on the grounds that he was an undesirable alien. Italy! The country of his birth! From there he joined a flight to Geneva where the same thing happened . . . On to France. There they kept him waiting in a dingy room for seven and a half hours before turning him away. It was unbelievable!

He was by this time exhausted and humiliated. And all the while the press danced attendance, recording his every embarrassment.

He had of course contacted Costa, who said there'd been a leak – and that the whole idea of the harrassment was to force him to return to America. But Costa had not been idle. He instructed Gino to fly to London where there was a slim chance he would be admitted. 'If not – try Israel – you understand me?'

Yeh. Gino understood him. What Costa was trying to say was that Israel would take him – but things had to be worked out. They had plenty of contacts in Israel. Plus Gino had made a very prudent contribution of one million dollars with more to come to a prominent Israeli children's charity.

He went through the motions of trying to get into England. He sat and fried in another little room while various officials came and went. He thought about his meeting with Dario and Lucky. It had not turned out like he had hoped. Dario, sulky and withdrawn. Lucky, as wild as ever. An emotional kid who didn't know *what* she wanted. It was a shame they had had to part bad friends – but he would be back soon – he would spend some time with her – make everything all right.

It turned out to be the same old story in England. Undesirable alien. Christ! They made it sound like he came from another planet!

Forty-two long weary hours after leaving America, Gino was granted entry – on a temporary visitor's visa – to Israel. He took up residence in a penthouse in the Dan Hotel for three months, and then moved to a house near the beach where he lived quietly with two bodyguards, a housekeeper, two Alsatian dogs and an occasional girl-friend.

He was waiting to go home.

Negotiations to arrange this were not proving easy.

As soon as Gino left, Lucky returned to the Bahamas, finished off her vacation with Craven, and then it was back to Washington and the same old routine. She was still seething with fury about her father's attitude towards her, and she was determined to think of some way to show him that he was wrong.

How dare he treat her like some dumb little kid. Women are too emotional for business huh? Well she would find a way to show *him*.

The Richmonds were embarrassed by Gino's publicity. *She* was an embarrassment to them. So when Costa sent her some papers to sign a few weeks later she decided to take a trip to New York and deliver them personally.

On the plane she read them through, and as she read she realized with a tingle of excitement that she had been appointed a director of Gino's companies and businesses. She glanced quickly at Costa's brief note again. ' . . . *You don't have to bother reading them . . . just sign by the pencil mark . . . purely a formality . . .* '

Don't bother reading them, my ass, she thought. If I'm signing, I'm reading.

She had booked a room at the Sherry Netherland, and after checking in she called Costa and said, 'Guess what? I'm in town. How about taking a starving girl out to dinner?'

'Why are you here?' he blustered. 'Where's Craven?'

'Craven is with his family in Washington where he belongs,' she said sweetly, 'I am here to do some shopping.'

'That's nice . . . ' Costa replied hesitantly.

'What's the latest news on daddy's situation?' she questioned.

'Slow,' he replied carefully, 'no more on the phone.'

'I understand. I'll see you later.' Instinct warned her to tread carefully with Costa. Play it wide eyed and innocent.

She was wide eyed and innocent all through dinner at Twenty-One. She ordered the duck as Costa advised, admired the dark wood panelling and the toys hanging from the ceiling, sipped prudently at her wine. 'I've never been here before,' she enthused, 'it's terrific!'

He was pleased that she liked his choice of restaurant.

'What do you think?' she inquired casually over prawn cocktail. 'When will Gino be back?'

He shook his head seriously, 'It's going to take a while, much longer than we anticipated.'

'How long?' she asked quickly.

'It's impossible to say.'

'Weeks? Months? *Years?*'

He shrugged. 'It could be a long time. Who can tell?'

Was he mistaken or did he see a smile hovering on her lips? She had certainly grown into a darkly beautiful young woman. It was strange to be sitting in Twenty-One with her. At first he was quietly ill at ease, but as the evening progressed she soon had him talking, reminiscing about the old days.

She was a good listener, interjecting with questions at just the right moments. Soon she was finding out more about Gino and his life than she had ever known before. She was aware of his rich period – after all, she had been born into it – but it was really fascinating to listen to stories about the old days – when he had had no money and lived in a beat up old room.

'How did you two meet?' she asked.

Costa immediately became cagey. She sensed something was up and dropped the subject.

Uncle Costa. She had known him all of her life – yet this was the first time they had ever sat down and had a proper conversation. She wondered what he was doing for sex now that Aunt Jen had died. Was he too old to bother any more? Was it difficult for a man to continue getting it up year after year, decade after decade? He was pleasant enough looking. Smallish, thinnish, grey hair on its way to heaven.

The good red wine had really loosened his tongue. He was talking of Leonora – Lucky's grandma. A forbidden subject over the years. Aunt Jen had always paled at the very mention of her name.

'Gino loved her very much,' Costa rambled, and then, as if realizing he was saying too much, he shut up.

'Uncle Costa?' she questioned artlessly, 'Remember the conversation we had just before Gino left?'

He nodded.

'You said that I'd have to sign a few papers – nothing to bother me. It was complicated – it would take a week to explain.'

He nodded again.

'Well I've got a week, and I'd be really grateful if you *would* explain things to me.'

How could he refuse? She was no longer the wild Lucky of old. She was a lovely sweet girl, with a genuine interest in things.

Day after day she came to his office and he began – slowly at first – because he thought her interest wouldn't last – to explain the workings of the various companies. 'Of course you're only a figurehead,' he said, 'you'll never be called upon to get involved.'

*Oh no? That's what he thought.*

'I'll send you things to sign . . . you can rest assured that whatever I send you has been checked out and approved by me.'

She nodded. Like a sponge she absorbed every bit of information she was given.

Craven called her angrily from Washington, 'When are you coming back?' he demanded.

'I'm not,' she replied coolly, 'our marriage is over. Please arrange to have my things packed and sent.'

Craven was more upset by what his father would say than by the thought of Lucky divorcing him.

Peter Richmond called her a day later. Casual politician's bullshit voice, 'Lucky? What are you thinking of? Come back and we'll discuss it.'

'There's nothing to discuss.'

'If you don't come here I'll have to fly in to see you.'

'Fine.'

She had told no one of her plans. *Her* divorce was *her* business. Costa did keep on saying, 'Shouldn't you be getting back to Washington?' But she just shook her head and murmured, 'No hurry.'

When Peter Richmond telephoned she arranged to meet him for dinner. She had been dining every night with Costa – probing and learning – so he was disappointed when she said she couldn't make it that night.

'I wanted to take you to a special place,' he complained.

'Tomorrow, Uncle Costa, I promise.'

'But it was arranged for tonight,' he fretted.

'Where?'

'Ah . . . it's a secret.'

'Tomorrow, then?'

'Yes.'

Peter Richmond wore his public gear of casual sports jacket, open neck shirt, and well fitting slacks. Man of the people. As he walked through the restaurant of the Sherry Netherland he waved and smiled at everyone as though they were all one big happy family.

Sitting at a table, watching his approach, Lucky felt slightly sick. At home he was a mini tyrant – all of his children were scared shitless of him. Only the indefatigable Betty took none of his crap. In public he was Mister Charm. In private Mister Shitheel.

'Hi, Peter,' she called acidly, 'you're late.'

'Am I?' Boyish surprise written all over his suntanned face. 'I am sorry. I hope you've ordered a drink.'

Couldn't the horse's ass see a hefty vodka right in front of her?

He sat down, greeted the wine waiter like a long lost friend and ordered himself a spritzer – combination of white wine and soda. 'Well, well,' he said leaning back in his chair and studying her. 'So the bird wants to fly.'

Her voice was steady, 'The bird never wanted to get trapped in the first place.'

'You have to be kidding, dear. Any bird would want to marry into the Richmond family.'

'Has anyone ever told you that you're full of shit?'

He bridled, but only for a moment. Over four years their relationship had been non-verbal. Now she had developed a mouth. 'You're just like your father,' he said coldly.

'Yeh. I guess I am. Only daddy would never have allowed himself to be conned into a boring marriage. I can see I'm going to have to develop balls – just like dear old daddy.'

'Christ! You're vulgar.'

'And you never put a foot wrong. It's a well known fact in Washington that you screw anything that moves.'

'You can't divorce Craven,' Peter said tightly.

'Can't?'

'No. It's impossible. I made an agreement with your father. Only he can give you permission. Only then would I allow it.'

'You really *are* full of shit. I'm almost twenty-one, you asshole, I can do what the fuck I like.'

'What a lady you are.'

'And what a phony creep *you* are.'

The wine waiter arrived with the spritzer and presented it to Peter with a flourish and a friendly, 'Nice t'see you in our town, Senator.'

The smile was back on Peter's face in a flash, 'It's certainly nice to be here.'

'You ready to order yet, Senator?'

'Marvellous idea.'

'I'll send the waiter right over.'

Idly Lucky dipped her finger into her vodka and twirled the ice cubes. 'What *did* Gino blackmail you with?' she asked curiously.

'I have no idea what you are talking about,' he said stiffly.

The waiter arrived with the menu, and they both ordered.

'I suggest we wait until your father gets back to town and we all sit down sensibly and discuss this divorce business in a civilized fashion,' Peter said. 'After all, if it's what you want, I don't see how he *can* object. And quite frankly – I myself would be relieved.'

'Well hot toasted titty for you! Only Gino is *not* coming back into town for a while – maybe a long while – so prepare yourself – I am divorcing Craven and I don't give a camel's crap what *anyone* says. Not even you.'

'We're going to Riccaddis,' Costa announced proudly as he drove his black Lincoln through the New York streets.

Lucky frowned. 'Riccaddis? Never heard of it, where is it?' Costa had been taking her to all the best New York restaurants and she was enjoying every minute of it. It was pleasurable to be out with a man who treated her in such an old world courtly fashion. Uncle Costa was a genuine antique and she loved him for it.

'Riccaddis is a very fine Italian restaurant. It's been around for over twenty years.'

'Really?' Lucky stared out of the car window. 'Where is it? New Jersey?'

Costa laughed softly, 'Don't be impatient, we're nearly there.'

'Can't wait!'

Costa had been unusually excited about the evening's excursion. He had refused to reveal where they were going until now. Somehow Lucky had known that Riccaddis was more than just another Italian restaurant.

She was right. As soon as they entered the small cozy place set in the middle of a run down neighborhood, Costa was afforded a king's welcome. An elderly woman greeted him with a warm hug. 'Costa! Why do you wait so long to see us?'

'Barbara! Always the same – always beautiful.'

'Older, greyer, tireder.' She stepped back and regarded Lucky in a kindly fashion. 'So,' she said, 'if I had not known you would not have had to tell me. She looks just like him.'

'Lucky,' Costa said, 'this is the famous Barbara Dinunzio – best pasta cook in the whole of New York.'

Lucky grinned and extended her hand politely to the elderly woman.

Barbara ignored the hand and hugged her. 'From Gino's daughter I expect a kiss. I have not seen you since you were five years old, but I remember you always. Come.' With her arm around Lucky's shoulder she guided her to a corner table where two men sat. One was grossly fat, he struggled to stand. 'Your Uncle Aldo,' Barbara said, 'when you were little he changed your diapers, taught you nursery rhymes in the old language. You remember?'

Lucky glanced around desperately for Costa. What had he brought her into? Why hadn't he warned her? 'N . . . not really,' she stammered, feeling out of place and awkward with these strangers who were all looking at her with such warmth and kindness.

'It doesn't surprise me,' said Barbara mildly, 'any child who went through what you did . . . Your poor beautiful mother.'

'You knew my mother?' Lucky asked quickly, and for some unknown reason her eyes filled with tears.

'We all loved your mother,' said Barbara softly, 'everyone did.' She touched her lightly on the cheek, 'Now sit – we will drink wine and talk of happier things.'

The other man at the table said, 'So . . . little Lucky. You know who I am?'

She shook her head.

He laughed. 'I'm Enzio Bonnatti – your Godfather. With Gino gone you got me t'look out for you. You want or need – y'come to me – never strangers.'

She stared at him. Was this old man really the notorious Enzio Bonnatti, her true Godfather? This man with sunken cheeks, deep set eyes, and a benevolent smile.

Costa was beside her now, 'Lucky, these people are Gino's closest and oldest friends. Be nice to them because they want to be nice to you.'

She had not quite understood what he meant at the time. But as the months passed she began to understand. Costa had taught her certain things – but there was so much to learn. To have a man like Enzio Bonnatti as her Godfather was a gift to take advantage of. She accepted the weekend invitations to his Long Island mansion, and enjoyed listening to the stories he had to tell.

The house was always full of different relatives and friends. His two sons, Carlo and Santino, attended on alternate weekends with their respective families. They did not speak to each other, a fact which both infuriated and saddened Enzio. 'A couple of clowns,' he called them, 'there are enough enemies in the world – family is blood and should be treated with respect.'

He took a strong liking to Lucky. Not only was she Gino's daughter, but she was sharp as any man and he admired her style.

She in turn quickly grew to respect him. He had strength and power – the qualities that impressed her most.

Soon she was dividing her time between the two old men. Costa in the city, and Enzio most weekends. Sex, once so important, didn't seem to matter any more. Drinking up the knowledge that these two men had to offer was far more important. She was enjoying herself and learning everything she wanted to know. It was enough to keep her satisfied.

One hot afternoon in New York, a contact arranged for her to go into the musty depths of a big daily newspaper. There she sat and studied the press clipping file on her father. Gino the Ram Santangelo. A vicious killer the newspaper called him.

There were headlines when he was arrested and tried for the murder of his own father. There was a small paragraph on page three when he was released years later with a full pardon.

She read about his first wife's death . . . and wondered. Was he everything they said he was? He was described as 'Infamous Bootlegger,' 'Violent Criminal,' 'Numbers Racketeer,' 'Notorious Gangster.' According to the newspapers he was a friend and associate of Lucky Luciano, Bugsy Siegel, all the big criminals of the day.

When she reached the clippings from the fifties she found a picture of herself. A small frightened girl being bundled into a car by a grim looking nanny. 'SANTANGELO CHILD DISCOVERS BODY OF MOTHER GRUESOMELY MURDERED IN GANGLAND REVENGE' screamed the headline.

Her mind clicked shut. She didn't want to look any more. She ran from the place upset and disturbed.

Her divorce went through with the minimum of publicity thanks to Richmond pull. Once Peter realized that there was nothing he could do to stop her, he cooperated in every way to get her out of the family as quickly as possible.

She was delighted. Costa was shocked. 'Your father will be very upset,' he worried.

'So we won't tell him,' she reasoned, 'that way he can't be upset can he?'

Costa nodded unsurely, and without mentioning it to her he phoned and told Gino.

'There is nothing I can do,' Gino said shortly, 'when I return I'll deal with things. You know I can't make waves while I'm here. *You* gotta take care of everything, and the most important thing you gotta take care of is gettin' me back to America.'

'I'm working on it,' Costa replied guardedly.

Gino was paranoic about communication. He felt that there was a wire tap on his phone, a survey on his mail, and that the quieter he stayed the better. 'Sure you are, I know, I know,' he sighed wearily. By special courier, Costa had sent him the information that he had gathered a team of expert tax lawyers who were looking into the whole situation and coming up with recommendations on how to move. It was nothing that could be dealt with in a hurry. The subject of Gino Santangelo was a delicate one. He had received so much publicity in his lifetime. Whatever he did was news. If a deal was to be worked out with the Internal Revenue service it had to be a watertight one that would stand thorough investigation at any level.

'So listen,' Gino added, 'you keep an eye on Lucky. I don't want her runnin' around New York like a wild one.'

'I'm with her all the time,' Costa assured his friend.

This was true. Lucky seemed happy enough to be in his company. He was glad that he had introduced her to Barbara and Aldo, and that she was spending time with Enzio. People like that were true friends of Gino's and would look out for her.

'I'll talk to you again soon,' he said warmly, 'you take care.'

Gino laughed dryly, 'Yeh, I'll take care not to overdose on gefilte fish and apple strudle! Jesus – what this food is doin' to my ulcer is nobody's business! Get me home Costa – this quiet life is no good for a man like me. Do it soon.'

Dario was due to arrive in New York any day after finishing the semester at the Art Institute. This fact didn't seem to please Lucky very much. She chipped away at Costa constantly. 'He doesn't want to come . . . It's stupid of Gino to force him . . . he just won't understand things . . . he's young for his age . . . immature . . .'

By the time Dario arrived Costa had been thoroughly brainwashed. Why *was* Gino forcing the boy to do something he didn't want to?

Lucky had moved out of Gino's large apartment where she had been staying. 'Why?' Costa asked. 'There is plenty of room for both of you to live there.'

'Gino wanted it to be Dario's. I'd sooner have my own place anyway.'

She found a nice little apartment around Sixty-First and Park and was installed by the time her brother arrived.

To survive in business you have to be tough, committed, ready to make instant decisions. Lucky had all the right qualities. Dario didn't. When he got to town Costa put him in a small office and gave him some minor chores to take care of. He screwed every one of them up, and merely looked indifferent when Costa berated him.

Costa was perplexd. What was there to teach a boy who did not want to learn? 'Why don't you relax,' he told him finally, 'get to know the city. We'll get together soon. In the meantime you take it easy.'

Dario did just that.

Eric had stayed in San Francisco sulking.

'When it's cool I'll send for you,' Dario had promised.

Now he began to sample the joys of being free. New York was not cool. New York was hot. Soon Dario forgot all about sending for Eric.

As the weeks turned into months Lucky was learning . . . acquiring every bit of knowledge she could. Her mind adapted quickly to the finer points of business. Costa was impressed. She asked intelligent questions and pinpointed significant discrepancies in contracts and legal documents that amazed him. She had an extremely sharp business head. Like Gino. She was direct, and blunt. Like Gino. She had every one of her father's business qualities. And when she told Costa that she wanted to handle certain matters that had arisen it was too late to stop her.

Gino had set up a syndicate of investors to finance the building of the Magiriano. Construction on the hotel had just begun, and the weekly payroll was vast. Since Gino's absence from America some of the finance had run dry.

'Jesus Christ!' Lucky exploded. 'Don't we have contracts with these people?'

Costa shook his head, 'No contracts . . . It was all done on a handshake basis.'

'They gave Gino their word didn't they?'

'Of course.'

'And what would *he* do if they didn't come up with the money?'

Costa cleared his throat nervously, 'He had his own . . . methods.'

'*You're* supposed to be running things for him . . . why don't *you* use his methods?'

'Some things are best left alone until the moment is right. You must wait for Gino.'

She stared at him hard. 'We can't wait – we don't know how long he'll be away – even *you* say it could be years. No,' she declared, 'the building must go on. If they gave their word they have to be made to keep it. Give me a list. I think I can work something out.'

He laughed in disbelief, 'Don't be a silly girl, these are hard men . . .'

Her eyes, black and icy cold. 'Don't ever call me a silly girl, Costa. You understand?'

He remembered Gino at the same age. So similar . . . so alike.

He sighed and said, 'Yes, Lucky.' And he knew then that there was no way he was going to stop her taking over while Gino was away. No way at all.

Lucky thought long and hard about things. Costa was a wonderful man, a brilliant lawyer. Excellent to deal with legal matters and the plodding work. But obviously not a man of action.

It was imperative that work on the Magiriano continue. She planned to make sure that it did.

She had noticed that on Sunday mornings Enzio Bonnatti spent a private hour or so in his study. During this time people came to visit him – staying sometimes for five minutes – sometimes for an hour. As they hurried away after the meeting there would always be a smile on their faces.

'What goes on?' Lucky asked Santino, the son she liked best. 'Who are all these people?'

Santino shrugged. He was short, prematurely bald, and constantly chewing on his nails, 'Favor time,' he said shortly, 'Enzio likes t'play God.'

'*I* want a favor.'

'So ask him.' Santino narrowed his small eyes, 'you – he'll never refuse. But expect to pay it back one day.'

She went to Enzio, sat on the corner of his desk, and requested his advice. 'Costa will not act,' she said after explaining the situation, 'But I want to. I am prepared to do whatever my father would do . . .'

Enzio chuckled, 'Gino never took no shit from no one – excuse my language. You want to be like him – why not? I lend you a couple of soldiers – you frighten the crap outta number one on the list – you ain't got no problems. Get my drift?'

She nodded, feeling the excitement creeping over her body like a rash.

Enzio looked at her shrewdly, 'Of course you want I should take care of it for you – my pleasure.'

She shook her head, 'If you can just let me have the assistance . . .'

He chuckled, 'You're Gino's daughter all right . . . he'd be proud of you. I tell you what I do. I give you two guys who'll back you every fuckin' inch of the way – 'scuse my language. You gotta remember though – you threaten – you gotta mean. Understand?'

'I understand.'

Where had Lucky learned street behavior? Was it in her genes?

She started off with the biggest investor, paying a visit to Rudolpho Crown, a slick haired, so-called investment banker who had once made a living at the track conning little old ladies with money to burn. Good fortune had smiled on him and he had married one of his old ladies who expired exactly six weeks after the wedding. 'She died of pleasure,' Rudolpho was fond of telling anyone who'd listen, 'hadn't gotten laid in twenty-two years!'

He inherited three million dollars, blew half on whores and good times, and went into business with the rest. He sat behind a massive desk in his office and leered insolently at Lucky while she discussed the money he had promised – but failed to put up.

'You gave your promise, Mr Crown,' she said coolly, 'you are part of a syndicate – if you try to drop out, others will follow and then work on the hotel will have to be stopped.'

'Sure,' he picked his teeth with the edge of a book of matches, 'I gave my word to Gino. And when he comes back I'll honor it.'

Her voice was very soft, 'It makes no difference where Gino is. You *gave* your promise – he wants it honored – now.'

Rudolpho grinned, 'He's hardly in a position to want anything. Word is out he won't be back for a long long time – if ever.'

She smiled very sweetly, 'Risk it, Mr Crown.'

'Risk what?'

'Risk waking up with your balls stuffed down your throat and your cock doing hot dog duty on the barbecue.'

He flushed a very dull red, 'Wash out your mouth, cunt, *nobody* threatens me . . .'

She stood, smoothed down the skirt of the well tailored suit she was wearing, smiled bleakly, 'It's not a threat Mr Crown. It's a promise. And I keep *my* promises. Just like my daddy.'

He did not believe her. He had no intention of putting money into a hotel without Gino Santangelo around to take care of things. Fuck her. So she was Gino's daughter. Big deal. A cunt with a mouth.

A week later he was woken at midnight by the touch of cold steel on his balls. He opened his eyes panic stricken. Two men were holding knives to his shrivelled penis. He started to scream, to cry, to beg.

He saw a shadow by the door and a woman's voice said, 'This is only a rehearsal Mr Crown. If your money isn't forthcoming immediately the first performance will be next week.'

Rudolpho Crown put his money up – fast. Other investors followed equally fast. The Magiriano was back in business.

Costa never could figure out how Lucky had done it. He suspected Enzio's involvement, but he never knew for sure, and Lucky certainly wasn't saying.

She seemed calmer, almost serene. She had felt the excitement of power and it was better than anything she had ever known. She, Lucky Santangelo, could handle anything now. Why not? She had proved herself capable.

Shortly after settling the business of the reluctant syndicate of investors Lucky flew to Las Vegas to see for herself the building progress being made on the Magiriano. Naturally enough she stayed at the Mirage, and naturally enough Marco was there to greet her.

She had finally found out who Bee was. Costa had told her the whole story. All about how Bee had taken Gino in when he was cut up and half bleeding to death and nursed him back to health. How she had faithfully hung around for the seven years Gino languished in jail.

'She sounds like a nice lady, why didn't they marry?' Lucky asked.

'They were going to, but after Marco it seemed she couldn't have any more children.'

Lucky was outraged. 'You mean he didn't marry her because she couldn't have kids? What a pig!'

When she heard about how Marco had grown up with Gino as good as his father she was unexplainably jealous. She greeted him coolly. It was the first time they had spoken in years.

'You look sensational, Lucky, really great,' he said.

'You look a little ragged yourself, Marco. Too much burning it at both ends?' Quickly she worked out how old he must be now. Forty-one. He was getting on. His exceptional good looks had not faded at all. He was still the most attractive man she had ever seen, and she *burned* to go to bed with him. It was the first time she had thought of sex for a long time. 'How come I'm not in Gino's suite?' she asked casually.

'I've taken his suite over . . . while he's away.'

'Oh *have* you?' She managed to make her tone mocking and amused.

He was disconcerted. 'How long are you staying?' he asked politely.

*Just as long as it takes to get you into bed.* She gestured vaguely, 'A few days, maybe a week.'

'Good. I want you to meet my wife. Maybe you'll have dinner with us tonight.'

*His wife!* 'How long have you been married?' she asked, hardly able to catch her breath.

'Exactly forty-six hours. You just missed the wedding. By the way, where's Craven?'

She felt he had betrayed her again and she hated him for it, her voice was icy, 'Didn't you hear? I got a divorce.'

'You did? Does Gino know?'

'It may amaze you Marco, but I am free, white and twenty-one. I can do what the fuck I like *without* asking Big Daddy's permission.' She paused and eyed him coldly, 'Maybe *you* have to jump – *I* don't.'

He started to laugh, 'You haven't changed – still the same old lovable Lucky!'

'Yeh. Still the same. A little sharper round the edges though – you'll soon find out.' Obviously he hadn't heard.

'I'll look forward to that.'

Their eyes clicked for just a second. She had never found a man that she couldn't get into bed if she wanted to. But did she still want him?

Yes. Goddamn it!

Helena, Marco's wife, was showgirl time. Six feet tall. Stacked. Flaming red hair. And a flaming red pussy, no doubt, fumed Lucky. She was – unfortunately – very beautiful.

The three of them met for drinks in the lounge. A combo

played Latin American music while waitresses in skimpy outfits served exotic cocktails. Lucky made a mental note that the place needed jazzing up. It was old fashioned and sleazy. She was sorry she did not have an escort. Marco still treated her like she was Gino's kid.

Wifey pie had big boobs that looked like they were no strangers to a jab or two of the old silicone. Lucky figured her to be in her late twenties, and hated her on sight. Unreasonable she knew, because Helena seemed genuinely nice.

Helena said, 'What a shame you couldn't've been here for our wedding – it was so quaint.'

Quaint! Whoever heard of a quaint wedding?

'Why?' drawled Lucky, 'did you have pixies for bridesmaids and toadstools for chairs?'

Helena laughed. She sounded like a drowning horse. The silicone shook and the red hair flashed.

'Tell me,' whispered Lucky, leaning forward conspiratorily, 'is your pubic hair the same wonderful color as the hair on your head?'

'Why no . . . ' began Helena, 'I did dye it once but it stung , . . ' She trailed off, not sure if Lucky was serious or not.

An idiot! Marco had married a beautiful raving idiot! What a disappointment when someone you have always wanted turned out to have appalling bad taste. What did she know of his personal taste anyway? Maybe he thought this bimbo was the best thing since fur lined jock straps. 'So . . . how did you two meet?' she asked crisply. May as well get the whole boring story.

Marco had been staring off into the gloom, but now he paid attention as Helena said, 'At my first husband's funeral. It was so funny . . . '

He silenced her with a glare, 'Want another drink, honey?'

Since Helena was clutching a mostly full Banana Daquiri this appeared to be a superfluous question. But Helena got the message. She wasn't *that* dumb. She changed the subject clumsily, 'I just *love* your outfit. Did you get it here?'

Lucky decided that she wasn't interested in *how* they had met, *why* they had met, or even *when* they had met. They *had* met. It was enough.

The evening went from boring to very boring.

When they dropped her off at her room around twelve, she couldn't wait to get back downstairs and cruise the casino. This time if she ran into Marco he couldn't buy her a sandwich, run to Big Daddy, and send her off to bed.

She spotted a tall dark cowboy with an unpermanent look. 'Can I buy you a drink?' she asked matter-of-factly.

He inspected her long and hard. Liked what he saw. 'I thought drinks were free when you're playin' the tables.'

She smiled, 'Not in my room.'

'You're not a—'

'Certainly not. The only currency you'll need is . . . talent.'

Together they boarded the elevator. She wasn't a whore. She wasn't a nymphomaniac. She just liked getting laid occasionally without all the bullshit and hassle of a long relationship. Men had been bedding casual pick ups since time began. Why shouldn't women? Besides, she *needed* someone tonight.

He stayed an hour. He *was* talented. But then she had an eye for talent. When he left he was mumbling about lunch the next day, she practically had to shove him out of her room. There had never been a man she wanted to stay. Never a kindred spirit.

She prowled around the room thinking of Marco and wondering what he had that made her want him so much. She had thought the cowboy would take away the hurt of him getting married. But he hadn't helped. Sexually he had been adequate. For once it wasn't enough.

She didn't get Marco on that trip. But when things began to happen, when she began to wield her new found power – that's when he finally started to notice her.

Back in New York she said to Costa, 'The Mirage looks like a tacky hooker on a street of high class call girls. Tino Martino headlining twice a year and a few exiles from bad TV shows *do not* make for scintillating entertainment.' She paused and lit up a cigarette, '*And* the place needs renovating – it's seedy, peeling paint, that dingy lounge. It needs jazzing up.'

Costa waved the smoke she was blowing in his direction out of his eyes, 'Marco takes good care of the place. If changes are needed I'm sure . . . '

She cut in on him sharply, 'Marco doesn't know his ass from a hole in the ground. Just married and reeling from too much pussy.'

Costa flinched. Where did she learn such expressions? It was all right for men to talk that way . . . But she was a girl . . . It wasn't right . . . proper.

'Marco has complete control. He runs everything – the money – everything. Gino trusts him implicitly. We cannot rock the boat.'

'Big deal. I am *the* major shareholder – I have more points than anyone. *I* want changes, and *I* plan to see that they're made. If Marco doesn't like it he can always quit.'

Costa regarded her solemnly. Had he created a monster? What would Gino say if he knew what was going on? Fortunately he didn't. He thought that everything was running smoothly, that Dario was learning the business, that Costa would know what to do if anything went wrong. He had no idea of Lucky's active participation in everything. And Costa did not feel inclined to tell him.

Over the following months, Lucky flew back and forth to Vegas with designers and decorators, planning the changes she wished to make at the Mirage and overseeing the building of the new hotel.

'What's going on here?' Marco screamed at Costa on the phone. 'She's disrupting everything. Get her off my back.'

'I can't,' Costa replied simply, 'She's the major shareholder, she can do what she wants.'

Simmering with fury, Marco noticed her all right. By the time he noticed her enough to want her, she was cool, business-like, and remote. She had no intention of sharing him with his wife.

Eventually the renovations that Lucky wanted took place. The Mirage acquired a new look. Fresh acts were hired for the lounge – no more tired girl singers in strapless dresses – but young rock groups who put a little meat in the place.

She hired a top P.R. firm to reactivate the hotel's image. 'We want to attract younger people,' she told an irate Marco, 'the place is beginning to look like a home for geriatrics!'

'Bullshit. It's the old ones who have the money to play. Our casino does top gross.'

'Yeh. And the hotel side has been losing money for the last ten years. You watch things change. Why shouldn't we make a profit on *both* sides of the business?'

She was right. Gradually business improved – dinner shows that had once played to half filled rooms were now booked solid. The restaurants were full again. The new style lounge attracted more and more people. Not only was the hotel now running at a profit – but the considerable casino takings soared also.

Satisfied, Lucky moved into other spheres of Gino's business empire. She had a magic touch. A knack of walking into a business and automatically smelling out the way for it to improve. Like Gino, she always sniffed in the right direction. She always went right to the top – the chairman, managing director, whoever Gino had appointed to run things. At first they resented her or patronized her. But when she pointed out that legally she had the right to do whatever she wanted – including fire them – they listened, complied and usually found out she was right.

In 1968 Gino had purchased a small cosmetic company as a favor to a friend. It lost money every year, and was trundling slowly towards bankruptcy. Lucky decided to make it her pet project. She changed the name to The Free Make-Up Co., hired new management, appointed herself as director, and said to Costa, 'You just watch me turn this business around.'

He watched. He was sure she could do it.

Occasionally she flew back to Vegas to check on the progress of the Magiriano. Slow. Slow. Slow. Problems – then more problems. Nothing she couldn't deal with.

Marco was always around to greet her cordially, give her the word on what was happening in town.

'Still married?' she would ask lightly, although her stomach would churn with the anticipation that he might have gotten a divorce.

'Sure am. And you? Still screwing around?'

'Give me a better hobby and I'll try it,' she drawled jokingly. She knew her casual sex life pissed him off.

Sexual tension between them was hot. She could feel it. She *knew* he could feel it.

One night he came on very strong. Helena was out of town visiting friends. They had dined together, talked a lot about old times – Gino – the Bel Air house – Dario. When she was at the door of her room he pressed her arm and said, 'I'll come in.'

She shook her head, 'No.'

'Why not?' He was surprised.

'I make it a habit to avoid married men.'

'I thought you didn't even bother with their names – let alone whether they were married or not.'

He was so close that she could feel his breath on her cheek. She wanted him more than she had wanted anyone in her life. Sweetly, she said, 'Take your smart ass remarks and stick them where they'll get the most laughs. Goodnight Marco. Sleep warm.'

She was in her room and the door was closed on him before she could weaken.

Oh God! Was this what love was supposed to be? A searing pain all over that either had you in the depths of gloom or grinning like a clown? The perfect opportunity to have him – and she had turned it down. Why?

Because when she had him she wanted him for keeps. That's the way it *had* to be. No other way.

And it *would* happen. She would *make* it happen.

Dario never did send for Eric, so after six months, Eric appeared one Saturday morning with two suitcases and many recriminations.

'I've been busy,' Dario sulked, 'you can't stay here.'

'Here' was Gino's luxurious apartment complete with live-in cook and daily maid.

'Why not?' demanded Eric, determined to insinuate himself into Dario's life again.

'Because you just can't . . . people will find out . . . Costa . . . my sister . . . '

'We lived together in San Francisco.'

'That was different.'

'Why?'

They argued for ten minutes, then reluctantly he was forced to let Eric in. He had no intention of allowing him to stay. He had discovered the joys of loving alone *and* of hunting alone. Who needed Eric any more?

Eric took one look around the sumptuous apartment and decided he had made the right move. He settled himself in and refused to budge.

Dario was angry and frustrated. He was having enough trouble with Lucky. All he needed was for her to find out he was gay.

The bitch had taken over. While he pottered around the office doing nothing very much, she queened it over everyone – and Costa let her get away with it. It wasn't that he particularly *wanted* to get involved, but it infuriated him that he was treated as a nobody – while his big sister got the treatment. 'Gino wanted *me* to learn the businesses,' he pointed out peevishly to Costa one day, 'not Lucky.'

'You want to learn, be here every morning at eight sharp. Prepare to finish seven, eight, nine at night.' Costa replied brusquely, 'that's what Lucky does.'

Dario had no intention of doing that. He liked to sleep late in the mornings, then drive his Porsche sports car down to the

Village and meet with friends. Every day he held court at a small Italian restaurant. The table in the corner was reserved especially for him, and sometimes as many as fifteen or twenty people would crowd round it. Money was no problem – whatever he wanted he just asked for – Gino had left instructions to that effect.

Yes, he had lots of friends, and he had no desire to share them with Eric. But Eric was not to be shifted. Once in, he was *there*.

'You can't stay,' Dario insisted.

'I have nowhere else to go,' Eric whined, 'I came all this way just to be with you.'

When he went to touch Dario it was all over. Dario attacked him with an uncontrollable violence he had never suspected he had in him.

Eric moaned in pain and delight. 'I didn't know you were into violence . . . Oh Darry, we'll be so happy together.'

As time passed Lucky worked hard and played hard. She was a resolute business woman, demanding and getting the best from the people she employed.

The small failing cosmetic company she had taken over was starting to do very nicely indeed. Her methods of obtaining new accounts were somewhat unorthodox – a little bribe here – a little threat there. She knew the product was good, and if she had to use a little persuasion to allow others to find out, it didn't bother her. Usually the Santangelo name worked wonders.

She flew back and forth to Las Vegas constantly, noting that Marco and the beautiful Helena were still firmly married. She still wanted him, never stopped wanting him, but it had to be on her terms.

Very rarely she thought of Gino whose empire she was taking over. She was building his hotel, realizing his dream – yet they had not spoken nor been in touch with each other at all.

A woman wasn't good enough to go into business huh? Too emotional huh? She would show *him*.

When Gino left he had offered her nothing. With Costa's help she was taking it all. Legally it was hers anyway . . . hers and Dario's. She thought about her brother and frowned. Such a screwed up boy. She wondered if and when he would ever straighten out. Poor blond beautiful Dario. What a waste . . .

Dario and Eric lived together uneasily, pursuing a life-style neither of them had ever experienced before. New York was full of new kicks . . . And Dario had the money to explore every avenue . . . Perversions, thrills, parties, clubs . . .

Together they ventured into the thriving underground world of the homosexual community. It was not all glamorous and romantic and eyes across a crowded bar. There was the sordid side. The meat racks, the quick sex, the beatings, and the sado-masochistic happenings. Eric found he was into all that. He dragged Dario along with him.

Soon they began to throw wild parties of their own in Gino's apartment – entertaining on a lavish scale with free coke and grass and everything else their guests required.

It wasn't long before stories began drifting back to Costa, who refused to believe what he heard. He informed Lucky – who wasn't surprised – she had long suspected.

'I'll go see him,' she told a worried Costa.

'We'll both go,' he said.

Lucky called up her brother and told him that she and Costa wanted to meet with him and would be at the apartment that afternoon.

Dario put down the phone. The fact that Lucky had taken control of the Santangelo Empire did not bother him that much. As long as he was left alone, and had access to un-limited funds he was satisfied. But now it sounded as if the bitch had found out his secret. She had spies everywhere.

He was confident that Gino would never get back to America anyway. Time was passing and nothing was settled. He wrote him a dutiful letter every few months and that was the extent of their contact. His father never replied, but Costa assured him the letters were received and enjoyed. After a while Dario stopped writing altogether and nothing was said.

'Eric, go out and stay out,' he told his friend. 'I'll meet you later.'

His sister. Lucky. She arrived looking cool and sharp and businesslike in a white suit. Costa – her lap dog – was with her of course.

She did not mince words, 'Things have got to change, Dario. You're playing out scenes in public should strictly be your own *private* affair. You get what I'm saying?'

'It would kill your father if he ever found out. Can't you see a doctor? Get yourself cured?' Costa fretted.

What did the old fart think it was? Measles? 'I can do what

the hell I like,' he said, glaring at Lucky, '*you* can't tell me what to do.'

She sighed, 'That's where you are very very wrong baby brother. If you don't want to cool down your activities – then I'll just have to see that things aren't quite so easy for you.'

'What do you mean?'

'You remember all those papers you signed?'

Yes, he remembered. Occasionally Costa or Lucky would ask him to come to the office to put his signature on some papers. He never read them, he just scrawled his name and ran. Now Lucky began to tell him in cool concise terms that he had signed everything over to her. 'I'm moving you out of this apartment to a smaller place, and putting you on an allowance. Maybe that'll get rid of some of your "friends."'

He glared at her. 'If you do that I'll call Gino.'

'Sure, go ahead. I know he'll be thrilled when he hears about you.'

Dario visibly paled. 'You can't do that.'

She raked him with a look that said it all, 'Don't worry, your secret is safe with me little brother. Just so long as you do what I want you'll never have to worry about *me* telling Gino. Oh – and cut out the drugs. A little grass is as far as you should go. Get it?'

Bitch! Bitch! Bitch!

But he would get her, he would think of a way. After all, he was a Santangelo too.

# Steven 1975

When Steven started work as an Assistant D.A. he soon proved himself to be a steely and successful prosecutor. At first, being on the other side of the fence was strange for him, but within a few weeks he knew it was what he had always been cut out to do. Prosecuting sons-of-bitches who sold drugs to children, bribed police officers, beat up on women, raped, tortured, murdered. Seeing these men locked away was the kind of job satisfaction he had always craved.

It did not take long for his reputation to spread, and defense lawyers would throw up their hands in despair if their client was unlucky enough to come up in court with Steven Berkely opposing.

Cops, on the other hand, were delighted if cases they had worked on long and hard were put in his capable hands. He was a winner. No slimey fish slipped through his tight net. Criminals got what they deserved. Steven did not play to lose.

He was incorruptible. A fact which reassured many an undercover investigator who had worked non stop for months to break a particularly difficult case. Especially as corruption seemed to be the order of the day – with everyone on the take from the neighborhood patrolman to the police captains.

Steven was not to be had. This he proved very early on in his new career, when he was approached outside the building where he lived one night by two men who informed him it would be to everybody's advantage if they – 'had a little talk'.

It did not take a genius to work out what was about to take place. Steven was in the middle of an extortion case – if all went according to plan, Loui Legs Lavinchi – a small time criminal – would get a ten or eleven year jail sentence at least.

'Sure,' he had agreed, thinking fast, 'We'll talk. Tomorrow morning – eight o'clock – here.'

The two men were surprised. They had heard he would be difficult, might need a little friendly persuasion. 'Why can't we talk now?' one of them asked.

He glanced around, 'Take my word for it – now's not the time. Tomorrow. OK?'

Nonplussed they watched him enter his apartment house.

Immediately he phoned his superior. Told him what he thought was about to happen. 'I want to be wired,' he insisted. 'let's get these two scumbags for attempted bribery.'

'Come on, Steven, you're a lawyer, not a cop, it could be dangerous.'

'Give me a good backup. I want to do it.'

And he did. A miniature listening device taped to his chest recording every word as the two men alternatively bribed and threatened him on Lavinchi's behalf.

When money passed hands, the backup team moved in, arrested the two men, and eventually they received jail sentences for 'Attempting to bribe a public official. Menacing and threatening the same said official.' Loui Legs Lavinchi went inside for twelve years, and Steven's reputation grew. He did not look back. For four years he did his job to the best of his ability enjoying every moment of it.

During that time he became very friendly with a young black

detective named Bobby De Walt. Bobby specialized in undercover narcotics busts. He was in his twenties, looked ten years
younger, wore outlandish street clothes, and his hair in an afro.
He was always horsing around and playing practical jokes.
Underneath the happy exterior lurked a very tough cop indeed.
Bobby De Walt had made more narcotic busts than anyone in
his unit of special detectives. And Steven had had the pleasure
of prosecuting on more than a few of them.

They made a strange looking pair when they ventured out on
the street together. Steven, so straight and good looking. Bobby,
wild and funky. Often they would sit in a bar near the court-
house talking until all hours. Sometimes they would go to a
restaurant. They enjoyed each other's company. They also enjoyed female companionship.

Steven was pleased and surprised one cold January night in
1975 when Bobby said, 'You gotta have dinner with me tomorrow – I found the top fox in the world, man. I'm gettin'
married.'

Steven was curious. Bobby had never struck him as the marrying type. When he met Sue-Ann he understood immediately.
She was nineteen years old, with curly hair, a sweet smile and
an even sweeter disposition.

Bobby wasted no time in fixing up the wedding. Within a
month Steven found himself in a pleasant Queens church acting
out the role of best man. It was there he met Sue-Ann's cousin,
Aileen. He noticed her at once. She was tall, well groomed,
attractive. She worked as an interpreter at the UN and lived
with her parents in a pleasant brownstone on Seventy-Eighth
Street.

He took her out four times, and when she refused to go to bed
with him on the fourth date he dropped her. Nicely.

He continued to date, but he did not forget her. Aileen was
the only girl who had ever turned him down. The rest were
always available – however nice – however respectable. And
while he realized that this was quite acceptable in the day of
the pill and women's lib – as the months went by he still thought
about Aileen.

Age seemed to have caught up with Carrie all of a sudden.
When she looked in her mirror she saw the same face, the same
smooth skin – only a few lines here and there to belie her more
than sixty years. The thing was, she felt old inside. A kind of
dead feeling that she couldn't seem to shake.

What had her life been for? How depressing that for the

last thirty-two years she had been living a lie. Even her own son could not be told the truth. *Especially* her own son, who spent *his* life fighting the very people she had grown up with. The pushers and junkies, whores and pimps. *They aren't all bad Steven. Sometimes people do things because there is no other way out.*

Often she would lie in bed all morning and let her mind wander back. Whitejack . . . What a man . . . How she had loved him for a time . . . When it had been good it had been very good. She and Whitejack and Lucille . . . The old jazz joints . . . Smalls Paradise . . . The Cotton Club . . . fancy clothes . . . dancing and hot hot loving . . . Good days at first . . . Until Dolly . . . Big white fat Dolly . . . and the drugs . . .

She brought her arms from under the covers and searched for the old needle marks . . . the scars. So faint . . . you could not see them at all unless you knew they were there.

Her mind drifted back over her time in the institution. She could remember very little of those long blank years.

Then she thought of Bernard and smiled. He had known everything about her and still he had loved her.

Elliott was so very different. She was his trinket, his possession. He had married her for his own reasons. Maybe he had suspected, seen something in her eyes. In the privacy of their designer decorated bedroom he had always treated her like a whore.

And the horrible thing was that she had put up with it, accepted it, and by doing so encouraged him to continue to act that way. The thought of having no money or position, had tied her to him like an invisible rock.

And now he was old. His sexual demands were less. One day he would be gone altogether and the thought frightened her. *She didn't want to be alone. She couldn't face life alone.*

The telephone interrupted her thoughts. She considered ignoring it, just letting it ring. But then it occurred to her that it could be Steven, so she picked it up quickly.

'Carrie? How are you?'

Jerry Meyerson. Of course. Not a week went by that he didn't call. How flattering that a thirty-six year old boy should be in love with her. She sighed wearily, 'Hello Jerry, and how are you today?'

'*I'm* great. *You* sound terrible.'

'I'm just a bit low.'

'Good. I am just the person to cheer you up. Lunch. The Four Seasons.'

'Not today Jerry . . . '

'Yes. Today. I have a sensational divorce case that I know you'll want to hear all about. It'll make you laugh . . . make you cry . . . It'll chase the blues away.'

She thought about her new Saint Laurent suit and decided that getting up and getting out *had* to be better than lying in bed all day.

'I'll see . . . '

'Perfect. One o'clock. Don't be late.'

Bobby De Walt had been working on a case for months. His wife, Sue-Ann, pregnant with their first child, saw little of him. Steven dropped by their house a lot and kept her company.

One night when he arrived at the small tract house he found Aileen there. They had not seen each other in eight months. She looked as surprised to see him as he was to see her.

They both looked to Sue-Ann, who shrugged nonchalantly, 'I didn't know *either* of you was comin' by tonight.'

'I can't stay long,' Aileen decided swiftly, 'just popped in to see how you were getting along.'

'I can't stay long either,' Steven said quickly.

'I'm sure you can both stay long enough to eat,' Sue-Ann murmured, smiling her sweet smile and laying out dishes of hot juicy spare ribs, corn fritters, and German style potato salad.

Steven's taste buds went into overdrive. 'Maybe I've got time for just a bite,' he said, sitting at the table.

Aileen had not eaten all day. She looked at the food, then at Steven, then she too sat down.

'I have to call my mother,' Sue-Ann said, leaving them alone.

'So . . . how have you been?' Steven asked, chewing on a delicious spare rib.

Aileen helped herself to a generous portion of corn fritters and replied, 'Busy. And you?'

'The same.' He thought about their last meeting. A movie. Dinner at a good Chinese restaurant. Then, casually, he had said, 'Let's go back to my place.' So confident had he been that she would say yes that he was already driving there.

'No,' she had said, 'I don't think so, please take me home.'

He had done so, and outside her front door he had said, 'I don't think I should call you again. I'm not looking for any serious involvements and . . . '

He had missed her. She was nice to take out. She would have been the perfect girl to take home to Carrie.

He chewed on another rib and said, 'You been going out a lot?'

She smiled faintly, 'Enough. Something I do never seems to get me past the third or fourth date.'

He grinned, 'Don't you mean something you *don't* do?'

She picked up a rib and nibbled on it delicately.

He decided she was definitely worth another try. 'How about a movie next week?'

She looked at him demurely, 'I'm no different, Steven. I still have the same . . . principles.'

'I wouldn't want it any other way. How about Tuesday?'

Sue-Ann waddled back into the room. She was in her seventh month of pregnancy and carrying big. 'Well, you two?' she inquired. 'Are you going to get together again, or have I been cooking all day for nothing?'

Steven was in court on a case when he heard. The whisper went around and reached him in fragments. Bobby De Walt had been made while working on his latest assignment. He had been set upon by two men in the basement of a Harlem tenement, stabbed and beaten badly. He had staggered out into the street, collapsed, and was now in Emergency. Steven asked for an adjournment and rushed right over to the hospital.

Sue-Ann was there, her sweet face swollen with tears. She clung to him and whispered, 'Why my Bobby? Why?'

Steven searched out the intern who had seen Bobby when he was brought in. 'How bad is it?' he asked.

'Not great. He lost a lot of blood from the stab wounds – got a couple of broken ribs. If he's strong he'll make it.'

'Oh – he's strong all right.'

Aileen arrived in the evening flushed and breathless, 'I came as soon as I heard. How is he?'

'Hanging on,' Steven said grimly.

Bobby hung on for two days, and then he rallied and began to recover. Seventy-six stitches patched together his body. His ribs were taped up, but he was smiling again.

The weeks and months that followed were not easy for Bobby. He was itching to get out of the hospital and back on the street. 'Screw it man, I wanna get back in action,' he complained to Steven, 'I was so close – so goddamn close.'

'Too close.'

'There ain't no such thing as too close.'

Steven spent a lot of time with the De Walts and so did Aileen. She was a very strong and supportive lady. Gradually he fell into the habit of picking her up after work if he was free and they would go over to Sue-Ann and Bobby's together. It was a routine he liked.

'You two should get married,'. Bobby joked, 'you look good together – sorta right.'

The thought had not occurred to Steven before, but he decided to introduce Aileen to Carrie one of these days and see what she thought.


Bobby – once on the road – made a rapid recovery. Sue-Ann gave birth to a lovely little baby girl, and Bobby felt the time had come for him to get back into action. He came into Steven's office one day simmering with information, facts, figures and a red hot anger that he had been so close to busting wide open one of the biggest cases of his career. 'Listen,' he said, 'I got enough for an investigation into the whole goddamn stinking rotten Bonnatti operation. He's the guy at the top – he runs it all – and I think we can nail him.'

'What makes you so sure?' Steven asked, his interest aroused. Nailing the notorious Enzio Bonnatti was any prosecutor's dream.

'Because I got street instincts.' Bobby said, roaming around the office, 'I got dudes I can subpoena. I got witnesses. I got connections with a lot of people who want to see Bonnatti go down. I *know* I was close to hitting on the big time. Who do you think wanted me out?'

'You think it was Bonnatti's people made you?'

'I'm sure it was. They got connections. Somebody blew my cover.'

Steven tapped on his desk thoughtfully. 'So what are you saying?'

'I'm saying we should go for a special commission to investigate Bonnatti. If you wanted to do it – head up the commission – nobody would turn you down – not with your reputation.'

Steven realized this was true. Twice before he had been asked to head special investigative commissions on certain matters. He had turned both opportunities down because the subjects had not grabbed him. Enzio Bonnatti was the lowest of the low. A violent criminal who had started off as a bootlegger in Chicago in the twenties and now controlled a very large part of

New York vice. Narcotics and prostitution were his big two.
'He's been indicted before . . . ' he said slowly.

'Yeah, an' always bought his way out. Or blown away
witnesses. Or somethin's come along to keep him on the streets.'
Bobby couldn't keep still, his skinny body was in perpetual
motion. He slammed his fist angrily down on the desk. '*You*
could get him. You got the style to do it, man. You go after
someone, I ain't *never* seen you lose. What d'y'say?'

'I say I'll look into the idea. That good enough for you?'

Bobby began to laugh, 'Man, you just said yes. You look into
that son-of-a-bitch's life and you won't let go until you got him.
I *know* you.'

'You think so?'

'Sweetheart. I would bet my left ball on it. And *that* I do
not bet lightly!'

# Lucky 1975.

Spotlights shot skywards. Illuminated fountains spelled out
'The Magiriano' in myriad cascades of water. A line of limou-
sines snaked their way to the entrance. The hotel was like a big
white Moorish castle. Impressive. Magnificent. Unusual.

Marco, in a new black silk dinner jacket, roamed the lobby,
his sharp eyes taking in everything. She had done it. The kid
had done it. It had taken her five long years of trouble and
problems and graft and strikes and threats – but she had come
through with one hell of a hotel.

Little Lucky. She was Gino's daughter, all right. A true
Santangelo. If Gino could see what she had achieved he would
be proud.

Of course, he, Marco, had helped her. Steered her in the
right directions, provided her with backup and protection, seen
that she didn't step on the wrong toes.

What a learner! She had a way of dealing with things that
always turned out right. She had a computer ticking away in
her head that worked out deals and percentages faster than
anyone he had ever known.

He spotted Skip, the rangey looking PR Lucky had hired,
hurrying towards him. Quickly he turned his back and walked

in the other direction. The guy was a deadly pain – full of smart ass fast talk. Marco knew she had taken him to bed, and the very thought made him angry. Why was she always taking guys to bed like some two bit tramp? What she needed in her life was a man . . . After all, what kind of men had she known? Craven Richmond. A real nothing. Good looking studs who passed in the night. Tennis pro's. Dumb actors. Pretty boys. He had seen them come and he had seen them go. Gino would have a blue fit if he ever got word of her activities. Still . . . tramp or not Marco wanted her . . . had wanted her for a long time . . . and tonight would be the night . . .

Beautiful Helena had been sent, objecting, to LA. 'Have a vacation, sit around the pool at the Beverly Hills and buy up Saks – you deserve a break.'

'But Marco, it's the opening . . . I've got a new dress, I can't be away for the opening . . .'

'Yes you can. I'll be too busy to look after you anyway.'

*Bye bye Helena. Only on a temporary basis. Lucky Santangelo and I have some unfinished business to take care of.*

Lucky stood under the icy needles of her shower and noted with satisfaction that today the water *was* ice cold. Yesterday it had been luke warm. 'Teething problems, Ms. Santangelo,' everyone had assured her. 'Don't worry, it'll be fixed.' Bow. Scrape. Ass kiss. Oh, how they catered to her! Oh, how she loved it!

She stepped from the icy water into her own personal bathroom. Sumptuous by any standards. Carpeted in white llama skin, jungle murals on the walls, alabaster fixtures and fittings.

She wrapped herself in a terry cloth robe and padded into her bedroom. Stark. Modern. Only the bed luxurious. Black silk sheets and tiger skin covers.

She sat on the bed and called down to the switchboard. 'No calls for an hour. I don't care *who* it is.' Then she stood, removed her robe, turned off the lights, and slid between the decadent black silk.

As soon as she closed her eyes a million things rushed into her head fighting her need for sleep.

She thought about what her yoga instructor had taught her. Turn off – inch by inch. First the toes, then the feet, the calves, the thighs . . . Impossible. She was too excited.

Naked under the sensual touch of the bedclothes she thought about who would be sharing her bed with her tonight. It didn't matter, really. They were all the same, handsome dark givers of pleasure. Interchangeable. Transient studs.

Except Marco of course. Dear married Marco. Son-of-a-bitch Marco. She desired him as much as ever, but for keeps, and he still showed no signs of dumping gorgeous Helena.

Goddamn it! She couldn't possibly sleep. She got out of bed and walked into the living-room. Huge plate glass windows led out onto a terrace. One press of a button and they slid open. She strolled outside, still naked. It was only seven o'clock, and the Vegas air was hot after the coolness of an air conditioned room.

What a triumphant evening it was for her. The opening of Gino's dream hotel – the Magiriano – and she alone had made it happen.

She pushed her hands into her long dark hair, piling it on top of her head. Then she let it fall and sighed deeply. Lucky Santangelo. Yeh. They had thought they were dealing with pussy – they had learned – the hard way – they were dealing with a Santangelo.


Costa had arrived the week previously. He could hardly believe that the day had finally come. Christ! The problems of getting the hotel built had been monumental. Lucky had dealt with them all – seeing the hotel completed had become her life.

She had surrounded herself with the best – Marco – who had learned personally from Gino. He had run the Mirage for nine years – a tight foolproof operation. He was all set to do the same at the new hotel. And of course had his people around him who had become Lucky's people too. They were all in the same family. All looking after Gino's interests.

And then Lucky had a powerful patron in Enzio Bonnatti – her Godfather – who counselled and advised her.

She had learned to be careful. She never moved without the personal attendance of her driver, Boogie Patterson. Boogie was very low key. Thin to the point of emaciation. Long haired. Always dressed in scruffy chinos and an old army jacket. He was twenty-eight-years-old, a Vietnam veteran, and a crack shot.

Lucky liked him because he never talked. It was bad enough that she had to have a bodyguard, a talkative one would have been impossible.

Yes, Costa reflected, Lucky certainly knew what she was doing. Not like Dario, the pervert as Costa secretly called him.

What was going to happen to the boy? What was going to happen when Gino found out?

If he ever did. The prospects of getting him back to America were gloomy. Costa had moved every way he could, tried everything. But with the upheaval in Washington, due to the Watergate scandal – and then Nixon resigning – nobody felt secure any more. Legal maneuvers. Bribery. Threats. He had talked to powerful friends of Gino's – people who owed him big favors – judges, politicians, high up connections in the police department. *Nobody* wanted to get involved. The Gino Santangelo tax case was still hot. The IRS wanted him back all right – they wanted him back so they could fry him.

The whole system was corrupt, yet Costa could not find a way. Five years was a long time to keep trying. If it took him forever he would do it. Gino depended on him. *He would do it.*

A cut in his life style infuriated Dario, but not enough to spur him into any sort of action. He had continued his existence to please himself. The parties were a little less wild, the drugs did not flow quite so freely, but he still did more or less what he liked, ignoring Lucky and Costa's occasional lectures. Who the fuck did they think they were anyway? He didn't have to answer to them.

One day he had landed up getting himself arrested. Stupid really. Some dumb kid had issued a complaint about being tied up, beaten, and raped by a group of men. The incident had taken place at Dario's apartment. He remembered it vaguely – Eric had brought the kid home – a sixteen-year-old freak who had loved every minute of it. Dario hadn't even joined in – he had been busy in the bedroom with a very straight married man who came out of the closet once a month with a vengeance.

Shit! Getting hauled down to the joint for something he hadn't even done.

Costa straightened it all out. White faced and angry he had told Dario, 'Enough. No more. You will respect the Santangelo name.'

Then he and bitch sister had cut his allowance down to a pittance and told Eric to get the fuck out of town. Not that Dario minded that. Eric going – it was a relief in a way.

When he received an invitation to the opening of the Magiriano he couldn't make up his mind whether to go or not.

Costa phoned and said, 'You have to attend, it's expected.'

By whom exactly? Bitch sister? 'I can't make it,' he had said shortly. Then he began to think about it, and decided that his not going was probably exactly what Lucky wanted. He decided he *would* go. Maybe he could think of a way to ruin her evening. Why not? She deserved it.

Lucky walked to the very edge of her terrace and leaned over. The view was staggering – a shimmering city of lights – a neon paradise. Soon she must get dressed and go downstairs to greet her guests. They were coming from all over for the opening. It was an event worthy of the stars putting on their glad rags and making the trek to Vegas.

Costa had told her so many times about the night the Mirage had opened. 'It was wonderful – Gino was like a king,' he had reminisced, eyes gleaming.

Well tonight she would be like a queen. In a black Halston dress with diamond and emerald jewelry she had gifted herself with. She didn't need men to give her presents. She didn't need men period. Well only occasionally . . . for medicinal purposes. She laughed softly to herself and walked back inside.

After completing an elaborate make-up she slid her naked body into the black Halston. It was perfect – a sensuous river of silk jersey, clinging and erotic.

She brushed her long jet hair and held it back on each side with ebony combs.

She was twenty-five-years-old. She had power, she had control, she had everything she had always wanted.

Except Marco.

One day she would have him . . . And maybe when it finally happened she wouldn't want him any more . . . Maybe . . .

Marco greeted Enzio Bonnatti personally with a warm clasped handshake. The old man was accompanied by his son Carlo, and a vacuous blonde who nobody bothered to introduce. Two bodyguards hovered in the background.

'Lucky's thrilled you made the trip,' Marco said respectfully, 'I'll buzz her, let her know you've arrived.'

Enzio nodded. 'Yes. I wanna see her. Wanna sit down with both of you.'

His voice had got old along with his body and Marco had to strain to hear what he was saying. He remembered Gino taking him to see Enzio Bonnatti for the first time. He had been seven-and-a-half, but he could still recall how impressed he had been.

He escorted Enzio and his party to the best table in the room.

Three bottles of his favorite scotch were already in place, and dishes of smoked roe, pistachio nuts, and cold chicken livers stood at the ready.

Enzio smiled, 'You got my favorite things. Lucky arrange it?'

Marco nodded, 'Of course.'

Enzio was beaming now, 'The kid never forgets anything – that's why she's a winner . . . not like her brother – whatshis-name. I keep on hearing things . . . What you think, Marco? Is the kid a fairy? Is it true what I hear?'

He shrugged, 'I don't know. I never see him.'

'Gino. He'd beat the bones from his body . . . Any man would do the same if a son of his . . . '

Enzio's words trailed off as a very stacked blonde passed by, 'Who's the one with the tits?' he asked, ignoring a sharp glare from his girlfriend.

Marco grinned. The old guy never stopped looking. 'I don't know. If you like I can find out . . . '

'So find out. Maybe an old man can do her a favor or two . . . '

Dario took a cab from the airport. No car to meet him. Why should there be? He was only the son, what did *he* matter. He conveniently forgot that he had not told anyone he was coming.

The cab driver said, 'I heard this joint cost more money than Caesar's and the Hilton put together. What d'ya think of that?'

Dario said nothing. He stared out the window and considered his position. He received a lousy allowance of two hundred and fifty bucks a week. His Porsche was five-years-old now. The rent on his apartment and a couple of charge cards were paid by the office. But that was it. That was fucking it.

'I like Circus Circus myself,' the cab driver continued, unper-turbed by his passenger's silence, 'y'can have a good time there – take the kids – nobody bothers ya.'

It was true, Dario thought, that nobody bothered him. As long as he stayed quietly out of the way he was free to pursue the life style that he wished. Since Eric there had been nobody permanent. He enjoyed sex with casual pick ups. No involve-ments. Just fresh street sex with dark haired boys. Since Eric there had been no more blonds. He didn't want to screw or be screwed by a mirror image of himself. There had been no more wild parties either – he didn't want to be cut off com-pletely – and that's what both Costa and Lucky had warned if there was any more trouble,

'You wanna get out here?' the cab driver asked when they reached the sidewalk outside, the long driveway. 'If I get in that line of cars we'll still be sittin' here tomorra.'

Dario paid the fare and got out, carrying his dinner suit in a plastic bag over his arm. The cab roared off, and he stared at the neon lit hotel in the distance. A sparkling white palace. It must have cost millions and millions to build. And he got a lousy two hundred and fifty a week.

Things were going to have to change. Tonight.

Resolutely he walked towards the hotel.

Lucky did not usually feel nervous. But tonight was different. Special. She was dressed, ready, and shivering like a fourteen-year-old on her first date.

When the door buzzer rang, she jumped. 'Who is it?' she called.

'Costa.'

She opened up the door and hugged him. 'I love you,' she said emotionally, 'for giving me the chance to do what you *knew* I could do.'

He hugged her back. She twirled around the room. He had never seen her look so vibrantly beautiful. 'Champagne,' she sparkled, 'now I know you don't drink it – but just for tonight – for me.'

'The bubbles give me indigestion . . . ' he began.

'Nonsense,' she objected, handing him a glass, 'let's drink to the Magiriano, may its casino outgross any other in the whole of Las Vegas!'

They clinked glasses, then Costa said, 'And to Gino – who planned the whole thing.'

She turned away from him, her face clouding over, 'Don't try to spoil my evening.'

'Lucky.' Costa said softly, 'without your father none of this would have been possible. You can't keep up this grudge against him forever.'

'Why not?' she demanded.

'Because one day he'll be coming back and taking over. And then you'll have to learn to accept him and his ideas.'

'He'll never come back,' she said airily, 'it's been too long – they'll never let him back.'

'I'll see to it that they do.'

She stared at Costa blankly, and silently wondered how she could convince him that Gino was better off staying where he was. The door buzzer prevented her from saying anything.

'It's Skip.' a voice called through the door, 'I wondered if you're ready to come down yet. Got a whole bagful of celebrities that I want you photographed with.'

She threw open the door and regarded the fast talking public relations man coldly, 'I told you,' she said patiently, 'no personal publicity.'

'I know, but I thought tonight , , , Being the opening and all . . . '

'No, Skip. Definitely not.' She closed the door firmly in his face. Why had she ever gone to bed with the creep? He came as fast as he talked. She turned to Costa and held out her arm, 'Let's go see if it's all holding together I've had nightmares this past week that the whole place will collapse in a heap of rubble and I'll be sitting in the middle stark naked with everyone screaming "schmuck – we told you a woman couldn't do it!" '

Costa took her arm and escorted her to the door. 'Lucky,' he said solemnly, 'One thing they'll never call you is schmuck. I can promise you that.'

Marco watched them approach. Lucky, electrifying in black, her eyes full of arrogant wildness, her breasts partially exposed in the revealing dress she wore. Costa, a proud old man, clinging to her in a possessive way.

He strode towards them as they paused in the doorway. The party had been going on for some time, an impressive turnout of superstars, producers, tycoons, sports personalities, hookers, con men, entertainers of all sorts.

Marco reached Lucky, kissed her chastely on the cheek, 'You look . . . very ordinary,' he joked.

She grinned. 'Where's Helena?'

'Funnily enough she's not here.'

'Why not?'

He held her eyes intently, 'You *know* why not.'

'I do?'

'It's a special night isn't it?'

'You're still a married man.'

'Listen.' he leaned close and his voice was very low, 'I think it's about time you made an exception.'

Her heart was beating like she had just got through jogging ten times round Times Square. 'I never make exceptions,' she murmured huskily But she knew she would. Tonight.

'There's always a first time, isn't there?'

Their eyes clicked together like dry ice sticking to skin.

'Is Enzio here yet?' Costa asked impatiently, not liking what he sensed was going on.

'Yeah – arrived a few minutes ago. I was just going to buzz you.'

'Come on, Lucky,' Costa said, 'let's go see him.'

She smiled, 'Sure.' Lightly she touched Marco on the hand, 'Later.'

Warris Charters observed carefully from his staked out position at the bar. An older slyer Warris Charters. Forty-one to be exact. He looked different. For a start he had dyed his hair black *and* his eyelashes. He had also developed heavy debauched pouches under his eyes and his perfect teeth had spread, leaving nasty ageing gaps.

The last nine years had not been kind to him. Being thrown out of the Cannes villa in a raging storm had not been good for his health. He had developed a dangerous case of pneumonia and ended up in a charity ward in a local hospital. He nearly died, not that any one would have cared.

As soon as he was better he attempted to contact Olympia. An impossible task. When the parents of a rich girl want her to vanish – she vanishes – and tough shit to anyone who tries to find her. After a while he gave up looking and moved in with a friendly hooker working the end of season tourist trade. In December he moved to Paris with her where she had forgotten to mention that she had a resident pimp. Warris ended up in the hospital again, this time with two broken ribs.

He finally limped home to Madrid where he took up with his old group of friends. Pushers, junkies, hopheads. He made a living arranging live sex shows, and then raised the money to make a porno movie. The male star dropped out at the last minute and Warris stepped in – hence the dyed hair. He had *some* scruples. Also a mother someplace . . . Wouldn't do to get recognized.

The movie was a vague hit in Europe. It gave him enough money to get back to America, where he made more of the same in a converted garage in Pasadena. Stars were not hard to find. Girls flocked to LA to make it in the movies. Some of them were not too particular about which movies. He made a passable living, had an erotic sex life, and all the while longed to become legitimate again. He still had the script of *Kill Shot* – Pippa's movie, but now his – because who could ever prove otherwise? The writer was dead seven years – he had done a little checking up.

*Kill Shot* was still a viable commercial property as far as he was concerned. Of course it needed a few changes here and there . . . But the story was a grabber. Time had not changed that.

He had thought long and hard about how to get it together. Financing a movie was like walking a tightrope backwards across the Grand Canyon – not easy. And then one day it had all fallen into his lap like a golden shower. He was in Vegas with a black hustler and her card sharp boyfriend. They had been cruising the hotels, when the black hustler had pointed a boney finger and said, 'You see that jive ass chick over there. That's Gino Santangelo's daughter. Can ya dig it? They say she's got balls like her old man. Wow! I'd sure like to lick 'em!'

Warris had looked. And double-taked. And looked again.

Lucky.

It couldn't be.

It was.

Lucky Saint. Lucky Santangelo.

*Pippa must have known. Why hadn't the dumb cunt told him?*

Then it all started going click click click in his head. When Pippa had first handed him the script she had told him it was a true story. The life story of Gino Santangelo. Who knew anything about Gino Santangelo then? The only news Warris ever read was in *Variety*. But the name had stuck over the years. Like Mickey Cohen, Meyer Lansky, it was a name you knew but didn't really know . . .

He had made it his business to find out everything he could. When he had enough information he decided to go to Lucky with the script and have her get it to her father. His hunch was that Gino would either want it made – in which case he would be happy to finance it. Or he wouldn't want it made – in which case he would be happy to finance any other script of Warris' choice with the provision that all copies of *Kill Shot* were destroyed.

It was a no lose situation. And Lucky was the connection to make it happen. Only it had to be done on a personal level – and she wasn't easy to get to. Finally he had managed to buy an invite to the opening night party from a part time porno queen who was a permanent fixture on Tiny Martino's guest list. He had paid her a hundred bucks and thrown in a fuck for good measure.

Now here he was, ready and waiting to make his play. And

what a play it was going to be. An ace. Either way he would win.

Dario checked into the hotel, took a shower, put on his dinner suit, and made his way downstairs.

He saw no one he knew, and no one knew him. He went to the bar and ordered a scotch. Christ! Who needed this? He just wanted to talk to his bitch sister and get the hell out.

Rudolpho Crown grabbed Lucky by the arm as she passed by his table. He was drunk, his slick hair hanging over his forehead in sweaty strands – 'We did it, little lady, we did it,' he slurred.

She pulled her arm away abruptly. There had not been one month when Rudolpho Crown had not been late with his money. During the long months of the union strike he had tried to back out altogether, and she had been forced to remind him of her original threat. Now it was all drunken leers and 'We did it'.

'Aren't you gonna sit an' have a drink with me an' my friends?' he slobbered. 'They all wanna meet you. They all heard lots an' lots about you.'

She inspected his friends briefly. The men seemed like a bunch of cheap hoods and she didn't like the look of any of them. The women at the table resembled Hollywood hookers on a bad night. 'Sorry, I can't stop now,' she said, a chill in her voice, 'have a good time.' She moved on past their table.

Costa muttered, 'I don't like that man.'

'Who does?' Lucky replied. 'But his money ain't bad.' She waved at Tiny Martino, who was with a fifteen-year-old movie tot and her mother.

'Disgusting!' Costa breathed.

Lucky laughed, 'No – just life.'

Enzio rose to greet her. He enveloped her in an affectionate hug. 'Congratulations!' he breathed, 'you did it.'

Her eyes sparkled, 'I did, didn't I?'

'You sure did. But I kinda always knew you had it in you.' He raised his glass of Jack Daniels, 'Never doubted you, Lucky – not for one friggin' minute – 'scuse my language.'

The next few hours she was on a high. She was Queen all right, and loving every minute of it. She table hopped, danced, chatted. Somewhere along the way Dario appeared, and she was genuinely glad that he had come, 'Why didn't you call? Let me know you could make it?'

He seemed stiff and ill at ease. 'I want to talk to you,' he said tightly.

'Come sit with me later,' she suggested before being swept off for another dance.

She mingled with the famous and the infamous. Danced, ate, drank, had a wonderful time. At midnight she personally threw the first pair of dice on the top crap table and started things rolling. The doors were opened to the general public, and the invited guests were all ushered into the 'White Room' where English rock soul superstar – Al King – entertained them. He had a throbbing rasping voice that brought chills to her spine. He was white but he sang soul the way it should be sung – black and hot and searingly sensual.

Afterwards there was a fireworks display around the M-shaped swimming pool, and the younger wilder guests stripped and flung themselves into the pool. Lucky was tempted to join them. But she knew it wouldn't look good. Knew that she must control her wilder impulses. She had worked for and won respect. Couldn't blow *that*. Couldn't become dumb available pussy.

So she stood beside the pool, and smiled, and watched, and knew that the evening was a raging success.

Dario skulked around the sidelines of the party, brooding. *Come sit with me, indeed.* The bitch hadn't sat all night.

He watched her, standing by the pool, glittering with jewelry that must have cost a small fortune. *Who did she think she was?* It was childish, but he had a sudden strong desire to go and push her into the water. He decided to do it. Why not? She was so full of herself, swanning around the place like a queen bee.

He started forward, but as he reached her she turned and said, 'Dario. There you are. I was looking for you.'

Liar!

'It's been such an impossible night, why don't we have break-fast in the morning?'

He bit down sharply on his lower lip, 'I wasn't planning on staying that long.'

She raised a sardonic eyebrow, 'Oh? And what pressing engagement do you have to hurry back to?'

Bitch! Bitch! Bitch!

'OK, breakfast,' he mumbled, 'there's plenty I have to say.'

'Good. It'll make a nice change. Ten o'clock, the Patio restaurant.'

He stared at her, his blue eyes bitter and full of jealousy.
Then he opened his mouth to say something cutting.

Warris Charters chose that particular moment to make his
approach. He strolled between them, his voice honeyed with
fake charm, 'Little Lucky Saint! Who would have thought it!'

She looked at him blankly, 'Who are you?'

'Who am I? You *have* to be joking.'

She glanced quickly to the shadows. Boogie was there should
she need him. 'Are we going to play guessing games or do you
want to tell me your name?' she asked sharply.

He ignored the sharpness in her voice. 'Are you going to
honestly say you don't remember me? I taught you to drive. I
taught you a lot of things. You, me, Olympia – the three
musketeers.'

She peered at him. 'Jesus Christ! Warris fucking Charters!
What stone did you crawl out from? And what happened to
you? You look *terrible*!'

Dario took a good look at the object of his sister's insults. He
didn't look so terrible to him. Rather handsome, actually. And
the bags under his eyes were sexy as hell.

'Nice to see you haven't changed,' said Warris dryly.

'Oh, I've changed all right. You can be sure of that.' She
paused, then added thoughtfully, 'What do you want, Warris?'

'Why should I want anything?'

'*Come on.* Cut out the "I'm just here to say hello" bullshit.
What do you want?'

He glanced quickly at Dario, 'A private talk.'

She indicated the party going on around them, 'I'm not in the
mood for private talks. Some other time.'

'I have something you'll want to see . . . ' he stopped meaningfully. 'Your father will want to see.'

What could Warris Charters have that could possibly be of
any interest to her or Gino?

'I'm not interested.'

'You will be when you know.'

'So stop playing Mister Secret and tell me,' she waved vaguely
towards Dario, 'it's OK – he's my brother – you can talk.'

Warris took a second look at the surly blond boy. He had
noticed him earlier sitting by himself at the bar, and had wondered if he was an actor . . . and if so if he would be interested
in doing a little porno work. Good thing he hasn't asked! 'I
have a film script. It's the story of your father's life. I think
he should see it before I go into production.'

She yawned, 'So send it to him – nobody's stopping you.' She saw Costa and waved, 'Goodnight Warris – *wonderful* to see you again.' She was off in Costa's direction without a backward glance, leaving Dario and Warris standing together.

'Shit!' muttered Warris angrily.

Dario sensed that there might be a way to get to Lucky here. He wasn't sure how . . . But he certainly intended to find out. He stuck out his hand, 'I'm Dario Santangelo,' he said, 'maybe *I* can help you.'

She had hardly seen Marco all night. A smile across the room, a look. He was working the room as she was. Being nice to the right people, spreading the charm, keeping a sharp eye on everything that went on.

When she was introduced to Al King, the singer, Marco had miraculously appeared by her side and steered her gently to Enzio's table. Al King had a reputation. So did she. Marco was determined to keep them apart.

Five minutes later Al King had three attentive women swarming all over him. Lucky noted with a grin that Marco had supplied a brunette, a redhead, and a blonde, just to make sure he hit the jackpot. He needn't have bothered. However attractive they were she did not like going to bed with stars. They were doing you such a big favor – sharing the hallowed organ that millions of women lusted after. The hallowed organ had usually done a touch too much mileage, needed careful direction and excellent reviews. The performance was never up to standard, especially in the close ups.

Enzio had his blonde girlfriend sitting on one side of him, and the young lady with the large breasts who had attracted his attention earlier, on the other. 'You satisfied?' he asked Lucky warmly.

'It couldn't be better.' She glowed.

'Good, good.' He leaned forward and whispered in her ear, 'You know who that dirty shit Crown brings here tonight?'

Automatically she twisted her head and stared at Rudolpho Crown's table across the room. The occupants were drunk and loud. 'Who?'

Enzio made a face. 'Maybe it's better I don't tell you now.'

'Who?' she demanded.

'He brings with him the Kassarri twins.'

She felt herself go cold, 'I don't believe you.'

His tone was mild. 'You think Enzio Bonnatti lies?'

'No, no, I didn't mean that. It's just that I don't believe it's possible he would do such a thing.'

'Yeah. It's possible. The man is a stupid fuck. Maybe he don't know. I'll have someone fill him in on the facts of life .. '

The Kassarri twins. Pinky Banana's sons from his first marriage. Lucky had never met them. She never wanted to meet them. Their father had murdered her mother. And Gino had disposed of Pinky . . . She had forced it out of Costa . . . Enzio had told her also . . .

'How dare they set foot in my hotel,' she flashed. 'I want them thrown out . . . *now*.'

'Let the bums stay – the evening is nearly over. Why spoil it with those turds? Don't worry, they won't come back. I'll deal with it for you – they'll *know* not to come back. My favor.'

She kissed him on the cheek, 'Thank you, Enzio.' She glanced once more over to Rudolpho Crown's table. What a pig he was. He *deserved* to have his prick cut off.

It was four o'clock in the morning, and the party was still going strong. But Lucky knew it was time to leave. She sought out Costa and whispered, 'I'm going to bed. It was a fantastic evening wasn't it?'

'Wonderful!'

'Why are you hanging around anyway? It's long past your bedtime.'

'I want to be able to tell Gino about this night from start to finish. I plan to stay until the last person leaves.'

Gino. Gino. Gino. Goddamn Costa for always reminding her.

'Sure, have fun,' she said coolly, 'see you tomorrow.'

She took the private elevator to her penthouse apartment. Boogie silently accompanied her, checked out the place for any intruders, then returned to his room in the back. His quarters were separate, but if she needed him all she had to do was press any one of several strategically placed panic buttons and he would be there within seconds.

Her mind was whirling. Why had Rudolpho brought the Kassarri twins to *her* hotel? What did Dario want now? Had she been right to dismiss Warris Charters without a second thought?

She kicked off her Charles Jourdan shoes, and selected an album to play. Marvin Gaye's *What's Going On.* The warm sensual sounds filled the apartment, relaxing her.

How long would it take Marco to appear? Five minutes? Ten? Certainly no longer.

With a deft flick of her wrist she undid a hook, and her expensive Halston fell to the floor. She picked it up, walked into her bedroom, and selected her oldest and most favorite denim work shirt from the closet. It was the same shirt she had been wearing for ten years. Marco had seen her in it often . . . but not recently.

In the bathroom she carefully removed every bit of make-up, took off her jewelry, vigorously brushed her long dark hair and braided it neatly. She looked fourteen-years-old. Scrubbed and clean and prepared to face the man she had loved for so many years.

When he knocked on her door she was ready. 'What took you so long?' she asked softly.

'I was only fifteen minutes . . . Hey, look at you. What have you done?'

She grinned. 'I put the clock back. Like it? You're seeing the real me.'

He looked perplexed. This was not the sensual beauty he had been with minutes before. This was a young girl he hadn't seen in a long time. 'Jesus, you look like a little kid.'

'That's what you used to call me – you and Gino.'

He was completely thrown.

She put her hands on her hips and faced him. Long bare tanned legs spread apart, head on one side, a dangerous glint in her black eyes. 'Hey, mister – you wanna play doctor?'

He laughed. 'You're nuts. You're making me feel like a dirty old man.'

'So come on. Be dirty. Tonight's an exception. If you stay married, no more exceptions.'

'Lucky.' He took her face in his hands and kissed her very very slowly.

She responded with ten years of passion, her tongue exploring his lips, teeth, the inside of his mouth. She felt his body against her grow satisfyingly hard. 'Let's make tonight an exception to remember,' she whispered.

They continued to kiss, until lazily, without hurrying, his hands drifted down to her breasts, holding them through the denim shirt, tracing their outline, feeling for the nipples and rolling them through the worn material.

'Nice,' she murmured, 'veree veree nice.'

'You can say that again.'

'Oh, I will . . . I will!'

He undid her shirt slowly, but didn't attempt to take it off, just let it hang open while his hands roamed around inside.

'You're driving me insane!' she said at last. 'Let's get naked and get it over with.'

'I'm not the dentist for crissakes.'

'Oh, God, Marco! *I can't wait.* I've waited *ten fucking years.*'

He acted so quickly she hardly knew what had hit her. His clothes were off, she was over his shoulder and dumped on the middle of the bed, and he was inside her screwing her with an intensity that made her nervous for his health.

Then all at once she didn't care about his health or anything else for that matter. She was coming so hard and so fast that she thought she might die of pleasure. And he was coming too with a roar of delight. They were bathed in sweat, joined together, and both laughing.

'Don't ever order me around again,' he said, 'look where it gets you.'

'Everywhere I've always wanted to be.' She propped herself up on one elbow and stared at him. His body was deeply tanned and covered with a light smattering of black hair. Lightly she ran her fingers over his chest. 'Do you *know* how long this has been my dream? Do you have *any* idea?'

He shook his head and smiled.

She brought her mouth down onto his chest and began to feather kiss him. Across his nipples, over his stomach, down towards his cock which immediately began to show signs of life. She paused before taking him into her mouth. 'What about you, Marco? How long have you wanted me? When I was a kid, when you used to drive me around – did you want me then? Did you lust after my girlish body?'

'You were the biggest pain in the ass I ever met.'

She took his half aroused cock into her mouth and carefully dug her teeth in.

Panic hit his face. 'Hey!'

Innocently she said, 'I'm not going to bite it off. Why would I do a nasty thing like that?'

He sat up and bundled her into his arms and began to kiss her again. Truthfully she could admit that she had never enjoyed kissing before. With Marco it was something else. The tip of his tongue was a real weapon of pleasure, and when he left her mouth alone and brought it down to her nipples, she knew she had died and gone to heaven. Words of love wanted to pour out of her mouth. But she knew she must wait . . . He was still married . . . Goddamn it! *Why* was he still married?

She pushed him away and reached for a cigarette, at the same time pulling up a sheet to cover herself.

'Did you know the Kassarri twins were here tonight?' she asked tightly.

'Yes,' his voice was guarded, 'I didn't want to spoil your evening.'

'If someone had told me earlier we could have had them thrown out . . . '

'Sure. And had Rudolpho screaming about his friends being badly treated. It was an accident – I guess he didn't know.'

'Enzio said he'll make sure he does know.'

'Good.' He extracted the cigarette from between her fingers and deposited it in the ashtray. Then he peeled down the sheet. 'Come here, kid.'

The second time they made love was leisurely and thrilling. Gradually they were starting to know each other's bodies – which positions, pressures, angles pleased, which didn't.

She watched him like she had never watched a man before. His eyes were greenish grey with thick black lashes. His hands were big. His body hard – no soft places . She found a scar on his thigh and wanted to know how it had got there. He started to talk about his life. It was the first time he had opened up to her and she was drinking in every minute. She heard about the things he had done, the restlessness he had always felt until his mother encouraged him to go to Gino. Marco shrugged, 'She was right. I hadn't seen him in years – yet he welcomed me back like I was his son. He's a great man – you must be proud he's your father.'

She had never discussed her relationship with Gino with anyone. It was private. 'Hmmm . . . ' she mumbled. 'Tell me about when you were little. You know, when Gino lived with you and your mother. What was he like then? What was she like? Why didn't they ever marry?'

'Hey – I thought we were talking about me.'

She jumped off the bed, 'Why don't we forget about talking and take a shower – see what comes up.'

He groaned. 'Nothing's gonna come up. I'm forty-five and whacked out. I think I'd better crawl off and get some sleep.'

She had been to bed with a lot of men. Never once had she ever wanted any of them to stay. Now she didn't know what to say or how to handle the situation. She only knew that *no way* could she let him go. 'Sleep here and you'll get a free breakfast.' she joked flippantly. But he was already getting off the bed and hunting around for his clothes.

Oh, God. Where did they stand now? What was going to happen? Why didn't the bastard *say* something?

She suddenly felt very vulnerable standing there naked with

her hair in stupid braids. He was pulling on his trousers. 'I guess I'll take a shower, then,' she said, waiting for him to stop her.

He yawned. 'Good idea.'

Forlornly she walked into the bathroom and stepped under the shower. Would he be gone when she came out? Would the next time be business as usual?

Christ! She had *never* felt like this in her life! Wanting him all those years had been one thing – but actually having him was another.

He came into the bathroom dressed, his clothes pulled on casually.

There was a bottle of shower gel beside her. Pretending not to have seen him, she grabbed at it quickly, and squeezed liberal amounts over her body, then began to massage it into her breasts.

'Wow!' he said, 'I saw a porno movie where a girl did that once.'

'Has your wife got silicone boobs?' she inquired sweetly.

He burst out laughing. 'Massaging your tits and thinking of Helena. Is there something I should know about you?'

Angrily she stomped out of the shower, nearly slipping. 'You're such a smart ass.'

He handed her a towel. 'What does that make you?'

'How many times do you do it in a night with *her*?' Even as she said the words she could hear the jealous twang in her voice and hated herself for it.

'Cool down.' He had stopped laughing. 'For someone with *your* record I wouldn't start asking those kinds of questions.'

She was furious, 'My record? What do you mean by *that*?'

'You ball a lot of guys – that's what I mean.'

'I'm single. Why shouldn't I? I bet *you* didn't keep it tucked up beside you at night when you were single.'

'That's different.'

'What's different?'

'I'm a man.'

'Christ! Now you *sound* forty-five. It's all right for a man to screw around but not for a girl – is that what you're trying to say?'

He scowled, 'You know the rules.'

'What fucking rules?' She was yelling now. 'Who fucking made 'em? *Men* – that's who.'

'Calm down, babe. It's nothing to get in a fight over.'

'But I *want* to get in a fight. I *want* you to understand me.'

'I understand you . . . '

She was speaking evenly now, 'No, you don't. But you will. I *like* good looking guys – if I have nothing better to do I take them to bed because I *like* sex. I am not a nympho or a hooker. I go to bed on my terms – and mostly I never see them again because that's the way *I* want it.' She paused d erratically. 'Now tell me, Marco. How many girls have you taken to bed just for an evening's fun – 'cos you liked their tits or ass or they had long legs. Be honest, how many?'

He shrugged vaguely. 'A lot.'

'And how many did you see again?'

A smile crept onto his face. 'OK, OK. I know what you're saying.'

She let the towel drop, went to him, and put her arms around his neck, 'Thank Christ for that!'

His hands began to roam. 'But you don't need no other guys right now – 'cos you got me – Right, little Lucky? Right?'

'You're pinching my ass!'

'Right, babe?'

Relief flooded through her body. She had him. Tomorrow they would worry about Helena. 'Take your clothes off and come back to bed,' she murmured.

He picked her up and carried her over to the shower. 'Hey . . . about that porno movie I saw . . . I forgot to tell you about the thing she did with the soap . . . really something . . . Maybe we should try it . . '

'Maybe we should . . . ' she agreed happily.

He was pulling his clothes off. 'Maybe we will . . . '

'Hey, I thought you said two was your limit.'

'Lady – you are just about to make me one hell of a liar!'

Rudolpho Crown and his party spilled out of the hotel at dawn. They were rowdy and vulgar. A cocktail waitress on her way home found herself grabbed and thoroughly groped by the five men, while their girlfriends screamed with laughter. A young couple suffered a barrage of obscene insults. One of the women in their party peeled down the top of her dress and shimmied her large naked breasts in the face of a doorman.

Rudolpho was convulsed. It was the funniest thing he had ever seen.

Salvatore Kassarri, the uglier of the twins, whacked him firmly on the shoulder, 'You gotta gold mine here. You wanna sell out your investment?'

He shook his head happily. It had been a grand evening.

Every fucking dollar he had reluctantly parted with was going to pay off. And how. That Lucky Santangelo broad had really done it. He had one great big piece of the finest fucking hotel he had ever seen.

Salvatore whacked him again. 'I don't think you heard me. You wanna sell?'

Rudolpho was too drunk to hear the note of menace in his voice. The Kassarri twins were big time. Rudolpho was only too happy to be able to entertain them. They were based in Philadelphia, where their tentacles of crime stretched in all directions. A few weeks previously a friend had brought them into his office, and they had expressed an interest in putting a steady supply of money into one of his hot investment schemes. He was delighted.

'Wait a minute,' Pietro the younger brother had said, 'doncha have a piece of that new hotel that's opening in Vegas?'

Rudolpho was pleased to be able to invite them to the opening. He chartered a plane, the Kassarris supplied the girls, and here they were. And what an evening it had been!

Rudolpho had a suite in the Magiriano, but the twins were booked into the Sands, and now there was talk of a private party, and he didn't want to miss out. 'I don't want to sell,' he said, laughing.

Salvatore Kassarri kicked him in the leg – hard.

Rudolpho was so surprised that he just stood there, his mouth hanging open like a fish.

Salvatore laughed and punched him in the stomach – hard. 'Just jokin' around, havin' fun. You don't mind, huh?'

Drunk as he was, he did mind. 'Cut that out . . . ' he began.

Salvatore smashed into his balls with something that felt like a shard of steel.

Rudolpho groaned, threw up, bent double, gasped for breath.

'You wanna sell out, doncha?' Salvatore asked mildly.

Rudolpho could not believe that this was happening to him. The time that Lucky Santangelo had come to his house and threatened him had been enough. But this was ridiculous. They were in front of a hotel. They were with a group of people – none of whom seemed to notice what was going on. It was daylight, for God's sake.

Pietro had hold of his arm, and Salvatore was on the other side. The other two men were getting the cars, the women stood around chatting.

'What the shit's going on?' he gasped.

'Nothin' partner,' said Pietro grinning and displaying nicotine stained teeth. 'We're just gonna take a little ride an' finalize our deal. You won't lose out – we'll give you back your original investment.'

'But I don't want to sell.'

'No?' Pietro was cheerful, 'Maybe you'll change your mind.'

'I won't change my . . .'

Salvatore grabbed his balls through the thin material of his trousers – 'Don't make any quick decisions,' he said squeezing and twisting, 'life is funny . . . who knows what you'll wanna do tomorra?'

As the Kassarri twins bundled him into a car, he blacked out. Rudolpho Crown was a coward. He would sell. Eventually.

Lucky stirred in her sleep and reached out. Her hand touched Marco's chest. She smiled and woke up. She didn't know what time it was and didn't particularly care. She only knew that this was the happiest day of her life.

Lightly she began to play with his nipples, licking the tips of her fingers and rubbing back and forth.

He groaned, and she watched his hard-on grow beneath the sheet. Lazily his eyes flickered open.

'I love you,' she said, 'and I want you to divorce your wife. *Christ! All the things she wasn't going to say were out in the open – just like that.*

'Yeah,' he replied, 'Sure. And you can stay away from other men or I'll break your beautiful neck.'

She couldn't make up her mind if he was kidding or not. Was it all going to be this easy? 'You'll really divorce Helena?' she asked tentatively.

'Listen, kid,' he sat up, his expression serious, 'I knew I was going to divorce Helena a week after I married her.'

'Huh?' She couldn't believe what she was hearing.

'You walked out of my life as a spoiled kid a long time ago. You walked back in, and I knew one day it was going to be you and me.' As he said it he realized that what he was saying was the truth.

Her eyes narrowed, 'You did?'

'I did.'

'Then why *the hell* didn't you tell *me*? Give me a sign. *Something?*'

'I gave you plenty of signs. You didn't want to know about me – you were too busy selecting talent. Besides – can you imagine Gino if I looked in your direction?'

She knelt on the bed, her long black hair unruly and wild,

'Hey – let's not forget about your wife. What was *I* supposed to do? Just ignore her?'

'You did last night.'

'So did you.'

'Jesus Christ, Lucky. We've wasted so much goddamn time . . .'

'Your fault.'

'I'll make up for it.'

She hugged him. 'We both will.'

They began to kiss. He pushed her away laughing, 'I've got to take a piss.'

'Oh really? I just thought I'd got incredibly fortunate!'

'Stay right where you are. Don't move.'

As if she would. She wanted to pinch herself to make sure she wasn't dreaming.

When he climbed back into bed he regarded her gravely. 'I'll tell you something that I think you should know. If you're just fucking around – then you're fucking with the wrong guy. You do understand that, don't you?'

'Yes, sir.'

'I just thought I should tell you.'

'*Yes, sir!*'

'That's what I like – a show of respect.'

She dived under the black silk sheets. 'I'll show you respect – I'll show you respect where it *really* matters!' She had such a passion for him. It wasn't just sex – although that was incredibly good. It was something more . . . It was caring about him – what he did and how he felt. He was going to belong to her, and she was going to belong to him. Just the way it should be.

When they finished making love she was grinning like a dummy. 'When can we tell everyone?' she demanded.

He stretched and placed his hands behind his head. 'I'll have to break it to Helena first . . . things haven't been that great between us. She's . . .'

'Dumb?'

'No. Don't sound like a bitch. She's just more interested in herself than anything else. She's beautiful and . . . boring I guess. I'll set her up in a house in L.A. or New York — wherever she wants. It'll take a month or two.'

Lucky looked alarmed. '*A month or two?* I can't wait that long!'

He began to laugh, 'So I'll fly to L.A. later today and tell her. Does that satisfy you?'

'*You* satisfy me. Oh God! You satisfy me more than anyone in my whole life!'

It was another hour before he was dressed and ready to leave. They talked, they giggled, they grinned like a couple of crazies.

Marco shook his head. 'I don't believe this. I knew it would happen, but I didn't know it would be like this.'

'Tell me about it – like what?' she asked eagerly.

'Like . . . Jesus . . . *I* don't know. I'm forty-five-years-old and I feel like I'm just finding something special out. You make me feel like a fucking IDIOT!'

She kissed him, roaming his mouth with her tongue, until he pushed her gently away and said, 'I've got to do *some* work sometime today. Like take care of business – remember?'

She grinned, 'Why don't you just shift your ass then, lover?'

After he left there was no way she could remove the smile from her face. She dressed quickly in white jeans and a soft silk shirt. Tinted shades covered her shining eyes. If this was being in love someone should bottle it – they'd make a fucking fortune!

Dario sat quietly in the Patio restaurant toying with his fork – pushing bacon and eggs across the plate and thinking of his encounter with Warris Charters. It had been different – *that* was for sure. He had never met anyone quite like him before.

'What's this script you were talking about?' he had asked, after introducing himself.

Warris angrily watched Lucky walk away. 'Your sister is a cunt, did you know that?'

Dario smiled, 'I'm glad to meet someone who agrees with me.'

After that they got along just fine. Warris decided that if he couldn't hit on Lucky to talk to her father, then the brother would do just as well. He told him about *Kill Shot*. About his plan to either produce or abort – whatever Gino wanted – as long as he was willing to pay. 'Can you arrange for me to get the script to your old man? Find out which way he wants to play it?'

Dario nodded. He had not taken his eyes from Warris' face . . . there was something decadent there . . . something sexual and bitter and hard . . . something he wanted . . .

They had spent the rest of the evening talking, and the more he talked the more interested Warris had become. Then two girls had horned in on their conversation, two sad sack hookers with long hair and curvy bodies. Warris' interest had waned in Dario, his arm had crept around the shortest girl, and he had said, 'This one's for me . . . that all right with you?'

Dario had felt a sharp twinge of jealousy. Warris hadn't realized . . . didn't know . . .

'Sure,' he said casually, 'when will you get me the script?'

'How about noon tomorrow? Where will you be?'

'In a plane on my way back to New York.'

'You're leaving that soon?'

'There's nothing for me to hang around here for.'

It was as if Warris had finally sensed what Dario was . . . what he wanted . . . Their eyes met. Warris wondered why he had been so slow in realizing. His arm dropped from around the girl, and he said, 'Beat it honey, not tonight. I got business.'

She left, complaining, dragging her friend with her.

Silently Warris stared, 'You should have told me.'

Dario could feel the excitement building inside him. 'Why?'

'Then we'd both have known where we were.'

'Do we know now?'

Slowly Warris had nodded.

Dario smiled as he remembered the rest. He pushed the eggs around his plate some more and glanced at the entrance to the restaurant. Breakfast, Lucky had said, the Patio, ten o'clock. It was now ten-thirty and still no sign of her. But of course it was only *him* she was meeting. What did *he* matter?

Abruptly he clicked his fingers for a waitress. He was not hanging around any longer. He wasn't one of her lackeys ready to sit around and wait. Besides . . . Warris had said he didn't have to beg for more money. He had said there were other ways to get what was rightly his.

The waitress handed him a check. 'You have a nice day now,' she smiled.

He planned to. Warris had invited him to stay for a while in Los Angeles. 'You help me and I'll help you . . . ' he had said, 'together we can both come up stinking of money – *your* money, Dario. It's just as much yours as hers and we'll figure out a way to get a big chunk.'

He hurried from the restaurant. He was meeting Warris at the airport at eleven-thirty and he didn't want to be late.

Rudolpho Crown sprawled on the back seat of a fast moving Mercedes limousine as it raced along the desert highway. The smell of new leather made him want to vomit . . . But he couldn't even do that, there was nothing left to bring up.

He craved a glass of water – coffee – anything to remove the taste of stale bile from his mouth. Painfully he sat up, but he was separated from the driver by a curtained glass panel.

A low moan escaped his lips, every bone in his body was bruised and aching, but it was the dull throbbing pain in his crotch that really worried him. Rudolpho Crown had always fancied himself as a great cocksman. If there was anything permanently wrong in *that* department . . . It did not bear thinking about . . .

He closed his eyes and moaned again. Who would believe what he had gone through? *Who would believe it?*

The Kassarri twins. So nice. So polite. Coming to his office and giving him creamed bullshit about all the money they were going to put his way.

Jerking him off. Coming with him to Vegas. Supplying five pieces of ass and telling him he had his choice.

He had his choice, all right. The brunette with legs that finished under her armpits – only he never got to stick it to her did he?

The Kassarri twins. They lived up to their reputation. They took him for a ride and in the end he was *begging* to sign his piece of the Magiriano away – begging and pleading and crying and grovelling like some sort of animal.

They had the papers ready, all drawn up and legal. They had witnesses to his signature who no way would ever admit that he had only signed under duress. When it was all taken care of he had been bundled in the Mercedes and sent on his way.

'The driver'll take you to Los Angeles,' Salvatore said non-chalantly, 'you can catch a plane to New York there. Only no calls. We got things to take care of an' you make one motherfuckin' call an' you're a dead man.'

What did they think he was? A fool?

He moaned again and clutched at his balls. Money. Shit! He had been better off hustling a living at the race track.

Enzio Bonnatti and his entourage stood at the entrance to the hotel while their bags were loaded into a long sleek Lincoln Continental.

Lucky stood with them. 'I wish you could stay longer, all this way for just one night – it seems ridiculous.'

'When you get to be my age you know what's good for you – and what's good for me is my own friggin' bed – 'scuse my language.'

'Weren't you comfortable last night?' she asked quickly,

He laughed, a throaty rasp, 'Sure. Why shouldn't I be? You had the only kind of pillow I like – two bottles of my favorite mineral water beside the bed – chocolate in the refrigerator. How you know all these little things?'

She laughed in return. 'I make it my business to find out.'

He leaned forward and kissed her on both cheeks. 'You're a good girl.'

'I'm not a girl, Enzio.'

'So what are you, an old man? To me you are a girl. But first you are a Santangelo – and that counts for much. When Gino gets his ass back . . .'

'I'll be in New York next week,' she interrupted quickly. 'Can we have dinner?'

He smiled, 'She asks – can we? You don't need to ask Lucky, you're like family.'

'I know.' She hugged him warmly, 'Thank you for coming, it meant so much.'

'I hadda see for myself the job y'did.'

'And were you impressed?'

'Y'got a winner. Makes the other place look like a dump.' He climbed into the Lincoln.

Lucky stood and watched the car out of sight, then realized it was past noon, and there was so much to do. So far she had done nothing except spend an idle hour with Enzio before his departure. Marco had dropped by to pay his respects to the old man, and she had looked at him, wanted him, and loved him so much that it almost hurt. Why couldn't she tell everyone about them? Why couldn't she climb to the top of the hotel and make a loudspeaker announcement for the whole of Las Vegas to hear?

*Goddamn it Marco – tell Helena and then I can tell the world.*

What would Gino think when he heard? If only he had fixed it for her to marry Marco instead of Craven Richmond . . .

Marco had bid Enzio a fond goodbye, and then he had winked at Lucky and said, 'I'm dropping by the Mirage – why don't we meet for a late lunch at two in the Patio?'

'Sure.' She had tried to keep her voice casual in front of everybody, but surely the way she was glowing all over was giving the game away.

'Lucky.' Skip was bearing down on her, waving an envelope. 'I thought you'd want to see the photos from last night – they just came in.'

'I'd like to, Skip, but I'm running late on everything.'

'Oh,' he looked disappointed, 'I was hoping we could grab an early lunch and I could fill you in on some of my plans. The press reaction is . . .'

'Why don't you have a memo typed up and send it up to me with the photos? I'm two hours late for a meeting with my brother and that's the *least* of my problems.' She hurried into the lobby and looked around. The place was nicely busy. What to do first? Track down Dario? If he could wait two hours another twenty minutes wouldn't hurt. She *had* to see Costa immediately, and there were a whole lot of employees she wanted a personal word with and several urgent phone calls to return.

What she *wanted* to do was spend the day in bed with Marco. What she *wanted* to do was spend the rest of her *life* in bed with Marco.

'Ms Santangelo . . . Paging Ms Santangelo.' The loudspeaker message came across loud and clear.

She walked over to the main reception desk and picked up the phone. 'Yes?'

'Lucky Santangelo?'

'Who is this?'

'Lucky. This is one of your new business partners.'

'What?'

'You heard.'

'Who *is* this?'

'Just wanted to let you know.'

'What?' Whoever was on the line hung up. She slammed the phone down and snapped at a startled desk clerk, 'Tell the switchboard I *do not* want to be paged unless it is urgent. And *all* calls are to go through the office first.'

The desk clerk nodded admiringly, 'Yes, ma'am.'

Stupid phone call. Goddamn moron on the switchboard. 'Get me Dario Santangelo on the line.'

'He checked out, ma'am.'

'When?'

'Around an hour and a half ago.'

'Are you sure?'

'I sent his bill through to the office to be comped myself.'

'OK. Thank you.' If Dario couldn't be bothered to wait it wasn't *her* problem, she would catch up with him in New York.

She thought about Marco, shivered, and couldn't wait until two o'clock when they would be together again.

●

The Kassarri twins celebrated with a magnum of champagne and two well endowed hookers who had no objection to sharing.

While they indulged in the pleasures of the flesh their enforcers were out working. Rudolpho Crown's piece of the Magiriano was not enough to satisfy them. There were other members of the syndicate who could be persuaded to sell. Not that they would get any money up front – like Rudolpho they would have to wait for their investment to be returned.

Salvatore Kassarri squeezed the full buttocks of the woman in his bed and said, 'You love it, don't you? You love getting fucked by a man like me?'

'Yes,' the hooker replied dutifully, 'you are some big man.'

Salvatore turned his attentions to the woman underneath his brother on the next bed, 'And you? How about you?'

'Ohhh yesss . . . you are both real sex machines.'

Sex machines! He leered. *They* could talk – two cunts who put it out day and night for money. Usually he wouldn't dream of paying. But today was different . . . today the whores were being useful . . .

A knock on the door. 'Room service,' a voice announced.

'Come in,' he shouted.

The floor waiter opened up the door with his pass key and wheeled the trolley laden with food into the room. He stopped abruptly when he saw what was going on.

Salvatore picked up a twenty dollar bill from the bedside and waved it at the man. 'That's OK. Take no notice – bring me over the check to sign.'

The waiter had interrupted a lot of scenes in his time – twenty years on the floor – you saw plenty – but he had never seen anything like this. Pietro Kassarri and friend kept right on bouncing up and down. Salvatore Kassarri was stark naked, and so was the woman lolling beside him.

The floor waiter couldn't wait to get back to the kitchen to tell *this* story.

Salvatore signed the check with a flourish. 'What time you got, pal?'

The waiter consulted his watch, 'Ten after two, sir.'

Lucky lit another cigarette and said, 'It's not like Marco to be late, he said two o'clock and it's twenty after.'

Costa took a sip of hot sweet tea and regarded her carefully. 'I spoke with Gino this morning,' he announced.

It was almost as if she didn't hear him, 'Oh yes?' she said distantly.

'One of these days you will have to face up to the fact that he is your father. That everything you have achieved was only made possible because of . . .'

She wasn't listening. She refused to listen. Why was he always carrying on about Gino?

Across the restaurant she noticed Boogie in agitated conversation with someone. Idly she watched, purposely not listening to Costa. It looked like one of the parking boys – what was a parking boy doing in the restaurant? Have to put a stop to *that*.

'Eventually,' Costa continued, 'Gino *will* come back, and then you are going to have . . .'

Boogie was heading swiftly across the restaurant towards her. He moved like a panther, sure-footed – fast – silent. As he approached she felt a slight chill of apprehension. Something was wrong. She was standing before he reached her, 'What is it?'

His face was blank. 'There's been a shooting outside.'

'A shooting? What do you mean?'

Costa joined in, 'What happened?'

Boogie shook his head. 'I don't know. Someone got shot, I want to get you upstairs Lucky – *now*.' He already had a steel grip on her arm.

She tried to shake free. 'I don't want to go upstairs – ' she began.

'Yes. Take her upstairs,' Costa ordered. 'I'll find out what's going on.'

'Goddamn it!' she flashed, 'I *am not* going upstairs. Will you let go of me!'

Boogie looked quickly to Costa, who gave an imperceptible nod. He released her arm.

She was furious. Who the hell did Boogie think he was working for anyway? 'Let's go find out what's going on,' she said shortly.

The man, lying on the hot asphalt ground could not see or hear much of anything. They say that when you are dying your life flashes before you. Not so. Not so at all. Pain had taken over his entire body. A blinding relentless pain caused by the three bullets that had smashed into him as he walked towards the entrance of the hotel. Pain was taking him on a wild trip, a short trip, and soon it would be all over. He choked for breath. His last breath. And as he went he heard her agonized scream.

'M . . . A . . . R . . . C . . . O. Oh n . . . ooo. OH GOD . . . nooooooo . . . M . . . A . . . R . . . C . . . O . . .'

# Book Three

## Thursday, July 14th, 1977, New York

Wearily Lucky reached the last flight of concrete stairs. Although it was only seven in the morning the heat was already settling over the city. She felt filthy and in desperate need of a shower.

The stairs led into the basement garage. Once there she headed for her car, a small sleek bronze Mercedes. She dumped her large bag on the hood, and began the ritual search for her keys. As she scrambled through the contents of her bag, she got more and more aggravated. The goddamn keys weren't there!

In a fury she tipped the bag upside down and everything fell out. No apartment keys, no car keys.

Suddenly she remembered emptying her bag out in the elevator when she had been desperately looking for her lighter. Idiot! She must have forgotten to put the keys back. Now they were probably lying on the floor of the elevator.

It was just too much. 'Goddamn it!' She kicked the car.

Steven, who had just entered the garage, paused. 'What's the matter?'

'I left my keys in the elevator. Can you believe it?'

'How could you do a stupid thing like that?'

'How could you do a stupid thing like that?' she mimicked furiously. 'I did it purposely of course – so that you would be forced to give me a ride. I mean – like we haven't spent enough time together, right?'

He sighed. 'Come on.'

She piled everything back in her bag and followed him to his car It was a two-year-old Chevrolet.

He unlocked the doors and she slumped into the passenger seat. 'Put the air conditioning on,' she demanded.

He ignored her and started the car, revving the engine gently.

'Put on the air conditioning,' she repeated.

'No. This car needs to run at least ten minutes before I can do that.'

'Why?'

'Because otherwise it stalls,' he explained patiently.

'So how come you don't buy a new car?'

'I happen to like this one. You don't mind do you?'

Silently he drove the Chevrolet up from the underground garage. The streets were alive with people hurrying in all directions. 'Where do you live?' he asked politely.

She yawned, not bothering to cover her mouth. 'Sixty-First and Park. But it's no good dropping me there, I don't have my apartment keys, and the maid doesn't get in until ten.'

'Surely the janitor has a set?'

She shook her head. His mouth tightened. He had just about had enough of her. 'So where then?'

'Where do *you* live?'

'Why?'

She extracted a cigarette from her pack and angrily jammed the car lighter in. 'Christ! It doesn't matter. I was only going to ask if I could hang out there until ten o'clock – but forget it. I wouldn't want to put you to any trouble.'

'No trouble,' he said tightly, wondering why she didn't ask to be dropped at a friend or relation's house.

'Thank you.' The lighter popped out, she pressed it to her cigarette and dragged hungrily.

In silence he drove to his apartment. The traffic signals were not in operation, so it was more or less a slow crawl.

He thought about all the work he had in front of him. The Bonnatti investigation was just about reaching a peak. Two years of checking out a man's life. Enzio Bonnatti – a street kid who over the years had turned into one of the biggest criminal bosses around. Prostitution, pornography, gambling, and drugs. Not to mention murder, extortion, and bribery.

It had not been easy persuading people to talk. Fear hung heavy. But a few had been persuaded. Bobby De Walt made sure of that. A few key witnesses who would be able to put Bonnatti away forever. Steven had his witnesses safely hidden away. And now it was just a question of finishing off the papers that would indict Bonnatti and bring him up for trial.

Carefully he parked his Chevrolet in front of the brownstone where he lived on Fifty-eighth and Lexington. Once a year there was a parking spot right outside – and today was it. Seemed like a good omen after the wasted night.

Lucky yawned again. 'We're practically neighbors,' she announced, stretching luxuriously. 'I'll be able to jog home at ten o'clock.'

What was he going to do with her for three hours? Why did he have to be Mister Nice Guy? Why couldn't he just tell her to go find someone else to hang around?

He got out of the car, but before he reached her side she was out, stretching again and saying, 'I'm hungry. Are you hungry? Have you got any *food*?'

She didn't honestly expect him to cook her breakfast did she? 'There's eggs if you want to make them,' he said curtly.

She followed him down the steps of the house. 'I can't cook.'

'Not even eggs?'

She shrugged vaguely. 'I guess I don't have that womanly touch in the kitchen. I've just got to *look* at uncooked food and it turns to –'

'Don't tell me.'

The brownstone was divided into four apartments. Steven had the basement. Carrie was always trying to get him to do something with it but he liked it just the way it was, plain and stark – dark wood, leather couches, a huge old desk, shelves crammed with books, and his one extravagance – incredible quadraphonic hi-fi equipment and an impressive collection of blues and soul records.

Lucky looked around. It was not what she'd expected. But then she didn't quite know what to make of Steven anyway. He was certainly one of the best looking men that she had ever seen. The thing was – men that attractive were usually full of conceit and arrogance. This guy was different. He honestly did not seem to be aware of quite how knockout he was. Of course, that didn't change the fact that he was an uptight pain in the ass.

She was experiencing a strong desire to lure him into bed. Get beneath the covers with him and see if she could thaw him out a little.

She almost laughed aloud. What a switch! It was always the guys who were raring to go. All she had to do was stroll into any singles bar and men were hitting on her from all sides, like pussy was going out of style and they had to be sure to grab a piece fast. She liked the anonymity of singles bars. The going in and choosing a partner and not even knowing his name.

No name. No pain.

'Why don't you sit down,' he said. 'I'll boil some water for coffee.'

'Are you gas or electric?'

'Gas.'

'Fortunate.'

'Yes.' He walked into the kitchen.

She sat on the leather couch and wished that she felt better. There was so much on her mind . . . so many things to deal with . . .

She closed her eyes for a minute. *Gino was coming back . . . Any moment . . . Any day . . .*

*I don't want to be a little girl again . . . Please daddy . . don't take it all away from me . . . Please . . .*

Her eyes snapped open quickly. *Christ! What's the matter with me? Nobody – but nobody is taking anything.*

Steven came back into the room. He had removed his jacket, and seemed more relaxed. 'The kettle is on, it takes a while. I'll put a record on for you while I dive under the shower.'

She nodded, her eyelids heavy, threatening to close again, just for a second, only for a second . . .

He leafed quickly through some albums and picked out one of his favorites. At least she had good taste in music, he'd try her on a little vintage Marvin Gaye. The *What's Going On* album was a classic. He put the disc on the turntable, and hurried to strip off his clothes and stand under the luxury of a cold energizing shower.

She was almost asleep when the sound came wafting through her consciousness. Marvin Gaye. *What's Going On.* Christ! Marco. The night they had made love. Pledged themselves to a future together. Marvin Gaye on the record player. *What's Going On* repeating again and again . . . The memories came flooding in before she could even attempt to stop them.

Marco. She never allowed herself to think about him. He was locked away in a corner of her mind she refused to visit. He was dead . . . gone . . .

Marco . . . Marco . . . Marco . . .

She could still hear her own screams. Still see his body lying on the black asphalt. Still remember the blood pumping out of him. Out of *her* Marco . . . her love . . .

And the people grouped around his body – staring and chattering as though he was just another Las Vegas sight. Fat hags in grotesque sundresses, ratty little kids, and florid men in polyester suits.

*One of them was taking a picture. Aiming his fucking Instamatic and taking a snapshot.*

Like an animal she had sprung, clawing the camera from his sweaty grasp, smashing it to the concrete and screaming over and over – 'Bastard ... bastard ... bastard ...'

Boogie had pulled her off the surprised tourist, and she sank to the ground, lifted Marco's head and cradled him on her lap.

And all the while the blood pumped out of him ... slowly ... Surely ... irrevocably ...

'I love you baby ... I love you ... *I love you ...*' Somehow she thought if she said the words enough times he wouldn't go ... wouldn't leave her ...

'He's dead, Lucky,' Costa said grimly. 'He's dead.'

'Fuck off!' she screamed, her face a twisted mask of pain, 'Just fuck off! He's going to be all right ... he'll be fine ...'

The ambulance and the police arrived at the same time.

'We have to get him to a hospital,' she wailed. '*Please!* Hurry! Every second counts.'

'He's gone, miss,' muttered the ambulance attendant, touching her gently on the arm.

She threw his hand off angrily. 'How the hell do *you* know? You haven't even *tried* to help him.'

Lucky saw the Marco she had been with that morning. She did not see the inert body. She did not see that half his face was gone – a pulp of blood and bone. She did not see the huge pool of blood around her.

A seasoned detective was moving into the picture with several cops in attendance. He began issuing instructions, calling for the crowds to be cleared and witnesses to be detained. 'Who is she?' he asked. 'Get her away from the victim and find out what the hell happened.'

A young policeman stepped forward to oblige. When he tried to separate her from the body she hit him so hard that he fell back in a state of shock.

Boogie moved then. He was strong as steel, in spite of his wasted appearance. He pried her away from Marco and half carried, half dragged her towards the entrance to the hotel.

The rest was a blur as far as she was concerned. A blur of faces and voices, doctors and nothingness. She retreated to a place she had visited once before. A quiet place where nobody bothered you. She remembered when her mommy had gone away ... It had been the same then.

She woke up in a private clinic twenty-four hours later, opened her eyes, and said sharply, 'What is this place? Why am I here?'

A nurse, dozing in a chair, sprang to attention, 'Oh Miss Santangelo . . . just a minute, please . . . ' She dashed from the room.

Gingerly she sat up and checked out her body. She thought she must have been in an accident. Casting her mind back she could remember the opening night party of the Magiriano . . . She could remember Enzio, and Costa, Marco, Warris Charters, Dario, a roomful of stars. She could remember the whole goddamn evening . . . then – nothing.

A white coated doctor came hurrying into the room.

'Why am I here?' she demanded. 'Did I have an accident?'

'More a traumatic experience Miss Santangelo. You've been sedated. Mr Zennocotti is on his way. I think it best if he explains.'

Costa arrived. Explained.

Now . . . two years later . . . Marvin Gaye and *What's Going On* and she was finally allowing herself to remember the real truth and the real pain.

She began to cry, deep, wracking sobs. The vengeance she had asked for had not been enough. But there had been no Marco to turn to for guidance and advice. No Marco upon whom she had depended so strongly. She was responsible for many things, but when it came to the smooth trouble free running of the two hotels, he was the one to make it all happen.

Of course, Enzio Bonnatti had been wonderful. He had personally selected two of his best men to run things in Vegas, and by the time she was out of the clinic they were installed and taking care of everything. This suited her fine. She didn't want to stay in the gambling city. She wanted to return to New York. She thanked Enzio profusely and asked him if he would mind continuing to look after things for a while.

'Sure,' he said. 'Do what y'havta do, Lucky. My guys'll handle the operations. We'll work a deal.' And then he had personally made it his business to have his people track down Marco's killer.

Two weeks after the shooting he told her, 'We got the guy – some dumb pisser who held a gambling grudge. You'll read about the bastard in tomorrow's paper.'

Lucky had read how a Mr Mortimer Sauris had burned to death in his automobile – a freak accident – the papers said. 'The cock-sucker died slowly,' Enzio had explained, ' 'Scuse my language.'

Enzio had been such a tower of strength. Lucky thought

grimly of the Kassarri brothers, and their attempt to take over the Magiriano, shortly after Marco's death. Enzio had said he would deal with it. A few weeks later he told her – 'Rudolpho Crown . . . the Kassarris . . . some of those other bums who invested in the syndicate . . . they're out. I got paper says it's all ours.'

She was pleased, but she still had no interest in ever returning to Vegas. She couldn't bear to be anywhere that reminded her of Marco.

Money from the Mirage continued to filter through in the normal way. A series of couriers picked up bags of cash and ferried them to various cities, where the money was laundered, made legitimate, and then finally it would turn up in one Santangelo enterprise or another. Money flowed up from the Magiriano in the same way, until one day Enzio summoned Lucky to his Long Island mansion and said, 'I gotta surprise for you. I'm involved in a deal that could mean big bucks for all concerned. I included your take from the Magiriano – trust me, Lucky.'

'I trust you.' She smiled.

Costa objected the moment he heard. When it came to money he was naturally suspicious of everything and everybody. Sometimes Lucky was just not responsible. Gino would never trust anyone with his money, not even an old loyal friend such as Enzio. Lucky was too young to realize the power and importance of the simple dollar.

'*Come on*,' she argued, 'we're talking about Enzio here. He's like my father for God's sake. Are you saying he'd try and cheat *me*?'

'I'm merely saying, why change the Mirage operation when it has worked successfully for over twenty years?'

'This is different – it's an investment. Besides, we don't need the income right now. Let Enzio do it his way. We'll take what we want when we want it – no problem.'

Marvin Gaye. Singing. Filling the room with memories. Opening and unlocking her mind.

God! But she had loved Marco. Why had she denied herself the pleasure of remembering quite how much?

Steven walked back into the room. He was wearing faded Levi's and a denim work shirt. His black hair was wet and curly and his feet bare. 'Did you check out the kettle?' he asked. Then he took a good look at her and added, 'Are you feeling OK?'

She had stopped crying and felt remarkably calm, like a heavy weight had been removed from her shoulders. 'Sure. I feel fine.' She rubbed under her eyes to remove any traces of smudged mascara, 'It's just that particular record happened to get me going on some locked up memories.'

'I'm sorry. If I'd known, I . . . '

'Shit!' She laughed sharply, 'You couldn't have known could you? Why are you always so goddamn polite?'

Just when he began to think that she wasn't so bad she always hit him with a zinger. For a moment she had looked like a forlorn little girl, then the mouth had gone into action and she was super-bitch again. A spoiled New York ballbreaker. 'I thought at least you would have stretched yourself and made the coffee,' he said coldly.

'*I'm* the guest,' she pointed out.

'Uninvited,' he couldn't help replying.

Quick to take offense she leaped off the couch. 'If I'm putting you to any trouble . . . ' she began.

He ignored her, walked into the kitchen. The water in the kettle was almost boiled away. 'Black? White? Sugar?' he called out.

'Black. No sugar. You don't mind if *I* use the bathroom do you?'

He did mind. 'Go right ahead.'

She found the bathroom. It was a mess. Damp towels on the floor, hair in the sink, a razor, deodorant and breath freshener mixed up with toothpaste and toothbrush on the side of the bath. It pleased Lucky – the fact that he wasn't Mr Perfect everywhere he went.

She closed the door, investigated the contents of his medicine chest, then decided to take a bath. Why not? He had said she could use the bathroom, hadn't he?

In the kitchen Steven gulped a mouthful of steaming hot coffee and picked up the phone. It was too early to call Carrie or Aileen. It was never too early to call Bobby.

'Hey, man, what's happenin'?' complained Bobby. 'I bin tryin' to call you half the night.'

'Would you believe I got trapped in an elevator over at Jerry's office building.'

'Yeah, I'd believe it – the whole city's gone nuts. You'd better let Aileen know you're OK. I ain't quit buggin' her on the hour every hour.'

'Is she all right?'

'Sure. She was home when it happened – the only place to be. The streets are like a jungle, man.'

'Right. Look, Bobby, I just walked in – just wanted to let you know I'll see you around ten-thirty. We'll talk then.'

'You think today's the day?' Bobby asked anxiously.

'We got a good chance. If not today, tomorrow for sure.'

'I can't wait to nail that dirty bastard. I have nightmares he'll get word of what's going down and skip town.'

Steven glanced towards the door. 'Bonnatti will never skip. He'll figure his lawyers will get him off like they been getting him off for more years than you've been alive. We've got him Bobby, don't worry about it.'

'Yeah, I know – I know. I just get nervous that's all.'

'Don't. I'll see you at ten-thirty. He replaced the receiver and drank the rest of his coffee. His stomach growled, reminding him that he was hungry. He was damned if he was going to fix breakfast for Lucky, he'd sooner stay hungry.

Where was she anyway? She'd been in the bathroom long enough. So much on his mind and yet having her in his apartment was throwing him off balance. He glanced at his watch. It was still only seven-thirty. Time was dragging. He went to the bathroom door and knocked loudly. 'What are you doing in there?' he yelled.

'Taking a bath,' she yelled back. 'Wanna come in and join me?'

Hurriedly he backed away from the door. She had such a smart ass mouth on her. He really should call her bluff and walk right on in and see what she would do *then.*

He knew what she would do then. Lucky wasn't the kind of girl to bluff. When she said something she meant it. In their short acquaintance he had learned *that* much about her.

He went into his bedroom and switched on the portable radio, listening to the latest news ' . . the consequences were appalling. Nearly three thousand people have been arrested for looting. The arsonists had a field day. In some parts of the city fires burned so brightly that electric lights were hardly missed. In Manhattan . . .'

Luxuriating in lukewarm water, Lucky grinned to herself. She felt fantastically high and full of energy. Allowing herself to finally remember the truth about her and Marco did not depress her at all. In fact, after the initial tears she felt strangely euphoric. It proved that she could love, feel, *care* for another person – For two years it had been all short sharp one nighters with good looking men who she never wanted to see again. Sex was in. Relationships were out. Marco would have wanted more for her – she knew that now.

Her mind was buzzing with plans for the future. With Gino due back to town she had to act fast. Enzio had kindly taken over in Vegas – but the Magiriano was hers – and now was the time for her to resume control. Otherwise Big Daddy would come back . . . walk in . . . take over . . . And she would be the kid again. The dumb little emotional female.

Costa had been right, she should never have let the hotel slip from her grasp. But it was no problem . . . Enzio would understand . . . And now was the time to collect the money due her. Costa had been checking out the figures . . . but of course legitimate figures only told a fraction of the story. By Costa's conservative reckoning Bonnatti owed them over a million dollars and if the investment he had made with the money on her behalf was half as good as he said it was – then that million dollars could have doubled. Not bad for sitting back and doing nothing.

Lucky's very considerable energies over the previous two years had gone into building The Free Make-Up Co. into one of the biggest cosmetic companies in America. She enjoyed playing tycoon and had really created a phenomenon in the cosmetic industry. Now she was ready to return to Vegas.

The bath water was turning uncomfortably cold. She immersed herself totally, then climbed out, shaking her wet curls like a wild mongrel.

The only towel appeared to be Steven's damp one on the floor, so she opened up the door and put her head out. 'Hey,' she shouted, 'Who do you have to screw around here to get a clean towel?'

He fixed hot buttered toast and scrambled eggs mixed up with chunks of ham.

Lucky, wrapped disconcertingly in a towel, wolfed them down like she hadn't eaten in years. 'You're really a great cook,' she said admiringly. 'Any time you want a job . . .'

'What as? Your houseboy?'

'Whew! You're really uptight. Are you always this tense?'

She stared at him, liking what she saw, aware of the fact that she had spent more time talking to him than with any of her one nighters. How about a relationship? She was game if he was.

He noticed her staring, and busied himself eating.

'Did anyone ever tell you . . . ' she began.

The phone rang, cutting off her words.

Steven picked it up with a curt, 'Yes?'

She watched him as he talked to someone – sounded like a girlfriend from his side of the conversation. He had great skin, such a magnificent color – smooth and chocolatey – like a six weeks on your back suntan. And his black hair was even darker than hers. Tight jet curls that glistened. His eyes were ever so slightly elongated – cat eyes, glass green, deep, and sensual. She wondered what his ancestry was. He was certainly no hundred per cent black.

He covered the mouthpiece of the phone, 'Why don't you go get dressed?' he hissed.

She nodded, but made no attempt to move. If he thought she was climbing back into her filthy clothes he could think again. When he got off the phone she was going to borrow something of his.

'No, it's just the radio,' he said, glaring at Lucky. 'Sure honey, sure. I'll call you later.' He slammed down the receiver. 'Thanks for the privacy.'

She widened her eyes. 'Why didn't you tell me?'

'I didn't think I had to spell it out.'

'I can't get dressed anyway. My clothes stink. I thought maybe you could lend me something and I'll jog on out of your life. I can always sit outside my apartment – I know I'm not welcome here.'

He was easy to read. As soon as she said anything negative he responded by being polite.

'I said it's OK for you to stay.'

'But I don't want to be in your way.'

Big sigh. 'You're not in my way.'

'Good.' She stood up. The towel barely covered her. He started to look, jerked his eyes away.

'Can we go check out your closet?' she asked innocently, pretending she hadn't noticed him looking.

'I won't have anything to fit you . . . '

'I don't want a suit, for crissakes! Just an old shirt, some jeans I can roll up, and a belt to keep 'em from falling down. Actually, that shirt you've got on would do nicely.' She grinned, 'Now I'm taking the shirt off your back.'

He couldn't help smiling. There *was* something about her . . .
He wished she'd put some clothes on . . . her naked body under
the skimpy towel was getting him horny . . . God! what was he
thinking of? Since Aileen had finally allowed him to make
love to her there had been no one else. If you had a good
satisfying relationship with a woman, you didn't need anyone
else . . .

They were in the bedroom now. He found her a pair of jeans
that had shrunk in the wash, and a rope belt she could tie
around her waist.

The shutters in the small bedroom were closed against the
morning sunlight. The room was hot and stuffy. The atmosphere oppressive.

'Give me your shirt, I'll go get dressed in the bathroom,' she
said.

He started to undo the buttons, aware of the fact that there
were a dozen other shirts he could have lent her. She moved
close to take it, and without either of them uttering a word they
began to kiss, at first tentatively – then, as they both realized
it was a mutual act, more passionately.

Steven forgot about Aileen, forgot about everything except
a strong unbeatable need for this beautiful wild woman with
the black opal eyes. Slowly he began to back her towards the
bed.

She felt lightheaded and unreal. So much had happened in
such a short time. Memories of Marco . . . And now this . . .
Somehow she knew that no way was Steven going to be just
another one nighter.

She fell back on the bed willingly, allowing the towel to
slip from her body. He was struggling with the zipper on his
Levi's. She reached up to help him.

The phone rang.

It was as though an alien presence had entered the room.
Steven froze.

'Ignore it,' she whispered.

'I can't.' He reached for the receiver, 'Who is it?' he asked,
his voice husky.

Aileen, dressed and ready for a brisk walk to the UN building, said, 'Steven? You sound busy. I thought I might stop by
and fix you some breakfast. You must be starving after your
ordeal, and . . .'

Guilt swept over him like a giant wave. What was he doing?
He jumped quickly off the bed. 'I'm not hungry . . . got a lot of
papers to check . . .'

'Are you all right?'

Aileen knew him well. Too well. 'Sure. Just tired and overworked.'

'Then a good breakfast is just what you need. I'll stop at the market and be there in half an hour.' She hung up before he could object further.

Lucky sensed that for now it was over. She rolled onto her stomach. 'Girlfriend?'

'Fiancée.'

'I didn't know people still did things like that.'

'Like what?'

'Get engaged.'

He pulled the zipper up on his Levi's and walked to the closet, where he selected another shirt. 'She's coming over,' he said.

'I heard.'

'I'm sorry.'

'Are you?' She wondered if he really was, or if he was just saying it to be polite. Goddamn it! Why had the phone interrupted them anyway. She got off the bed, covering herself with a sheet, 'I guess I'll get dressed and hit the road. I wouldn't want to embarrass you.'

'Hey, Lucky.' He went to her and held her by the shoulders, staring into her eyes intently. 'I don't know what's going on . . . Something's happening I don't know what, but I do know that I want to see you again. Can I?'

'I hate men who ask for things.' She snatched up the borrowed clothes and slammed into the bathroom.

He frowned. He didn't need any complications in his private life, and yet he knew that he had to see her again. She was unfinished business, and all his life Steven had never left any loose ends. He wandered into the kitchen and fixed two mugs of coffee. She emerged from the bathroom, grinning. 'You like?'

'I like.'

'Think I could start a new fashion?'

'Why not?'

'Maybe I'll market it. Call it the Big Baggy Look.'

He watched her seriously, trying to read her, wondering how she really felt under the flippant façade. 'Here,' he handed her a mug, 'I made coffee.'

'No, thanks, gotta split. Gotta hot date with a Danish pastry. I'll probably stack on five pounds just waiting to get into my apartment!' She picked up her Gucci bag. 'Why don't

I just stuff my old clothes in here and get out of your life. It's really been . . . interesting.'

'What's your phone number?' he asked impulsively.

'Why?'

'Because I want to see you again.'

She laughed. 'You just want to make sure you get your clothes back, right?'

'I want your phone number,' he repeated.

She looked at him quizzically, 'I got your number – *I'll* call *you*. If a woman answers, I promise I'll hang up!'

'What's your last name?'

'So you can look me up in the book? Forget it, I'm not listed.' She touched his cheek lightly, 'but I will call – honestly.'

'I want you to,' he paused and stared at her meaningfully, 'I really do.'

'I know,' she murmured softly. 'After the time we've had together how could you possibly resist me?'

Her phone was ringing when she finally got into her apartment. Problems at one of the Free Make-Up Co. production plants. The emergency generator had gone out and there was a panic going on. She barely had time to take another shower and slip into fresh clothes when one of her managing directors picked her up and drove her over to the plant.

She had wanted to relax, contact Enzio, sleep, but by the time she got home again it was already five in the afternoon. She was exhausted – too exhausted to do anything about anything except collapse on top of her bed and fall into an immediate sleep.

She dreamed about Marco, which was pleasing, and Steven, which was confusing, and Gino – which brought her awake with a heart thumping jolt. Gino. Coming back. Taking over. Christ! She had to get back to Vegas fast.

She consulted her watch. It was just before seven. She had fallen asleep fully dressed. Quickly she changed into a short cotton shift, fixed herself some iced tea, and phoned Enzio.

'He's out,' a surly maid informed her. 'Won't be back 'til late.'

She tried Costa, but there was no reply. She contemplated phoning Steven, but then decided it was too soon. Too soon for what? She shivered slightly and grinned. Steven was something else. Steven was special. She didn't want to blow it.

The phone rang and she snatched it up, hoping it was Enzio

returning her call. It wasn't. It was Boogie Patterson, her ex-bodyguard driver – dear quiet Boogie who had wanted to come with her to New York but who she had discouraged because Boogie spelled Las Vegas and blood and memories. He had stayed in Vegas, and started his own limo service, bankrolled by her. They were rarely in contact but they were friends.

'Hey – Boog. How *are* you? What's happening?'

'Lucky,' he said, his voice straining in a call box, the sound of slot machines heavy in the background, 'I have to talk to you.'

'Good timing. *I* was going to call *you*. I'll be in Vegas – maybe tomorrow – and I'll need you to meet the plane.'

'*You're* coming here?' His voice hardly spelled out welcome.

'Sure. It's been long enough. I'm coming back.'

'Don't.'

'What?'

'I'm headin' for the airport now. There's things you should know. Things I only just found out . . . '

Aggravation crept into her tone, 'What things?'

'Lucky . . . I know you'll find this difficult to believe – but Enzio Bonnatti is not the friend you think he is.'

'Boogie, what's the matter with you? Are you stoned? Do you realize what you're saying?'

'Yes. I realize.' He paused meaningfully. 'And you should realize this. No way did Mortimer Sauris put the hit on Marco – no way at all. Bonnatti burned the wrong man. And that's only the beginning.'

'What?' she gasped, sudden cold chills shivering down her spine.

'I'll see you soon – no more on the phone. There's a can of shit opening up, and it stinks. Don't say a word to anyone until we talk – you understand? *Not to anyone.*'

'I understand. Wire me your flight number.' Dully she hung up the phone.

*Marco . . . Marco . . . Baby, I'll get them . . . whoever it was, I'll personally get them. I promise you that.*

## Thursday, July 14th, 1977, New York

A six million dollar pay out to the Internal Revenue bought Gino Santangelo the right to return to America. Everything nice and legal. And so it should be, it had taken long enough to work out. Long delicate negotiations that had gone on forever with Gino screaming long distance to Costa, 'Pay 'em – I don't care what it costs. Pay the bastards whatever it takes to get me back.' It *had* cost, but paying the money was no real problem. After all, as long as it kept on flowing . . . and it did.

Now he was back, and Costa was waiting for him in his suite at the Pierre. The two old friends embraced affectionately.

'It's good t'see you – bum!' Gino exclaimed. 'Lost a little hair, I notice, but you still look like you could go a round or two.'

Costa smiled. 'And you. Always the same – you never alter.'

'Why should I change, my friend? When I go I plan to take my teeth, my hair – everything. Why not?'

Costa nodded. Gino had not changed at all. He still looked exactly the same. Dark and suntanned, his hair as thick and black as ever, no gut protruding over his trousers. Unconsciously Costa pulled his own stomach in.

'I wanna eat,' Gino said. 'Why don't you order room service while I get outta my clothes and into something comfortable.' He headed towards the bedroom, 'I want a big fat juicy American steak. And french fries. And some red wine. You order – I'll be with you in a minute.'

Costa nodded, and went to the phone while Gino checked out the bedroom. It was nice. But it was not home. Now that he was back he wanted a home. No more hotels, he was too old for them. He thought about his friend, Costa. Contrary to what he had said, the man did not look good. He looked his age and more besides. Grey skinned, weary eyed, fatigued. Gino had left everything in his control – perhaps it had been too much. For all of his seven years exile, Gino had purposefully avoided becoming involved in what was happening in America. He knew that he couldn't handle the frustration of hearing about what was going on and not being in a position to do anything about it. 'You take care of things,' he had told Costa. 'You need anything – go to Enzio.' As long as the money continued to arrive he was satisfied. A different courier made a deposit in one of his numbered Swiss bank accounts weekly – and things progressed smoothly. Then Marco was hit, and the money had stopped coming. It was the worst time. There he was, trapped in a foreign country, powerless to do anything, filled with rage and a helpless fury. Marco had been like a son to him ... like a son ... And he could do nothing to avenge his murder. He had sent instant word to Enzio. He wanted justice. Immediately. Within days word filtered through that justice had been done, and the money began to flow again. Gino felt he owed a great debt to Bonnatti.

Of course, even in Israel, rumors reached him about Lucky. He was aware of the fact that she had become a part of his business empire. He was not aware of the extent of her involvement.

Quickly he changed his clothes, swapping his dark suit for a cashmere sweater and comfortable slacks. The sooner he heard everything the better. He was back and rarin' to go.


Sal regarded the sleeping form of Dario Santangelo – he certainly was a pretty one with his pale blond hair and perfect features. Pretty and valuable. And why shouldn't she pick up a nice chunk of bread for something that was thrown in her lap?

She had been working hard since giving him the two turquoise capsules – capsules that would guarantee a straight twelve hours solid sleep.

First she had removed the body of the dark haired boy from the apartment. Lugging him down the service stairs slung over her shoulders like a sack of flour. In the underground garage she threw him on the back seat of her old Chrysler, and covered him with a blanket. The power cut was making her job easy. Everyone was busy doing their own thing. She drove fifteen blocks and dumped him in an alley. Then she returned to Dario's apartment, cleaned up the mess, and slung *him* over her shoulders.

Sal had the strength of two men. By the time she put Dario in the back seat of her car she was scarcely out of breath. She hummed softly to herself as she drove all the way out to Queens.

Ruth was up and waiting for her. Gorgeous Ruth, ex-showgirl ex-hooker – with one side of her face so badly scarred by acid that no man would look at her. Who needed men when Sal was around?

'Everything OK hon?' Ruth asked anxiously.

'Peachy,' Sal replied, kissing her gently on the bad side of her face. 'We got a guest. Make up a bed an' I'll tell you the scam.'

Ruth did just that. Together they stripped off all of Dario's clothes and put him between the sheets.

'Who is he?' Ruth whispered.

Sal stared at the sleeping figure. 'If I play it right he's our house in Arizona. Either that or he's dead.'

Elliott Berkely finally departed for his office. 'I want you to think seriously about our getting out of here for a few weeks,' he admonished before leaving.

'Yes, I will,' Carrie replied unenthusiastically.

*No. Impossible. Not until I find out who's blackmailing me. Not until I deal with the situation.*

She spent an uncomfortable day nervously pacing the apartment, jumping every time the phone rang.

She was short with Steven when he phoned, not telling him of her ordeal the previous evening.

'I'll call you tomorrow,' he said at last, sensing her reluctance to carry on a conversation. 'You know I may have good news about that investigation I'm working on.'

'Mmmm . . . that's nice. Tomorrow, then.' She hung up the phone fast. Didn't want to block the line. It rang again almost immediately, and she snatched it up.

'How would you like a nice strong charge of electricity?' a voice leered.

'Oh, Jerry. What do you want?'

'What do I want? What kind of a greeting is *that*? I want . . .'

She was not listening as he listed what he wanted. Dear sweet Jerry. Dear sweet *young* Jerry. He had a crush on her which never seemed to fade.

'Jerry, I'm very busy today,' she interrupted. 'Can I call you back?'

'When?'

'Soon.'

'Promise?'

'Yes.'

Jerry was possessive, almost like a lover. He treated her like the princess she was supposed to be. The vast difference in their ages didn't seem to bother him.

At five o'clock the phone rang. It was a pay station. Her heart began to pound relentlessly. 'This is Carrie Berkely,' she said clearly. 'Who is calling?'

'Tomorrow. Twelve noon. Same place,' a muffled voice whispered.

'Just a minute – ' she began, but the line clicked dead in her trembling hand.

The two old friends had been talking in Gino's suite for hours. Costa hesitant at first, but more confident as he got into his story.

Gino did not interrupt. He watched and listened intently noting once again how old Costa had become and thinking to himself – *the guy must be getting senile because I just do not believe what I am hearing.*

What he was hearing was the story of Lucky's rise to power. And it was unbelievable that the wild young girl he had last seen in 1970 was a cool, tough, clever businesswoman, who had taken over *and* done pretty good – or so it seemed. The way Costa told it Lucky could walk on water if the feeling took her. He spoke proudly, telling the story of her struggle to build the Magiriano – the death of Marco – Enzio Bonnatti's help and assistance.

'Are you tellin' me,' Gino questioned unbelievingly, 'that we've seen no money from the Magiriano for almost a year – not one fuckin' red cent?'

'I thought I explained,' Costa said ploddingly. 'After Marco's murder, Lucky didn't want to stay in Vegas so Bonnatti stepped in. A temporary measure. Then came the investment business. Now that you're back . . . '

'You bet your fuckin' ass now that I'm back! Jeeze Costa! I told you to go to Enzio if you needed help. I didn't tell you to hand him things on a fuckin' plate. You know what he's like with the drugs an' the whores . . . Jesus! I don't need those connections in *my* hotels.'

'No problems we can't settle. Enzio will withdraw whenever we want.'

'You wanna bet on that, Costa? You wanna put money on it? You couldn't put your own people in? You couldn't shift your ass to reorganize things and keep control? You and my smart ass daughter. I don't believe this. What about Dario? You don't mention him.'

Costa shrugged mournfully. 'He has no interest in the business.. '

'What's *that* supposed to mean?'

Costa wiped the sweat from his brow with a clean white handkerchief. 'I think Dario needs help.'

'Help?' snapped Gino. 'What are you talkin' about?'

'He has . . . sexual problems,' Costa continued hesitantly.

'What problems?' Gino laughed sharply, 'Too much pussy, huh? Since when was *that* a problem?'

Costa squirmed. He had hoped that he wouldn't have to be the one to tell Gino about Dario's predilections, but the truth had to be told. 'Dario is a . . . uh . . . he likes . . . boys . . . '

'Boys?' Gino frowned, his entire face darkening with fury, 'BOYS? Are you fuckin' tellin' me the kid's a fairy?'

Costa nodded miserably.

'I don't believe it!'

'Unfortunately it is true.'

Gino got up from the chair he was sitting on and stalked around the room, furiously hitting his fist into the palm of his hand. 'So what you're fuckin' tellin' me is that I got a pretty boy for a son – a daughter with cement balls swingin' between her legs – and you gave away my hotel. Is that it?'

'I didn't say that about Lucky,' Costa interjected quickly. 'She's a wonderful business woman – quick – a mind like a razor. She's like you, Gino, you should be proud of her. Without her the Magiriano would not exist. I think that when the two of you get together . . . '

'Where is Dario?' His voice was like ice.

Costa had forgotten all about Dario and his frantic phone call. But Sal should have taken care of things by now. 'He's in the city. He has an apartment near the river. Shall I arrange a meeting?'

'Don't arrange nothin'. Just give me his address. I'll take care of him.'

Costa shuddered. He wouldn't want to be in Dario's shoes. But still, *someone* had to show the boy some sense. If Gino ever found out about the pornographic movie Dario had starred in . . . Lucky had taken care of *that*. It had cost, and she had been as angry as Costa had ever seen her . . . but she had taken care of it. Maybe he *should* tell Gino. If he found out elsewhere . . . Some other time perhaps. Right now he was in no mood to hear about his son's movie career.

'So where's Lucky?' was his next question.

'She has her own apartment too. Sixty-first and Park.'

'I thought she'd be living in my place.'

'That was sold . . . six years ago. I have two realtors standing by when you're ready to decide where you want to live.'

Gino's eyes were deadly. 'She didn't sell the East Hampton house did she?'

'No. Of course not.'

'And it hasn't been touched?'

'Absolutely not.' Costa remembered a heated discussion with Lucky about the house. She had wanted to sell – for once he had blocked her way.

'Maybe I'll live there,' Gino said unexpectedly. 'I kinda got used to livin' in a house . . . '

'Good idea,' Costa agreed, relieved that he was no longer screaming. 'Of course, it'll need a great deal of work.'

'So what? I'll take a drive tomorrow – have a look at the place. You got me a good driver?'

'The best. He was working with the Vittorrio family in Chicago – came into town a year ago. Enzio's personal recommendation.'

'Enzio's personal recommendation, huh?'

'He's delighted about you coming back.'

Gino stared thoughtfully into space. 'Delighted. I bet.'

Costa cleared his throat, 'Enzio says whenever you're ready to meet. Two weeks, a month, whenever you're ready. He knows you'll want time to settle in, get used to being back. He –'

'What the fuck is the matter with you?' Gino screamed suddenly. 'You losing your marbles or what? I'm back. As of this minute I'm back. I don't like what's bin goin' on. I want a meet arranged with Enzio for tomorrow. And when I've found out what the fuck he's up to *then* I'll deal with Lucky an' Dario.' He paused and glared. 'They know I'm in town yet?'

Costa once again mopped his forehead, 'I thought it best to wait, tell them when you actually arrived. Now with the power cut . . . the city has been in a turmoil . . . I haven't spoken to either of them since yesterday.'

'That's good – that's OK. Don't tell 'em yet – I want to surprise them.'

Costa nodded weakly. He could keep no secrets from Lucky.

'I'm tired now,' Gino said dismissively. 'I want to get a good night's sleep.'

'Certainly,' Costa said quickly, watching his old friend pace around the room like a caged lion.

'Arrange the meet with Bonnatti. I want it tomorrow. No excuses.'

'I'm sure Enzio will be only too happy to . . . '

'Yeh, yeh. We'll see.' He walked to the window and stared out. 'It's strange bein' back,' he mumbled, almost to himself.

'It'll seem so at first – ' Costa began.

'Shit! One day and I'll feel like I never bin away.'

Costa could believe that. He nodded his agreement, then said, 'So, nothing else for tonight then?'

Nothing else. He had heard enough for one day. He wanted action, not more talk. 'You go home, Costa.'

'I'll do that. I *am* tired. Russo's in the adjoining room should you want him.'

'Yeh, I know, I know.'

Russo was Gino's appointed bodyguard, again recommended by Enzio. All the old guys were gone. Retired or dead. Russo wasn't of the old school, he was only in his twenties, sharp and well dressed. Gino had already decided he didn't look like he could hit a fly on the wall.

He walked Costa to the door. 'Hey, take no notice of my screamin', I know y'did your best.'

Costa left hurriedly. It was past seven o'clock and he needed to have a long serious talk with Lucky. Once she realized that her father was indeed back . . . Well, *something* would have to be worked out. The two of them were just going to have to learn to live together.

Gino watched his friend depart, lit a cigar, and paced restlessly around the room. Why hadn't the idiot told him about Lucky and Dario sooner? What the fuck was he waiting for? Then he remembered why: his own instructions. *Don't bother me with anything, just get me back.* Shit! Something was wrong. He felt it. It was a physical feeling, a gut reaction to something in the air.

But what?

He would have to wait and see. Just be extra careful and watchful – which reminded him. He picked up the phone and requested a number. An hour later he had a new driver and a new bodyguard. It wasn't that he didn't appreciate Enzio's personal recommendations, but rule number one was surround yourself with people whose loyalty was to you – and you alone.

The years in exile had not dulled his senses. If anything he felt fitter and more alert than when he had left. Seven years was a long time to sit still in one place, but Israel hadn't been so bad . . . A nice house, the sea, the beach, his dogs. An occasional female visitor when he felt like it.

During the third year of his exile he had met a woman. No spring chicken. In her early forties. But what did a man of his age need spring chickens for? They gave him indigestion with their silly questions and bouncing around.

The woman he met was an attractive widow with swept up blondish hair and clear blue eyes. It surprised Gino when she told him she was Jewish – she didn't *look* Jewish. Israeli girls were devastatingly gorgeous – but all that smoldering darkness had never appealed to him. He liked his women fair. Rosaline Glutzman was fair. She was also a great cook, a great listener, and a great lay for a man who no longer wished to do it ten times a night. She moved in at his invitation, and stayed until he departed, never once making demands of any kind.

He had not asked her to accompany him back to New York. She had not asked if she could. They had parted like two civilized people. He had given her a full length mink coat. End of *that* episode.

Now he found himself wishing he *had* brought her with him. Rosaline would have been the perfect person to talk to about Dario and Lucky. His children. Two strangers.

Lucky. What was she like now? From all accounts just like him. He smiled grimly. Was it so bad to be just like him? He remembered her as a little girl, always strong, always wild. Always so much sharper than Dario.

He frowned. A son of his a fag? It *had* to be a mistake. Costa was confused somewhere along the line.

He stripped down to his shorts and lay on the bed. The room was still hot, in spite of the fact that the air conditioning had resumed service.

What the fuck was Bonnatti up to? Word had reached Gino that he and the Kassarri twins were tight. Enzio knew how he felt about the Kassarri family. But what did he care? With Gino out of the country all he had to contend with was a girl, and a senile old fart – *excuse me Costa but it's true.*

Taking over the Magiriano must have been easy. Especially with Marco out of the way. The true test of Enzio Bonnatti and his loyalty and friendship would be how easily he relinquished control of the two Vegas hotels. Costa seemed to think it would be easy. Gino wasn't so sure. His instinct told him trouble. His instinct had never been wrong.

He closed his eyes, and Lucky and Dario were back in his thoughts. Lucky and Dario. They danced across his mind like two puppets on a string until eventually he fell into a troubled sleep.

## Friday, July 15th, 1977, New York — Morning

Lucky slept badly, waking every hour to check out the time. She dismissed Costa when he phoned right after Boogie with a curt 'Tomorrow. I don't want to be bothered now.' He did not try and pursue the conversation. It was not the right moment to tell her that Gino was back; he knew that by the tone of her voice.

Since she was up early anyway, she decided to go to the airport and meet Boogie's flight. The suspense was driving her crazy. She called down to the doorman for a cab, then had the cab take her over to the basement garage where her Mercedes waited. As she was opening it up with a spare set of keys she saw a note stuck on the windshield. Tearing it open quickly, she read the neat script — *'I'll give you three days — then I'm checking out your license plate and calling you — Steven.'*

She couldn't help smiling. He must have made a special trip to leave her message. She *would* call him . . . She *wanted* to call him . . . Just as soon as she found out what Boogie had on his mind.

Gino was up at six, dressed and breakfasted by seven, on the phone to Costa soon after. 'Well?' he demanded. 'What time is the meet with Bonnatti?'

'Enzio suggests one o'clock. A restaurant he frequents in Brooklyn. It has a garden — he says you'll enjoy the cassatta. He also says — '

'What's wrong with Riccaddis?'

'Nothing's wrong,' Costa replied nervously. 'If you would prefer it, of course I will speak to Enzio and — '

'Good. Riccaddis — at two o'clock. I'll see you there.'

Dario struggled to wake up but his eyelids were holding him back — they felt so very heavy . . .

It was early, he knew that — he could hear garbage being collected and the sound of kids going to school. He wasn't in his apartment . . he didn't know where he was . . . slowly he drifted back into a deep sleep.

Downstairs in the kitchen Sal kissed Ruth lightly on the cheek and said, 'You sure you know what to do?'

Ruth nodded, and smoothed down the top of her dress, 'I know exactly what to do.'

'Good,' Sal said, holding up two fingers firmly crossed for luck, 'go to it then.'

Carrie arose before Elliott – an unusual occurrence, but one that had happened two days in a row. This time she dressed down in a plain black pants suit with no accompanying jewelry. She brushed her glossy hair thoroughly, and twisted it back in a tight knot. She was ready and set to go at eight o'clock in the morning.

'Carrie,' Elliott snapped testily, 'where are you off to?'

'A new gym – marvellous place.'

'I want to get out of here today and you're off to a new gym.' She attempted a smile, but felt that it was frozen on her face. 'I'll be back before lunch.'

He snorted with disgust, 'I don't know what's the matter with you lately – ever since the blackout . . .'

'Nothing's the matter with me. I just like to keep healthy.'

'I'm making reservations for the Bahamas. Be prepared to leave tonight.'

She nodded obediently *Maybe. Only maybe.*

'How are you getting to the gym?' he inquired, just as she reached the front door.

She stopped for a moment, her mind blanking out. 'I'll walk,' she said at last. 'It's only a few blocks.'

'Where?'

'Oh . . . near,' she replied vaguely, opening the door and hurrying from the apartment.

Out on the street she took a deep breath and headed for the subway. Her nerves were taut. The sooner this meeting was over and done with, the better.

Steven was always up by six-thirty. He had a routine that he didn't like to deviate from. An ice cold shower, half an hour of punishing calisthenics, then fresh orange juice, wheat germ, bran flakes, honey, hot coffee, and he was ready for anything and anyone.

Today he was ready for Enzio Bonnatti. Today was the day the papers would be ready to serve. Two years of meticulous punishing work was finally reaching a peak. A peak which both elated and frightened Steven. Elated him because a man like Bonnatti deserved to spend the rest of his miserable life behind bars. Frightened him because even now so much could go wrong.

He finished dressing and thought briefly about his own life. Aileen – so much a part of it. So capable, organized, and attractive. Perfect wife material.

One night in an elevator with a kooky ballsy girl called Lucky – and he knew that Aileen was not for him. He did not wish to spend the rest of his life with her – it was as simple as that.

He sighed deeply. How to tell her – that was the thing.

Enzio Bonnatti woke with the lingering feel of a hangover. His mouth tasted of stale chicken turds, the back of his head ached, and his body felt stiff and unclean. It had been a good evening though . . . Plenty of fine red wine and lusty blonde females prepared to do whatever he wanted. Women. What *puttanas* they all were. Nothing new about that. He had always known it. But somehow – in the seventies – they had changed. They almost seemed to *enjoy* the fucking and the sucking and the other things. He could remember a time – not so far off – when only the whores indulged in perversions. Now it seemed that women liked sex – actually *liked* it. It was almost enough to ruin his watching pleasure. In the future, he decided, girls recruited for his entertainment must be of a more innocent nature altogether. Virgins, perhaps. Were there any left?

He raised his sleep mask and indulged in an early morning fit of coughing. Then he pressed the buzzer beside his bed and summoned to his presence Big Victor, personal bodyguard for over thirty-five years.

A busy day lay ahead. Gino Santangelo was back in town and there was a lot of work to do.

Lucky watched Boogie's plane arrive. Then she waited impatiently until he came sloping through the arrival gate.

He hadn't changed. Still the same old Boog – skinny, long haired – dressed in tight jeans and his battered old army jacket.

She ran forward and hugged him, an impulse which seemed to embarrass him. Boogie was not big on emotional gestures.

He looked around with slitted watchful eyes. 'Anyone know I was coming in?'

'You told me not to mention it – and frankly, Boog, who do I know that gives a shit any way? Now *what* is this all about?'

He took her by the arm, his strong fingers digging in. 'The sooner we talk, the sooner you're going to be one wise girl.'

'Let's go, then. My car's outside. We can talk on the way into town.'

'I'll drive. When you hear what I've got to say you're liable to freak. Lucky – you have been played for dumb pussy.'

The words struck home. Her eyes gleamed black and deadly, her tone pure acid, 'Tell me about it, Boog – I can't wait.'

The morning newspapers announced Gino's arrival back in America. Not headlines – page three of the *New York Times.*

Gino read the article and threw the newspaper down in disgust. It sure as hell blew him surprising Lucky and Dario. He called up Costa and instructed him to arrange an afternoon meeting with his children. Children. What a joke. A fag and a ballbreaker. Yet the thought of seeing them again excited him more than he cared to admit.

Lucky and Dario. The offspring of his marriage to Maria. Sweet beautiful Maria. Every time he thought of her the pain was as fresh as the day it happened. Her murder would linger in his mind until the day he went to join her. Maria. So soft, so gentle. Why hadn't Lucky turned out like her mother?

He spent a busy morning on the phone, renewing old acquaintances, letting the right people know he was back – to stay. Listening, absorbing, hearing rumor, gossip, and truth. By the time he was ready to set off for his lunch with Enzio he had learned a lot – more than enough to make him certain that Enzio was not going to relinquish his hold in Las Vegas without a fight.

Well, if it was a fight he wanted, Gino was ready. He had taken steps to reinforce his position, and Enzio Bonnatti – if he was smart – would back down before a confrontation. Gino Santangelo always won. It was a fact of life.

This time Carrie drew no second glances. She was black in a black neighborhood – so what? No expensive trinkets adorned her person, although the sunglasses which shielded her eyes had cost over a hundred dollars at Henri Bendel.

The subway was an experience – hot, dirty, smelly, and crowded. How many years since she'd ridden the subway? Enough to make her aware of the enormous difference in her life style from that of the ordinary person. *You're lucky Carrie* – she told herself – *You are living the American dream*

*– You have money – style – position. Yet she was a fake wasn't she? She was living a lie. Her whole background was a lie.*

It was long before twelve o'clock. She wished that it was long after. Apprehensively she went into a drug store, took a stool at the end of the counter, and ordered a coffee.

'Gonna be a scorcher today, hon,' remarked the skinny woman behind the counter, lazily scratching her armpit, 'hotter than Muhammad Ali's mouth!' She cackled loudly at her own joke, 'I sure 'nuff *love* that boy's mouth!'

Carrie smiled weakly. Another three hours to wait.

Warris Charters missed bumping into Lucky Santangelo at Kennedy Airport by half an hour. His flight from Los Angeles was early, and he was in exceptional good spirits. The morning paper carried news of Gino Santangelo's return to America, and the timing couldn't be better.

He smiled to himself. It had taken long enough but he had done it – finally *Kill Shot* was to be made – and no thanks to Dario Santangelo, although indirectly Warris reluctantly supposed that he *was* in a way responsible.

Warris reflected on the events of the past two years. Dario. A blond beautiful boy with an enormous sexual appetite. Useless when it came to contacting his father re the script. Jealous, insecure, kinky. God! Warris had known enough women with those qualities. Dario – after moving in uninvited – became Mister Possessive. *That* kind of relationship he didn't need – especially when there were no bonuses to go along with it. The only Santangelo quality Dario had was his name. Gino and Lucky were the two with the power and the money. He soon found *that* out.

When he realized that there were no advantages to Dario's sharing his life – he put him to work. And how he loved the work. Dario Santangelo became David Dirk – porno movie star supreme – a vocation he seemed to have been made for. The only disadvantage was that Dario/David could not get it up for any female thespians – fellow male actors were the only lucky ones.

'You're not easy to cast.' Warris complained. 'Heterosexual movies are the ones that make the big bread.'

'So write me a movie,' Dario replied airily.

It wasn't a bad idea. Warris did just that. He called it *Cowboy Cruiser* and it was an immediate smash on the porno circuits. Dario, a better looking Robert Redford on the screen, had every faggot from coast to coast falling desperately madly in love. Fan mail began to arrive at the seedy Pasadena studio by the sackload. Dario had made it. He was a Movie Queen.

It was a short lived career. Early one morning two men arrived at the Marina del Rey apartment Warris and Dario shared. They were the kind of men you did not argue with, so when they said that Mr Bonnatti requested their presence – pronto – neither of them demurred. Obedient as two puppies straight out of dog training school, they accompanied the two men to Las Vegas where the infamous Enzio Bonnatti received them in a penthouse apartment on top of the Magiriano.

He minced no words. To Dario he said, 'You get your faggot ass back to New York an' you *keep* it there. I ever see your face in one of them movies again, an' you don't have no face. Get it?'

Dario got it. He fled to New York without so much as a goodbye.

'You,' said Enzio to Warris, when Dario had departed. 'Got any idea who I am?'

'Mr Bonnatti,' he replied smoothly, 'I've been a fan of yours all my life.'

Enzio nodded and grunted. 'I can take it I ain't gonna get any trouble from you, then?'

Warris threw up his arms noncommitally, 'Mr Bonnatti, whatever you want, name it.'

'I got the blond faggot's sister breathin' down my neck. She wants the movie – so *I* gotta get the movie. The negative an' *all* the prints an' *no* bullshit deals or you'll be pushin' cactus in the desert. You savvy?'

He nodded gravely, 'Of course I'll be reimbursed.'

Enzio laughed loudly, 'Yeah – sure. You gotta good touch. You direct that junk?'

'I wrote it, directed it, cast it. *That* junk is cleaning up, as I'm sure you know.'

'Yeah, yeah. I know.' Thoughtfully Enzio picked his nose, 'I want you to write a movie for me. Plenty of tits, ass, an' blonde cooze with drippin' boxes. You get the picture?'

Warris got the picture.

'I'll finance the whole thing – how much will it cost?'

'I have no shortage of people willing to finance anything I care to do,' he said mildly, 'after the success of *Cowboy Cruiser . . .*'

'So what d'y'want?' snapped Enzio. 'Don't fuck me around with speeches I don't need. Spit it out'

His eyes gleamed, 'I want to make a legitimate picture – a

script I have called *Kill Shot*. I'm sure it's a subject that will
interest you once you read the property . . .'

That conversation had taken place four months previously.
And in those four months Warris had been busier than he'd
ever been. Enzio Bonnatti had *loved* the idea of making a movie
based on Gino Santangelo's life, only he wanted a few changes
here and there. Just small changes – such as the friend and
mentor of Gino becoming a superhero, and Gino himself becoming a petty violent hood.

Warris agreed to all changes. Screw Enzio Bonnatti – once
the picture was under way Warris would do it *his* way. He had
waited ten years to do it his way.

In the meantime Bonnatti had put up all pre-production
costs, and had agreed to a four million dollar budget. Warris
had got together a first class crew, and an exciting cast of un-
discovered talent. The stumbling block was the female lead. He
knew who he wanted. Bonnatti had other ideas. The trip to
New York was to finalize the flow of finance and settle on
which girl would get the part. With shooting due to commence
in ten days there was no time to screw around.

Whistling softly to himself Warris left the airport by cab.
Under his arm was a can of film containing a test done by *his*
girl. Once Bonnatti saw her there would be no more argument.

Ruth hurried into the large supermarket complex. She was used
to the looks she received – first admiration – because she was –
had been – a great looking girl. Then – shock – horror – embarrassment. They got a look at the disfigured side of her face
and it was all over.

'Hey, cutie – ' a guy started to say. His words came to an
abrupt halt as she walked by.

She took no notice. Dumb asshole. What did he know? She
paused by a pay phone and took a deep breath. Dario Santangelo was asleep in her bed. Sal thought they were sitting on a
mint – Ruth was smart enough to know different. Never mess
with the big boys – rule one for survival in the big city. Sometimes Sal could be a dumb asshole too.

She extracted some coins from her purse and began to dial a
number. 'Victor,' she whispered, 'it's Ruthie. I got something
I want you to help me out with . . .'

The street was not familiar in the daytime. But Carrie found
the meat market and stationed herself outside, jumping every
time anyone walked within a yard of her.

Her eyes swept to the left and the right, anxiously picking out faces, walks, attitudes. *Who the hell was putting her through this torture? She would kill them. She would get hold of another gun and kill them.*

She wasn't looking for a car, so she took no notice of the white Eldorado that swept to a stop in front of the market. She didn't even hear her name called the first time. The second call grabbed her attention, and she stepped towards the car.

The occupant was hidden behind the safety and anonymity of black tinted windows.

'Who are you?' Carrie hissed.

The rear door swung open. 'Get in,' murmured the same voice as her telephone caller. 'Quickly please.'

Boogie had been talking non-stop for an hour. Boogie, who was usually reluctant to string two sentences together.

Lucky listened, not interrupting once as he told his story in a flat expressionless monotone. She believed everything he said. Boogie would never lie to her – he had no reason to. A fury began to build in her as he spoke. A cold hard fury that she knew she was powerless to control. Dumb pussy. That's what Boogie had said she had been taken for – and Boogie was right. Dumb fucking pussy.

They were back in her apartment now, and she went to a locked drawer in her desk and silently removed a small tin box. Expertly she rolled a joint, lit up, dragged deeply, and passed it on to Boogie. Pot calmed her, cleared her mind. It did not make her mellow and giggly, it had exactly the reverse effect. She didn't use it all the time only when she really wanted to be extremely alert and sharp.

Boogie was concluding his story. He stared at her knowingly, 'I had to tell you, didn't I?'

'Absolutely.'

He stretched his lean and lanky body, 'I thought so.'

They were both silent then, finishing off the joint, busy with their own thoughts.

'How are you going to move?' he ventured.

'Like a black widow spider,' she replied coldly. 'Silently, stealthily – and anyone who gets in my way will get their ass crushed.'

## Friday, July 15th, 1977, New York — Afternoon

'So,' Gino beamed, 'Enzio, my friend, I bet you never dreamed we would be breaking bread together again – here – in Riccaddis – with all our loyal paesanos around us.'

'Gino, my friend. It is something I have thought about every day since you left.'

'Of course you have. Why not? We grew up together – grabbed the world by the balls together – honored each other in every way.' He raised his wine glass, 'We've had our differences along the way – but nothing we couldn't sort out. I drink to us Enzio – you and me. Two old war horses who have survived with dignity and good faith.'

Enzio picked up his glass and clinked it with Gino's. The two men drank.

'Tell me,' said Gino offhandedly. 'What is this investment you have made with my money from the Magiriano?'

'Ah . . . ' Enzio studied his short blunt manicured nails. 'I'm glad you asked. You came back so suddenly it was quite a surprise. I am not prepared . . . I want to show you papers . . . figures . . . I have done a wonderful thing for you.'

'How wonderful?' Gino asked mildly.

'You'll see. Later this week I'll have everything ready.'

'Good, good.' He toyed with a forkful of spaghetti. 'I appreciate all you have done, Enzio. Taking over in Vegas, looking after Lucky . . . I understand you have been like a father to her.'

Enzio smiled, his teeth were badly decayed, he had a fear of the dentist that prevented him from doing anything about them. 'She's a true Santangelo, Gino. You gotta be real proud of her.'

'I am Enzio, I am. But let us not forget that she is also a woman – the weaker sex. Too bad that some people will always be around to take advantage.'

Enzio's right eye flickered, an affliction he had always possessed – a sure giveaway that he was about to tell a lie. 'No one would dare take advantage of Lucky with me around,' he boomed, 'no one.'

'No, not with you around, my dear friend – because you would do as I would do, should it ever happen. You would squash that person underfoot – like a bug – like vermin. Am I right?'

Enzio did not reply. He stared at Gino, and Gino stared right back.

'Tomorrow,' said Gino slowly, 'I shall be taking steps to reinstate my people in my hotels.' His finger crept up to the faded scar on his face and he rubbed it gently. 'You will tell your people to cooperate – let's do this thing smoothly. No sense in waiting – huh, my friend? huh?'

Carrie did not recognize the old woman sitting in the back of the white Eldorado, but she got in the car anyway. After all that's what she had come up to Harlem for – to find out.

The air conditioning was going full blast, and the black tinted windows made the interior strangely dim. A curtained partition separated them from the driver.

As soon as she got in, the car sped away from the curb. A nervous sweat broke out all over her body, she could feel the dampness under her arms, between her thighs, the palms of her hands. She managed to keep her voice strong – 'Who are you?' she repeated, 'and what do you want?'

The old woman laughed, a strangely sad sound. She was fat, wrapped in a voluminous white caftan, with plump beringed fingers drumming nervously on her knees. She sported unflattering large white sunglasses, dyed black hair worn in a Spanish upsweep, and a slash of obscene scarlet lipstick. Her olive skin was wrinkled and liver spotted, and her chin hung in crepey folds. A sickly sweet perfume filled the air. 'You don' remember me?' the woman appealed in a raspy whisper.

'I don't *know* you,' Carrie said desperately. 'For God's sake tell me what you want. I don't have a lot of money but . . . '

'Ha! You don' have a lot of money. Look at you, honey – you *stink* of money.'

'How much do you want?'

The woman's voice softened. 'I don' wan' your money. Baby Steven, he certainly growed into one fine lookin' man.'

Alarm filled Carrie's voice. 'What do you know about Steven?'

'I remember heem – you don' remember me.'

The raspy voice struck a chord. Carrie's mind ticked over furiously. The accent . . . something about the accent . . .

'I loved heem . . . he was my baby too. When you ran out on me you took little Stevie.' The woman sighed wearily, 'But I don' blame you, Carrie . . . I don' blame you. You done so good for yourself, you became a beeg somebody . . . you – '

'Suzita?' she whispered in shocked amazement, '*Suzita?*'

The woman grinned, 'I got a leetle fat . . . a leetle old. Time stood still for you . . . Me,' she shrugged, 'I been a workin' woman all my life.'

Carrie felt like bursting into tears. This obese old crone couldn't be Suzita. Young vibrant Suzita with a body grown men used to fight over. Fate had been cruel indeed.

'I ain't got you here to blackmail you,' Suzita said quickly, 'I guess eet must look that way to you.'

Carrie was confused, a million thoughts kept rushing through her mind. 'Why? After all this time? How did you find me?'

'I never lost you, honey,' Suzita said matter-of-factly. 'I followed your life – right after I see some photo spread on you een a magazine a couple years after you left. Eeet made me feel good, knowin' you had got away. Not many get away from Bonnatti . . . not many . . . '

Bonnatti. The sound of his name brought back cruel memories. Bonnatti treating her like a table, a chair, a piece of meat, an inanimate object to play with.

Bonnatti. The master. Treating everyone like dirt.

'Suzita,' she said softly, 'these last days you have put me through hell. I was outside the market on Wednesday night . . . I waited . . you never came . . . I was assaulted . . . arrested . . . It was a nightmare. Please tell me what you want with me and let me get on with my life.'

'Yeah, sure, I know. We have nothin' een common anymore. You're a lady – I'm a whore still running a house for Bonnatti. So why wouldya wanna spend any time with me?'

'For God's sake!' Carrie implored. '*Tell me what you want.*'

Suzita played with the rings on her fat fingers. 'I wanna warn you, ees all.'

'Warn me?'

'Yeah. About the Bonnatti investigation.'

'What investigation?'

Suzita raised her large white sunglasses and peered at Carrie incredulously. Her eyes were raisins in dusky sour dough skin. 'The investigation your son ees conducting.'

An electric jolt struck Carrie. *The investigation your son is conducting.* She had known Steven was working on something, but security had forbidden his mentioning any names. He had confided in no one. Not even Jerry knew.

'You didn't know,' stated Suzita.

Blankly she shook her head.

'Sheet!' exclaimed Suzita. 'Well, Bonnatti knows . . . an' he ain't worried.'

'What do you mean?'

'I ain't the only one followed your life . . . '

She felt the vomit rise in her throat.

'Bonnatti *knows* who Stevie is. It's kinda givin' heem a charge. When he's up there before the grand jury, he's gonna tell 'em about you . . . Can you imagine what'll happen to Stevie's case? With you for a mother he'll be laughed out of court. Bonnatti's lookin' *forward* to it . . . it's like the openin' of a show an' he's plannin' eet real good. He has everythin' on you – drugs – pictures – hospital records – everythin'. He even has those old snapshots of Stevie with all the girls when he was just four years old. Cute little boy in a white silk romper suit standin' on a table . . . '

Carrie slumped back into the seat.

Lucky sat cross legged in the middle of her bed, eyes closed, fingers pressed deeply against her temples. Enzio Bonnatti. Her Godfather. Her mentor. The man she had confided in – loved. The man who had replaced Gino in her affections.

Enzio Bonnatti. Vile snake in the grass. Murderer. Killer. Marco's assassin – if not by actual hand – by command. 'Finish Marco,' he must have said. 'He's the only one knows what's goin' on. The girl and Costa are easy meat. They'll back off – they ain't got the brains to stay.'

How right he had been. How he must have gloated when she handed him everything on a plate. Him and the Kassarri twins – *sons of her own mother's killer*.

And she never suspected a thing. Dumb little Lucky Santangelo. Dumb pussy.

If it wasn't for Boogie she still wouldn't have been any the wiser. Boogie – who had picked up certain information eavesdropping on two Chicago hoods riding in the back of his limousine ten days previously. Boogie had just heard bits and pieces, a few names – dates – but enough to interest him – enough to get him wondering about Enzio Bonnatti and his loyalty to Lucky. Enough to spur him into doing a little investigating of his own.

He had found out plenty. Easily. He had a friend in the police department who checked out the files on Marco's murder. Perpetrator unknown – the file was marked. And there was a long police report about certain suspects who were brought in. The Kassarri brothers were questioned, but their alibi was watertight. A hired enforcer of theirs was questioned, arrested, released on bail, and killed by a hit and run driver before he appeared in court. Mortimer Sauris was a small time gambler who hadn't even been in town when Marco was gunned down. He had a history of welshing on bets. He wasn't looking to put out anyone – but a lot of people were looking to put out him.

Marco was assassinated by the Kassarri brothers on direct orders from Enzio Bonnatti. It was no big secret.

Lucky's fingers pressed her temples harder. Why hadn't she realized what was going on? Why hadn't she suspected?

Christ! She jumped off the bed abruptly. She knew what she had to do.


Costa was sweating freely when they left Riccaddis. All his life he had liked things peaceful. Now that Gino was back, peaceful was a thing of the past.

'That dirty son-of-a-bitch,' Gino muttered, as soon as they were in the car. 'That dirty filthy lying fuckhead.'

'What is wrong?' Costa asked uneasily. 'He agreed with everything you said. He did not argue.'

'You gettin' senile, Costa? *I'm* the one that's bin away – and *you're* the one don't know from nothin'.'

'You think he plans to cheat us?'

'Wake up, old man. He plans more than a cheat. He plans a hit. I know. I can read it in his eyes.'

Costa was genuinely shocked. 'You think that Enzio – your friend for so many years . . .'

'Be quiet, Costa. You blow sunshine out your ass don't mean everyone's the same. I must think. I must have peace. And I must double my security. He plans a hit. *I know it.*'

'But Gino . . .'

'What, Costa? What? You think these things don't happen?'

'I only . . .'

'Did you arrange a time for Lucky and Dario to meet me?'

'Er . . . I tried to reach them –'

'Don't *try*, get them to the hotel. If Enzio plans to blow me away – then maybe Lucky will be next. Who knows? I want them at the hotel as soon as possible. Personally bring them.'

Costa nodded, and his sweat flowed freely.


Enzio climbed into the back of his brown Pontiac with the bullet proof windows and the sound system that cost more than the whole goddamn car. Viciously he shoved in a Tony Bennett tape, and to the strains of 'I Left My Heart In San Francisco' he said to Big Victor, 'It's time. Arrange it. And I don't want no fuck ups.'

'I got an idea, boss,' said Victor, saliva bubbling in his mouth as he spoke.

'What?'

'Whyn't we use the boy? This Dario. If he did the hit there could be no fingers pokin' at you. Santangelo's gotta lot of big friends wouldn't be happy if you was involved. We use the boy ... they can't say nothin'.'

'You're fuckin' A right!' exclaimed Enzio – 'The boy is at the house now, right?'

'Just like you told me, boss,' smirked Victor. He made a mental note to see that Ruthie was taken care of. She was an OK dame – she'd made the right move when it mattered. Called her old uncle and asked his advice. Big Victor had sensed an advantage in getting hold of Gino Santangelo's son. 'Stay away from home. I'll have my boys take care of it,' he told her. 'You done a good thing calling me.'

'What about Sal? They won't hurt her?'

So what? Victor wanted to say – You'd be better off without that shit tough dike. ' 'Course not, sweetie,' he had assured her, 'Go home tonight, it'll all be taken care of.'

'When we get back to the house bring him to me,' Enzio decided. 'You know somethin' Vic? If the kid does the hit it's the perfect answer.'

'That's what I said, boss.'

'No. That's what *I* said.'

Carrie left Suzita's car on the corner of 109th Street, and rode a cab back to her apartment. She dismissed the maid and locked herself in Elliott's study, where she sat and stared at the glass fronted cabinet displaying his gun collection. What did she know about guns? Hardly anything. Enough to take one of the smaller ones down, load it, use it. Only Suzita wasn't the victim she had in mind. Suzita had come to warn her – God knows why when all those years ago she had just run out on her.

Enzio Bonnatti was the victim she had in mind. Enzio Bonnatti – who, according to Suzita, lived in a highly protected Long Island mansion from where he ran his network of crime and vice.

She stared at the guns, and her stare settled on a .38.

Very slowly she stood up, walked to the window and tipped the key to the cabinet out of a vase.

The choice was simple. Steven's career or Enzio's life.

There was no choice.

Urgently Costa rang the bell outside Lucky's apartment. He had tried to call her all morning with no success. Likewise his attempts to reach Dario. During lunch he had tried to call them both again. He had left messages all over, but neither had returned his calls.

Now he stood outside Lucky's door and prayed for her to be home. The time had come for her to face up to reality. Gino was back. No mistake about it.

At last a shuffling noise, and the door was opened on a security chain. 'Costa?' questioned a voice.

He was alarmed. Where was the maid? Who was in Lucky's apartment?

'Yes,' he said shortly.

The door was thrown open and Boogie Patterson stood there.

'What are you doing here?' Costa asked sharply.

'He's visiting. I'm allowed visitors aren't I?' Lucky strolled out from the bedroom in a short robe.

'I have been trying to reach you all day,' he said pompously.

'I was out – then I switched the phone off. What's on your mind?'

'Have you seen the newspapers?'

'No. Why?'

He took a deep breath. 'Your father is back,' he said, diving straight in, 'and he wants to see you.'

Dario was confused. What the hell was happening in his life? He sat in the kitchen of Enzio's house drinking cup after cup of hot strong coffee while two hoods lounged around watching him.

'I want to go home,' he stated peevishly. It was the fourth time he had said it.

'We'll take y'home,' one of the hoods said, his name was Russo, 'just soon as you given your proper thank-yous to Mr Bonnatti.'

'I don't know what the hell's going on,' Dario muttered. He had woken up in the back of a car with Russo beside him and the other man driving. His last memory was of Sal feeding him pills. Neither Russo nor the other man had felt free to give him any information. He didn't dare ask what had happened to Sal or the boy he had stabbed.

When they arrived at the house, Russo had said, 'This is Mr Bonnatti's residence. He helped y'out of a jam. When he says it's OK we'll take y'home.' That's the only information he had received.

He scowled, and took another mouthful of the steaming coffee. 'Can I make a phone call?'

'I don't – '

A third man burst into the kitchen then. A fat man in a sweaty suit with gravy stains on the lapels. 'Dario!' he exclaimed, as though they were old friends. 'Last time I saw you was in Vegas. Remember?'

He stared. Yes. The fat man had been with Enzio Bonnatti when he had summoned Warris and himself to his presence. 'Get back to New York,' Enzio had commanded, and the fat man had personally put him on a plane.

'Listen, what the hell is going on around here?' he asked hotly.

'You had a few problems. Mr Bonnatti heard – figured you was family – decided we should help y'out. Come. He'll see you now.'

Enzio Bonnatti sat on an overstuffed damask covered armchair picking at pistachio nuts from a glass bowl. 'Sit,' he commanded, as though he was talking to a dog.

Dario sat. He knew when not to argue. Enzio Bonnatti might look like somebody's grandfather, but his voice, his eyes, the way he cracked his knuckles when he made a command – they all told another story.

Silence filled the room while he looked Dario over. Finally he said, 'I don't like to waste time – never have. I'll give you the story and tell you what I want.'

Dario nodded.

Enzio squeezed a pistachio nut from its tight shell and popped it in his mouth. 'Somebody sent that fairy into your apartment to kill you. You got smart. You did away with him before he could do the same to you.'

Dario blinked quickly. It seemed he couldn't make a move without fucking Bonnatti finding out.

'Y'know somethin'? I never had you figured for smart,' Enzio paused, 'but you did the right thing.' He popped another nut and reached for a glass of mineral water. 'So – you do away with the fairy – call Costa Zennocotti – and he gets Sal to clear up the mess. Only what happens then?'

'That's what I'd like to know,' Dario mumbled.

'Sal kidnaps you!' Enzio announced dramatically. *'The person that Costa sent to help you kidnaps you.'*

Dario sat forward on his chair and eagerly strained to hear more.

'Why?' Enzio boomed. 'Ask yourself, why?' He paused, stared meaningfully, then continued in hushed tones. 'Because your family wants to get rid of you. You get my meaning? They want to dump you – push you out of the way – bury you ten foot under. Gino and Lucky – they want you dead, Dario, dead. You understand boy? Dead.'

Dario took a deep breath. So it *had* been Lucky all along.

Costa felt a lot better when Lucky agreed to a meeting with her father. She seemed a little strange, but that was only to be expected.

'Come to the hotel with me now,' he pleaded. 'Gino is waiting.'

'I can't come now,' she replied coolly. 'I have some calls to make. But I'll be there later – I promise.'

Costa glanced quickly at his watch. It was almost two-thirty. 'Four o'clock at the Pierre then?' he asked anxiously.

'Fine. I'll be there. Don't worry, I will, honestly.' She pecked him quickly on the cheek – he looked so tired and worried and old. He would look even worse if he knew what she knew . . .

Costa hurried over to his office.

'Ah, Mr Zennocotti,' said his secretary, 'I have Dario Santangelo on the line. He's called twice before.'

Costa snatched up the phone. 'Dario? Where are you? I was trying to reach you. Is everything all right?'

'Everything's cool. I've been hangin' out with some friends. Hey – I read that Gino's back. I want to see him.'

'And he wants to see you. Can you be at the Pierre by four?'

'Sure.' He hesitated for just a second. 'Will Lucky be there?'

'She will be. It would be nice if now that your father is back the two of you could get along. I do think – '

'Later.' Dario hung up the phone.

Enzio, sitting in his overstuffed armchair watching, said 'Well?'

He took a deep breath. 'Four o'clock, the Pierre, they'll both be there.'

Enzio nodded. 'Then you'll do what you have to do,' he said softly, 'won't you, Dario?'

Gino paced the floor of his suite, his mind racing. He needed this aggravation like he needed bleeding piles. A show of strength was imperative. Bonnatti had to know – up front – that he wasn't going to give an inch. Not one goddamn inch. The two hotels in Vegas were his – sure Bonnatti had a piece of the Mirage, but that was all, only a piece of the cake.

Unfortunately Bonnatti had an army – but a mob had never been Gino's style. Big business was his style, dealing with the right people, having key connections who could do him a lot more good than an army of goons.

By the time Lucky arrived at the hotel he had made enough calls to ascertain that a big investigation was going on. Any day now, Bonnatti was going to be indicted. Enzio had wriggled his way out of a lot of indictments, but this one looked like the real thing.

He smiled grimly. If Bonnatti was put away it would solve a lot of problems. Better get the money he owed him fast . . .

Costa preceded Lucky into the room and then vanished into the bedroom. Gino stared at his daughter. It was a shock because it was almost like looking in a mirror. As she had grown, so she had grown more like him. The eyes were exactly the same – black opal pools – and the jet hair – and the set of her jaw – the full sensuous mouth – the brilliant white teeth. Christ! But she wasn't him. She was beautiful like a wild black orchid.

He could see at once that this was not the spoiled girl he had left behind. This was a woman, Self-assured, confident . . .

He smiled and held open his arms. 'Lucky!'

She was taken aback. Did he honestly expect it to be that easy? One hug and an affectionate 'Lucky'?

Her voice was stilted, she ignored his open arms and said, 'Hi, Gino. Welcome back.' *Dumb. Dumb. Dumb. Why had she said welcome back when she didn't mean it?*

He stared at her quizzically and tried to turn his arms into a gesture – a shrug. 'Well, well,' he said, 'look at you – all grown up.'

She regarded him coldly. 'I thought I was all grown up when you married me off at sixteen.'

He made a face, 'So it didn't work out. But it kept you out of trouble – right? You goin' to hold a grudge forever, kid?'

She spotted a bottle of scotch on a table and walked towards it. 'Can I fix you one too?' she asked stiffly.

'Not at this time of the day.'

She poured herself a hefty glass of the amber liquid and deliberately took a long drink.

Gino did not take his eyes off her. 'I guess we'd better talk,' he said at last.

She was unnerved by his steady stare. 'Yes,' she said defiantly, 'a lot of things have changed while you've been away.'

'Yeh?' he questioned mildly.

'Yeh.' She tried to return his stare but couldn't hold the look. She walked to the window and gazed out. 'I'm involved now. I'm a part of it.'

'So I heard.'

She turned to face him, her black eyes blazing, 'I can tell you this – no way are you shoving me out – *no way*.'

Riding up in the elevator Dario licked his lips. They were dry and cracked. He picked at a hangnail and tried to think rationally. Enzio Bonnatti was right. It was him or them. Why let the two of them go on making his life hell? *Sending people into his own apartment to kill him.* It was shocking. How could he go on living that way? Never knowing who had been sent to get him. Never knowing if a casual pick up would suddenly produce a knife. Never knowing his future.

Enzio Bonnatti *was* right.

Still . . . to kill his own flesh . . . to murder in cold blood . . .

'Why me?' he had asked Bonnatti.

'Because you have everything to gain an' nothin' to lose,' Enzio replied. 'Besides, Gino's suspicious – none of my boys could get close. Don't fuck up – do the job properly – there'll be a car waiting for you when you leave the hotel – a ticket to Rio – and a million dollars cash when you arrive. Friggin' beat that.'

'How do I know – ' Dario began.

'That you can trust me?' Enzio laughed his throaty laugh. 'You don't. You're takin' a chance – but it's a better chance than your sister or father will give you. You can bet on *that* little fact of life.'

By four o'clock in the afternoon Steven was getting jittery. He had spent the entire day tying up loose ends and waiting for the papers to be processed. He wanted to be there when they arrested Bonnatti. He wanted to see the look on his face when they put the cuffs on, read him his rights, and hauled him down to the station.

A man like Bonnatti would immediately try for bail. Steven had plans to block *that* little move.

He and Bobby sat around his office drinking endless cups of coffee and waiting for the call to tell them everything was ready.

'Shit man!' exclaimed Bobby. 'I figured the two years of work was tough, but I'm sweatin' piss today just waitin' to see that motha's face.'

Steven nodded. 'Tell me about it.'

'What d'y'say. Another cuppa java?'

He shook his head and yawned. 'How long does it take to check out a license number on a car?'

'About five minutes. I got a friend in the department. What's the number?'

Steven read out the number of Lucky's Mercedes from the piece of paper he had scribbled it down on.

'You wanna see action, I'll show you action,' Bobby joked, picking up the phone.

Five minutes later he had the name of the company the car was registered to 'Who you trackin'?' he asked curiously.

'Just . . . someone.' Steven muttered, thinking of Lucky and wanting to see her again very much indeed

'Well *someone's* car belongs to the Free Make-Up Co. – I have an address if you want to track *someone* further.'

'Not right now.'

'Does Aileen know about *someone*?'

'Why don't you just shut up, Bobby, and get us another cup of coffee.'

'Right on boss man, right on.'

The meeting between Lucky and Gino was not going well. She was full of too much anger to even consider reconciling with her father. He was mild, and friendly, but the more he spoke, the nicer he was – the more it made her feel that he was talking down to her, playing her along.

'Vegas is mine,' she snapped finally. 'I'm going back.'

'A little late in the day.'

'What do you mean?'

'Come on, Lucky – you seem like a smart girl. You *gave* Vegas to Bonnatti – *handed* it to him. You think he'll just step down with a smile?'

'I know how to handle him.'

He laughed aloud. 'I came back not a moment too soon. Don't you realize that Bonnatti is no longer our friend?'

Two red spots burned brightly on her cheeks. Even Gino
knew . . . Before she could say anything there was a knock on
the door. Costa hurried from the bedroom to get it.

Dario stood in the doorway, slim and blond and innocent
looking. 'Hi, everyone,' he said. 'Good to see you.'

At two o'clock in the afternoon Carrie rented a car from Hertz.
At three o'clock in the afternoon she was parked near the gates
to Enzio Bonnatti's mansion.

She sat in the car, her purse beside her, the gun in her purse.
She was waiting. She didn't know what for. She only knew that
if she waited long enough she would summon the courage to
do something about the monster who lived only yards from
where she was sitting.

Wafris Charters checked into the Plaza Hotel. Why not? Enzio
Bonnatti was paying.

He had a sauna, a massage, a manicure. On two occasions he
phoned the Bonnatti mansion but both times Enzio was un-
available. At three-fifteen he phoned again and Enzio spoke to
him.

'I have some film I'd like you to see,' Warris said, relieved
that Enzio had finally taken his call. In the movie business you
could never be sure of *anything*.

'Good,' said Enzio, 'I wanna see it. An' I got an idea for a
new ending that'll *kill* you.'

'Shall I come out now?'

'You gotta car?'

'No. I was going to rent one.'

'Don't bother. I'll send one of the boys for you. Russo –
he'll pick you up around six. Be ready.'

Warris hung up with a smile on his face.

Lucky wasn't pleased when Dario showed up. Who'd invited
*him?* This was supposed to be a business meeting and it was
turning into a family reunion. Shit! She had things to do. She
didn't need this.

Dario and she were no longer on speaking terms. Since the
porno movie – and the subsequent embarrassment – their relationship was null and void.

The atmosphere in Gino's suite was strained to say the least.
Dario tried to play it nice and easy, but the pressure of the
small gun in the ill fitting holster under his arm was bothering
him more than a little. Perspiration beaded his top lip.

'Take off your jacket,' Gino urged. 'Make yourself comfortable.'

'In a minute,' replied Dario. *In a minute I'm going to blow your brains out. Who first? If I hit bitch sister first what will Gino do? And vice versa?*

Sweet Jesus! Bonnatti had just shoved a gun at him and said 'Do it.' But how? Who first, for crissake? Who first?

'I have to be going,' Lucky said abruptly.

*Hit her first. She was the one who had given him the most trouble.*

Automatically his hand reached for the gun. *Rio. A million dollars. Freedom.*

'Gino,' Costa came walking in from the bedroom, 'would you like me to order something from room service?'

*Goddammit!* Costa! He wouldn't be able to take the three of them out. *Goddammit!* Why hadn't Bonnatti told him what to do about Costa?

It was all getting too confusing. He would do it – sure he *would* do it – but another time. Tomorrow. The day after. Bonnatti would understand. He would *have* to understand. Rio could wait a day or two. The million dollars would still be there. His hand slid away from the gun. Gino was staring at him strangely – like he *knew*.

He rushed towards the door, 'I gotta go, something I forgot to do . . .' he mumbled.

They were all staring at him now. All three of them. His hand, slippery with sweat, slid on the door knob.

'Hey – ' Gino began, 'what's the matter with you? I want to talk to you. I want – '

He got a grip on the knob and ran from the room. He could hear Gino yelling after him, but he didn't look back. He raced to the emergency stairs, just as Bonnatti had said he should. He stumbled down them two at a time, his breath labored, the goddamn leather holster digging uncomfortably into his armpit.

*What was he running for? He hadn't done anything.*

Gradually he slowed down. By the time he reached the first floor he was breathing normally.

He walked from the hotel calmly and looked around. Across the street he saw Russo and nodded to let him know everything was all right.

Russo caught the signal and imperceptibly returned it.

Then something happened that Dario didn't understand. He was standing in front of the hotel in broad daylight waiting for

Russo to cross the street and walk him to the car, wherever it was, when suddenly somebody pounded him on the back. Jesus! Hard like a boneshaker.

He turned to see who it was, opened his mouth to speak, and blood came bubbling out.

Surprise crossed his face. He began to fall. People were screaming. I'm dying, he thought. I've been shot. By the time he hit the sidewalk he was dead.

Steven bent laboriously over his desk intently going over statements, records, papers he had checked a hundred times before. Anything to pass the time.

Bobby slid into the office. 'Hey, man, what are you on to?'

Steven looked up. 'Just going over things.'

'No, I mean what are you on to with the car, the Mercedes? I found out who it belongs to.'

'Who?'

'Does the name Lucky Santangelo ring any bells?'

'Lucky . . . Santangelo,' Steven said slowly.

'Daughter of *the* Gino Santangelo who just got back into town yesterday. Friend and associate of Bonnatti – although we couldn't fix anything on him, he's not into the drug scene or vice racket. Very connected, though.' Bobby perched excitedly on the side of Steven's desk, 'Come on – share it.'

For a moment there was silence. 'Are you *sure?*' he asked at last.

'When Bobby De Walt has information he's *sure,* man.'

He thought about Lucky and frowned. *Why hadn't she told him?* Why should she have told him? He hadn't offered any information about himself, had he?

But of course she must have known who he was. Must have arranged the whole thing to see what she could find out.

*Arranged a city power cut?* His imagination was going berserk. It was just a coincidence.

'Foxy lookin' chick,' Bobby remarked. 'Got her picture on file. Bonnatti's her Godfather – she was involved in openin' up the Magiriano in Vegas. Come on Steven, what you know, man?'

He gestured vaguely. 'Nothing.'

'*Nothing?* So why you trackin' her car?'

'Christ! If I find out she's Bonnatti's partner I'll let you know,' he said sharply. He was inexplicably upset. How could he possibly get involved with Gino Santangelo's daughter?

The office buzzer sounded. 'Yes?' he snapped.

'Your mother is here to see you, Mr Berkely. And the message just came through that the papers you were waiting for are all ready.'

'Thanks, Sheila. What's my mother doing here?'

'I don't know. Shall I send her in?'

'Yeah, I guess you'd better.' He jumped up from behind the desk and made a thumbs up sign at Bobby. 'We're in business – let's get it on.'

Bobby gave a whoop of delight.

Carrie entered the room and Steven grabbed her in a wild bear hug – 'Ma, I sure appreciate you taking the time out at last to check out where I work – but I got an emergency. Why don't you drop by tomorrow. I'll buy you lunch.'

'Steven,' she said in a strangled voice, 'I have to talk to you.'

'Not now, beautiful. I'm sorry but I am just about to get the best charge of the year. A strong shot of P.S.'

'Personal satisfaction, Mrs B.,' laughed Bobby.

'It's important,' Carrie said in a low voice. 'I wouldn't have come here if it wasn't very important.'

'So I'll drop by and see you later.' He reached for his jacket and slung it over his shoulder.

Bobby edged close to him. 'Your old lady don't look so good,' he whispered.

Steven took a look at Carrie. She wasn't her usual groomed self. 'Later,' he said, kissing her lightly, 'I promise. Now why don't you go on home and get some rest – you're not lookin' like your usual self. You got a car?'

Wanly she nodded. 'Give me the key to your apartment. I'll wait there,' she murmured, trying to control the insane trembling that was taking over her body.

'Oh! *I* got it,' he said, 'you had a fight with Elliott.'

She did not reply. She did not trust herself to speak.

He fished in his pocket and produced a key, 'I'll be at least a couple of hours, make yourself at home,' he said, handing it to her. 'C'mon, Bobby – let's go to it.'

She watched her son leave, and she wondered for the hundredth time if she had made the right decision. Sitting in the car outside Enzio Bonnatti's house had given her a lot of time to do a lot of thinking. What was her plan? March right on up to the front door, ask to see Bonnatti, and shoot him dead. That was the way it would happen in a movie – but life was a little different from the movies.

There were a lot of 'could she's.'

Could she get a face to face confrontation with Enzio?

Could she use the gun? Could she actually shoot another human being down in cold blood? Could she escape to her car and get away unseen?

Gradually, as she sat in the hot rented car with the air conditioning shut off and the sweat soaking her body she realized how impossible her whole scheme was. And as she realized that, so she thought of other alternatives.

There was only one.

Tell Steven the truth. Tell him everything.

Once she made that decision she felt alive, rejuvenated. She started up the car and headed for the city without a backward glance.

Steven had a right to know. And whatever happened she would tell him.


'What the fuck is the matter with that kid?' Gino stormed. 'You know what? He actually looked like he was reaching for a piece. Did you get that action, Costa?'

'No, I didn't see that.'

'I did,' said Lucky. 'I wouldn't put anything past Dario.'

'I don't understand what's goin' on,' Gino said excitedly. 'My own kid carryin' a piece in here. Get him back, Costa. I think it's about time I straightened the little pansy out.'

'Oh,' said Lucky, 'I think you've left it a bit late to straighten him out. If you had paid more attention to him when he was a teenager I – '

Gino whirled on her. 'And who do you think you're talkin' to?'

She flushed, but she didn't back down. 'You. I'm talking to you. When Dario and I were little we *had* no family life. Shut up in that Bel Air mausoleum like a couple of lepers. We weren't allowed friends. We couldn't go out to the movies like other kids. If we went shopping one of your heavies had to go with us. No wonder Dario is screwed up today.'

He glared at her. 'Terrible life you had. A beautiful home. The best that money could buy.'

She raised her voice excitedly. 'Money. Who cares about money? I wanted *you* when I was growing up. I wanted you to *care* – to be with me. I wanted you to be a proper father.'

Her words cut into him like a knife. 'I always did the best for both of you,' he growled, 'the best I knew how . . . '

'Well, it wasn't enough,' she said triumphantly.

Police sirens wailed in the street outside. Costa went to the window and tried to see what was going on.

'Get the fuck out of here and bring Dario back,' Gino screamed at him. Costa left hurriedly.

Lucky sighed. 'I'm going,' she said. 'You and I . . . we just can't communicate – we never could.'

'You talk about me bein' a proper father,' he steamed. 'How about *you* bein' a proper daughter? Runnin' away from school. Screwin' anything in pants. Going from – '

'*I didn't*,' she interrupted – incensed with fury. 'And even if I did, so what?'

'So what? she says. *So what*.' He shook his head sadly, 'You're right, Lucky. You an' I – we just aren't on the same wavelength. Why don't you go. Seven years an' not even a lousy postcard *That's* a daughter.'

'*You* didn't write me,' she accused fiercely.

He felt very very tired. Someone was pounding on the door. 'Who is it?' he barked.

'It's Costa, let me in – quickly.'

Lucky picked up her purse. For some stupid unknown reason she wanted to cry.

Gino opened up the door, and Costa burst in, white and trembling. 'Dario's been shot,' he gasped, 'outside the hotel. He's dead.'

'Holy Christ!' Gino cried out. 'Holy mother of Christ!'

Lucky stood transfixed.

Suddenly Gino clutched at his chest and staggered towards the couch. A low moan escaped his lips.

'What is it?' Lucky asked urgently, '*What is it?*'

He moaned again, his face grey. All at once he looked every one of his seventy-one years.

'I . . . think . . . it's . . . my . . . heart . . . ' he mumbled, 'you'd better . . . get . . . me . . . a . . . doctor . . . fast . . . '

## *Friday, July 15th, 1977, New York – Evening*

Enzio flicked the remote control on the bedroom television changing channels fast and furiously, pausing at each news report.

'Honey,' complained the sugary blonde, bouncing up and down on his king size bed clad only in peach colored silk french knickers. 'I want to watch *The Dating Game.*

'Will you get dressed for crissakes,' he growled. 'I seen enough of your tits to last me a month.'

She pouted. 'Thought you liked baby's titties.'

'Get dressed, you dumbo broad. I got this guy comin' 'specially to see you all the way from Hollywood. Now go get dressed an' shut up.'

She crawled off the bed, still pouting, admired herself in the mirrored wall, and flounced into the bathroom.

Enzio scowled, and switched channels again. Goddamn cooze – only good for one thing. But he liked to have a piece that knocked 'em dead when he walked into a restaurant, and this was the best one yet. Imogene. Eighteen. A former Playmate of the Month. Forty-two inch bazookas that beat anything he had ever handled.

The dumb broad wanted to be a movie star. So he'd make her a movie star. Big deal.

'Vic,' he bawled out loudly, 'where the frig is the report on Gino and Lucky? I mean it should be on the news by now shouldn't it? They got the Dario shootin' on.'

Big Victor lumbered into the room, 'Beats me, boss. Maybe they ain't got discovered yet.'

'You talk straight outta your asshole. They're in a hotel. People don't get shot in a hotel without someone findin' 'em. A maid, a nosy dame in the room next door – *someone*.'

'Beats me, boss.'

'Is that all y'can say for shit's sake? You *sure* the job was done?'

'Oh, yes, boss, I'm sure. Russo got the signal from Dario himself, just like was arranged.'

'Where is Russo?'

'He'll be here any time now. He's bringin' out that movie producer – pickin' him up at the Plaza like you said.'

'OK.' Enzio's attention flickered back to the screen. A severe looking newscaster was reporting on the shooting outside the Pierre. She wasn't a bad looker – a bit on the skinny side. He squinted and imagined her in the nude. 'Vic, do me a favor, call the Pierre – tell 'em to check out the Santangelo suite – then hang up. Do it from a pay station.'

Big Victor nodded. 'Good idea, boss.'

'*My* idea. I'm the only one ever *has* any ideas around here.'

'I love you daddy.' She had whispered the words crouched over him in the ambulance. 'You're going to be all right – I know it. You'll be fine – honestly.'

He had not responded verbally – an oxygen mask was clamped down over his nose and mouth, but his black eyes had met hers, held, and told her that she was forgiven.

She had stayed beside him all the way to the hospital, held onto his hand tightly, wanted to say so much, and hoped that it wasn't going to be too late.

Once at the hospital, he was rushed through to emergency. Costa arrived shortly after. Lucky could see that he had been crying by his red rimmed eyes. She squeezed his arm. 'He'll be fine, I can feel it.'

After a while she managed to get hold of the doctor treating Gino. His long thin horseface was grave. 'Your father has suffered a severe coronary thrombosis.'

'Is he going to be all right?' she demanded fiercely.

The doctor coughed, covering his mouth politely. 'It's too soon to tell. The medical term for what your father has is Arteriosclerosis. This is a condition that affects the heart through hardening of the coronary arteries. These may be either narrowed or actually occluded. In an occlusion . . .'

As the doctor droned on, she found herself thinking of Gino as he had been when she was young. Throwing her up in the air, hugging her, kissing her. She was filled with so much love for that man – *and* for the man who lay in a hospital bed struggling for his life.

The doctor was concluding his speech. 'So you see, Miss Santangelo – things can go either way. Both narrowing and occlusion can be compatible with a reasonably active existence in many patients for quite a few years. We have excellent new drugs to retard the clotting of the blood, and other measures have improved the outlook considerably.' He shrugged noncommitally. 'In your father's case we just cannot tell right now how much damage has been done. If he gets through the night, then the outlook is hopeful.'

Hopeful. *Hopeful.* What did *that* mean?

She stared at the doctor, hating him with a passion. What did he care whether Gino lived or died?

'Thank you doctor,' she said tightly.

'His condition seems stable at the moment . . . If you would care to go home we can call you if there is any change . . .'

As if she would want to go home. 'Can I see him?' she asked in a low voice.

'For a moment I suppose, although the quieter the patient is kept –'

'Thank you.'

Gino lay, white as a sheet, in an austere hospital bed. A drip was attached to his arm, his eyes were closed.

A nurse sat in attendance, a big boned woman who said – as soon as Lucky entered the room – 'No visitors. This is a very sick man.'

'This man is my father,' Lucky blazed, 'and the doctor said I could see him. Would you wait outside, please.'

The nurse flared strong nostrils but said nothing. She got up and marched from the room, her whole demeanor signalling disapproval.

Lucky took up a position beside the bed. She was crying, although she didn't notice the tears falling. She clutched Gino's hand and whispered, 'I'm sorry it had to take something like this to make me realize how much I love you. We *can* communicate – if we both try – and I *want* to try. I withdrew from you because that's what you did to me. I had to reject *you* first so that you couldn't reject me. I *love* you. You're my father. And I *want* you to live more than I've ever wanted anything in my life.'

His eyes flickered and opened, 'Do me a . . . favor,' he mumbled, 'save . . . the emotions . . . 'til I can . . . deal with 'em.'

His voice was so very weak, but she heard the words, knew he understood, and a grin spread over her face. 'Anything for attention, huh?'

'Yeh . . . Anything, kid.'

His eyes closed again, and for a while there was silence. She held firmly onto his hand, and it was almost as if she could feel the love and understanding flowing between them like a psychic force.

He said something. She leaned closer to hear, his voice was hardly more than a whisper.

'Dario . . . ' he mumbled, 'family . . . honor . . . the . . . Santangelo . . . name.'

'Yes?'

'You . . . deal . . . with . . . it . . . Lucky.' He gasped for breath. 'You . . . take . . . revenge . . . for . . . both . . . of . . . us. Bonnatti's . . . the . . . one . . . Bonn . . . '

'Nurse!' screamed Lucky, *'Nurse!'*

Warris Charters was spruced up and ready to go. California chic. Light tan slacks, a Giorgio Armani jacket, Gucci loafers, Optique Boutique shades. *Finally. Finally. Finally.* It was all coming together.

He finger-waved the front of his hair in the mirror, and descended to the lobby of the Plaza Hotel.

Lucky left the hospital, her step purposeful. She had already decided what she had to do earlier that day. What had taken place since only confirmed that it was necessary.

She went straight to her apartment where Boogie waited. 'Listen, I'm real sorry about what happened . . . ' he began

'Yes,' she said. 'It changes a lot of things. I'm not ready to take on Bonnatti right now I need time. Why don't you go back to Vegas. We can talk again in a week or so, figure out which way to move.'

He stared at her. 'I thought you were a doer, not a talker.'

'I thought so too. But right now I have to get my head together. I'm so upset, Boog . . . There was no love lost between Dario and me, but he *was* my brother . . . '

'Who hit him?'

'I'll find out.'

He made a helpless gesture. 'Well . . . if there's nothin' I can do.'

'Yes, there is something,' she said matter-of-factly. 'I want a contract on the Kassarri brothers.' She paused and lit up a cigarette. 'Get me the best. There's a hundred thousand dollars for results. Fifty thousand a twin. Cash. Can you arrange it? I want it done immediately.'

'You'd trust me with a hundred grand?'

'I trusted you with my life didn't I?'

Silently he nodded. 'I can arrange it. What about Bonnatti?'

'We'll wait on that.'

As soon as he left, she changed her clothes. White seemed suitable, sensuous folds of a Halston silk jersey dress that she hadn't worn before. She applied fresh make-up and brushed and shook her jet curls. From a locked drawer she took the fine gold chain with the tiny diamond and ruby locket that Gino had given her on her fifth birthday. She opened the locket and gazed at the picture of Gino and her. How alike they looked – even then. She smiled softly and put the locket on. It fitted tightly – like a choker. Next she took from the drawer the diamond earrings he had given her on her sixteenth birthday. They sparkled like the day she had received them sitting in Las Vegas with Gino and Marco . . .

*Oh Marco. Tonight I will not only take revenge for Gino – but for you too my darling – you too.*

She inspected herself in the mirror.

She was ready.

Imogene was ready.

Spandex pants and what she called a boob tube was ready? 'Take that shit off,' boomed Enzio. 'You look like somethin' that just got fucked by the Mexican army.'

'I didn't know there was a Mexican army,' frowned Imogene.

Big Victor watched her undulate out of the room and licked his lips. Sometimes . . . when the boss was finished with them . . .

'I don' understand it,' Enzio snarled, 'seven o'clock an' nothin' on the friggin' news. You call the hotel?'

Big Victor nodded. 'The nine o'clock news'll have it for sure,' he soothed.

'It better – or friggin' heads'll roll around here.'

Warris sat on the rear seat of Enzio Bonnatti's black, extra large Mercedes, and reflected on what it must be like to be rich. Not a couple of million dollars rich but the real thing – unlimited funds. Je . . . sus! What a dream! And if *Kill Shot* took off it could be more than a dream, it could be a fucking reality!

He leaned forward and tapped on the tinted glass separating him from the driver. The glass slid open.

'How long before we're there?' he asked.

The strong smell of pot came wafting into the back of the car.

'Not long,' the driver said casually, a hood in a black suit and shirt, with sly narrow eyes.

'You always turn on when you drive?' Warris asked in a friendly fashion – hoping that perhaps the driver might offer him a drag. His answer was the glass sliding firmly shut.

He leaned back against the rich leather, and drummed his fingers against the can of film on the seat beside him. Soon . . . Soon . . .

'This OK honeypuff?'

Enzio narrowed his eyes and looked Imogene over. She had changed into a red blouse that knotted underneath her mammoth breasts, and with it she wore an unfashionable red mini and knee length white boots.

'I suppose so,' he spat. It didn't matter *what* she looked like really If he wanted to use her he would, no matter what Warris Charters said. Charters was a pawn, a front man. The film would be made the way Enzio wanted – or not made at all.

Big Victor appeared in the doorway, 'He's here,' he announced, 'Where d'ya want me to put him?'

Lucky drove her small bronze Mercedes like a seasoned racing driver. She dodged in and out of the early evening traffic expertly Teddy Pendergrass serenaded her through the stereo speakers and she smoked continually, lighting each cigarette from the butt of the last. She knew the road to Enzio's house inside out. If she closed her eyes her car would automatically take her there. How many weekends she had taken refuge at the house. Stayed in the guest bedroom. Swam in the pool. Shared meals with Enzio and whichever son he was talking to that particular weekend. She had been the daughter he had never had. Or so he had said.

Dirty lying slime. She had trusted him. How he must have been laughing behind her back.

Her mouth was set in a grim line as the small car raced towards his house.

Steven and Bobby rode along in the back of the squad car. Destination: Enzio Bonnatti's Long Island residence.

'How do you feel, man?' crowed Bobby.

'Pretty goddamn good,' replied Steven, 'but I'll feel even better when we have him.'

'Got a lil coke for baby?' Begged Imogene, hanging onto the sleeve of Enzio's quilted smoking jacket.

He shook her off. 'For shit's sake. The man is here that I want you to meet.'

'I know babee    But I do want to make a good impression. So pl  . .ease . . for baby?'

He made a face. The younger generation used drugs like *his* generation used to use booze. 'In my bureau. Just one snort. I don't want you comin' in all glassy eyed.'

'Sweetie – coke makes me *sparkle.*'

'Your tits give you all the sparkle y'need. Now hurry up.' He walked out of the room, uncomfortable in the smoking jacket that had cost six hundred bucks but felt more like a straight jacket. Fashion. Made in Italy. Who gave a fast fuck?

In the library Warris admired bookshelf after bookshelf of fine books. He was frankly amazed. Who would have thought Enzio had the culture to surround himself with such a great collection

'Wanna drink?' Big Victor asked. 'Enzio'll be right in.'

'White wine on ice,' Warris replied, repelled by the look of the fat man.

Big Victor's mouth fell open. 'Huh?'

'White wine. Is that a problem? With some ice in the glass.'

'Yeah. I know wotcha mean. But I open a bottle, who drinks the rest?'

Warris did not believe what he was hearing. 'Make it a vodka then,' he said, adding sarcastically, 'if the bottle's open, of course.'

Big Victor glared.

At that point Enzio walked into the room.

Warris wanted to laugh, the old man looked ridiculous in a quilted satin jacket that threatened to swamp him. 'Where did you get that jacket?' he asked immediately.

'Y'like it?' Enzio preened.

'On you – anything would look good.'

Sitting in the back of the patrol car Steven's mind began to tick over. With Bonnatti's arrest it would almost be like starting all over again. So much work lay ahead – but it was the kind of work he looked forward to.

Somehow Lucky kept on drifting into his thoughts, and he wondered what it would be like with a girl like her.

Had to stop thinking about her. Had to get her *out* of his mind.

Lucky Santangelo. Would it matter if he saw her just one more time?

Yes. It would matter. He was thinking like a moron. Better forget her . . . forget those black opal eyes . . . that long lithe body . . . those wide sensual lips . . .

'Hey, man,' interrupted Bobby, 'nearly there!'

Lucky zoomed by the guard at the gate with a cheery wave. She knew all the boys and they all knew her. A hunch told her that only Enzio and those close to him would know of his deceptions.

She parked out front and headed for the main door. Two sharp rings and Big Victor was staring at her, his ugly mouth hanging open in amazement. 'Lucky?' he questioned, like he wasn't sure it was her.

'The very same,' she replied lightly, 'Why? Do I look different?'

'Uh . . . no. We wasn't expectin' you.'

'I'm on my way to a party close by – figured I'd pay my respects to the man. He's around isn't he?'

Big Victor swallowed loudly. Somebody had fucked up and Enzio was not going to be happy.

She strolled into the house, 'He's not busy is he?'

'Uh, yeah . . . he's busy.'

'Oh? Anyone I know?'

Big Victor stared at her. She was cool as a cucumber, all dressed up. Maybe she hadn't even been at the Pierre. Maybe she didn't even know about Dario. 'Whyn't you wait in the front room. I'll tell Enzio you're here.'

'Sure thing. Hurry up though Vic, this is a hot party I've got ahead of me, and I don't want to miss a moment.'

He stared at her some more, followed her into the living-room, saw her sit down, and then departed, shutting the door behind him.

'If we could run the film of my girl . . . ' Warris said, 'all I want you to do is look.'

'Yeah. I'll look,' Enzio said expansively, 'but I got somethin' for *you* ta look at'll knock *both* your friggin' eyes out.'

'Wonderful,' Warris murmured politely, planning the small role he would quickly add to the script for Enzio's girlfriend. 'You said you had a screening room . . '

'*This* is the screenin' room,' Enzio crowed triumphantly. 'Y'see all these shitty books? Watch this.' He pressed a couple of buttons on the wall and the bookshelves slid out of sight revealing a projector at one end of the room and a screen at the other. 'Snazzy, huh?' he boasted.

'You mean those books aren't real?'

'Naw . . . fakes. Pretty clever, doncha think?'

Warris nodded and headed for the projector to thread his film.

Big Victor waddled into the room and held a whispered conference with his boss.

'OK,' said Enzio loudly. 'You get everythin' ready Warris. I got somethin' come up – but I'll be back soon. Set it all up.'

'Oh! You gave me a fright!' shrieked Imogene, staring at Lucky who had padded silently into the bedroom. 'Who are you?'

Lucky smiled, Enzio's taste went from bad to worse. She

had never seen this deformed dog before. Must be his new discovery.

'I'm the Avon lady,' she said, still smiling.

Imogene giggled. 'Are you with the Hollywood producer?'

'Sure thing. Enzio sent me up here to share a little of that coke you're so greedily imbibing.'

'Inwhat?'

'Snorting noney. Have you had enough?'

Imogene's eyes widened. 'Why? Is Enzio getting impatient?'

'He said that if you don't get that chubby little ass of yours downstairs *tout suite* he will *personally* deal with you. Now we all know what *that* means don't we?'

Imogene hurriedly dropped the tiny gold coke spoon she was using on a thin line of white powder. 'You can have the rest,' she said generously.

'You're too kind.'

The girl wiggled off, and without hesitating Lucky went straight into Enzio's private bathroom. She opened the cabinet where he kept twelve bottles of equally revolting different aftershaves, and there – in position – was one of the three guns he kept in his bedroom suite. He had boasted of this fact to her one Sunday lunchtime a long time ago. 'Any fucker comes t'get me on the crapper an' I'm ready,' he had bragged. ' 'Scuse my language.'

'Hi,' simpered Imogene. 'You the producer?'

Warris stared at the girl. She was larger than life. He had never seen anything like her.

'Yes,' he managed, 'and you're . . . ?'

'Imogene. *I'm* gonna star in your movie!'

'Where is she?' roared Enzio.

Big Victor gazed around the empty room in amazement. 'I don't know, boss. I put her in here. Maybe she left – she said she had this hot party to go to.'

'And you don't think she knew anything?' Enzio inquired disbelievingly.

'She was cool, boss. Dressed real nice. She had nothin' on her mind 'cept havin' a good time.'

'You're *sure*?'

'I know people, boss. I studied people all my life.'

Timing was imperative. Lucky checked that Enzio's gun was

loaded, then slowly, deliberately tore the front of her beautiful Halston dress open. Next she picked up the phone, dialed the nearest police station and gasped out a frenzied, 'Please help me – come quickly – I've been attacked . . . ' She sobbed out the address and hung up.

Her timing was impeccable. She knew it. Adrenalin was bursting her veins.

*Gino . . . Marco . . . This is it.* She ran to the top of the stairs and yelled, 'Enzio. I'm up here.'

Enzio turned to Big Victor. 'What the frig is she doin' upstairs?'

Big Victor threw open his arms. '*I* don't know, boss. You know Lucky, she treats this place like a second home.'

'Could she have been carrying?'

'No way. She's got on one of those real skimpy dresses wit nuthin' underneath. She wasn't even carryin' a purse. I'm tellin' you boss, she knows from nuthin'.'

'Hmmm . . . ' He frowned, not fully convinced. 'Then what does she want?'

'Whyn't we go see?'

'No,' said Enzio quickly. It wouldn't do to lose face. Let Victor think he was nervous of some stupid little bimbo. 'I'll handle her – you go see to that Warris guy – give him a drink – tell him I'll be right there.'

'I gave him a drink, boss.'

'So give him another one,' Enzio snapped impatiently, 'this ain't prohibition, y'know.'


Gino Santangelo stirred in his hospital bed and opened his eyes. The pain was gone. The horrible dark pain that had gripped him around the chest with a sickening intensity.

He tried to sit up, but something was holding him back – some goddamn contraption on his arm.

The nurse, noticing movement, leaped to attention. 'Mr Santangelo, please, don't try to move.'

'Why not?' The words rang out clearly.

She had never been asked such a question before. Patients under her care were usually docile and quiet. 'I'll fetch the doctor,' she said primly.

He watched her, a smile hovering on his lips. 'Hey, nurse, Has anyone ever told you, you got a beautiful ass!'

She fled from the room.

*

Enzio mounted the stairs slowly. If Lucky was still around did that mean Gino was too? Had that little Dario creep funked? Worse – had he told them?

'Lucky,' he called out, 'where are you?'

'In your bedroom,' her voice sang out. 'Your girlfriend dragged me up here for some coke.'

'Friggin' cunt!' he muttered. Imogene had two things going for her. Big tits and a new level of stupidity. He entered the bedroom.

'I'm in the bathroom,' Lucky called gaily. 'I want to show you something.'

He reached the bathroom door and realized too late. He had been had.

Abruptly he stopped and stared at Lucky. His own gun sprouted from her hands. 'We can talk – ' he began to say.

'Never underestimate the power of a woman, old man,' she said evenly. 'This is goodbye from Gino and Dario and Marco . . . *especially* Marco. Oh – and of course me.'

She pulled the trigger, and the first bullet smashed into his stomach, spilling his guts all over the golden carpet.

The second caught him in the neck as he was falling.

The third he didn't feel.

It was all over for Enzio Bonnatti.

In the distance Lucky could hear the scream of police sirens. *'OK Marco?'* she whispered, *'OK babe?'*


As the car carrying Steven, Bobby and the two arresting detectives approached the Bonnatti estate one of the detectives said, 'There's something going on. It looks like someone got here before us.'

Steven felt his stomach turn to lead. Up ahead he could see the flashing lights of two police cars. 'Shit!' he exclaimed, because instinct told him that his moment of triumph was not to be.

A uniformed cop had taken over guard duty at the gate. He help up his hand to halt the car.

'What's happening?' Steven asked excitedly, leaning from the car and flashing his ID.

The cop shrugged. 'There's been a shooting. Some girl hollering rape shot Bonnatti.'

The leaden feeling in Steven's stomach increased. 'Is he dead?'

'Wouldn't you be if you had three bullets in you?'

'Jesus H. Christ.'

'Amen,' said Bobby.

'Let's go up to the house,' decided Steven.

'Yeah,' agreed Bobby. 'At least we can look at the body.'

Wrapped in a blanket, seated in the kitchen, Lucky answered the detective's questions as best she could. 'I was so surprised when he grabbed me,' she said, her eyes full of tears. 'Please understand – this man has always been like a father to me.'

The cop nodded his head sympathetically.

'He . . he was like an animal. He ripped at my dress – grabbed for my breasts,' she broke into sobs. 'It was horrible – horrible!'

'I know this is tough ma'am. But what happened then?'

'I knew he kept a gun in the bathroom – he had shown me many times. I ran to get it. He followed me. It all goes blank then.'

'But you shot him?'

'Only to protect myself.'

'Of course.'

Steven checked out the body. He didn't stare as Bobby did, one quick glance was enough. 'Where's the girl?' he asked.

'In the kitchen,' replied the police photographer. 'What a looker!'

At the bottom of the stairs in the hall stood a cow faced blonde of astronomical proportions, a fat man, a narrow eyed hood, and a suntanned middle aged man who looked about ready to burst into tears.

The flotsam and jetsam of Enzio Bonnatti's life.

'Let's get 'em down to the station, take their statements,' a burly cop said, shepherding them together.

'I wanna lawyer,' insisted the blonde.

'What do you need a lawyer for sweetheart?' asked the cop, leering at her obvious assets. 'You ain't done nothin', have you?'

Steven strode into the kitchen. Lucky looked up Their eyes met. For one instant it looked like she was going to greet him, but she didn't. Her eyes hooded over, she said nothing.

'Is this the suspect?' he asked, unable to keep the surprise out of his voice.

'What is it, Kennedy airport in here?' rasped the investigating detective. 'Who are you?'

Steven produced his ID 'Steven Berkely,' he said, loud enough for her to hear. 'DA's office.'

She stared at him, her black eyes impassive, revealing nothing.

'You guys certainly move fast enough,' complained the detective.

'I've been conducting a special investigation on Bonnatti. Came down with the papers to arrest him.'

'Well you're too late.'

'I can see that. Listen, can I speak to you for a moment?'

The detective sighed, and got up from his seat at the table. The two men walked to the door.

'What's the situation?' Steven asked in a low voice.

The detective cleared his throat. 'The old bastard tried to rape her – looks like a simple case of self-defense to me.'

'Just wanted to know.' Steven glanced over at Lucky one more time. Her eyes were downcast. 'Guess there's nothing.I can do to help then.'

'Help!' snorted the detective. 'Since when did you guys do anything to help?' He walked back to the table, sat down, and began making notes on a weathered pad.

Suddenly Steven felt the blaze of her eyes again. He returned her gaze.

Very slowly she mouthed, *'Hello, Steven,'* and then equally slowly she mouthed, *'Goodbye, D.A.'*

He wanted to say something – anything. Knew that he couldn't.

She smiled wanly, and just as he was beginning to feel as crushed as she must be, she winked. A true, ballsy, Lucky Santangelo wink.

Goddamn it! Two solid years of work down the .drain and she winked.

He almost smiled.

Only almost.

# Epilogue

The funeral of Enzio Bonnatti was a grand affair. He was buried in a solid bronze casket that cost ten thousand dollars.

They came from all over to pay their respects – those who could afford the notoriety of being seen at such a man's burial. His blood relatives wore black, his two sons in suits they had worn only a day before to the double funeral of the Kassarri twins in Philadelphia.

Enzio lay in an open casket for three days at the Long Island mansion, while friends, relatives, and business associates paid their respects.

Gino Santangelo was not among them, but that was only because he was confined to bed by his recent heart attack. He sent flowers, though, a massive bank of chrysanthemums, with a note that read – *To my friend Enzio. Each step takes us on to the next. Gino.'*

Father Ameratti, who laid the body to rest, gave a moving speech. 'Enzio Bonnatti was a gentleman,' he said, 'almost to the end.'

Steven, already shattered by what had happened, returned to the city and the cool sanctuary of his apartment.

His mother, Carrie, waited there for him. 'Steven,' she said, 'I have a story to tell you. I want you to sit down and hear me out.'

When he heard, it was almost as if his life were broken into a thousand tiny pieces. He had always been so proud of his heritage, of the father he had never seen.

She spared him no details, telling him everything right from the beginning.

'Who is my father, then?' he had demanded. *'Who is he?'*

'I don't know,' she replied simply. 'There were two men the night you were conceived. One I went with willingly . . . the other . . . ' she shrugged helplessly, 'He forced me.'

'Do you know their names?' he asked brutally.

'It wouldn't help you to know . . . '

*Tell me their names.'*

'Freddy Lester . . . He was a society boy  . . . I don't know much about him.'

'White?'

She nodded.

'And the other?'

'Gino Santangelo.'

It took Steven a long time to recover from the shock. He threw up his work and went to Europe, where he bummed around for three years. Eventually he met a girl, a beautiful black girl who worked as a model. She wasn't Zizi, or Aileen, and most of all she wasn't Lucky.

He still thought about Lucky.

Sometimes.

Carrie divorced Elliott. She gave up the money, position, and style, and settled in a modest house on Fire Island. It was within walking distance of the home she had shared with Bernard.

When Steven came back to America in 1980 he went to see her. 'I understand,' he said. It was enough.

Warris Charters returned to Hollywood. Showbiz had dealt him another dirty blow – but there was always tomorrow.

He took with him forty-two inch Imogene and made her a star.

She stayed with him until this event took place. Then she dumped him for a twenty-two-year-old black basketball star.

He shot them both in a Hollywood motel and ended up in jail where he became king of the heap.

Warris had finally found a position for himself.

Costa Zennocotti retired. He bought himself an oceanside apartment in Miami Beach and took Gino's advice. A man needed sex. To give it up was to give up a part of life. He met a friendly divorcee who did his cooking, and an even friendlier call girl whom he visited once every two weeks.

He had a winning combination at last.

Lucky Santangelo got off scot free. Her case never even came to court. 'One of the advantages of havin' the right friends,' Gino explained.

They were inseparable, father and daughter. They renovated the East Hampton house and lived there half the year, the rest of the time they spent in Vegas. Lucky in her penthouse suite atop the Magiriano. Gino in his luxurious apartment at the Mirage.

Often Lucky thought of Marco – and what might have been.

Sometimes her thoughts would drift to Steven.

But she was happy. She had Gino. And together they could own the world.

*The World is full of Divorced Women*

I would like to thank the following women,
Divorced, Married, or Otherwise . . .

    JAN
    HAZEL
    JOAN
    EVIE
    LUISA
    SHAKIRA
    JOANNA
    CHRIS
    CAROLYN
            *and*

        JOHNY!

# 1

'Are you bored with sex?' Mike had asked the other day.

'Bored?' Cleo James had replied, her voice guilty, 'of course not.' But she was bored by him, by the way he always made the same predictable moves, by the way he always touched her in exactly the same places in exactly the same way.

It was the beginning of summer in New York, a time when it is still pleasant to walk the streets. Cleo stood in a fitting-room at Saks and stared at her reflection in the mirror. She had discarded her own clothes and was trying on a beige suede dress. The dress had been altered for her the previous week and it now fitted perfectly; but still she stared in the mirror, seeing a slim girl with long straight dark hair, big eyes, a wide mouth.

Cleo wasn't really thinking about the dress. The dress was fine. She was thinking about her husband, Mike. She was thinking about him *screwing* that other girl.

At the onset of their relationship, sex with Mike had been fantastically exciting. Now he seemed stuck in some strange set ritual.

He never wanted to try anything new.

He never wanted to do anything different.

Marriage had changed him.

He did not turn her on any more, and she never had been good at pretending.

They didn't row much. In fact, hardly ever. They had discussions where they talked things out and analysed situations.

Mike was an executive with a record company. He was thirty-six, seven years older than Cleo. Attractive in a free rangy way with his Che moustache and come-on eyes. They had been married four years. A modern marriage where infidelity certainly shouldn't be the end of the world.

'Did you fancy her?' How many times had Cleo asked him that question, her stomach in knots waiting for his reply.

'Sure.' Mike would laugh and make a joke of it. 'I even fucked her a few times.'

Ha. ha. not very funny. Cleo thought. and she never questioned further. She didn't want to know.

Now she knew. She had seen him.

Mike was her second husband, the first a vague memory when she was eighteen. She loved Mike. but not the white heat of love she had felt when they were first together.

'It looks great, huh?' The salesgirl popped her head round the door.

'Yes. it's fine.' Cleo replied. But it wasn't fine that she'd caught Mike today. It wasn't fine that his lean naked body had been bent in such obvious enjoyment. It wasn't fine that the busty blond beneath him was one of her best friends.

She unzipped herself out of the beige fringed suede and handed it to the girl to take away to wrap.

Are you bored with sex? Why had he asked her that? She wasn't doing anything different. Were her sexual moves as predictable as his?

Perhaps the gradual lull in their sex life was her fault. But she knew it wasn't. It was Mike who had changed.

She had been unfaithful once. One man. one time. It had been beautiful, but at the same time sordid. She had made sure it was only once.

They had money, not vast amounts, but enough to satisfy most material demands. Mike was successful. Cleo worked for magazines as a freelance interviewer. They didn't need the money she made. but she enjoyed working. she loved her job.

She dressed slowly. dark brown gauchos. Sonia Rykel sweater. Biba boots. Gucci leather belt. Oliver Goldsmith brown-tinted sunspecs to cover her prune shadowed eyes.

She collected her package and walked out into the Fifth Avenue sunshine. She was supposed to meet Ginny for lunch and it was too late to cancel. The last thing she felt like doing was having lunch with Ginny—Ginny of the 'baby blue eyes. blond curls. and vast sexual appetite.

'Ginny's a bird brain.' Mike had said many times. But then he always had disparaging comments to make about most of her friends—including Susan. the blond wriggling about under him that very morning.

Maybe he had also had Ginny. It wasn't an implausible

thought. Ginny was a notoriously easy lay, but she was also the last of the great talkers, and if she had been with Mike full details would be all over town.

'I think you stink!' an old woman hissed at Cleo as she passed on by, and Cleo took no notice of the old biddy who launched away up Fifth Avenue waving a flowered parasol before her. New York was full of nuts, and you just ignored them and hoped that one day you wouldn't get raped or robbed or attacked or shot. New Yorkers were immune to the violence amongst them, only the tourists moved uneasily. Cleo felt like a New Yorker, although she had only lived there for the four years since marrying Mike. She was actually from London, a place she had hardly moved out of before—only as far as Europe for a weekend tan.

She wrestled with a blue-suited businessman for a cab, and won. Then she sat back and tried to untense herself. She didn't want to arrive at lunch in a neurotic state, ready to pour out the whole stupid story to Ginny.

The whole thing was so goddamn ridiculous. Why did she feel so bad about it? It was just one of those things that went on every day. It was perfectly understandable.

But screw him for choosing one of her friends. And double screw him for letting her catch them at it.

She half wished she had never met Mike, and she definitely wished she had never married him. Mike had been the one that had insisted on getting married, Cleo would have been happy just living with him. Her whole attitude upset him, he was used to being with girls whose ultimate goal was the thin gold ring on their wedding finger. He couldn't understand the fact that Cleo didn't care. It was a blow to his ego. He insisted that they got married. If they weren't married now it would all be a lot easier. She had one bad marriage behind her, she didn't want to make it two. . . .

The restaurant was small and noisy. Ginny was already there, sitting at a table sipping a martini and exchanging glances with a well-known actor who was seated close by.

'Boy, would I like to handle him!' she enthused as Cleo sat down. Ginny was an agent, thirty, plumpish, divorced, not unattractive in a girly way. 'Hey, you look very good today. I like the boots, where did you get the boots?'

'The Biba Boutique. I had to go back three times to get my size. Who's the extra seat for?'

'Susan said she'd try to join us. I had the most fantastic night last night; went to that new disco down the Village with Bob, and *guess* who came in. Cy Litva. You remember what that bastard did to me last time—well, I tell you when I saw the little fink I went hot and cold—but I was cool, just smiled, y'know. I looked very good, had on my Saint Laurent shirt, and a darling pair of hot pants, and were they ever hot! Well . . .'

Ginny talked a lot. She told of each sexual encounter in detail and with great enjoyment. She didn't notice that Cleo was hardly listening.

Cleo was thinking—Susan will not be joining us, Susan would not have the nerve to join us, because even if Susan hadn't seen her walk unexpectedly into Mike's office, Mike certainly had.

She remembered the morning yet again. She had been near his office, and decided to pop in and surprise him. His receptionist was not there, so she had just walked right through. She had surprised him all right. They were on the large studio couch. Susan was naked, lying with the back of her head towards the door. Mike, astride her, stared right at Cleo.

She just stood there unsure of what to do. It seemed like hours. It was actually only a few seconds before she turned and walked quickly away. Mike never broke his movement. What a bastard! The least he could have done was climb off.

' . . . so we had this really fantastic scene, one of those slow wild things that just builds and builds and goes on for ever, and—hey—here's Susan. Let's order, I'm starving.'

Susan White was a tall girl with thick long blond hair which hung in a heavy curtain past her shoulders. Her hair, and her large accommodating breasts, were her best features, and she was well aware of that fact. She wore a soft pink angora sweater tucked into trousers. She was an actress, not really successful, but she worked quite consistently in off-Broadway productions.

It struck Cleo with much irony that Mike hadn't told Susan about their being discovered that morning. That would be just like him, weak, frightened of a scene. Either that or Susan was a better actress than Cleo had ever given her credit for, because she was approaching the table full of smiles. 'Have I had a morning!' she announced, flopping down in her chair. 'Two auditions, both on opposite sides of town. I'm exhausted!'

'Those auditions must really take it out of you,' Cleo murmured, 'all that taking off of your clothes.'

'Huh?' Susan stared.

'I mean it is another nude role, isn't it?' Susan had recently been in a play where she had had to strip off and simulate masturbation. The play had only run three nights.

'I'm not *typed* you know,' Susan said irritably, 'anyway actresses don't have to strip at auditions. It doesn't matter what your body is like, it's the play that matters.'

'Oh sure,' Cleo said. 'Susan, I never thought I'd hear *you* coming out with that tired Hollywood claptrap.'

'Let's order for crissakes,' Ginny interrupted; 'if I have a salad for lunch does that mean I can go mad tonight and gorge myself? Cy's taking me to eat Russian, and I *love* eating Russian. Hey—that conjures up a mental picture of a guy's dick covered in sour cream. Delicious—do you think he'd dig it?'

'Your conversation always reminds me of a college girl who finally got it for the first time the night before,' Cleo said coldly.

Ginny shrugged. 'It's always the first time for me,' she giggled.

'How's Mike?' Susan asked, a shade too casually.

Cleo fixed her with green angry eyes, but her voice was even. 'What the fuck sort of childish game are you playing, Susan? If this is the best acting ability you've got I can understand how you ended up playing with yourself in some fleapit off Broadway.'

'What's going on?' Ginny asked blankly, putting down the menu. 'What's with the insults?'

Susan muttered, a dull red flushing her face, 'I don't know, I only asked how Mike was, I—'

'Cut it out, baby,' Cleo said, rising from the table. 'Fuck my husband if you want, but don't take *me* for an idiot. Sorry about this Ginny, I'll talk to you later.'

Susan said, 'But . . .'

Cleo didn't wait to hear. She was out of there. She was in the street. She was walking with tears blinding her eyes. She was cursing because her eyelashes were falling off.

I have blown my cool, she thought. Not only have I blown my cool but the whole of New York will know about it because of Ginny Sandler's big big mouth.

Where has all my women's lib good sense gone to?

Live and let live.

Fuck and let fuck.

Well, it was probably all for the good. It had certainly shaken Susan up.

What a fool Mike was not to have told her.

What a fool Mike was period.

She composed a letter to him in her mind. 'Dear Mike—While we have lived together and loved together for several years I would now like to terminate this agreement. I feel that I have outgrown you, both mentally and physically, and we have nothing left to offer each other except a future of indifference. I wish you much happiness with Susan big boobs. Sincerely yours—Cleo.

P.S. I never knew big tits were your hang up.

P.P.S. I never knew you liked girls who played with themselves.

P.P.P.S. I guess I just never knew.'

Her tears had stopped, and under cover of her shades she peeled off the falling eyelashes and wrapped them in a tissue.

She would go home and repair her makeup, bath and change. She would also pack. She had been due to leave the following morning on an interview assignment in London, but she would leave tonight. She would take the coward's way out and stay in a hotel for the night and not face Mike. She didn't want to see him, he would only lie. She wanted time to think.

She ran for a cab, lost it, and waited for a bus.

## 2

The girl had blond hair, bubbly and curly and streaked with little patches of orange.

Her face was very pretty, very painted.

False freckles abounded. Little brown dots painstakingly sketched on early in the morning.

Each extra eyelash was fixed individually. China blue eyes were surrounded by China blue eye shadow.

Her own eyebrows had been shaved off and replaced with clever arched strokes of soft brown pencil.

Full pouty lips were made more so by two different shades of pale lipstick, and over the top liberal helpings of lip gloss.

Clever shading fined her slightly plump cheeks down, and her skin was softly burnished all over by an out-of-the-bottle sun tan.

She wasn't very tall, only about five foot three, but the enormous clogs she was wearing added a good six inches. They were green with red stripes, and she wore them with bright green tights and rolled up to the knee faded blue jeans. She had a tiny waist, slightly exposed as the skimpy halter top sweater left a gap of four inches. She wore no bra, and her breasts, perky and upright, bounced engagingly through the thin material.

She strolled through Harrods, swinging an outsize canvas bag in one hand, and stuffing chocolates—Maltesers—into her ever open, ever moist mouth.

Her name was Muffin, but all the photographers called her Crumpet.

She was twenty, and had found fame as a respectable nude model. Respectable meaning that her nude or semi-nude poses advertised everything from bras to men's shirts in all the best magazines and newspapers.

Muffin was oblivious to the stares, she was used to it.

She stopped at the sunglasses counter and tried a pair on. They were large and round, pink tinted.

Muffin liked them. She glanced surreptitiously around, no

one appeared to be watching, so calmly she walked away from the counter, glasses stuck firmly on her nose.

She jammed some more Maltesers into her mouth, crumpled the empty packet and let it fall to the ground. Then humming softly to herself she went out of the front entrance and asked the doorman to get her a cab.

It was raining in London, but Muffin attracted a cab immediately. She lived on the top floor of a large house in Holland Park. She shared the studio apartment with her boyfriend, Jon Clapton. He was the photographer who had discovered Muffin when she was seventeen, and had moved her in with him as soon as they had persuaded her parents in Wimbledon that it was O.K.

'We're going to get married,' Jon had assured them, 'just as soon as I get my divorce.'

'Anybody home?' Muffin called, as she let herself in. Scruff, the mongrel dog she had found wandering the streets, barked confirmation that he was indeed home. 'Want to go for a walk, fella?' she inquired, looking on the message pad by the phone to see if Jon had left her any notes. He had been asleep when she had left that morning.

'*Terrazza*—nine o'clock,' he had scrawled, 'get tarted up, it's the Schumann Calendar deal.'

She screwed up her face in distaste. She hated all the business dinners he got together.

'We *have* to do them,' Jon would patiently explain, 'it's the personal touch these old geezers like. So what if they touch you up with their eyes, they're going to see all of you in the photos anyway.'

'Photos are different,' she would argue.

'All right, forget it. Be just another dreary little model girl with nice tits. I'm making you a *personality*, a *star*.'

Muffin had to agree that he was right. She was being offered money now that a year before she had only dreamed about.

Jon handled everything. They had a joint bank account and all monies they both earned went into that.

Jon was a successful photographer, and on deals they did together they were paid royally.

The calendar deal was important. Schumann Electronics put

out a fabulous calendar each year using twelve different girls. Jon's idea was that they just use Muffin, with him taking the photographs. Twelve incredible naked Muffins.

The deal was nearly set, but Klauss Schumann was in London and wished to meet Muffin before the contracts were signed.

'Forget about the walk, doggie,' she sighed, 'mama's got to start gettin' it all together.'

Jon Clapton arrived at *Terrazza* at eight. He was tall and skinny, twenty-six years old, with long dirty blond hair and surprisingly innocent good looks. He had found the innocent look extremely useful when dealing with people. Underneath the clean-cut looks lurked a brain of crystal cunning.

Klauss Schumann waited in the bar, a middle-aged German in a shiny blue suit.

'Hello,' Jon said warmly, 'you're early and I'm five minutes late, sorry about that. What are you drinking?'

Klauss was drinking vodka and bitter lemon. Jon ordered rum and coke.

'Muffin will be a bit late,' Jon explained, although actually he had told her not be there until nine. He wanted some time alone with Schumann. 'In the meantime I thought you might like to flick through these.' He handed Klauss a leather folder containing a series of photos of Muffin.

There was Muffin on a swing, coyly crossing her legs, naked.
There was Muffin bending down, bottom in the air, naked.
There was Muffin on the beach, in a car, on a boat, all naked.
There was Muffin in a large hat and nothing else.
Muffin in fine black tights and nothing else.
Muffin in thigh-length white boots.

'She's a lovely girl,' Klauss said thickly.

'Yes,' Jon agreed, 'and she always looks so wholesome. Even the women love her. There's nothing rude about her, that's the great thing.'

Klauss nodded, and flicked through the photos again.

'We have to have a final decision by tomorrow,' Jon said quickly. 'Other important clients are after her and I must let them know.'

'Of course. Of course. I know you have worked out all the

details with our PRs. But I thought as I was in town I should meet with you both. However, I'm sure the answer is yes.' He picked up the photo of Muffin in the white boots. 'Such a charming girl . . .'

Yeah, Jon thought, a charming little raver, who if it wasn't for me would be finished by now, or perhaps would have never got started.

He remembered how they met. At a skating rink of all places.

It was 1972 and he was doing a series of picture articles 'Birds around London'. Muffin had been at the skating rink, plump and toothy. She was wearing an orange sweater, and Jon had thought, 'great pair of knockers', so he had done a few photos of her. They turned out all right, so he had taken her down to Brighton to do some bikini shots. She had just left school and was taking a typing course.

'Waste of time,' Jon told her, 'bird like you stashed behind a desk.'

She came to his studio to see the contacts, and he suggested there was a lot of bread in nude modelling.

'My parents would be furious,' she giggled. But in no time at all she was out of her clothes, and he shot five rolls of film, and then in no time at all she was in his arms and they made it on the floor and he had asked, 'What's a nice little girl from Wimbledon doing being so experienced?'

'I've had five fellas,' she had announced, 'one boyfriend a year since I was twelve!'

Within two months Jon had left his wife, and Muffin had lost ten pounds of baby fat.

Within six months Jon had started Muffin's career rolling, and she moved in with him.

They had an understanding relationship. From the start Jon told her, 'Look, you're young, lots of good things are going to happen for us together, so don't let's blow it.'

'You're not exactly old,' she had remarked.

'I know,' Jon agreed, 'but I've got a wife and two kids and I know what it's all about. Here's the situation, either of us want to screw around it's cool. Only there's a rule. One time only with the same person. Understand?'

Muffin had nodded.

'Oh, and we tell each other about it, O.K.?'

Muffin agreed. It sounded a terrific rule.

And it worked. In the two years they had been together Muffin had slept with three men, one time with each, and she had told Jon all about it.

In turn he had told her about the three girls he slept with. Actually there had only been one other, but he didn't want Muffin becoming too sure of him.

'Ah, this must be the young lady now,' Klauss announced.

Jon turned to watch her entrance. Smiling, pretty, everyone turning to look.

Muffin had come a long way from the plump little girl at the skating rink.

# 3

Cleo went home, packed, bathed and changed, and was back at the office by four. There was an urgent message for her to call Mike, and two calls from Ginny. She didn't return either of them. She checked through arrangements for her trip, and made a few business calls.

At five Russell Hayes sent a message to see if she was free to come up to his office. Russell was the owner editor of the magazine *Image* that was sending Cleo to Europe. He was a thin nervous man who had a disconcerting habit of biting his nails—two or three at a time. He wore pink shirts and cramped Italian suits, and after three wives he had settled for a parade of statuesque girlfriends who called for him at the office.

''Lo, Russ,' said Cleo. She was feeling very down. 'What's going on?'

'Just wanted to know if you had any problems.'

'Everything's under control. I'm all packed and ready to go. In fact, big surprise, I've got my suitcase with me and I was wondering if there was any chance of getting a plane tonight?'

Russell tapped a silver pencil on his desk-top. 'Don't mess up my plans for you, sweetie. They're all set to take very good care of you tomorrow, cars are arranged both ends, also I am superstitious—*never* change a flight. Anyway, I want you to come to the Richard West party with me. You *did* promise.'

Cleo had forgotten all about it. *Image* Magazine had bought the serial rights to Richard West's book.

Russell smiled a quick bunched-up smile. 'The West book will be a winner—*Sex—an Explanation*—what could be a better title?' He added pointedly, '*I* thought of it you know.'

'I know.' she said with a smile. She liked Russell, they had a good business relationship. although at one time he had tried to make it more. She had joked him out of it, and now she felt they were real friends.

'Is Mike coming to the party?' Russell asked. He and Mike were also close friends.

'Why?' Cleo countered.

'What do you mean—why?'

'No, he's not coming.'

'Is everything all right with you two?'

'Now that you ask . . .' she hesitated, 'no it's not. Everything stinks.'

'I've been through three, I know the signs.' He walked around the desk and put his arm around her.

'It makes me feel such a failure,' she said helplessly.

'Tell me about it.'

She shook her head. 'If I talk about it I'll probably start crying. Anyway, it's over, and I've moved out. and oh God, that reminds me. I've got to book into a hotel for tonight.'

'You can stay with me if you want.'

'We're friends, right? I need friends, so a hotel will be better.'

'I'll have my secretary fix it, don't worry about a thing.'

The buzzer on his desk rang and the receptionist told him Dr Richard West was downstairs.

'Send him up.' Russell said. 'Cleo, you can meet him, and we'll all go over to the party in my car. How's that?'

'Fine. Can I use your bathroom?'

'Help yourself.'

She shut herself in the little oak-panelled room adjoining

18

Russell's office and stared at herself in the mirror. Her makeup was perfect, having only been freshly applied that afternoon. She added a touch more prune eyeshadow, it made her oval face paler.

'You've got the most incredible skin,' Mike had told her the first time they met.

She combed her long dark hair and remembered the first time Mike undressed her. The original hang-up was purely sexual, and when the sex stopped being exciting the rot set in.

How long could a relationship like that last? For how many years did one have to pretend it was the greatest thing in the world? Oh, sure it was great, but there were other things, things that Mike didn't want to know about. Children. Cleo sighed. She had always loved kids, and had always imagined she would have plenty. It had seemed sensible when Mike had said they should wait. She wasn't one of those women who relished the thought of all those dreary months blown up like a balloon. So when he said let's wait, she agreed with him, thinking in terms of a year or two. It gradually dawned on her that Mike didn't even like children, let alone want any of his own.

When she asked him one Sunday, in bed, after making love, he said, 'Yeah, sweetheart, I can't say I'm overboard about the idea. Like some little monster interfering in our lives—who needs it? And I *do not* get horny over pregnant ladies—they turn me right off.' Had that been the moment when things began to go sour?

Cleo went back into Russell's office and he introduced her to Richard West.

'You don't look like your picture on the book,' she said.

He nodded agreeably. 'I know. But if the picture on the book looked like me we'd have trouble giving the book away.'

She smiled. He was O.K. Not a neurotic. She hated neurotic authors.

He was a man of medium height, slightly too heavy, with thick sandy hair cut too short. The suit he was wearing was horrible, and the matching shirt and tie didn't help. In spite of it all he was attractive in a way he obviously wasn't aware of. She wanted to tell him he had lips like Mick Jagger, thick sensual lips on the face of a middle-aged sex expert.

19

'I think we should go,' Russell said.

They were the first there. Just them, and a room full of waiters. Russell fussed around magazine displays, re-arranging.

Richard frowned, 'I hate these things,' he said, 'they make me nervous.'

Cleo smiled. 'Just be nice to everybody, you never know who you're talking to. And throw in a lot of quotes—you know—kind of racy statistics.'

'What constitutes racy statistics?'

'Well—figures. Like how many times a man can—er—make it in twenty-four hours. Things like that. Titillation for the potential reader.'

'Couched in more professional terms I take it?'

She laughed. 'Oh yes—*much* more professional.'

Ginny was one of the first guests to arrive. She rushed over to Cleo who was talking to a book reviewer.

'Can I interrupt?' she asked brightly.

'Sure,' said the book reviewer. 'I must go and find Dr West, there are several points I want to discuss with him.'

'I bet!' Ginny replied, tossing blond curls and looking round the room. 'Who's here? Anyone I have slept with or should sleep with or might want to sleep with?'

'Is that what you barged in to ask me?'

'No. Actually *why* didn't you return my call? I mean I just don't believe the scene at lunch with you and Susan, it's not like you to make scenes, and poor Susan was in a *terrible* state. She swears that nothing has gone on with her and Mike.'

'Oh, come on, Ginny—she may bullshit you, but I am here to tell you I *saw* them together.'

'*Saw* them together—what is that? Just because you saw them together doesn't mean the next step is a good healthy fuck. She did mention they had a coffee one day. But she swore to me on her mother's life that nothing went on, honestly Cleo, I think—'

'Will you shut up a minute. I *saw* them together—naked—screwing—at Mike's office this morning.'

'Oh,' said Ginny, and she was silent for the shortest of times, then—'That no good lying bitch! Swearing on her mother's life. Just wait 'til I see her . . . I just can't get over it. You must feel awful, I should have guessed *you* of all people wouldn't make a scene over nothing. I'm sorry, I'm really—'

'Enough, Ginny. I don't want to talk about it. It doesn't matter, it really doesn't matter. I have packed, and I'm leaving for London tomorrow. I just want some time to think things out.'

'What does Mike say about it all? He can't possibly have a thing about Susan. Big girls were never his scene, and let's face it, great tits she may have, but the IQ of a five-year-old. In fact I think—'

'Ginny, I don't want to talk about it, and I'd appreciate it if you wouldn't discuss it all over town. Come on, I'll introduce you to Dr West.'

'Oh, all right. I always fancied comparing notes with an expert at the game.'

They walked across the room.

'Richard, I'd like you to meet a friend of mine—Ginny Sandler. Ginny's an agent.' Cleo smiled as she spoke. The smile was becoming very weary on her face. She wondered if Mike had reached home yet and realized that she had moved out.

'Hello, Ginny,' Richard said warmly, shaking her hand.

'I was thinking we might make a movie sale on your book,' Ginny said as Cleo moved off. 'They buy titles you know. *Sex—an Explanation*—it could be a sort of groovy skin flick— like educational. Or even a Julie Andrews starrer with her as a school marm. There's lots of possibilities. You're not represented, are you?'

He shook his head.

'Then I'm going to take you over and we'll grow rich together.' She took his arm. 'About that chapter on enlarged clitorises— there were one or two things I wanted to ask you about that.'

Cleo felt suddenly tired. She had had enough of small talk, and smiling, and being nice to people who bitched as soon as you were two feet away.

She looked around for Russell. He was with a group which included his latest girlfriend, a redheaded giant named Florinda.

She edged over. 'I'm very tired,' she whispered. 'What hotel did you book me into?'

'Christ!' Russell banged his forehead with the palm of his hand, 'I forgot!'

'Thanks a lot.'

'Don't worry though, I told you I've got a spare room, lots of spare rooms in fact.'

'Russell—'

'Surely after all this time you can trust me?' He acted offended. 'I'll call my houseboy and tell him you're on your way. I won't be back until late, and unless you fancy sharing a bed with me and Florinda, you'll be left very much alone.'

She felt too tired to argue. 'Well, if you're sure . . .'

'Of course I'm sure. Your suitcase is already in my car. I'll take you out to the chauffeur, he'll drop you at my place, and then come back for me.'

'If Mike turns up here—'

'My lips are sealed.'

Impulsively Cleo kissed him on the cheek. 'It's good to have a friend like you.'

He laughed nervously. 'I've told you before, if ever you and Mike split I'm very available.'

She nodded. He may make himself available, but he just wasn't her type.

Russell lived in a sprawling penthouse with incredible views over the city. Cleo had been there on social occasions and thought to herself what a great apartment. Now, seeing it devoid of people it seemed like a set out of a movie.

The houseboy let her in and showed her to an orange tented bedroom, adjoined to a bathroom that featured a sunken bath big enough for six. Silently the houseboy demonstrated how the bath could be turned into a thermal whirlpool.

Cleo nodded. The last thing she felt like was a thermal whirlpool bath.

The houseboy pointed out various switches. One for music, or tapes, or TV.

It was one hell of a guest room. She glanced at the titles of books piled neatly on the bedside table. *Erotic Art, The History of Erotica, Sexual Understanding*. She started to smile. Oh

22

Russell! What a disappoinment you turned out to be. Where was the stack of *Playboy* magazines?

Sure enough they were piled on a glass table next to the loo.

She pushed the button for the tapes. and Isaac Hayes came on at his most horny. What was Mike doing now? He would have arrived home. Would he realize she had gone?

If he checked the bathroom he would. No more feminine clutter

If he looked in her closets he would. No more favourite clothes.

Perhaps she *should* have left a note. No. The hell with him. Let him wonder. By the time he got around to looking for her she would be in London.

She wanted to sleep. but sleep wouldn't come. Her thoughts were too active. darting this way and that.

Repeatedly the scene with Mike making love to Susan flashed before her eyes. If only he had stopped. rolled off. But no. he had stared at Cleo, stared right through her. and just kept on grinding away.

Bastard. Didn't want to spoil his fun. Fuck now—argue later.

Well she had screwed that little game. She just wasn't around to argue with: and Mike would hate that. Mike was a talker. a reasoner. Keeping it all to himself would choke him.

Good. Let him choke. Let him discuss it with Susan bird brain.

An hour must have passed when she heard her door open and someone tiptoed in. She clicked on the bedside lamp. It was Russell.

'I just wanted to check that everything's all right,' he said lamely.

She pulled the sheet up. 'Fine. I can't seem to sleep. What are you doing home so soon?'

'I was worried about you. Thought you might like a little conversation.'

'Where's Florinda?'

'Sent her home.'

'You shouldn't have done so on my account.' Oh Christ, he's going to launch an attack.

23

He sat down on the side of the bed. 'What do you think of this room?'

'It's very modern.'

He nodded. 'You could stay here when you get back from Europe.'

'That's very kind of you.'

'You're a beautiful woman. Cleo. And what is more, an intelligent one. You and I could have a very fine relationship together.'

We couldn't, she replied silently. Aloud she said, 'It's getting late, Russ, I think I'll try and get some sleep.'

'You still love Mike, I know that, I'm not a fool. But you and I could have a different kind of relationship, a more mature one. Mike's not the man for you, he still has a lot of growing up to do.' He leaned forward and kissed her, a practised, insistent kiss.

She couldn't struggle, as under the sheet she was naked. So she accepted his kiss, and with both hands firmly pulled the sheet around her.

With a sudden movement he rolled on top of her. She wrenched her mouth away from his. 'Get off, Russell, please!'

His body was moving up and down, his eyes tightly closed. He still wore the striped Italian suit, the pink shirt, the polished shoes.

Cleo lay rigid under the sheet.

At the moment of his climax, he muttered, 'I've always loved you, always . . .' He shuddered to a stop and Cleo couldn't help thinking about his suit, it must be ruined. Good.

He lay still for a few moments, and then quietly he clicked the bedside lamp off, whispered goodnight, and was gone.

Cleo leapt out of bed and locked the door. She didn't know whether to laugh or cry.

The perfect end to a perfect day.

## 4

'You were great!' Jon said, 'absolutely perfect. The Schumann Calendar is going to be all ours by tomorrow. Takes care of our holiday problems this year.'

Muffin giggled. 'He didn't half give me a few funny looks. Honestly, sometimes I feel more naked than any of my photos when these old fellas gaze at me.'

He patted her on the knee. 'Doesn't bother you does it?'

'Sometimes it makes me feel a bit sort of funny . .'

'Pie face. your boobs are famous, and they'd all like to have a grope. Enjoy it, revel in it. One day you'll be a little old lady in Wimbledon and then you'll be wishing you were a young piece of—'

'Jon!'

He put his arms around her and kissed the lip gloss off her full pouty lips. She snuggled up against him.

He pulled her blue denim frilled skirt up from behind and slid his hands under her tight-fitting bikini pants. 'Beautiful bum . . .' he mumbled.

'Your hands are freezing!' she complained, but she didn't try to move them.

'I'm going to take your knickers off, little girl.'

Muffin gasped, china blue eyes widened. 'Oh please sir! I'm just an innocent country maiden, please do not molest me!'

Jon peeled the pants off her. 'O.K., country maiden, let me into your forest.'

'But sir . . '

The phone rang.

'Shit!' said Jon.

Muffin answered it, slowly unbuttoning the white camisole top she was wearing. 'It's your wife,' she hissed, sticking out a small pink tongue and marching out of the room.

He picked up the phone. 'Jane? What do you want now?'

He hadn't lived with her for three years but she still depended on him for everything. All right, he didn't mind supporting his kids, but why did he have to keep her and her layabout boyfriends?

She wanted more money. She always wanted more money.

He had bought her a little house in Putney, gave her twenty-five quid a week, *and* paid all the kid's bills.

She was a rotten mother. He saw the children every weekend and they always looked filthy.

'Look after them yourself if you think your little dolly bird can do any better,' Jane would sneer when he criticized.

Jon would have liked to have taken her up on her offer, but there was no way Muffin could cope with two small children. Muffin was just a kid herself. Plans for a divorce were well under way, but financial hassles kept on holding it up.

Jon agreed to send her another fifty. Fucking leech. So much for young romantic love. *Never* marry young. Even better—*never* marry.

Muffin was at her dressing table carefully peeling off single eyelashes and placing them on a Kleenex. He ruffled her hair. 'Get lost!' she muttered. Jane on the phone never put her in a good mood. It reminded her of the divorce that Jon had promised and so far failed to get.

# 5

Mike James smoked long, thin, black cigarettes. They were better for you than ordinary cigarettes, and cheaper than cigars. Actually the main reason he smoked them was because they had style, and Mike always had been a man who liked style.

That was why he was mad that Cleo had caught him with Susan. If there was one quality Susan did not possess it was style. She was just a schlock with a great body. Sometimes the lure of a pair of sensational knockers proved too much for even the most discerning of men.

After being discovered by Cleo. Mike got rid of Susan quickly. She went with a smile and a wink. 'See you again soon, honey.'

Oh, the loyalty of women. The only thing you could trust them with was your cock, and that was only on a temporary basis!

He regretted the fact that he hadn't waited to ball Susan. Waited only a matter of days until Cleo was safe and sound in Europe. But his motto in life had always been 'do not do tomorrow what you can do today'.

He thought of a million 'if only's.'

If only he had locked the office door.

If only he hadn't sent his secretary out for coffee.

If only Cleo had knocked. Jesus, she *never* called in on him at the office, now she would think he spent his entire time there screwing.

He paced around his office. Cleo was certainly not going to take kindly to the fact that she had caught him with one of her friends. It would have been better if he had been straddling a stranger aboard the office couch. That would have been bad enough—but this . . .

Susan had been giving him the come-on for some time. He had lunched her the previous week, and they were both aware of what promises 'come to my office for coffee' offered.

It was one thing your wife finding out about another woman, but actually catching you at it—well, that wasn't a good scene. Not unless you had in mind a cosy threesome, and Cleo would never go along with *that*, indeed he wouldn't want her to. Sex with Cleo was beautiful. Cool, calm, satisfying Sex with other women was different, more raunchy, rougher. He could use them in a way he didn't care to use Cleo. He had used Susan. It meant no more to him than a morning's fun.

From the very beginning things had been different with Cleo. She had come into his life at a time when he had decided that the life he led was perfect. He worked hard at a job he liked. He had a nice apartment. A Ferrari A lot of different girlfriends. In fact he felt he was personally living out the *Playboy* dream.

Cleo came along and proved to him that it was just a wet dream after all.

She didn't want to get married. She was independent. She asked him for nothing. After six months of living together he insisted. 'If you really love me you'll prove it by marrying me,' he had said.

How many girls had said that to him in the past . . .

So they got married, and it was great. Four years of living with an intelligent, beautiful girl. A very modern marriage.

Surely Cleo had never imagined he was faithful? No one was faithful. She wouldn't expect him to be.

Of course *she* probably was, well naturally. Women *were* different, they didn't have such needs. Anyway he just knew that Cleo wouldn't deceive him with another man, it wasn't her scene. He kept her happy sexually. He kept her happy in every way. Anyway he'd fucking kill her if she ever screwed around. But of course she never would.

Sometimes they discussed other women. He had often said he fancied this one or that one, and they had both laughed about it. Cleo was probably laughing now. When he got home later she would be laughing . . .

'Got no bloody taste, that's your problem,' she would say. And they would talk about it, and laugh about it; and later they would make love . . .

Yes, Mike decided, that was the way it would be. Cleo was far too clever a woman to make a big deal out of this.

Maybe the best thing to do would be not to mention it. Just ignore the fact that it had ever happened. No—he wouldn't get away with that. Cleo would want an inquest. She was entitled to one and he was quite prepared to eat humble pie.

After all she was the woman he loved, and he was going to have to prove it to her.

Perhaps it was a good thing that he had finally been caught. Now it would have to stop, and maybe what he really wanted after all was a one woman relationship.

## 6

Cleo did not feel safe until she was on the plane, in the air, on her way to London.

It wasn't crowded, and she sat in an aisle seat. The middle seat was vacant, and the window seat was occupied by a male singer that she vaguely recognized as Shep Stone. He was taking nervous swigs out of a Tiffany hip flask, and as soon as they were airborne he lit up a joint which he calmly smoked hidden behind a *Time* magazine.

Cleo was in no mood for conversation, and fortunately it seemed he felt the same way.

She was angry, humiliated, disgusted. Russell Hayes' behaviour was really chickenshit. He had appeared that very morning like nothing had happened. He was smiling and dapper and full of business-like conversation. They had eaten breakfast together, silently as far as Cleo was concerned. But it hadn't phased him one bit. He had insisted on coming to the airport with her. Paid her excess baggage. Bought her ten new magazines and an ugly toy dog. When they parted he tried to kiss her, but she moved her face and he just got her cheek.

'Last night was wonderful,' he whispered.

What did you say to a man like that? She tried to smile a goodbye, but after years of being fairly good friends she suddenly hated him, and her smile turned sour.

'Don't feel guilty, darling,' Russell said reassuringly. 'Everything will work out for the best.'

She boarded the plane in a mild fury. Christ! What an egotistical shit! Sweet, kind, funny old Russ. One of Mike's best friends. A hell of a best friend *he* turned out to be. A hell of a friend *Susan* turned out to be.

'Can I borrow one of your magazines?' Shep Stone leaned across and asked.

'Sure.' She dumped all ten of them on the middle seat.

'Going to London?' he inquired.

What a stupid question considering that's where the plane was headed. 'Umm,' she mumbled.

'Been there before?' he persisted.

'Yes,' she replied coldly. What was it about planes that gave men the impression you were there for an immediate pick-up?

'Lovely city,' he said. 'I've been there many times. Are you a New Yorker?'

She turned to stare at him. 'Look, I have an awful headache. Do you mind if we sit this one out?'

'Huh?'

'Have a magazine, a hostess, anything. But please, a little silence.' She turned away, but not before he had managed a hurt expression.

Shep Stone was quite well-known as a singer of romantic ballads, but he had never really made it big. He was thirty-five with brown hair and a nice smile. Not exactly an Andy Williams, but heading that way.

Cleo shut her eyes and tried to regain her thoughts. She was going to London to start on the series of interviews *Image* magazine had commissioned. It was to be headed 'Who's Afraid of the Big Bad Wolf', and it was to be an in-depth, probing analysis, of five famous eligible male movie stars.

'You'll do the five most horny guys,' Russell had said. 'You'll do a great job, baby. We'll run it over five issues.'

Cleo had liked the idea. She was good at interviews, although she was usually more into politicians or businessmen. 'Actors are so overdone,' she had said at first. 'What more is there to say about someone who's said it all three hundred times before?'

Mike had encouraged her. 'It'll be good for you, a change of pace is just what you need. Your stuff is always so serious.'

So she had said yes. The money was good. A couple of weeks in London at the Connaught. She could see her mother. A few days in the South of France, and maybe Rome.

'Did my smoking bother you?' Shep Stone asked anxiously. 'If it did I'm sorry. I don't usually need that stuff, but goddam it, I'm scared of flying. Isn't that ridiculous?'

Cleo sighed patiently. She found it extremely hard to be rude to people. In print it was easy, but in person she chickened out. 'It didn't bother me, I guess I'm just tired.'

'Would you like a drink? It will pick you up.'

She nodded. May as well give in, now the plane was on its way he was determined to talk.

And talk he did. All the way across the Atlantic. She heard about his career, his three wives, his two children, his financial position, his political beliefs; and finally, of course, his sex life. 'I like women,' he explained, 'maybe I like them too much. I started making it when I was eighteen. That's late, isn't it? Well, anyway . . .' The plane ran into a sudden storm, and Shep ran into a sudden silence. 'I hate flying,' he said, producing the Tiffany hip flask and gulping mammoth slugs. At the same time he was fiddling round in his pocket searching for another joint.

The plane was bouncing around like a ping-pong ball. Shep lit up and took a couple of heavy drags. 'Doesn't make any difference,' he said morbidly, 'booze, drugs. I still stay as sober as the pilot.'

He offered Cleo the joint, and she took it. She inhaled deeply. Pot agreed with her, gave her a much better high than drinking. She and Mike had enjoyed the occasional joint together.

The pilot's voice suddenly came crackling through the loudspeaker system.

'Oh my God!' Shep gasped, clutching the armrests tightly. 'We're going to crash!'

The pilot apologized for the bad weather, explained that the weather was equally bad over London, asked everybody to fasten their seatbelts, and explained that they would shortly be landing in Frankfurt.

'Sonofabitch!' Shep muttered, and remained in a nervous huddle until they landed.

Cleo summoned the hostess and discovered that it would be a stopover for the night in Frankfurt. She didn't mind. She knew that Mike would be phoning her as soon as she arrived at the Connaught. This would give him another night of stewing.

Let him stew.

# 7

Muffin and the Japanese girl stood back to back. They were of the same height, but every other detail of their physical attributes was different.

They were both naked, and both held aloft champagne glasses.

'That's terrific, girls,' Jon said, adjusting his Nikon. 'Hey Annie,' he called to his assistant, 'rub some more ice cubes on their nips, they're getting a bit depleted.'

Annie rushed forward with a small ice bucket and rubbed an ice cube across the Japanese girl's nipples. They sprang erect immediately.

Muffin stuck her chest forward. 'Me next please, my thrill for the day!'

John said, 'Bum in a bit. Muff, right leg slightly more bent, I'm getting a flash of the fuzz. That's beautiful, darlings. Beautiful!'

He worked quickly, the sounds of Bobby Womack belting out over the stereo system. After six rolls of film he was satisfied. 'That's it, girls.'

Muffin yawned and stretched. 'I'm beat!' She and Kamika, the Japanese girl, went into the dressing-room.

'Charlie and I, we get a divorce,' Kamika said, slipping into a shirt and trousers.

'Shame!' Muffin said. 'You've only been married—what? A year?'

'One year, seven days,' Kamika said precisely. 'He fart all day, he fart all night. No longer can I stand it.'

'Yeah, well all fellas fart,' Muffin said sagely.

'But not in time to music!'

Muffin giggled. 'Sorry. Kam, but you're so funny!' She wriggled into skintight jeans and a sweater, and stuck her new sunglasses into her hair.

'Very nice glasses.' Kamika remarked.

'You like them. they're yours.' Muffin handed them over.

'No. I couldn't. Please . . .'

Muffin insisted. 'Compliments of Harrods,' she said with a sly laugh.

Jon was still working, photographing a tall blond who posed silently in a long slinky nightgown. Muffin kissed him on the cheek. 'See you later, sweetie.' She waved at the tall blond. 'Hands off him Erica, he's taken.'

She had the afternoon before her. It was a rare treat, most days she hardly had time for lunch.

There was a variety of choices. She could go home, and take the dog for a long walk in the park. Or she could go shopping. Or she could go to a movie.

Then again she could drift down to the *Carousel* for lunch, there were bound to be a lot of her mates there. She could have a gossip and a chatter and find out who was doing what to whom.

Erica said, 'You and Muffin are still going strong I see.'

'Legs a bit more together, that's it, fine, lovely.' Jon clicked away. 'Yeah, we're still together.'

'I'm amazed.'

Jon grunted. 'Right leg forward a bit, not too much. Perfect! Why are you amazed?'

Erica shrugged. 'I just never thought a girl like that would be a long-term prospect.'

'Head back, and don't be bitchy.'

She threw her head back. 'Would *I* be bitchy.'

'Yeah. You're the original bitch.'

'You didn't think that when we were together.'

'I gave you one four times a few years ago, so that doesn't make you an expert on what kind of girl I want to spend my time with.'

'Jon Clapton, you're a liar! It was at least six times.' She posed provocatively. 'Want to make it seven?'

'You're a married lady, Erica.'

'You were a married man the last time. This will make us even. Anyway, I'm getting a divorce.'

'Thanks for the offer but no thanks. Be a darlin' and slip into the black satin job while I change the film.'

'Bastard!' she muttered. 'You just don't want to blow your

bread and butter. Who do you think the two of you are? Justin and Twiggy?'

'Belt up and get changed.'

John lit a cigarette. Justin and Twiggy. that was a laugh! He and Muffin were going much further than that.

The *Carousel* was packed. Muffin squeezed in with Jan and Brenda.

'Where you bin. girl?' Brenda inquired. 'Want to hear my new song?'

'How's the boyfriend?' Jan asked. 'I haven't seen him since Africa.'

'He's fine.' Muffin replied. biting on a stick of celery. 'Oooh—who's that?' She pointed at a slight blond boy in skin-tight chamois leather.

'Forget it.' Brenda said. 'I've had it. and girl—it's quick and small!!'

They all laughed.

Muffin said, 'I was working with Kamika this morning and she's getting a divorce.'

'What's the matter. her old man gone off Japanese food?' Brenda laughed. 'By the way. isn't it about time we were all dancing at your wedding?'

Muffin smiled. 'Soon.' she promised.

Jon better get his finger out. He had been promising to divorce his wife for long enough. If things went on for much longer she was going to look like a fool. Anyway, she wanted to be Mrs Clapton. Mrs Jon Clapton.

# 8

'Take it easy. Calm down.' Russell Hayes said. 'I know she's a wonderful girl, but if it's not to be. it's not to be.'

'I don't need your half-ass philosophies.' Mike said shortly.

34

'Christ almighty! All I did was screw some moon-faced blond, and Cleo vanishes off the face of the earth.'

'If I had a wife like Cleo.' Russell said primly. 'I don't think I'd feel the need to screw around.'

'Balls! You were married three times and you still tried to stick it into anything that moved!'

'Yes. but I wasn't married to Cleo.'

'Keep it up, Russ. and I'll think you and Cleo had something going.'

Russell sipped his drink and didn't say anything.

'I don't understand her.' Mike said shortly. 'To take off without even discussing things with me. I mean she's treating me like some sort of boyfriend. I'm her husband goddamn it! She can't just walk out on me without a word.'

'Why not?'

'What do you mean—why not? She's mine. We're married. We're *tied* to each other in every way.'

'Except sexually,' Russell commented dryly. 'Or so it would seem.'

'Whose side are you on anyway?'

'I can see both points of view. My personal opinion is that perhaps you're not suited. perhaps this is the best thing.'

'Bollocks! A quick fuck ain't gonna end *my* marriage.'

Russell shrugged. 'Perhaps the choice won't be yours. Anyway—you've been whoring around so long you were bound to get caught eventually.'

'Oh. you're a great friend, very reassuring. Look, when I can *find* her. *talk* to her, everything will be all right.'

'I hope so,' said Russell insincerely, 'I really hope so. But knowing Cleo I wouldn't count on it.'

'What do you mean by that snide remark? If anyone knows Cleo it's me.'

'Perhaps you don't know her as well as you think you do.'

'Jesus, Russell. what is it with you? Anyone would think you were happy about what's going on.'

'What will be will be . . .' Russell repeated sagely.

'Yeah—and I'll tell you what will be. I'll find her, talk to her, and everything is going to work out just fine.'

Mike went home. Russell really pissed him off with his slippery smile and pompous manner. What did he know about serious relationships? Three failed marriages had taught him exactly nothing.

He placed another call to the Connaught. Mrs James had *still* not checked in.

He missed her. The apartment seemed so strange without her. He studied their wedding photo in their one and only silver frame. Cleo. That face. Those eyes. That beautiful slim body with the smooth skin. Long legs. Small feet. Tiny hands. Everything about her was understated. Mike liked that, there was nothing obvious about Cleo.

The first time they had met at a rock party in London, there had been one of those instant sexual attractions that they were both aware of. He had wanted to drag her into the nearest bed and make love without exchanging so much as a word. She knew it. He knew it. Instead they had allowed themselves to be introduced, and they had chatted lightly whilst their eyes met and carried on their own private conversation.

Later, after the party, after a drink at a discotheque, he had suggested his hotel. Cleo had politely declined.

Mike had been prepared to wait. There were certain games to be played, rules to be followed before he was allowed into her bed. He understood. He waited.

When they became lovers she came to live with him in New York. It was a temporary arrangement, Mike was not prepared to settle for anything less than marriage.

So what had gone wrong? What had led him into other beds and other bodies?

There had been no other women when he and Cleo were living together. Three weeks after they married it had all started.

Mike had always found women were very attracted to him, and came on strong. He could not recall exactly how many others there had been but he knew it was a lot. He could remember only a few of them. Fanny, because she had given him a dose of the clap. Brook, because she was only sixteen and forgot to mention the fact until they were actually doing it. Linda, who claimed he got her pregnant and demanded a thousand dollars abortion money. And of course, Susan, Cleo's good friend Susan.

Sex with Cleo was incredible. perfect. But somehow there were things he wanted to do that he didn't want to do with her. She wasn't some girl he was living with. she was his wife and deserved to be treated as such. Respect. an old-fashioned word. but a word he wanted to apply to his wife. He didn't want to make heavy demands on her. so almost as a service he turned to other women. It became a habit—like smoking; and like smoking he found he couldn't give it up.

Up until now he had always been discreet. What Cleo didn't know. she couldn't possibly be angry about. He felt guilty. but only because he had the misfortune to be caught. and life was just not complete without Cleo. He needed her. He wanted her. And he desired her in exactly the same way it had been when they had first met.

So where was she? How could she do this to him?

It wasn't fair, didn't she have any feelings? How could she just leave him hanging? If she knew him at all she knew that he would want to talk. explain.

What she was doing to him now was punishment enough.

Angrily he picked up the phone again and dialled the international operator. 'I want a person to person call to London, England. Mrs Cleo James . . .'

# 9

The hotel in Frankfurt was full of good old German efficiency. It was early evening and what with the drinks and the pot Cleo felt in fairly good shape.

Shep Stone became a different person when his feet hit firm ground. At the airport he organized them a private car. At the hotel he said, 'See you in the bar at eight.' He took it for granted they would dine together.

Cleo took a leisurely bath and washed her long dark hair. She let it dry naturally and it surrounded her face with languid damp curls. To achieve the straight effect she had to dry her hair pulling it all the time with a brush. She couldn't be bothered, Shep would just have to accept her *au naturel*.

She put on a soft grey silk shirt and a pin-stripe suit tailored for her in New York. Round her neck she hung the jade horn Mike had given her last Christmas, and on her fingers a mixture of thin ivory and jade rings.

'You look really terrific,' Shep told her as he stood to greet her in the bar. He too was wearing grey, a suit with a strange short jacket piped with braid. Mike called them 'bum freezers'.

They dined in the hotel restaurant which was located on the roof and had good food and an awful cabaret.

Shep was charming and attentive. Cleo knew that he fancied her. She knew that at the end of the evening there would be the inevitable invitation for a drink in his room. She had already made up her mind to accept.

Well why not? When it came to discussing things with Mike she wanted to be on even territory. Shep Stone was an attractive man. Mike had screwed Susan. She would have Shep. Fair is fair.

Sure enough he went through the expected ritual of conversation. 'How about a nightcap in my room?'

Somehow she would have preferred the more honest, 'How about a fuck in my room?'

They took the elevator down to his room where Shep summoned room service and ordered champagne. At least he had some class, although champagne always reminded her of the time Mike had opened a bottle on their water bed, deliberately poured it all over her naked body, and spent the rest of the evening licking it off her. She smiled at the memory and Shep took that as a signal to get started. He ripped off his 'bum freezer' jacket, and gripping her tightly by the arms started to kiss her. Long, hard kisses. They reminded her of Russell and the unfortunate previous evening. She wriggled free.

'What's the matter?' he asked, offended. 'I got bad breath?'

Saved by a short sentence. Cleo knew she could never go to bed with a man who asked 'I got bad breath?'

'I have a headache', she said. If he could say 'come to my

room for a nightcap'. she could certainly say, 'I have a headache.'

She thought he was going to be cool about it, but he suddenly unzipped his fly, and his cock, red and erect, popped out. 'Just a little head.' he pleaded.

She was furious. Christ! Two of them in so many days. She stalked to the door and let herself out, nearly bumping into the waiter with the champagne.

Back in her room she called the desk. 'Take me off the plane to London in the morning, please, book me on the first plane to Paris, with a connecting flight to London.'

Shep Stone could shiver and shake his own way to London.

# 10

Sunday lunch time with Muffin's family was a drag. Jon hated it, and it always managed to put the usually happy-go-lucky Muffin in a grim mood.

Lunch in Wimbledon at the small, neat, ever-so-respectable semi-detached house that Muffin had grown up in.

There was Mum, a plump youngish woman with worn hands and straggly curls. Dad, honest and jovial. Ben and Josie, ten-year-old twins. Penny, Muffin's twin sister younger by eight minutes. And Penny's husband, Geoff.

It was the relationship between Penny, Geoff, and Muffin, that caused all the tension.

When she was fifteen Muffin had dated Geoff a few times, then she didn't hear from him again. When Penny brought him home months later and announced that they planned to be married Muffin was furious. He had been pinched from right under her nose by her own sister. She had never forgiven her. She was a reluctant bridesmaid at the wedding. Shortly after, she met Jon and moved out.

Muffin became a personality and Penny became the mother of one fat baby and another on the way. The relationship between the two sisters did not improve. Penny did not approve of her sister's nude modelling, she thought it was disgusting, and made a point of telling anyone who would listen. 'Geoff and I may not be rich,' she would say, 'but Geoff would rather see me *dead* than stripping off in public.'

Geoff remained silent on the subject. He was rather chuffed at having a famous sister-in-law.

Muffin took much pleasure in criticizing her twin's appearance. 'You're too fat. Why don't you do something with your hair? If you had your front teeth capped you'd look much better.'

Penny would reply maliciously, 'Well, there's nothing we can do about our short fat legs is there?'

Reluctantly Muffin had to agree. Perfect boobs, pretty face, tiny waist, lovely little ass, but she was *still* stuck with stumpy legs. Anyway, nobody seemed to notice her legs.

Lunch was invariably stringy roast lamb, lumpy gravy, burnt roast potatoes, and watery peas. Muffin could remember when it was her favourite meal, that was before her taste buds had been developed at all the best London restaurants.

One of the newspapers had requested a fashion spread on Muffin with her family. They were all quite excited about it, that is all except Penny, who had only agreed to be in the picture on condition she was paid. Jon had personally decided to pay her. It would look a bit odd having photos of Muffin and her family without her twin sister.

In the front room there were suitcases of clothes. Matching jeans outfits for Josie and Ben. Sports casuals for Dad. A silk shirtwaist dress for Mum. Maternity outfit for Penny. And for Muffin full length calico, frilled and flounced, low cut and pretty. Lately she was in as much demand clothed as unclothed.

After lunch the entire family went off to get changed, and Jon started to set up his equipment. He would have preferred to work in his studio, but the paper had specially requested an at home shot.

Geoff stood around watching, the two-year-old baby clinging to his legs. Although he and Jon were about the same age they had never had much to say to each other. They had nothing in common except the sisters. Geoff was a window-cleaner, apparently satisfied with his work. His only ambition was to operate a little firm of his own—an ambition he did nothing to achieve.

'You got a lot of gear,' Geoff remarked. He was slightly taller than Jon, but not quite so thin.

'Yeah,' Jon nodded, cursing privately that he hadn't thought to bring an assistant.

'Me, all I need's a bucket and cloth and I'm away.'

'Great,' Jon muttered, fiddling with an umbrella he was attaching to one of his lights.

'I wouldn't have thought it would take all this larking about just for a couple of snaps.'

Jon didn't bother to reply. Christ—if he and Muffin ever got married this moron would be his brother-in-law. A sobering thought. How the hell had Muffin ever managed to go out with Geoff in the first place?

'Caught a bird in the bath the other day,' Geoff said cheerily, 'mind you—I think she was looking to get caught, she *knew* I was in the house. I'm always coming across them in their knickers and bras. I could do myself some good if I wanted to. Little one the other day she . . .'

Jon tuned out. He wasn't interested in what he termed as wishful crumpet conversations. Muffin had told him that nothing had ever happened with her and Geoff. If it had, would he be jealous? No, he decided, the past was the past, even if it did keep on hanging around.

Muffin came bouncing in. 'Ready,' she trilled.

Self-consciously the rest of the family trailed behind her.

'Cor!' exclaimed Geoff, 'smashing looking group.'

Penny glared at him. 'This outfit is horrible,' she complained, 'the trousers are too long.'

'You all look very nice,' placated Jon, and he started to try and organize them into a family group.

It wasn't easy—everyone kept shuffling around, Penny kept complaining, and the baby clinging to Geoff started to scream.

Silently Jon vowed never to get involved in one of *these* scenes again. Muffin minus the family was quite enough thank you.

It was a long hard afternoon.

Later, at home, when they were in bed, Jon said to Muffin—'How did you ever manage to go out with that idiot?'

'Who?'

'Your brother-in-law.'

'Oh. Geoff,' she giggled, 'He's very good-looking.'

'Good-looking?'

'Yes. Well, he was, I guess he doesn't look so good now. Nagged into an early old age.'

'Did he give you one?'

'One what?' Wide, innocent, little girl eyes.

'Don't play silly buggers with me, fat ass.'

'Don't call me fat ass.'

'Why? Is it a sensitive spot? Here, give me a handful.' He grabbed her roughly. She was wearing a shortie nightie with matching pants, and he ripped them off her.

'You swine!' She kicked him. 'They cost me five quid at Fenwicks.'

He pinned her down easily. 'I'll give you a fiver.' he spread her legs and entered her. 'Think this will be worth a fiver?'

'It's a good job you've got a big dick otherwise I'd be furious with you!'

# 11

June in London is an unpredictable month. Sometimes cold, sometimes hot and sticky.

Cleo arrived in the midst of a mini heatwave. Heathrow airport was in chaos due to a bomb scare, and it was impossible to get a taxi. She travelled into the centre of London on an airport bus sweating in the Gatsby style suit that had been just right during the changeover of planes in Paris.

What a lot of trouble to have gone to just to avoid one stupid singer. She sheltered behind tinted glasses and surveyed the English in a heatwave from the bus window.

Every little patch of green they drove past was littered with half naked bodies. Businessmen in rolled-up shirtsleeves and crumpled trousers. Secretaries in old-fashioned mini skirts and sweaters with bra straps showing. Long legs, short legs, hairy legs—they were all on show.

Mike had fabulous legs for a man. Long and straight, not too heavy, lovely curved calves with a light smattering of dark hairs. As a matter of fact he also had a fine set of balls, tight and hard.

Cleo couldn't help smiling to herself as she thought about Mike striding around their apartment naked. Men looked so vulnerable when the hard-on was gone, and so horny when it was there.

'I like your style,' had been one of Mike's favourite lines to her.

'And I like your balls—figuratively speaking that is!' had been her reply.

The bus rattled and shaked its way towards the Brompton Road air terminal. It was late afternoon, another day past. Cleo felt like she had spent the last few days in limbo, as indeed she had. She wanted a bath, and a visit to the hairdresser. She wanted to unpack and phone old friends. She wanted to drop in and surprise her mother. She wanted to shop at Biba, Harrods, and Marks and Spencer. Four years was a long time to have been away.

There were numerous messages for her at the Connaught. Mike had phoned at least five times, and there was an international operator's number to call immediately she checked in. Russell Hayes had called twice. Ginny Sandler once.

There were flowers waiting from Shep Stone with a humble note of apology. Why had she ever told him where she was staying?

She stripped off her Gatsby suit and headed for the shower. She felt inexplicably horny. Was it the hot weather or just the thought of her unfaithful shit-faced husband's lovely legs and tight balls?

Mike had always claimed that the hot weather turned her on. They had made love the previous week and it had been short and boring.

'I think we should pop down to Puerto Rico for a few days,' Mike had said. 'get some rest and sunshine '

'When I get back from my trip.' Cleo had replied. Maybe in Puerto Rico they could talk about starting a family.

The phone rang and she decided not to answer it. She was still wet from the shower and not ready to get involved in any hassles. Whoever it was would call back.

She dressed in plain trousers. a silk shirt. and tied her long dark hair back. Then she unpacked. realizing that if the hot weather continued she had brought all the wrong clothes.

After her clothes were put away. her makeup and toiletries laid out. and her notepads and files and tape recorder stacked neatly on the desk. she felt better.

'You're so organized.' Mike was always mocking her. He stepped out of his clothes leaving them on the floor. His desk was a clutter of junk. The bathroom awash when he was finished in there.

Cleo wondered wryly what their apartment looked like now after three days of her absence. The only thing Mike bothered to clean was his Ferrari.

'I love you.' he had informed her one day, "cos you're the only girl I know that cleans my toothbrush.'

'An old English custom.' she had replied sweetly.

She too had been brought up to do nothing for herself. Middle class English family with a series of maids who picked up after her. Only child like Mike. Spoilt rotten like Mike. Then at eighteen a runaway marriage to a scruffy layabout who thought he had found himself an heiress. She had learned then. No maids to pick up after you when you're squatting in a derelict house. No one to spoil you rotten when you didn't have enough money to eat.

A year had been long enough to teach Cleo the facts of life. At nineteen she got a divorce and started to write for magazines. Within a couple of years she had got herself a good reputation and plenty of work. She met Mike when she was doing a piece on an American pop group who were with his company. Mike came to London for their launching. They met at the press party.

At the time Cleo was sleeping with an extremely attractive disc jockey. He wanted to marry her. Mike was going through his rounds of different beautiful girls. They met and stuck. Cleo went back to America with him, he introduced her to Russell Hayes and she became *Image* magazine's special lady reporter. She also eventually became Mrs Mike James.

'You and I are going to make it work forever,' Mike had told her on their wedding night, 'just the two of us—forever.'

The phone rang again, and she picked it up hesitantly. 'Yes?'

'Cleo? At last. Did you get my flowers? I thought we could have dinner.'

'Who is this?'

'It's Shep, baby. Shep Stone.'

She sighed. Give, and they would take. Run, and they would follow.

'I'm sorry,' she said, 'but you have the wrong approach.'

# 12

'Shit!' exclaimed Mike James as he banged the phone down yet again. Where the hell was Cleo?

He was late for an appointment. He grabbed his leather jacket and stormed out of the apartment. No breakfast. No fucking. This sort of life was not good for a man.

He rode the elevator down to the car park in the basement. He didn't usually take the Ferrari out on a week-day, but he was late, and getting a cab was impossible, and anyway he wanted to.

The Ferrari waited gleaming and shining in its parking bay. Nine years old and still looked like new. It was a Five Hundred Superfast, a great model.

Mike patted the bonnet lovingly and climbed in. He started

the engine and magic sounds filled his ears. He relaxed. Whatever else he still had his beautiful baby.

He pushed in a tape to listen to a new group. and steered his car carefully through the snarling New York traffic to his office. His thoughts were of Cleo. He was remembering the last time they had made love. It had been a very quick event. Short and sweet. It had been good for him—let's face it a come is a come. But how had it been for her? Maybe he should have spent more time at the beginning getting her in the mood. she hadn't been exactly ready. But she had been ready at the end. he could always manipulate her to a beautiful climax. And no faking—he always checked that out. there were ways to tell when a woman was faking.

Their sex life was pretty good. No. that certainly couldn't be the reason she had run off. He could understand it if she had caught him screwing Susan and she wasn't getting any herself. But he had plenty to go around. Plenty.

Of course. Cleo did have some hang up about having children. but they had discussed it. and she had finally agreed with him that it would be best to wait. God. he had seen what kids had done to other people's marriages Anyway. he was not yet ready to share Cleo with a small person who would infringe on their lives.

Hampton Records was a chrome and glass building filled with blue jeaned secretaries and bearded young men. Everyone was on first name basis from the boy who delivered the mail to Eric B. B. Hampton—president and founder of Hampton Records.

Mike went straight up to B. B.'s office.

B. B. consulted a solid gold watch. 'Dragging your ass again' he commented.

'Fuck you.' Mike replied cheerily.

'Ooh baby. that would be a sight to see!'

B. B.'s secretary brought in black coffee for Mike. and a huge chocolate milk shake laced with rum for B. B.

'Be a nice girlie, run down to Charlie O's for a selection of Danish.' B. B. requested.

The secretary looked unsure. 'Mary Ellen told me no. absolutely no. She said no food for you 'til after twelve-thirty.'

Mary Ellen was B. B.'s girl friend.

B. B. picked up the solid gold clock on his desk and twiddled the dials until it read twelve-thirty.

'O.K. now. little smart ass? Make sure you include a few with cherries.' He smacked his lips and leered at Mike. 'I love those little ripe cherries. don't you?'

Mike grinned and nodded.

'Hey,' said B. B., 'the deal is this. With all the advance publicity working for us and Cassady out of it, I think we should bring the Little Marty Pearl Europe gig forward. I feel now's the time.'

'Yeah,' Mike said slowly, 'be a good one for the new record. In fact the timing's great.'

'Before I put my ear to the instrument I wanted to check out with you that you can go along on the trip. I think it's important you be there.'

Mike nodded. 'I guess there's nothing I can't postpone. When?'

'Soon as soon. I'll let you have dates later today.'

'Great.'

Little Marty Pearl was Mike's own personal discovery. 'Let's ride with the weeny bopper market.' B. B. had instructed his five top executives a year previously. And Mike had obediently scouted around and come up with Little Marty Pearl. He had spotted him on a television commercial. liked the look of him, tracked him down, and been delighted to discover that Marty had a plaintive simple voice that all the little girls would love. Of course the voice was secondary. it was the looks that really mattered, and Marty got an A-plus for looks. He was every mother's idea of Mister Teenage America. He was medium height, with calf-like brown eyes. freckles, tousled blondish hair, and perfect teeth. Little Marty Pearl was supposed to be sixteen, but actually he was going on nineteen, a closely guarded secret.

Mike had guided him through three super hit records, and in America he was a big star. So far he had not yet cracked the European market, but they all had high hopes at Hampton Records that his new record *Teenage High* would be the one.

Mike smiled to himself. Convincing Cleo to come back was going to be a whole lot easier when he surprised her in London.

# 13

'We're in, Muff!' Jon shook her awake, waving a contract in her face. 'This came this morning, all it needs is your sweet little signature.'

Muffin yawned and rubbed her eyes. Jon was already searching around for a pen.

'I knew we were in as soon as Klauss the German started eyeballing your fanny in the photographs. He was drooling. Timed the whole thing perfectly. The pictures, then you making your entrance late. Perfect! Here, sign where the cross is.'

'I want to pee.' she said in a whiney voice, ignoring the pen that Jon was offering her. She wriggled out of bed and went into the bathroom.

He sat on the side of the bed and scanned the contract yet again. What a deal he had got for them!

In the bathroom Muffin splashed her face with cold water and stared at herself in the mirror. The face that launched a thousand products. She stuck out her tongue at her reflection. Without makeup she looked disgustingly like her sister.

'Come on, Muff,' Jon called. 'I want to get this contract in the post.'

She emerged from the bathroom. 'Jon,' she said sweetly, 'how's your divorce going?'

'What?' he questioned shortly.

'D I V O R C E.' she spelt it out.

'You know the problems.'

'Yeah. Bread—right?'

'Yeah. Right. Why?'

'Why hassle over money? We'll have plenty if I sign this contract.'

'Sure.'

'O.K. Settle with Jane, give her what she wants.'

He sighed impatiently. 'You know that's impossible. She wants fifty quid a week. the house, *and* all the kid's schooling, doctors, all that.'

'If I sign we can afford it.'

'Yeah, for a couple of months. But it's a lifetime deal. Who knows what I can afford next year.'

Muffin narrowed her eyes, 'I'm sick of waiting, I'll wait forever. I want you to settle with her, work it out. I want to get married. You *promised* we would get married. I'm not signing anything until you settle with Jane.'

'Now listen, Muff, don't be stubborn, don't be silly.'

She climbed back into bed. 'I mean it,' she said, 'and I won't be conned either. I want to see the papers from the solicitors before I sign anything.'

He frowned. She had him by the short and curlies and she knew it.

'Look, Muff . . .' he began.

She replied by burying her head beneath the covers.

Jon knew when he was beaten.

# 14

Butch Kaufman was the first actor on Cleo's list.

Butch Kaufman, a blond-haired, blue-eyed, all American sexy film star.

He had achieved fame as the star of a long running TV soap opera. 'Like being in um er prison for six years,' was the way he put it.

He was twenty-eight and had starred in six major blockbuster box office smash hits in the last four years. Along the way he had collected and discarded two wives. 'Never um er marry an actress,' was the way he put it.

He was currently in England filming, and Cleo met with him at the studio on her first day in London.

A lunch was arranged by an anxious press lady with fluttery hands who obviously planned to join them until Cleo told her politely but firmly that she only ever conducted interviews on a nobody else present basis. The press lady was put out, but *Image* was an important publication and she didn't want to blow it. She fussed round Butch, settling him in his seat, and then reluctantly she left with a departing whisper in his ear.

'What did she say?' Cleo asked.

'She um er told me you eat movie stars for breakfast.'

Cleo smiled. 'You're lucky then we didn't meet for breakfast.'

Butch laughed, and the ice was broken.

Cleo clicked on her tape recorder and started in with the questions.

An hour and a half later they parted friends.

'How long you um er here for?' Butch inquired.

'Just a week.'

'Maybe we could grab a bite to eat one night.'

'Maybe,' Cleo nodded. He wasn't a super stud, he was a pussy cat.

She sat back in the studio car that drove her back to the Connaught and played the tape over. There was some good stuff, he was interesting and funny.

At the hotel the temporary secretary she had hired was waiting.

'Transcribe this.' Cleo tossed her the tape. When she had it all typed out she would select the best quotes and write the story.

'Your husband called from America,' the secretary said. 'Would you call the International operator.'

'I have got to go out,' Cleo replied, 'if he calls again tell him to try again tomorrow.'

She took a taxi to Eaton Square. It was four o'clock and her mother was expecting her for tea.

Stella Lawrence was an immaculate woman of forty-eight. She was groomed from her short, chic, ash blond hair, to her waxed, thin, perfect legs. She greeted her daughter with an impersonal peck on the cheek. 'Wonderful to see you, darling.'

Stella had remarried rather well when Cleo's father had died of an unfortunate heart attack seven years previously. She had found herself a Greek shipping tycoon. It suited her that her twenty-nine-year-old daughter had gone off to live in America.

'You look magnificent,' Cleo said dutifully.

Stella smiled distantly. 'Do I? Do I really. darling? I'm such an old bag I'm amazed I'm still in one piece.'

Cleo suddenly realized that Stella had indulged in a face lift. There were no visible scars, but Cleo knew. could tell. 'How's Nikai?' she asked.

'Busy as ever. He wanted to see you, but he had to fly to Athens.'

'Oh, I'm sorry.' She suddenly felt incredibly scruffy and unattractive. Her mother had always somehow managed to make her feel like that.

'What about Mike?' Stella inquired. 'Is he going to join you here?'

It would be nice, Cleo reflected. to have the sort of mother one could confide in, but Stella wouldn't understand, she never had. Stella enjoyed men for their money. and their admiration of her. Stella wasn't interested in men as human beings.

'I don't think he will. Work pressure—you know.'

Tea was wheeled in on a trolley by a uniformed maid.

Cleo found herself eating all the wafer thin sandwiches and three cream cakes, while Stella just sipped at a cup of lemon tea.

'You'll get fat, dear,' Stella remarked disinterestedly.

She wondered if she could leave right after tea. Stella gave her a massive inferiority complex.

Later, back at the hotel, Cleo wrote her piece on Butch Kaufman. It pleased her, she hoped it had bite and humour. She wanted reaction to it, so she decided to take it along with her that evening. She was dining with an old friend. Dominique Last. They had been out of touch for four years. and she was looking forward to meeting her friend's husband, Dayan. Dominique had described him as 'big and handsome and clever'. He was an Israeli businessman. and they lived in a house in Hampstead, and had a baby of eighteen months.

Dominique looked as sensational as ever. She was a small compact girl with masses of red curly hair, and full seductive lips. They met in the bar of the Connaught, and the two women hugged.

'Show me a picture of the baby.' Cleo demanded.

Dominique nudged her husband. 'You've got the pictures.' He shook his head. 'Oh God. you're so stupid!' she exclaimed, and Cleo noted a look of anger pass between them.

Dayan was indeed big and handsome as Dominique had described him. But what about the clever? Married only three years and already clever had changed to stupid.

'I thought we would eat at *Mr Chows*.' Dominique announced over a campari and soda. 'Cleo. you look *so* well, and I do love your hair that way.'

Cleo's hair was a mild freakout of curls as she had still not had time to get to the hairdressers. 'It's a mass of frizz. What hairdresser do you go to now? I feel like such a tourist,' she said.

'Christine at Main Line. She's fabulous, you'll love her. Now tell me, I'm dying to know. how was Butch Kaufman? Is he divine?'

Cleo hesitated. Dominique seemed so different, sort of wound up and on show. She decided against displaying the Kaufman interview tucked safely in her shoulder bag.

'He was nice. sort of ordinary.'

'Ordinary!' Dominique hooted with laughter. 'You really are too much.'

So are you, Cleo thought, marriage seems to have changed you into a petulant bitch.

'We'd better go,' Dayan said, 'or we'll be late for our table.'

'Go get the car, darling, we'll meet you outside.' As soon as Dayan was out of sight, Dominique confided, 'He's so bloody boring, I don't know what's happened to him. He makes me want to scream. I'm seriously thinking of divorce.'

Cleo showed her surprise. 'But you seemed so happy—'

'Happy,' Dominique snapped, 'with him? He's only interested in the baby and TV. In that order. He has no interest in me or what I think or how I feel.'

'But you've only been married such a short time.'

'Yes I know. But we can't all find instant sex and happiness like you and Mike. I mean it, Cleo. I'm fed up, absolutely fed up.'

52

Dayan reappeared. 'The car's outside.'

At *Mr Chows* they were joined by Dayan's best friend, a thin wiry man by the name of Isaac. Dominique and Isaac spent the rest of the evening in close conversation. Cleo attempted polite talk with Dayan, but the intimate looks flashing between Dominique and Isaac were creating an uneasy situation.

It was with relief that Cleo arrived back at her hotel. She lay on her bed and thought about Mike. They had never reached that married limbo land of calling each other stupid in public. Indeed, Cleo didn't think that Mike *was* stupid. Surely if you put down your partner as an idiot you were putting down yourself for marrying them in the first place?

She sighed. Maybe it was time to talk to Mike. Maybe it was time to work things out

# 15

The trip was all set. Jet out of Kennedy the very next day. Mike James was pleased. Everything was going to work out perfectly. He could do the business he had to, get that out of the way. And then he and Cleo could spend a little time in London together. It would be romantic getting together in the city where they had first met.

He showered, and naked, started to sort out the clothes he thought he might take.

The doorbell rang, and he knotted a blue towel round his waist and went to answer it. Maybe it was Russell dropping by to commiserate. Well, there would soon be nothing left to commiserate about.

It was Cleo's good friend Susan. Susan of the big boobs and thick blond hair and unsuccessful acting career.

'Mike,' she said dramatically pushing past him, 'I'm so upset, so distraught!'

He trailed her into the living-room where she picked up a

cigarette package from the coffee table and shook out his last cigarette. She placed it between quivering lips and turned to him for a light.

He wondered how she managed to walk around without getting arrested. Mammoth unbra'd bosoms in a faintly transparent white shirt.

'I don't want to be responsible for breaking up your marriage,' Susan wailed, tears filling heavily mascaraed eyes. 'Cleo's my friend, my dearest friend.'

'Yeah, well . . .' Mike said lamely.

'I'm not a marriage breaker,' Susan said primly. 'I'm not even promiscuous.'

No, you just like fucking a lot—Mike thought. And why not? Nothing wrong with it. The name of the game was not getting caught.

'You haven't broken up any marriages,' he said kindly.

'I haven't? But I thought Cleo had left, gone.'

'Only on a business trip. Everything is cool, Susan. Cleo understands.'

'Oh!' Susan sat down deflated. 'I mean I heard—'

'Never believe everything you hear.'

'Ginny told me it was all over. I wouldn't have wanted to be the cause of anything so—well y'know—drastic.'

'I guess we picked the wrong place, wrong time.'

'I guess so,' Susan flicked her hands through her long blond hair. 'But it was nice, wasn't it?'

'It was very nice.' And it had been until Cleo had appeared at the office door. God, the shock of it. It was amazing really that he had been able to stay on the job.

Susan was wearing an unfashionably short skirt, and was it—Mike stared—yes it was—stockings and suspenders. He felt himself stir under the towel. And of course she immediately noticed, good little nymphomaniac that she was. Well, there was no hiding a hard-on under a towel. He remembered her body, ripe and luscious and juicy.

She licked full red lips. 'I wish you weren't married,' she said throatily.

Mike flicked the towel undone. 'Be a good girl, everything off except stockings and shoes.'

Susan smiled understandingly and stood up. Like a stripper she shed her shirt and skirt.

He had known she wouldn't be wearing any panties.

After all, he was battling with Cleo about Susan already. One more time wouldn't make any difference. And anyway—he *needed* it, it was purely a medicinal fuck.


After, Susan demanded a cigarette. Mike slipped on some clothes and went downstairs to get some from the corner drugstore.

He felt physically refreshed, but he hoped it wouldn't be long before he could get rid of good friend Susan. She was like rich cream cakes, you wanted them when you saw them, and felt sick when you had had them.

God, what was it with him? Why did he have such insatiable urges?

When he returned—surprise surprise—Susan was fully dressed and ready to leave.

'You really are a motherfucker!' she said daintily. 'Cleo phoned from London. It seems to me that she doesn't understand at all. She left you no message, and the message she gave *me* I wouldn't repeat.' Susan snatched the pack of cigarettes from him and made a good exit.

Mike swore to himself softly, he had done it again. But then of course you couldn't expect a girl who wore no panties to have the intelligence not to answer other people's phones.


# 16


Muffin posed prettily for the hordes of photographers. Legs crossed, shiny lips moistened, sweet bouncy tits straining at the neckline of her red gingham blouse.

A crowd had gathered in the usually quiet English park to watch her being photographed.

'Who is she?' a nanny inquired of a young photographer.

'Muffin,' he replied, as if that was explanation enough.

'She's got fat legs,' the nanny muttered to no one in particular. '*I've* got better legs than her.' She walked off pushing her pram disconsolately.

'Isn't she lovely,' a travelling charlady remarked, pausing to watch.

'Cor, I don't 'arf fancy 'er,' said a fourteen-year-old schoolboy to his friend.

'Yer,' agreed the friend, 'she looks a real wanker's special!'

'How about a few with the lucky lad,' one of the photographers asked, and Jon was reluctantly pushed in to the picture. He felt like a right fool. Behind the camera was his scene, but anything to make Muffin happy.

'We'll announce our engagement,' she had finally compromised, and signed the contract.

It had cost him six hundred quid for a lousy engagement ring. And God knew what it would cost him when Jane saw the engagement pictures. One thing he hadn't been able to change about Muffin was her stupid conventional working-class background. Marriage had been on her mind the moment they had moved in together. Christ, before you knew it she would be wanting kids.

'Smile,' one of the photographers demanded, 'you look dead gloomy.'

Jon attempted a smile. Muffin snuggled close to him and gave him a secret grope. He *felt* dead gloomy. Who needed a divorce to be rushed straight into another marriage?

A woman reporter with red hair and glasses asked, 'How does it feel to be engaged to every man's fantasy?'

'Great,' Jon managed a smile. 'Wait 'til you see the new calendar we'll be doing together. We're thinking of having a competition to find out what twelve fantasies your average guy in the street would like to have Muff portray.'

'What a good idea,' the lady reporter said. 'Perhaps our newspaper would be interested in organizing it.'

He perked up. 'I'm sure we could work something out.'

Muffin celebrated with lunch at the *Carousel* for a table full of mates. She didn't have what could be termed as any close

56

friends, but a certain select group of models were the closest to her.

Kamika, on her right, said, 'I hope it work out O.K. for you.'

Muffin grinned, 'I want babies, lots of babies!'

'You told Jon, darling?' inquired Erica. 'I don't get the impression he's in line for another family just yet.'

Muffin giggled. 'I'll surprise him!'

Beautiful black Laurie hooted with laughter. 'Some surprise, baby! Who *needs* all that crap. Nappies, washing, dirty little brats always buggin' you.'

'Children can be more than nappies and washing,' Kamika intoned primly.

'Bullshit!' exclaimed Laurie.

'Ladies, ladies,' said Erica sweetly, 'I'm sure our little Muffin knows what she wants.'

'I had the most incredible new guy last night,' Laurie announced, anxious to impart her news at the first opportunity.

'I didn't know there was such a thing as a *new* guy,' Erica said.

'Maybe not to you, baby,' Laurie retorted swiftly, 'we all know you've been through everyone!'

Muffin smiled dreamily. Soon she would be out of all this bitchy competition. 'Good key and lock?' she asked encouragingly.

Laurie laughed happily. 'Fantastic! Good solid stuff!'

'Japanese say quality not size that matter,' Kamika remarked.

'Yes, we all know that old wives' tale,' interjected Erica, 'if that was the case you'd still be married.'

'I get no divorce because of *size*,' Kamika explained patiently, 'I divorce because of *farting*.'

They all dissolved in laughter.

'Have I got a guy for you, Kam,' said Laurie brightly. 'He's got a prick the size of a cigarette, and terrific manners!'

Later Jon joined them, and they lolled around the restaurant until four-thirty, at which time Muffin insisted that they all come back to her place for tea.

'You can't even boil a kettle,' said Jon in the car, 'what's with the hostess bit?'

'I'm going to learn to cook,' she said excitedly, 'I'm going to turn you on with tasty little gourmet meals. Hang on a sec, stop at Lyons and I'll pop in and get some tea bags and cakes.'

Jon sat in the mini and waited. Jane had been a terrific cook. Great breakfasts, eggs, bacon, fried bread, the lot. Home-made teas. All the good cooking in the world couldn't hold a marriage together. Jane had turned from a free-thinking pretty young student into an unnattractive nag. Four years and two kids and he had a changed woman on his hands. He had decided then that marriage was definitely not his scene. However, his hands were tied, so marriage it would have to be. He loved Muffin as she was, he just hoped a thin gold band on the finger wasn't going to turn her into a split personality.

'Got buns with sticky jazz on top,' Muffin announced, bouncing back into the car. Passersby stopped to stare at her. The familiar face that they couldn't quite place. 'Why don't we buy champagne instead of tea?'

'Easy on, I spent every last penny cash on the ring.'

'We do have money in the bank, don't we? Let's make a cheque. Stop at Harrods.'

'I feel like tea.'

She pouted. 'You aren't half mean.'

'Yeah. That's why we've still got money in the bank.'

Erica had collected a boyfriend on the way, and Laurie asked if she could phone her fantastic new guy and ask him over.

'It's turning into a party,' Muffin said excitedly. 'I'm going to phone a few more people.'

Jon made a face at her.

By six o'clock the place was jammed. Jon had gone out for half a dozen bottles of cheap wine, and a new Barry White record was blaring on the stereo.

Jane phoned in the middle of it all. Jon could hardly hear her.

'I've changed my mind about the divorce settlement,' she screamed down the phone. 'I just caught a flash of your little tramp's ring in the evening paper. Christ, you must be rolling in it, and I'm sitting here like a pauper. Go on, enjoy your party, don't worry about your kids, I can't even buy them winter coats. You rotten bastard, you stinking . . .'

Jon replaced the receiver.

Problems. Always problems.

# 17

Cleo and Dominique lunched at *Rags*, a restaurant club in Mayfair. Dominique started the lunch with a vodka martini.

'Pretty good for a girl who didn't used to drink,' Cleo remarked.

'I do a lot of things I didn't used to do,' Dominique fluttered her hands nervously.

'So I noticed,' Cleo said dryly.

'Well it's all right for you,' Dominique was suddenly petulant, 'interesting job, glamorous life in New York. You get out, meet famous people. How would you like to be stuck in a house in Hampstead, with a baby, and an au pair, and a husband that takes you for granted.'

'Don't forget the lover.'

Dominique reddened. 'You always did know me better than anybody. But don't blame me. Isaac *cares* about me, Dayan wouldn't know the difference if I dyed my hair blue and posed naked for the *Sunday Times!* I gave up a terrific job to marry him, and now I feel I've wasted nearly three years.'

'Hardly a waste if you have a lovely baby to show for it.'

'I'm going to divorce him,' Dominique confided urgently.

'What are you waiting for then?'

'It's not easy. Isaac doesn't have any money, and I don't know if I could get my old job back. What I really need is a super rich man to come along and bail me out.'

'Charming! It's all down to economics now.'

Dominique adjusted a curl and smiled at a nearby acquaintance. 'I suppose it is. Listen, Cleo, Dayan doesn't even like sex any more. Give him a choice—*Match of the Day* or me, and guess which he would pick. He was practically a sex maniac when I married him. Thank God for my afternoons with Isaac or I'd go mad.'

'Cleo!' Shep Stone placed a triumphant hand on her shoulder. 'Quite a coincidence.' He stood by the table, a pleased smile suffusing his face. 'Did you like the flowers?'

'Lovely,' Cleo replied. Dominique was kicking her under the

table, so she added, 'Oh Shep. I'd like you to meet a friend of mine—Dominique Last—Shep Stone.'

Dominique fluttered her eyelashes. 'I've seen you on television, *loved* your last record.'

Shep regarded her with sudden interest, his smile broadened. 'I ain't Sinatra, but I manage to jog along.' He shot a look at Cleo to gauge her reaction to the fact that he was indeed a star. She had taken to studying the menu.

'How long are you here for?' Dominique inquired, and without even a pause for breath, she added, 'Why don't you join us?' She snapped delicately manicured fingers. 'Waiter! Another chair over here, please.'

The waiter rushed a chair over, but Shep still stood.

'I'm with some business associates.' He stared at Cleo, hoping she might press him to be seated, but she resolutely continued with the menu. 'Maybe just for a minute then.' He sat himself down.

Cleo stood up. 'I'm going to the loo,' she announced.

In the sanctuary of the ladies' room she stared at herself in the mirror angrily. God, it wasn't enough that she had problems of her own—problems that might be eased if there was only someone who cared enough to listen. But on top of everything else she had been lumbered with the one man that she had absolutely decided she couldn't stand. She had a vivid picture of him in her mind, red-faced and pleading, unzipping his fly and demanding 'just a little head'.

Dominique had asked him to join them, let Dominique be the one to get stuck with him.

Mind made up, she went to the reception desk and left a note for Dominique. Called away on business. She would probably be furious, but that was just too bad. I am sick of being nice to people, Cleo thought, the nicer you are the more you get taken advantage of.

She left enough money to settle the bill and taxied off on a shopping trip.

Two pairs of Yves Saint Laurent shoes, three silk shirts, one pair of Oliver Goldsmith sunglasses tinted green, and a Chloe dress later, she felt a lot better. Ease the tension by releasing some hard earned cash, there was nothing like it.

All her life Cleo had wished to be slightly tougher with people. She was the one that got stepped all over. People did not respect weakness, they sniffed it out like aromatic coffee, and then they trampled all over you.

'Can't you *ever* say no to a party?' Mike had often admonished. 'We never get any time at home, it's one goddam party after another.'

'I tried to say no,' she would murmur, 'but they insisted.'

When pushed far enough she could be tough. In her writing she was tough. With Mike she planned to be tough. Christ! The nerve of him. She had hardly left the country and he had moved Susan big boobs in. Well let him keep her there. Let him hump her until his tongue fell out. It proved she had made the right move.

Divorce was on her mind. One quick simple divorce.

# 18

'Geoff's coming over this morning to do the windows,' Muffin announced.

'He's what?' Jon inquired.

'Coming to clean the windows,' Muffin replied patiently, sticking out her toes and painting the nails in intricate white and green stripes.

'Why?'

'Because he said he wanted to. Said he was going to be in the district and would pop up and do them.'

'Jesus!! Don't know why you want *him* up here. He's verging on being a complete moron.'

'He's quite nice really.'

'Oh, he's quite nice really,' Jon mimicked her, 'and was he quite nice when you were going out with him?'

'I only went out with him a couple of times.'

'Oh yeah, that's right, your sister whipped him from under

your nose.' Jon finished dressing He was unaccountably angry.

Muffin sat cross-legged on the bed intent on the art job she was doing on her toes.

'You'd better get dressed,' Jon said irritably, 'can't greet your window-cleaner in your baby dolls, or is that the whole idea?'

She giggled. 'Don't be silly. If I'd known you were *jealous* I would have said no.'

'I'm not jealous.'

'It's just that the windows haven't been touched for ages, and I thought it was sweet of him to offer.'

'Sweet,' Jon said morosely. He had other problems to worry about. Jane. Their agreement. She was taking him to the cleaners, and because of Muffin's stupid insistence about marriage there was nothing he could do except agree.

'I'm off then,' he said. 'Thanks for the breakfast.'

Muffin bounced off the bed. 'Why didn't you say?'

'You knew I had to be at the solicitors at ten o'clock.'

'I'll make you something now.'

'Haven't got time.' He relented and kissed her on the nose. 'Get dressed,' he admonished, feeling under her shortie nightie, 'and put on knickers.'

When he left, Muffin resumed painting her toes. When they were finished she got out her makeup case and started on her face. She was dotting on the last of her freckles when the doorbell rang.

Scruff started to bark, and Muffin quickly inspected herself in the bathroom mirror. She ran a brush through her orange-tipped blond curls, and sprayed on some Estée perfume. Then, still in her skimpy nightie, she answered the door.

Geoff stood there looking slightly embarrassed. He wore blue dungarees with a bib front, a check shirt, and he carried a ladder and large bucket.

'Morning,' he said, 'this is your friendly neighbourhood window-cleaner.'

'Morning,' Muffin grinned, 'you'd better come in.'

She had arranged the whole thing. She had phoned Geoff and complained about the fact that their windows were in a terrible state and that they just couldn't get anyone and could he possibly come over and not to mention it to Penny as she would only think it was a liberty to ask.

Geoff had agreed. Muffin had said Tuesday morning would be perfect. She knew that Jon had an early appointment with his solicitor. She had worked the whole thing out carefully.

It still hurt the way that Geoff had used her. She had been fifteen, an impressionable age. He had picked her up in a cinema queue, bought her a ticket and a packet of crisps, chatted her up. Sat next to her and caressed her breasts, stuck his tongue in her ear, tried to explore under her skirt. The excitement of necking in a cinema at fifteen was hard to beat, especially with a good-looking older man. Geoff at the time was twenty-two. He had walked her home, and arranged another date.

Again the cinema, again the hot sticky unbearably exciting groping. He had undone her bra, practically got her knickers off. After, they had gone for a Wimpy, and he had said, 'Tomorrow night, John Wayne.'

With hammering heart she had met him the next evening. The back row, the same routine. But when finally he managed to jam a finger inside her she had whispered, 'I'm only fifteen, I'm a virgin.' He had moved his hand rapidly, then a few minutes later he had said he was going to get some chocolates.

That was the last she saw of him until Penny brought him home as her prospective bridegroom.

The agony she had felt at that time was secret and private. She had never told anyone. Then Jon came along, and when he made love to her the first time he didn't even realize she was a virgin. She had told him she had had lots of boyfriends. He liked her. He rescued her.

Moral. Girls who fuck are more popular.

Muffin had worked on it.

She became an extrovert. She became famous. She fell in love with Jon. Now they were to be married, but before that, well there was just one little matter to be resolved. A matter of pride. 'Cup of tea?' she asked.

'Never say no,' said Geoff.

She moved around the small kitchen aware of the fact that her nightie was almost transparent.

Geoff sat awkwardly on a chair and remarked, 'Nice little dog—come 'ere, fella, come on, boy.'

'How is Penny?' Muffin asked sweetly. She remembered her sister on her wedding day saying 'Geoff says he never even kissed you, is that true?' And she remembered herself replying, 'Yeah. True. He did stick his fingers in my drawers though.' Penny had stamped off to the altar red-faced and furious.

'She's fine,' Geoff said cheerily, 'fat and fine.'

'I wish she'd do something about herself. After the baby she should go on á strict diet.'

'I expect she will.'

Muffin yawned, 'Oh—I had such a late night. Lots of wine and lots of love,' she smiled softly, 'know what I mean?'

'Yeah.' He grinned. 'I think I do.'

'I get letters from complete strangers wanting to make love to me. They carry on about my face and my body.' She sat down. 'Hey, remember John Wayne?'

'Did *he* write to you?'

'No, stupid. John Wayne. The back row. Please, sir, I'm only fifteen.'

'Pardon?'

'Us.'

'Us?'

'When I was a silly little kid.'

It finally dawned on him. 'You mean when I took you out. Cor, when I see your picture all over the newspapers it doesn't seem real.'

'It was real. I didn't half fancy you.'

He took a loud gulp of his tea.

'Did you fancy *me*?' she persisted.

''Course I did.'

'Then why did you run out on me?' She whined plaintively, her bright blue eyes suddenly and unexpectedly filling with tears.

Geoff stared down at his tea. 'You was fifteen, only fifteen. Know what a bloke can get for interfering with a girl of fifteen?'

'But Penny was the same age,' she accused.

'Yeah, well that was different, wasn't it? I never touched her, never laid a finger on her until we was married.'

'Charming! What was I, the trailer?' She tugged down her nightie angrily, then blurted out, 'You know you're not nearly as good-looking as you were then. You used to look like Steve McQueen, now you look like Michael Caine gone wrong.'

He stood up. He was very tall. 'I never thought I'd have a chance with you,' he announced, 'not after you became famous and all that.' He was edging round the table towards her. 'Jon's a nice bloke, I wouldn't want to take any liberties.' He grabbed hold of her. 'Give us a kiss, darlin', give us a little encouragement.'

As his hands started to explore under her nightdress she sat perfectly still. This was it. This was the moment she had been waiting for. This was the man who had given her the first orgasm she had ever experienced while fiddling around under her sweater in the local Odeon.

He was at it again. Fiddle. Fiddle. Fiddle. His technique hadn't changed much. She squirmed more with aggravation than excitement.

'Take it easy,' she complained, 'you're not tuning a television!' She noticed the bulge in his jeans and it didn't look that big. Jon was big. Jon had a terrific technique.

'I think you're a smashing little bird,' Geoff was mumbling, 'a real little darlin'.'

She pushed him away. Poor Penny, she hadn't got hold of any big deal.

Businesslike, she stood up. 'I'm going to get dressed,' she announced. 'You'd better start on the windows, Jon will be back in a minute.'

# 19

Ramo Kaliffe, Arabian film star extraordinary. Dark curls tipped with grey, olive skin, broody black eyes, and a voice tinged with Eastern promise.

Cleo met him in the bar at the Dorchester. He clutched her hand, stared into her eyes, and muttered, 'You are very beautiful.'

She had her opening line for the story. Ramo Kaliffe has a voice that sounds like hot molasses buried in sticky treacle. His eyes are as hot as desert sands, red-tinged like the sunset.

Cleo smiled to herself, and he took it as a sign that she liked compliments and launched into his full display.

How she longed to say, 'Shall we cut the bullshit, Mr Kaliffe, and get down to a really interesting interview?'

Butch Kaufman had told her that underneath the Desert Arab lurked a thoroughly likeable, very Westernized, amusing man.

An hour and a half later she found him, and soon he was telling a series of funny stories against himself.

When finally she clicked off the tape recorder and said she had enough he insisted that she join him and some friends for dinner. She agreed. He was nice, he was funny, and he was devastatingly attractive, bloodshot eyes and all.

It had been a confusing day. Mike and Susan were on her mind, and she couldn't shake off the feeling of disappointment. One lay with a girl like that—O.K. But moving her in? Definitely not O.K.

Dominique had phoned, she was delighted, in fact she didn't even mention the fact that Cleo had absented herself in such a fashion from lunch.

'Shep Stone is the most exciting man I have ever met,' Dominique enthused. 'He's vibrant and strong, and so down to earth for a star.'

'I take it you like him.' Cleo's sarcasm was ignored.

'I think this is the man I have always been waiting for. I did something with him today that I have never done before.'

'What was that?'

'I slept with him!' Dominique announced dramatically.

'You've done that before.'

'Not an hour after meeting,' Dominique replied coldly. 'The vibrations were too strong, neither of us could resist. We were both helpless. We went to his hotel and fell upon the bed like two people possessed.'

'It's not called possession, it's called frustration.'

'I didn't think you would understand. It's probably never happened for you like this. I'm leaving Dayan.'

'What about Isaac?'

'What about him?' Dominique said irritably. 'He was just a passing fancy. Shep means everything to me.'

'My God, you sound demented. Are you sure Shep feels the same way about you?'

There was a pause, then, 'I think so. I'm almost sure. I mean nothing was said, but after, he had to rush and I had to get home. It was too beautiful to spoil with words. That's why I'm phoning, Dayan will be home in a minute and I can't seem to reach Shep, so I thought that maybe you could phone him and say I'll meet him for lunch tomorrow.'

'I'm not phoning him. If you can't reach him leave a message.'

'Thanks a lot. I thought you were a friend.'

'I am a friend, not a message service. And take some advice from me, don't leave Dayan until you check out with Shep that he wants you to. I suggest you also ask him about his current wife and the two that went before.'

'You're jealous,' Dominique accused. 'I wondered why you disappeared at lunch. Couldn't take the fact that he fancied me and not you. Really, Cleo, since you got back I find you very changed, I—'

'Oh for Christ's sake!' Cleo slammed the phone down.

Had she changed? Maybe for the better if it meant getting a clear view of someone like Dominique.

Ramo's friends for dinner included Butch Kaufman with a frizzy haired girl; and a small Danish blond who eyed Cleo suspiciously and hung tightly on to Ramo's arm.

They went to *Trader Vics* and feasted on spare ribs and Indonesian lamb roast. Navy grogs were the drink of the evening, and Cleo soon felt that very special glow that one gets from good food, interesting company, and turn-on booze.

Ramo divided his attention between Cleo and the small blond, likewise Butch and the frizzy haired lady.

Cleo thought—it's time to even up the score. Butch or Ramo? She liked them both. They were both attractive in different ways. Neither as attractive as Mike though. Mike had the most amazing eyes, and the most amazing balls.

I'm drunk—Cleo thought—no rash moves while I'm drunk.

But later, when they all went to *Tramp*, crushed against Ramo on the dance floor she decided she would have one of them. Like a man she felt horny, and like a man she would pick a suitable mate and screw just for the sheer sensual pleasure of screwing. No strings. If Mike could do it and enjoy it she saw no reason why she couldn't.

The only problem was which one. Ramo was fun, but a little obvious, and not too particular. He had already had the small blond earlier in the day, a fact that the small blond had insisted on confiding.

Butch was a more promising proposition. He had a stud reputation, but if you wanted to screw what better than a stud?

The girl with the frizzy hair was so stoned that she wouldn't even notice if Butch vanished.

Ramo asked her to dance, and pulling her towards him with a firm grip he suggested a threesome. 'You, me, and the little Dane.'

Cleo declined, 'Not my scene.'

'You a married lady?' Ramo questioned.

'Why?'

'Married ladies usually love threesomes.'

'Including their husband or not?'

Ramo threw his head back and laughed. 'I like you. Shall I get rid of the blond and make beautiful love to you?'

Cleo couldn't help smiling. Here at last was a truthful man.

Back at the table Butch was throwing her moody looks while his frizzy haired friend danced by herself on the packed dance floor.

'You going with lover boy?' he inquired.

'No, I'm coming with you.'

Butch nodded. 'Great. Let's go.'

He was renting an apartment in Mayfair. It was all plush leather and dimmed lights.

'Not my um er style,' Butch drawled. 'In L.A. I've got this great beach house in Malibu. Sea swirling about at your front door, sun, sand. You get up in the morning, straight in the ocean for a swim, jog along the beach, barbecued bacon for breakfast. Can't beat it. Do you smoke?'

Politely he offered her a joint. Politely she accepted it.

'My stand-in scores the best grass in town,' he said proudly, 'good huh?'

She nodded. It was good, very good to just relax and let all her tensions hang out.

'I guess you're always being told how beautiful you are. When you came to interview me you blew my mind. How come you're not into the model actress bag?'

'Why should I be? Are girls with looks supposed to all follow the same ballgame?'

'Nope. Guess not. Prettiest girl I ever knew was a schoolteacher.' Slowly he leaned over and undid the buttons on her silk shirt.

She leaned back and drew strongly on the joint, letting the smoke drift in a slow swirl towards the ceiling.

He undid her bra which clipped at the front, and she shrugged it off. Then she stood up and unzipped her St Laurent trousers and stepped out of her brown lace bikini pants.

Butch stood up too and stripped off his clothes.

They smiled at each other, then he pulled her very close, and quietly, with their hands, they explored each other's bodies.

They made love standing up until both their bodies were covered with a thin film of sweat.

'You've got to be fit to do it this way,' Butch gasped.

Cleo's eyes were shut, a half smile hovered round her lips.

'Hey, baby? What do you think? Together?' Butch asked.

She arched back even further. A purely physical fuck. Like Mike she could enjoy it too. 'Any time you're ready.'

Together they came, then collapsed on the floor laughing.

'Jesus!' Butch exclaimed, 'you are too much. No sobbing and moaning and I love yous.'

'Did you want them?'

'Hell no.'

She dressed. 'It was lovely, I'm going home now.'

He shook his head in admiration, 'Miss Cool. Will I see you again?'

'Around.'

She took a taxi back to the hotel. It was true. A woman could enjoy it as much as a man.

She felt free, high, very confident.

O.K. Mike. If we've got anything left to work out let's work it out on equal terms.

She ignored the phone which began to ring, and went to sleep.

# 20

The weeny boppers were out in full force at Kennedy airport. Small, sweaty, pubescent little figures darted here and there, screaming and wailing. One tiny little blond stood quietly sobbing.

Mike reviewed the scene with customary amazement. He had seen it many times before but it never failed to amaze him. Where did they all come from in their minis and their boots and their Marty Pearl emblazoned sweaters? What about school? What about their parents? What kind of life did they lead that they could just forget everything and spend a day running around Kennedy airport hoping for a glimpse of their idol?

They were all so young. 'I'm eleven,' one little girl had lisped proudly when he had inquired. Eleven! He was no stranger to the way these girls got treated if singled out for attention by any of the pop groups or their entourage. Eleven!

They were travelling by commercial jet. There was Marty. His backing group. His manager. His dresser. His publicity man. His mother. And of course Mike.

The hostesses were flashing bright smiles and serving drinks. Little Marty Pearl ordered a scotch and his manager laughed and said, 'What a joker!' and changed the order to orange juice.

Lately, Little Marty Pearl was getting rather pissed off at still being sixteen.

When the flight was under way, and Omar Sharif was chasing Julie Andrews on the cinema screen, Little Marty's manager, Jackson, came and sat himself down next to Mike. He was a youngish guy with prematurely grey hair and watery blue eyes.

'The kid's getting impossible.' he remarked glumly. 'I try to isolate him. but what you gonna do—he's gonna be nineteen in two months.'

'You're doing a great job. His reputation is clean as a whistle. Doesn't drink. Doesn't smoke. Doesn't fuck. What more do you want?'

'It ain't easy, Mike. One of these days I'm just not gonna be able to tell him what to do. Besides, everywhere we go we got groupies climbing up the wall. Caught one giving the electrician a blow job the other day in the hope that he'd take her over to Marty.'

Mike laughed. 'Maybe the time has come to find him an official girlfriend.'

'She'd get torn to bits. Listen, the kid is getting very randy. I've thrown a couple of professional pieces his way in the last month and he's lapped it up. At least hookers keep their mouths shut. We can't afford a girlfriend yet—the fans just wouldn't like it.'

Mike shrugged. Little Marty Pearl's sex life was really not his problem. Cleo was his problem. No way was he going to allow four years of pretty incredible marriage to be swept out of the way like so much garbage. He would go straight to her hotel. Surprise her. Make love to her. They would forget about the past. He would promise to be a good boy. and she would agree that it would be stupid for a girl like Susan to come between them.

In future, Mike decided. if he felt like playing around he would be very very careful. Discreet, that was the word.

Jackson said conversationally. 'Last time I was in London I had the best piece of ass this side of heaven.'

'Oh yeah.' Mike replied politely.

Jackson's watery blue eyes filled with emotion, 'Fat juicy little redhead. Stoned shitless, but what a lay!'

'You going to see her this trip?'

'Naw.' Jackson shook his head in disgust. 'don't even know her name.'

'Excuse me, Mr Jackson,' Little Marty Pearl's mother was standing in the aisle. Emma Pearl was a woman of forty who looked a great deal older. Her husband was dead, and Marty was an only child.

'Yeah?' Jackson looked her over with the resignation he usually felt for her requests.

Emma Pearl plucked nervously at the collar of her dress, 'I was wondering if the accommodations arranged include adjoining suites for me and Little Marty. I was most disturbed in Philadelphia when I found myself on a different floor of the hotel.' Her voice started to rise, 'After all, Mr Jackson, *you* know that Little Marty likes me to be near. He *needs* me near him. He—'

'Sure,' Jackson cut her off, 'I'm sure it will all be fine in London. No problem.'

'You know I don't like to be a bother, Mr Jackson. You know I never cause trouble. But Little Marty likes me near him.' Emma Pearl bit on her lower lip nervously. 'He wants me by his side.'

'Quite right.' Jackson nodded reassuringly, and Emma Pearl went back to her seat on the plane. 'Piss off, you old crow,' Jackson muttered in her wake. 'Jesus!' he exclaimed to Mike. 'We gotta do something about her. Marty's bugging the crap out of me—get rid of her—keep her away—stop her following me. She still thinks he's fucking thirteen.'

'Why is she on the trip then?'

'"Cos Marty ain't got the balls to tell her he's a big boy now. He expects her to come along and stay out of the way. And who's supposed to keep her out of his way? Guess who? Schmuck face, yours truly, that's who.'

Mike nodded, 'Relatives always turn out to be a drag. I guess a mother is better than a wife though.'

'Maybe. The mother scene is bad enough. The wife scene I don't wanna even imagine! Gives me bad vibes, know what I mean?' Jackson tailed off, suddenly remembering that Mike was married.

In London it was raining, and in spite of the fact that Little Marty had never had a hit record outside of America, there was a massive crowd of young girls waiting to greet him.

'We set up 'bout a hundred,' Jackson remarked enthusiast-ically, 'but there seems to be nearly a thousand.'

There was a fleet of cars to meet them, and Mike managed to push past the photographers and crowds, and commandeered a car to himself. He had plans to head straight for Cleo's hotel. There was nothing he could do for Little Marty, he was surrounded by people ready to deal with his every whim. Really Mike was only along on the trip to keep an executive eye on things. And of course, as far as he was concerned, to meet and make up with Cleo.

In the car he rehearsed his opening lines. Should he apol-ogize? Explain? Lie?

Actions always spoke louder than words. He would give her some action.

He smiled to himself. He always *had* been known as the man with the answer to every problem.

# 21

Jon Clapton was worried. He had committed himself. He had arranged to sign a large chunk of himself in payments to his soon-to-be ex-wife.

One hundred quid a week she had finally demanded, plus the usual benefits such as children's school fees, doctor bills, dentist bills. He had baulked at holidays. Surely on a hundred quid a week she could scrape enough together to manage a couple of weeks in Brighton.

Cow! Bitch! Women!

It had been a long haul to pull himself up into the money, and now that he was nearly there Jane would be hanging round his neck like a financial albatross.

However. It would be worth it. Now he would be free to marry Muffin, and Muffin stood for money. Together there would be no stopping them. The Schuman Calendar deal alone would take care of their monetary affairs for the next year at least. And after that, well who knew? Muffin had incredible potential.

He hadn't told her yet the full scope his plans for her. Dancing lessons. Singing lessons. Drama coaching. She had natural talent. With a little bit of polishing she could become a star. She already had the name. Everybody knew her. Her picture appeared in one or the other national papers practically daily. Comedians made jokes about her on television. She received hundreds of admiring letters a month.

Jon was confident she had what it takes to become much more than just a sexy body and a pretty face.

Today was an important day for Muffin. A journalist on one of the big daily papers had requested an interview with her. It was important that now she started to come across as a personality, and Jon had coached her in how she should behave.

'Anthony Private is a prick,' he had warned her, talking of the journalist who was to do the interview, 'he'll try to charm the knickers off you with his small chat, but just remember that he's a bitch, probably a closet queen, and jealous as hell.'

'Will I fancy him?' Muffin had asked coyly.

'Only if you fancy skinny geezers with glasses and thin mean lips. Oh, and do me a favour, Muff, if he tries to give you one the answer is very definitely no.'

'Yes,' said Muffin.

'Yes?' questioned Anthony Private incredulously.

'Yes,' confirmed Muffin, 'I was thirteen.'

'That seems awfully young,' Anthony mumbled unsurely.

'How old were *you* then?'

'Me?' Anthony Private coughed nervously. '*I'm* interviewing *you.* I don't think how old I was is really relevant.'

'Just curious. I bet you were a late starter.'

Anthony reddened and quickly changed the subject. 'How do you feel about thousands of men ogling your naked body every day?'

'Chuffed.'

'Pardon?'

Muffin openly yawned. She had spent an hour and a half over

74

lunch with Anthony Private, and she was bored. He asked stupid questions in a stupid high-pitched voice, and she was amazed that this was the man who had a full page weekly in a national daily paper.

'If looking at me in the buff turns old geezers on then I'm chuffed. Like it's a giggle, right?'

Anthony threw her a disdainful look. 'How does your father feel?'

'You have a cold sore on your lip,' Muffin pointed out accusingly, 'you know what that comes from don't you?'

'No, I don't,' said Anthony irritably, 'and I don't want you to tell me either. What about your father?'

'*He* doesn't have any cold sores; and I've got a lovely mum.'

'Christ!' Anthony heaved a sigh of despair, and called for the bill. 'What are you doing now?' he inquired of Muffin.

'Having lunch with you,' she stated in surprise.

'I mean now—when we leave here. Are you going home?'

She shrugged. 'Hadn't thought. Why?'

'I would like to see where you live. Get a sort of background picture.'

'Oh, all right. Come back for coffee. But I'm telling you now—no nooky.'

'I can assure you I wouldn't dream of it.'

'No, I didn't think you would!'

Over coffee at Muffin's Holland Park flat Anthony Private snapped, 'Do you make a lot of money doing nothing?'

'Pardon?' Muffin asked. She was not used to people who were arrogant and sly and jealous.

'How much money do you make a year?'

Jon had often instructed her never to discuss the money that they made, so she said hesitantly, 'I'm not really into money, my boyfriend sort of takes care of that side of things.'

'Women's lib would love you,' said Anthony dryly. 'What do you think of your looks?'

'I should like to be taller, you know, sort of a Verouchka type lady. And I should like to have longer thinner legs.'

Anthony Private stood up. 'O.K.,' he said, 'I think I have everything I want.'

Muffin smiled nicely. She sensed that he didn't like her, but she didn't want him to know that the feeling was mutual.

'Goodbye.' She scooped up Scruff and walked her guest to the door. 'See you again I hope.'

When he was gone she burst into tears. She didn't know why, he just made her feel sad. After a while she recovered, and full of new energy she stomped off to Harrods. If you were into shoplifting Harrods was *the* place.

# 22

'Mrs James,' Mike told the receptionist confidently.

'Mrs James checked out this morning.'

'She can't have.'

'I can assure you that she did.'

'Where has she gone?'

'I'm sorry, sir. I'm afraid I cannot reveal information about our guests' movements unless they request that we do so.'

'I'm her husband.'

'I'm sorry, sir. Mrs James left no forwarding address, but she will be returning to us on the twenty-fourth of this month.'

'That's three days. You mean you have no idea where she's gone?'

'Sorry.'

'Can I get a room?'

'I'm sorry, sir. We are fully booked.'

'Jesus H. Christ!'

He deposited his suitcase with the hall porter, and made his way to the bar. What timing! A mad dash all the way across the Atlantic and she was gone. He didn't even know where to.

Russell Hayes would probably know. She had obviously taken off to interview someone. He had known that she wasn't going to stay in London the entire time, but he had thought at least a week.

Now he couldn't even get a room in her hotel. He would be forced to join the Marty Pearl entourage over at the Europa. A drag.

He swallowed two fast scotches to drown his disappointment He was really starting to miss her. Badly. In fact so much that if Susan hadn't presented herself at his apartment and made herself readily available then he wouldn't even have bothered to get himself laid. For the first time in years he was off casual sex. He was concentrating on building up one hell of a hard-on for his own wife.

He took a taxi over to the Europa where there were lots of little girls milling about outside. There was a suite booked for him, and he placed a call to Russell in New York. Then he got through to Jackson on the house phone to find out how everything was going.

'A breeze,' Jackson informed him, 'gonna tuck Little Marty up for the night, and then I'm gonna find myself a nice tight little piece of English country. You wanna join me?'

Mike declined. He felt tired, a touch of jet lag. And besides he wanted to try and find out where Cleo was.

Russell Hayes did not call back for an hour.

'I don't know where she is,' he informed Mike, 'as long as she mails her stuff in on time she's a free agent.'

'Thanks a lot. You're a big help.'

'If you find her have her call me.'

'How can I find her?'

'I don't know, she's your wife. Call her mother, her friends.'

'Thanks Russ. I can always depend on you for fuck all.'

He didn't know where to contact her mother. He couldn't remember any of her friends. In fact her life before he had met her was a closed book, one he had never bothered to open.

He called down to room service and had them send up a menu. There was nothing he felt like. He certainly did not feel like sitting alone in a hotel room all night. He pulled on his leather jacket and went out.

In the hotel corridor a bizarre sight greeted him. Mrs Emma Pearl was sitting on a cushion outside the door to her son's suite. She jumped up nervously when she saw him.

'What are you doing?' he inquired incredulously.

77

'I am seeing that Little Marty is all right.'

'Oh.' he said. 'I see.' He paused for a moment. glancing along the corridor to see if they were being observed. They were not. 'Why are you *outside* his room?'

Emma Pearl blushed. ashamed of her own eccentricity. 'He doesn't want me inside.'

Mike nodded. The woman was obviously mad. 'Where's Jackson?'

'He has gone out for dinner. They have all gone out for dinner. They have left Little Marty alone. and frankly. Mr James. I just don't think it's right. Why. only five minutes ago a dreadful blond girl tried to get into his room. She said he had sent for her. Of course I knew she was lying and I got rid of her. If I hadn't been here she would have probably got in. Mr James. he's only a young boy. and idolized by these stupid girls. He shouldn't be left alone.'

'Mrs Pearl, he's nearly nineteen.'

Emma rolled her eyes wildly. '*We* know that. Mr James. But to the world he is sixteen. and sweet sixteen he must stay.'

Mike shrugged. At that moment the door to Marty's suite was flung open and Little Marty himself stood there. He was a short boy with a cowlick of blondish hair falling on his forehead. and big brown eyes. Clad in a white towelling dressing-gown he had none of the strut of the boy who appeared on stage in skintight white leather and high heeled studded boots. A rash of angry red spots was gathering on his chin. He had been about to scream abuse at his mother. but upon seeing Mike he quickly shut up.

'Hey, Marty,' said Mike. 'I thought you were having an early night. You've got a real bastard tomorrow.'

'Yeh,' agreed Marty. 'I was.' He glanced expectantly along the corridor. 'Tell my ma to get off to bed. Mike.'

'That's just what I was doing. Come along. Mrs Pearl. Marty's going to get some sleep. he's perfectly safe.' He led her off towards the elevator. winking at Marty. 'Get to bed.'

Mrs Pearl said in a tired disappointed voice. 'I'm not even on the same floor. I *told* Mr Jackson I wanted to be near my boy.'

'Sure,' Mike soothed, 'you stay in your room for tonight and I'll see what I can arrange for tomorrow.'

He deposited her on the floor above, and then took the elevator down to the lobby. 'Which is the young lady for Mr Pearl?' he inquired at reception. They pointed out a blue-jeaned blond waiting for a taxi.

Mike went over to her. 'It's O.K. now,' he said, 'Marty's waiting.'

She gave him a toothy grin. 'You sure? Some batty old lady is guarding his room.'

'The coast is clear.'

'Thanks, sugar.'

She wriggled her way over to the elevator and he admired her ass.

Poor Little Marty. What use was it being a pop star if you couldn't even get laid in peace?

# 23

The flight to Nice, in the South of France, was very pleasant. Cleo made sure that she didn't sit next to any unattached men. Instead she found herself next to a very pretty lady who was celebrating her divorce by taking a holiday.

'I had seven years of misery,' she confided to Cleo, 'just me, him, and his bloody mother. I saw more of *her* than I did of *him!*'

At Nice Airport Cleo hired a car, a small grey convertible. She had wanted to drive along the coastal road but the summer traffic was so bad that she changed her mind and switched to the autoroute.

Just under three hours later she arrived in St Tropez. Hot and dusty she checked into the Byblos Hotel.

She had a cold bath and put on the bikini she had purchased in a hurry before leaving London. She attempted to phone the office of the film company whose star she had arranged to interview. No one who seemed to know anything about it, so she decided to phone back later.

She felt awkward going out to the hotel pool alone. Women on their own always seemed so vulnerable. Other women summed them up as potential rivals, and men summed them up on their probable bedability. Baby—you've come a long way was bullshit. Women were still the second classes of the world. Judged on their looks. Judged on their morals. A man who screwed around was 'clever old Fred'. A woman was still regarded as an old scrubber.

Ten minutes after settling on a mattress, applying sun tan oil, and ordering a long cool drink, the first man appeared. He was short and extremely hairy.

'Just arrived?' he questioned in English tinged with cockney.

'No,' replied Cleo coldly.

'Oh. I thought you had.' He squatted down next to her. 'Want a drink?'

'I have a drink.' She got up, dived in the pool, and left him squatting. She stayed in the pool until he left.

The next arrival was French with a deep mahogany oiled body. He didn't waste any time. 'You like to have good evening dancing tonight?'

She ignored him.

He made a face and drifted off, to be quickly replaced by a blond German who hovered beside her and commented on how boring it must be to have men chasing her all the time. She ignored him too, and word must have gone around because after that she wasn't bothered any more.

After two hours of sun she went inside and tried to phone the film company again. This time she got the publicity man, and an appointment was made for her to meet Sami Marcel for lunch the following day.

'Tahiti beach, one o'clock,' the publicity man said. 'We shall be filming there all morning, so if you want to come by earlier and watch the action just do so.'

Great. St Tropez. Alone. No desire to be with anyone. But what was there to do alone?

Female on her own. Instant pick-up. Already proved.

There was no alternative but a long and boring evening in her hotel room.

Sami Marcel was tall, sinewy, and ugly in a way that was devastatingly attractive. He had horse teeth, a large nose, fleshy lips, and he was the current heart-throb of France.

Cleo had taken the publicity man's advice and arrived at Tahiti Beach early to watch them shooting. She and several hundred other ladies. The area in which they were filming was roped off, and Cleo had to literally fight her way through to reach the location. She used her school French, and the publicity man came over and helped her over the ropes.

'Sami's a great guy,' he told her swiftly, 'got a reputation for being a pain in the ass, but believe me, he's a lot of fun.'

The film crew was American. It was Sami's first American film, and as such quite important for him.

They were shooting a scene that involved Sami walking alone along the water's edge. He was wearing white trousers rolled up around the ankles. His chest was bare, and a large gold disc hung round his neck.

In her mind Cleo composed the beginning of the story she would write. 'Sami Marcel looks like he should smell strongly of garlic. According to his legion of girl friends he does.'

It was boring watching the filming. Take one. Sami strolling along. Cut. No good. Break. Take two. Sami strolling along. Cut. Sami sneezed. Take three . . . and so on and so on.

Cleo lay back on the sand and slipped her shirt off. The sun was hot, and she closed her eyes and enjoyed it. It would be nice to have come here with Mike. He loved the sun, he could lay unmoving for hours. She wondered if he would take Susan to the sun. She wondered if he missed her. Probably not as much as if he lost his bloody Ferrari.

The call came to break for lunch, and she looked around for the publicity man. He came puffing up looking harassed.

She put her shirt back on over her bikini. 'We have an hour, right?' she asked briskly.

'Yeah, well Sami usually takes a short break before lunch, but I'll take you over to the restaurant, he shouldn't be long.'

The restaurant was at the back of the beach. Wooden tables, striped umbrellas. and tight-assed waiters.

There was one long table in the middle set up for about twenty people. and the publicity man sat Cleo at it.

'Hey.' she objected. 'I have to interview Sami on his own, I told you that from London.'

'Yeah. I know. We'll work it out. Sami has to be handled, he's been treated badly by the press.'

'What do you mean—he has to be handled? I arranged to interview him and everything was supposed to have been set up.'

The publicity man looked sheepish. 'He's a difficult guy, he's moody. I'm sure when he meets you he'll give you some time.'

'Gee. thanks a lot.' Her tone was cold with sarcasm. 'I just don't work this way. I've come all the way from London for this interview and now I'm supposed to take my chances that he'll give me a few minutes.'

'I'm sorry. I'm sure it will work out.'

'Bullshit. You are just not doing your job properly. If Sami Marcel doesn't like interviews say so up front. Don't drag people down here on spec. It won't do you. the film. or Sami any good.'

Some of the crew from the beach were sitting down. The director. The cameraman. The continuity girl.

Cleo was really furious. Oh God—was she going to do a scorcher on Mr Marcel. If he thought he was badly treated by the press wait until *she* had finished with him.

He arrived after half an hour. A brunette nymphet on one arm, and a curly blond on the other. Both girls were wearing just the tiniest bottom half of their bikinis. The brunette was compact and small, with boyish suntanned bosoms. The blond was more ample with bouncy breasts that still featured white marks from the recent confines of a bikini top.

On looking around Cleo realized that most of the females in the restaurant were topless, and there was a dazzling array of unfettered breasts. Big ones, small ones, perky. droopy. Take your choice.

Sami sat opposite her, his girlfriends clinging to an arm each. His horse teeth were extremely white, and his eyes were black and broody.

The publicity man said nervously. 'Sami, this is the lady I was telling you about. *Image* Magazine, remember?'

Sami ignored him. He listened to the whispers of the blond on his left, and absently stroked the shoulder of the girl on his right.

Cleo leaned foward. 'Monsieur Marcel,' she said firmly, 'my name is Cleo James. I'm from *Image* Magazine, and it was arranged that I should interview you.'

Sami's eyes swept over her without a flicker of interest. 'Why are you all bundled up in a shirt?' he demanded. 'Where are your titties?' He banged on the table, acquiring an admiring audience. 'Put them on the table, woman, where they belong!'

Cleo felt the blush sweeping over her face like a wave. What a pig. She tried to ignore his rudeness, to keep her cool.

'Sami,' the publicity man attempted a laugh that was stillborn in his throat, 'don't joke. Miss James is with *Image* Magazine. It's a biggie in America,' desperately he added. 'A real biggie.'

'And her titties?' Sami inquired, 'are they—how you say—biggies too?' He roared with laughter, and the girls on either side of him laughed too.

Cleo had recovered her composure. 'Monsieur Marcel,' she said sweetly. 'When you see fit to expose your balls maybe I'll join you and take off my top. Until that time comes why don't we just both keep our clothes on.'

Sami narrowed his eyes. 'A woman should not talk like that,' he said sternly. 'A woman should be soft, pleasurable.' He looked around the table to make sure everyone was listening, then continued expansively. 'A woman should be feminine, sweet, quiet. A woman should be a mother when required, and a whore when required. Most women seem to combine those qualities admirably.'

'Do they?' Cleo asked sarcastically. She had managed to switch her small Sony tape recorder on and was getting every word.

'But of course,' he fingered the blond's bouncy breast and her nipple hardened under his touch. 'Women are beautiful playmates to be loved and to be kept in their place.'

'And what—in your opinion—is their *place*?'

'Oh, at home, in the bedroom, the kitchen,' Sami said vaguely. 'They are decorative creatures, they don't belong in man's domain.'

Cleo laughed, 'You have the strong aroma of a male chauvinist pig.'

Sami did not like to be laughed at, 'You must be a lesbian,' he stated.

Cleo laughed even louder. 'Jesus! You really are too much. Is any woman who doesn't agree with your philosophies supposed to be a dyke?'

Sami stared at her, his thick lips pursed together with disapproval. 'I think you are frustrated.' he said shortly, 'I think you need a man to make love to you. To fuck you properly.'

'Fuck you too.'

Sami stood up from the table, his eyes flashing angrily. 'You have a mouth like a sewer.'

Cleo was unperturbed. 'Just following the great master.'

Sami's mouth twitched nervously, then with a sudden angry gesture he strode away from the table.

The publicity man was sweating. 'You shouldn't have done that.'

Cleo treated him to a look of scorn, 'Listen, I *do* what the situation calls for, and this situation was caused by your incompetence.' She stood up from the table. 'Anyway, as it happens it all worked out O.K. I'm sure I have a most enlightening interview. Thanks for lunch.'

She walked back to her car.

Monsieur Marcel look out!

# 24

'He's a rotten, stinking, filthy swine!' Muffin screamed. 'An uptight, stupid, limp dick idiot! I hate him, Jon, *I hate him.*'

'Stop screaming. Calm down.'

'You'd be bloody screaming.' Muffin picked up the newspaper she had flung on the floor in her fury. 'Listen,' she said shrilly. Short, Fat, and Rich! And that's only the heading! How would *you* like to be described as short, fat, and rich?'

'I wouldn't mind the rich.'

Muffin narrowed her blue eyes. 'Can I sue him?'

'What for?'

'Well, detrimental treatment, damage to my character, *you* know what I mean.'

'Don't be silly.'

'Why is it silly?' She thrust the newspaper in his face. 'Read it again, read the insults, and look at the picture, three years moulding away in their files. *I don't look like that any more.*'

'It's not *that* bad, Muff.'

'Oh, isn't it? Isn't it?' She started to cry. 'How can I go out and face people? How can I go to the cleaners?'

'The cleaners?'

'Yes, the bloody cleaners. They know me there, they cut out my pictures. How can I ever collect my suede skirt?'

'When you are in the public eye,' Jon explained patiently, 'you must expect all sorts of publicity. True. Untrue. Good. Bad. Just read it and if it's bad forget it. Everyone else does.'

'I want to take out a full page ad in *Private Eye*. I want it to say Anthony Private is a Prick—in big black type. I *mean* it, Jon.'

'O.K.,' he humoured her. 'Although why waste the money? Anyone who's ever read his page *knows* he's a prick. They expect him to write like a bitchy college queen, that's why they read him. I *did* warn you.'

Muffin stripped off her nightdress and stretched in front of the bedroom wall mirror. 'I am *not* fat. Can *you* see any fat?'

'No way. Just a gorgeous pair of bristols and a grabable bum.'

'What do you mean by grabable?'

'Well, y'know. Nice. Comfortable.'

'You mean fat.'

'I don't mean fat.'

An hour later they were both dressed, ready to leave the apartment, and not talking.

All the fury and hate and hurt that Muffin had felt towards

Anthony Private had somehow manoeuvred itself in Jon's direction.

'You're a shit,' she hissed at him as they headed for the studio, 'I don't even *want* to marry you any more.'

'Promise?'

'Yes, I bloody promise. And you can take your bloody Schumann Calendar deal and shove it.'

'Great. I'll do it without you. I'll take some other little dolly on all the locations. Erica likes Barbados, maybe I'll try Erica.'

'They want *me*.'

'They'll settle for someone else.'

'You're a bastard.'

'Big word for such a *little* girl.'

'I can understand why Jane hates you.'

At the studio Jon busied himself with his equipment and his assistants.

Muffin put herself in the hands of the hairdresser, makeup artist, and fashion lady. They were due to shoot a record album cover. Muffin and Little Marty Pearl. She had been most excited at the prospect of meeting him, but Anthony Private had spoiled all of that, and Jon had double spoiled it.

Muffin sulked quietly as her body was made up with a sponge and pancake makeup. She was fed up with taking her clothes off. Fed up with holding her stomach in, sticking her tits out, stretching on tiptoe to make her legs seem longer.

'That's nice, darling,' said the camp boy, who was applying her body makeup. He was indicating her heart-shaped pubes. She had shaved them into a heart shape for a magazine glamour shot.

'Thanks,' she said glumly.

The boy bent down. 'Be a sweetie and open up your legs, don't want patchy thighs, do we?'

She stood with her legs apart while the boy fussed around with his pancake and sponge. Good job he was a fag as he had a bird's eye view.

'Have you seen Little Marty yet?' asked the boy, a note of excitement creeping into his voice. 'I hear he's gay.'

'Cor blimey, according to you everyone's gay!' exclaimed Muffin. 'You'll be telling me about Prince Philip next.'

'Oh. Is he?'
'Don't be daft.'

Little Marty arrived with his mother and Jackson.

He was dressed from head to toe in white fringed buckskin. He immediately disappeared with the makeup artist to have his spots covered.

Jackson approached Jon, shook him by the hand, and said, 'This is gonna be great, absolutely great.'

Jon agreed. 'Terrific idea,' he said. 'Muffin's never been on an album cover before. Was it your idea?'

'Yeah, sort of.' Jackson forgot to mention it had all been arranged by the English P.R. whose firm handled Marty's records in England.

Muffin emerged from the dressing-room. She was wearing thigh length very high-heeled white leather boots, and a white Stetson cowboy hat. That was all.

'Holy shit!' exclaimed Jackson.

Mrs Emma Pearl shot out of the chair at the back of the studio. 'Mr Jackson!' she complained in a shrill voice, 'that girl is *naked*. Get her out of here before my Little Marty sees her.'

Jackson's patience was wearing thin with Mrs Emma Pearl. He took her firmly by the arm and led her outside to the chauffeured limousine. He placed her inside and instructed the driver to take her back to the hotel. She was complaining loudly. Let her bitch to Little Marty later. Right now he needed her out of the way.

He rushed back inside and quickly cornered Jon. Muffin had wandered back into the dressing-room.

'The piece?' Jackson asked breathlessly. 'She put out?'

Jon laughed. 'For me—yes. For you—no. She's my girlfriend, we're getting married.'

'Oh, Jesus! I'm sorry, didn't know.'

'Don't worry about it. I'm used to men falling about over her. She's terrific, isn't she?'

'Really something. She a model, actress, or what?'

'I thought you knew all about her. I thought that's why you wanted her on the album cover.'

'Yeh, well, details—y'know. We just got in from the States

87

yesterday. I knew they'd lined up a great broad for the shots—I didn't know she was *that* great.'

Jon was pleased with the American's reaction. It proved everything he thought about Muffin. She had Instant Impact. Universal Appeal.

'Muff's *the* most famous model in England. She's a household name. This year we want to launch her in other activities. TV. Movies. That sort of thing.'

'You her manager?'

'Yes. I handle everything she does.'

Jackson nodded. 'Any contacts in the States yet?'

Jon shook his head. 'Not yet. I was thinking of taking her over there later this year.'

'Maybe I can help you. You gotta approach Stateside with a lot of clout. You gotta come in with balls. Know what I mean?'

'Well, when they see Muffin . . .'

'Not enough, take it from me, I should know. When I first got hold of Little Marty he was a farm hick. Nice boy. Nice looks. Nice voice. Without me he'd still be shovelling shit down on the farm. I gave him the works, made him a star. You and I should have a little talk about your girlfriend, I got ideas, money ideas.'

'I'm always ready to talk money.'

Jackson clapped him on the shoulder. 'Good boy, you've got a nose that sniffs in the right direction I can see. Why don't you and the girlfriend come along to Marty's reception tonight? After, we can have dinner. What ya say?'

'Terrific. We'll be there.'

'Listen, kid, you don't want to be snapping pictures all your life. No offence—I know you're good, but I can steer you and the little lady right where the bread is. You stroke my balls, I stroke yours. You dig?'

Jon nodded. He didn't much like Jackson, but he sensed there might be a deal somewhere, and it would be good to have the right connections in America.

Muffin reappeared, and Jon introduced her to Jackson. She had thrown a silk shawl around her nakedness but it wasn't concealing much. She was still furious with Jon, and kept on fixing him with dark and moody stares.

'Hey,' suggested Jackson, 'maybe Muffin could bring a girl-friend along tonight.'

'What for?' asked Muffin balefully.

'Sure,' agreed Jon, who had the message. 'Any preferences?'

Jackson chuckled. 'Just the usual.'

Little Marty emerged from the dressing-room. He walked with a slightly put-on swagger. His boyish face was neatly blanked out with pale orange pancake.

Muffin shrugged the shawl off her shoulders and smiled.

Little Marty managed a blush that shone through his make-up.

'Hello,' said Muffin.

Little Marty's voice cracked suddenly, 'Hello.'

'What a great couple!' Jackson enthused. 'Don't they look perfect together?'

They did match very well indeed. Both short, in spite of mutual high-heeled boots. Both young. Both pretty. Jon had arranged a plain backdrop, and Little Marty was to stand face on to the camera, while Muffin, beside him, stood with her back to the camera, just turning her Stetsoned head.

'Fanfuckin'-tastic!' exclaimed Jackson. 'Just right, sexy without being obvious. Just the image my boy needs.'

Muffin left the studio before Jon. He had another photo session to do, and she wanted to go home, wash her hair, and generally prepare for the party Jackson had invited them to.

She looked forward to the party with an excited churning in her stomach. Little Marty Pearl. He was lovely!

'Can I see you later?' he had asked. 'Why don't you sneak over to my hotel after the party?'

'I don't see why not,' she had replied, 'not a word to anyone though.'

'Secret,' he had said, putting a finger to his lips.

'Secret,' she had giggled in agreement.

They had been posing for the record cover while this whispered conversation had taken place. As soon as Muffin had set eyes on Little Marty she had flipped. After seeing his photo in so many magazines, hearing his records, it was a real thrill to meet him in the flesh.

She had remained bad-tempered towards Jon. That way it would be easy to pick a fight at the party and walk out.

Her anger about the Anthony Private interview had evaporated. Jon was right. It was nothing to get excited about. the poor guy was just jealous.

Humming softly Muffin let herself in to the Holland Park flat. What should she wear for the evening's activities? Something sexy. Something great.

The phone rang and she picked it up. Silence on the other end. Muffin banged it down. The secret wanker strikes again! Jon said that there was an army of secret wankers who phoned pretty girls. 'It's the only way some geezers can get it off.' he had casually explained. If *he* picked up the phone and there was a silence he would sometimes yell down the receiver. 'Go on. my son! Have one for me!'

'You're disgusting!' Muffin would complain at the time. but she couldn't help laughing. and it certainly took the fear out of obscene phone calls.

The phone rang again. It was probably Anthony Private. now he *looked* like a secret wanker.

'Mrs Wilson's home for unmarried scrubbers!' Muffin said primly.

'Is Jon there?' It was Jane's voice. sharp and unfriendly.

'No'. She *hated* having to speak to Jon's wife.

'Is that—er—Muffin?' Jane made it sound like a dirty word.

'Yes. Who is this?'

'This is *Mrs* Clapton.'

'Oh. Jon's mother?'

'No. his wife. dear.'

'So sorry. I thought you sounded like his mother.'

'That's perfectly all right. dear. I thought *you* were the daily. 'Jon's out.'

'So you said. Tell him to give me a ring will you. Oh. and by the way. I saw your engagement pictures. What a laugh! You silly little girls will do anything for publicity. Jon's got no intention of getting married again—he told me it was only to keep you quiet. The divorce isn't even definite yet. did Jon tell you it was? Don't bank on it. dear. I might even change my mind. Bye bye.'

'Oh!' Muffin was left hanging on to the receiver as the line went dead. 'Oh, you horrible old bitch! He does want to marry me—he does.' She banged the phone down in a fury.

What kind of game was Jon Clapton playing with her now? She would show him. Oh boy, would she show him!

# 25

London was sunny when Cleo jetted in. She had spent the few hours on the plane writing an explosive piece on Sami Marcel. It was an indictment of all men who felt that women were just attractive objects to be used for men's pleasure. He had turned out to be the perfect male chauvinistic pig, and in a biting, sometimes humorous piece, Cleo had exposed Sami Marcel, and all men who were like him. She couldn't wait to get it typed up and sent off express to Russell.

She took a taxi to the Connaught, and although she was back a day early they were able to find her a room.

There were three urgent messages for her to call Dominique Last immediately she arrived. She phoned at once.

Dominique said, 'Thank Christ you're back. Can I come over?'

'I only just got here, I have some work to get sorted out.'

'Please. It's important. I must talk to you.'

'All right.' Cleo wasn't enthusiastic, but that hard-to-say-no streak was still prevalent.

Dominique arrived an hour later. Her red hair was hidden beneath a scarf, and her red eyes beneath sunglasses. She had obviously been crying.

Cleo felt a sudden rush of sympathy, and she decided to forget the things that Dominique had said to her a few days previously.

'You look awful!' she exclaimed. 'What on earth has happened?'

Dominique removed her sunglasses to reveal a heavy black eye. 'Look what the bastard did,' she said bitterly.

'Dayan?' Cleo questioned.

'No.' Dominique snapped, '*your* friend. That creep you fixed me up with.'

'Shep Stone?'

'That's the name of the impotent little bastard.'

Cleo sat down. 'I'm not really following this conversation. Last time I spoke to you he was the most exciting man you had ever met, and you were leaving your husband *and* your lover for him.'

'Can I get a drink?' Dominique took off her headscarf, and shook her long red hair free.

Cleo consulted her watch. It was four pm. 'I don't know if the bar is open.'

'Room service doesn't close. I'd like a scotch, a double.'

Cleo picked up the phone and ordered tea for herself and a drink for Dominique. 'So?' she questioned. 'Can I please hear what this is all about?'

Dominique sighed. 'As I told you, Shep forced me to sleep with him that afternoon after you introduced us. I suppose I was a bit tiddly. He took advantage of me. If you had stayed and not run out on me—'

'Let me remind you, it was *you* invited him to join us.'

'I thought he was your friend.'

'If I had wanted him to join us I would have been quite capable of asking him myself. Actually I can't stand him.'

'Well anyway, if you had stayed—'

'On the phone,' Cleo stated pointedly, 'you said you had a marvellous time with him, true love and all that, and that you were going to leave Dayan for him.'

'Nonsense,' said Dominique briskly, 'you must have misunderstood.'

'Bullshit!' Cleo exclaimed.

There was a discreet knock at the door, and a waiter came in with their order.

They waited for him to leave, and then Dominique said flatly, 'Anyway, I lost my diamond ring at his hotel, and when I went there the next day to retrieve it he hit me.'

'Just like that?'

'Yes. Just like that.'

Cleo poured her tea. She was speechless. Dominique should get some sort of award for liar of the year.

'So?' she questioned at last. 'What do you want *me* to do?'

'Arrange a meeting. I want to talk to him.'

'Talk to him! What about?'

'I want to have a private discussion. If you phone him he'll come here to see you. You will be out, and I'll be here. Simple.'

'Hey now, just hang on a minute. Why would you want to see a man that clobbered you? And much as I dislike Shep Stone, I never did imagine him as a woman beater. *Why* did he hit you?'

'I don't know.'

Cleo shook her head. 'Listen. Either be straight with me or let's just forget it.'

'You mean you won't help me?'

'Help you? Help you do *what*?'

'What I said.'

'Your story has more holes than a punchcard. Please don't come here and give me a bag full of lies and then try and use me.'

Dominique shrugged. 'I didn't think you would help me.' She drained her scotch in one fell swoop, and stood up, then evenly she said, 'You are a very jealous person, Cleo, you still can't get over the fact that Shep wanted me and not you.'

'Oh, come on . . .'

Dominique put her sunglasses back on, and her headscarf. 'You are jealous because I've got a home and a baby. You always were jealous of me. My hair, my figure. You always—'

Cleo stood up. 'Bye bye, Dominique.' She walked in the bathroom and slammed the door. Christ! This whole thing was so unfair. She had always tried to be a good friend, but look where it got you.

Russell Hayes. Good friend Susan. Now Dominique.

If you knew absolutely nothing about your *friends* what was it all about?

The phone rang, and when Cleo emerged she was glad to see that Dominique had left It was Butch Kaufman and he said,

'There's a slew of parties tonight, and I thought we might um er visit them together.'

'Great. I could do with some parties.'

'I'll pick you up at eight. Then maybe later a party of our own. My stand-in handed me something outasite today!'

'Maybe.'

'O.K., Miss Cool. See you later.'

# 26

Unable to decide which girl would be the most suitable, Jon finally rounded up both Erica and Laurie.

They all met at the Holland Park flat, and Muffin, who was still hardly speaking to Jon, greeted them with, 'Has he got a travelling fireman for you!'

'It's travelling salesman,' Jon remarked, 'visiting fireman.'

'Pooh!' Muffin stuck out her tongue, and bounced off to finish her makeup. She hadn't mentioned the phone call from his wife yet. She was saving that piece of information.

Erica was wearing a brown satin jump suit, slit down the front, revealing pale, interesting, small breasts. Her blond hair was parted in the middle and hung long and straight.

'You look lovely,' Jon said admiringly.

Laurie had emphasized the dark ebony of her skin with a red gypsy outfit. Her hair was freaked out Afro style, and her makeup was bright and arresting.

'Very tasty!' said Jon. He was pleased. Both girls looked sensational, and one or the other was bound to appeal to Jackson.

Muffin appeared in a white frilled blouse, tucked into white jeans, tucked into white boots. She immediately made the other two girls look ordinary by comparison.

'Saw the piece Anthony Private did on you this morning.' Erica smiled, 'What a bitch!'

'Yes, aren't you.' Jon took her firmly by the arm. 'That's one subject we are *not* going to discuss. Let's go.'

Muffin glared. Trust Erica to have seen the Anthony Private thing. Stupid old cow. She must be at least twenty-six, what did *she* have to laugh about. It had worked out well that Jon had wanted to bring Erica *and* Laurie to the party, they would keep him well occupied. Muffin had plans to enjoy herself, and those plans did not include Jon bloody Clapton.

She hummed a little song in anticipation of the good times ahead.

Mike James spent the day involved in one business meeting after the other. He wanted to get everything done quickly, so that when Cleo returned he would have nothing but time for her.

Free time. Talking time. Fucking time.

He was taken to lunch at a restaurant in Chelsea, and he amazed himself by not attempting conversation with any of the dozen or so very pretty girls who were also lunching there.

I am a reformed character, he thought. I can look a roomful of nooky straight in the eye and not give it a second thought. Well . . . Maybe a second thought. But that was all. Thinking not doing. An improvement on his former lifestyle.

He had a long talk with Jackson about Little Marty Pearl's mother. 'She's got to go,' he said, 'it's no good having her on this tour, send her back.'

Jackson was in complete agreement. 'It's as good as done.'

In the evening he went to the Little Marty Pearl party. Stay loose, he warned himself, don't get involved, let's see if you can do it for once.

There were a lot of girls there. Fat ones. Thin ones. Smart ones. Tacky ones. He stayed loose, he made idle chat, he even turned one smokey proposition down.

He felt proud and self-righteous. A faithful husband. A man who was saving himself for his wife.

'Hey,' called Jackson, when the party was in full swing. 'You gonna come to dinner with us?'

'I don't know,' said Mike, and he inspected the two girls on either side of Jackson. The blond appealed to him, so did the black girl.

'You met Jon—er Jon . . .'

'Clapton,' supplied Jon.

'Yeah. Clapton,' said Jackson. 'Jon photographed the album cover today—he's a good guy—great guy. This is Mike James, Jon. Mike's a top exec. at Hampton Records, a good guy for you to get to know.'

They shook hands, and Mike turned expectantly towards the blond.

'I'm Erica,' she said, extending her hand and holding on to his for just a moment too long.

Jackson whipped a quick arm around Laurie claiming ownership for the night. He knew about Mike James' reputation.

It wouldn't matter, Mike reasoned, if he got laid again *before* seeing Cleo. It wouldn't count. Anyway, she would never know, and what she didn't know she couldn't mind about . . .

'So where are we going for dinner?' he asked.

'You—as usual—look like an um er gorgeous person.'

Cleo sighed. 'Thank you, Butch. But I don't feel it. I feel uptight, and angry, and hurt.'

'Not with me?'

'Of course not with you.'

'Well, then?'

'Don't want to go into it, it's boring and dull. I just want to have a lovely enjoyable *selfish* evening.'

'I couldn't agree with you more. Together we shall be decadently selfish. Shall we forget the parties?'

'No, let's go. I feel like noise and music and watching people.'

She was wearing her new Chloe dress. It was silk jersey, and it draped its way in beguiling curves down her body. She also wore black silk stockings, and very high heeled strappy shoes. It made a change from always being in trousers. She knew that Mike would love the way she looked, he was always complaining that he never saw her legs. 'You have the best legs in New York,' he often nagged, 'and you keep them hidden like a Portuguese nun!'

Thinking of Mike made her narrow her eyes in anger He had

stopped phoning. Just like that. No messages. Nothing. It didn't take *him* long to accept the fact that she had gone.

She would have to start sorting out her future. She had two more actors left to interview for the series, and then what? She wasn't sure if she wanted to go back to New York. She wasn't sure if she wanted to continue working for Russell Hayes and *Image*.

'First the Dorchester,' Butch said. 'I promised I would show my face at the party for Little Marty Pearl. If you play your cards right I'll introduce you. He's sixteen, a virgin, and prettier than you!'

Jackson and Jon watched like proud parents as Muffin and Little Marty posed for pictures together.

'They make a cute couple,' Jackson remarked.

'Yeah,' agreed Jon absently. He was thinking it was a shame that he and Muff had announced their engagement, because a trumped-up romance between her and Little Marty would have been fantastic publicity. Also it had not helped the situation between him and Jane.

'You've got to watch out for my mother!' Marty whispered.

'Pardon?' whispered back Muffin.

'Just wait in the lobby. I'll call down for you when it's safe.'

Muffin giggled. 'Very cloak and dagger.'

'I really like you,' Marty said seriously. 'Do you like me?'

''Course I do!' she squeezed his arm, smiled for the photographers, and stuck out her incredible bosom.

Mike held on to Erica's arm and said, 'What is a beautiful looking girl like you doing getting herself fixed up with a dude like Jackson?'

'Jon's an old friend, I thought it might be fun. My, what horny eyes you have!'

'All the better to stare you down.'

'Down where?'

'You name it.'

'Naughty, naughty!'

'I like your blouse.'

'Blouse is such a sweet old-fashioned word.'

'I used it because I can see I'm with a sweet old-fashioned girl.'

'Ha Ha.'

'How would you feel about skipping out on the mass dinner and going off somewhere on our own?'

'Sounds like a good idea.'

Mike winked. 'I shall fix it. Just a quick word with Jackson and we shall be on our way.'

'My, what a fast way you have of doing things!'

'You ain't seen nothin' yet!'

'So,' said Butch, 'when the movie is finished it's back to the beach house and um er flake out time. If you're around L.A. you are more than a welcome house guest. I've got a girl that sort of lives with me there, but I can always move her out for a spell, she'll understand.' He helped Cleo out of the car. 'What do you think?'

'I've got no plans right now, Butch. I'm just going to wing it.'

A gaggle of girls sprang forward to get Butch Kaufman's autograph, and Cleo walked on inside the hotel. She stood in the lobby and watched a man approaching from a distance through the lounge. He looked very much like Mike. He had the same rangy walk. He was holding on to a tall blond, and as they got nearer she realized with a stomach lurching throb that it *was* Mike.

He had been talking to Erica, light sexy conversation designed to warm her up. Then he had spotted a pair of incredible legs, and as his eyes had travelled up to inspect the face of the owner of the legs he had realized—shit—it was Cleo!!

He abruptly stopped walking, but it was too late, she had seen him also. He pulled his arm away from Erica, and a man he recognized as the film actor Butch Kaufman entered the hotel and took *his Cleo* by the hand.

'Jesus!' exclaimed Mike.

'What's the matter?' asked Erica, 'Why are we stopping?'

While Mike tried to decide what to do, Cleo took the matter into her own hands, and came walking over with her escort.

'Hello, Mike,' she said. 'Glad to see you're making out O.K.'

98

He opened his mouth to reply, but hand in hand with Butch she was strolling off calm as you please. Bitch!! He had flown all the way across the Atlantic for *this!*

'Who was that?' asked Erica.

'Just my wife,' he said bitterly.


# 27


The desk clerk looked at Muffin suspiciously.

'I'm waiting for Mr Marty Pearl,' she said grandly.

'So are a lot of other girls,' he said, scratching his head and peering goggle-eyed down her neckline.

'Mr Pearl has invited me. I'll wait in the lobby, when he phones will you please let me know. My name is Muffin.'

'What?'

'Muffin. M-U-F-F-I-N.'

'You can't hang around in the lobby all night. Why don't you go outside with the other girls?'

'I am not a fan,' Muffin said crossly. 'I am a personal friend. Kindly let me know when he telephones for me to come up.' She flounced off to a seat where she could watch the desk, and let out a sigh of relief.

It had not been easy. After the photographic session with Little Marty at the party she had wandered around cleverly avoiding Jon. There were lots of people there who knew who she was, and so she chatted to this group and that, until at last Jon had cornered her and said, 'Come and be nice to Jackson, chat him up, throw on the charm. He could be just what we are looking for in America.'

'No!' she had snapped. 'I'm sick of being nice to people. I'm sick of you with your deals. *And* your lies.'

'Come on, Muff,' Jon had pleaded, 'this could be very important.'

'Don't care. Leave me alone.'

'You're being stupid.'

'If I want to be stupid, I shall be stupid, and you can get stuffed.'

They had glared at each other, and Jon had marched off back to Jackson, and Muffin had marched off to the front of the hotel and got herself a taxi.

Tomorrow she could make up with Jon *if* she felt like it. And *if* he had a good explanation for Jane's phone call.

Tonight she planned to do something *she* wanted to do for a change.

The desk clerk was beckoning her over. 'Suite 404,' he said, 'fourth floor.'

'Thank you. I *told* you he was expecting me.' She made her way over to the elevator. She had butterflies in her stomach. Ridiculous really, she could not remember the last time she had been *nervous*.

Little Marty was waiting for her at the door to his suite. He had on a short white towelling bathrobe and nothing else. 'Quick!' he whisked her inside, slammed the door, and locked it. Then he grabbed her and gave her a long and inexpert kiss.

'You make me *shiver!*' she exclaimed.

'You're really sexy!' he replied. 'Come on in the bedroom and see my records.'

They ran in the bedroom, holding hands, giggling. Laid out on the bed was an array of record albums all featuring Little Marty on the cover.

'I've made ten albums,' Little Marty claimed proudly, 'two of them golds.'

'Fabulous. Shall I take my clothes off?'

Little Marty watched in fascination as Muffin shed first boots then trousers, then top.

'You're so pretty,' he said, reaching for her perky upright breasts.

She undid the belt on his bathrobe. 'You've got a smashing John Thomas!' she exclaimed.

'John Thomas?'

'You know—your what not!'

'Oh. Gee, thanks. Shall I put a record on?'

'Yes. Terrific.'

Little Marty put on *Teenage High*, and Muffin squealed with delight.

'Shall we do it?' Marty inquired.

'Why not?' said Muffin, and she lay on the bed and parted her legs expectantly.

Carefully Marty climbed aboard. Verbally Muffin encouraged him.

He came quickly, but then so did she. So they put *Teenage High* back on and started again.

Within an hour they had repeated the performance four times, and Muffin gasped, 'You are superman! You are wonderful! I love you!'

And Little Marty said, remembering his previous sexual experiences with three dismal hookers, 'I think we should get married.'

'Yes,' said Muffin, the idea appealing to her. 'I think we should. Let's play sixty-nine and discuss it!'

# 28

Not being an avid drinker Cleo decided that the time had come to get very very drunk. For someone whose entire alcoholic intake was limited to small glasses of white wine, she switched with a vengeance to double scotches.

'Let's go back to my place and get very very stoned instead,' Butch suggested.

'I feel like getting good and drunk,' Cleo insisted. 'I am celebrating the end of my marriage, I want to do it with a bang.'

'That's just what I had in mind.'

'Sex maniac!'

They started the evening at the Little Marty Pearl party, then there was a drinks party in Fulham, then a film party in Mayfair where they bumped into Ramo, and he and two girls joined them.

By this time Cleo was well gone. The double scotches had been replaced with champagne, and then brandy, and now, somehow, they were all back in Ramo's hotel suite, and someone was popping ammis under her nose, and she was trying to tell them that she *hated* the smell—just hated it.

Where the hell was Butch? Someone was trying to peel her out of her Chloe dress, and she finally realized it was Ramo, and somewhat unsteady she got to her feet and insisted that she was taken home.

'But darling,' explained Ramo, 'Butch is in the bedroom with the girls, and so it is only you and me, and I want to make fantastic extraordinary love to you.'

'No.' She shook her head, everything took off in different directions and she felt filled with nausea. 'I'm going home.'

She wished that she had a home to go to. But the apartment in New York was no longer home, and until she got things sorted out it would have to be hotels.

She managed to make her way unsteadily downstairs, and was surprised to see it was almost light out. She had an eleven am appointment with English actor Daniel Onel, she was going to be in great shape for *that*. She got a taxi, and concentrated on not throwing up.

Outside the Connaught Mike paced up and down, white-faced and furious. 'It's five in the morning,' he accused, 'where the hell have you been?'

One thing Mike had never been short of and that was balls. *He* was accusing *her*.

She paid the cab while trying to ignore her soon-to-be ex-husband who was practically hopping up and down with fury.

'Well?' he demanded.

She squinted at him. 'Something about you missing . . . Ah, I know. Shouldn't you have a blond draped around you? Doesn't look right, Mike, no blond.'

'Are you drunk?'

'And tired. And I'm going to bed.' She walked into the hotel and he followed her. 'Go away,' she said.

'I would like to talk.'

'Go away and talk then, I'm not stopping you. I'm not stopping you doing *anything*.'

'Cleo, baby . . .'

Anger struck. The lying, conniving, unfaithful shit. 'Mike, baby . . . do me a favour and fuck off!'

She marched into the elevator, made it to her room, and promptly threw up.

So much for getting drunk.

The initial impact had been of the 'fuck you' variety.

Caught with his pants down—figuratively speaking that is—it had taken Mike at least an hour to be fully outraged.

'Who was that?' Erica had asked, and when Mike had replied, 'just my wife', he was suffering strong pangs of embarrassment at having been caught yet again.

It finally occurred to him—what the *hell* was Cleo doing hand in hand with a souped-up super stud like Butch Kaufman?

By that time he and Erica were sitting in the very same restaurant he had lunched in the previous day, and she was making conversations with various people at nearby tables who all seemed to be friends of hers.

'I wonder,' said Mike, 'if you'd excuse me?'

'Sure,' said Erica, imagining he was off to the men's room.

He left the table, found a waiter, settled the bill, and left. He had no pangs of regret about Erica. She would be all right, she was surrounded by friends.

He taxied back to the Little Marty Pearl party, but it was sadly depleted. All that remained were a few drunken journalists getting a free skinful.

He wandered around the hotel's public rooms, but could find no trace of Cleo, so he taxied over to her hotel, and found that yes indeed she had checked back in that very afternoon, but at the moment she was out.

He then spent an exciting evening waiting in the bar until it closed. Waiting in the lobby until at 2 am they politely asked him to leave. Waiting in the street until at approximately five minutes past five Cleo came wafting up in a taxi. Drunk. Sarcastic. Rude.

Now she had very nicely—oh yes, really stylishly, told him to fuck off. Language Cleo never used unless really pushed. Of course she was drunk, but what excuse was that when he had been waiting *all night long*.

Now she had vanished, gone to her room without even a goodnight. In the mood she was in he did not feel inclined to follow her. She was not in a forgiving mood. She was not in the right frame of mind for explanations.

Susan. Susan who? Oh *her*, well that was nothing, just a little slip, I felt *sorry* for her. It didn't mean anything.

Come back, Cleo. You looked sensational tonight. I saw your legs—Christ, but I get hard just thinking about you.

Back at his own hotel Mike restlessly paced the room. He would get a few hours sleep and go back to her. Maybe he would take her a present, she liked presents. Then, quietly, after she had forgiven him, he would find out what the hell she had been doing with Butch Kaufman until five in the morning.

# 29

Somehow Jon found himself out to dinner with Laurie, Erica, and Jackson. Not the most ideal of situations. Not a scene that was going to drive Muffin mad with joy. Anyway it was *her* fault. She was the one that had run off like a bad-tempered teenager.

They sat in *San Lorenzo*, the four of them. Very cosy. Jackson had taken a strong fancy to Laurie, and he was engaging her in a secret whispered conversation which was producing much giggling on her part, and much groping on his.

Erica sat straightbacked and aloof, the original long cool blond. They had found her already there, unconcernedly tucking into a plate full of lasagne.

'Mike James did a vanishing trick,' she explained, 'but I stayed because I am absolutely starving.'

*San Lorenzo* always had a scattering of spies for various gossip columns, and Jon knew that the next day there would be some snide mention of the fact that he was out with another girl. Not Muffin. Where was Muffin? Home in bed with an attack of the sulks no doubt. He would placate her later. Right now it was be nice to Jackson time. He was a key connection, a good guy to get in with.

'Where's Muff Muff?' Erica finally inquired, having finished the entire plate of lasagne.

'I don't know where you put it,' said Jon, shaking his head in amazement.

'Oh yes you do! Or have you got a short memory?'

Christ! He could never forget his scene with Erica. She was stark raving mad when it came to sex. A true raver. He would never forget that one blazing moment when she had clicked those perfect white teeth hard down on his cock, and he had thought—oh no! She's going to bite it off. I *know* she's going to bite it off. Wrenching free had left him with some nasty scars, and a firm belief that you left the long cool blonds well alone. Of course that had been before Muffin.

He was glad that Jackson had not chosen Erica, although according to Muffin, Laurie had some wild sexual habits. Nothing violent though. Jon had discovered that Muffin and her girlfriends spent *hours* discussing their various sex lives. No details were spared. Who did what to whom. How big was it. Was a guy a good performer. Did he go down. Muffin seemed to know intimate details about every male in town. Secondhand details of course. Talk about equality. Muffin and her group could destroy any guy with one sarcastic chorus of—'Small!!'

'I asked where Muffin had gone?' Erica said sweetly.

'She was tired,' Jon explained. 'It was a long tough day, so I sent her home.'

'Was she upset about the Anthony Private article?'

'Erica, would you be upset if you were the subject of a lead interview in a major daily newspaper? All due respect, my old sweet, you're a lovely model, but how often is your name mentioned next to your picture?'

'I don't need *personal* publicity. *I* never stop working.'

'O.K. Great. But Muffin's going to be more than just another model. Much much more.'

105

'You little Svengali you! You always were a terrific grafter. I believe you can do it too.'

'I can do it.'

Erica tapped long fingernails on the table. 'How about coming back to my place for coffee?'

'No, love.'

'Home to your investment?'

'Nope. Just home to my girl.'

Erica shrugged. 'In that case I know you'll excuse me if I take off and join some friends over there.' She stood up and smiled faintly. 'When you change your mind, Jon, give me a buzz. I'll always have a soft spot for you—know what I mean?'

Jackson and Laurie were still giggling and whispering. Jon could hardly see the evening culminating in a big business discussion, so he tapped Jackson on the shoulder and arranged to meet with him the following day.

Jackson winked lewdly. 'Thanks pally, tomorrow we'll sort things out.'

Jon nodded. Already he had decided what he wanted out of the American. He wanted know-all, and technique, and introductions to the people that mattered. After they had finished the Schumann Calendar photographs America was the place to be. In America Muffin would become world famous, and Jon—with a little help from his friends—would be right there with her. He would offer Jackson a piece of Muffin—a small per cent—well maybe a medium per cent. Jackson did not look like the sort of guy who would do something for nothing.

In America Jon felt he would finally be able to get away from Jane. What a relief not to have to listen to that whiney nagging voice complaining about how terrible her life was. Of course he would miss his kids, but they could come over for visits. By that time he would be able to afford a nanny to bring them over. It would be great. A house with a pool. Several cars. Servants. Lots of parties.

Jon smiled to himself. Life was going to be really good. He planted a kiss on Laurie's cheek. 'Be nice to my friend,' he instructed.

Laurie rolled her eyes. 'You betcha ass, baby face!' she said with a laugh

Well, it looked like Jackson was all set there. Jon hoped the American would remember who to thank.

He spotted Erica sitting with some friends and he threw her a cursory wave. He was quite flattered that she kept on propositioning him, but truthfully he just didn't fancy her any more. Home to Muffin. Pretty, cute, lovable, dumb, Muffin. Well no, she wasn't really dumb, that wasn't fair, she was just a bit childlike in her attitude towards life, and that was nice.

At twenty-six Jon was cynical towards women. He had been screwing them since he was fourteen, and he had been through a lot. When he was married to Jane he had just been starting out on his own as a photographer, and it hadn't been easy. He soon found out it could be a lot easier. Mabel Curson was the middle-aged editor of a woman's magazine, she was only too happy to put lots of work his way, and in return she wanted screwing at least once a week. In the fashion industry Jon found there were plenty of Mabel Cursons.

You could say he had slept his way up the ladder of success. Until Muffin. Muffin had been his passport to better things, and together they were making it work. It hadn't been necessary to service Mabel Curson in two years.

Jon let himself into the Holland Park flat quietly. Let Muffin sleep on her grievances, she would feel better in the morning. He greeted Scruff, and gave him a saucer of milk. Then he took his clothes off in the bathroom and made his way stealthily to bed.

It wasn't until he reached out to touch Muffin that he realized she wasn't there.

# 30

The phone woke Cleo early. She squinted at the clock and realized with panic that it was ten after ten. It had failed to sound its alarm bell at nine o'clock, or maybe she just hadn't heard it. Anyway, she felt terrible. An American operator was telling her to hang on, and she was parched with thirst, and had a raging headache.

'I can't hang on all day!' she snapped angrily down the phone, and when there was no response she slammed it down, got up, felt worse, forced herself into the bathroom and under a cold shower.

Her head cleared slightly and fragments of the previous evening came floating back.

Oh Christ! Ramo—naked and horny. Butch with two girls. Mike—or was that all a bad dream?

No time to wonder now. Eleven o'clock appointment. No time for breakfast. Fast makeup. Dress. Brush hair. Look shitty.

Gather up tape recorder, purse, notebook, pencils. Ten forty-five. Phone rings again. This time it's Russell Hayes loud and clear from New York. Wasn't it some unearthly time there?

'The stuff on Kaufman and Kaliffe is terrific,' he enthused.

Yeah! thought Cleo, and I could give you more stuff on both of them that would blow your mind. For instance, Ramo Kaliffe has a foot-long cock, that she *did* remember.

'Thanks, Russ.'

'I thought we'd use the Kaufman piece to open up with—going to send Jerry over to do the pics.' He paused, then—'Have you seen Mike yet?'

She glanced at her watch, she was going to be late. 'No. Listen, Russ, I—'

'Don't worry about anything. I'm here. I'm waiting, and if you want me to I can fly over.'

Oh shit! 'Everything is fine, no need for you to come over. I have to dash, I'm late for an appointment.'

'All right, my darling. I just wanted you to know I'm here if you need me.'

'Bye, Russ.' She banged the phone down.

My darling indeed. Sadly, after this assignment it would have to be farewell to *Image* Magazine and all who sailed in her. A shame, but inevitable.

It would be starting all over again—in everything.

She rang down to the front desk and asked them to get her

a cab. Ten fifty-five. If she was lucky she wouldn't be more than a few minutes late.

Daniel Onel lived in a small mews house in Belgravia. The front door was opened by a blond Danish au pair who smiled vacantly and ushered Cleo into an untidy living-room. 'He won't be long,' the au pair said in a thick accent. 'You want the coffee?'

Cleo nodded. 'Black. No sugar.'

The au pair slouched off and Cleo took stock of her surroundings. A large room, very modern, with black leather chairs and couch, and chrome and glass tables.

Daniel Onel had obviously been entertaining the previous evening, for the ashtrays were all full, and dirty glasses abounded. Record albums were littered across the floor, and a vase of roses had been knocked over and lay in a damp mass on the carpet.

'Why do you want to include Daniel Onel?' Russell had questioned when she had given him her list for 'Who's Afraid of the Big Bad Wolf'.

'Because he's a very talented man, and women find him attractive. A guy doesn't have to look like Bobby the Beach Boy to be a stud.'

'O.K.,' Russell had agreed, 'just asking.'

But why *had* she decided on Daniel Onel?

Because she wanted to meet him. Because he was her favourite actor. Because even though he was on the short side, wore glasses, and was nearing fifty, he had a charismatic personality that appealed to women.

She wished that she felt better. She wished that she could have stayed in bed all morning. Sometimes she almost wished she was like her mother and had never worked a day in her life.

In her marriage to Mike there had never been any question of her *not* working. Mike had always accepted without question the fact that she had her own thing to do. He believed in women's equality, and he didn't seem to have much respect for women who did nothing.

'Don't they get bored?' he had inquired about her married and idle girlfriends. 'What the hell do they *do* all day?'

'Oh, they go to the hairdresser, shopping, lunch with the girls,' she had replied.

'Scintillating!!'

Cleo had often wondered how he would feel when they had children—she wasn't about to give *her* babies away to a nanny. But of course that problem had never come up.

Daniel Onel came into the room. He was taller than she expected, and thinner.

He smiled, and said, 'Sorry about the mess.' He was wearing a paisley shirt open at the neck, black trousers, and white gym-shoes. His normally dark hair was dyed henna red for a film. 'You may as well know from the start I hate interviews,' he announced pleasantly. 'I find them boring for everyone concerned—you—me—and the poor schmuck who gets to read my opinions on everything from pot to sky diving.'

'Well . . .' said Cleo.

He held up a hand to silence her. 'However, I read a piece in *Image* that you did on Senator Ashton, and it was so good, unbiased and fresh, that I thought it just might be interesting chemistry for you and I to get together.' He took off his glasses and stared at her, 'Verbally that is.'

'Of course,' she stammered, suddenly unnerved by this strange man with his henna'd hair and white gymshoes.

'I must warn you,' he said abruptly, 'I do not want to discuss any of my wives except maybe the first one, and I do not have one solitary word to say on my last divorce. It was a terrible mistake—mind-blowing . . .' He lapsed into silence, and then bent suddenly to pick up the fallen roses and stuff them back in the vase.

The au pair came in with the coffee.

'Ah, Heidi,' greeted Daniel, 'have you meet Cleo James?'

'We sort of see each other,' said the au pair.

'Princess Heidi Walmerstein, may I present Cleo James,' Daniel gave a mock little bow. 'Here is a girl you could write about, poor little impoverished princess, arrived here with just the clothes she stood up in, and a few phone numbers of course, mine was one of them.'

Cleo sensed sudden tension.

Heidi said, 'Daniel, I go out now.'

'Good,' he said expansively, 'spend a little more of my money, have some of the fun you say you're not getting with me.'

'Oh Daniel!' exclaimed Heidi, 'do not always be to joking.'

'Do not always be to joking,' mimicked Daniel. 'You've been here six bloody months. Can't you get your English straight?'

Heidi scowled. 'I go now. Back in the later.'

'Christ!' he exclaimed, as he watched the small blond girl depart. 'I don't know how I stand her. She's too young, too dumb, and can't even master the Queen's English.'

'She's very pretty.'

'*Quite* pretty,' amended Daniel.

'I thought she was your au pair.'

He roared with laughter. 'You are forgiven for thinking that. Come to think of it she has got that fresh from Hendon look. But she *is* a princess, I've met the family.'

'How nice for you,' murmured Cleo, and sipped her coffee. It was unbearably strong. 'Ugh!' she exclaimed.

'Tastes awful, does it? Come in the kitchen and we'll make some more. Coffee is not one of Heidi's strong points, especially when it's for another woman. She nearly poisoned one of my ex-wives!'

The kitchen was in worse disarray than the living-room.

'This place looks like a shithouse,' announced Daniel.

'Don't you have a maid?'

'She comes and she goes. Right now she's gone as you can see.'

'There's places you can phone and they send up out of work actors and people like that.'

'Listen, love, if I had an out of work actor here do you think he'd be mucking around with a Hoover—no he bloody wouldn't—he'd be giving me an audition wouldn't he?'

The phone rang, and Cleo was treated to a one-sided conversation—Daniel's side.

'She's driving me batty.' Pause. 'Well of *course* I've told her.' Pause. 'She doesn't even *speak* it let alone understand it!' Pause. 'I know, I know. I must.' Pause. 'Yes it is, it's the bloody same every time. If I wanted to be treated like that I could find a bird

111

in Soho couldn't I?' Pause. 'All right, old matey, maybe later.'
Daniel hung up. 'I am going to tell little Miss Walmerstein to
pack up her bags and get out.'

'Look,' said Cleo earnestly, 'would you like me to come back
later?'

'No, certainly not. I told you it would be boring. It will be
just as boring later.'

Cleo made the coffee; this time it was drinkable. Daniel
produced a packet of digestive biscuits and they went back into
the living-room.

'Tell me about Senator Ashton.'

'You read all there was to tell.' She was really pleased he had
seen the piece she had done on the Senator. It was one of the
best things she had ever done. A week in Washington following
him around. Six hours of taped interviews—it was unheard of
for him to give that kind of time to a journalist. Russell had
said that the circulation of the magazine soared the week it
appeared. Mike had been really proud, and a television producer
had offered her an audition any time she liked for her own
interview show.

'Are you married?' Daniel asked.

'Yes I am.'

'Happily?'

'*I'm* supposed to be interviewing *you*.'

He threw wide his arms. 'Interview me. Ask me what you
like. Only don't ask me the usual bloody stupid questions.'

'Why don't you just talk. About anything you like.'

'What do I like? I'm not sure any more. I keep on getting
stuck with things I don't like. Bad marriages. Bad relationships.
Bad movies that I should never have done.'

'What *do* you want out of life?'

'I want a beautiful great bird who only cares about me. A
woman who is prepared to put me first. A faithful woman. An
unpossessive woman. A mother figure. A great lay. A fantastic
cook. A lady with a sense of humour. Do you think she exists?'

'If she does I want the male equivalent!'

He laughed. 'Problems too?'

'Who hasn't,' she sighed.

Daniel screwed up his face in a grimace of disgust. 'Life would

112

be so bloody simple if we didn't have to live it with other people.'

'Is that another way of saying Garbo's immortal line—I want to be alone?'

'Perceptive little thing, aren't you?'

Cleo blushed. Little thing indeed! She was five foot six inches tall and twenty-nine years old. Daniel Onel made her feel about fourteen. 'Why do you stay with Heidi if it's not the relationship you want?'

He shrugged helplessly. 'Habit. Loneliness. Have you any idea what it's like coming back to an empty house at night?'

'But surely you have plenty of friends?'

'Acquaintances,' he corrected. 'Fair weather friends who are only too happy to spend time with you if your last movie was a big success.'

'You must have close friends.'

'Have you?'

She thought of Dominique and Russell and Susan. 'I think I know what you mean,' she admitted.

'I have a few close mates. People I have known from the beginning. But they have their own lives to lead. Their own families . . .' he trailed off.

'What about your children? You must be close to them.'

'As they grow up they grow away in their own directions. I see Dick occasionally, he's eighteen now—he's got his own thing to do. Listen, love, I'm on my own, that's it. I'm forty-nine years old and I've fucked up my personal life and now I'm stuck with some little Danish raver whom I certainly do not love. No, I don't love her, but it's good for the old public image—know what I mean?'

Cleo nodded. 'I suppose so, but it seems such a waste. I mean, *somewhere* there is the right lady.'

'Do you want to find her for me?'

Why did he make her feel so *nervous*. 'I'm sure she's somewhere . . .'

He smiled cynically. 'Sure.'

'Your gymshoe's undone.'

He bent to tie it. His hair was ever so slightly thinning. It didn't matter. Nothing mattered. He was the most attractive man she had ever met. He hadn't even noticed that she was a woman. To him she was a notebook, pencil and tape recorder.

Cleo cleared her throat. 'Let's talk about your last movie,' she suggested. 'Is it true that you sent the producer a telegram saying that you would never work with him again?'

Daniel laughed. 'Do birds fly?'

# 31

Frantically Little Marty shook Muffin. 'Wake up,' he implored, 'my Ma is at the door and if she sees you—like pow!!'

Slowly Muffin opened her eyes. Sleepily she looked around. Where was she? Oh yes. 'Hi Marty,' she said, snuggling further under the covers. She had been having this fantastic dream all about sandy beaches and photographs of her dressed up in furs on the cover of *Vogue*. She wondered if Jon could arrange something like that—he was a very good arranger. Why did she always have to be naked with lots of tit and bum showing?

'Get up!' Marty hissed desperately. 'We'll have to hide you, it will only be for a few minutes.'

'Oh!' she exclaimed crossly, 'I'm so warm and comfortable.'

In the distance loud banging on the door could be heard, and Mrs Emma Pearl's piercing voice demanding to be let in.

'Come on!' Marty bundled her out of bed. 'In the bathroom, lock the door and don't open it unless I say to.'

'But I'm cold.'

'There are lots of towels in there. *Please*, babe, just for me.'

Still half asleep and yawning she allowed herself to be pushed into the bathroom.

Marty raced to the door of the suite. He opened it. Mrs Emma Pearl came bursting in looking suspiciously round.

'Who's here?' she demanded.

'No one's here,' protested Marty.

'Why did it take you so long to open the door?'

'I was asleep. Gee, mom, it's only eight o'clock, why d'ya wake me up so early?'

She peered through the door into the bedroom, and satisfied that it was empty, she collapsed sadly on to the couch.

'As if you don't know,' she shook her head, 'they are sending me back to America. A mother is bad for your image.' Her voice rose to a plaintive shriek. 'Since when has a mother been bad for *anyone's* image!'

'Yeah, mom.' Marty studied the floor. 'I have to go along with what they say—*you* know that.'

'And who will look after you? Who will see that you eat properly? Get enough sleep? Wrap up warm after a show?'

'Gee, ma, Jackson will take care of all that crap.'

'Already you are using foul language and I haven't even gone yet. What about girls?'

'What girls?'

'Any girls. Just stay away from them, all of them.' Mysteriously she added, 'There are diseases so terrible that I would not even mention them.'

'Yeah, ma.'

Briskly she stood. 'You are a good boy, Marty, in my heart I know that. I have to go now, but remember all that I have said.'

'Yeah, ma.'

She hugged him. 'Think of your mother, and don't forget to brush your teeth *three* times a day. Teeth are very important to you. Do not eat candy. Remember to keep your eyes up in photographs.'

'Goodbye, ma.'

Tears were streaming down her cheeks, 'Goodbye, son. It will only be a short parting.'

Marty shut the door on her. Oh God! Freedom at last! Freedom to swear, eat candy, stay awake all night, and most important of all—girls!! Well—girl. Muffin. Sweet. Adorable. Gorgeous. Sexy. Muffin!

Marty rushed to the bathroom and hammered on the door. 'All clear,' he yelled, 'let me in.'

Muffin had curled up on the bath mat and gone back to sleep.

'Let me in,' pleaded Marty, 'c'mon, honey, she's gone.'

'I wish you wouldn't keep waking me up,' Muffin mumbled, getting up and unlocking the door.

Marty pounced on her. 'Gottcha!'

Mike woke late, swore, and called Cleo's hotel, but he just missed her.

He shaved and dressed and brooded. He wasn't happy with the way things had developed. Not at all. In the past when he and Cleo had a falling out they sat down and discussed it, talked it out. Always they would come to some mutually acceptable agreement. Cleo was by no means stupid, she was sharp and intelligent and what the hell were all these bullshit games she was playing?

O.K., he had fucked around. O.K. he was ready to take his punishment.

There was a knocking at his door, and for one bright moment he thought it might be Cleo, but on opening it he found it was Jackson.

'Congratulate me!' Jackson boasted. 'Momma is at this very moment aboard a big beautiful jet bound for New York. I saw her on the plane *personally*.'

'Very good,' said Mike.

'And get a load of our coverage—not bad huh?' Jackson flung a pile of newspapers on the table, and a large picture of Little Marty with Muffin at the previous evening's party was on most of the front pages. 'That little broad certainly helped things along,' continued Jackson. 'Looks good with our boy doesn't she?'

'Yes,' agreed Mike. He really couldn't give a shit.

'Had a great piece last night,' confided Jackson: 'Hot English ass cannot be beaten—especially when it's laced with a little bit of Jamaica.'

'How's the bookings on the concert?' Mike inquired abruptly. The last thing he wanted to hear about were Jackson's sexual adventures.

'Going great, should be a sell-out by this afternoon.'

'What's Marty doing today?'

'I said he could sleep late, then it's lunch with some guy who's

116

gonna do a full-page interview in one of the nationals. Then more publicity. Photos in the park, a couple of interviews for the music papers, then over and out for the concert. I'm gonna get him up now. You wanna come along to the lunch?'

'You're kidding aren't you?'

Jackson ambled off, and Mike finished dressing. His plans were set. Off to Cleo's hotel and wait for her, and this time things were going to be set straight. No more hanging around. He must have been mad to let her get away with sending him away. Screw that type of treatment. No, this time it was all going to be different.

Humming to himself Jackson knocked on the door of Little Marty's suite. He was pleased with himself. Pleased with getting rid of the mother. Pleased with the publicity coverage. Pleased with his evening of fun with the inventive Laurie—although he was a bit pissed off that Jon Clapton hadn't warned him the girl would expect to get *paid*.

'Can't you do it for love?' he had asked her.

'Fuck love!' Laurie had drawled laconically. 'I don't get no money—you don't get no honey.'

So he had paid her, laid her, and it had been worth it.

Marty came to the door and inched it open. Jackson attempted to enter, but Marty blocked him.

'Hey, kid, the coast is clear. Mommy's gone a-flying.'

'I know,' said Marty, 'she came to say goodbye. Look—can you come back later?'

'Later?' Jackson consulted his watch in some surprise. 'Listen, kid, it's past twelve, we have an appointment at one, and by the time you dress and we make it to the car—'

'I'll meet you in the lobby at ten of one.'

Puzzled, Jackson stood his ground. 'Don't you want to see the papers? You made every one.'

Marty took the papers and started to shut the door.

'Hey, kid. What is goin' on? You got a little teeny bopper stashed under the bed in there?'

Marty reddened.

'Look, kid,' Jackson spoke in a kindly tone, 'flush her out and let's get it together huh? We got work to do. Let me arrange your sex life in future and then we get no morning stragglers. You point one out—hey, Jackson baby. I want the redhead— and I'll do the rest. That's what I'm here for. to look after you.'

'I'll see you in the lobby,' Marty muttered.

'O.K. If that's what you want. Wear the pale beige buckskin and don't be late. Oh and Marty, we'll let it go this morning, but in future all arrangements are down to me. We don't want momma back, do we?'

# 32

A day spent with Daniel Onel was exhausting. Especially—Cleo decided—if you had a mansized hangover and were also suffering from lack of sleep. She wished that she had spent more time on her makeup and choice of clothes.

She would have liked to have looked her best for Daniel. He was a complex, talented person. and she felt attracted to him, sorry for him, and strangely in sympathy with him. It seemed to her that here was a man who didn't quite know what he wanted, and yet was stretching out in all directions and coming up with all the wrong solutions.

Their meeting finally broke up when Heidi returned in the late afternoon with a group of her friends.

Daniel made a face. 'I have to entertain the United Nations he explained. 'Heidi only ever brings home fellow Danes or the lower echelons of the chinless-wonder set. A real fun group'

Cleo smiled. 'I only planned to stay an hour and I ve been here all day. I've got lots of good stuff,' she hesitated if you like I'll give you a ring when I've written it, and you can see it.'

He nodded. 'That would be great, Do that.' He took her h nd and held it tightly. 'I've really enjoyed our talk. I hope I didn bore you too much.'

'You didn't bore me at all.'

He still held her hand and she didn't attempt to pull it free.

'Daniel,' Heidi said petulantly, 'where do you be keeping the champagne?'

'Well . . .' said Daniel.

'Well . . .' replied Cleo.

They smiled at each other, and he squeezed her hand before she extracted it. 'I'll phone you,' she promised.

'I'll look forward to it,' he replied.

Of course I won't phone him, she thought, in the taxi on the way back to the hotel. I must have been mad to suggest it. Any fool knew that if you showed an actor what you had written about him before publication he would want the whole thing changed. Egos were delicate, and constantly surprised at what other people thought of them.

As she was paying the taxi outside the hotel, somebody grabbed her from behind, covering her eyes with their hands.

For one blind moment of panic she thought she was being mugged, and then a high girlish voice was shrieking—'You're never gonna guess who this is!!'

'Ginny!' Cleo exclaimed, 'what are *you* doing here?'

They hugged and Ginny said, 'Supposedly working. But actually screwing!'

'Who?'

'I'm in love,' Ginny said solemnly, 'with a married man yet; and I think he'll probably have to divorce his wife for me,' she giggled. 'True love mixed with lust. I didn't think it was possible!'

'Who is it?' Cleo demanded.

'Shall we retire to the bar, and I'll tell you *all* in lurid detail. We're staying here, I tried to call you—did you get my messages?'

'When did you arrive?'

'Only today. I'm supposed to see Ramo Kaliffe about a package the agency is getting together. Do I look thin and beautiful? I've lost five pounds, does it show?'

'Sure. You look great. Who's the guy you're with, Ginny?'

'Hold your breath and prepare for a surprise. Mr Sex Expert himself—Dr Richard West!'

'I do need that drink. Let's go up to my room and you can tell me all about it, or were you just going out?'

'I was going shopping—it can wait. I was only going to buy a long black sexy nightie. Richard's mad for me in black! So what is happening with you and Mike? Lovey dovey or daggers drawn? That Susan really turned out to be supercunt. What a liar!'

'It really is a lovely surprise to see you. How long will you be here?'

'Three days of suck and fuck! This guy wrote *Sex—an Explanation* and I'm having him explain it to me every inch of the way!'

Cleo smiled. Ginny Sandler really was outrageous. But she was a true original. 'How did you and Richard West get together?'

'*You* introduced us, at that party for his book—remember? I guess we just sort of hit it off. I lured him back to my apartment, plied him with grass—his first time can you believe? Forty-six years old and a pot virgin. It was some thrill turning him on. I felt like a dirty old lady showing him my etchings! Anyway it all started that night, and here we are! He's doing some book promotion things, and as I said, I'm here to grab Ramo Kaliffe on a deal.'

'Knowing you,' said Cleo laughingly, 'that's not the *only* place you'll be grabbing Ramo Kaliffe.'

'Cleo!' exclaimed Ginny in a hurt baby girl voice, 'I told you I'm in love. I am even being faithful for the first time in my life!'

'I don't believe it!'

'It's true! Honestly!'

They arrived in Cleo's room, and as usual the switchboard had a varied assortment of messages for her. Mike had called three times.

Ginny was prattling on about New York, and her new grand affair, and the fact that she absolutely refused to talk to *that* Susan.

Cleo was only half listening. She really wanted to be alone. She fancied getting into bed with a good book to take her mind off *everything*. A full night's sleep was what she needed Then in the morning perhaps her mind would be clear enough to think about Mike.

What was she going to do about Mike?

What did she *want* to do about Mike?

It was a difficult and painful decision, and one that would affect her whole future. Did she want to spend the rest of her life with a man that lied and cheated? Or did she want a chance to go it alone?

She just didn't know.

'Anyway,' Ginny was saying, 'I want you to have dinner with us tonight, y'know you can sort of slip Richard little items about what a marvellous girl I am and how kind and sweet and all that shit. He digs me, but like I want him to freak—y'know?'

'I'm sorry, I can't, Ginny. Maybe tomorrow, how would that be?'

'Great. Just great. Perhaps I'll try and fix you up with Ramo Kaliffe, how would *that* grab you?'

'Not at all. I have already met him, interviewed him, seen him in his full frontal glory, and that is enough thank you.'

Ginny laughed. 'You're such a kidder!'

Cleo smiled. If Ginny only knew! But she wasn't about to confide in her about Ramo and Butch. Confiding in Ginny would be like taking out a full page ad in *Variety!*

There was a knock at the door.

'Ah—the drinks,' said Cleo. She opened the door and there stood Mike.

They stared silently at each other, and then Mike grinned and held out his arms and said, 'Hello, baby!'

Cleo stepped back, avoiding his outstretched arms. He followed her into the room coming to a stop when he spotted Ginny.

'Michael!' exclaimed Ginny. 'Good to see you.'

'I didn't know you were in town.'

'That just goes to show you don't know everything! I'm part of the jet set you know.' She fluttered her long false eyelashes at him 'You're looking as gorgeous and horny as ever.'

Mike frowned. Cleo tapped her fingernails impatiently on the wall.

'I guess I'd better make a move,' said Ginny reluctantly.

'No,' Cleo was quick to reply, 'I have some more questions.' She turned coldly to Mike. 'Ginny and I are in the middle of some business.'

'I've hung around all day waiting to see you,' Mike pointed out.

'That's not my fault. I never said I was going to be here.'

'I think we should talk.'

'I don't think we have anything to talk about.'

'Oh come on, Cleo. We have everything to talk about.'

'Look, kids,' said Ginny, standing up, 'I think perhaps I should split . . .'

'Yes,' agreed Mike.

'No,' insisted Cleo.

'Jesus!' exclaimed Mike, 'when you want to be stubborn—'

'Stubborn? I'm just doing what I want to do. Isn't that the general pattern of our marriage?'

'I would like to talk to you—alone. I really don't think that's too much to ask.'

'Fine. Don't just come barging in here like you own me. Make an appointment.'

'Who with? Your fucking secretary?'

'If you're going to be sarcastic I don't think there is any point in us talking.'

'You are not making this easy for me, Cleo.'

'Oh I'm so sorry, what a shame.'

'I'll come back later when you are alone. I don't think you're being fair to Ginny, she doesn't want to be involved in our problems.'

'*Your* problems.'

'I'll be back later.'

'Don't bother.'

'Christ! You can behave like a spoilt bitch at times.'

'Fuck off, Mike.'

Again. Yet again. Furious, Mike marched out of the room. Who was this strange angry woman who kept on telling him to fuck off? It wasn't the Cleo he knew. The calm beautiful woman he married. The lady with style. What had he done to conjure up a complete stranger? A person who was not even prepared to

122

discuss things with him. All he had done was get caught in the act, and surely that wasn't a *crime*?

He went to the bar. He would wait an hour, give her time to calm down, get rid of Ginny. Then he would go back, and this time she would be reasonable, and they would talk, and everything would be O.K.

'Have you ever been to bed with Mike?' Cleo inquired casually as soon as he had gone.

'Huh?' stammered Ginny.

'It's a straight enough question. Have you?'

Ginny reddened. 'Cleo, I'm your friend. How could you ask such a thing?'

'Easy. We both know you're not the vestal virgin type. You like guys, you like screwing. Mike's *very* attractive, I wouldn't blame you. Let's be open with each other. I won't be mad.'

'I just don't know why you're asking me a question like that.'

'Perhaps because I thought it might be fun if you gave me a truthful answer.' She paused. Mike had called her a bitch, O.K. she would behave like a bitch. 'Listen, Ginny, Mike has done a lot of talking since he's been here . . Isn't there something you feel *you* should tell me?'

'That sonofabitch!' Ginny exclaimed. 'Jesus Christ, Cleo, the last time was *three* years ago. Three lousy years.'

Cleo felt like she had been kicked in the stomach. A sudden hunch had turned into horrible reality. She had tricked a so-called friend into confessing something that she didn't even want to hear about.

'I don't know why he told you,' Ginny resumed miserably. 'It was never anything serious—just a quick screw for old times' sake. After all,' she added, her tone becoming defensive, 'you and I were hardly friendly then, and I had known Mike long before he even met you.'

'So now it's you *and* Susan. What other good friends of mine has my darling husband been giving it to?'

'I don't know—' started Ginny.

'You *do* know. You know everything that goes on. I think you owe me at least a little information, I don't think you owe Mike anything—do you?'

'Oh God. I feel really bad about it. I mean I thought you *knew* about Mike.'

'Knew what?'

'Well, let's face it. He likes to fuck around. I thought you knew all about his little flings and just turned a blind eye. I thought you got so mad because you caught him with a *friend*.'

'He likes to fuck around,' Cleo stared blankly, 'and I guess everyone knows this, and I guess I'm like a schmucky wife in those TV soap operas who is always the last to find out.'

'It doesn't mean he doesn't *love* you,' Ginny said desperately, 'he's mad about you—everyone knows that.'

'Oh great. Everyone knows that, and everyone knows he likes to fuck around. Beautiful!'

'You know how it is. Some guys can never get enough—'

'You're making Mike sound like a male version of you.'

'There's nothing wrong with that!' Ginny said defensively. 'I am not ashamed that I enjoy sex.'

'Goodnight, Ginny.'

'Look, don't be mad at me, *I* didn't do anything.'

'No, you're just a great big bundle of cute blond fun, and why don't I just give you a kiss and say thank you for humping my husband.'

'Oh shit!' exclaimed Ginny, 'I'm sorry if I've upset you.'

Cleo stared directly at her. '*You* haven't upset me. You just surprise me. In fact I'm surprised at Mike's taste.'

'I am not staying around for the insults. If you want to throw insults remember those three black girls Mike put under contract at Hampton. Dogs, all three of them, only Mike didn't think so. And remember Fanny Mason, tacky sloppy Fanny, well from her there was a little gift of the clap that Mike wasn't too anxious to bring home to you. Oh, and of course you remember . . .'

Cleo walked as calmly as she could into the bathroom and closed the door on Ginny's diatribe. She did not wish to hear the details of Mike's infidelities. It was enough that they existed.

She sat on the floor and mused on the fact that this was the second time in as many days that she had had to seek refuge in the bathroom. First Dominique. Now Ginny.

Ginny yelled from outside the bathroom door—'I'm not

surprised Mike had to fuck around. You're so cool it must have frozen his prick every time you did it!'

Oh it was good to have friends. Warm, honest, understanding individuals who were always around when you needed them. There was no one she could talk to. Not her mother. Not Dominique. Not Susan. Not Ginny. Not even Russell. Male friends had about as much loyalty as female friends.

In a fit of anger she decided she would get on a plane, rush back to New York, and jump straight into bed with Russell. *That* would show Mike. *That* would be sweet revenge. But it was a childish thought, and one that she soon dismissed.

Instead she went to bed. A night's sleep was what she needed. She told the switchboard no calls, locked her door, took two sleeping pills, and before long she drifted into a deep and uneasy sleep.

# 33

Marty handed Muffin the papers. 'We made all the front pages.' Muffin squealed with delight, and studied the pictures with rapt enjoyment.

Marty coughed nervously. 'My manager is getting a bit uptight with me. I—er—don't want to tell him about us. He'll throw a stupid fit—you know—the fans won't like it—that sort of stuff.'

She nodded understandingly.

'I've got a day of publicity, and then a big concert tonight We could sneak off early in the morning and get married before they suspect. They can't do anything once we've done it. How do you get married here? Is it easy?'

She giggled. 'How should I know?'

Marty frowned. 'In the States you need blood tests, you have to fill out forms, I think you have to wait.'

'Let's phone Caxton Hall—that's where all the stars get married, they can tell us what we should do.'

125

'Terrific idea!' Marty beamed. 'Am I glad they got my Ma out of here, it would have been a real drag with her around—she follows me everywhere—even to the bathroom!'

He dialled the operator and asked for Caxton Hall. Muffin curled up on his lap. What would the girls say when they read about *this!* What would Jon say?

'Excuse me,' Marty was inquiring, 'can you tell me how one goes about getting married?'

'Well?' Muffin asked excitedly when he hung up.

'No sweat,' he responded happily. '*You* need a birth certificate, *I* need my passport. You go along to your local register office and give notice that we want to get married—you put down we have both lived in the area for over fifteen days—then one day must pass—then like—yeah! So we can get married day after tomorrow!'

'Oh Marty, that's wonderful!'

They rolled about on the bed kissing and laughing.

'Gee!' he sighed. 'I've got to get dressed and out of here. Now *you've* got to get it all together—think you can do it?'

'Of course I can do it.'

'We have to be really careful no one suspects. Maybe you'd better go home and like cool it—then we could talk in the morning. I'll call you. If you come back here tomorrow night then we'd be all set for first thing next morning.'

'But what can I say to Jon?'

'Just boogie along. Don't tell him anything.'

'You mean like nothing's happening?'

'Right on! We haven't seen each other since the party.'

'I spent the night at a girlfriend's.'

'You've got it. Now you have got to get to the register office and give notice. Isn't this wild?'

'Absolutely too much!'

'You'll soon be Mrs Pearl.'

'I don't know if I can last tonight without you.'

'Maybe you can get Jon to bring you to the concert.'

'I could watch you on the stage. I'd probably wet my knickers!'

'Gee, you're cute.'

*

126

'Where the bloody hell do you think you've been?' demanded Jon. 'I've been out of my head with worry.'

Muffin bent to greet Scruff who barked with excitement.

'Well?' insisted Jon.

'Very well thank you,' replied Muffin perkily.

'Cut that out,' said Jon in an enraged tone. 'I've even phoned the hospitals looking for you.'

'I stayed with a girlfriend.'

'Who?'

'None of your business.'

'Don't be so childish.'

'Don't be so nosey.'

'I'm late for an assignment, and *you* were supposed to be at the wig place at eleven, you'd better phone them and get down there now. We'll talk about this later, but I am here to tell you that I'm really pissed off.'

She threw him a sulky stare.

'I'll be back at five,' he stated, 'and we might have to meet Jackson—he's big stuff in the States so try and be a little more charming tonight. He could do us a lot of good in America, look what he's done for Marty Pearl.'

'Are we going to the concert?'

'I don't know.'

'I'd like to.'

Jon snorted. 'Anything *you* want.'

When he left, Muffin phoned her mother. 'I need my birth certificate.'

'Lovely pictures in the papers, dear. It's so nice to see you with your clothes on for a change. Daddy says—'

'Have you got my birth certificate?'

'Yes, dear. Auntie Hildy says . . .'

Muffin took a cab out to Wimbledon, and kept it waiting while she collected her birth certificate. Then she went straight to her local register office and gave notice of an impending marriage. High with excitement she kept the cab on to Harrods where she went on a marvellous shoplifting spree. Two pairs of tights. Blue-tinted sunspecs. A pair of stretch knickers.

For a grand finale she went in the record department and

pinched the latest Marty Pearl single. Triumphant, she then returned home.


'Tell me,' inquired Anthony Private, 'how do you feel about the eleven- and twelve-year-old girls who become completely out of control at your concerts?'

Marty glanced nervously at Jackson.

'We feel,' said Jackson expansively, 'that the kids are having a good time, y'know—letting themselves go.'

'Marty,' said Anthony Private pointedly, 'How do *you* feel about it?'

'We feel,' Marty's voice cracked, so he cleared his throat and started again, 'well—like we feel the kids are having a good time.'

'Yes, but don't you think that it could be dangerous? In fact it has been proved that it is dangerous. One young girl was crushed to death—'

'She wasn't at one of Marty's concerts,' Jackson pointed out quickly.

'I know, but all the same—'

'If he thought,' Jackson indicated Marty who was picking at a prawn cocktail, 'that one little girl ran the risk of getting hurt, well he would just stop there and then. Give it all up.'

'Would you, Marty?'

'Sure I would.'

Anthony Private pursed his lips and scribbled something in a notebook. 'What about sex?'

'What about sex?' boomed Jackson

'I thought it might be fun if Marty told me about his first experience.'

Jackson frowned. 'This is a very religious boy. *Very* religious. He feels that he is too young to become seriously involved, in fact he doesn't even date yet. Marty's heart belongs to his fans.'

'Are you saying that he's a virgin?' Anthony Private raised incredulous eyebrows.

'Is there anything wrong with that?' demanded Jackson.

'No, not at all.'

Marty pushed his shrimp cocktail away. He couldn't eat. A naked image of Muffin danced before his eyes.

128

'Do you miss not dating?' Anthony Private inquired.

'Oh no, sir,' replied Marty mechanically, 'I have thousands of lovely girls who write to me and send me pictures, and their letters and love are more than enough.'

'Yes,' said Anthony Private, 'of course.'

# 34

Ginny Sandler found Mike in the bar. She slid on to a stool beside him. 'Just to let you know that I'm not a complete bitch I thought I had better warn you.'

'What about?' asked Mike shortly.

'I confirmed your story. By the way, thanks a lot, Cleo and I *were* friends you know.'

'What are you talking about?'

'You and me.'

'You and me?'

'You told Cleo—right? Why, I'll never know. Anyhow *I* told her the last time was three years ago. I don't think mentioning our fuck of the month arrangement would be wise. By the way, I want to terminate that arrangement. I'm in love—true love. I am going to be faithful. Order me a martini will you?'

'You told her about us?' asked Mike incredulously.

'Yes. Didn't you?'

'No, you silly bitch, I didn't. She sussed you out, and of course you fell. You never did have any brains.'

'But a nice cunt, right? You never objected to your little monthly visit there.'

'Oh Christ!' Mike buried his head in his hands. 'Jesus Christ! She'll never forgive me for you.'

'Boy oh boy—you and your lady wife certainly have a nice way of putting things. Forget the drink—I'm going.'

Mike's mind was racing. Deny it. Deny everything. Ginny was just a troublemaker. A plump blond troublemaker. Cleo darling, would I even *look* at a woman like that? Yes I would, because I have been screwing Ginny Sandler since she was seventeen years old, and she is the most uninhibited fuck this side of heaven. A birdbrain. A fatso. A stupid cow. But an incredible fuck.

If he confessed that to Cleo what would she say? She wouldn't understand. Nor would she understand about the many others. And he couldn't blame her. So deny it was the only answer.

He went to the housephone and dialled her room. No reply. He went up in the elevator and hammered on her door. No reply. He wasn't surprised. He wrote her a note and slipped it under her door. Maybe tomorrow would be his lucky day.

Crowds of fans milled about outside the theatre where Little Marty Pearl was due to appear. Young girls giggled and shrieked hysterically, some of them were wearing Little Marty Pearl T-shirts, some carried banners declaring their love for him.

Mike got out of his hired car at the front entrance and inspected the souvenir stands hastily erected. The latest records were displayed nicely, banked by a massive array of Little Marty Pearl posters.

Security seemed good, massive strongarm men were everywhere. Mike met with the manager, and had a short and friendly chat, then he made his way backstage.

Little Marty sat stiffly in a chair in front of a dressing table. His face was a mass of orange pan cake, and a spread of Kleenex was tucked neatly into the collar of his white satin jump suit to prevent staining.

'How's it going?' asked Mike.

'O.K.,' said Marty. 'I'll be glad when it's over.'

'Sure kid,' agreed Mike. He peered in the mirror at his own reflection. He looked terrible. Tired, strained, and uptight. He knew what *he* needed.

Jackson bustled in. 'Mike baby, it's all lookin' good huh? Packed house, they love the kid over here. Wanna go to the press room for a drink? I got some guests. You gonna have dinner with us after?'

'What guests?' inquired Mike.

'You remember Laurie? Little black chicken I was tellin' you about,' he winked, 'and that photographer guy and his lady—the one in the pictures with Marty. Oh, and that blond you left sitting last night.'

'Erica,' stated Mike.

'I was never good at names.'

'I'd like a drink,' declared Marty.

'After the show,' dismissed Jackson.

'Now,' demanded Marty. 'Why not? My ma ain't here to complain.'

'Oh shit!' exclaimed Jackson, 'I knew I should have kept her around.'

'Just a scotch and coke,' pleaded Marty.

'Don't forget you can't take a piss in that outfit.'

'I won't forget.' He got up.

'Where are you going?' Jackson demanded.

'To the press room.'

'Sit down, *I'll* get you a drink.'

'Can't I see the people?'

'No. After the show. You can come to dinner if you're not too tired.'

Marty's face lit up. 'Gee, thanks.'

Mike went along to the press room and sought out Erica. In times of stress he found that sex was the only answer. 'I have a headache,' he informed her.

'You really are a shit,' she protested mildly. 'Why did you walk out on me last night?'

'Because I knew the chances were that I was going to rape you at the table, and I didn't want to put you in that kind of embarrassing position. Can I fuck you?' Honesty was going to be his new policy.

'My God, you certainly don't waste time.'

'Don't believe in it. Well?'

'I think you're a little too direct.'

'I think you're a very beautiful girl and a very modern girl. What's wrong with making love if two people want to?'

'Nothing. But—'

'But what?'

'But I didn't say that I wanted to.'

'But you do.'

131

'Do I?'

'You know you do.'

'It's showtime folks,' Jackson was saying, 'let's go. Someone will take you out to your seats. C'mon everyone.'

Mike put a hand lightly on Erica's arm. 'We're staying here.'

'Why?'

'Why do you think?'

'But I want to see the show.'

'You'll see a show.'

She laughed softly. 'You really are a horny bastard.'

'Isn't that the only kind?'

They waited until the room had emptied out, and then Mike locked the door.

'Hey,' objected Erica, 'there isn't even a sofa or anything.'

Mike put his hands on her shoulders and peeled down the thin straps of her dress. She was wearing no bra and he bent his mouth to her small breasts and sharp pointed nipples.

Obligingly she unzipped his fly. 'My God,' she whispered, 'it's jumbo jet time!' He pushed her to her knees. 'I'll ladder my tights,' she complained.

'I'll buy you some new ones,' he soothed.

'The floor is hard.'

'So am I baby, so am I!'

She opened her mouth and he pushed himself in. Oh, what a sensation. She had a way with her tongue, short feathery little strokes. He had to withdraw before it was too late.

He peeled the tights off her and the rest of her dress. Naked, she was very thin, with sparse blondish pubic hair.

'I want to be on top,' she demanded, 'you can have the floor.'

He hadn't undressed so he didn't mind. He lay flat and she climbed on top of him, then she opened her legs suddenly, and he penetrated her deeply. She knew what she was doing.

'Are you ready?' she whispered after a few moments

'Any Any Any time.'

'Now!!'

Almost together, she was slightly ahead. And in the background they could hear the stamping and screaming of the teenyboppers.

'I always did like a big ovation!' murmured Erica.

## 35

Muffin joined in the screaming, she couldn't help herself. All around her in the theatre girls were freaking out.

On the stage Little Marty strutted and postured and made obscene movements with his guitar.

'This is one sexy little boy!' Laurie exclaimed. 'Shakes that baby ass like a hot little piston!'

Jon remained unmoved. Jackson may have made this boy a star, but what did he have to offer? Good looking in an All American Boy Next Door way. A no talent, packaged in white satin and high heeled boots. His voice you couldn't hear above the girls' screams, and his guitar playing was of the strum strum pause variety.

But the girls liked him, were obviously mad for him, and adulation was the name of the game.

It occurred to Jon that Muffin could be in the same position. She could hold a tune, she could be taught to strum a guitar. What a great idea! Boys would go mad for her. He would suggest the idea to Jackson, maybe they could cut a record. One guest appearance on *Top of the Pops*—it was a fantastic idea.

Little Marty was working up to his finale. The orange make-up was running in streaky rivulets down his face. The white satin jump suit was straining at the seams.

Muffin was bouncing up and down in her seat. Laurie was screaming with excitement.

Jon shook his head in amazement. He had never expected two girls like Muffin and Laurie to get carried away by this teenage corn flake.

At last it was over, and mob hysteria reigned while everyone yelled for more. The noise was deafening.

'Come on,' hissed Jon, 'let's get out of here.'

'Where's Jackson?' pouted Laurie.

'I said we'd all meet at *Tramp*.'

'Oh goody,' enthused Laurie, 'I love going there.'

'Aren't we going backstage?' asked Muffin.

'And get involved in that mob scene. No thanks.'

Muffin scowled. 'I wanted to tell Marty how terrific his concert was.'

'I'm sure he's got a dressing-room full of people telling him that. Anyway, Jackson said he's bringing him to dinner.'

'Wow!' exclaimed Laurie, 'I want to get my hands on that sexy little sweetheart!'

Muffin bit back a swift retort. Oh, wouldn't Laurie be jealous if she knew about the previous evening. Only a day to go and they would *all* be jealous!

She felt a bit guilty about Jon, but he would just have to understand. He would probably be quite pleased after he got used to the idea. Deep down she knew that he had never really wanted to get married again. Jane had just confirmed her suspicions. She had forced him into a commitment by withholding her signature on the Schumann Calendar contract.

Jon would still look after everything for her. He would still take all her photographs. They would be business partners. And friends.

Yes, Muffin decided, it would probably be a big relief for Jon in the long run. They had had fun together. Made it happen together. But now she had met Little Marty Pearl, and it wasn't *her* fault that they had fallen madly in love. It only proved that she hadn't really been in love with Jon in the first place—well maybe in the first place—but certainly not now. And anyhow Jon didn't want to marry her—and Marty did. It made a difference to a girl.

The restaurant at *Tramp* was bustling with activity; however, Guido had saved the big table in the corner for Jon, and he settled there with Muffin and Laurie.

'I hope I'm not going to get stuck with the cheque,' Jon muttered to Muffin.

'Don't be so mean,' she snapped back.

'I don't know who you spent last night with,' said Jon peevishly, 'but whoever it was they haven't sent you home in a good mood.'

'I told you. I was with a girlfriend.'

'I don't know why you insist on lying. We have an arrangement. It's cool. One time with whoever you fancy.' But it wasn't cool. He was secretly furious. Now that they were supposedly engaged things should change. The arrangement they had was O.K. for two people living together, but it certainly wasn't going to be O.K. for his wife. When he got the business with Jackson cleared away he and Muffin were going to sit down and have a long talk.

'Hey!' exclaimed Laurie, 'isn't that Butch Kaufman at that table?' They all looked.

'Yes,' said Muffin, 'very fanciable.'

'Yes,' agreed Laurie, 'very.'

'Do me a favour and try and spend tonight concentrating on Jackson,' instructed Jon.

'I concentrated on him last night,' pouted Laurie.

'Well concentrate again, and I'll do a whole set of new photographs for you.'

'Oh, really? Just what I need. When can we do them?'

They arrived in a group. Little Marty, Jackson, Mike James, and Erica.

Jon manoeuvred Jackson next to him, so *he* was happy. Muffin manoeuvred Marty next to her, so *she* was happy.

'You've gone very quiet,' Erica said to Mike, 'didn't you want to come?'

'Got to eat haven't I?'

'That's charming! Very flattering.'

'If it's flattery you're after you're sitting with the wrong guy.'

She laid her hand lightly on his knee under the table. 'If earlier was an example, I'm not with the wrong guy. I was thinking that perhaps you might like to spend the night at my place.'

He nodded. Whatever gets you through the night. And he wouldn't get through the night for thinking about Cleo if he was on his own.

Muffin enthused to Marty, 'Your concert was terrific!'

Marty grinned and winked, and under the table they twisted their legs together.

135

'Gee thanks,' he grunted, 'the kids seemed to get a good buzz going.'

Jon said to Jackson, 'I've had this really interesting idea. Can you imagine Muffin on something like a TV special playing a guitar and singing?'

'Can she sing?' asked Jackson in surprise.

'Yes,' said Jon confidently.

'Then it's a good idea. No problem getting her a guest spot. I think . . .'

Laurie suddenly threw her arms around Jackson's neck and kissed him long and lingeringly on the mouth.

Jon frowned. Not now, Laurie. Later. Concentrate on him later.

Butch Kaufman was approaching the table. Big and blond, in blue jeans and a massive cable knit sweater.

'Marty, baby!' he greeted, 'great to see you. Hey, Jackson, it's all happening for you and the kid. Cannot pick up a paper without seeing that cocky um er little face.'

'Who you with?' Jackson inquired.

'Couple of cute little ladybirds.'

'Why don't you join us?'

'Sure. Why not. Hey Franco—bring my two lady-friends over here.'

More chairs were squeezed around the table, and Butch's two girlfriends appeared. They were a pop singer's wife, and a freaky black lady with dyed blond hair. They seemed more interested in each other than anything else.

'How's the movie shaping?' asked Jackson.

'Slow. I've been over here three months now, and I'm getting beachsick. Man, I really miss my little um er shack at Malibu. Up in the morning, straight in the ocean for a swim, jog along the beach, barbecued bacon for breakfast. Can't beat it.'

'Sure,' agreed Jackson. 'Do you know everyone here, Butch? Laurie, Jon, Muffin, Erica, and you know Mike James of Hampton Records, don't you?'

Butch shook hands with Mike earnestly, 'Never had the pleasure, but I know B. B. and Mary Ellen. What a couple!'

Laurie licked her lips. 'I saw *Romantic* five times,' she announced, 'it made me cry.'

'I saw it twice,' joined in Muffin. She squeezed Marty's thigh under the table to let him know her thoughts were still with him.

'How about that!' exclaimed Butch, flashing his famous smile. 'I got paid peanuts for that goddamn picture, and it's one of the biggest grossers of all time. I bumped into the producer the other day—how about giving me some of your action I asked him—I got paid shit. Tough *shit*—the guy said—tough shit! That guy has made millions from that film—millions!'

'It was so sad when you died at the end,' confided Laurie, 'you know it was so real.'

Butch beamed. 'That's why the film was a success, sweetheart.'

'Hey,' said Jackson enthusiastically, 'you thought any more about making a record?'

'I can't sing . . .' protested Butch.

'Can Lee Marvin? Rex Harrison? Telly Savalas? What ya think, Mike? Great idea huh? Butch Kaufman on the Hampton label. Wanna offer him a contract now?'

'You were with my wife last night,' Mike stated coldly.

'Pardon?' asked Butch, not sure if he had heard correctly.

'You were with my wife,' repeated Mike.

Butch tried desperately to remember the names of the two girls he had ended up in bed with the previous evening. It was a lost cause, because he had never got as far as finding out their names.

'I was?' he said at last, his smile cracking at the edges.

'Cleo is my wife,' Mike said icily.

'Oh, Cleo!' exclaimed Butch. 'Yeah. Great lady She's writing a piece on me for *Image*.'

'I know,' said Mike shortly, 'she told me all about it.'

'That's nice,' mumbled Butch nervously. How much had Cleo told the husband? 'She's a fantastic person. Have you um er been married long?'

'Four years,' Mike stated shortly. 'Didn't she tell you?'

'Nope. Well you know how it is with us actors, always talking about ourselves. I never did get into any *personal* conversations with Cleo. Hey, Jackson, can I borrow your girlfriend for a dance?'

'Sure,' agreed Jackson. Laurie jumped eagerly up from the table, and she and Butch went off together.

'What's with the jealous husband bit?' inquired Erica with an amused smile.

'I'm not jealous,' stated Mike. 'I just wanted to let that beach boy prick know where it's at.'

'Where *is* it at?'

'Never mind. Drop it.'

'Are you and your wife separated?'

'No, we're not.'

'You just go your own ways.'

'No we don't. Cleo is tired, she's sleeping, that's why I'm out without her tonight.'

'What does that make me?'

Mike shrugged. He was still burning with anger at Butch Kaufman's sneering grinning face. Of course Cleo would never have done anything with him—he knew that for sure. But the bastard had probably tried. Any man would want to try with Cleo.

'You made love to me,' said Erica, 'so why would it be wrong if your wife made love with another man? Fair's fair, isn't it?'

Mike treated her to a scathing look. 'Whatever I do is my own thing. Cleo's—different. She wouldn't be interested in making out with transient studs. She has me.'

'What utter conceit!'

He scowled, 'Call it conceit if you want. Cleo wouldn't cheapen herself, she has too much style.'

'Jesus!' exclaimed Erica, 'what a sweet old-fashioned boy you are at heart.'

'You know something?'

'What?'

'On a dressing-room floor you're a lot of fun, but sitting at a table spouting dumb opinions on subjects you know nothing about, you're a pain in the ass.'

Now that Butch had taken Laurie off to dance, Jon launched into a heavy conversation with Jackson. Muffin took the opportunity to whisper in Marty's ear, 'It's all fixed.'

138

'Wow!' he declared, 'It's certainly gonna blow everyone's mind.'

'I know,' she giggled and squeezed his knee, then let her fingers slowly creep up.

'Watch it,' warned Marty, 'you know what that's gonna make me do.'

'Put your napkin on your lap,' she whispered.

He did as she requested, and Muffin slid her hand underneath and got a grip on his satin encased hard-on. He had changed from his stage suit into blue satin trousers and matching shirt.

Muffin was fumbling around. 'Can't find the zipper,' she muttered.

'Isn't one.' groaned Marty.

'How do you pee?'

His voice was muffled, 'I take them off.'

'That's rude!' she exclaimed.

'What's rude?' inquired Jon, suddenly tuning in.

'Oh nothing.' Slowly, Muffin slid her hand out from under the napkin.

'I think we may go straight to New York after shooting the calendar stuff in Barbados,' Jon said. 'Jackson's got some ideas for you that could really work out.'

'Smashing!' replied Muffin. 'Doesn't that sound smashing, Marty?' And they both burst out laughing.

Jon scowled. He could not stand Muffin when she got in one of her silly childish moods.

# 36

Cleo woke early. She felt fresher, more alert, and more able to cope with everything. She ordered coffee, juice, scrambled eggs, and after gorging herself on that she sat down and wrote her piece on Daniel Onel.

Four down, only one to go. then her assignment would be finished and she would be free to do as she pleased.

She called the desk and told them it was O.K. to put through calls now. Then she phoned and requested a temporary secretary to do her typing.

The phone rang as soon as she put it down. Surprise, it was her mother, the impeccable Stella.

'We haven't seen you, darling,' announced Stella. 'Nikai is back from Athens so we thought a little dinner party would be nice.'

'That would be lovely,' lied Cleo. 'When did you have in mind?'

'Tonight, dear. About eight. Wear something pretty.'

The phone rang again. This time it was Mike. He was contrite. 'I'm phoning for that appointment you promised me.'

'That was *before* I had a heart to heart with *your* friend Ginny.'

'Oh come on, Cleo, we have to talk.'

'Why?'

'Well . . .' he stumbled for words, 'I want to explain . . .'

She laughed flatly. 'Explain what?'

'You know what I mean, the things you've heard.'

'And what about the things I've *seen*?'

'Nobody's perfect.'

'I'm not looking for perfection, I'm looking for truth, and frankly, Mike, I don't think that you're the man who can give it to me.'

'I can give it to you, baby, you *know* I can give it to you.'

'Oh, Mike. It's very sad. With you everything always comes down to sex and smutty innuendoes.'

There was a long silence, then he said, 'I need you, babe, I can't make it without you.'

'You managed before I came along.'

'You can be a hard bitch.'

'So I've been told.'

There was another silence. Finally Mike broke it with—'I've been thinking about things. I've been thinking that maybe we should go back to the beginning.'

'The beginning, Mike?'

'Start again. Right back to square one.'

'It's a little too late for that.'

'It's never too late,' he pleaded desperately. 'We could do all the things you always wanted. Like maybe start a family.'

'I'm sorry, things just aren't the same any more.'

'We could make them the same.'

'Not me, Mike, not me.'

He hung up then, and Cleo sighed. It was going to end with bitterness. What was the point of letting him trot out all his lies and excuses? It would be a painful experience for both of them. It was better that he should think of her as a bitch, that way she could assume the burden of his guilt and he would feel better.

The phone rang yet again.

'Cleo. This is Shep Stone. You'd better get that friend of yours off my back. She's causing me a lot of problems, she's nutty as a fruitcake, a real ding-a-ling.'

'What are you talking about?'

'Your friend, Dominique. She is some mad broad. She is accusing *me*, Shep Stone, of stealing her diamond ring.'

'Stealing?'

'You heard it right the first time. Look, I want to tell you the whole story, maybe you can clear it up. It's urgent. Can you have lunch?'

'I suppose so,' she agreed reluctantly.

'I'll pick you up in twenty minutes.'

'O.K.' Jesus! Yet another problem to be faced. What *was* going on? Before she could get as far as the bathroom to comb her hair, and touch up her makeup, the phone rang again. After this call she must tell the desk no more. It was getting ridiculous.

'Yes?' she said sharply.

'It's Butch. I'm at the studio. Why didn't you tell me you had a jealous husband.'

'You didn't ask.'

'*Funny*. I met him last night, and like he was um er very uptight. You tell him anything?'

'Not yet.'

'What do you mean *not yet*? He's the kind of guy goes right for the balls, and I still need mine.'

141

'Where did you meet him?'

'*Tramp*. He had a blond draped across him, but he sure didn't like the fact that you've spent time with me.'

'I'm sorry if he made you nervous.'

'Aw shit, I'm not nervous. Just thought I'd let you know. By the way, what *is* the scene with you two?'

'I'm getting a divorce.' It was the first time she had said it and it felt good. Her feelings towards Mike were becoming numb. He was so upset about their marital break-up that he already had a blond in tow.

'That's cool. Want to have some chow tonight?'

'Sorry, tonight is family night.'

'Only *you* would turn me down for your family. Tomorrow? Or are you babysitting for a friend?'

'Tomorrow would be great if I don't have to fly to Rome. I'm doing Paulo Masserini.'

'Rephrase that please.'

'I am interviewing Signor Masserini.'

'That's better. I have feelings too you know.'

'Oh shut up.'

'Hey—I hear you turned Ramo down. He's destroyed. It's the first time a lady has gotten a look at supercock in the buff and said no thanks.'

'There's always a first time. By the way, wasn't I supposed to be out with *you* that night?'

'Yeah. Don't know what happened, we were all so stoned. Anyway thanks . . .'

'For what?'

'For not digging the Arab. I love him like a brother, but I don't want you to.'

'I don't get it. It's perfectly fine for you to lurch off in the bedroom with two scrubbers, but it's good that *I* didn't indulge with Ramo. Why?'

'Because I'm a rat and *you* are a beautiful lady. And I believe in bullshit double standards which I really should shit on. Talk to you tomorrow. Ciao.'

She rang the reception to tell them no more calls. Her temporary secretary arrived to type up the Onel interview.

'Three copies,' Cleo instructed. One for New York. One for

herself. And maybe one for Daniel, she would have to think about that.

In the lobby Shep Stone waited. 'I'm flying tomorrow so I am *very* nervous,' he confided, 'and your girlfriend is not making life easy.' He took her by the arm. 'I've got a car and driver. I thought we'd go to *Terrazza*.'

'I can't stay long,' she warned.

Just as they were leaving Mike pulled up in a cab.

She pretended not to see him, but he pounced over and grabbed her by the other arm.

'Shep,' she said wearily, 'I'd like you to meet my husband, Mike James.'

'Mike!' greeted Shep. 'Haven't seen you in years. Cleo is *your* wife?'

'*My* wife. Where are you taking her?'

'We're going to lunch, got a little problem Cleo's helping me with.'

'Oh, really. Perhaps I'll join you.'

'Perhaps you won't,' interrupted Cleo sharply.

'I didn't know you were married to Mike,' Shep said accusingly. 'Mike and I go back quite a few years together.' He slapped Mike on the shoulder. 'How's it going, old pal? *I* didn't even know you were married.'

Cleo wondered blankly if it would have made any difference at all to Shep if he had known. Maybe she would have been spared the flash of that red and angry cock, and Shep's voice pleading, 'Just a little head!'

'Are you writing a piece on Shep?' Mike asked sarcastically. 'Are we on to singers now?'

'No,' she replied sweetly. 'We're eloping to the nearest office couch we can find.'

'We met on the plane over,' Shep confided. 'She helped me through the journey, you know how I am about flying.'

Mike ignored him. 'I want to talk, Cleo.'

'Then she introduced me to her girlfriend, pretty girl, but nuts!' continued Shep, oblivious to the atmosphere.

'If we don't talk I'm not going to leave you alone. I'm going to follow you everywhere, and cramp every horny little bastard's style.' He glared at Shep.

'O.K.', she sighed. 'We'll talk.'

'Now?'

'Tonight. Only I want you to promise me that if we talk, that's it—no more phone calls, visits, or contacts.'

'You'll change your mind after we talk.'

'Just promise me, Mike.'

'All right, I promise. What time?'

'Seven-thirty, eight.'

'I'll see you then.'

'You going to lunch with us?' Shep asked in a falsely jovial voice.

'No, he's not,' responded Cleo firmly. 'Come along, Shep, if you have problems you'd better tell them to me, otherwise it will be time for me to go.'

'Later, then,' said Mike warmly. 'Take care of my old lady, Shep, she's very very special.'

In the car Shep repeated accusingly, 'You didn't tell me you were married to Mike James.'

'You didn't ask. If I remember correctly on our initial meeting you were rigid with fear, and after that all our conversations were about you.'

'You should have told me,' he insisted.

Cleo frowned. What a boorish man Shep Stone was. She tuned out as he launched into a running commentary of the first time he and Mike had met.

Of course it was inevitable that she would have to sit down and talk it out with Mike. You couldn't just brush four years with someone aside without an exchange of words. There were things to be settled. Possessions to be divided. A divorce to be arranged. She did not want a penny from him. He could have their apartment, their furniture. Most of it was his anyway. She wasn't even sure if she wanted to go through the trauma of dividing up possessions. These three Diana Ross albums are mine—you can have the Marvin Gaye. In her mind she had a plan. A plan of freedom.

Wouldn't it be great to have one suitcase that contained everything you needed? You could just wander around the world. Take yourself wherever you fancied. Interview anyone that struck you as interesting. She had enough money to get by. She

144

could sell the interviews. Russell would probably want to buy them for *Image*. and if not there were plenty of other magazines. After her interview with the Senator she had had plenty of offers. It was an idea that appealed to her immensely.

At the restaurant Shep made a lot of noise greeting the waiters, and generally revelling in the fact that everyone recognized him.

They both ordered spaghetti and white wine, and finally he confided, 'I balled your friend you know. She's very pretty. Like it was her suggestion, and I'm a red-blooded American male so I wasn't about to say no. We went back to my hotel and made love, and that was that. You see I'm a married man, and I can't afford to get involved.'

'Of course,' agreed Cleo sarcastically.

'Well, after that, she started to bug me with phone calls, and I tried to put her off nicely, but she wasn't having it, and the next day she burst in on me while I was in the middle of talking to my wife on the phone. and shit—I had to fight her off. She wanted to grab the phone and tell my wife everything. I had to get off the phone quick, and in the scuffle your friend got herself a black eye. It was an accident, but goddamn it she was like a wild cat.' He paused to gulp down some wine. 'Anyway.' he continued, 'she got excited and started ripping off her clothes, and by this time I knew she was bad news so I didn't want to do anything. This made her even more angry, and she started screaming about a diamond ring and accused me of *stealing* it, I'd never even *seen* any goddam ring. Anyway I finally got her calmed down, and the only way I could do it was by making love to her. I didn't want to, but there was *no other way*—she was screaming about getting the police and phoning all the papers. I *had* to do it. I can't afford that kind of publicity. I have a family image.'

'You should have thought about your family in the first place,' Cleo pointed out.

'I know that now. I made a mistake.'

'Yes, your mistake was that you went to bed with someone who wanted more than just a quick fuck.'

'I don't need a lesson in morals,' he snapped. 'I have learnt my lesson. I finally got her out of there, and I left word at the desk *no more* calls from, her, *no more* visits.' He fished in his pocket and pulled out a telegram. 'This morning I got this.' He handed the telegram to Cleo, and she read it slowly.

'PHONE BY SIX OR I WILL CONTACT THE POLICE AND YOUR WIFE AND THE NEWSPAPERS. DOMINIQUE.'

'My wife is in bed expecting a baby next month,' Shep mumbled. 'She's had two miscarriages, so this time they've kept her in bed. No excitement. No worries. If this gets to her . . .' he trailed off miserably.

Cleo shook her head sadly. 'Why didn't you think of your wife earlier?'

'I wasn't doing anything to hurt her.'

Is that what Mike was going to say?

'You must help me.'

'Yes, I suppose I must. Only I'm not helping *you*—I'm helping your wife. *You* make me sick.'

He averted his eyes.

'I'm not promising that I'll be able to do anything,' she added. 'Dominique has seemed a bit strange lately, but I'll go over and try and talk to her. Can you lend me your car and driver?'

Shep cheered up. 'Of course. Anything.'

# 37

'I think,' Jon announced, when they arrived home from *Tramp*, 'that we are well in there, Muff.'

'Pardon?' she yawned.

'With Jackson. The Americans. It will be red carpet for you all the way when we get there.'

'Oh.'

'Is that all you've got to say—oh? You should be dancing around with excitement. This is just the connection I've been looking for. Come here little girl, I want to feel your connections!' She was bending to pet Scruff, and Jon sneaked up behind and goosed her.

'Stop it!' she said crossly.

He laughed, and started to pull down her polka dot bikini panties.

She stood up quickly. 'I said *stop* it.'

'You're not still mad about that article? *I* didn't write it.'

'I'm not mad about anything. I'm just tired.'

'After your night of screwing,' he snapped.

'I wasn't screwing. I was with a girlfriend.'

'Oh, don't play that record again.' Jon felt surprisingly high. Everything was slotting nicely into place. His divorce. The Schumann Calendar. Jackson. 'Let's take some pictures,' he suggested.

'What pictures?'

'Personal pictures, for fun.'

'I don't feel like it.'

'Come on, you'll enjoy it.'

'I won't.'

'Where are the last Polaroids we took?'

'I threw them away.'

'You what?'

'I cut them up in tiny pieces and got rid of them.'

'Why?'

''Cos they were dirty.'

'Dirty!' he snorted. 'They were fun. After all they were only for us to see.'

'I don't want close-ups of your great big thing!'

'You wanted them when you were taking them.'

'That was different.'

'Let's take some more.'

'No.'

'Why not?'

'I told you, I don't want to.'

He shrugged. 'What did Laurie tell you about Jackson?'

'Nothing.'

'What do you mean—nothing. You and Erica were in the ladies' loo with her for twenty minutes.'

'Erica was telling us about Mike James.'

147

'What about him?'

'He did it to her on the dressing-room floor while we were all watching the concert.'

Jon grinned. 'Good old Erica, true to form.'

Muffin had started to undress. She was down to her sweater and panties.

Jon was sitting on the bed. 'Come and sit on my knee,' he instructed.

'Why?'

'I want to give you one.'

'I don't feel like it,' she retorted primly. She pulled her sweater over her head. Jon made a quick move, imprisoning her head in her sweater, and caressing her bosom with his free hand. She squealed with anger. He laughed, and manoeuvred her on to the bed.

'I can't breathe!' she pleaded.

'You are my prisoner, little girl,' declared Jon, pulling down her panties.

'You're a bloody swine!' mumbled Muffin.

'So I am,' he agreed, undoing the zip on his jeans and shaking himself free.

'Let me go,' she demanded.

'Not until I have had my way with you, woman.' He entered her, and she wriggled about vigorously. 'Ten strokes of the whip,' he laughed, 'or shall we make make it twenty?'

There was no response. Muffin enjoyed games. In fact it was *she* who usually instigated them.

'How's it feel getting raped?' Jon joked.

Muffin remained silent, but he could feel her approaching a climax, and he joined her in her efforts.

'You really are a swine,' she complained after.

'What's up with you? You loved it.'

'I didn't want it.'

'Yes, but you got it and you loved it.'

'Well, don't tell anyone then.'

'Who am I going to tell? The Queen?'

'I want to go to sleep now.'

'I'm not stopping you.' Jon shook his head.

Sometimes Muffin could be such a funny little thing.

Jackson, Laurie, and Little Marty rode back to the hotel together. When they arrived Jackson confided to Marty, 'I gotta surprise for you.'

'Gee, thanks. What is it?'

'Go to your room and wait, when I knock three times let me in.' Jackson wheezed with laughter, and nudged Laurie conspiratorially. 'I'm a telling you, boy, it's something gonna blow your little old mind. Take it from your old Uncle Jackson.'

'I like surprises,' remarked Marty, 'when I was a little boy my daddy once surprised me with a piano—that was before he died of course.'

Jackson laughed drunkenly. 'This ain't no piano, but I'm here to tell you it's got legs—yeah baby! Legs! You like chocolate ice-cream, son?'

'You know I do, Jackson. Only I'm not supposed to order it on account of my skin.'

Jackson doubled up with laughter. 'This dish will knock your zits right out.' He hugged Laurie. 'Right, baby? Am I right?'

'You sure are!' she giggled.

Marty went up to his suite, took off his satin outfit, and put on his towelling bathrobe. He hoped that Jackson's surprise was something to eat. He would give anything for a cream topped banana split, or a double chocolate sundae. He wondered if Muffin liked things like that. He hoped she did, because when they were married instead of proper meals they could have ice cream feasts. There would be no one to stop them. Jackson couldn't go around telling him what to do when he was married.

There were three distinct knocks at the door, and Marty went to answer it.

Laurie stood in the corridor stark naked apart from 'Present from Jackson' daubed across her breasts in bright red lipstick.

'Jesus Christ!' exclaimed Marty in a cracked and startled voice.

'No. Just Laurie baby,' and she giggled, and sauntered into the room. 'Come over here, sugar, and I'll teach you how to behave like a *star!*'

## 38

Cleo had never visited the house in Hampstead where Dominique lived, but Shep's driver seemed to know the street so it didn't take them too long to reach it.

It was a nice looking house with a short drive-way and flower beds neatly kept. Two cars were parked in the driveway, and a baby's pram stood empty outside the front door.

'Will you wait please,' Cleo instructed the driver, 'I won't be too long.'

She hadn't yet decided what she should say to Dominique. Perhaps if she explained about Shep's wife, or maybe if she could just make Dominique see what a worthless animal Shep really was. If Dominique started to insult her again she would just ignore it. Their friendship went back a long way, and Dominique was obviously going through a difficult time. Deep in thought she rang the bell.

Dayan answered the door. It hadn't occurred to her that he would be home. He looked upset. He looked like he had been crying. He stared at Cleo without a flicker of recognition.

'I'm Cleo. Cleo James, Dominique's friend. We met the other night, remember?'

'Yes,' he said at last. 'I remember.'

She stood uncomfortably on the doorstep waiting for him to invite her in, but he didn't move or make a welcoming gesture, he just stood there with a dour air of finality.

'Can I come in?' she asked at last.

'How did you know?' questioned Dayan. 'Did she tell you?' He suddenly started to sob, burying his face in his hands.

'I'm sorry,' stammered Cleo, 'I don't know what's going on. Has something happened? Is Dominique here?'

At that moment Isaac appeared. He looked gaunt and worried. He took his friend by the arm and gently guided him inside the house. To Cleo he made a gesture of silence, and she waited with a sudden horrible sense of foreboding while Isaac took Dayan off.

He returned in a minute. 'Dayan is very shocked,' he explained. 'We all are.'

'What has happened?' asked Cleo urgently.

'I'm sorry. I thought you knew. I thought that was why you came.'

'Knew what?'

'Dominique killed herself this morning.'

'Oh my God! I don't believe it . . .' she felt her knees start to buckle and the blood rush from her head.

Isaac held her and helped her inside. 'Sit down,' he said softly, 'I'll get you some brandy.'

She sat on a chair in the hall, and buried her head on her knees. It was unbelievable. Someone like Dominique wouldn't kill herself.

Isaac returned with a brandy, and she gulped it down.

'Why?' she questioned.

He shrugged. 'Nobody knows. She went through depressions, she had tried it before.'

'But she was so young. She had—everything.'

'Everything,' agreed Isaac.

'How did she do it?'

'It's best that I don't tell you. It wasn't very—nice.'

'Who found her?'

'Dayan. He phoned me and I arrived at the same time as the police. He has no one here you know. All his family are in Israel. I don't know what he will do.'

'Where is the baby?'

'The nanny took her out.'

'Did she leave any notes? Any explanation?'

He shook his head. 'Nothing. She was on tranquillizers, sleeping pills. Any little thing could set her off into one of her black moods.'

'I wish I had known. I don't think I was very sympathetic towards her. If I had known she was ill—'

'How do you think I feel?' he interrupted. 'I could have helped her more than anyone, but instead I just complicated matters. We were lovers you know '

'Yes, I know. She told me.'

'A few days ago I told her we must quit. I loved her, but

151

Dayan is my best and dearest friend and I couldn't do it to him any longer. She was furious, she couldn't accept any kind of rejection.'

Cleo nodded. 'I know.'

'She told me all about the American. I think she thought it would make me jealous—it did. Last time I spoke to her she told me she was going to the States with him. Was she?'

'He was married. More rejection. I guess it all added up.'

'I suppose so. God, I feel I should have done *something*. But what?'

'I don't know. I feel the same way. But I didn't know she was depressed, I thought she had just changed.' Cleo stood up. 'Shall I go and see Dayan?'

'I think it is best if he's just left alone.'

'I would like to come to the funeral. If there is anything I can do—'

'I'll tell Dayan.'

In a daze she made her way back to the car. She wanted to cry. She wanted to sob the way Dayan had done. But she couldn't, no tears would come. Just blankness, and a numb feeling of disbelief.

Back at the hotel she telephoned Shep. 'Your problems are over,' she told him.

'Great!' he exclaimed. 'I knew you could do it. What happened? What did she say?'

'She didn't say anything. She killed herself this morning.'

Quietly Cleo replaced the receiver. Yes, you bastard, she killed herself, and you gave her more than a little help. I hope you choke on the next woman you pull in for an afternoon hump.


Stella was immaculate in a black Yves St Laurent dress, her short ash-blond hair newly styled by Ricci Burns.

'You look like sisters,' enthused Nikai as he greeted Cleo. 'Nobody would believe Stella is your mother.'

'Don't be riduculous, darling,' admonished Stella, 'everyone knows I'm an old bag!' She slipped a thin arm through Mike's and flirtingly trilled, 'And how's the second most attractive man I know?'

'Who's the first? I'll kill him,' mocked Mike.

'My husband of course,' laughed Stella. 'Cleo darling, Mike is looking absolutely marvellous, what have you been doing to him?'

Cleo wanted to say—He's been fucking a lot of blonds, mummy. That always brings out the best in him.

Instead she smiled vaguely and admired a new star ruby and diamond ring that her mother was featuring.

'A present from Nikai,' confessed Stella. 'He spoils me, don't you, darling?'

Nikai agreed happily. 'If I didn't spoil you somebody else would.'

Oh, what a mistake to have come, thought Cleo. What a boring egotistical woman her mother was. All she craved out of life were presents and compliments and a certain amount of adoration. Fuck her; and fuck Nikai; and fuck Mike too.

'You look tired, darling,' observed Stella.

'I am tired. I had a lousy day. Do you remember my friend Dominique?'

'The pretty girl with the lovely red hair?'

'That's right. She killed herself today.'

'Oh dear, how awful. Mike darling, would you pour me out a teensy weensy martini, it's all mixed in the jug on the table.'

Was that it, Cleo wondered. Oh dear, how awful. Was that going to be Stella's only comment on Dominique? She had *known* her, *remembered her*. Even Mike, when she had told him earlier, had shown more concern than that, and he hadn't even *known* Dominique.

'I think,' said Stella, 'that after dinner we should be really naughty and pop along to *Annabels* for some of their delicious bitter chocolate ice cream.'

'Unbelievable!' muttered Cleo.

'What, darling?' questioned Stella.

'Nothing. You wouldn't understand.'

'How about a game of backgammon, Mike?' inquired Nikai. 'You do play, don't you?'

'Sure.' Mike glanced over at Cleo to see if she minded.

'Go ahead.' After leaving the house in Hampstead the rest of the day was a blur. She had phoned Shep. Checked through her

153

article on Daniel Onel which had been typed out. Made a couple of business calls. Then she had gone out and wandered around Hyde Park.

She had quite forgotten about Stella's dinner, and also her arrangement to meet and talk to Mike. When he had turned up at her hotel there had been only one answer. Take him along to Stella's. After all he was still her husband, it would not look odd as Stella knew nothing about their problems.

So here they were; and she felt trapped. Her only family; and it didn't matter one little bit if she never set eyes on any one of them again. Why should you have to like someone just because they were your mother?

Ever since she could remember Stella had made her feel ugly and inferior and stupid. Isn't your mother young! Friends from school would exclaim in envy and surprise. Isn't she beautiful! And so she bloody well should be. She spent every waking hour at the masseur or the hairdresser or the beauty salon or the dressmaker or the health farm.

When other kids' mothers were tramping round the zoo with them, or struggling to manoeuvre a small boat round the pond in Regents Park, Cleo's mother would be getting her winter suntan in Jamaica. 'Don't bring your friends home,' Stella was apt to complain, 'they're so noisy, I can't have my rest.'

Somehow Cleo struggled through the dinner. She had to admit that she was glad Mike was there. He turned on his full wattage charm and saved the evening. Stella loved him. He told her how young and desirable and gorgeous she was all through dinner.

When the suggestion of *Annabels* came up again Cleo declined. 'It's been a lovely evening,' she lied, 'but I'm so tired I just wouldn't be able to stay awake.'

'You should take a daily dose of wheatgerm and honey,' Stella admonished, 'it gives you lots of energy and does wonders for your skin.' She peered closely at Cleo. 'You are getting to an age, dear, when you should be looking after your skin.'

What was it Ginny used to say—a mouthful of sperm a day keeps the doctor away—and beats the shit out of face creams!

'Goodnight, Stella.' Cleo kissed her on the cheek.

'Goodnight, darling, and do write when you get back '

'You never reply.'

154

'I just never find the time, darling. But write anyway, I like to hear from you.'

In the car Mike said, 'My hotel or yours?'

'I don't suppose you would understand if I said I just wasn't up to talking tonight.'

'I don't suppose I would.'

'O.K.,' she shrugged helplessly. 'Your hotel.'

He instructed the driver and they rode in silence both immersed in their own private thoughts.

Mike was gaining his confidence back. His hotel, that was a good sign. Once he got her upstairs, once they got to talking, once they got their clothes off . . .

He certainly couldn't take much more of being without her. The previous long night spent at Erica's apartment had begun to pall. Erica, it turned out, was very kinky indeed. Almost too kinky for Mike's rich and varied tastes.

He had sneaked out early in the morning while she still slept.

They rode up in the elevator in continued silence until Cleo said, 'This isn't a good idea, Mike, it's only going to end in a screaming match.'

'You're wrong,' he shook his head. 'We can work it out, we always have before.'

'We always worked things out that involved the two of us.'

'All I ask is a chance to explain.'

He opened the door of his hotel room and ushered Cleo in. Sitting on the sofa reading a magazine and wrapped in a bath towel was Erica.

# 39

Muffin feigned sleep until Jon had left their flat. Rotten bastard, making her do it with him the previous evening. She hadn't wanted to—he had *forced* her. It could almost be called rape.

She had arranged with Little Marty to meet him at his hotel at seven.

'It will be cool by then.' Marty had instructed. 'I'm recording all day, and I'll tell Jackson I'm tired if he wants me to do anything in the evening.'

Muffin packed a few things. She wanted to get out of the flat long before Jon came home. She planned to buy an outfit to get married in. White would be nice, something frilly and virginal.

When she was made up, dressed, packed and ready, she scrawled a short note for Jon. 'Gone to a friend's. Will phone you tomorrow.' That would stop him from worrying. It was a shame really that she couldn't invite him to her wedding, but of course that was out of the question.

The phone rang as she was leaving the flat. It was Laurie. 'Come to lunch,' she insisted, 'I've got mind-blowing news!'

'What?' questioned Muffin.

'Too good to tell you over the phone.' boasted Laurie, 'you just won't believe it! I want to see your face. Two o'clock at the *Carousel*—O.K.?'

'O.K.'

Lunch with the girls would be fun. But it would also be tempting. She was bursting to tell *someone* about herself and Little Marty Pearl, but to tell the girls would only mean trouble. They couldn't be trusted. They would *race* to tell Jon, and then Jon would try and stop her, and it would all become boring. Who could she tell?

Her mother. She could tell her mother. She could swear her to secrecy. Bubbling with excitement Muffin took a cab out to Wimbledon.

'Two visits in so many days,' remarked her mother, 'it's not my birthday.'

'I know, mum. Have you ever heard of Little Marty Pearl?'

Her mother wiped workworn hands on a dish cloth. 'Take a look in the twins' room. Little Marty Pearl's picture is all over the walls.'

'Really? How terrific. Mum, don't faint, but I'm going to marry him.'

'So is Josie, but I've told her she's got to wait until she's sixteen.'

'Mum, I'm *serious*. I'm going to marry him. We're getting married secretly tomorrow morning. We met at a photo session and he's lovely and we fell in love.'

Muffin's mother sat down heavily. 'What about Jon?' she asked at last. 'You're engaged to Jon.'

'He doesn't mind,' lied Muffin airily. 'He quite understands. He never wanted to get married anyway.'

'Well . . . it all seems so sudden. Why tomorrow? You're not in trouble are you?'

Muffin giggled. 'Of course not, mum. Don't be so silly.'

'I always thought you'd have a white wedding, flowers, and Josie and Penny as bridesmaids. A nice reception at the townhall, all our relatives. Auntie Annie, Uncle Dick—'

'Mum! Is that all you've got to say?'

'It's a shock, dear. A disappointment. I was so looking forward to a nice ceremony, a *church* ceremony.'

'Oh, mum!'

'I can't help how I feel, dear. I can't hide my feelings. Your father will be disappointed too. We're both so proud of you, and it would have been—'

'All right, mum,' Muffin interrupted, 'no need to go on. Perhaps you'll change your mind when you come and visit me in Marty's house—*our* house—in Hollywood.'

'Has he got a house in Hollywood?'

'I expect so. Anyway if he hasn't we'll *get* one. A big house with a swimming pool. And we'll have two cars and lots of cute little dogs. And I won't have to take my clothes off in photos any more. Imagine that!'

'There's a lovely photo of you in the *Sun* this morning. Your hair looks lovely. Do you want to see it?'

Muffin never turned up at the *Carousel* for lunch. She was deflated by her mother's lack of enthusiasm, and after leaving there she went shopping for a wedding outfit. She found what she wanted, a tiered and frilled white calico ankle length dress. It had a chemise top which plunged alarmingly, and a matching shawl.

'Aren't you Muffin?' the girl in the shop asked.

'Yes.' agreed Muffin.

'I would have thought you would have got all your clothes for free, someone famous like you.'

Her mood improved. It was nice to be regarded as someone famous.


'Well?' inquired Jackson, digging Marty in the ribs. 'Was that a present or was that a present?'

'Thanks, Jackson,' said Marty lamely.

'I told you I'd take care of things in future.' he winked. 'I tested out the goods myself first. Hot stuff. A little soul food is good for you. You want her again tonight?'

'No!' said Marty hastily. 'I want to get some sleep tonight. Let me sleep late tomorrow too. I think I've got jet lag, I really feel flaked.'

'Not used to it, huh?' Jackson laughed. 'Not used to hot nooky as your bedtime snack.'

'Guess not.'

'I understand. I'll book you a call for twelve tomorrow. We're visiting the factory that makes your records—then we've got a photo session and we tape a kid's TV show. Nothing heavy.'

'I'll see you in the morning then.' said Marty. He glanced at his watch, it was six-thirty.

'If that's the way you want it, kid. By the way, that was a good session today.'

'Mike didn't seem to think so.'

'Mike's having personal problems. Take it from me, it was good. Things are moving just the way we want them to.'

I hope so, thought Marty. I hope Muffin turns up. I hope we make it tomorrow without getting found out. I hope by tomorrow night I'll be a married man.

'Goodnight, kid,' said Jackson.

'Goodnight, Jackson,' said Marty. When I am a married man I do not want you to call me kid any more. I am going to drink and swear and whore around just like all the other married men I know.

'Sure there's nothing you want?' asked Jackson.

'Nothing,' replied Marty.

'See you in the morning, then.'

## 40

The shock of finding Erica sitting calmly in his hotel room was too much for Mike to take.

Cleo took off immediately. 'Some other time.' she threw at him when he attempted to follow her, 'like in a year or two.'

He tried to argue but it was no use. so he let her go and went back to his room where Erica still sat.

'What the fuck do you think you're doing here.' he exploded 'Get up. Get out. Piss off.'

Erica put down the magazine and shrugged. 'I thought you would be *pleased*. I thought I would *surprise* you.'

'You surprised me all right. And you've fucked me up with my wife. Just get dressed and *out*.'

'Suppose I don't want to go?'

'Suppose I said I could make you go?'

'Make me.'

'Don't fuck around. Don't you know when you're not wanted? Just move it out of here—and fast.'

'You wanted me last night.'

'And I had you. And I don't want more, so just get it together and *out*.' His anger was like a tired throb. It seemed whatever happened was wrong. Since Cleo had caught him with Susan there had been a trail of disasters. Now this. Cleo would never forgive this. It was the final straw.

Erica stood up and undid the tie on the bath towel she was draped in. It fell around her ankles. Slowly she brought her hands up and started to massage her nipples until they stood out erect.

Mike watched.

'Want to join me?' she breathed huskily.

'No,' he snapped, but he couldn't help watching.

Her hands moved down to her stomach, caressing herself lovingly. Then she parted her legs, 'Come on,' she pleaded.

Mike stood unmoving.

She knelt down on the floor and parted her legs further. She started to groan and her movements grew more frantic. 'Please!' she begged him.

He didn't move.

She was nearly there. and suddenly he could stand it no more. The hell with it all. He unzipped his trousers and walked over to her. Roughly he thrust himself into her mouth, and as he did so she shuddered to a climax.

He gripped the back of her head, and rocked himself quickly back and forth. Three or four strokes and he was there. He held her head tightly nearly choking her.

'Is that what you wanted?' he growled when he was finished.

'Oh, yes!' she sighed.

'Good. Now you can get your clothes on and get out.'

He was aghast. What came over him? Did he have no control? What if Cleo had relented and come back? Christ! He really was a shit. Maybe Cleo was right to want to leave him. Maybe it wasn't in him to change. Maybe he didn't really want to.

He turned his back while Erica dressed.

'Are you sure you want me to go?' she whispered.

He ignored her. He didn't turn around until he heard the door close.


Cleo wondered if Mike had done it purposely. My hotel or yours? That had been *his* question. He must have known that there would be a girl waiting at his, so why had he taken her there? It was almost as if he *wanted* her to catch him.

She didn't understand him. It was just another shitty move in a week of shitty moves.

Anyway it had saved a long and painful conversation. There would be no conversations now, there would just be polite legal communications, and then a nice quick divorce. She would even be prepared to fly to Reno if that would make things quicker.

It all hit her at once. Dominique's death. The final realization that things with her and Mike really were over.

She got into bed and found that she couldn't sleep at all. Her mind was racing in a hundred different directions. The more she tried to sleep the more impossible it became.

In the morning she got a call to confirm her interview with Paulo Masserini, so she phoned the airline and booked herself on the next flight to Rome. She felt terrible, but she didn't want to cancel the interview, she just wanted to get it over with.

Mike phoned, but when she heard his voice she quietly replaced the receiver without saying anything. She wasn't even upset, just disappointed. Once she had loved him. Now she just felt sorry for him.

On an impulse she telephoned Daniel Onel before leaving. 'I finished the piece,' she told him.

'Did you?' he questioned vaguely.

'Yes. I think you'll like it. Look, if you like I'll drop it off to you on my way to the airport.'

'Are you going back to America?'

'No, I have to go to Rome to interview Paulo Masserini.'

'You have my sympathies.'

'Do you want to read the piece or not?'

'Certainly. Can I change it?'

'No changes. The original has already been sent to New York.'

'I don't think I'll bother then. It will only frustrate me.'

'Oh.' She was deflated. 'So I won't bother to drop it off then?'

'Thanks for the offer, love, but there is really no point to it. If I hate it I'm powerless—I couldn't stand that.'

'I don't think you'll hate it.'

'*You* wouldn't—*you* wrote it.'

'All right then,' she paused, 'I guess I'll send you a copy of the magazine when it appears.'

'You're very sweet.'

Very sweet indeed. Why hadn't he wanted to see her? Why had she wanted to see him?

It was much too soon to be thinking of getting involved with another man. Anyway Daniel Onel was very much involved already, she knew that; and anyway she had only ever met him once.

However there was something about him . . . just something . . .

## 41

Muffin never had been able to write properly. She had a large childish scrawl which actually aggravated Jon as much as the contents of the note. Sometimes he felt that he was living with a six year old. She couldn't even spell friend.

He read her note through twice, and then crumpled it into an angry ball and threw it down the toilet.

He had planned a special evening. Champagne, a bottle of which he had brought home with him. Flowers, a big bunch of pink roses—her favourite. And two airline tickets for Barbados booked for three days later.

Now she had ruined it all. Staying with a friend indeed! Did she take him for a fool? She was shacking up with some guy, and while one night was just about acceptable—two nights certainly weren't.

He racked his brain to think who it could be.

She had recently worked with Dave Ryle, and he was a bastard with the ladies. If Dave Ryle was moving in on Muffin . . .

Who would know?

Erica knew most things that were going on. He phoned her, but there was no reply. So then he phoned Dave Ryle, and made some vague inquiries about a new camera on the market. Casually he finished up with—'Oh by the way, is Muff there?'

Dave gave a dirty laugh. 'La Crumpet doesn't put it about over here—more's the pity. You lost her then?'

'No,' assured Jon, 'she's just late home. I thought she might have dropped by your studio to see the contacts of the session you two had last week. She mentioned that she might.'

'If she appears, me old son, I'll tell her you're waiting.'

'Thanks, Dave.' And he imagined them in a naked clinch laughing at the fact that he had phoned.

He tried Erica again. Still out.

He was more than slightly put out. He was furious. When Muffin came giggling home tomorrow he was going to give it to her straight. No more other guys—agreement or no agreement. And if she didn't like it . . . Oh God, what if she didn't like it?

Early in the morning when they were deciding that perhaps a couple of hours' sleep would be a good idea, Muffin snuggled up to Marty and said, 'I shouldn't have spent the night with you.'

'Why?'

''Cos I'm going to be a bride today, and we should have spent the night apart.'

'Wow!' sighed Marty, 'look what we would have missed!'

'Wow!' agreed Muffin, 'you're right!'

Neither of them could sleep, and eventually Muffin got up and started the long and elaborate ritual of getting herself together for an occasion.

She bathed, and shampooed her hair. Then while it was drying she started on her makeup—which on days when she wanted to look really special took at least an hour. When every false eyelash, and freckle, and glosser was in place, she put up her hair in heated rollers.

Marty, meanwhile, was peering at a new and angry crop of red spots on his forehead. He decided that the best form of coverage was to put a light make-up base over his entire face. He wondered if Muffin's heated rollers would do anything for his hair. Sexual activity seemed to equal limp and lifeless hair. He asked her, and with enthusiasm she carefully put rollers around the front part of his hair.

'Do you know,' announced Muffin, 'I once tried to dye Jon's eyelashes—they're so pale. Anyway he was furious—absolutely mad with rage. I think men should be into beauty stuff—it's fun. Shall I dye *your* eyelashes?'

'Not this morning,' Marty replied quickly.

'Oh no, not this morning, silly. I thought maybe on our honeymoon. Where shall we go for our honeymoon?'

Marty had actually thought no further than the marriage ceremony. A honeymoon hadn't occurred to him. They would get married, come back to the hotel, tell Jackson, and then Jackson would take over. Jackson made all his arrangements, and when he was a married man Jackson would have to treat him with a

163

little more respect. Of course Jackson wouldn't be thrilled—but it would be too late for him to do anything about it.

'I don't know,' he said vaguely. 'I've gotta finish this tour thing.'

'O.K.,' agreed Muffin brightly, 'we'll have a delayed honeymoon. How about Hawaii?'

'Yeah.'

'It looks so super on TV. You know—*Hawaii Five O*—and Steve McGarret, and all those fellas in a boat. Come here, I'll take your rollers out.'

When they were both finally ready they left the hotel by the back entrance. They were hardly an inconspicuous pair. Marty in his white buckskin suit with a magnificent quiff of hair— the rollers had worked beautifully. Muffin, like a pretty painted doll in her long frilled calico dress. They held hands and giggled nervously

It was a short taxi ride to the register office, and it wasn't until they arrived that Muffin realized they had forgotten to acquire two witnesses.

'We could ask two people from off the street,' Marty suggested.

Muffin grimaced, 'I wouldn't like *that*.'

'What then?' snapped Marty. He could feel a nervous rash breaking out all over his body. Oh God—what would Jackson say? He just wanted to get it over and done with.

'I know. I'll phone a couple of girlfriends.'

'Can they get here *quickly*?'

'I'll tell them it's a matter of urgency.'

A tall thin lady appeared and ushered them into a small anteroom. She offered Muffin the use of a phone.

Muffin phoned Kamika first. For a model Kamika was most dependable, and trustworthy. She promised to be there in fifteen minutes. Muffin then tried to decide whether to contact Erica or Laurie, theirs were the only other phone numbers she knew off by heart. Of course they were both bitches, but how much harm could they do at this late hour?

She finally decided on Laurie. She didn't tell her anything, she just requested that she got there immediately without a word to anyone.

Marty had started to chainsmoke.

'I didn't know you smoked,' stated Muffin in surprise.

'Jackson doesn't let me. Bad for the vocal cords. Did you get two friends?'

'They're on their way.'

The tall, thin lady had been staring at them in silence for some time. She suddenly said, 'The photographers will be here soon, do you want us to allow any of them in?'

'What photographers?' asked Marty in alarm.

'The newspapers.'

'Oh shit! How do they know?'

The tall, thin lady lowered her eyes in embarrassment. 'I'm sure *I* don't know.'

Marty jumped up. 'We can't wait for your friends, Muffin. If somebody has told the press, Jackson will be down here like a flash.'

'But we have to have two witnesses.'

'*She* could be one.' He indicated the tall, thin lady. 'Couldn't you?'

'No. I have to be able to receive people, answer the telephone. I work here. The registrar wouldn't allow it.'

'Does he allow you to tip off the papers?'

'*I* didn't tell them.'

'Oh, sure . . .'

At that moment Kamika arrived. 'What urgency?' she inquired. 'I have no breakfast, no time for makeup.'

'Kam!' Muffin fell upon her with relief. 'I'm getting married.'

'Where is Jon?'

'Not to Jon, to Marty. I want you to meet Little Marty Pearl.'

Kamika shook her head in amazement. 'I don't understand . . . Yesterday, at lunch Laurie said that she and . . .'

'Laurie will be here in a minute,' interrupted Muffin.

'Laurie?' questioned Marty, a confused blush spreading under his makeup.

'You English girls are so—liberal,' said Kamika. 'In Japan . . .'

'Why ask Laurie?' snapped Marty.

'Why not?' snapped back Muffin.

'Well, she's er—well she's Jackson's friend.'

'I didn't tell her anything.'

'It was stupid to ask her.'

'*So sorry.* I didn't exactly have a huge bloody choice.'

Laurie burst in then, clad in a button through jeans dress which concealed little. 'Hey. The streets are alive with photographers.' She raised her shades. 'Marty! What are *you* doing here. Jesus! I must take a pee. Muffin baby, what *is* going on?'

'We're getting married!' Muffin declared triumphantly. 'Marty and me.'

'Whaaaaaat?'

'Let's go,' said Marty quickly, 'let's do it and get out of here.'

'I'll show you through,' said the tall, thin lady primly.

'I'm *nervous!*' exclaimed Muffin.

Laurie shook her head. 'I guess I'm just dreaming. This is unreal.'

'Laurie,' asked Kamika, 'did you not say at lunch yesterday that you and—'

'Shush! We're at a wedding, Kam. Let's just cool it with the gossip.'

They all trooped into the room where the marriage was to take place. The registrar appeared, and without further ceremony he proceeded with the legalities of getting married.

Fifteen minutes later it was all over. Marty had forgotten to purchase a wedding ring, so Kamika slipped hers off and lent it to him to put on Muffin's finger.

'I just don't believe this whole thing!' whispered Laurie. 'If I had known what was happening I'd have dressed for the occasion.'

'We're married!' Muffin exclaimed, as they left the room. 'I'm Mrs Marty Pearl.' She hugged Marty who appeared to be in a daze. 'Let's go back to the flat and celebrate!'

'What flat?' asked Laurie.

'My flat.'

'What about Jon? Doesn't he mind?'

'Oh creeps! I forgot about Jon. He doesn't know.'

'Doesn't know! Oh baby, I want to go home.'

'I think I go home too,' joined in Kamika.

'O.K.,' pouted Muffin. 'Let's go to the Dorchester, Marty that would be fun. I've always wanted to go there for breakfast.'

Outside they were besieged by photographers.

'Wow!' exclaimed Muffin, 'now I *really* feel famous!'

# 42

'Do you mind if I smoke?' asked the fat man on her left.

Cleo smiled. Right on cue—she had known exactly when he would deem it the right moment to strike up a conversation.

The fat man took her smile as encouragement. 'I'm not the world's best flyer,' he confessed.

'I bet you're not the world's best anything!' she muttered.

'Pardon?' He was not sure that he had heard her correctly.

'You should really go on a diet,' observed Cleo, 'too much cholesterol. A middle-aged man like you is asking for a heart attack.'

The man reddened. 'Excuse me.' He headed for the back of the plane where he could chat up a stewardess without fear of being insulted.

Cleo yawned. In the morning she had felt terrible, now she felt good for the first time in days. She felt free. She felt exultant. Was this the way you were supposed to feel when you decided to get a divorce? Probably not—but the hell with it. She felt great! Perhaps going without sleep was good for you.

A British pop group was aboard the plane, and they were reeling up and down the aisles generally annoying everyone. There was one, about nineteen, with long black freaky curls and horny green eyes. Cleo smiled at him. He smiled back.

Oh how sweet to be a baby-snatcher!

If she was Ginny she would chat him up without further ado. He must be at least ten years younger than her.

He kept on passing by in his too tight jeans and sequinned jacket.

The fat man returned and squeezed back into his seat without a word.

Cleo got up and went to the back of the plane where she leafed through the magazine rack. Long black freaky curls appeared and studied her through cynical nineteen-year-old eyes.

'Wanna joint?' he finally asked in American cockney tones.

'Here?'

'Naw. We can squeeze in the john together. I can give ya more than a joint.' He winked hopefully.

An airborne fuck! A fantasy that Mike had always wanted to play out. But going with strangers had never been her style, tempting as the offer was. 'No, thanks.' She smiled to show that there was no animosity.

'O.K.,' freaky curls shrugged. 'Just thought it might be a groove.'

And well it might have been. Perhaps with Daniel Onel it might have been more than a groove—but then again screwing in aeroplanes was probably not Daniel's scene. There she went again—thinking about Daniel.

There was a car at Rome airport to meet her and take her to her hotel. The publicist for Paulo Masserini met her in the lobby and confirmed her appointment with the star at four o'clock.

Reports were that Paulo Masserini was a conceited egomaniac, but at least he seemed to be an organized one.

She was getting bored with interviewing actors. There was not enough meat on the bones to make a meal, and she was hungry for a politician. Ramo, Butch, Sami, Daniel, now Paulo. Some women would give anything just to meet those men, but they were only ordinary people, who by their looks and talent and charisma had been propelled into positions of great fame. A man who achieved things with his brain was a far more interesting proposition.

Still, she could not complain. Butch Kaufman had helped her make up her mind about her future. Daniel Onel had made her realize that Mike was no longer the most interesting and attractive man around. In retrospect Mike had stopped being that a long time ago.

Paulo Masserini was all that everyone had said he would be.

Tall, blondish, fortyish. With blue eyes that pierced right through you, and an Italian flavoured accent that smoothed over you like milk chocolate.

He kissed Cleo's hand, ordered her a Pernod and milk—because that was what he was drinking—and launched into a thousand and one stories about how witty, handsome, and sexy he was.

God, he was boring! For once in her career Cleo was unable to summon up that fixed look of interest that convinced the person who was being interviewed that they were indeed irresistibly interesting.

Openly she yawned, and when her cassette tape came to the end she couldn't be bothered to turn it over.

What a way to make a living. She needed a holiday. Interviewing actors was enough to make anyone need a holiday.

After two hours his wife arrived to collect him. She was a large lady of mammoth dimensions. She looked more like his mother than his wife. He did not seem anxious to go, and there followed a short, loud argument in Italian.

Cleo sat blankly through it. She didn't have an interview, there was nothing he had said that was remotely interesting enough to write about.

Or maybe it was her. Maybe she was losing her touch.

At last his wife led him away into the protective custody of his white Rolls Royce.

'He is a marvellous man!' the publicist said loyally.

'Quite a talker,' observed Cleo.

'But interesting.'

'Of course.'

'You have a good interview?'

'I'm sure I have more than enough.'

'Oh. There is a message for you. Signor Kaufman will be arriving at the hotel by six. He is expecting you to dine with him.'

They sat in a pavement restaurant.

'I er um didn't think that a lady who was just about to get a divorce should spend the night alone in Rome.'

'That's very thoughtful of you.'

'Not so thoughtful. I've been dying for a plate of decent spaghetti in weeks.'

'How did you know where I was?'

'A little detective work.'

'Was it difficult to get away? What about the movie?'

'I had two days off. I didn't tell them—there would only have been a hassle. Anyway we'll be back in the morning. Jeeze, but this wine is *good!* So tell me about pain in the ass Masserini? Still as full of bullshit as ever?'

'I guess so. Let's face it—an actor is an actor. I think I have a lousy interview.'

'Don't insult the profession by calling Masserini an actor. He's a lump of Italian pigshit.'

'You really like him don't you?'

'I really like you.' Butch stared at her searchingly. 'What do you say?'

'About what?'

'About us? Like er um how about giving things a try?'

'What things?'

'Like Malibu—the house. Living together. Moving in. Having a few laughs.'

'We hardly know each other.'

'Don't give me that sweet old-fashioned girl crap. I think we could make things happen together. What's to lose?'

'I thought you had a girl living with you.'

'She's just a friend—nothing heavy. I would like to play at being heavy with you.'

'I'm just climbing out of a marriage.'

'Climb in with me. I finish the movie in a week—we could fly back to L.A. together. No hassles, just fun.'

She laughed. 'This is so sudden . . .'

Butch laughed. 'Whoever is writing your dialogue must be fired immediately! Finish your spaghetti and we'll go to a disco and get chased by the papperazzi.'

Being with Butch made her feel safe. He was the sort of man you could be involved with without being involved with. And most important—he was totally honest.

Later, in bed, she considered his proposition. A few

weeks—maybe even months—lying around in Malibu could be just what she needed. She could see lawyers in California to arrange her divorce. She could stop work for a while and just relax. Butch was nice, easy to be with, they got along. What was there to lose? He was also a stud in bed, and maybe that's what she could do with right now. A little ego boosting in that direction after Mike was just what she needed.

In the morning she said, 'O.K. Let's give it a try, Mister Kaufman.'

He grinned. 'Good decision. We can have some laughs, see what happens . . .'

'Yes,' she agreed, 'we'll see what happens.'

# 43

The jostling crowds terrified Marty. People pushing and shoving, and photographers yelling for him to look their way.

Where had all these people come from? They were running in all directions, joining the back of the crowd, craning to see what was happening. A girl clung on to Marty's sleeve, he brushed her off. Where was his car? Where was Jackson?

Realization dawned. There was no car. There was no Jackson.

Muffin was unconcernedly posing for the photographers, she didn't seem to mind the crush, she didn't even appear to be aware of it.

Marty pulled her back inside the register office and slammed the door shut. He was perspiring and out of breath.

'What's the matter?' asked Muffin, slightly annoyed at being yanked out of the spotlight.

'Those crowds, they're dangerous.'

'Don't be so silly!'

'Call us a taxi,' Marty informed the tall, thin lady. 'Is there a back way out?'

'I like having photos taken,' pouted Muffin.

Marty didn't reply. His stomach hurt. He had a mild ulcer that played up under strain. His mother usually carried his pills for him. Now Jackson probably had them.

The taxi arrived, and they were ushered out the back way, but photographers had gathered there also, and there was more shoving and pushing.

'This is fun!' exclaimed Muffin, eyes sparkling.

'I've got a belly ache,' complained Marty.

Their taxi was followed, and more pictures were taken outside the Dorchester.

'I'm going to eat a huge breakfast,' announced Muffin, 'eggs, bacon, sausages, and champagne!'

'I feel sick,' declared Marty.

Waking up was never the best time of the day for Jackson. He usually had a hangover, and a million and one minor problems to deal with.

His immediate problem on this particular morning was how to get rid of Erica. He had encountered her leaving Mike James' room the previous evening, and since he was alone, he had automatically invited her to his room for a drink. One of Jackson's mottoes was never pass up a going opportunity. Of course, after polishing off a very fine bottle of brandy, they had ended up in bed. She was a maniac! Dangerous. Even Jackson wasn't ready for a repeat performance. He just wanted to get her awake and out.

He slid quietly out of bed, and grabbing some clothes locked himself in the bathroom.

Ruefully he examined his body. He was a mass of bites and scratches. He ached all over. Talk about a hungry woman! She acted like there hadn't been a man in years. Perhaps Mike James wasn't all he was cracked up to be. He had been dying to ask her, but talking was not part of her curriculum.

Quickly he dressed. Would Erica be wanting money like Laurie? *She* should be paying *him*.

The phone beside the bed began to ring, and before Jackson could reach it, Erica stretched out a long naked arm and picked it up. 'Yes?' she breathed.

Jackson removed it from her. 'Hello,' he snapped, 'Jackson here.' And then he wished he hadn't. He wished he had stayed in bed asleep.

Jon didn't sleep at all. He was so annoyed at Muffin's behaviour that he stayed up all night brooding about it. By morning he had bloodshot eyes, and he didn't feel at all like getting it together and photographing a fashion session.

He was just about to pick up the phone and cancel, when it rang.

It was Laurie. 'I think I should tell you.' she said.

'What?'

'After all I'm just as much *your* friend as Muffin's.'

'What?'

'And I really don't think she's being very fair.'

'Is it Dave Ryle?'

'Huh?'

'Nothing. What do you want to tell me?'

Laurie took a deep breath, 'Muffin and Little Marty Pearl just got married.'

'Don't be stupid,' responded Jon in disgust. 'Is she there with you? Is this her idea of a joke?'

'It's a fact, Jon. I was *there*. They just got married.'

'Are you serious?'

''Course I am. I wouldn't joke about something like this. I think it's—'

'Where are they?' he asked urgently.

'I think they said they were going to the Dorchester for a wedding breakfast. I didn't go. I—'

'Is Jackson with them?'

'He doesn't know. That's the whole point—no one knows. They—'

Jon hung up. That bitch! That dirty little bitch. How could she do this to him?

He phoned Jackson and a girl answered. It was Erica.

'He just rushed out of here,' she drawled, 'What *is* going on?'

Jon was already dashing out of the flat.

*

Marty's pains were getting worse, and when he saw Jackson come striding into the restaurant his only thought was that he would be carrying his stomach pills.

'You little cocksucker!' smiled Jackson, pulling up a chair, and waving amicably at a couple of reporters who had taken up residence at a nearby table. 'I told you, you get a hot nut it's *me* you run to. *Me*—not little Miss Golden Tits.'

'I've got my ulcer pains,' complained Marty. 'Can I have my pills?'

'I'll stuff your goddamn pills up your goddamn ass. What the fuck game do you call this? Because I call it marrying yourself right out of a job.'

'Morning.' chipped in Muffin brightly. 'Someone got out of bed the wrong side today.'

'Shut up, you little cunt. Do you *know* what you've done?'

'I want my pills.' whined Marty. He was thoroughly fed up with the whole thing, and he was glad that Jackson had arrived to take care of everything.

'Don't you call *me* names,' asserted Muffin. 'Marty, did you hear what he called me?'

'Where's your boyfriend?' demanded Jackson. 'Does *he* know about this?'

Muffin scowled.

'Jesus! You are two stupid kids! Whatever got into you both? Jesus!'

'We love each other,' declared Muffin.

'I am gonna get the cheque, and the three of us are gonna walk nicely out of here, and when I get you back to the hotel, Marty, I am personally gonna break your scruffy little neck.'

Marty hung his head. Where was all the respect he was supposed to get now that he was a married man?

Languidly Erica reached for the phone and asked for Mike James' room. 'I'm in the hotel,' she informed him.

'So?'

'So I thought you might like me to pay you a visit.'

'Don't push it.'

'Yes or no?'

174

He was silent. Cleo had just hung up on him. He sighed. 'Please yourself.'

'I always do.'

Jon caught them just as they were about to get into the car.

'Do join us.' intoned Jackson. 'you can beat the shit out of her. while I strangle this cute little prick.'

'I wish you would stop being rude!' complained Muffin.

Jon climbed into the car.

'My stomach hurts!' moaned Marty.

'Make the most of it. son.' said Jackson. 'right now that's the *least* of your problems.'

Muffin attempted a smile at Jon. 'Don't be mad. she said sweetly. '*you* never really wanted to marry me anyway.'

It was true. He couldn't deny it. But he *would* have married her. To protect his investment he *should* have married her.

Jackson said. 'I gotta plan.'

'What?' asked Jon. He was deflated.

'Annulment.' announced Jackson triumphantly, 'we got them early. Annulment—the only answer.'

'But . . .' began Muffin.

'No buts.' insisted Jackson. 'annulment. O.K., Marty?'

'Yeah,' agreed Marty miserably. 'can I have my pills now?'

# 44

Mike James checked in at the Pan American desk and handed the counter clerk two tickets for New York. He was glad to be going home. He hoped they had taken good care of his Ferrari.

Erica stood behind him. She looked cool and classy in a pale green midi suit. her blond hair smooth and shining. She had been booked to do a TV commercial in America; they needed a long cool English blond and she had been picked immediately. Mike had suggested they travel together. In fact he had suggested that she could stay in his apartment. Erica had not objected. In fact she had been delighted.

What the hell—Mike had thought—Cleo wasn't coming back—so he might as well enjoy himself. Erica would be fun to take around New York. A new face. What the hell . . .

A day earlier he had seen Little Marty Pearl and Jackson safely off on their European tour. Oh, and Mrs Emma Pearl had been recalled from America and was with them also. When last seen she had been stuffing Marty with stomach pills, and complaining about dirty foreign foods. Mike laughed at the thought.

Cleo was a bitch. He should have realized it long ago. Selfish, conniving, cold, hard. Good riddance.

Erica had more style in her little finger.

Fuck you, Cleo James—running off with a superstud like Butch Kaufman. Fuck you—bitch.

Later in the day there was a flight leaving for Los Angeles.

Muffin arrived at the airport wearing a see-through peasant blouse, and faded jeans tucked into outrageous wedge-heeled boots that appeared to be made out of the American flag.

'Hey—Muffin!' the photographers called—'Over here. Turn sideways. Beautiful! This direction, darlin'!'

Jon organized the luggage and sorted out the travel documents—visas, passports, tickets, etc. It had been a tough week—but thank Christ for Jackson. After his initial fury he had calmed down and taken complete control of the situation. Quietly he had taken Jon to one side. 'You don't want these two babies shitting on you do you?' he had inquired. 'No way,' Jon had stated. 'Then no sweat,' Jackson replied, 'I'll deal with it.' And he had.

Muffin had been a bundle of scorned girlhood. Marty had been relieved. Jackson had pulled all the right strings.

'What was the *real* story with you and Little Marty Pearl?' a photographer was asking.

Muffin dimpled cheekily. 'Like I've said a million and one times, it was just a joke—a silly joke that misfired.' She turned

176

to hug Jon. 'This is my man, always has been, always will be. We're going to marry soon, aren't we, sweetie?'

Jon disentangled himself. 'Sure,' he agreed, 'we'll be shooting pictures for a calendar spread that Muffin is doing, then who knows . . .'

'Is the marriage with Little Marty legally off?' asked a reporter.

'It was never legally on,' replied Jon. 'It was declared null within a couple of hours. Look, fellas—we've been through this all week. You know the facts. Can we drop it now?' He took Muffin firmly by the arm and led her away.

'*You are hurting my arm*,' she complained. 'You don't own me.'

'I own your contract for the calendar deal, so just shut up and come on.'

'Pig!' she muttered.

'Can it, Muff. Don't vent your childish little temper on me. *I* didn't marry you one minute and wriggle out of it the next. You're lucky you were saved from that teeny bopper wonder so quickly.'

'Shitty socks!'

'Listen. We're going to Hollywood. We're going to stay in a beautiful house all arranged for and paid for by Jackson. We're going to shoot some incredible pictures. *Then* we go to Barbados. What more could you want? Relax. Enjoy it. We're going to have an incredible time.'

'Pooh!' said Muffin, and stuck out her tongue.

Once Muffin had passed through, the photographers turned their attention to Butch Kaufman, who had just arrived.

Cleo left him to be photographed, and perused the magazine stand. She saw a newspaper with a picture of Shep Stone hugging a pretty woman on the front page. The copy read 'Shep Stone 39 greets his wife dancer Mary Lou 22 who arrived from Florida today.'

Mary Lou looked in the pink of health. Certainly not eight months pregnant. Certainly not just recovering from a miscarriage. So much for Shep Stone and his lies. He had fooled her. And what had he done to Dominique?

Cleo sighed, most people thought only of themselves. She had attended Dominique's funeral. Shep Stone had not even sent flowers.

The latest edition of *Image* was on the magazine stand, and she bought two copies. 'Who's Afraid Of the Big Bad Wolf' was advertised on the cover, and Russell had opened the series up with her piece on Butch. 'If you are after American prime stud . . .' her article began. Is that what she had been after? Is that what she had got?

'Hey, baby,' Butch came rushing over, 'don't want to have your er um photo with me—huh? All those guys are asking me who's the mystery lady, who's the pretty girl with the long sexy legs. Then Daniel Onel arrived and they turned their lenses on him. You had a lucky escape.'

'Daniel Onel—here?'

'Yeah. He's on the same plane—staying at the Beverly Hills for a couple of weeks. I told him to come by the house. You don't mind do you?'

'No, I don't mind.' She turned to look, and sure enough there was Daniel trying to brush his way past the photographers, and there was his Danish au pair princess posing happily.

Cleo smiled. Perhaps Los Angeles would turn out to mean more than she had hoped.

Daniel suddenly saw her, and for a moment he stared, and that stare meant everything.

'Come on, baby,' drawled Butch, 'we've got an um er plane to catch.'

# Los Angeles
# Six Months Later

## 45

Life with Butch had its advantages.

Like—an easy time lying in the sun with nothing much to do except concentrate on getting an incredible suntan.

Like—no taxing conversations. He and his friends drifted easily through life discussing nothing more serious than surfing and health foods.

Like—Butch did all the cooking on his trusty Hitachi barbecue. And all the shopping. He actually *liked* being recognized at the supermarket.

Like—sex.

Life with Butch also had its disadvantages.

Like—wondering if seeing that your inner thigh tanned exactly the same colour as the rest of you was really that important.

Like—being bored to death with his bunch of brainless friends.

Like—endless barbecued steaks, chicken and salad. And never any cookies or candies in the house as Butch refused to buy them on the grounds that they were poison.

Like—sex.

And then there was the Beverly Hills social scene. Occasional little sorties into town to attend parties that Butch thought he should be seen at. After all he was an actor—and actors had to put themselves about—flash the profile and remind everyone that they still existed and had not vanished in a puff of celluloid.

Cleo had never looked so good in her life. She hardly recognized herself. Was this finely muscled suntanned creature really her? This lady full of boundless energy stuffed full of barbecued steaks and health food. This woman who jogged patiently along the beach next to Butch. Who did push ups and leg bends and yoga. This woman who had not written one solitary word since arriving in California.

Her body was active. Her mind was lying dormant. She didn't care. She needed this break in her life. A period of limbo where she could try and decide what she *really* wanted to do.

Mike was but a distant memory—a *divorced* distant memory.

No longer a part of her. And now that he was permanently gone she didn't even miss him. Perhaps she had never really loved him in the first place. Perhaps it had been his cock she had loved—his long thin weapon of pleasure and his tight hard balls. When she had heard how indiscriminate he had been with his equipment . . . Well . . .

Butch was no husband substitute. He was someone to coast along with. Nothing heavy or binding. Although lately he had taken to calling her 'my old lady'—and that irritated her. She didn't belong to him just because she had chosen to share his house. She was nobody's old anything.

Every month she received a six-page letter from Russell Hayes. Gossip about mutual acquaintances, a few funny comments on his latest statuesque girlfriends, and always, at the end of the letter, a request to know when she was going to start work again. She sent him a postcard in return. A view of the beach with a few scrawled lines of greeting. It was good to know that Russell had returned to the 'good friend' category, and was no longer lusting after her body. She giggled when she considered Russell lusting after anyone, and Butch, ensconced beneath a giant sun reflector—all the better to capture the best of the March rays—said, 'What was that babe?'

'Nothing,' she replied lazily, turning her body on the slatted wooden boards of the front deck of Butch's house.

She wondered why they were still together. She was hardly his type. Before her they had all been seventeen with enormous boobs. Once she had questioned him about this.

'You got class and intelligence,' he had replied, 'can't beat *that*, babe.'

As far as she knew he didn't screw around. And if he did—well she didn't much care. It wasn't that sort of relationship.

She was quite prepared to sleep with another man if she could only come across one that she fancied. The only vague contender was a friend of Butch's who lived up the beach. Another movie star with shifty eyes and a sly grin. A good actor with an Oscar in his kitchen to prove it. But he was a bastard with a capital B. And so stoned most of the time that he didn't realize he was a bastard. Cleo steered warily clear of him.

Occasionally her thoughts turned to Daniel Onel. She had

seen him twice, nothing to get excited about. Once, while shopping on Rodeo Drive, she had recognized him strolling towards her. Quickly she had crossed the street, she didn't know why.

The second time they had attended the same party and exchanged a brief hello. To Cleo's annoyance he didn't seem to *remember* her, his greeting was very vague. Then it occurred to her that maybe he hadn't liked the article she had written on him. Actors were funny about seeing the truth about themselves in print. The hell with him anyway—he was just another ageing egotistical movie star—probably as boring as all the rest if you got to know him. She hadn't got to know him. She had wanted to at the time, but she hadn't. Conveniently he faded gradually from her thoughts—although she couldn't help reading about him.

Butch had a passion for movie magazines, and they littered the house full of juicy gossip about which superstar was doing what to whom. Photos of himself he cut out, and a secretary pasted them into a series of giant scrapbooks. He had tried to persuade Cleo to appear in a photo spread with him, but she had steadfastly refused. She had looked through his scrap-books, she had seen the endless layouts of Butch partaking in a variety of activities with numerous busty females.

'I don't want to join the photographic tits and ass club,' she had joked when he sulked about her refusal.

'You'll change your mind,' he had said confidently.

Oh no I won't—she had replied silently.

So what did she read about Daniel? Items of great interest. The fact that he was into yoga—who wasn't? The fact that he was a vegetarian—nothing new about *that*. The fact that his favourite colour was green. His hobby was reading. He was most comfortable in casual clothes. Hated cats. Loved cars. And his favourite pastime appeared to be women.

After the Princess got dumped there was a never-ending supply of different females in his life. From fifteen to fifty they were photographed with him everywhere he went. You certainly could never accuse him of having a type. All shapes, sizes and colour hues seemed to suit him just fine. He was hardly the womanizing type—but he certainly seemed to be enjoying a riotous success.

'Hey babe,' drawled Butch, interrupting her lazy thoughts.

'Yes?' she questioned shortly. Butch's 'hey babes' always heralded a request, and she didn't feel like getting up and making him a tuna fish sandwich or whatever it was he was going to ask.

'I guess we're makin' out pretty good,' Butch stated, throwing an arm across her stomach and stroking her finely muscled flesh the way he knew she enjoyed.

'I guess,' she agreed. 'Why? What's on your mind?'

'I like you—you like me. We're a couple—a real couple. You understand what I'm saying?'

She knew what was coming. Every so often he mentioned marriage. She wasn't interested in marriage. Why was it when you told a guy you were in no way anxious to get married *that* was the time it became his strongest desire in life.

She had explained to Butch how she felt. Two marriages behind her. Who needed it? She was surprised he kept on pushing—after all he had two ex-wives—hadn't he learned his lesson?

Butch removed the sun reflector from around his face and placed it on the ground—a sure sign that he wanted a *serious* conversation.

Cleo sighed. She liked him—he was undemanding, easy to be with, a sexual athlete, and fun. She did not love him. She had no wish to become any further involved than she already was. In fact she knew the time had come to be moving on—all this sun and health was stupefying her brain. She needed to be stimulated mentally for a change.

'What's on your mind, Butch?' she asked again.

He laughed. He had a boyish laugh—one of his most endearing qualities on the screen. 'You always know when I got somethin' to say,' he chortled, 'like I could never *lie* to you—you'd pick up on it in a minute.'

The sun disappeared behind a cloud and she shivered, sat up, hugged her knees to her and gazed at Butch expectantly.

'I never lied to you, babe,' he said sheepishly, 'there's just somethin' I never got around to tellin' you.'

'What something?'

'Like I gotta daughter,' he said quickly.

'A daughter! Why didn't you tell me? How old is she?'

'*That's* why I never told you . . . She's er um . . . thirteen.

'Thirteen! But Butch—you're only twenty-eight youself.'

'Yeah, I was a child father.'

She shook her head in amazement. 'So where is she?'

'S'why I'm tellin' you, babe. She's gonna be here—tomorrow. Her mommy is sendin' her out from New York—figures I should take a little er um responsibility.'

'And who is mommy? Your first wife?'

'Hell no. Had the kid five years 'fore I got married the first time.'

'This is some bombshell. You with a thirteen-year-old daughter. I just can't believe it!'

'You'll believe it all right—she looks just like me.'

'When do you see her? And how come you've never mentioned her before?'

'I always visit them when I make New York. Shelley and me—that's the kid's mother—always got along good. I lay a lot of bread on her—see that everything's nice and tight.'

'Does the kid have a name?'

'Vinnie. She's a little tomboy—cute as hell—wants to get into movies. Course I gotta tell everyone she's my *sister*—can't blow the image. Hey Cleo—you'll love her, I just know it.'

They talked long into the night. Cleo was fascinated that Butch had managed to keep it a secret so long. He told her everything. How Shelley had been a rich girl of thirteen living in a high class apartment building with her family. He had delivered the groceries once a week—and finally he had been delivering more than groceries when Shelley's mother was out. Hot sticky afternoons of passion atop the best living-room couch. Fast but fun. Fumbling with French letters, disposing of them down the waste disposal unit after the deed was done. Then the weeks of agonizing while Shelley waited to get her period—and waited and waited . . .

Her elder sister took her to a doctor and the dreaded pregnancy was confirmed. Butch threw away his stock of rubbers in disgust. Shelley wanted the kid. She actually wanted it—and nobody could talk her into an abortion although they all tried.

Butch was summoned by her father. 'You're too young to get

married,' he snorted in disgust, 'but you get the hell out of my little girl's life or I'll have the police after you.'

Terrified, Butch had hitched across country to California, and there he had stayed—drifting into acting, two marriages, and stardom. He and Shelley had always kept in touch. They were real good friends. After his first marriage broke up they had even talked about marrying each other—but it had seemed too much like incest. They were brother and sister now—why spoil it?

Shelley was into ballet dancing. At twenty-six she suddenly wanted a career, she had been through three marriages and wanted something lasting. She had called Butch and said, 'I'm sending Vinnie out to you, it's about time *you* had your turn at playing daddy.'

He hadn't argued. It was the first time in thirteen years she had asked anything of him.

Cleo was quite excited at the prospect of a child arriving. She hoped that they would get along—it certainly wouldn't be *her* fault if they didn't. Already she was making plans. Disneyland, and Magic Mountain. A trip around Universal studios, maybe a drive up to San Diego to visit Sea World. These were all things that Cleo had promised herself to do, but somehow—alone—it didn't seem like fun.

In bed Butch stroked her body in his usual expert way. His tongue, starting on her mouth, drifted down to her breasts, her stomach, her thighs.

She moaned softly. It wasn't time to move on—not yet anyway.

Mike James swore quietly to himself. How did you get rid of them? Moving in seemed to be an easy enough process. One day it was a hairbrush and a few jars of makeup—the next—all of their life's possessions. Clothes, magazines, hair dryers, photographs. Jesus! When would he learn?

Since Erica three girls had taken up what they obviously intended to be permanent residence—and each time it seemed to get more difficult to persuade them to pack up their things and go.

Erica had been the easiest. Six weeks of gradual boredom on

186

both sides and then Erica had announced she was moving in with Jackson.

Mike had not been sorry. He had even helped her pack, and when she begged to come back. two weeks later. Samantha was already in residence. Samantha of the slidey green eyes and strange exotic body odour. She had lasted a month. Then Tulea, a sweet. docile. very pretty Philippine girl. Three months—perhaps a record. She had cried when he asked *her* to go. Cried for a week. All very upsetting. so Annie Gamble. raunchy independent model girl had seemed like a good thing at the time.

Annie was no longer a good thing. Talk about demanding! Equal orgasm wasn't in it. She wanted equal everything, including a drive of his Ferrari. *Never.* He asked her to go.

'When I find another apartment.' she replied dismissively, studying her beautiful face in the mirror. and applying silver eyeshadow. 'Let's trip out and boogie. baby.'

He had no desire to do anything with Annie any longer.

It didn't seem to bother her. She eased herself into a silver cat suit. thigh-length boots. and went out to boogie without him.

He sulked around the apartment. taking stock of her numerous possessions. and finally went to bed with a plan forming in his mind. The plan was to buy a large trunk, wait until Annie was out. pack all her things. change the locks. and hey presto—he would be a free man again. And this time he really had learned his lesson. No more moving in. Fuck and out. Better still—go to *their* apartment—don't even let them through the door.

Satisfied with his solution he finally fell asleep, only to be woken by Annie at four o'clock in the morning. She was attempting to get some action out of his fast asleep penis. 'Come on. baby.' she crooned. 'mama is feelin' mighty horny.'

Mike drew away angrily. She reeked of booze and sweat, and the hell with her. He wasn't some sex object to be used at her convenience.

'You're all fuckin' faggots at heart.' Annie mumbled in disgust. and reeled off into the bathroom, where the sound of her plastic vibrator filled the air.

Annie was the worst of them all. Very beautiful—but so what?

*She* acted like the man with her independence, sexual demands, and total dedication to her own pleasure.

Mike thought of Cleo—he often did. And he had a horrible feeling that he would never find another woman like her.

The next morning he bought a trunk—a large one. And as soon as Annie left the apartment he started to pack it.

*This* one would never be allowed back.

# 46

'Open your legs,' requested the photographer in a matter-of-fact fashion.

Muffin pretended she hadn't heard. She smiled in her cute girlsy fashion, and thrust her pretty little tits out even further.

'Hey,' said the photographer, 'these pix are for *Hard* magazine. *You* know what they want. Be a good girl—after all you're getting paid a lot of bread for a few shots of pussy. Bring your knees up—let them fall open—come on sweetpuss.'

The sun was blazing down on the gleaming luxurious swimming pool. Muffin, lying naked on a sunbed beside it, reluctantly obeyed. Legs up, slightly open. She knew what he wanted. Christ—she had been doing it for the last five weeks. She had *had* to do it. Who wanted straight nude stuff any more? Who wanted a pretty face and a beautiful body?

Forget that scene—it was over. If a girl didn't open her legs for a camera it was forget-it time. No work. No bread. And Jon leeching off her like a fucking ponce. There was no money left. Everything had gone sour. The great American dream had turned into this.

'Wider,' said the photographer. 'Come on—you've got a beautiful snatch—what are you trying to hide it for?'

Wider. Sure. He wasn't a photographer. He was a fucking gynaecologist.

Muffin wished she had smoked a joint or sniffed some coke

before the session. Jon had promised to get her some. Big promise. Nothing. Some husband.

'Why don't you throw your hand across your thigh.' suggested the photographer, 'let it trail—yeah—let the fingers loose—yeah—that's it—great!'

Click. Click. Click. He stopped to change his film.

Muffin stared up at the cloudless blue sky. Everyone complained about the smog in Los Angeles. What smog? Sweat was forming on her body. She felt sticky and dirty. Very dirty.

At first it had all been so great. Jackson—true to his word—had set them up in a magnificent house on Summit Drive—five minutes from the very centre of Beverly Hills. For six weeks they had languished in the sun. swimming in their own pool, playing tennis on their own court. entertaining a variety of Jackson's friends. Jon had started the calendar pictures—incredibly innocent shots compared to what she was doing now. Then Barbados. Three weeks of pleasurable work—and glowing with success they had returned to L.A.. where Jackson had said he would set about getting Muffin work. He was happy to let them move back into the same house—but this time at an enormous rental.

Jon had agreed. Jon had dollar signs weaving in front of his eyes. Jon was convinced she was going to be the biggest thing since sliced bread. Jon had swept her off to Mexico with a pile of friends and finally married her. Only by now she knew it wasn't love. It was called protecting your investment.

Oh yes—in Los Angeles she had grown up. She had changed from a dizzy little dummy into a disillusioned resilient hard nut.

Los Angeles was full. Pretty. Beautiful. Exotic. Erotic. Legs. Tits. Ass. You name it—you could get it.

Muffin was no big deal in America. Couldn't sing. Couldn t act. Couldn't dance. A lot of their money went on lessons. She still couldn't sing. act or dance.

When the money started to run out she suggested that they went back to London.

'Are you kidding?' Jon had said in total amazement. 'How can we go back as failures? *You* might be able to do it—but *I* certainly couldn't. We'll make it here if we just hang on.'

Hanging on, to Jon, meant staying in the house. And

somehow the rent had to be paid. Eventually he had suggested she did some layouts for the girlie magazines. 'Just once or twice—the money will keep us going.'

She hadn't really realized what she was letting herself in for. The first session Jon photographed her himself. He got her very stoned, and it was all sort of hazy fun. When she opened her legs it was for him not the camera—and in the middle he had made love to her—and she hadn't realized how she had been conned until she saw the photos . . .

There was no going home to Wimbledon now. She blushed with shame that her father might see them. Oh God! Jon was a bastard. She finally understood why his first wife had always said that he was.

The American dream. Open your legs and I'll show it to you.

The photographer had reloaded and was ready to start again. 'Let's go sweetpuss,' he said briskly, glancing at his watch. 'I've got two more sessions to shoot today. Open up those pearly gates!'

'Move your arm,' the girl giggled in clipped British tones. 'You're hurting me!'

Jon obliged, extricating his arm from around her thigh.

'My leg's gone to sleep,' she complained, lifting it up and shaking it. 'Ouch! Pins and bloody needles.'

They were entwined naked on the floor of her mobile dressing room. Jon with Diana Beeson—English movie actress—two films to her credit and all the producers clamouring for more.

She was twenty-eight. A ladylike sex symbol. Long dark curls, cat eyes, a luscious mouth. She had been in Hollywood for eight months and had a reputation for being hard to get into bed. Many had tried. Most had failed.

It had taken Jon with his baby-faced charm seven days.

Diana caressed his flaccid penis affectionately. 'We have another ten minutes before they come knocking on my door,' she suggested.

Ten minutes. Get it up you fool. Don't blow it.

He rolled on top of Diana and started to nibble her erect nipples.

She sighed happily. She was a very beautiful girl. He thought of Muffin. Thought of the photos he had taken of her. Miraculously he was hard, and mounted Miss Beeson and gave her what she required.

She laughed. She moaned. She came.

She got up off the floor and checked her appearance in the mirror. She brushed her luxurious dark hair and slipped a bathrobe over her nude body. She blew him a kiss.

'When they knock tell them I've popped along to makeup, all right luv?'

She didn't wait for an answer. She was gone  Very independent lady, Miss Beeson. Very successful. With the right man behind her . . .

Jon got up and stared at his skinny body in the mirror. No muscles. Bones sticking out here and there. He could still pull whenever he wanted to.

Diana had left her mark. Two deep scratches across his rib cage. It didn't matter. Muffin wouldn't notice. She didn't notice anything any more. she was always too stoned. He remembered with a flash of guilt that he had promised to get her a joint before her photographic session. Shit. She would be really pissed off and more whiney than ever. Whatever happened to the Muff he used to know? Whatever happened to his sweet little girl?

Hollywood. That's what happened. And all the accompanying bullshit that went to her dumb little head.

He scowled at himself in the mirror. If only she had listened to him. He *could* have made her a star.

Too late now. Posing for snatch shots. Christ! She had *really* blown it. Conveniently he forgot that it had been *his* idea in the first place. Anything to pay the rent on the fucking palace Jackson had saddled him with. Fuck Jackson. And fuck his drugged out friends.

Slowly Jon pulled on his clothes. He knew he had to dump Muffin before she dragged him down with her. If only he hadn't married her . . . How easy it would be . . . When was he going to *learn?*

Now. if he could only move in with Diana. Get a quickie divorce. She had a nice beach house. simple but comfortable. Not the kind of house a future star should be living in. He would soon change that.

191

It had been a clever stroke on his part to get in touch with some of his contacts in England. Middle-aged lady photo editors were only too pleased to commission some work from him. And one of them had wanted a cover story on Diana Beeson.

A phone call. Diana had agreed. Now all week he had been on the set photographing her.

As soon as he saw her he had known that she could be his new passport to the big time. Carefully, subtly, he had planned to have her.

Seven days wasn't bad for a girl who was supposed to be very hard to get. Not bad at all.

Now, if he could only figure out what to do with Muffin . . .

# 47

Cleo was excited. For the first time in months she had something to look forward to. Butch's revelation about having a thirteen-year-old daughter had startled her at first, but now suddenly, inexplicably, she was delighted.

When Butch drove off to the airport she cleaned the house. The place was filthy—house cleaning had never figured high on either of their lists. The room that Vinnie was to have, had no more than a bed and bureau. It was not too late to pretty it up. On impulse Cleo dashed out to her car and drove into Beverly Hills. She went straight to Robinsons where she perused the linen department and chose candy striped sheets and matching frilled coverlet. Then on her way out she passed the toy department and spotted a large Snoopy dog. Little girls were *never* too big for Snoopy.

Pleased with her purchases she piled them in the back of her car, and headed home. On the way she stopped at the supermarket. Why not get some cookies for a change? And candy, and ice-cream and fudge nut brownies. Butch called them 'poison foods'—but Cleo was sure that Vinnie wouldn't feel the same way. Vinnie. Funny name for a girl. Short for—what? She had forgotten to ask Butch. She put her foot down on the gas hard—maybe she would just make it home before them. Time to set the room up, get it looking pretty.

Butch's car was not out front. Good. She had made it first. Quickly she parked, staggered from the car, and piled high with packages, let herself in.

Rock music assailed her senses. The loudest hardest rock she had ever heard. Jesus, where was it coming from? It was impossible.

'Hey—' she called out, but her voice was drowned in the sound.

She dumped the packages on the kitchen table, explored further, the noise drumming into her head like a hammer. The living-room was empty.

'Butch?' she called weakly. Where the hell *was* he.

She walked into Vinnie's room. Empty. Only one place left. Their bedroom, and yes—that *was* where the ear shattering music seemed to be coming from. She threw open the door. A blonder version of Butch sat in the middle of the bed. A female blond version, with flowing silky hair and firm jutting breasts, barely concealed by the bikini she was wearing. Bright tough little blue eyes stared in an unfriendly fashion. A tape recorder propped between her legs issued forth the awful noise, and she was engaged in painting her toenails a glittering shade of gold. A cigarette—grass?—dangled from full jammy lips. *This* was Vinnie? *This* was his *child?*

'Who're you?' the girl asked in a gravelly voice.

Cleo couldn't actually hear the words, she lip-read them.

Vinnie, having asked the question apparently lost interest in the answer, and returned to painting her toenails, cigarette ash scattering over the bed.

For a moment Cleo was speechless—then anger took over at the blatent *rudeness* of this grotesque child person. She stepped briskly forward and slammed the Off button on the nerve-racking sound.

'Wassamatter?' drawled Vinnie, 'dontcha like to get it on?'

'I guess you're Vinnie,' she stated, hoping that maybe—please God maybe—she might be wrong.

'I guess I am.' replied the girl. studying Cleo through narrowed eyes. 'so—I'll try again—who're you?'

Hadn't Butch told her? Surely he couldn't be *that* dumb. With a sinking feeling she realized that he could.

'My name's Cleo.' she said tightly. attempting a smile, 'and I live here. Actually that's my bed you're spread out on.'

The girl made a clicking sound through her teeth—a sound that indicated amusement. 'So you're the latest huh? You sure don't look like the others. Aintcha kinda skinny for Butch?'

Cleo swallowed anger and attempted to remain cool. 'Where is your father?' she asked politely.

'He hadda go inta town.'

Yes—she thought grimly—I bet he did. What a goddamn coward. 'Well.' she said brightly. 'I guess we'll start by getting you settled in your own room. Come along—bring all your things.'

'I'm jake here. Butch said I could go where I wanted.'

'I don't think Butch had it planned we would sleep three to a bed.'

'I'm not gonna *sleep* here.' Vinnie said scornfully. 'I'll move offa here in time for you to screw.'

'You'll move off now!' snapped Cleo.

'Jeeze! Are you uptight!' Vinnie dragged deep on her cigarette and stubbed it out in an ashtray. Then she picked up her tape recorder and nail polish. and slid off the bed. Without another word she exited through to the living-room. and from there through the screen doors to the wooden deck. The tape recorder was clicked on and the heavy rock blasted out.

Cleo sat on the side of the bed. She couldn't believe it—just couldn't believe it. Was this what thirteen-year-old girls were like today? Was this *monster* the sweet little daughter she had been expecting? God! How wrong could you be?

Somehow she had a strong feeling that it wouldn't be long before she was moving on.

Butch did not return until after six. He breezed into the house like nothing could possibly be amiss. Kissed Cleo casually on the cheek. and swept Vinnie up in an affectionate bear hug. 'How's my little beauty?' he crowed proudly.

Vinnie struggled free. 'For crissakes don't hand me that shit you hand out to all your girls.'

Butch laughed. 'Watch your mouth, shortstuff.'

'Aw—shove it.' Vinnie retreated to the beach.

'Great kid,' Butch enthused, 'spunky—just like her um—er good old dad.'

'And where has her good old dad been?' Cleo asked coldly.

'Didn't I tell you? Had a meeting with Lew Margolis over at Paradox. You know something—the new rewrite on *Surf Stud* is not that bad. If they up the bread I just might be tempted.'

'Butch—why didn't you tell me Vinnie was so—well—so precocious?'

He opened up a can of beer. swigged from it, wiped his mouth with the back of his hand. 'She is?' His surprise was genuine.

'Don't tell me you haven't noticed. Lolita isn't in it. And why didn't you tell her about me?'

He smiled boyishly. 'I knew the two of you would get along just fine.'

Cleo raised her eyebrows, 'You know something, Butch? You're more stupid than even the newspapers give you credit for.'

'Hey . . . Come on babe . . .'

'I mean it. If you think for one sweet minute I'm going to have little Lolita running wild all over *this* house—well—*babe*—just think again.'

He went over to her, enclosed her with his arms. 'Hey . . . easy. Give the kid a break. She's disorientated. A coupla days and we'll all be one big happy family!'

Two days later Cleo was packing her suitcases. Enough was enough. Vinnie was impossible to live with—no wonder her mother had wanted to get rid of her. She smoked. drank, swore. She was untidy, dirty, inquisitive, searching every closet and drawer in the house. She was rude. insulting and surly. And Cleo had considered it the final straw when she came across 'sweet little Vinnie' screwing the attendant from a nearby gas station on *her* bed. 'Out!' she screamed.

'*You* get out,' Vinnie had retorted. 'this is my dad's home and I'm a minor. *I'm* the one that stays—so *screw you*, lady.'

There was a certain logic in what she had to say. Butch was out. Cleo decided waiting to discuss it with him was a waste of time—as far as he was concerned Vinnie was Little Miss Cute Ass. So she began to pack.

Moving on was no great wrench. Six months of baked brains was enough for anyone.

# 48

Karmen Rush was one of the new style movie stars. Exotic, rich, talented and ugly. She compensated by surrounding herself with beautiful men, and throwing the best, most bizarre parties in Hollywood. If you weren't invited to Karmen's you just didn't exist.

Jon manoeuvred an invitation to the latest bash. A late-night party to welcome superstar Al King to Hollywood.

'I don't want to go, I'm beat.' Muffin had complained. Several quaaludes later she changed her mind.

It upset Jon to see her so dependent on pills and drugs, but then again if that's what kept her going . . . Besides a little grass or coke never hurt anyone. Half of Hollywood was stoned out of their heads most of the time—and they still managed to take care of business. Jon did not indulge. He wanted to keep his head crystal clear at all times. He had noticed that Diana wasn't averse to a little snort of coke occasionally. He would soon get her off *that* kick.

'Are we nearly there?' Muffin questioned, 'I'm famished.'

Jon was driving their rented Cadillac. Muffin's photographic fee for her day's work would have to go on the latest payment. The car was the last thing he wanted to lose. 'Five minutes,' he said, 'don't worry, it will probably be the best meal we've had all week.'

Karmen Rush lived in a huge glass house on the Malibu Colony. Guards saw them through to the private estate, and then Jon surrendered the car to a muscle-bound parking attendant.

The magnificent house was already teeming with guests. Loud rock music issued forth from every corner. A Charlie Chaplin movie played soundlessly on a plain white wall. Perspex tables, supported by sculptures of naked men, groaned under the abundance of food.

Muffin headed in that direction first. She stuffed her mouth with egg roll and chunks of crabmeat, spare ribs and giant prawns. The food was delicious. Satisfied, she turned and looked around for Jon. He had vanished into the crowd. It was not unusual, he always seemed to leave her alone at parties. The thing she hated about Hollywood was the fact that she didn't seem to know anyone. In London, at any party, she had known *everyone*. And she had always been the centre of attention. Here she was just another pretty girl in a city brimming over with pretty girls. She grabbed a glass of champagne off a passing tray and looked around.

One side of the house was totally open to the beach, and she noticed that here and there parts of the ceiling rolled back to reveal the sky. Some house.

She gulped her champagne down and wandered out onto the sand.

Jon surveyed the scene quickly. Who would it do him the most good to talk to? He spotted Butch Kaufman, a face he hadn't seen since London. He went straight over.

Butch was friendly, introduced him to his sister, Vinnie, and then said, 'Look after her for me, will ya? I gotta take a piss.'

Vinnie glared at him. 'Look after me,' she sneered, 'who are you anyway?'

'Name's Jon.'

'Got any grass?'

'You don't look old enough to be—'

'Aw—cut out the lecture. You got any or not?'

The girl didn't look any older than fifteen, in spite of the skin-tight black satin outfit. 'Not. said Jon. He had heard of young but this was ridiculous.

'So screw you then,' replied Vinnie, 'guess I'll just have to find someone that has—and that ain't gonna be difficult with all these freaks around ' She teetered off on extremely high heels.

Jon looked around again. Thought he spotted Warren Beatty. Wasn't sure. Then he saw Diana, and headed straight in her direction.

Muffin seemed to have got herself involved with a spikey-haired rock star and his entourage. The fact was he knew who she was—coming from England and all. He also knew all about her brief marriage to Little Marty Pearl. 'That guy's a cunt.' he announced dismissively. 'Right fellas?' His entire entourage nodded. 'What you doin' here anyway?'

'I got married. I'm doing photographs.'

'Naughty naked ones. eh? I always did think you had the best tits in the business!'

'It's not her tits they're photographing any more.' interrupted one of the entourage. 'Didn't you see this month's *Core?*'

'Missed that.' the rock star said. 'Maybe I can get me a personal view. What you say. Muff?'

She felt mortified. Now everyone would know. It was one thing doing the photos—that was bad enough. But to actually meet people who had *seen* them. ''Scuse me.' She pushed her way out of the group. Tears were stinging her eyes. the effect of the Quaaludes was wearing off. She just wanted to get out of there.

So where the hell was Jon? Where the hell was her wonderful husband?

'What's your star sign. lover?' A stoned redhead had accosted Jon—squeezing between him and Diana.

'Do go away. darling.' said Diana coolly.

'You a Scorpio?' slurred the redhead. 'gotta fine me a Scorpio.'

'Well run along and find him somewhere else,' snapped Diana 'this one's taken.'

The redhead swayed away.

'I do believe you could have had her.' Diana smiled. 'What do *you* think?'

Jon grinned. 'I think it's about time I moved in with you.'

'Oh yes? And what about your wife?'

'I married her in Mexico—a quick divorce—no problem.'

Diana surveyed him quizzically. 'I'm not going to marry you,' she said, an amused smile hovering on her extremely sensuous lips.

'I wasn't asking you to,' he replied, 'but I'd be good for you—you know that.'

'Hmmm . . . Maybe.'

He put on his best young and innocent expression. 'Don't take too long to make up your mind—somebody else might snap me up . . . A nice young English lad like me . . .'

She laughed. 'Knock it off, Jon. I am not impressed by the baby-faced looks.'

He dropped the expression at once. Wouldn't do to push it. One thing about Diana—she wasn't dumb.

Muffin was in the line of fire when several people were pushed in the swimming pool which snaked sinuously through the centre of the house. She couldn't swim, and was dragged out spluttering and choking by Keeley Nova, Karmen's dress designer boyfriend. He took her to a bedroom, waited while she stripped off her soaking wet clothes, and then leapt on her.

'Stop it!' she objected, struggling. 'I thought you said you were going to get me some dry clothes.'

'Don't you want to fuck?' he asked in surprise. 'I'm not with Karmen for the length of my nose you know.'

'Honestly!' she snapped wrapping herself in a handy bedspread. 'If Karmen Rush is your girlfriend—this little scene wouldn't exactly thrill her.'

'Where do you think she is, chicken? She's fucking her brains out with Al King right this very moment.'

Muffin widened her eyes. 'Don't you mind?'

He shrugged. 'Why should I? She does her thing—I do mine. It's a mellow situation. Hey—who are you anyway?'

'Muffin.'

'That's a name?'

'Have you got some clothes for me or not?'

199

He stood back and surveyed her, squinting through stoned eyes. 'You'll never get into any of Karmen's things. She's like a stick and three feet taller than you.'

'Thanks a lot.'

'You'll have to make do with one of my sweaters and a pair of shorts. What do you do?'

'I'm a model.'

He fell about laughing, '*You're* a model. Jesus! I'd never put you into any of *my* clothes.'

'In England I was *the* top nude photographic model.'

Keeley was busy rummaging through a closet—finding her some things to put on. 'No kidding? You interested in movie work?'

'What kind?' she asked suspiciously.

'Beautiful stuff, sweets. I gotta friend could make you a star and multo bread. If you're interested give me a call and I'll arrange a meet. She'd like you, oh yeah, she'd freak out over a baby like you . . .'

Diana said, 'I am going to go home. I have an early call, and this party is getting distinctly rowdy.'

Jon grinned. He loved her clipped English accent and prep school words. Very classy. And contrasted beautifully with her sensuous looks. 'I'll walk you out to your car,' he offered.

'Don't bother darling. I think I see a certain short person reeling out of a bedroom—dressed in a most *peculiar* outfit. Isn't it your child bride?'

Jon followed Diana's gaze. It was indeed Muffin. Christ—what was she dressed up in? He scowled.

'See you tomorrow, sweetie.' Diana edged her way out through the crowds.

Jon pushed his way over to Muffin and grabbed her roughly by the arm. 'What the hell are you wearing?'

'I fell in the pool.'

'Can't you do anything right? Come on, we're getting out of here—I've had enough.'

## 49

Cleo took a room at the Beverly Wilshire hotel. A temporary move, far too expensive to make it permanent. Not that she would even want to. It was decision time. Time to decide what she wanted to do with her life. Bumming around for six months had not produced any answers.

She telephoned Russell in New York. He couldn't have been more thrilled. 'I'm flying out,' he informed her. 'Richard West has written a new book and I want to tie up the rights. I'll be there tomorrow and we can discuss your future.'

She hung up the phone thoughtfully. Yes, she did have a future, and it was about time she started looking after it.

She surveyed her clothes: two suitcases full of bikinis, shirts, jeans. She needed to go shopping. She looked like a beach bum herself—what with the tan and the tangled mass of jet curls. A manicure wouldn't be a bad idea either, and maybe a haircut—get rid of all the frizz and look like a person again.

She couldn't help giggling quietly to herself. If her mother could see her now—the ever-elegant Stella. 'What have you done to yourself?' Stella would exclaim in horror. 'You look like a gipsy. And your skin—don't you know what the sun *does* to your skin!'

Russell arrived accompanied by five Gucci suitcases.

'How long are you here for?' Cleo asked in surprise.

'As long as it takes to bring you back to New York,' he replied smugly.

'I didn't say I was coming back.'

'You will when you hear what I have to offer you.'

Oh God! She hoped it wasn't his body.

They went to dinner at *Matteos*. and Russell regaled her with stories of mutual friends. Tactfully he waited until the coffee to mention Mike. At the same time Cleo observed a group of five come in and settle at the next table. Three women. Two men. One of the men was Daniel Onel.

She could hardly concentrate on what Russell was saying. For some stupid insane reason her stomach was doing flips and her mouth was dry.

' . . . so the dumb bastard drinks too much, screws around too much—and frankly—looks dreadful.' Russell paused for breath. 'I don't think he'll ever get over you, and who can blame him. Would you care for a brandy?'

She jumped, 'What?'

Russell pursed his lips. 'Weren't you listening to me?'

'My mind was wandering.'

He nodded knowingly, 'Yes. Divorce is upsetting, I'll never forget *my* first one . . .'

Once again her thoughts drifted as Russell launched into the long and boring saga of his first divorce. She had heard the story of all three of his divorces. So had everyone else in the office.

What was it about Daniel Onel that made her into a nervous wreck? He was certainly no matinee idol. Not even a Jack Nicholson. He was hovering on the brink of fifty, really quite ordinary looking. But, oh God, something about him . . . He turned her on with a vengeance. And she wasn't the only one who felt like that if the newspapers and magazines were anything to go by. Reports of Daniel and his women abounded. Only recently he had been splashed all over the front pages announcing an engagement to a dark-haired neurotic superstar. That had lasted exactly five minutes.

Cleo moved surreptitiously to see who he was with. At that precise moment he left the table and saw her.

'He-llo,' he greeted, smiling warmly. 'How are *you?*'

Suddenly she was glad she'd had her hair cut, bought a new dress, bothered about her appearance for a change. 'I'm fine.' She couldn't think of anything else to say. Oh God—if she couldn't think of something he would be gone.

'I was just thinking . . .'

'Er, do you know . . .'

They both started to speak at the same time. 'You first,' said Daniel, laughing.

Cleo smiled, took a deep breath, 'I was only going to ask you if you knew Russell Hayes—my editor. Russell owns *Image* magazine.'

'I don't think we've met,' Daniel shook him warmly by the

hand. 'What are you two doing now? I was just going to phone my housekeeper and warn her that I'm coming back to run a movie. The new Woody Allen. Why don't you join us?'

Daniel lived in a rented house on Benedict Canyon. By Hollywood movie star standards it was simple—but comfortable and nice—and as soon as Cleo walked in she knew that she was going to stay the night.

The other two couples were business. A major director and his girlfriend, and Lew Margolis—chairman of Paradox Television studios, and his wife Doris Andrews—a movie star famed for her 'nice girl' roles.

Russell was very impressed. 'I spot at least three exclusive interviews here,' he hissed at Cleo. 'See what you can tie up.'

She had no intention of tying anything up. She wasn't working for Russell again—not yet anyway.

The Woody Allen movie was another gem. Cleo laughed and tried to relax, but she was only too aware that Daniel was within touching distance, and she wanted to touch him desperately. Angrily she brushed Russell's hand off her leg when he attempted to place it there. He didn't try to put it back.

At the end of the movie Daniel offered Irish Coffees. Cleo sipped hers slowly, trying to keep her eyes off Daniel, but not succeeding. Somehow their eyes kept on meeting and conducting a silent conversation of their own. Then Doris Andrews said she was tired, and the director said he was off early on a location scout, and everyone started to make a move.

Daniel glanced at Cleo, 'Why don't you stay on,' he suggested quietly, 'I'd like to talk to you.'

'O.K.' she agreed.

'What about your friend. Shall I see if Lew can give him a lift?'

'Either that or he can take my car.'

'Good idea. Shall I tell him or will you?'

Russell was not at all pleased. 'I can stay with you,' he insisted.

'No.' Cleo was firm. 'I have to talk to Daniel alone. I promised.'

'Talk?' sneered Russell.

'Or fuck,' replied Cleo, suddenly angry. What business was it of his?

Russell departed, angry and affronted.

'Did he think he was going to end up in your bed?' Daniel asked.

'I don't know and I don't care.' She stared at him, willing him over to her.

They stood very close together, not touching, just having an eye to eye confrontation.

'Did you want to stay?' he asked.

'What do you think?'

His lips were like fire, burning down on hers, and creating a sensation of excitement and abandon that seemed to have been buried for quite some time.

She wasn't aware of the clothes slipping from her body. But she was aware of the way his fingers traced every outline of her form, creating exquisite electric shocks of ecstasy.

She struggled to get his clothes off. Tore at his shirt, ripped the zipper on his trousers. 'I want you so, so badly,' she murmured. 'I've wanted you for months and months. It seems like for ever.'

He touched her breasts, played with them gently, fingered her nipples until she wanted to scream. She wanted to beg him to make love to her.

She reached for his balls. It was always exciting feeling the body of a new man. The surprise of each penis. Whoever said they were all the same in the dark was lying. Every one was a revelation. Size, texture, smell, taste. Daniel's was small, but beautifully formed. No Butch Kaufman—somehow she knew it wouldn't matter.

She knelt in front of him and took him in her mouth. He groaned his pleasure, then drew her head away, and knelt on the floor with her. Together they fell on the carpet, rolling over and over, laughing, enjoying every beautiful minute. Then he mounted her, thrusting himself in. She rose to meet him, clinging her legs tightly around his back. Immediately she started to come. He wouldn't let her go. It was agony and ecstasy. Usually she needed time between orgasms, she couldn't bear to be touched. Daniel clung on to her, and then suddenly it was all right again—in fact it was more than all right—it was goddamn *marvellous*. A heightened sensation of sexual energy and power.

Daniel felt the change in her, and rolled over so that she was on top of him. Now her mind, brain, and body concentrated on only one thing. He was guiding her buttocks, slow . . . slow . . . then fast . . . faster . . . His cock was the greatest organ of pleasure she had ever known. Then suddenly she was coming again. An uncontrollable orgasm that swept over her in exhausting waves of intense delight. And she was screaming as loud as she could.

Then Daniel was joining her. Squeezing her ass. And she could feel his glorious juices pumping into her.

This wasn't screwing. This was nirvana.

'Oh my God!' At last he let her go. 'Oh my good God!' She lay on the floor motionless.

'Enjoyable?' he asked quietly.

'Absolutely unbelievably!'

He started to touch her again.

'Enough!' she protested.

'When you're having fun it's never enough.'

'Please . . .'

He didn't listen to her objections. He brushed over her nipples lightly, then his fingers were between her legs, opening her up, making way for his tongue which was an object of great delicacy.

'No more . . . please . . . no more . . .' But even as she said it she surrendered herself to his delicious probings, and when she reached orgasm for the third time it was incredibly gentle and beautiful and totally draining.

She couldn't help herself, she drifted into sleep, and when she awoke an hour or so later she found that Daniel had put a cover over her and a pillow under her head.

She sat up, alone and suddenly embarrassed. She had wanted to talk to Daniel, communicate—not fall into his arms like every one of his highly publicized romances probably did. And it wasn't even a first date—truth was it wasn't a date at all.

Now she knew the secret of his magnetism. He was a wonderful lover—certainly the best *she* had ever experienced. He was a sensualist. a man who actually liked a woman's body and didn't make certain plays and moves because that is what *Playboy* magazine *told* him to do.

It was dark in the living-room. and the floor was getting to be an uncomfortable resting place. She got up and gathered her clothes together.

Daniel was asleep in the bedroom. It niggled her slightly that he could just fling a cover over her and leave her out in the living room.

She stared at him. He slept soundly. snoring very softly.

She was at a loss. What to do? Crawl into bed with him? Or go back to her hotel?

What would he expect her to do? Was this just one night of good sex. or was it the beginning of a relationship?

She had never felt so out of control in her life. Usually *she* called the shots. Damn Daniel. He was making her feel like a teenager.

She decided to dress and go home. It seemed to be the safest bet. And yet . . . She had a passionate longing to pull all the covers off him and have *her* feast. She wanted him in her mouth enclosed and warm . . . She wanted to suck the juices out of him as he had done to her.

She dragged the covers down. He was wearing pyjamas. It made him seem somehow vulnerable. She eased her hand into the bottoms—feeling for him—playing with him until he started to come to life in her hand. She slid her head down. took him half in her mouth teasingly—licking and caressing with her tongue.

'You're beautiful.' she murmured.

'I'm awake.' he mumbled.

'Good.' She drew him over with her until she was lying on the bed and his penis was in her mouth.

Now it was his turn to try and protest. But she had him, her hands on his ass to prevent his escape. He began to pump into her mouth. but every time he got near the peak she forced him to withdraw and wait.

'What are you doing to me!' he protested.

She laughed softly. 'Beautiful suffering. Remember? You taught me, now I'll play too.'

When she did let him reach his climax it was an explosion. 'Oh Jesus Christ! That was the *best!*' he exclaimed, 'The absolute *best.*' He slid down next to her and she fitted into his arms.

'I'd like you to stay the night,' he said. 'Think you could manage that?'

'Yeah. I guess so. Nobody at the Beverly Wilshire is going to miss me.'

'Except maybe your friend.'

'Russell? I told you—he's business not pleasure.'

He hugged her, 'And me?'

'Pleasure of course. What do you think—I'm going to write a story about our night together?'

'I *am* slightly paranoid about reporters. That's why I fought getting involved with *you.*'

'We're involved?'

His hands were exploring her body again. 'What do *you* think?'

She laughed softly, suddenly very secure and warm in his arms. 'I think I wanted you that first day I came to interview you.'

'Mutual.'

She was delighted. 'Really? But you were so offhand when I called to show you the article—'

'Which I quite liked,' he interrupted.

'Why only quite?'

'Because I just don't like reading about myself period. But to get back to you . . . Well, the timing was off . . . I had Heidi to get rid of—'

'And a million others since.'

'Don't believe everything you read.'

'Would half be a fair estimate?'

'Are you jealous?'

'Of *course* I'm jealous.'

'Don't be. Anyone to while away a lonely night.'

'Oh thanks . . .'

He kissed her, 'Not you, idiot. I've been saving you since the day you crossed the street to avoid me. That's when I knew you were the girl for me.'

'I never even thought you saw me.'

'I saw you—like I saw you at that abysmal party with Butch Kaufman. What the hell were you spending your time with a dumbhead like him for?'

'Waiting for you.' And as she said it she knew that it was true.


Mike James found that having no live-in playmate was almost as bad as having one.

Living alone was a drag. It was peaceful, quiet, and very, very lonely—not to mention boring.

He employed a maid to come in and do the work. She was a tight lipped Irish lady who appeared at nine o'clock. cooked him a solitary breakfast, and then cleaned the apartment to horrible perfection. When he returned from the office in the evening the place smelt of disinfectant and leather polish. The toilet was always filled with a white foam cleanser. Everything in the fridge was hygienically sealed beneath virgin tin foil.

He hated it. He yearned for the smell of woman. Something was missing in his life, and he wasn't sure what. Since getting rid of Annie—a nasty scene, she had scrawled obscenities all over his front door—he had dated girls carefully and kept to his new rule of not bringing them home.

This meant evenings in their apartments if he wished to get laid. This meant sitting through tasty gourmet dinners for two recommended by *Cosmopolitan* or *Glamour* magazine. This meant instant indigestion and stomach ache. This meant his sexual performance wasn't up to his usual standard. This meant shrill girlish voices complaining. This meant—shit.

Mike was not leading the perfect life.

Russell had called to tell him he was flying to the coast to see Cleo.

'So?' Mike had replied shortly. 'She's nothing in my life any more. We're divorced.'

'Then you won't mind if I try my luck?' Russell had replied.

Bastard. Cleo would never look at you. Bastard. Mike had forced himself to remain non-committal. 'Do what you like.'

Russell had flown off in high spirits, and Mike had sulked.

If it wasn't for Cleo maybe he could have settled down with one of his live-in playmates. But he had Cleo to compare them

# 50

At first Muffin could not believe that Jon would do such a thing to her. But as the days passed it became increasingly obvious that the short terse note he had left her was true.

She sat in their luxurious mansion and waited for him to come back. Oh she knew Jon had changed in Hollywood—they both had—but to have changed to such a degree that he could just dump her. Leave her alone to face all their debts and bills—it was downright cruel.

She had exactly twenty-six dollars and fifty cents, and that was it. Not even enough to pay her fare back to England—hardly enough to keep her in food for more than a few days. And the bastard had even taken their car—the rented Cadillac that *she* had been posing for porno pictures to keep up the payments on.

She had never been alone in her life. Never had to fend for herself and make decisions. From the day she had moved away from her family Jon had always been there. Jon, who had always professed to love her so much. Yeah—he had loved her—just so long as she was making good bread. Muffin realized for the first time that Jon had been *using* her, promoting and pushing her in every direction. And *that* was why he had been so angry when she had married Little Marty Pearl. Losing a good investment—only in Hollywood the investment turned out to be a dud. In Hollywood she just couldn't cut it. Too many pretty girls, and sexy bodies, and what made *her* special?

Jon had left her in the same way a racing driver would abandon a defunct car—a tennis player a broken racket. She should have realized what a bastard he was. Hadn't his first wife, Jane, said so a million and one times—and when he left

Jane it had been with two little kids. If he didn't care about his *children* what chance did *she* have?

Jon bloody Clapton—with his blond innocent good looks, and his scrawny body. Honestly! How could she have fallen for such a bastard! Three and a half years of her life she had wasted with him, and where had it gotten her? Exactly nowhere. Exhibiting her snatch in a bunch of filthy magazines. Charming!

Thinking about Jon was not going to pay the bills, and she didn't even have enough money to do a moonlight skip. Where exactly could she skip to on twenty-six dollars?

She didn't know who to turn to. Somehow all the friends they had made had been Jon's. She didn't even have a girlfriend to help her out.

She sat and thought. There was Little Marty Pearl—now a big television star on a weekly spectacular with his sister—the two of them all teeth and smiles, they looked like a very glossy toothpaste commercial. He probably wouldn't appreciate getting a call from her. They hadn't even spoken to each other since the fateful day of their short marriage.

Then there was his manager, Jackson. But he gave her the creeps, and if she asked him for help he would want *plenty* in return. She may flash for pictures, but she certainly wasn't ready to fuck for anything. Some of her Wimbledon background stayed firmly with her. You had to draw the line *somewhere*.

She couldn't think of anyone else who might help her, and she realized the only thing she could do was pose for some more of those photographs. The open your legs and smile variety.

The thought depressed her. No Jon to get her stoned and in the mood. No Jon to sweet talk her through the session.

Rummaging through her clothes she came across the shorts and shirt Keeley Nova had lent her. She tried to remember what he had said to her. Something about . . . make you a star . . . plenty of money . . .

He seemed like an O.K. guy. Maybe it was worth a phone call. After all—they hadn't cut off the phone—not yet anyway.

'You are a sonofabitch,' drawled Diana, 'haven't you even phoned?'

Jon was busy massaging her back. She had a lovely back.

'Nope.' he replied patiently. 'if I call she'll cry and whine and beg me to come back. Believe me, it's better this way. She's got a lot of friends, she'll manage.'

Diana sighed. 'You know best, darling. And God knows you've put up with so much. I think you've been a positive martyr—no other man could have stood it.'

Sadly Jon said. 'Yes, it was tough. And he was glad he'd laid it on as thickly as he had. Diana had been more than sympathetic to his tales of Muffin's other men, drunken orgies and pornographic exhibitions. He had even shown her a picture of Muffin au naturel—au very naturel indeed. 'I begged her not to pose for photos like these.' he told Diana. 'but she just does what she wants.'

Diana had held his hand and consoled him. 'Move in with me, darling. No man should have to stand for that sort of behaviour.'

Now she was worried that maybe it had been a hasty move. She wanted to be certain that Muffin wouldn't publicly complain. After all . . . that sort of publicity . . . who needed it?

'Turn over.' Jon said.

'You have incredible fingers,' Diana murmured, doing as he asked.

'All the better to touch you with.' He shook a few drops of baby oil on to her stomach and started to massage it in.

'Delicious!' Diana sighed luxuriously. 'Who knew that when I got you I got the best masseur in town too! My God! Just think of the money I'll save!'

The Rush mansion was a magnificent sight in the daytime, sprawling along the ocean front like a series of white bizarre monuments. Karmen had started off owning one house, and during the course of her fame had purchased the neighbouring six, and joined them all together making one wide strange incredible mansion. Karmen's house was almost as famous as she was.

Nervously Muffin paid the cab off with the last of her money. She certainly hoped the trip was worth it. Keeley Nova had been very friendly on the phone. He remembered her, and when she had asked him if he had been serious about introducing her to someone who could 'make her a star' he had laughed and said, 'Sure—if you got what it takes you got it made. Come on by the house around four o'clock.'

So here she was, pretty and pert in satin jeans and an off-the-shoulder frilled blouse. Her hair was freshly washed, and cascaded in tangly orange-tipped curls. Her makeup emphasized her wide China blue eyes, and pouting full lips.

Under her arm she carried a large portfolio of her photographs. Glamour nude stuff, none of the open leg variety.

There was a long cord by the massive double front doors. She pulled it, and loud chimes rang out, and a lot of dogs started to bark.

After a while Keeley appeared. 'Had to chain the monsters up,' he explained. 'If they don't like you . . .' he shrugged explicitly, and pantomimed a slit throat.

Muffin shivered as she followed him into the house. He was wearing white jeans, that was all, and his back was covered in fresh talon-like scratches. She felt uneasy. There was a strange atmosphere in the house.

'How you 'bin?' he asked.

'Fine.'

'I'm glad you called, took me up on what I said. Sit down—you wanna snort some coke? The lady ain't ready for you yet.'

Muffin collapsed onto a cushion; there was no normal furniture as such.

Keeley squatted down beside her and produced a narrow phial of cocaine. He tipped some carefully into a small silver spoon and handed it to Muffin. She pinched a little between her fingers and snorted it up her nose. It was a tickly sensation, but she had tried it several times before and the effect was wonderful.

Keeley did the same, sighing with pleasure.

'I brought some pictures with me . . .' she ventured, handing him her portfolio.

He leafed quickly through the book. 'You photograph good,' he commented, 'but this job is more than tits 'n' ass.'

She was silent. How much more? He had mentioned making her a star, and a lot of money. But how?

212

Suddenly a voice screamed throughout the house. A perfectly pitched—'Keeeeeellleeyyy!'

He jumped to attention. 'The lady is ready.' he said. facial muscles taking off in a nervous spasm. 'Come with me little girl. Money, fame, everything I said. Let's go audition, babe. Let's see if you got what the lady has been looking for.'

It pained Jon to discover that not only did Diana have an agent, to whom she was paying ten percent of her earnings, but she also had a business manager who peeled off a further fifteen per cent!

'Ridiculous!' he exclaimed. 'The guy's a rip off merchant.'

'Nonsense.' replied Diana. 'He's a perfectly legitimate, highly recommended, *very good* businessman.'

'Who recommended him?' scowled Jon.

'Daniel Onel, and *he* hasn't done too badly.'

Jon couldn't argue with that. Everyone knew that Daniel Onel, Diana's current co-star, was now one of the richest actors in Hollywood since moving his base from England—land of crippling taxes.

'I still say.' grumbled Jon, 'that paying out twenty-five per cent of your income is a load of bollocks. *I* could handle your career, and it wouldn't cost us a penny.'

Diana burst out laughing. 'Jon darling—as a lover I adore you, but if you think I am foolish enough to put my financial affairs in your hands—just forget it.'

'I did all right for Muffin.' he argued.

'Oh yeah?' replied Diana, 'And what do you both have to show for it?'

He shut up. Couldn't argue with the truth. It would take time to soften Diana up. At least he had a roof over his head, and all the bills were paid. But what to do when the next payment on the Cadillac became due? And how about when Diana finished the movie she was working on and wanted to go out at night? Somehow he did not think that Diana was the sort of lady who would take kindly to picking up the cheque.

Karmen Rush lolled in the centre of a huge triangular bed.

The room was entirely black—walls, cushions, thick fur rugs. Daylight zoomed in through the top—there was no ceiling, just a vast expanse of sky. Indian sitar music drifted into the room from various hidden speakers.

'Hello,' husked Karmen, in a deep, almost masculine, voice. She held up her hand to indicate silence. 'Don't speak until I switch on the recorder—I want to catch every word. Who knows . . . One day our first conversation might be worth a fortune.'

Muffin gulped. She was stunned and speechless anyway. She hadn't expected to meet Karmen Rush. Wow—what would they make of *this* whole scene back in Wimbledon!

Keeley said, 'Shall I stay or go?'

Karmen crushed him with a look. 'Get out. I don't want *you* on tape. Go make a jug of blackcurrant juice.' She fixed Muffin with a moody look. 'Come and sit on the bed, let me get to know you. Let me see if our vibes are in tune.'

Keeley gave her a little shove, and gingerly Muffin approached the bed and balanced on a corner.

She couldn't help staring at Karmen. The woman was—well—weird looking, with her whiter than white face, dramatic Egyptian eye make-up, and slashed blood red lips. She was wearing some sort of caftan—black naturally. And her jet hair hung in multiple braids around her head.

Muffin had always been a fan of hers. Karmen Rush had the most beautiful incredible singing voice. She was also one of the few bankable female stars in the world.

'How old are you?' Karmen asked.

'Twenty,' mumbled Muffin.

'Fortunately you look younger,' observed Karmen, studying her through slitted eyes.

'Oh yes,' agreed Muffin quickly, 'people are always telling me I look *much* younger.'

'Did Keeley tell you anything?'

'Not really . . . I brought some pictures.' She handed the book to Karmen, who took her time studying each photograph intently. Suddenly Muffin wished that Jon was with her. She felt out of her depth and very much alone.

'I like your body,' Karmen stated matter of factly, 'slightly plump, but I like that. The audience will like that. Little Miss

Ordinary—a girl they can identify with. Take your clothes off dear. and walk around the room for me.'

The request was unexpected. Muffin hesitated.

'You're not shy. are you?' Karmen questioned coldly.

'No, of course not. I just sort of wondered . . . well, what kind of job am I auditioning for?'

'A lot of money, a lot of fame. Are you interested in those two things?'

'Yes . . . But . . .'

'We are two women here together.' Karmen's voice was more gentle. 'I am not regarding you as a piece of meat, but I must see your body.'

'Sure,' Muffin's voice sang with false bravado. She stood up and unzipped her satin trousers, wriggling out of them in what she hoped was an unconcerned fashion. Then the blouse, peeling it down, until she was totally exposed.

Karmen stared at her. 'Walk around.' she commanded.

Muffin followed her bidding, wondering why she felt more naked than she ever had in her entire life.

'Perfect breasts.' Karmen observed, 'short legs. I like the combination. I like your face.'

'Can I dress?'

'Not yet. I need to see more.'

'More?'

'Muffin dear.' Karmen spoke deliberately slowly, 'I think you are the girl I have been looking for.'

'Yes?' Muffin didn't know if she should be pleased or not. This whole scene was weird. Parading around starkers in front of a movie star. Maybe it was all a put on. What job could Karmen Rush possibly have for her?

'Yes,' agreed Karmen. 'I am directing a film—a marvellous story about an ordinary little girl who comes to Hollywood—and the things she has to go through to achieve fame.'

This was more like it. Muffin could see herself in a part like that.

'Of course it's going to be a very honest film,' Karmen continued, 'the *real* story of what it's all about. And I should know—I've been there and back twenty times before I finally made it.' She sat up. her eyes gleaming. 'I wrote the script myself. I have one of the best lighting cameramen and a small tight crew. We are ready to begin—but we have not found the right girl. You could be that girl. You could be as big a star as me in your own way.'

Muffin had caught some of Karmen's enthusiasm. But still . . . what was the snag? There must be one, there always was.

'Do you want the part?' Karmen asked.

'Yes, of course. But . . .'

'If every detail is perfect the job is yours. Our camera will be very . . . probing. You saw *Deep Throat?*'

'No.'

'You missed nothing. Ugly bodies, ugly women. Whoever auditioned them did not do a thorough job.'

'It was a pornographic movie, wasn't it?' Muffin asked. Jon had seen it and come home laughing.

'What is pornography? Life is pornography. Our movie will be *beautiful* pornography. *You* will be beautiful.' Karmen stood up. 'Muffin, dear, you will make a lot of money, I promise you that. You will live here in your own section of the house—the movie will all be shot here. Six weeks of your time and instant fame. Trust me. Believe me I know. I *will* make you a star. But first—'

'What?' Excitement was flooding through Muffin. She *could* be a star. Karmen Rush was saying so, and somehow she *trusted* her.

'I must look between your legs. I must see if you are as perfect there as everywhere else. After all—my movie is called *The Girl With the Golden Snatch*, and it wouldn't do to disappoint, would it now?' Karmen reached towards her, lightly touching her breasts. 'Lie down, sweet little girl. Let the audition begin.'

## 51

At Daniel's invitation Cleo moved in with him. She debated for some while as to whether she was doing the right thing or not. Straight from one actor to another. Surely that wasn't a wise move?

But no way could anyone possibly compare Daniel and Butch. They were so utterly different. Butch had been a resting space while she recovered her strength. Daniel was a whole new life. Besides which, she loved Daniel, a fact which was painfully nice. Since Mike there had been no one she had contemplated sharing her life with—on a permanent basis that is. Now there was Daniel.

She felt reborn. Happy, enthusiastic, and ready to work again. Only after a six month lay off she was not exactly in demand. Of course there was always Russell. She hadn't seen him since her first night with Daniel—he had checked out of the hotel, flown back to New York, and left her an uptight note.

*Image* magazine could no doubt hand her some interesting assignments in Los Angeles, and she was *so* ready to work. Daniel was out all day on the movie he was shooting—and three weeks of wandering around Beverly Hills alone, and catching afternoon movies, was almost as stupefying as the beach.

The evenings and weekends compensated. Daniel was an exciting companion. Witty, informative, inquisitive, and charming. Never boring, always alert and interesting and amusing.

And of course there was the love-making. Long drawn out evenings of discovering each other's bodies all over again. Passionate hours of sheer sensual delight. Daniel was a master—*the* master.

Cleo phoned Russell early on a Monday morning. She timed the call to catch him as he entered the office—New York time being three hours later. He tried to be cool, but she knew he was secretly pleased.

'I'd like to do some exclusives,' she suggested. 'Any idea?'

'Had your fling with that senile actor?' He had to be snide.

'He's only eleven years older than you.'

'And twenty years older than you,' Russell retorted quickly.

'Let's drop the subject, Russ. I'm in no mood for an argument.'

'No argument—just advice.'

'No thanks.'

'He's a three-time-married loser neurotic bum.'

'So are you, but we're still friends—right? Now—what do you have for me?'

He sighed, and promised to phone her back with some suggestions.

She knew that he would, and sure enough he was on the phone again within an hour.

'Richard West,' he suggested. 'They're making a film of *Sex—an Explanation.* I'd like to have his thoughts on the way they are going about it. You know the sort of stuff I want—is the writer getting screwed as usual etc. etc. Sort of a sex expert Joseph Wambaugh.'

'Did Richard West do his own screenplay?'

'I think he worked on a couple of drafts.'

Cleo laughed dryly. 'I thought *Sex—an Explanation,* was a sort of sexual textbook. Do tell—what's the plot?'

'That's for you to find out. You want the assignment?'

'Sure. Anything else?'

'Your old boyfriend—Butch Kaufman. That should be an easy one for you.'

'I interviewed Butch already—in the 'Big Bad Wolf' series. Remember?'

Russell indulged in a short coughing fit, then, 'Of course I remember—that series pulled in more readers' letters than the office could cope with.'

'So? Why Butch?'

'Because if you read your morning papers out there, you would see that Butch Kaufman has signed for a movie called *Surf Stud,* and that his co-star is his thirteen-year-old sister, Vinnie. Good stuff, Cleo, and you *do* have an inside track.'

Oh boy—if he only knew *what* an inside track!

'I'd like fifteen hundred words on Dr West, and around an eight hundred-word piece each on Butch and his sister.'

'And you want it by tomorrow, right?' she intercepted.

'The weekend will do.'

'Oh—great. That gives me a full four days.'

'I can remember the time you interviewed in the morning, wrote in the afternoon and had it in by the next morning.'

'That's when I was young and in action.'

Russell gave a nasty laugh. 'I don't notice any changes.'

By the time Daniel arrived home from the studio Cleo had all the interviews arranged. Dr Richard West would see her at his house in Beverly Hills the following morning. A publicist for the film company had been the intermediary. 'Dr West doesn't give interviews, but because of his relationship with the editor of *Image* he will be glad to oblige,' the publicist said.

Cleo wondered how Dr West's relationship with Ginny Sandler was progressing.

Butch, she called directly.

He was distinctly off. She couldn't blame him, maybe she *should* have left a note. Once she mentioned 'interview' and *Image,* his voice perked up considerably, and he agreed to see her at two o'clock the following day.

The thought of interviewing sweet little Vinnie filled Cleo with mirth. Now it was *her* turn—and the pen was mightier than that Lolita brat's tiny little voice any day.

It occurred to her that she did have a pretty good exclusive story. The fact that Vinnie was daughter not sister—headline making stuff. Should she use it? Yes—the reporter side of her said. No—the personal side insisted. It was a confidence between lovers. But still . . . It *was* tempting.

Daniel was exhausted but loving. 'Only two more days on the movie,' he said, 'then I thought a short vacation before the next. How about the Bahamas? Ever been there?'

It hadn't occurred to Cleo that once she started working again Daniel might not be working himself. Actors, between movies, were what is politely known as a pain in the ass. Worried about the film they had just completed. Worried about the one they were about to do.

Daniel, of course, would be different.

'Lovely,' she said. 'How long for?'

'Ten days, a couple of weeks.' He was peering in the mirror studying his face.

'Guess what I did today?' she asked brightly.

'Got any tweezers, luv?'

'Er . . . yes.' She found him the tweezers and began again. 'Daniel? Do you know what I did today?'

Industriously he started to pluck away at some hairs on the bridge of his nose. 'What?'

'I . . . I went back to work.'

Somehow Daniel tweezering his face irritated her. 'I called Russell, told him I was ready, and—'

'Did you ever make love to him?'

'What? *No*—of course not. I *told* you that.'

'Why call him? There are plenty of other magazines—*Los Angeles*—*People*—*Newsweek*—'

'I know. But well . . . I have a special connection with *Image*.'

He laughed sarcastically. 'Yes. I'm beginning to realize that.' Stoically he continued to pluck his eyebrows.

'For crissakes.' Cleo snapped, 'Can't you do that in the bathroom?'

He stopped abruptly, threw the tweezers at her, and walked out of the room.

She was stunned. Followed him through to the living-room. 'What's the matter with *you?*'

'*Me*,' he shouted in reply, 'more like *you*.'

'I don't shave my *legs* in front of you. I can't help it if I think some things should be private.'

'Christ almighty! What kind of a sanctimonious statement is *that!*'

'I believe in being honest.'

'Yes? So why don't you admit you made it with Russell Hayes?'

'Oh Daniel! How many times do you want me to tell you? I didn't. You *know* I didn't.'

'Sure.'

Suddenly they were embroiled in a screaming row. Their first argument, and so ridiculous that after they had screamed themselves out they couldn't help laughing, and then they were touching, and peeling each other's clothes off. Suddenly they were both caught up in the intensity of their love-making.

'We have something special together,' Daniel whispered softly, when they lay moist and warm in each other's arms.

'Yeah, a passion for the floor!' giggled Cleo. 'Can't we try a bed for a change?'

'Let's get married,' Daniel suggested quietly. 'We could do it in the Bahamas next week. I promise you we'll spend our honeymoon in a bed!'

Cleo was more than surprised. She hadn't considered marriage with Daniel. She hadn't considered marriage with anyone. Butch had mentioned it on occasion, but it had been a jokey thing—a proposition she had never taken seriously.

Extracting herself from Mike had set up one giant barrier against marriage. Who needed a little bit of paper that led to lies and deceit? Who needed 'belonging' legally—when not to be tied by law seemed to lead to a much more honest relationship? If she and Butch had married they would be embroiled in a big hassle now. Who owned what. How to split the money. As it was she had just been able to pack up and go. And Butch had not been able to feel it was his right to come running after her.

She would never forget Mike's face as he chased her around London. 'You're mine—you bitch!' his expression had said. 'So get right back into this marriage where you belong.'

Oh no. She didn't want to go through *that* again. Not with anyone. Not even with Daniel.

And yet—in two months time she would be thirty years of age. And she wanted a child. And she wouldn't mind at all it being Daniel's child. In fact . . .

'I don't think we should spoil everything by getting married,' she murmured, snuggling close to his body, and running her fingers through his furry chest. 'We've both been through it enough times to know better. We love each other. I don't think we need a piece of paper to prove it.' She moved her hands down to where she knew he would be ready for her. 'But I would love to have your baby—our child. Daniel? Can we?' She didn't wait for his answer. She slid on top of him and guided him inside her.

The next morning she threw away her supply of birth control pills. In the heat of the moment, the night before, Daniel never *had* answered her. but she was sure it was the right thing to do A baby was a far more personal bond that a marriage contract

Dr Richard West did not resemble the ordinary-looking. unas suming. middle-aged man that Cleo had met in Russell's office nearly a year previously. He had changed considerably. Gone was the short sandy hair. Gone was the heavy body. Gone were the unstylish clothes. The only thing that seemed to have remained were the Mick Jagger lips. Somehow they looked more at home in a deeply tanned face. the eyes obscured by tinted shades. A heavy beard covered his chin. and his hair—now incongruously blond streaked—grew thick and long. He was wearing white tennis shorts and a tee shirt. all the better to show off long tanned legs. and nicely muscled arms.

'Hi there.' he greeted. 'good to see you again. Come on in and pop a few vitamin pills.'

Gone was the charming reticence. California and the whole success trip could claim yet another victim.

'I hardly recognized you.' Cleo confessed. over a breakfast of prunes. yoghurt. wheat germ. and rose hip tea. 'You must have lost at least twenty pounds.'

'I got my body together along with my head.' Richard confessed. 'I shed thirty-two pounds of unnecessary body weight. and forty-two years of unmitigated garbage from my mind. I am a new man. In tune with my real needs for the first time in my life.'

She sipped the rose hip tea. it didn't taste bad at all. 'Do you still see Ginny Sandler?' she asked.

Richard frowned. 'Ginny was not a woman who knew what she wanted in life. To her. sex was the ultimate. She never considered her mind. just her genitals.'

'But you write about sex—'

'Not any more. My new book is called *A Trip Around The Inner Brain.* Tell me Cleo. have you ever taken acid?'

She staggered out of his house two hours later bogged down with his pontificating. Boring. But she did have a wonderful interview, and she couldn't wait to write it. What a number she could do on him—a real tongue in cheek piece.

She wished that Butch wasn't on the agenda next. because

her mind was alive with ideas. But still. it was all on tape—and later she could let it all pour out. Russell was right He knew her. He knew that once she got excited about something there was no stopping her.

She felt exhilarated as she drove towards the beach. Suddenly her life seemed to be fitting into place. Daniel. Work. A baby. She felt alive again, no longer a stupified beach bum.

Butch regarded her through slitted blue eyes. his little boy hurt expression prominent. 'You let me down,' he whined. 'takin' off without so much as a fast goodbye.'

Funny. when they had lived together she had never actually noticed the whine in his voice. But it was there. coming through loud and clear.

'I did plenty for you.' he continued. 'I took real good care of you. Got you away from that schmuck you were married to. Gave you a home and plenty of fantastic lovin'. Jeeze. Cleo, look in the mirror. You never looked so good in your life. And you can thank *me* for that—I relaxed you—made you a real beautiful woman.'

She sighed. 'Butch.' she interrupted, 'let us not forget you *wanted* me to come and live with you. I was not some charity case you took pity on. You came to Rome and asked me to move in with you. No ties on either side. Plenty of laughs. Remember?'

'Aw . . . shit . . . Cleo. Whyn't you move back? We were doin' O.K. together. Vinnie will be workin', so she won't be around to bug you. What d'ya say? Shall we give it another crack?'

She shook her head. 'It wasn't Vinnie. she was maybe the catalyst—but I was ready to move on. Let's face it Butch—we gave each other everything we had to give—and I'm sorry—for me it wasn't enough.'

He made a face. 'First time a woman walked out on me in my *life.*'

She touched him lightly on the arm. 'There's always a first time. You *know* we would never have made it as a permanent fixture. Can we be good friends?'

His face cracked into a grin. 'Occasional lovers?'

She grinned back. 'I don't think so. I had in mind more of a brother sister deal. Wouldn't it be nice for you to have *one* female you didn't feel obliged to screw?'

'Hey, that's not such an um er bad idea.'

'You could tell me all your problems.'

'Yeah, can I start now?'

She indicated her tape machine. 'Tell you what, give me an interview first, then I'll give you an hour problem time. Deal?'

'You always were a classy lady. I gotta say this, when you dump a guy at least you do it with style!'

Butch loved talking about himself. It was, without a doubt, his favourite pastime. He had a carefully worked out interview persona, but with Cleo he was more natural and genuinely at ease. After six months of living with him she knew most of his views on everything from the Pope to the President. What she wanted from him were some provocative quotes.

Halfway through the interview he grabbed her in that old familiar way. 'Let's screw,' he suggested, 'for old times' sake.'

'Let's not. I'm working.'

'I just cancelled the interview.'

'Cancel your hard-on instead. We're at the good friends stage. Remember?'

'If I don't, I know you'll er um remind me. Hey—what's with the rumour about you and Onel?'

She clicked off the recorder. 'Where did you hear that?'

He laughed, 'Can't keep secrets in this town. I hear you moved in with him.'

'So?'

'Don't get defensive with me, lady. I just wouldn't have thought he was your bag . . . I mean—'

'You mean after a big horny stud like you—why the hell would I look at a guy like Daniel Onel?'

'Somethin' like that.'

She smiled, a special smile. 'That's one secret you can't find out.'

'Yeah,' he grimaced. 'So he's a good actor—that don't make for the perfect relationship. Now you and I, we had somethin' different. Like really mellow and steady. I—,

Vinnie interrupted them. She appeared on the slatted deck

and planted herself firmly between them. She was wearing sawed-off jeans that clung like second skin, and a skimpy halter top barely concealing her pubescent breasts.

'You gonna interview me or not?' she demanded. 'I gotta date. I can give you fifteen minutes then I gotta split.'

Butch chuckled proudly. 'She's a star already.' he tapped her on the bottom. 'watch the way you talk to this lady.'

Vinnie threw him a scathing look. 'He tell you about the new girl living here now? Outasite! Biggest tits I ever saw, and she's only nineteen. Must make *you* feel kinda ancient.'

'Will you shut up.' Butch interrupted. 'You need your ass spanked.'

Vinnie gave him a challenging look. 'You gonna do it, daddy dear?'

Butch stood up. 'She's all yours.' he said to Cleo. 'Try to get some sense out of her—you know she's not as smart as she makes out. She's really just a sweet—um—er—misunderstood little girl.'

Vinnie rolled her eyes heavenwards. 'What garbage!'

Butch winked at Cleo and headed for the house. 'See you later.'

Vinnie slouched into his chair. 'Didn't he tell you?' she pursued.

'Tell me what?' asked Cleo. inserting a fresh tape into her portable machine.

''Bout his new piece of gash.'

'I love your vocabulary.'

'She's *gorgeous.*'

'Good.'

'Aren't you mad?'

'Why should I be?'

Vinnie shrugged. '*I* don't know. Don't you love him?'

Cleo burst out laughing. 'Vinnie! Where on earth did you learn great big sentimental words like love?'

The girl scowled. 'Don't make fun of me.'

For the first time Cleo felt a sense of compassion for the objectionable child woman. The girl actually had feelings. 'I'm not making fun of you. Just relax. Vinnie. Let's talk. Let's see if we can get some communication going here.'

Two hours later Vinnie was still talking. It appeared tha
nobody had ever listened to her before. Mommy was pretty
rich, and spoiled, and into men and group sex. Daddy was the
big movie star who patted her on the head and thought she was
cute as hell but for crissakes don't tell anyone she was his
daughter.

Vinnie was the classic case of too much too soon. Now she
was to become a movie star herself, and Cleo had no doubt
that the child would create a very successful world of celluloid
fantasy.

'Sure, I'll be a star,' Vinnie said. 'I got the looks. I got the
talent. Tatum and Jodie can go suck. I'm gonna be the biggest.'

'Yes,' Cleo agreed, 'I think you will be.'

'Hey.' Vinnie's usually sullen expression brightened. 'You
ain't half bad, you know that? This bimbo he's moved in is
dense, but a real nothing. She'll last five minutes. You gonna
move back?'

Slowly Cleo shook her head. If she had learned one thing in
life it was that there was no going back. She leaned forward and
touched Vinnie lightly on the hand. 'I wish I had bothered to
get to know you when I was here. You're not nearly as bad as
you'd have everyone believe.'

Vinnie actually blushed. 'Oh yes I am,' she replied defiantly.
'You bet your ass I am.'

When Daniel arrived back from the studio, Cleo was right in
the middle of her piece on Vinnie and Butch. She looked up
from her typewriter and blew him a kiss.

'I'm beat,' he announced. 'If Diana Beeson could act it would
make everyone's day a hell of a lot easier.' He sat down in a
leather chair and proceeded to remove his shoes. 'Any tea?'

'Mrs K's in the kitchen,' she replied absently.

'That sonofabitch, Mark Hughs, can't direct himself out of
a paperbag,' Daniel complained. '*I'm* practically directing the
goddamn picture.'

'Sweetheart,' she said softly, 'do you mind if we talk later? I
must finish this, and I'm losing the thread.'

'What are you doing?' he asked, getting up, and peering over
her shoulder.

Instinctively she covered the paper. She *hated* anyone reading her work in progress.

'So *sorry*,' he said sarcastically. 'I didn't realize Ms Rex Reed needed total privacy. Do let me know when you're finished. I wouldn't *dream* of disturbing you further.' He stamped out of the room.

'Daniel,' Cleo called after him. 'Daniel? Come back, don't be so silly . . .'

She heard the kitchen door slam, and the sound of him talking to his housekeeper. He was being petty. He would just have to understand about her work. After all, when he was reading a script, silence had to prevail. That he had made very clear right from the beginning. And if one of his old movies was on television the only time you could breathe was in the commercial.

She contemplated following him to the kitchen and making peace. But then she would *never* get back to the typewriter, and it would only take her another hour or so—and goddamn it—working again was such a *kick*.

# 52

It was not the ordeal Muffin had expected it to be. She had left the rented house, packed up her two suitcases and just moved out. Straight in with Karmen, Keeley, and the monster dogs. Straight into the title role of *The Girl with the Golden Snatch*.

Karmen said her qualifications were the most perfect she had ever seen. 'She should know,' Keeley said, 'she's bin auditioning for six months.'

Muffin had thought the matter out as best she could. She was alone in Hollywood. Jon had abandoned her. She had no money. What choice was there really?

Karmen offered her a place to live. A starring role in a movie. Money. Friendship.

Of course it was a porno movie. But if she showed everything in photographs for a little bit of money—then why not show it in movies for a lot?

She made her decision, and within a day of auditioning had moved into the Malibu mansion where she was given her own room, the run of the house, and a script to study.

When she read the script she almost changed her mind. The storyline was familiar. Girl meets boy. Loses boy. Gets boy in the end. In between girl goes to Hollywood to make her fortune and gets propositioned by everyone and everything from a midget stuntman to a Great Dane dog. The point of the story was the girl maintains her sweet innocence throughout every one of her ordeals.

The other point was every ordeal would be shot in detail. Every detail. Close up detail.

'Don't worry 'bout a thing,' Keeley assured her. 'I'll set you up so good you won't care *what* you're doing. In fact you'll get a kick out of it.'

True to his word on the first day of shooting he greeted her with a combination of pills that made her feel absolutely incredible.

Karmen had a studio built on to the side of her house, and most of the film was to be shot there. She had assembled a small crew of professionals—and Muffin established immediate rapport with them. In two days of shooting she didn't have to remove one item of clothing, and by the time she *did* have to she felt she was among old friends.

Karmen was so encouraging and supportive. Always praising her, making her want to do better. 'I love your accent,' she would say. 'Just a little more emphasis when you say no in that scene. That's it sweetheart—that's exactly what I want. Clever girl.'

Somehow Muffin slipped naturally into the role. And when the time came to indulge in things she had only ever indulged in in private—well strangely enough it was enjoyable. It was a turn-on. It was exciting.

'You're beautiful,' Karmen never tired of telling her. 'A little golden puppy dog. Do you *realize* how many guys are going to fall insanely in love with you?'

228

Muffin hadn't thought about *that*. Revealing herself to so many men . . . and all of them horny . . . and wanting her . . . her . . . *her*.

She giggled at the thought.

Halfway through the movie Karmen summoned her to her bedroom one night. She lay back in the big bed thoughtfully pulling on a joint. 'Keeley and I thought you deserved some fun. You've been working so very hard, little one, we thought you should relax.'

Muffin shivered. She had been expecting them to approach her, but it was still a surprise.

'Come here,' said Karmen lazily. 'That's if you want to. No one around here is going to force you to do anything you don't want to.'

Muffin did want to. Very much.

Keeley walked out of the bathroom. True to his original boast Karmen was not with him for the size of his nose.

Muffin glanced at him and quickly looked away.

Karmen smiled a very knowing smile.

'Shall I tell Keeley to go?' she asked softly.

Muffin nodded.

Diana Beeson was a bitch. Jon found that out in no uncertain terms. And what was worse was the fact that she was an intelligent bitch. He couldn't talk her round, string her along, or get her to do anything she didn't want to.

He had moved in with her, and she expected service with a smile. 'Go to the supermarket, Jon.' 'Fill the car up.' 'Go buy the trades.' 'Fetch my cleaning.' 'Walk the dog.' Instead of moving in as her manager and taking over, he was chief gofer. *And he didn't like it. It was not what he had had in mind.* Apart from which he had no money and she was as tight as the proverbial drum.

It occurred to him that he had better move on. But where to? It was no good going until he had something better lined up. The way things were, staying with Muffin would have been better than this. He wondered briefly how Muffin was making out. His guilt was minimal at abandoning her. She would be alright. All she had to do was call up Jackson and he would come running—he had always had a hot nut for Muffin. And she could do worse than Jackson.

'Jon!' The sound of Diana's impatient call from the bedroom. 'Come and zip me up. sweetie. will you. And do hurry. otherwise we'll be late. and you know how I hate being the last to arrive.'

Another boring party. Now that Diana's movie was finished she wanted to go out every night She loved the parties. the attention she always received. the propositions from the local stud talent. And Jon trailed behind her. the unknown idiot, boyfriend of the star. It was not a role he was happy in. But until something better came along it would have to do.

Muffin had never imagined herself involved in a sexual relationship with a woman. Oh sure—she knew all about it. You were not a model in London without finding out a thing or two about life. Some of the girls had been very dykey—fed up with randy. grabbing men. Extolling the virtues of how different a female liaison could be had been one of their main topics of conversation. She remembered a certain location trip to Spain where Erica and Kamika had indulged right in the same room as her! 'Come and join us. Erica had urged. But Muffin knew that if Jon ever found out he would kill her. Anyway—the idea just did not appeal.

With Karmen it was a whole different trip. Karmen. with her broody Egyptian eyes. and thin erotic body.

Karmen, with her low enticing voice and scented black bedsheets.

Karmen excited Muffin as much as any man ever had. And the things she did in bed surpassed anything any man had done to her.

Muffin felt more protected and loved than she had felt in her entire life.

When the movie was finished Karmen threw a big party to celebrate. First she took Muffin on a shopping trip to celebrate, and they glided through Beverley Hills. along the Strip. and to several obscure exciting clothes boutiques. in Karmen's all-black Mercedes. Karmen was treated like a queen by all and sundry, and she played the part to the hilt.

Keeley travelled with them, dancing attendance, jumping at Karmen's every wish.

Muffin enjoyed every second of it. Because she was with *the* Karmen Rush, she too was treated with reverence and respect. Suddenly she was somebody again. It was great and she loved it.

'Just wait,' Karmen husked, 'within months they'll all know who you are. They'll be asking for *your* autograph. Just you wait, little sweet thing, and you'll see how right I am.'

Jon was surprised to see Muffin at the Karmen Rush party. She looked good too, prettier and bouncier than he had seen her in ages.

He hoped she wouldn't spot him, didn't want a whole big scene. Diana would not appreciate that. Diana liked to keep a low profile as far as her personal life was concerned. So low in fact that in a recent cover story for *People* she hadn't even mentioned his existence. Bloody marvellous. What was he—the invisible man? After all he *was* living with the bitch.

'Is that wifey pie I spot hovering around the great Karmen?' Diana questioned.

'Where?' asked Jon insincerely.

Diana raised her eyebrows, 'Right in your line of vision, darling. The one with the boobs.'

'Oh yeah,' he agreed, with a suitable note of surprise in his voice.

'Are you going to talk to her?'

'Why should I? I'm divorcing her, aren't I?'

Diana shrugged, 'Do what you like, it makes no difference in *my* life.'

It bloody wouldn't. Why couldn't she be jealous like normal people? He looked around the room searching for Jackson. Better make peace with him about running out on the rent for the house. He couldn't see him. Oh well . . .

Diana had drifted independently off as usual. Jon turned sharply and collided with a woman. The drink she was carrying spilled down her ample cleavage. 'Oh shit!' she said sharply.

He recognized her at once. She was April Crawford, a fiftyish movie star of past glory—recently and very publicly divorced from her fifth husband.

'Why don't you goddamn look where you're going?' April snapped.

'Sorry,' said Jon quickly, turning on the boyish look and English accent full wattage. 'Can I get you another drink?'

April looked him over—a sharp head to toe scrutiny. Her face relaxed into a smile. 'Why not? Double scotch on the rocks. Light on the rocks—and why don't you join me?'

'I'd like that,' he replied quickly. At the very least he could get a cover picture out of it. April Crawford always had been, and always would be, news. He smiled. 'Why don't you sit down and I'll fetch it to you.'

'Yeah,' replied April, winking, 'why don't I.'

Muffin saw Jon at the party and she couldn't even be bothered to go over and tell him what a bastard she thought he was. He didn't matter in her life any more. He was past news, over and finished. Keeley had told her that Jon would be the one that got chased for all their unpaid debts. That would teach him a lesson.

After half an hour of partying. Karmen got bored. She never did stay at her own parties. A brief appearance was all that was necessary. She took Muffin by the hand and led her into the famous black bedroom. They locked the door, settled on the vast bed, and switched on the closed circuit television system. Scenes of the party filtered onto the screen.

'The only way to attend,' Karmen murmured. 'Pour the brandy, pass the cocaine. You and I will have our own kind of party.'

## 53

Daniel suffered from depressions. In the Bahamas Cleo got her first taste of his illness. He took to his bed for almost the entire trip, just lying there and gazing into space.

At first she tried to joke him out of it. 'Come on, get up. If you don't get a suntan people will think we spent our entire time here screwing!'

No response. Daniel was totally uncommunicative.

She tried sympathy. He responded to that alright. He burst into racking sobs and didn't stop for an hour.

She tried anger. 'For crissakes get up. What *is* this crap?'

In the end she just left him alone. As soon as she stopped taking any notice of him he got up.

'I get these black attacks,' he told her solemnly. 'I just can't do anything. Can't function at all.'

'What about when you're working?' she asked crisply.

'Funny, it doesn't seem to happen then.'

'Hmmmn . . .' She was sceptical.

Once up again, Daniel was his usual charming self—and they were out and about playing golf, swimming, snorkling, eating delicious dinners under the stars, and gambling.

His good humour lasted exactly two days, and then a new problem arrived. He became impotent. After two nights of incredible lovemaking he suddenly couldn't get it up.

'Don't worry,' Cleo soothed, 'it's nothing. Happens to everyone some time or other.'

'Yes—you *would* know that,' Daniel raged. 'How many lovers have you had? Fifty? A hundred? Two hundred?'

'Including you, five actually,' she replied calmly. 'And how about you? How many princesses, movie stars, and other transient ladies have passed through *your* talented hands?'

In no time at all they were in the middle of an insult-throwing row. They seemed to be getting rather adept at arguments.

By the next day Daniel's good humour had returned along with his hard-on. They made long leisurely love in the morning, and then sat out by the pool. Everything was fine until Daniel accused Cleo of flirting with the pool boy—a finely muscled lad who was all of eighteen. Cleo, of course, denied it. But they were soon embroiled in another fight, and right in the middle of it all she found herself thinking—What the hell do I need this for? This guy is nuts. Jealous. Insecure. Petty.

She left him alone in the hotel for the afternoon and went off on her own. When she returned he was full of apologies. They dined in the hotel restaurant, and in the middle of their dinner a vacuous pretty blond came and sat herself down. She was Swedish introduced herself as Ingmar smiled patronizingly at Cleo. and proceeded to hold a lengthy and intimate conversation with Daniel.

Suddenly Cleo realized what was going on. Shades of darling ex-Mike. Ingmar featured the same self-satisfied smile as Susan big tits used to wear Ingmar had recently been laid. and with a burning anger Cleo realized that it was by Daniel. that very afternoon.

'You sonofabitch!' she hissed. pushing her chair away from the table and getting up. 'You *bastard!*'

'What's the matter. darling?' Daniel asked innocently.

'Don't give me that *shit!*' She stalked back to their suite. Daniel soon followed.

Cleo was packing. Throwing her things into a suitcase with venom.

'I don't understand . . .' he began.

'I thought you at least were different . . . But you're all the same, the whole bloody lot of you.'

'What am I supposed to have done?' He stood there misunderstood and confused.

'You know what That . . . that . . . person. You gave her one. didn't you? This afternoon. right in this very room.'

He started to laugh. 'Of course not. How could you possibly think that?'

Angrily she glared at him. 'Sixth sense. I'm not an idiot you know.'

'Baby. baby. baby.' he put his arms around her. 'Sixth sense indeed! What kind of an opinion do you have of me anyway? Do you honestly think I would do a thing like that to you?' He was still laughing. and kissing her. and pushing her hand towards his crotch. 'Here. feel this. It's yours—all yours. If it goes anywhere else you'll be the first to know!'

'Oh Daniel!' She could feel her anger collapsing. She touched his face softly. It had been a ridiculous thought.

His hands were sliding inside her dress. and within moments she had forgotten all about Ingmar and thoughts of leaving.

It was a sexual thing. But it was also more. She loved Daniel.

234

Depression, moodiness, jealousy, and all. She really loved him.

'Dynamite!' Russell shouted down the phone. 'The piece on Butch and Vinnie is a gem. We're running it as the cover story next issue. Where have you been? I've been trying to contact you for weeks.'

'The Bahamas. Daniel wanted a rest.'

'You might let me know when you take off. In-house reaction on your two stories is so strong that everyone in the goddamn place is coming to me with ideas on who you should do next. What we want to do is make your piece a regular spot—you know what I mean, a two or three page in-depth interview. I think—'

'Hang on Russ. I don't want to be tied to a weekly thing.'

'You will, when I tell you the fee involved. When can you fly here and discuss everything?'

She was tempted. 'I don't know.'

'Get here as soon as possible.'

'I'll call you back on it.'

'Don't vanish again.'

'Wouldn't dream of it.' Thoughtfully she hung up. Even more thoughtfully she ran her hands down her body. Her breasts felt swollen. Was that good or bad? She grinned to herself. She would have to find out. Being pregnant was a whole new experience.

Daniel lay out by the tennis court reading scripts. Now she had things to tell him. But telling him about the baby had to be a very special moment. She would savour the news to herself until the time was right.

'Hey—guess what?' she said, squatting on the grass beside him.

'What?' he mumbled, immersed in a script.

'*Image* loves the stuff I did—they want to offer me all sorts of money to write a weekly interview piece.'

'That's nice.'

'It's more than nice. They want me to fly to New York to discuss terms and things.'

Daniel placed the script carefully on the grass. 'Who is they? That pimped up editor or whatever he is?'

'Well Russell runs the show . . .'

'Why don't you tell me the truth about Russell? I know you've slept with him.'

'I haven't. I keep on telling you that,' she sighed, 'and anyway, even if I *had*, what difference would it make?'

He got up. 'So you have?'

'No I haven't.'

'Go to New York,' he snapped, 'if that's what you want to do.'

'I would like to—'

'So go. I won't stop you.'

'But I don't want you to mind. Why don't you come too?'

'I hate New York. How long will you be gone?'

'Two days.'

He picked up the pile of scripts and headed for the house.

She followed him. 'You do understand don't you? I *have* to work, it's important to me—and Daniel, if it's important to you about us getting married—well, I was thinking . . . Why don't we?'

'What happened to your "I don't think we should spoil everything by getting married" speech?'

'I changed my mind. I love you. I have my reasons which you will be the *first* to know about.'

'Tell me.'

'When I get back.'

'When are you going?'

'I thought the sooner the better. Tomorrow morning, and I'll be back before you know it.'

Russell said, 'Cleo's coming to town.'

Mike concentrated on the ball. They were playing squash—a weekly game they had together.

'What happened to the old actor?' he replied casually.

'I don't know, maybe he's still around. But Cleo is definitely into working again.'

'For you?'

'For the magazine. Did you read her cover story on the Kaufmans?'

'No,' lied Mike. He had devoured every word of it. She was writing well. He wished she wasn't. He wished that she had faded into obscurity. He didn't want to be reminded of the beautiful intelligent woman who had once been his wife.

'Great stuff,' said Russell, slamming a shot against the wall. 'She seems to have acquired a sharp edge she never had before.'

'She always had a sharp edge,' said Mike bitterly, 'only she kept it well hidden.'

'Don't be bitter,' chided Russell, 'it's about time the two of you were friends.'

'Let's quit,' Mike threw his racket down none too gently. 'I need a drink.'

'We have the court for another fifteen minutes,' protested Russell.

'So play with yourself. I've had it.'

Mike left Russell at the sports club and went to a bar where a lot of the models and photographers hung out. He was too early, the place was nearly empty.

He needed a little company. He needed a little fucking.

He moved on to another bar used by the show business group. And who should he run into but Ginny Sandler, all girlish blond curls and plumpness.

'Mike!' she squealed, as if London had never happened. 'One day in this town and I bump into *you!*'

Ginny had moved to Los Angeles, and was an extremely powerful and important agent. Mike had read about her success in the trades.

'You look wonderful, Ginny,' he said, eyeing her opulent boobs escaping from the confines of a hardly buttoned silk shirt.

She introduced him to the group she was with and ordered him a drink.

'Mikey,' she whispered, a hand straying to his thigh, 'you are looking vereee tasty,' she giggled, 'but then you always did.'

Ginny he could take home. Ginny would no more think of moving in than taking up knitting. She took her fucking like a man—straight.

'Are we going to—' he began.

'Of course!' giggled Ginny. 'Don't we always?'

Cleo had missed New York. She didn't realize it until she wa
riding in the cab from Kennedy airport, and then, suddenly, sh
knew how much she had missed the hustle and grind of the city

It occurred to her that she hadn't even bothered to book a
hotel room—but she figured *Image* could do that—and this time
she would check that there were no screw-ups landing her in
Russell's penthouse apartment.

The cab passed right by the Hampton Records building, and
she thought fleetingly of Mike. She had no hard feelings toward
him any more. She felt exactly nothing in that direction.

Russell was waiting anxiously to greet her. He wore a new
Italian suit, and pink striped shirt. 'Welcome back!' he
exclaimed. 'Here—you like it?' He thrust the next issue of *Image*
at her. A picture of Butch and Vinnie adorned the cover, and
a yellow star proclaimed—'Cleo James—special exclusive story
on Butch Kaufman and sister.'

'Well?' questioned Russell.

'I like it,' Cleo grinned. Name on the front of the
magazine—she had never had *that* honour before.

'This is just the start,' said Russell happily. 'Remember that
piece you did last year on Senator Ashton? As you know he's
running as a presidential candidate in the next election—and
guess who will have an upfront exclusive? It's all been arranged.'

'But that's so far ahead—'

'So what? Now you're back in action you don't plan to fade
away again do you?'

Slowly Cleo shook her head. Daniel was just going to have
to accept the fact that he was marrying a working girl.

So much happened in such a short time, that before Cleo knew
it a week had passed. Russell wanted her to do an on-the-spot
interview with a deposed foreign king, and she could hardly turn
*that* down. Then a top book publisher requested a meeting and
offered her a hefty advance to do a book of interviews on
prominent people. It was an offer she could hardly refuse. Then
*Women's Wear Daily* wanted to do a story on *her*.

Everyone loved the Butch and Vinnie piece. and publicists were calling *Image* saying that this celebrity and that celebrity would like to be interviewed by Cleo James.

It all just seemed to come together at once.

'My celebrity reporter.' Russell grinned. 'Someone on the magazine will have to interview *you* next.'

She called Daniel to explain. Each phone call his voice grew colder and colder. After three days she felt a bit silly telling him every day she would be back the next. So she decided to just ride with what was happening and make it up to Daniel when she got back. After all. when he heard about the baby . . . Well she knew he would be as thrilled as she was. Meanwhile New York was such fun. Visiting old restaurants. new shows. boogieing at *Studio 54* with a young gay copywriter from the magazine.

Russell drove her to the airport. Her book contract was signed and sealed. and a six month contract with *Image*. She felt great. But she missed Daniel. and couldn't wait to surprise him with all her good news.

At the airport Russell suggested magazines and candy. and that was *all* he had suggested the whole trip. It was a relief. At last she could really relax with him. A newspaper headline caught her eye. It caught her eye because it was accompanied by a photograph of Daniel. He was not alone in the photo. He was with Swedish Ingmar from the Bahamas.

Calmly Cleo purchased the paper—the headline was enough to give her the whole story.

### ENGLISH ACTOR DANIEL ONEL WEDS
### SWEDISH HEIRESS IN SECRET CEREMONY

Silently Russell took her arm. 'Shall we forget about the plane?'

Dumbly she nodded.

Goddamn Daniel. Was he that insecure that he couldn't have waited a few extra days?

# 54

Karmen was more excited about *The Girl With the Golden Snatch* than any of the multi-million-dollar epics she had starred in. The film was her baby, and she nursed it carefully through every stage.

The finished product was everything she had hoped for. It had comedy and humour, an interesting story, and the best looking cunt in Hollywood. Muffin was sensational. When she opened her legs for the close-ups every man in America was going to fall instantly in love.

Karmen was delighted, only sorry that she was unable to attach her name to it. A porno movie directed by Karmen Rush would guarantee disaster for her public image. Of course it was not exactly a secret, people in the business knew—Natasha Mount—credited as director—was Karmen Rush. It was a well known fact. Only no one could prove it.

Diana and Jon were at a producer's house for dinner one night. About twelve people were present and it was a convivial meal. For once they had not argued before coming out, but Jon knew his time was almost up. He had already spent a couple of afternoons photographing April Crawford—and he felt that if things got desperate he would find a bed in that direction—more than a bed, but it wouldn't be the first time he had obliged a lady in the older age group. Diana was treating him as nothing more than an unpaid lackey, and he wasn't going to hang around for the final kick out. If nothing else turned up . . . Well April *was* a star . . . had been a star . . . And with him to guide her . .

'Movietime, folks,' their hostess was clapping her hands excitedly. 'We have a preview tonight.'

They all trooped into the screening room.

Diana was paying too much attention to an ageing writer. Jon had a nasty feeling the man would be his successor.

Their host was passing round brandies and laughing. 'You're not going to *believe* this film,' he announced to all and sundry. 'You just will not believe it!'

The lights dimmed, and a golden sunset flickered onto the screen. Very beautiful.

Jon was trying to see if Diana had physical contact with the ageing writer seated on her left.

A roar of laughter went up and Jon glanced back at the screen. James Bond-type music was blaring forth, and spelled out in girls' naked bodies sprayed gold was the title, *The Girl With the Golden Snatch*.

In a Busby Berkeley routine the girls changed position, and *Starring Muffin* appeared on the screen.

'Oh, my God!' laughed Diana. 'Don't tell me wifey has become a movie star!'

Muffin strolled across the titles, naked and gold. She lay down on the sand, opened her legs, and the camera panned in.

'Christ!' said Diana reverently. 'Whatever made you divorce *that!*'

'He's here again,' said Keeley.

Muffin grinned. It was the fourth time Jon had attempted to see her.

'I think it's about time we had the shit kicked outa him. I know a coupla dudes get their jollies doin' that kinda thing. What ya say?'

'I say today I'll see him.' Muffin jumped up and surveyed herself in the nearest mirror. 'Show him in, Keeley.' She fluffed her hair a little, licked her shiny lips. She had just completed a photo layout for *Macho* magazine. She knew she looked adorable.

Muffin loved her new notoriety. Karmen had been right, as the movie started to take off all over America, so her fame began.

Karmen, away on a location trip, called her daily. They had a wonderful relationship, warm and caring and very, very sexual.

Muffin giggled at the thought. The only bad news in her life now was that she would have to move out of the Rush mansion. It didn't look right her staying there. Now that she was famous (well nearly) separate abodes were the order of the day.

Keeley walked back in, an anxious Jon behind him.

'Shall I stay?' asked Keeley.

'It's O.K.,' said Muffin. 'he won't be staying long.' She stared at Jon. 'You look ever so skinny.' she remarked. 'your old lady not feeding you?'

Jon ignored her question. 'My little Muff!' he exclaimed admiringly. 'How about *you* then?'

'How about me?'

'I saw the movie.'

'Somehow I thought you had.'

'It seems that all our plans for you worked out.'

'What plans?'

'The singing. dancing. acting lessons I made you have.'

She yawned. *You* made me have them. *I* paid for them.'

'It was our money.

'What's up Jon? What do you want?'

He ventured closer. 'Nice greeting.'

'Almost as nice as your last goodbye. Remember? Leaving me stuck in that house with all the bills and no car.

'You can't drive.

'I can now. I can do lots of things I never did before.' She walked over to the bar and opened up a can of Seven Up.

He followed her. 'Can I have a drink?'

'Help yourself.'

'You're being very cold.'

'I can be what I like. We're divorced. or did you forget?'

'What did they pay you to do that film?'

'None of your business.'

He sighed. 'You never did understand money. You're probably getting taken for the ride of your life.'

'Oh no. I *had* that ride already '

He slid his arm around her waist. 'You need looking after. I've missed you like crazy. I was nuts to go—I just had this stupid idea that you'd manage better without me—and you did.'

'And I still can.' She moved away from him. swigging from the can of Seven-Up.

'Listen Muff. I know you're bugged with me and I don't blame you. But I made a mistake—just like the one you made with Little Marty Pearl ' He paused. followed her across the room. grabbed her. 'You and I belong together.' He felt her incredible tits and realized that he *had* missed them. No one had tits like

242

Muffin. 'We're a team. I can look after you like nobody else—in *every* way.'

She was silent, allowing him to fondle her and to feel her nipples harden.

'Pack up your things,' he whispered, his hand sliding down the front of her shorts. 'I've got some very exciting things planned for you.'

She didn't say anything. She was waiting for the amazing jolt of excitement she felt when Karmen touched her. It didn't come. His hand was between her legs and it didn't come. His fingers were exploring further and it didn't come.

She stared at the bulge in his jeans. So what?

Roughly she moved his hand and stood back—hands on hips—surveying him with scorn.

'Piss off, Jon. I'm not the same dumb bunny you married. You're not taking another free ride with me. So just piss off—and don't bother coming back.'

# 55

At first, when Cleo had read about Daniel marrying, she had been destroyed, in a state of shock. Russell had been very kind. He had insisted she stay in his apartment—no strings—and this time there had been no strings, and she had been grateful for that. Somehow he had arranged for her things to be sent from California—she hadn't asked how—she didn't even want to hear Daniel's name mentioned.

Within a week she threw herself into work with a vengeance, telling no one of the fact that she was pregnant. She found a pretty little apartment, went on occasional one-off dates, and for the first time in her life realized that she was quite capable of managing on her own. She did not need a permanent man. She could get along very nicely without one. It was strangely exciting having to go it alone. And somehow fulfilling.

Russell was very supportive. He was always there in case she needed him, and when it turned out her supposed pregnancy was a false alarm, it was *his* shoulder she cried on.

'But you should be pleased,' he stated, after she had confided in him.

She shook her head sadly. 'I wanted Daniel's baby.'

He was very matter of fact. 'If it's a baby you want *I'll* marry you.'

She couldn't help laughing. 'What is this hang up everyone has with marriage? You don't need to be *married* to have a baby.'

'I'll be happy to oblige either way,' he offered nervously.

'Oh, Russ, you're very sweet. I appreciate all your kindness—but find yourself a big tall model girl. You and I can never be anything but the *best* of friends.'

'Why?' He was piqued.

'Because it's a question of chemistry. Our chemistry is of the platonic friend variety. We've already discussed it a hundred times and both agreed.'

'I never agreed.'

'Oh yes you did.'

Work was her salvation. Things were going very well, and then suddenly, out of the blue, she was invited to do a television pilot. A fifteen minute face-to-face interview show. She knew that at least eight other people were being considered for the job, and after the pilot she forgot about it, and got on with the other things in her life. It came as a great surprise to her when she was picked to do the show

'I just can't believe it!' she told Russell, and grabbed at the opportunity.

They went out to celebrate.

'I feel I'm at the threshold of a whole new life,' she enthused. 'Television is such a great challenge.'

She threw herself into her new job with boundless enthusiasm, and the show was an instant success. She had a television presence that made her an immediate celebrity.

The loss of privacy was a jolt Being recognized in the supermarket and street by total strangers who felt they had every right in the world to talk to her. And then there were all her new-found friends. People she had only met once, briefly—maybe with Butch, or Mike, or when she was writing for *Image*. Suddenly, according to them, she was their best friend. It was all very startling. But she weathered it, accepted it, and eventually began to enjoy it.

A month after the show was a weekly event, Daniel got divorced.

Ingmar stated to any newspaper that would listen that Daniel Onel was an impossible and difficult man. She then demanded a three million dollar divorce settlement.

Cleo could just imagine Daniel pacing around his house in his gym shoes and dyed hair screaming about the unfairness of it all.

She did think of him often. Sometimes he came to her in dreams, and they were back together, and oh so happy. Maybe it wasn't such an impossible thought that one day they might be together again. It was a feeling she had.

He was like a magnet. Sure he was difficult. But she could have handled him, if she had been willing to concentrate all her energies in his direction. She understood him. She didn't love him because of *who* he was, but because of *what* he was. And the moodiness, depression and petty jealousies were a part of him. The timing had been wrong for their affair. She had jumped from Butch's bed to Daniel's with no space in between. She had needed a freedom on her own terms that Daniel hadn't understood.

Maybe now things could be different. Maybe . . .

Mike followed Cleo's every move. He watched her on television, read about her in magazines, and had vague casual conversations with Russell about her. It irked him beyond belief that his dear friend Russell was spending so much time with his ex-wife. Were they screwing? It was a question which haunted Mike. He didn't think he could stand it if they were.

Russell, of course, was giving nothing away. He was as tight-mouthed and smug as ever.

Eventually Mike knew that he would have to see Cleo, and he devised what he thought was a fiendishly clever plan. Russell had mentioned that she was to tape several shows in Los Angeles, he had even mentioned the date she was going.

Mike had a business trip to L.A. he had been postponing. It didn't take too much detective work to find out what flight Cleo would be taking. He booked himself on to the same one.

Perfect. An accidental meeting. Natural and nice.

He didn't even mention to Russell he was going—wouldn't do to give the game away.

Cleo decided she would call Daniel when she arrived in L.A. Why not? Then again. why yes? She *still* hadn't made a firm decision. Yet she had to know how she really felt about him. She couldn't continue in the limbo land of not really knowing what she wanted. Did she still love him? Didn't she? How did *he* feel about *her*?

It was no use pretending. She had to know.

She hadn't exactly been pining for him—there had been other men. Only one she had actually slept with. Her director on the show who looked ever so slightly like Daniel. Now that was sick. She needed to know her true feelings so that she could get on with the rest of her life. It was as simple as that.

On the plane she enjoyed the celebrity treatment. She was travelling alone. her crew had gone on ahead.

The TV show was enjoying excellent ratings. and Cleo had to admit that she loved doing it more every programme.

The thrill of each new guest. The research—done for her—but she still read every author's book. saw every actor's film, read up on every politician.

She was meeting so many new and interesting people. It was a job that was never boring.

She opened up her Vuitton briefcase. There was an art book to study, a record by a new girl rock sensation. a folder on *Surf Stud* and another on *The Girl with the Golden Snatch*. She was going to Los Angeles to tape two specials. One on Muffin—current porno superstar—and the second on Butch and Vinnie. *Surf Stud* had become *the* cult movie. and Vinnie *the* new teenage star. Funny how the Kaufmans drifted in and out of her life.

She wondered how Vinnie was making out with all her new found fame. Probably loving every minute of it. and acting in an even more obnoxious way—if that was possible So far the Kaufmans had managed to maintain the brother/sister image.

It would be interesting to see how long they could keep it up—and *she* wasn't going to be the one to give them away.

She opened up the folder on *The Girl with the Golden Snatch,* and leafed through a series of stills from the movie. Hmmm . . . Naked was no longer naughty. It was boring as hell. All those acres of bums and tits, and a few stiff pricks for good measure.

She had to admit though that Muffin was certainly something. Sort of a teenage Marilyn Monroe type—dumb and cunty—the type that appealed to most men.

'Cleo?'

She glanced up. Standing in the aisle was Mike.

'Hey—what a *surprise!*' he exclaimed, availing himself of the empty seat next to her, and shaking his head in amazement. 'Of all the places to bump into each other! You going to L.A.?'

'If I'm not, I'm on the wrong plane,' she said drily, and shut the folder.

'Do you mind if I sit here?' he asked.

'It looks like I have no choice.'

'Hey,' he said quickly, 'it's a long time ago. At least we can be friends now, can't we?'

She stared at her ex-husband. Horny-looking Mike—with the come-on eyes and black curly hair. He was a very attractive man. A man she had once loved to distraction. A man she now felt absolutely nothing for. No hate. No recriminations. Yes, they *could* be friends.

She smiled. 'Why not?'

He was pleased. He summoned the stewardess and ordered champagne.

'This is a celebration,' he told Cleo, 'it's been a long time.'

They talked casually about mutual acquaintances, what was happening over at Hampton Records, Russell, Cleo's TV show, family.

'It's really *great* to see you.' Mike fixed her with his incredibly sexual eyes. 'I have missed you more than you could ever possibly believe.' His hand reached over and covered hers.

Oh Christ! She had fallen into a trap. She didn't need this. Deftly she moved her hand away and stood up. 'Got to visit the loo.' She squeezed past him. Damn Mike being on the same plane. He never had been a good loser—he probably would only consider their marriage over if *he* had been the one to walk. Yet it was over. Irrevocably. She had a piece of paper to prove it.

She stayed in the toilet for a while. She knew Mike—knew exactly what the next conversational tack would be. In a way it was flattering that he obviously still wanted her—but not *that* flattering. He still wanted her because *she* didn't want him. Shit! What bad luck to be on the same plane. If indeed it was luck. She wouldn't put it past him to have arranged the whole thing . . .

It occurred to her that there was a way of stopping him dead in his tracks, before he said things he would regret. She made her way back to her seat.

He stood attentively to let her pass, making sure there was body contact as she did so.

'Still got the sexiest ass in the world,' he leered, the confidence of a successful cocksman deep in his voice.

'Your lines haven't improved. In fact they're getting even cornier.'

'Ain't nothing wrong with a sexy ass.'

'Yeah. Ass. That's all women are to you aren't they?'

'Hey—come on—I was joking. Can't you take a joke?'

She stared at him, and wondered how they had ever survived four-and-a-half years together. 'I'm getting married again, Mike. It's a secret at the moment, so I'd appreciate it if you wouldn't tell anyone. Even Russell doesn't know about it. But I thought you should.'

He was stunned. This piece of news was totally unexpected. Cleo. *His* Cleo getting married again. He could feel the anger rising within him. She was a bitch. He had always known it.

He attempted to keep his voice steady and light. Mustn't let the bitch know she had gotten to him. 'Who's the lucky guy then?'

She was dismissive and secretive. 'No one you know.'

He was furious. She had let him sit next to her for the whole frigging flight making a fool of himself. He tried to think of something that would hurt. Came up with Ginny. 'I was thinking of giving the marriage scene another try myself,' he said, casually.

'Oh, yes?'

'Well . . . you know how it is. Lonely nights—lonely beds—even if you've got three girls shacked up with you.'

'I've never had that problem myself.'

She was a cutting bitch. 'I've been spending a lot of time with Ginny.'

'Ginny?' she couldn't keep the amusement out of her voice.

Not quite the reaction he had expected. 'Yes—Ginny.' he pushed on regardless, 'She's a very warm and giving person. I've always had a lot of feeling for her.'

Cleo wanted to say. 'Yes—so I discovered in London.' Instead she said, 'I hope you'll both be very happy.'

Then, fortunately the seat belt sign flashed on, and their conversation came to a halt.

Neither spoke again until the plane landed, and they were ready to disembark.

'See you around, Cleo,' said Mike. He had already spotted a ripe and luscious redhead moving down the aisle. She looked like she could entertain him for an evening or two. He set off after her.

Cleo remained seated for a few minutes while the plane emptied out.

Mike and Ginny. It couldn't be true, could it? Mike's taste had always been so much more up-market. But then Ginny was probably the perfect companion for him. Two sex maniacs together. What could be better.

She suppressed a smile. Poor old Mike. The same tired old lines. Briefly she felt sorry for him—but only briefly. He was a big boy. He could look after himself.

Once installed in the Beverly Hills hotel Cleo found she had itchy fingers to use the phone.

Daniel.

He was on her mind.

Constantly.

Funny. It was all the other guys that came running. Daniel merely got married behind her back without so much as a word of explanation. It was a *very* shitty thing to do. After all they *had* been living together, planning their own marriage.

It made absolutely no difference to the way she felt about him. She wanted to see him—dyed hair and all.

A woman answered the phone. Young, unfriendly, with a distinct English accent. Coldly, 'I'll see if he's here.'

A pause. Then Daniel. 'How are *you*?'

His voice brought back every good memory. 'I'm fine. You?'

'The same.'

She laughed softly. 'Is that good or bad?'

'It depends.'

'I'm in Los Angeles.'

'Oh. You finally came back.'

'Yeah, it took me a little time. How did the marriage go?'

'Quickly.'

His replies were sparse to say the least. 'Are you alone?' she asked.

'No.'

'Can you talk?'

'No.'

'You're not married *again* are you?'

'No.'

She took a deep breath. 'Daniel, do you want to see me?'

'Of course.'

'So call me back when you *can* talk. I'm at the Beverly Hills.'

After hanging up she couldn't concentrate on anything. Her director called her about dinner but she hedged her way out of it.

Daniel did not call back. His secretary called at approximately 5 p.m. and in a very businesslike tone stated that Mr Onel wondered if she was free for lunch the following day, and if she was he would see her at *Ma Maison* at one o'clock.

Terrific. Lunch. And *Ma Maison* was not exactly the most private place in town.

Disgusted, she took a sleeping pill and went to bed.

Daniel was waiting when she arrived. Suntanned, and about eight pounds thinner. He looked good. He would never be a matinee idol, but he was the best looking man *she* had ever seen.

She had dressed carefully. White. His favourite colour. Not too much makeup. She was as nervous as a girl on her first date.

He stood as she approached the table. 'Hello Cleo,' he said.

She was immediately lost in his eyes. He seemed to be returning the silent signals racing back and forth. She knew at once he was as nervous as she was.

They ordered some food, picked at it. Gulped down the wine.

'Who are you living with?' she asked softly.

'A girl.'

She attempted to laugh. 'I was hoping you hadn't switched to boys.'

'A girl who's always around. Sweet, unambitious, concerned only with me.'

'Never runs off to New York. Right?'

'Right. Ingmar was a mistake—but we both know—you and I—we would never have worked things out.'

There was a lump in her throat. 'We wouldn't?'

He took her hand and held it gently. 'You know we wouldn't. Let's not kid ourselves, I am a very selfish man—I need someone on call twenty-four hours a day. I need a yes-lady—and you are a lot of things—but a yes-lady—never.'

'What is a yes-lady, anyway?'

'Someone who's always there telling me how wonderful I am. Fucking stupid isn't it? But I need that in my life.'

The lump in her throat refused to go. 'Yeah, it's stupid.'

'You're beautiful, intelligent, and quite rightly you want a career. I could never handle that. I'd go out of my mind with jealousy.'

'I never did anything to make you jealous.'

'Of course you didn't. It wasn't your fault that I imagined you screwing your way around New York. At home now sits Jilly. She is twenty years old, passive, and dedicated to me. She tells me I'm the best actor in the world, the best lover, the best everything. I am her life. I don't care about her that much, but I *do* need her. You—I cared about much too much.' He squeezed her hand, 'Do you understand what I'm saying?'

Her voice was very low. 'I think so.'

'Of course if you wanted to give your career up . . .' he trailed off, 'but you don't do you?'

'Don't answer for me.'

'I've seen you on television. You love it—you come alive.

251

You're like me—you have to express yourself in many ways,' he shrugged, 'nothing wrong with *that*.'

'But you couldn't take it—'

'I'm being honest with you. That's what our relationship was about wasn't it? We *were* always honest with each other weren't we?'

'What about Ingmar?'

'I never had her in the Bahamas. She turned up in L.A. when you were in New York. I was lonely, mad at you. She was around. Getting married was a horrible mistake. I just wanted to get my own back on you.'

'For what?'

'For leaving me.'

'Oh Daniel,' her eyes filled with tears. '*I* think we could make things work.'

A waiter was hovering, pouring more wine. She blinked back tears. This was hardly the place to break down.

'Damn!' The waiter had spilled some wine on Daniel's grey gaberdine trousers, and was now trying to rub it off. 'Leave it alone, man,' Daniel stormed. 'Bloody careless.' He grimaced at Cleo. 'Just had them made—first time I wore them.'

'Try water. It's white wine, won't stain.'

Industriously he soaked his napkin in water and dabbed at the offending stain. Somehow Cleo felt that if Jilly was around she would produce an instant solution. After all, a totally dedicated twenty-year-old girl would *never* allow his precious new trousers to remain stained.

She stood up. 'I have to go,' she said quickly.

He stopped rubbing. 'Yes, I understand. It was nice seeing you again.'

Only nice?

'Maybe we can have lunch again,' he continued, his attention now torn between her and the stain.

'Why not?' Why yes?

She left the restaurant, blinked in the sunshine. Well, that was that. At least Daniel knew what *he* wanted. And it obviously wasn't her.

So . . . she was free . . . All options open.

Daniel was right—a yes-lady she could never be. And if that

was the kind of woman he would be satisfied with . . . Well maybe he wasn't the man she had thought he was.

She went back to her hotel, slipped off the white outfit, lay on the bed, lit a cigarette and called her director. 'I'm available,' she said. 'What's happening?'

'Nice of you,' he replied. 'You're sure?'

'You sound pissed off.'

'I *am* pissed off. You come to L.A. and vanish. We have a show tomorrow. If you can spare the time, tonight we are dining with Muffin. You *do* want to talk to her before the show don't you?'

'Tell me where and when and I'll be there.'

'I'll pick you up at seven-thirty.'

'I'll look forward to it.'

'And Cleo?'

'Yes.'

'It will be nice to see you again. You've been avoiding me since—'

'Later.' She put the phone down.

True. She had been avoiding him since they had slept together. But it wasn't *his* fault he looked ever so slightly like Daniel. And anyway—he was younger by at least twelve years, and better looking, taller, smarter, and he didn't dye his hair, and he wasn't a fucking egomaniac.

She sighed. Time to start forgetting Daniel. Definitely time.

# 56

Muffin had moved from the Rush mansion. She now lived in a fantasy Spanish Palace of pink brick and tile situated in the very centre of Beverly Hills. She did not live alone. Three miniature dogs cavorted through the house, and oriental twin maids tended to her every need.

In residence also was a young man named Buff. He was not

unlike Jon in appearance—skinny. blond. boyish. But Buff had no control over Muffin's new found fortunes. he was merely installed as a sort of Keeley figure—just around for the size of his cock.

Karmen and Muffin still shared a more than intimate relationship. but for appearances' sake they kept separate houses. Now that Muffin was *the* current porno superstar. she could no longer afford to share a house with Karmen. It wouldn't look right. People would talk. And Karmen had a formidable reputation to protect.

Cleo arrived at the house in a white chauffeured Cadillac.

Buff came out to greet her. His tight jeans emphasized the reason he was Muffin's live-in boyfriend. 'Hi.' he mumbled 'good t'see you again.'

They had all spent a drunken evening together the previous night. Cleo. with her director. and producer. Buff. with Muffin.

Cleo remembered the evening with a thin smile. Her producer and director had been in a nervous sweat at meeting Muffin 'What do you say to a broad whose pussy has been seen on every screen in the country?' the producer had asked. perplexed.

'Hello puss might be good.' Cleo had replied drily.

'Don't joke around. This girl has the most famous snatch in the country!'

'Why does that make you nervous?'

'Jeeze! I don't. *know!*'

This was the same producer who had met heads of state. senators. movie stars. and not flinched at all.

'The male malady.' Cleo had said cuttingly. 'a terror of cunt.

'You really know how to turn a pretty phrase.' her producer had replied. disgusted. Then he had shut up.

As it turned out Muffin had been a delight. Full of girlish giggles and innocence. Cleo had liked her immediately.

Dinner had been at *Trader Vics*. and the navy grogs had flowed at an alarming rate. Everyone had a good time. Even Cleo. She had decided that her director did not resemble Daniel one little bit—and when they were in bed together later, it was only the influence of the navy grogs that made her cry out 'Daniel!' at her moment of climax.

The camera crew were already at Muffin's house. setting up

and getting things together. Her director greeted her with a more than friendly kiss. Apparently calling out another man's name at orgasm was not the kind of thing to put *him* off.

She pushed him away in an offhand fashion, and the makeup girl came at her with a powder puff.

Cleo thought about the interview as she glanced around the living-room—it was all thick pile carpets and huge cushions. Virgin white. Of course. Very predictable.

Muffin was news. *The Girl with the Golden Snatch* was the biggest grossing porno movie of all time.

Cleo had, of course, seen the film. As porno films went it wasn't bad. But as porno stars went, Muffin was sensational. A child woman, with a totally beautiful body. Nothing tacky about Muffin, she lived up to every word in the somewhat crude title.

It was going to be difficult to attack such a sweet little golden bunny. But attack she must. Her viewers would expect it. They knew her opinions on the way women were used in the massive pornography industry. Only three weeks previously she had taken to task the editor of a sick porno magazine. At the end of the confrontation the man had been a nervous wreck. As a crusader on women's rights Cleo had become something of an overnight phenomenon. She came across as witty, sharp, cutting and intelligent. Also beautiful. The combination was dynamite.

Muffin wafted into the room dressed in white broderie anglaise frills from head to toe.

She was a superstar—just as Karmen had assured her she would be.

'Hi Cleo,' she greeted, in carefully cultivated baby girl tones. 'Are you ready for me?'

'Five minutes—they're setting up now.'

Muffin walked to the mirrored bar, and studied her image in the pink tinted glass. She licked her lips and fluffed out her hair. 'The Prettiest Girl in Porn' *Newsweek* had labelled her in a recent cover story. She wouldn't argue with *that*. She had done pretty good for a little dumb English girl who had been abandoned penniless in big bad Hollywood. Pretty goddamned good. And nobody had been more surprised than Jon bloody Clapton.

It had given her extreme satisfaction telling him exactly what he could do. He had not believed that she wasn't the same pliable sweet dumb little Muff. It had taken Keeley and two strong-arm friends to convince him.

Diana Beeson had kicked him out—and for a while April Crawford had kept him. The last Muffin had heard was that his visa had run out, and he had been forced to return to England. Good riddance.

'All set, Muffin,' Cleo called out. 'Why don't we sit on the couch.'

Muffin joined her, and giggled inanely.

'Don't be nervous,' Cleo said reassuringly, 'just make believe the two of us are having a private chat.' She glanced over at her director. 'Ready, Phil?'

He nodded.

Cleo stared straight into the camera, her face alert and sincere.

'Hi, this is Cleo James talking to you from Los Angeles—city of dreams, city of angels—and a city that runs one of the largest pornographic industries in the world. Whatever your kink, you can get it here. Right now I am sitting in the home of Muffin—your average pretty girl next door porno star.'

The camera panned back to include Muffin in the shot.

Cleo turned to her and smiled. 'Hi, Muffin. Welcome to the show.'

Muffin dimpled in return. 'It's *my* pleasure,' she lisped sexily.

'Yes,' Cleo said, the smile sliding from her face, 'that's exactly what I wanted to talk to you about . . .'

She turned back to face the camera. 'Tonight ladies and gentlemen, our subject is pornography. Do we want it? Can we take it? And why the hell don't we get rid of it?'

Cleo was back on the screen. It felt good. Somehow she knew Daniel was right. This was where she really belonged.